Female Sleuths Megapack

Lady Molly of Scotland Yard, Loveday Brooke and Amelia Butterworth

Baroness Orczy

C. L. Pirkis

Anna Katharine Green

Copyright © 2014 Enhanced Ebooks

All rights reserved.

ISBN-10: 1497433134
ISBN-13: 978-1497433137

CONTENTS

LADY MOLLY OF SCOTLAND YARD

by Baroness Orczy

1	THE NINESCORE MYSTERY	1
2	THE FREWIN MINIATURES	13
3	THE IRISH-TWEED COAT	25
4	THE FORDWYCH CASTLE MYSTERY	37
5	A DAY'S FOLLY	49
6	A CASTLE IN BRITTANY	61
7	A CHRISTMAS TRAGEDY	75
8	THE BAG OF SAND	90
9	THE MAN IN THE INVERNESS CAPE	102
10	THE WOMAN IN THE BIG HAT	115
11	SIR JEREMIAH'S WILL	130
12	THE END	142
	WHO WAS BARONESS ORCZY?	180

THE EXPERIENCES OF LOVEDAY BROOKE, LADY DETECTIVE

by C. L. Pirkis

1	THE BLACK BAG LEFT ON A DOOR-STEP	154
2	THE REDHILL SISTERHOOD	187
3	A PRINCESS'S VENGEANCE	203
4	DRAWN DAGGERS	216
5	THE GHOST OF FOUNTAIN LANE	231
6	MISSING!	246

THE AMELIA BUTTERWORTH MYSTERIES

by Anna Katharine Green

1	THAT AFFAIR NEXT DOOR	265
2	LOST MAN'S LANE	417

LADY MOLLY OF SCOTLAND YARD

THE NINESCORE MYSTERY

1

WELL, you know, some say she is the daughter of a duke, others that she was born in the gutter, and that the handle has been soldered on to her name in order to give her style and influence.

I could say a lot, of course, but "my lips are sealed," as the poets say. All through her successful career at the Yard she honoured me with her friendship and confidence, but when she took me in partnership, as it were, she made me promise that I would never breathe a word of her private life, and this I swore on my Bible oath–"wish I may die," and all the rest of it.

Yes, we always called her "my lady," from the moment that she was put at the head of our section; and the chief called her "Lady Molly" in our presence. We of the Female Department are dreadfully snubbed by the men, though don't tell me that women have not ten times as much intuition as the blundering and sterner sex; my firm belief is that we shouldn't have half so many undetected crimes if some of the so-called mysteries were put to the test of feminine investigation.

Do you suppose for a moment, for instance, that the truth about that extraordinary case at Ninescore would ever have come to light if the men alone had had the handling of it? Would any man have taken so bold a risk as Lady Molly did when–But I am anticipating.

Let me go back to that memorable morning when she came into my room in a wild state of agitation.

"The chief says I may go down to Ninescore if I like, Mary," she said in a voice all a-quiver with excitement.

"You!" I ejaculated. "What for?"

"What for–what for?" she repeated eagerly. "Mary, don't you understand? It is the chance I have been waiting for–the chance of a lifetime? They are all desperate about the case up at the Yard; the public is furious, and columns of sarcastic letters appear in the daily press. None of our men know what to do; they are at their wits' end, and so this morning I went to the chief–"

"Yes?" I queried eagerly, for she had suddenly ceased speaking.

"Well, never mind now how I did it–I will tell you all about it on the way, for we have just got time to catch the 11 a.m. down to Canterbury. The chief says I may go, and that I may take whom I like with me. He suggested one of the men, but somehow I feel that this is woman's work, and I'd rather have you, Mary, than anyone. We will go over the preliminaries of the case together in the train, as I don't suppose that you have got them at your fingers' ends yet, and you have only just got time to put a few things together and meet me at Charing Cross booking-office in time for that 11:00 sharp."

She was off before I could ask her any more questions, and anyhow I was too flabbergasted to say much. A murder case in the hands of the Female Department! Such a thing had been unheard of until now. But I was all excitement, too, and you may be sure I was at the station in good time.

Fortunately Lady Molly and I had a carriage to ourselves. It was a non-stop run to Canterbury, so we had plenty of time before us, and I was longing to know all about this case, you bet, since I was to have the honour of helping Lady Molly in it.

The murder of Mary Nicholls had actually been committed at Ash Court, a fine old mansion which stands in the village of Ninescore. The Court is surrounded by magnificently timbered grounds, the most fascinating portion of which is an island in the midst of a small pond, which is spanned by a tiny rustic bridge. The island is called "The Wilderness," and is at the furthermost end of the grounds, out of sight and earshot of the mansion itself. It was in this charming spot, on the edge of the pond, that the body of a girl was found on the 5th of February last.

I will spare you the horrible details of this gruesome discovery. Suffice it to say for the present that the unfortunate woman was lying on her face, with the lower portion of her body on the small grass-covered embankment, and her head, arms, and shoulders sunk in the slime of the stagnant water just below.

It was Timothy Coleman, one of the under-gardeners at Ash Court, who first made this appalling discovery. He had crossed the rustic bridge and traversed the little island in its entirety, when he noticed something blue lying half in and half out of the water beyond. Timothy is a stolid, unemotional kind of yokel, and, once having ascertained that the object was a woman's body in a blue dress with white facings, he quietly stooped and tried to lift it out of the mud.

But here even his stolidity gave way at the terrible sight which was revealed before him. That the woman—whoever she might be—had been brutally murdered was obvious, her dress in front being stained with blood; but what was so awful that it even turned old Timothy sick with horror, was that, owing to the head, arms and shoulders having apparently been in the slime for some time, they were in an advanced state of decomposition.

Well, whatever was necessary was immediately done, of course. Coleman went to get assistance from the lodge, and soon the police were on the scene and had removed the unfortunate victim's remains to the small local police-station.

Ninescore is a sleepy, out-of-the-way village, situated some seven miles from Canterbury and four from Sandwich. Soon everyone in the place had heard that a terrible murder had been committed in the village, and all the details were already freely discussed at the Green Man.

To begin with, everyone said that though the body itself might be practically unrecognisable, the bright blue serge dress with the white facings was unmistakable, as were the pearl and ruby ring and the red leather purse found by Inspector Meisures close to the murdered woman's hand.

Within two hours of Timothy Coleman's gruesome find the identity of the unfortunate victim was firmly established as that of Mary Nicholls, who lived with her sister Susan at 2, Elm Cottages, in Ninescore Lane, almost opposite Ash Court. It was also known that when the police called at that address they found the place locked and apparently uninhabited.

Mrs. Hooker, who lived at No. 1 next door, explained to Inspector Meisures that Susan and Mary Nicholls had left home about a fortnight ago, and that she had not seen them since.

"It'll be a fortnight to-morrow," she said. "I was just inside my own front door a-calling to the cat to come in. It was past seven o'clock, and as dark a night as ever you did see. You could hardly see your 'and afore your eyes, and there was a nasty damp drizzle comin' from everywhere. Susan and Mary come out of their cottage; I couldn't rightly see Susan, but I 'eard Mary's voice quite distinck. She says: 'We'll have to 'urry,' says she. I, thinkin' they might be goin' to do some shoppin' in the village, calls out to them that I'd just 'eard the church clock strike seven, and that bein' Thursday, and early closin', they'd find all the shops shut at Ninescore. But they took no notice, and walked off towards the village, and that's the last I ever seed o' them two."

Further questioning among the village folk brought forth many curious details. It seems that Mary Nicholls was a very flighty young woman, about whom there had already been quite a good deal of scandal, whilst Susan, on the other hand—who was very sober and steady in her conduct—had chafed considerably under her younger sister's questionable reputation, and, according to Mrs. Hooker, many were the bitter quarrels which occurred between the two girls. These quarrels, it seems, had been especially violent within the last year whenever Mr. Lionel Lydgate called at the cottage. He was a London gentleman, it appears—a young man about town, it afterwards transpired—but he frequently stayed at Canterbury, where he had some friends, and on those occasions he would come over to Ninescore in his smart dogcart and take Mary out for drives.

Mr. Lydgate is brother to Lord Edbrooke, the multi-millionaire, who was the recipient of birthday honours last year. His lordship resides at Edbrooke Castle, but he and his brother Lionel had rented Ash Court once or twice, as both were keen golfers and Sandwich Links are very close by. Lord Edbrooke, I may add, is a married man. Mr. Lionel Lydgate, on the other hand, is just engaged to Miss Marbury, daughter of one of the canons of Canterbury.

No wonder, therefore, that Susan Nicholls strongly objected to her sister's name being still coupled with that of a young man far above her in station, who, moreover, was about to marry a young lady in his own rank of life.

But Mary seemed not to care. She was a young woman who only liked fun and pleasure, and she shrugged her shoulders at public opinion, even though there were ugly rumours anent the parentage of a little baby girl whom she herself had placed under the care of Mrs. Williams, a widow who lived in a somewhat isolated cottage on the Canterbury road. Mary had told Mrs. Williams that the father of the child, who was her own brother, had died very suddenly, leaving the little one on her and Susan's hands; and, as they couldn't look after it properly, they wished Mrs. Williams to have charge of it. To this the latter readily agreed.

The sum for the keep of the infant was decided upon, and thereafter Mary Nicholls had come every week to see the little girl, and always brought the money with her.

Inspector Meisures called on Mrs. Williams, and certainly the worthy widow had a very startling sequel to relate to the above story.

"A fortnight to-morrow," explained Mrs. Williams to the inspector, "a little after seven o'clock, Mary Nicholls come runnin' into my cottage. It was an awful night, pitch dark and a nasty drizzle. Mary says to me she's in a great hurry; she is goin' up to London by a train from Canterbury and wants to say good-bye to the child. She seemed terribly excited, and her clothes were very wet. I brings baby to her, and she kisses it rather wild-like and says to me: 'You'll take great care of her, Mrs. Williams,' she says; ' I may be gone some time.' Then she puts baby down and gives me £2, the child's keep for eight weeks."

After which, it appears, Mary once more said "good-bye" and ran out of the cottage, Mrs. Williams going as far as the front door with her. The night was very dark, and she couldn't see if Mary was alone or not, until presently she heard her voice saying tearfully: "I had to kiss baby—" then the voice died out in the distance "on the way to Canterbury," Mrs. Williams said most emphatically.

So far, you see, Inspector Meisures was able to fix the departure of the two sisters Nicholls from Ninescore on the night of January 23rd. Obviously they left their cottage about seven, went to Mrs. Williams, where Susan remained outside while Mary went in to say good-bye to the child.

After that all traces of them seem to have vanished. Whether they did go to Canterbury, and caught the last up train, at what station they alighted, or when poor Mary came back, could not at present be discovered.

According to the medical officer, the unfortunate girl must have been dead twelve or thirteen days at the very least, as, though the stagnant water may have accelerated decomposition, the head could not have got into such an advanced state much under a fortnight.

At Canterbury station neither the booking-clerk nor the porters could throw any light upon the subject. Canterbury West is a busy station, and scores of passengers buy tickets and go through the barriers every day. It was impossible, therefore, to give any positive information about two young women who may or may not have travelled by the last up train on Saturday, January 23rd—that is, a fortnight before.

One thing only was certain—whether Susan went to Canterbury and travelled by that up train or not, alone or with her sister—Mary had undoubtedly come back to Ninescore either the same night or the following day, since Timothy Coleman found her half-decomposed remains in the grounds of Ash Court a fortnight later.

Had she come back to meet her lover, or what? And where was Susan now?

From the first, therefore, you see, there was a great element of mystery about the whole case, and it was only natural that the local police should feel that, unless something more definite came out at the inquest, they would like to have the assistance of some of the fellows at the Yard.

So the preliminary notes were sent up to London, and some of them drifted into our hands. Lady Molly was deeply interested in it from the first, and my firm belief is that she simply worried the chief into allowing her to go down to Ninescore and see what she could do.

2

AT first it was understood that Lady Molly should only go down to

Canterbury after the inquest, if the local police still felt that they were in want of assistance from London. But nothing was further from my lady's intentions than to wait until then.

"I was not going to miss the first act of a romantic drama," she said to me just as our train steamed into Canterbury station. "Pick up your bag, Mary. We're going to tramp it to Ninescore—two lady artists on a sketching tour, remember—and we'll find lodgings in the village, I dare say."

We had some lunch in Canterbury, and then we started to walk the six and a half miles to Ninescore, carrying our bags. We put up at one of the cottages, where the legend "Apartments for single respectable lady or gentleman" had hospitably invited us to enter, and at eight o'clock the next morning we found our way to the local police-station, where the inquest was to take place. Such a funny little place, you know—just a cottage converted for official use—and the small room packed to its utmost holding capacity. The entire able-bodied population of the neighbourhood had, I verily believe, congregated in these ten cubic yards of stuffy atmosphere.

Inspector Meisures, apprised by the chief of our arrival, had reserved two good places for us well in sight of witnesses, coroner and jury. The room was insupportably close, but I assure you that neither Lady Molly nor I thought much about our comfort then. We were terribly interested.

From the outset the case seemed, as it were, to wrap itself more and more in its mantle of impenetrable mystery. There was precious little in the way of clues, only that awful intuition, that dark unspoken suspicion with regard to one particular man's guilt, which one could feel hovering in the minds of all those present.

Neither the police nor Timothy Coleman had anything to add to what was already known. The ring and purse were produced, also the dress worn by the murdered woman. All were sworn to by several witnesses as having been the property of Mary Nicholls.

Timothy, on being closely questioned, said that, in his opinion, the girl's body had been pushed into the mud, as the head was absolutely embedded in it, and he didn't see how she could have fallen like that.

Medical evidence was repeated; it was as uncertain—as vague—as before. Owing to the state of the head and neck it was impossible to ascertain by what means the death blow had been dealt. The doctor repeated his statement that the unfortunate girl must have been dead quite a fortnight. The body was discovered on February 5th—a fortnight before that would have been on or about January 23rd.

The caretaker who lived at the lodge at Ash Court could also throw but little light on the mysterious event. Neither he nor any member of his family had seen or heard anything to arouse their suspicions. Against that he explained that "The Wilderness," where the murder was committed, is situated some 200 yards from the lodge, with the mansion and flower garden lying between. Replying to a question put to him by a juryman, he said that that portion of the grounds is only divided off from Ninescore Lane by a low, brick wall, which has a door in it, opening into the lane almost opposite Elm Cottages. He added that the mansion had been empty for over a year, and that he succeeded the last man, who died, about twelve months ago. Mr. Lydgate had not been down for golf since witness had been in charge.

It would be useless to recapitulate all that the various witnesses had already told the police, and were now prepared to swear to. The private life of the two sisters Nicholls was gone into at full length, as much, at least, as was publicly known. But you know what village folk are; except when there is a bit of scandal and gossip, they know precious little of one another's inner lives.

The two girls appeared to be very comfortably off. Mary was always smartly dressed; and the baby girl, whom she had placed in Mrs. Williams's charge, had plenty of good and expensive clothes, whilst her keep, 5s. a week, was paid with unfailing regularity. What seemed certain, however, was that they did not get on well together, that Susan violently objected to Mary's association with Mr. Lydgate, and that recently she had spoken to the vicar asking him to try to persuade her sister to go away from Ninescore altogether, so as to break entirely with the past. The Reverend Octavius Ludlow, Vicar of Ninescore, seems thereupon to have had a little talk with Mary on the subject, suggesting that she should accept a good situation in London.

"But," continued the reverend gentleman, "I didn't make much impression on her. All she replied to me was that she certainly need never go into service, as she had a good income of her own, and could obtain £5,000 or more quite easily at any time if she chose."

"Did you mention Mr. Lydgate's name to her at all?" asked the coroner.

"Yes, I did," said the vicar, after a slight hesitation.

"Well, what was her attitude then?"

"I am afraid she laughed," replied the Reverend Octavius, primly, "and said very picturesquely, if somewhat ungrammatically, that 'some folks didn't know what they was talkin' about.'"

All very indefinite, you see. Nothing to get hold of, no motive suggested–beyond a very vague suspicion, perhaps, of blackmail–to account for a brutal crime. I must not, however, forget to tell you the two other facts which came to light in the course of this extraordinary inquest. Though, at the time, these facts seemed of wonderful moment for the elucidation of the mystery, they only helped ultimately to plunge the whole case into darkness still more impenetrable than before.

I am alluding, firstly, to the deposition of James Franklin, a carter in the employ of one of the local farmers. He stated that about half-past six on that same Saturday night, January 23rd, he was walking along Ninescore Lane leading his horse and cart, as the night was indeed pitch dark. Just as he came somewhere near Elm Cottages he heard a man's voice saying in a kind of hoarse whisper:

"Open the door, can't you? It's as dark as blazes!"

Then a pause, after which the same voice added:

"Mary, where the dickens are you?" Whereupon a girl's voice replied: "All right, I'm coming."

James Franklin heard nothing more after that, nor did he see anyone in the gloom.

With the stolidity peculiar to the Kentish peasantry, he thought no more of this until the day when he heard that Mary Nicholls had been murdered; then he voluntarily came forward and told his story to the police. Now, when he was closely questioned, he was quite unable to say whether these voices proceeded from that side of the lane where stand Elm Cottages or from the other side, which is edged by the low, brick wall.

Finally, Inspector Meisures, who really showed an extraordinary sense of what was dramatic, here produced a document which he had reserved for the last. This was a piece of paper which he had found in the red leather purse already mentioned, and which at first had not been thought very important, as the writing was identified by several people as that of the deceased, and consisted merely of a series of dates and hours scribbled in pencil on a scrap of notepaper. But suddenly these dates had assumed a weird and terrible significance: two of them, at least– December 26th and January 1st followed by "10 a.m."–were days on which Mr. Lydgate came over to Ninescore and took Mary for drives. One or two witnesses swore to this positively. Both dates had been local meets of the harriers, to which other folk from the village had gone, and Mary had openly said afterwards how much she had enjoyed these.

The other dates (there were six altogether) were more or less vague. One Mrs. Hooker remembered as being coincident with a day Mary Nicholls had spent away from home; but the last date, scribbled in the same handwriting, was January 23rd, and below it the hour–6 p.m.

The coroner now adjourned the inquest. An explanation from Mr. Lionel Lydgate had become imperative.

3

PUBLIC excitement had by now reached a very high pitch; it was no longer a case of mere local interest. The country inns all round the immediate neighbourhood were packed with visitors from London, artists, journalists, dramatists, and actor-managers, whilst the hotels and fly-proprietors of Canterbury were doing a roaring trade.

Certain facts and one vivid picture stood out clearly before the thoughtful mind in the midst of a chaos of conflicting and irrelevant evidence: the picture was that of the two women tramping in the wet and pitch dark night towards Canterbury. Beyond that everything was a blur.

When did Mary Nicholls come back to Ninescore, and why?

To keep an appointment made with Lionel Lydgate, it was openly whispered; but that appointment–if the rough notes were interpreted rightly–was for the very day on which she and her sister went away from home. A man's voice called to her at half-past six certainly, and she replied to it. Franklin, the carter, heard her; but half an hour afterwards Mrs. Hooker heard her voice when she left home with her sister, and she visited Mrs. Williams after that.

The only theory compatible with all this was, of course, that Mary merely accompanied Susan part of the way to Canterbury, then went back to meet her lover, who enticed her into the deserted grounds of Ash Court, and there murdered her.

The motive was not far to seek. Mr. Lionel Lydgate, about to marry, wished to silence for ever a voice that threatened to be unpleasantly persistent in its demands for money and in its threats of scandal.

But there was one great argument against that theory–the disappearance of Susan Nicholls. She had been extensively advertised for. The murder of her sister was published broadcast in every newspaper in the United Kingdom—she could not be ignorant of it. And, above all, she hated Mr. Lydgate. Why did she not come and add the weight of her testimony against him if, indeed, he was guilty?

And if Mr. Lydgate was innocent, then where was the criminal? And why had Susan Nicholls disappeared?

Why? Why? Why?

Well, the next day would show. Mr. Lionel Lydgate had been cited by the police to give evidence at the adjourned inquest.

Good-looking, very athletic, and obviously frightfully upset and nervous, he entered the little courtroom, accompanied by his solicitor, just before the coroner and jury took their seats.

He looked keenly at Lady Molly as he sat down, and from the expression on his face I guessed that he was much puzzled to know who she was.

He was the first witness called. Manfully and clearly he gave a concise account of his association with the deceased.

"She was pretty and amusing," he said. "I liked to take her out when I was in the neighborhood; it was no trouble to me. There was no harm in her, whatever the village gossips might say. I know she had been in trouble, as they say, but that had nothing to do with me. It wasn't for me to be hard on a girl, and I fancy that she has been very badly treated by some scoundrel."

Here he was hard pressed by the coroner, who wished him to explain what he meant. But Mr. Lydgate turned obstinate, and to every leading question he replied stolidly and very emphatically:

"I don't know who it was. It had nothing to do with me, but I was sorry for the girl because of everyone turning against her, including her sister, and I tried to give her a little pleasure when I could."

That was all right. Very sympathetically told. The public quite liked this pleasing specimen of English cricket-, golf- and football-loving manhood. Subsequently Mr. Lydgate admitted meeting Mary on December 26th and January 1st, but he swore most emphatically that that was the last he ever saw of her.

"But the 23rd of January," here insinuated the coroner; "you made an appointment with the deceased then?"

"Certainly not," he replied.

"But you met her on that day?"

"Most emphatically no," he replied quietly. "I went down to Edbrooke Castle, my brother's place in Lincolnshire, on the 20th of last month, and only got back to town about three days ago."

"You swear to that, Mr. Lydgate?" asked the coroner.

"I do, indeed, and there are a score of witnesses to bear me out. The family, the house-party, the servants."

He tried to dominate his own excitement. I suppose, poor man, he had only just realised that certain horrible suspicions had been resting upon him. His solicitor pacified him, and presently he sat down, whilst I must say that everyone there present was relieved at the thought that the handsome young athlete was not a murderer, after all. To look at him it certainly seemed preposterous.

But then, of course, there was the deadlock, and as there were no more witnesses to be heard, no new facts to elucidate, the jury returned the usual verdict against some person or persons unknown; and we, the keenly interested spectators, were left to face the problem—Who murdered Mary Nicholls, and where was her sister Susan?

4

AFTER the verdict we found our way back to our lodgings. Lady Molly tramped along silently, with that deep furrow between her brows which I knew meant that she was deep in thought.

"Now we'll have some tea," I said, with a sigh of relief, as soon as we entered the cottage door.

"No, you won't," replied my lady, dryly. "I am going to write out a telegram, and we'll go straight on to Canterbury and send it from there."

"To Canterbury!" I gasped. "Two hours' walk at least, for I don't suppose we can get a trap, and it is past three o'clock. Why not send your telegram from Ninescore?"

"Mary, you are stupid," was all the reply I got.

She wrote out two telegrams—one of which was at least three dozen words long—and, once more calling to me to come along, we set out for Canterbury.

I was tea-less, cross, and puzzled. Lady Molly was alert, cheerful, and irritatingly active.

We reached the first telegraph office a little before five. My lady sent the telegram without condescending to tell me anything of its destination or contents; then she took me to the Castle Hotel and graciously offered me tea.

"May I be allowed to inquire whether you propose tramping back to Ninescore to-night?" I asked with a slight touch of sarcasm, as I really felt put out.

"No, Mary," she replied, quietly munching a bit of Sally Lunn; "I have engaged a couple of rooms at this hotel and wired the chief that any message will find us here to-morrow morning."

After that there was nothing for it but quietude, patience, and finally supper and bed.

The next morning my lady walked into my room before I had finished dressing. She had a newspaper in her hand, and threw it down on the bed as she said calmly:

"It was in the evening paper all right last night. I think we shall be in time."

No use asking her what "it" meant. It was easier to pick up the paper, which I did. It was a late edition of one of the leading London evening shockers, and at once the front page, with its startling headline, attracted my attention:

MARY NICHOLL'S BABY DYING

Then, below that, a short paragraph:—

"We regret to learn that the little baby
daughter of the unfortunate girl who was
murdered recently at Ash Court, Ninescore,
Kent, under such terrible and mysterious

circumstances, is very seriously ill at the cottage of Mrs. Williams, in whose charge she is. The local doctor who visited her to-day declares that she cannot last more than a few hours. At the time of going to press the nature of the child's complaint was not known to our special representative at Ninescore."

"What does this mean?" I gasped.

But before she could reply there was a knock at the door.

"A telegram for Miss Granard," said the voice of the hall-porter.

"Quick, Mary," said Lady Molly, eagerly. "I told the chief and also Measures to wire here and to you."

The telegram turned out to have come from Ninescore, and was signed "Measures." Lady Molly read it aloud:

"Mary Nicholls arrived here this morning. Detained her at station. Come at once."

"Mary Nicholls! I don't understand," was all I could contrive to say.

But she only replied:

"I knew it! I knew it! Oh, Mary, what a wonderful thing is human nature, and how I thank Heaven that gave me a knowledge of it!"

She made me get dressed all in a hurry, and then we swallowed some breakfast hastily whilst a fly was being got for us. I had, perforce, to satisfy my curiosity from my own inner consciousness. Lady Molly was too absorbed to take any notice of me. Evidently the chief knew what she had done and approved of it: the telegram from Measures pointed to that.

My lady had suddenly become a personality. Dressed very quietly, and in a smart close-fitting hat, she looked years older than her age, owing also to the seriousness of her mien.

The fly took us to Ninescore fairly quickly. At the little police-station we found Measures awaiting us. He had Elliot and Pegram from the Yard with him. They had obviously got their orders, for all three of them were mighty deferential.

"The woman is Mary Nicholls, right enough," said Measures, as Lady Molly brushed quickly past him, "the woman who was supposed to have been murdered. It's that silly bogus paragraph about the infant brought her out of her hiding-place. I wonder how it got in," he added blandly; "the child is well enough."

"I wonder," said Lady Molly, whilst a smile—the first I had seen that morning—lit up her pretty face.

"I suppose the other sister will turn up too, presently," rejoined Elliot. "Pretty lot of trouble we shall have now. If Mary Nicholls is alive and kickin', who was murdered at Ash Court, say I?"

"I wonder," said Lady Molly, with the same charming smile.

Then she went in to see Mary Nicholls.

The Reverend Octavius Ludlow was sitting beside the girl, who seemed in great distress, for she was crying bitterly.

Lady Molly asked Elliott and the others to remain in the passage whilst she herself went into the room, I following behind her.

When the door was shut, she went up to Mary Nicholls, and assuming a hard and severe manner, she said:

"Well, you have at last made up your mind, have you, Nicholls? I suppose you know that we have applied for a warrant for your arrest?"

The woman gave a shriek which unmistakably was one of fear.

"My arrest?" she gasped. "What for?"

"The murder of your sister Susan."

"'Twasn't me!" she said quickly.

"Then Susan is dead?" retorted Lady Molly, quietly.

Mary saw that she had betrayed herself. She gave Lady Molly a look of agonised horror, then turned as white as a sheet and would have fallen had not the Reverend Octavius Ludlow gently led her to a chair.

"It wasn't me," she repeated, with a heart-broken sob.

"That will be for you to prove," said Lady Molly dryly. "The child cannot now, of course remain with Mrs. Williams; she will be removed to the workhouse, and–"

"No, that shan't be," said the mother excitedly. "She shan't be, I tell you. The workhouse, indeed," she added in a paroxysm of hysterical tears, "and her father a lord!"

The reverend gentleman and I gasped in astonishment; but Lady Molly had worked up to this climax so ingeniously that it was obvious she had guessed it all along, and had merely led Mary Nicholls on in order to get this admission from her.

How well she had known human nature in pitting the child against the sweetheart! Mary Nicholls was ready enough to hide herself, to part from her child even for a while, in order to save the man she had once loved from the consequences of his crime; but when she heard that her child was dying, she no longer could bear to leave it among strangers, and when Lady Molly taunted her with the workhouse, she exclaimed in her maternal pride:

"The workhouse! And her father a lord!"

Driven into a corner, she confessed the whole truth.

Lord Edbrooke, then Mr. Lydgate, was the father of her child. Knowing this, her sister Susan had, for over a year now, systematically blackmailed the unfortunate man–not altogether, it seems, without Mary's connivance. In January last she got him to come down to Ninescore under the distinct promise that Mary would meet him and hand over to him the letters she had received from him, as well as the ring he had given her, in exchange for the sum of £5,000.

The meeting-place was arranged, but at the last moment Mary was afraid to go in the dark. Susan, nothing daunted, but anxious about her own reputation in case she should be seen talking to a man so late at night, put on Mary's dress, took the ring and the letters, also her sister's purse, and went to meet Lord Edbrooke.

What happened at that interview no one will ever know. It ended with the murder of the blackmailer. I suppose the fact that Susan had, in measure, begun by impersonating her sister, gave the murderer the first thought of confusing the identity of his victim by the horrible device of burying the body in the slimy mud. Anyway, he almost did succeed in hoodwinking the police, and would have done so entirely but for Lady Molly's strange intuition in the matter.

After his crime he ran instinctively to Mary's cottage. He had to make a clean breast of it to her, as, without her help, he was a doomed man.

So he persuaded her to go away from home and to leave no clue or trace of herself or her sister in Ninescore. With the help of money which he would give her, she could begin life anew somewhere else, and no doubt he deluded the unfortunate girl with promises that her child would be restored to her very soon.

Thus he enticed Mary Nicholls away, who would have been the great and all-important witness against him the moment his crime was discovered. A girl of Mary's type and class instinctively obeys the man she has once loved, the man who is the father of her child. She consented to disappear and to allow all the world to believe that she had been murdered by some unknown miscreant.

Then the murderer quietly returned to his luxurious home at Edbrooke Castle, unsuspected. No one had thought of mentioning his name in connection with that of Mary Nicholls. In the days when he used to come down to Ash Court he was Mr. Lydgate, and, when he became a peer, sleepy, out-of-the-way Ninescore ceased to think of him.

Perhaps Mr. Lionel Lydgate knew all about his brother's association with the village girl. From his attitude at the inquest I should say he did, but of course he would not betray his own brother unless forced to do so.

Now, of course, the whole aspect of the case was changed: the veil of mystery had been torn asunder owing to the insight, the marvelous intuition, of a woman who, in my opinion, is the most wonderful psychologist of her time.

You know the sequel. Our fellows at the Yard, aided by the local police, took their lead from Lady Molly, and began their investigations of Lord Edbrooke's movements on or about the 23rd of January.

Even their preliminary inquiries revealed the fact that his lordship had left Edbrooke Castle on the 21st. He went up to town, saying to his wife and household that he was called away on business, and not even taking his valet with him. He put up at the Langham Hotel.

But here police investigations came to an abrupt ending. Lord Edbrooke evidently got wind of them. Anyway, the day after Lady Molly so cleverly enticed Mary Nicholls out of her hiding-place, and surprised her into an admission of the truth, the unfortunate man threw himself in front of the express train at Grantham railway station, and was instantly killed. Human justice cannot reach him now!

But don't tell me that a man would have thought of that bogus paragraph, or of the taunt which stung the motherly pride of the village girl to the quick, and thus wrung from her an admission which no amount of male ingenuity would ever have obtained.

THE FREWIN MINIATURES

ALTHOUGH, mind you, Lady Molly's methods in connection with the Ninescore mystery were not altogether approved of at the Yard, nevertheless, her shrewdness and ingenuity in the matter were so undoubted that they earned for her a reputation, then and there, which placed her in the foremost rank of the force. And presently, when everyone—public and police alike—were set by the ears over the Frewin miniatures, and a reward of 1,000 guineas was offered for information that would lead to the apprehension of the thief, the chief, of his own accord and without any hesitation, offered the job to her.

I don't know much about so-called works of art myself, but you can't be in the detective force, female or otherwise, without knowing something of the value of most things, and I don't think that Mr. Frewin put an excessive value on his Englehearts when he stated that they were worth £10,000. There were eight of them, all on ivory, about three to four inches high, and they were said to be the most perfect specimens of their kind. Mr. Frewin himself had had an offer for them, less than two years ago, of 200,000 francs from the trustees of the Louvre, which offer, mind you, he had refused. I dare say you know that he was an immensely wealthy man, a great collector himself, as well as dealer, and that several of the most unique and most highly priced works of art found their way into his private collection. Among them, of course, the Engleheart miniatures were the most noteworthy.

For some time before his death Mr. Frewin had been a great invalid, and for over two years he had not been able to go beyond the boundary of his charming property, Blatchley House, near Brighton.

There is a sad story in connection with the serious illness of Mr. Frewin—an illness which, if you remember, has since resulted in the poor old gentleman's death. He had an only son, a young man on whom the old art-dealer had lavished all the education and, subsequently, all the social advantages which money could give. The boy was exceptionally good-looking, and had inherited from his mother a great charm of manner which made him very popular. The Honourable Mrs. Frewin is the daughter of an English peer, more endowed with physical attributes than with worldly goods. Besides that, she is an exceptionally beautiful woman, has a glorious voice, is a fine violinist, and is no mean water-colour artist, having more than once exhibited at the Royal Academy.

Unfortunately, at one time, young Frewin had got into very bad company, made many debts, some of which were quite unavowable, and there were rumours current at the time to the effect that had the police got wind of certain transactions in connection with a brother officer's cheque, a very unpleasant prosecution would have followed. Be that as it may, young Lionel Frewin had to quit his regiment, and presently he went off to Canada, where he is supposed to have gone in for farming. According to the story related by some of the servants at Blatchley House, there were violent scenes between father and son before the former consented to pay some of the young spendthrift's most pressing debts, and then find the further sum of money which was to enable young Frewin to commence a new life in the colonies.

Mrs. Frewin, of course, took the matter very much to heart. She was a dainty, refined, artistic creature, who idolised her only son, but she had evidently no influence whatever over her husband, who, in common with certain English families of Jewish extraction, had an extraordinary hardness of character where the integrity of his own business fame was concerned. He absolutely never forgave his son what he considered a slur cast upon his name by the young spendthrift; he packed him off to Canada, and openly told him that he was to expect nothing further from him. All the Frewin money and the priceless art collection would be left by will to a nephew, James Hyam, whose honour and general conduct had always been beyond reproach.

That Mr. Frewin really took his hereto idolised son's defalcations very much to heart was shown by the fact that the poor old man's health completely broke down after that. He had an apoplectic fit, and, although he somewhat recovered, he always remained an invalid.

His eyesight and brain power were distinctly enfeebled, and about nine months ago he had a renewed seizure, which resulted in paralysis first, and subsequently in his death. The greatest, if not the only, joy the poor old man had during the two years which he spent pinned to an invalid chair was his art collection. Blatchley House was a perfect art museum, and the invalid would have his chair wheeled up and down the great hall and along the rooms where his pictures and china and, above all, where his priceless miniatures were stored. He took an enormous pride in these, and it was, I think, with a view to brightening him up a little that Mrs. Frewin invited Monsieur de Colinville—who had always been a great friend of her husband—to come and stay at Blatchley. Of course, there is no greater connoisseur of art anywhere than that distinguished Frenchman, and it was through him that the celebrated offer of £8,000 was made by the Louvre for the Engleheart miniatures.

Though, of course, the invalid declined the offer, he took a great pleasure and pride in the fact that it had been made, as, in addition to Monsieur de Colinville himself, several members of the committee of art advisers to the Louvre came over from Paris in order to try and persuade Mr. Frewin to sell his unique treasures.

However, the invalid was obdurate about that. He was not in want of money, and the celebrated Frewin art collection would go intact to his widow for her life, and then to his heir, Mr. James Hyam, a great connoisseur himself and art dealer of St. Petersburg and London.

It was really a merciful dispensation of Providence that the old man never knew of the disappearance of his valued miniatures. By the time that extraordinary mystery had come to light he was dead.

On the evening of January the 14th, at half-past eight, Mr. Frewin had a third paralytic seizure, from which he never recovered. His valet, Kennet, and his two nurses were with him at the time, and Mrs. Frewin, quickly apprised of the terrible event, flew to his bedside, whilst the motor was at once despatched for the doctor.

About an hour or two later the dying man seemed to rally somewhat, but he appeared very restless and agitated, and his eyes were roaming anxiously about the room.

"I expect it is his precious miniatures he wants," said Nurse Dawson. "He is always quiet when he can play with them."

She reached for the large, leather case which contained the priceless art treasures, and, opening it, placed it on the bed beside the patient. Mr. Frewin, however, was obviously too near death to care even for his favourite toy. He fingered the miniatures with trembling hands for a few moments, and then sank back exhausted on the pillows.

"He is dying," said the doctor quietly, turning to Mrs. Frewin.

"I have something to say to him," she then said. "Can I remain alone with him for a few minutes?"

"Certainly," said the doctor, as he himself discreetly retired; "but I think one of the nurses had better remain within earshot."

Nurse Dawson, it appeared, remained within earshot to some purpose, for she overheard what Mrs. Frewin was saying to her dying husband.

"It is about Lionel—your only son," she said. "Can you understand what I say?"

The sick man nodded.

"You remember that he is in Brighton, staying with Alicia. I can go and fetch him in the motor if you will consent to see him."

Again the dying man nodded. I suppose Mrs. Frewin took this to mean acquiescence, for the next moment she rang for John Chipps, the butler, and gave him instructions to order her motor at once. She then kissed the patient on the forehead and prepared to leave the room; but just before she did so, her eyes lighted on the case of miniatures, and she said to Kennet, the valet:

"Give these to Chipps, and tell him to put them in the library."

She then went to put on her furs preparatory to going out. When she was quite ready she met Chipps on the landing, who had just come up to tell her that the motor was at the door. He had in his hand the case of miniatures which Kennet had given him.

"Put the case on the library table, Chipps, when you go down," she said.

"Yes, madam," he replied.

He followed her downstairs, then slipped into the library, put the case on the table as he had been directed, after which he saw his mistress into the motor, and finally closed the front door.

2

ABOUT an hour later Mrs. Frewin came back, but without her son. It transpired afterwards that the young man was more vindictive than his father; he refused to go to the latter's bedside in order to be reconciled at the eleventh hour to a man who then had no longer either his wits or his physical senses about him. However, the dying man was spared the knowledge of his son's irreconcilable conduct, for, after a long and wearisome night passed in a state of coma, he died at about 6.00 a.m.

It was quite late the following afternoon when Mrs. Frewin suddenly recollected the case of miniatures, which should have been locked in their accustomed cabinet. She strolled leisurely into the library—she was very fatigued and worn out with the long vigil and the sorrow and anxiety she had just gone through. A quarter of an hour later John Chipps found her in the same room, sitting dazed and almost fainting in an arm-chair. In response to the old butler's anxious query, she murmured:

"The miniatures—where are they?"

Scared at the abruptness of the query and at his mistress's changed tone of voice, Chipps gazed quickly around him.

"You told me to put them on the table, ma'am," he murmured, "and I did so. They certainly don't seem to be in the room now—" he added, with a sudden feeling of terror.

"Run and ask one of the nurses at once if the case was taken up to Mr. Frewin's room during the night?"

Chipps, needless to say, did not wait to be told twice. He was beginning to feel very anxious. He spoke to Kennet and also to the two nurses, and asked them if, by any chance, the miniatures were in the late master's room. To this Kennet and the nurses replied in the negative. The last they had seen of the miniatures was when Chipps took them from the valet and followed his mistress downstairs with the case in his hands.

The poor old butler was in despair; the cook was in hysterics, and consternation reigned throughout the house. The disappearance of the miniatures caused almost a greater excitement than the death of the master, who had been a dying man so long that he was almost a stranger to the servants at Blatchley.

Mrs. Frewin was the first to recover her presence of mind.

"Send a motor at once to the police-station at Brighton," she said very calmly, as soon as she completely realised that the miniatures were nowhere to be found. "It is my duty to see that this matter is thoroughly gone into at once."

Within half an hour of the discovery of the theft, Detective Inspector Hankin and Police Constable McLeod had both arrived from Brighton, having availed themselves of Mrs. Frewin's motor. They are shrewd men, both of them, and it did not take them many minutes before they had made up their minds how the robbery had taken place. By whom it was done was quite another matter, and would take some time and some ingenuity to find out.

What Detective Inspector Hankin had gathered was this: While John Chipps saw his mistress into the motor, the front door of the house had, of necessity, been left wide open. The motor then made a start, but after a few paces it stopped, and Mrs. Frewin put her head out of the window and shouted to Chipps some instructions with regard to the nurses' evening collation, which, in view of Mr. Frewin's state, she feared might be forgotten.

Chipps, being an elderly man and a little deaf, did not hear her voice distinctly, so he ran up to the motor, and she repeated her instructions to him. In Inspector Hankin's mind there was no doubt that the thief, who must have been hanging about the shrubbery that evening, took that opportunity to sneak into the house, then to hide himself in a convenient spot until he could find an opportunity for the robbery which he had in view.

The butler declared that, when he returned, he saw nothing unusual. He had only been gone a little over a minute; he then fastened and bolted the front door, and, according to his usual custom, he put up all the shutters of the ground-floor windows, including, of course, those in the library. He had no light with him when he did this accustomed round, for, of course, he knew his way well enough in the dark, and the electric chandelier in the hall gave him what light he wanted.

While he was putting up the shutters, Chipps was giving no particular thought to the miniatures, but, strangely enough, he seems to have thought of them about an hour later, when most of the servants had gone to bed and he was waiting up for his mistress. He then, quite casually and almost absent-mindedly, when crossing the hall, turned the key of the library door, thus locking it from the outside.

Of course, throughout all this we must remember that Blatchley House was not in its normal state that night, since its master was actually dying in a room on the floor above the library. The two nurses and Kennet, the valet, were all awake, and with him during the whole of that night. Kennet certainly was in and out of the room several times, having to run down and fetch various things required by the doctor or the nurses. In order to do this he did not use the principal staircase, nor did he have to cross the hall, but, as far as the upper landing and the secondary stairs were concerned, he certainly had not noticed anything unusual or suspicious; whilst when Mrs. Frewin came home, she went straight up to the first floor, and certainly noticed nothing in any way to arouse her suspicions. But, of course, this meant very little, as she certainly must have been too upset and agitated to see anything.

The servants were not apprised of the death of their master until after their breakfast. In the meanwhile Emily, the housemaid, had been in, as usual, to "do" the library. She distinctly noticed, when she first went in, that none of the shutters were up and that one of the windows was open. She thought at the time that someone must have been in the room before her, and meant to ask Chipps about it, when the news of the master's death drove all thoughts of open windows from her mind. Strangely enough, when Hankin questioned her more closely about it, and she had had time to recollect everything more clearly, she made the extraordinary statement that she certainly had noticed that the door of the library was locked on the outside when she first went into the room, the key being in the lock.

"Then, didn't it strike you as very funny," asked Hankin, "that the door was locked on the outside, and yet that the shutters were unbarred and one of the windows was open?"

"Yes, I did seem to think of that," replied Emily, with that pleasant vagueness peculiar to her class; "but then, the room did not look like burglars—it was quite tidy, just as it had been left last night, and burglars always seem to leave a great mess behind, else I should have noticed," she added, with offended dignity.

"But did you not see that the miniatures were not in their usual place?"

"Oh they often wasn't in the cabinet, as the master used to ask for them sometimes to be brought to his room."

That was, of course, indisputable. It was clearly evident that the burglar had had plenty of chances to make good his escape. You see, the actual time when the miscreant must have sneaked into the room had now been narrowed down to about an hour and a half, between the time when Mrs. Frewin finally left in her motor to about an hour later, when Chipps turned the key in the door of the library and thus undoubtedly locked the thief in. At what precise time of the night he effected his escape could not anyhow be ascertained. It must have been after Mrs. Frewin came back again, as Hankin held that she or her chauffeur would have noticed that one of the library windows was open. This opinion was not shared by Elliott from the Yard, who helped in the investigation of this mysterious crime, as Mrs. Frewin was certainly very agitated and upset that evening, and her powers of perception would necessarily be blunted. As for the chauffeur: we all know that the strong headlights on a motor are so dazzling that nothing can be seen outside their blinding circle of light.

Be that as it may, it remained doubtful when the thief made good his escape. It was easy enough to effect, and, as there is a square of flagstones in front of the main door and just below the library windows, the thief left not the slightest trace of footprints, whilst the drop from the window is less than eight feet.

What was strange in the whole case, and struck Detective Hankin immediately, was the fact that the burglar, whoever he was, must have known a great deal about the house and its ways. He also must have had a definite purpose in his mind not usually to be found in the brain of a common housebreaker. He must have meant to steal the miniatures and nothing else, since he made his way straight to the library, and, having secured the booty, at once made good his escape without trying to get any other article which could more easily be disposed of than works of art.

You may imagine, therefore, how delicate a task now confronted Inspector Hankin. You see, he had questioned everyone in the house, including Mr. Frewin's valet and nurses, and from them he casually heard of Mrs. Frewin's parting words to her dying husband and of her mention of the scapegrace son, who was evidently in the immediate neighbourhood, and whom she wished to come and see his father. Mrs. Frewin, closely questioned by the detective, admitted that her son was staying in Brighton, and that she saw him that very evening.

"Mr. Lionel Frewin is staying at the Metropole Hotel," she said coldly, "and he was dining with my sister, Lady Steyne, last night. He was in the house at Sussex Square when I arrived in my motor," she added hastily, guessing, perhaps, the unavowed suspicion which had arisen in Hankin's mind, "and he was still there when I left. I drove home very fast, naturally, as my husband's condition was known to me to be quite hopeless, and that he was not expected to live more than perhaps a few hours. We covered the seven miles between this house and that of my sister in less than a quarter of an hour."

This statement of Mrs. Frewin's was, if you remember, fully confirmed both by her sister and her brother-in-law, Lady Steyne and Sir Michael. There was no doubt that young Lionel Frewin was staying at the Hotel Metropole in Brighton, that he was that evening dining with the Steynes at Sussex Square when his mother arrived in her motor. Mrs. Frewin stayed about an hour, during which time she, presumably, tried to influence her son to go back to Blatchley with her in order to see his dying father. Of course, what exactly happened at that family interview none of the four people present was inclined to reveal. Against that both Sir Michael and Lady Steyne were prepared to swear that Mr. Lionel Frewin was in the house when his mother arrived, and that he did not leave them until long after she had driven away.

There lay the hitch, you see, for already the public jumped to conclusions, and, terribly prejudiced as it is in a case of this sort, it had made up its mind that Mr. Lionel Frewin, once more pressed for money, had stolen his father's precious miniatures in order to sell them in America for a high sum. Everyone's sympathy was dead against the young son who refused to be reconciled to his father, although the latter was dying.

According to one of the footmen in Lady Steyne's employ, who had taken whiskies and sodas in while the interview between Mrs. Frewin and her son was taking place, Mr. Lionel had said very testily:

"It's all very well, mother, but that is sheer sentimentality. The guv'nor threw me on my beam ends when a little kindness and help would have meant a different future to me; he chose to break my life because of some early peccadilloes—and I am not going to fawn round him and play the hypocrite when he has no intention of altering his will and has cut me off with a shilling. He must be half imbecile by now, and won't know me anyway."

But with all this, and with public opinion so dead against him, it was quite impossible to bring the crime home to the young man. The burglar, whoever he was, must have sneaked into the library some time before Chipps closed the door on the outside, since it was still so found by Emily the following morning. Thereupon the public, determined that Lionel Frewin should in some way be implicated in the theft, made up its mind that the doting mother, hearing of her son's woeful want of money, stole the miniatures herself that night and gave them to him.

3

WHEN Lady Molly heard this theory she laughed, and shrugged her pretty shoulders.

"Old Mr. Frewin was dying, was he not, at the time of the burglary?" she said. "Why should his wife, soon to become his widow, take the trouble to go through a laboured and daring comedy of a burglary in order to possess herself of things which would become hers within the next few hours? Even if, after Mr. Frewin's death, she could not actually dispose of the miniatures, the old man left her a large sum of money and a big income by his will, with which she could help her spendthrift son as much as she pleased."

This was, of course, why the mystery in this strange case was so deep. At the Yard they did all that they could. Within forty-eight hours they had notices printed in almost every European language, which contained rough sketches of the stolen miniatures hastily supplied by Mrs. Frewin herself. These were sent to as many of the great museums and art collectors abroad as possible, and of course to the principal American cities and to American millionaires. There is no doubt that the thief would find it very difficult to dispose of the miniatures, and until he could sell them his booty would, of course, not benefit him in any way. Works of art cannot be tampered with, or melted down or taken to pieces, like silver or jewellery, and, so far as could be ascertained, the thief did not appear to make the slightest attempt to dispose of the booty, and the mystery became more dark, more impenetrable than ever.

"Will you undertake the job?" said the chief one day to Lady Molly.

"Yes," she replied, "on two distinct conditions."

"What are they?"

"That you will not bother me with useless questions, and that you will send out fresh notices to all the museums and art collectors you can think of, and request them to let you know of any art purchases they may have made within the last two years."

"The last two years!" ejaculated the chief, "why, the miniatures were only stolen three months ago."

"Did I not say that you were not to ask me useless questions?"

This to the chief, mind you; and he only smiled, whilst I nearly fell backwards at her daring. But he did send out the notices, and it was generally understood that Lady Molly now had charge of the case.

4

IT was about seven weeks later when, one morning, I found her at breakfast looking wonderfully bright and excited.

"The Yard has had sheaves of replies, Mary," she said gaily, "and the chief still thinks I am a complete fool."

"Why, what has happened?"

"Only this, that the art museum at Budapest has now in its possession a set of eight miniatures by Engleheart; but the authorities did not think that the first notices from Scotland Yard could possibly refer to these, as they had been purchased from a private source a little over two years ago."

"But two years ago the Frewin miniatures were still at Blatchley House, and Mr. Frewin was fingering them daily," I said, not understanding, and wondering what she was driving at.

"I know that," she said gaily, "so does the chief. That is why he thinks that I am a first-class idiot."

"But what do you wish to do now?"

"Go to Brighton, Mary, take you with me and try to elucidate the mystery of the Frewin miniatures."

"I don't understand," I gasped, bewildered.

"No, and you won't until we get there," she replied, running up to me and kissing me in her pretty, engaging way.

That same afternoon we went to Brighton and took up our abode at the Hotel

Metropole. Now you know I always believed from the very first that she was a born lady and all the rest of it, but even I was taken aback at the number of acquaintances and smart friends she had all over the place. It was "Hello, Lady Molly! whoever would have thought of meeting you here?" and "Upon my word! this is good luck," all the time.

She smiled and chatted gaily with all the folk as if she had known them all her life, but I could easily see that none of these people knew that she had anything to do with the Yard.

Brighton is not such a very big place as one would suppose, and most of the fashionable residents of the gay city find their way sooner or later to the luxurious dining-room of the Hotel Metropole, if only for a quiet little dinner given when the cook is out. Therefore I was not a little surprised when, one evening, about a week after our arrival and just as we were sitting down to the table d'hôte dinner, Lady Molly suddenly placed one of her delicate hands on my arm.

"Look behind you, a little to your left, Mary, but not just this minute. When you do you will see two ladies and two gentlemen sitting at a small table quite close to us. They are Sir Michael and Lady Steyne, the Honourable Mrs. Frewin in deep black, and her son, Mr. Lionel Frewin."

I looked round as soon as I could, and gazed with some interest at the hero and heroine of the Blatchley House drama. We had a quiet little dinner, and Lady Molly having all of a sudden become very silent and self-possessed, altogether different from her gay, excited self of the past few days, I scented that something important was in the air, and tried to look as unconcerned as my lady herself. After dinner we ordered coffee, and as Lady Molly strolled through into the lounge, I noticed that she ordered our tray to be placed at a table which was in very close proximity to one already occupied by Lady Steyne and her party.

Lady Steyne, I noticed, gave Lady Molly a pleasant nod when we first came in, and Sir Michael got up and bowed, saying, "How d'ye do?" We sat down and began a desultory conversation together. Soon, as usual, we were joined by various friends and acquaintances who all congregated round our table and set themselves to entertaining us right pleasantly. Presently the conversation drifted to art matter, Sir Anthony Truscott being there, who is, as you know, one of the keepers of the Art Department at South Kensington Museum.

"I am crazy about miniatures just now," said Lady Molly in response to a remark from Sir Anthony.

I tried not to look astonished.

"And Miss Granard and I," continued my lady, quite unblushingly, "have been travelling all over the Continent in order to try and secure some rare specimens."

"Indeed," said Sir Anthony. "Have you found anything very wonderful?"

"We certainly have discovered some rare works of art," replied Lady Molly, "have we not, Mary? Now the two Englehearts we bought at Budapest are undoubtedly quite unique."

"Engleheart–and at Budapest!" remarked Sir Anthony. "I thought I knew the collections at most of the great Continental cities, but I certainly have no recollection of such treasures in the Hungarian capital."

"Oh, they were only purchased two years ago, and have only been shown to the public recently," remarked Lady Molly. "There was originally a set of eight, so the comptroller, Mr. Pulszky, informed me. He bought them from an English collector whose name I have now forgotten, and he is very proud of them, but they cost the country a great deal more money than it could afford, and in order somewhat to recoup himself Mr. Pulszky sold two out of the eight at, I must say, a very stiff price."

While she was talking I could not help noticing the strange glitter in her eyes. Then a curious smothered sound broke upon my ear. I turned and saw Mrs. Frewin looking with glowing and dilated eyes at the charming picture presented by Lady Molly.

"I should like to show you my purchases," said the latter to Sir Anthony. "One or two foreign connoisseurs have seen the two miniatures and declare them to be the finest in existence. Mary," she added, turning to me, "would you be so kind as to run up to my room and get me the small sealed packet which is at the bottom of my dressing-case? Here are the keys."

A little bewildered, yet guessing by her manner that I had a part to play, I took the keys from her and went up to her room. In her dressing-case I certainly found a small, square, flat packet, and with that in my hand I prepared to go downstairs again. I had just locked the bedroom door when I was suddenly confronted by a tall, graceful woman dressed in deep black, whom I at once recognised as the Honourable Mrs. Frewin.

"You are Miss Granard?" she said quickly and excitedly; her voice was tremulous and she seemed a prey to the greatest possible excitement. Without waiting for my reply she continued eagerly:

"Miss Granard, there is no time to be more explicit, but I give you my word, the word of a very wretched, heart-broken woman, that my very life depends upon my catching a glimpse of the contents of the parcel that you now have in your hand."

"But–" I murmured, hopelessly bewildered.

"There is no 'but,' she replied. "It is a matter of life and death. Her are £200, Miss Granard, if you will let me handle that packet," and with trembling hands she drew a bundle of bank-notes from her reticule.

I hesitated, not because I had any notion of acceding to Mrs. Frewin's request, but because I did not quite know how I ought to act at this strange juncture, when a pleasant, mellow voice broke in suddenly:

"You may take the money, Mary, if you wish. You have my permission to hand the packet over to this lady," and Lady Molly, charming, graceful and elegant in her beautiful directoire gown, stood smiling some few feet away, with Hankin just visible in the gloom of the corridor.

She advanced towards us, took the small packet from my hands, and held it out towards Mrs. Frewin.

"Will you open it?" she said, "or shall I?"

Mrs. Frewin did not move. She stood as if turned to stone. Then with dexterous fingers my lady broke the seals of the packet and drew from it a few sheets of plain white cardboard and a thin piece of match-boarding.

"There!" said Lady Molly, fingering the bits of cardboard while she kept her fine large eyes fixed on Mrs. Frewin; "£200 is a big price to pay for a sight of these worthless things."

"Then this was a vulgar trick," said Mrs. Frewin, drawing herself up with an air which did not affect Lady Molly in the least.

"A trick, certainly," she replied with her winning smile, "vulgar, if you will call it so—pleasant to us all, Mrs. Frewin, since you so readily fell into it."

"Well, and what are you going to do next?"

"Report the matter to my chief," said Lady Molly, quietly. "We have all been very severely blamed for not discovering sooner the truth about the disappearance of the Frewin miniatures."

"You don't know the truth now," retorted Mrs. Frewin.

"Oh, yes, I do," replied Lady Molly, still smiling. "I know that two years ago your son, Mr. Lionel Frewin, was in terrible monetary difficulties. There was something unavowable, which he dared not tell his father. You had to set to work to find money somehow. You had no capital at your own disposal, and you wished to save your son from the terrible consequences of his own folly. It was soon after M. de Colinville's visit. Your husband had had his first apoplectic seizure; his mind and eyesight were somewhat impaired. You are a clever artist yourself, and you schemed out a plan whereby you carefully copied the priceless miniatures and then entrusted them to your son for sale to the Art Museum at Budapest, where there was but little likelihood of their being seen by anyone who knew they had belonged to your husband. English people do not stay more than one night there, at the Hotel Hungaria. Your copies were works of art in themselves, and you had no difficulty in deceiving your husband in the state of mind he then was, but when he lay dying you realised that his will would inevitably be proved, wherein he bequeathed the miniatures to Mr. James Hyam, and that these would have to be valued for probate. Frightened now that the substitution would be discovered, you devised the clever comedy of the burglary at Blatchley, which, in the circumstances, could never be brought home to you or your son. I don't know where you subsequently concealed the spurious Engleheart miniatures which you calmly took out of the library and hid away during the night of your husband's death, but no doubt our men will find that out," she added quietly, "now that they are on the track."

With a frightened shriek Mrs. Frewin turned as if she would fly, but Lady Molly was too quick for her, and barred the way. Then, with that wonderful charm of manner and that innate kindliness which always characterised her, she took hold of the unfortunate woman's wrist.

"Let me give you a word of advice," she said gently. "We at the Yard will be quite content with a confession from you, which will clear us of negligence and satisfy us that the crime has been brought home to its perpetrator. After that try and enter into an arrangement with your husband's legatee, Mr. James Hyam. Make a clean breast of the whole thing to him and offer him full monetary compensation. For the sake of the family he won't refuse. He would have nothing to gain by bruiting the whole thing abroad; and for his own sake and that of his late uncle, who was so good to him, I don't think you would find him hard to deal with."

Mrs. Frewin paused awhile, undecided and still defiant. Then her attitude softened; she turned and looked full at the beautiful, kind eyes turned eagerly up to hers, and pressing Lady Molly's tiny hand in both her own she whispered:

"I will take your advice. God bless you."

She was gone, and Lady Molly called Hankin to her side.

"Until we have that confession, Hankin," she said, with the quiet manner she always adopted where matters connected with her work were concerned, "Mum's the word."

"Ay, and after that, too, my lady," replied Hankin, earnestly.

You see, she could do anything she liked with the men, and I, of course, was her slave.

Now we have got the confession, Mrs. Frewin is on the best of terms with Mr. James Hyam, who has behaved very well about the whole thing, and the public has forgotten all about the mystery of the Frewin miniatures.

THE IRISH-TWEED COAT

IT all began with the murder of Mr. Andrew Carrthwaite, at Palermo.

He had been found dead in the garden of his villa just outside the town, with a stiletto between his shoulder blades and a piece of rough Irish tweed, obviously torn from his assailant's coat, clutched tightly in his hand.

All that was known of Mr. Carrthwaite over here was that he was a Yorkshireman, owner of some marble works in Sicily, a man who employed a great many hands; and that, unlike most employers of labour over there, he had a perfect horror of the many secret societies and Socialist clubs which abound in that part of the world. He would not become a slave to the ever-growing tyranny of the Mafia and its kindred associations, and therefore he made it a hard and fast rule that no workman employed by him, from the foremost to the meanest hand, should belong to any society, club, or trade union of any sort or kind.

At first, robbery was thought to have been the sole object of the crime, for Mr. Carrthwaite's gold watch, marked with his initials "A. C.," and his chain were missing, but the Sicilian police were soon inclined to the belief that this was merely a blind, and that personal spite and revenge were at the bottom of that dastardly outrage.

One clue, remember, had remained in the possession of the authorities. This was the piece of rough Irish tweed, found in the murdered man's hand.

Within twenty-four hours a dozen witnesses were prepared to swear that that fragment of cloth was part of a coat habitually worn by Mr. Carrthwaite's English overseer, Mr. Cecil Shuttleworth. It appears that this young man had lately, in defiance of the rigid rules prescribed by his employer, joined a local society–semi-social, semi-religious–which came under the ban of the old Yorkshireman's prejudices.

Apparently there had been several bitter quarrels between Mr. Carrthwaite and young Shuttleworth, culminating in one tempestuous scene, witnessed by the former's servants at his villa; and although these people did not understand the actual words that passed between the two Englishmen, it was pretty clear that they amounted to an ultimatum on the one side and defiance on the other. The dismissal of the overseer followed immediately, and that same evening Mr. Carrthwaite was found murdered in his garden.

Mind you–according to English ideas–the preliminary investigations in that mysterious crime were hurried through in a manner which we should think unfair to the accused. It seemed from the first as if the Sicilian police had wilfully made up their minds that Shuttleworth was guilty. For instance, although so many people were prepared to swear that the young English overseer had often worn a coat of which the piece found in the murdered man's hand was undoubtedly a torn fragment, yet the coat itself was not found among his effects, neither were his late master's watch and chain.

Nevertheless, the young man was arrested within a few hours of the murder, and–after the formalities of the preliminary "instruction"–was duly committed to stand his trial on the capital charge.

It was about this time that I severed my official connection with the Yard. Lady Molly now employed me as her private secretary, and I was working with her one day in the study of our snug little flat in Maida Vale, when our trim servant came in to us with a card and a letter on a salver.

Lady Molly glanced at the card, then handed it across to me. It bore the name: Mr. Jeremiah Shuttleworth.

The letter was from the chief.

"Not much in it," she commented, glancing rapidly at its contents. "The chief only says, 'This is the father of the man who is charged with the Palermo murder. As obstinate as a mule, but you have my permission to do what he wants.' Emily, show the gentleman in," she added.

The next moment a short, thick-set man entered our little study. He had sandy hair and a freckled skin; there was a great look of determination in the square face and a fund of dogged obstinacy in the broad, somewhat heavy jaw. In response to Lady Molly's invitation he sat down and began with extraordinary abruptness:

"I suppose you know what I have come about–er–miss?" he suggested.

"Well!" she replied, holding up his own card, "I can guess."

"My son, miss–I mean ma'am," he said in a husky voice. "He is innocent. I swear it by the living–"

He checked himself, obviously ashamed of this outburst; then he resumed more calmly.

"Of course, there's the business about the coat, and that coat did belong to my son, but–"

"Well, yes?" asked Lady Molly, for he had paused again, as if waiting to be encouraged in his narrative, "what about that coat?"

"It has been found in London, miss," he replied quietly. "The fiendish brutes who committed the crime thought out this monstrous way of diverting attention from themselves by getting hold of my son's coat and making the actual assassin wear it, in case he was espied in the gloom."

There was silence in the little study for awhile. I was amazed, aghast at the suggestion put forward by that rough north-countryman, that sorely stricken father who spoke with curious intensity of language and of feeling. Lady Molly was the first to break the solemn silence.

"What makes you think, Mr. Shuttleworth, that the assassination of Mr. Carrthwaite was the work of a gang of murderers?" she asked.

"I know Sicily," he replied simply. "My boy's mother was a native of Messina. The place is riddled with secret societies, murdering, anarchical clubs: organisations against which Mr. Carrthwaite waged deadly warfare. It is one of these–the Mafia, probably–that decreed that Mr. Carrthwaite should be done away with. They could not do with such a powerful and hard-headed enemy."

"You may be right, Mr. Shuttleworth, but tell me more about the coat."

"Well, that'll be damning proof against the blackguards, anyway. I am on the eve of a second marriage, miss—ma'am," continued the man with seeming irrelevance. "The lady is a widow. Mrs. Tadworth is her name—but her father was an Italian named Badeni, a connection of my first wife's, and that's how I came to know him and his daughter. You know Leather Lane, don't you? It might be in Italy, for Italian's the only language one hears about there. Badeni owned a house in Bread Street, Leather Lane, and let lodgings to his fellow-countrymen there; this business my future wife still carries on. About a week ago two men arrived at the house, father and son, so they said, who wanted a cheap bedroom; all their meals, including breakfast, they would take outside, and would be out, moreover, most of the day.

"It seems that they had often lodged at Badeni's before—the old reprobate no doubt was one of their gang—and when they understood that Mrs. Tadworth was their former friend's daughter they were quite satisfied.

"They gave their name as Piatti, and told Mrs. Tadworth that they came from Turin. But I happened to hear them talking on the stairs, and I knew that they were Sicilians, both of them.

"You may well imagine that just now everything hailing from Sicily is of vital importance to me, and somehow I suspected those two men from the very first. Mrs. Tadworth is quite at one with me in wanting to move heaven and earth to prove the innocence of my boy. She watched those people for me as a cat would watch a mouse. The older man professed to be very fond of gardening, and presently he obtained Mrs. Tadworth's permission to busy himself in the little strip of barren ground at the back of the house. This she told me last night whilst we were having supper together in her little parlour. Somehow I seemed to get an inspiration like. The Piattis had gone out together as usual for their evening meal. I got a spade and went out into the strip of garden, I worked for about an hour, and then my heart gave one big leap—my spade had met a certain curious, soft resistance—the next moment I was working away with hands and nails, and soon unearthed a coat—the coat, miss," he continued, unable now to control his excitement, "with the bit torn out of the back, and in the pocket the watch and chain belonging to the murdered man, for they bear the initials 'A. C.' The fiendish brutes! I knew it—I knew it, and now I can prove the innocence of my boy!"

Again there was a pause. I was too much absorbed in the palpitating narrative to attempt to breathe a word, and I knew that Lady Molly was placidly waiting until the man had somewhat recovered from his vehement outburst.

"Of course, you can prove your boy's innocence now," she said, smiling encouragingly into his flushed face. "But what have you done with the coat?"

"Left it buried where I found it," he replied more calmly. "They must not suspect that I am on their track."

She nodded approvingly.

"No doubt, then, my chief has told you that the best course to pursue now will be to place the whole matter in the hands of the English police. Our people at Scotland Yard will then immediately communicate with the Sicilian authorities, and in the meanwhile we can keep the two men in Leather Lane well under surveillance."

"Yes, he told me all that," said Mr. Shuttleworth, quietly.

"Well?"

"And I told him that his 'communicating with the Sicilian police authorities' would result in my boy's trial being summarily concluded, in his being sent to the gallows, whilst every proof of his innocence would be destroyed, or, at any rate, kept back until too late."

"You are mad, Mr. Shuttleworth!" she ejaculated.

"Maybe I am," he rejoined quietly. "You see, you do not know Sicily, and I do. You do not know its many clubs and bands of assassins, beside whom the so-called Russian Nihilists are simple, blundering children. The Mafia, which is the parent of all such murderous organisations, has members and agents in every town, village, and hamlet in Italy, in every post-office and barracks, in every trade and profession from the highest to the lowest in the land. The Sicilian police force is infested with it, so are the Italian customs. I would not trust either with what means my boy's life and more to me."

"But–"

"The police would suppress the evidence connected with the proofs which I hold. At the frontier the coat, the watch and chain would disappear; of that I am as convinced as that I am a living man–"

Lady Molly made no comment. She was meditating. That there was truth in what the man said, no one could deny.

The few details which we had gleaned over here of the hurried investigations, the summary commitment for trial of the accused, the hasty dismissal of all evidence in his favour, proved that, at any rate, the father's anxiety was well founded.

"But, then, what in the world do you propose to do?" said Lady Molly after a while. "Do you want to take the proofs over yourself to your boy's advocate? Is that it?"

"No, that would be no good," he replied simply. "I am known in Sicily. I should be watched, probably murdered, too, and my death would not benefit my boy."

"But what then?"

"My boy's uncle is chief officer of police at Cividale, on the Austro-Italian frontier. I know that I can rely on his devotion. Mrs. Tadworth, whose interest in my boy is almost equal to my own, and whose connection with me cannot possibly be known out there, will take the proofs of my boy's innocence to him. He will know what to do and how to reach my son's advocate safely, which no one else could guarantee to do."

"Well," said Lady Molly, "that being so, what is it that you want us to do in the matter?"

"I want a lady's help, miss–er–ma'am," he replied, "someone who is able, willing, strong, and, if possible, enthusiastic, to accompany Mrs. Tadworth–perhaps in the capacity of a maid–just to avert the usual suspicious glances thrown at a lady traveling alone. Also the question of foreign languages comes in. The gentleman I saw at Scotland Yard said that if you cared to go he would give you a fortnight's leave of absence."

"Yes, I'll go!" rejoined Lady Molly, simply.

2

WE sat in the study a long while after that—Mr. Shuttleworth, Lady Molly and I—discussing the plans of the exciting journey; for I, too, as you will see, was destined to play my small part in this drama which had the life or death of an innocent man for its dénouement.

I don't think I need bore you with an account of our discussion; all, I think, that will interest you is the plan of campaign we finally decided upon.

There seemed to be no doubt that Mr. Shuttleworth had succeeded so far in not arousing the suspicions of the Piattis. Therefore, that night, when they were safely out of the way, Mr. Shuttleworth would once more unearth the coat, and watch and chain, and then bury a coat similar in colour and texture in that same hole in the ground; this might perhaps serve to put the miscreants off their guard, if by any chance one of them should busy himself again in the garden.

After that Mrs. Tadworth would hide about her the proofs of young Shuttleworth's innocence and join Lady Molly at our flat in Maida Vale, where she would spend the night preparatory to the two ladies leaving London for abroad, the following morning, by the 9.0 a.m. train from Charing Cross en route for Vienna, Budapest, and finally Cividale.

But our scheme was even more comprehensive than that and herein lay my own little share in it, of which I tell you presently.

The same evening at half-past nine Mrs. Tadworth arrived at the flat with the coat, and watch and chain, which were to be placed in the hands of Colonel Grassi, the chief police officer at Cividale.

I took a keen look at the lady, you may be sure of that. It was a pretty little face enough, and she herself could not have been much more than seven or eight and twenty, but to me the whole appearance and manner of the woman suggested weakness of character, rather than that devotion on which poor Mr. Shuttleworth so implicitly relied.

I suppose that it was on that account that I felt unaccountably down-hearted and anxious when I bade farewell to my own dear lady—a feeling in which she obviously did not share. Then I began to enact the rôle which had been assigned to me.

I dressed up in Mrs. Tadworth's clothes—we were about the same height—and putting on her hat and closely fitting veil, I set out for Leather Lane. For as many hours as I could possibly contrive to keep up the deception, I was to impersonate Mrs. Tadworth in her own house.

As I dare say you have guessed by now, that lady was not in affluent circumstances, and the house in a small by-street off Leather Lane did not boast of a staff of servants. In fact, Mrs. Tadworth did all the domestic work herself, with the help of a charwoman for a couple of hours in the mornings.

That charwoman had, in accordance with Lady Molly's plan, been given a week's wages in lieu of notice. I—as Mrs. Tadworth—would be supposed the next day to be confined to my room with a cold, and Emily—our own little maid, a bright girl, who would go through fire and water for Lady Molly or for me—would represent a new charwoman.

As soon as anything occurred to arouse my suspicions that our secret had been discovered, I was to wire to Lady Molly at the various points which she gave me.

Thus provided with an important and comprehensive part, I duly installed myself at Bread Street, Leather Lane. Emily—who had been told just enough of the story, and no more, to make her eager, excited and satisfied—entered into the spirit of her rôle as eagerly as I did myself.

That first night was quite uneventful. The Piattis came home some time after eleven and went straight up to their room.

Emily, looking as like a bedraggled charwoman as her trim figure would allow, was in the hall the next morning when the two men started off for breakfast. She told me afterwards that the younger one looked at her very keenly, and asked her why the other servant had gone. Emily replied with due and proper vagueness, whereupon the Sicilians said no more and went out together.

That was a long and wearisome day which I spent cooped up in the tiny, stuffy parlour, ceaselessly watching the tiny patch of ground at the back, devoured with anxiety, following the travellers in my mind on their way across Europe.

Towards midday one of the Piattis came home and presently strolled out into the garden. Evidently the change of servants had aroused his suspicions, for I could see him feeling about the earth with his spade and looking up now and again towards the window of the parlour, whereat I contrived to show him the form of a pseudo Mrs. Tadworth moving about the room.

Mr. Shuttleworth and I were having supper in that same back parlour at about nine o'clock on that memorable evening, when we suddenly heard the front door being opened with a latchkey, and then very cautiously shut again.

One of the two men had returned at an hour most unusual for their otherwise very regular habits. The way, too, in which the door had been opened and shut suggested a desire for secrecy and silence. Instinctively I turned off the gas in the parlour, and with a quick gesture pointed to the front room, the door of which stood open, and I whispered hurriedly to Mr. Shuttleworth.

"Speak to him!"

Fortunately, the great aim which he had in view had rendered his perceptions very keen.

He went into the front room, in which the gas, fortunately, was alight at the time, and opening the door which gave thence on to the passage, he said pleasantly:

"Oh, Mr. Piatti! is that you? Can I do anything for you?"

"Ah, yes! zank you," replied the Sicilian, whose voice I could hear was husky and unsteady, "if you would be so kind—I–I feel so fainting and queer to-night–ze warm weazer, I zink. Would you—would you be so kind to fetch me a little—er—ammoniac—er—sal volatile you call it, I zink—from ze apothecary? I would go lie on my bed—if you would be so kind—"

"Why, of course I will, Mr. Piatti," said Mr. Shuttleworth, who somehow got an intuition of what I wanted to do, and literally played into my hands. "I'll go at once."

He went to get his hat from the rack in the hall whilst the Sicilian murmured profuse "Zank you's," and then I heard the front door bang to.

From where I was I could not see Piatti, but I imagined him standing in the dimly-lighted passage listening to Mr. Shuttleworth's retreating footsteps.

Presently I heard him walking along towards the back door, and soon I perceived something moving about in the little bit of ground beyond. He had gone to get his spade. He meant to unearth the coat and the watch and chain which, for some reason or another, he must have thought were no longer safe in their original hiding-place. Had the gang of murderers heard that the man who frequently visited their landlady was the father of Cecil Shuttleworth over at Palermo?

At that moment I paused neither to speculate nor yet to plan. I ran down to the kitchen, for I no longer wanted to watch Piatti. I knew what he was doing.

I didn't want to frighten Emily, and she had been made to understand all along that she might have to leave the house with me again at any time, at a moment's notice; she and I had kept our small handbag ready packed in the kitchen, whence we could reach the area steps quickly and easily.

Now I quietly beckoned to her that the time had come. She took the bag and followed me. Just as we shut the area gate behind us, we heard the garden door violently slammed. Piatti had got the coat, and by now was examining the pockets in order to find the watch and chain. Within the next ten seconds he would realise that the coat which he held was not the one which he had buried in the garden, and that the real proofs of his guilt—or his complicity in the guilt of another—had disappeared.

We did not wait for those ten seconds, but flew down Bread Street, in the direction of Leather Lane, where I knew Mr. Shuttleworth would be on the lookout for me.

"Yes," I said hurriedly, directly I spied him at the angle of the street; "it's all up. I am off to Budapest by the early Continental to-morrow morning. I shall catch them at the Hungaria. See Emily safely to the flat."

Obviously there was no time to lose, and before either Mr. Shuttleworth or Emily could make a remark I had left them standing, and had quickly mixed my insignificant personality with the passers-by.

I strolled down Leather Lane quite leisurely; you see, my face was unknown to the Piattis. They had only seen dim outlines of me behind very dirty window-panes.

I did not go to the flat. I knew Mr. Shuttleworth would take care of Emily, so that night I slept at the Grand Hotel, Charing Cross, leaving the next morning by the 9.0 a.m., having booked my berth on the Orient Express as far as Budapest.

3

WELL, you know the saying: It is easy to be wise after the event.

Of course, when I saw the older Piatti standing in the hall of the Hotel Hungaria at Budapest I realised that I had been followed from the moment that Emily and I ran out of the house at Bread Street. The son had obviously kept me in view whilst I was still in London, and the father had travelled across Europe, unperceived by me, in the same train as myself, had seen me step into the fiacre at Budapest, and heard me tell the smart coachman to drive to the Hungaria.

I made hasty arrangements for my room, and then asked if "Mrs. Carey," from London, was still at the hotel with her maid—for that was the name under which Mrs. Tadworth was to travel—and was answered in the affirmative. "Mrs. Carey" was even then supping in the dining-room, whence the strains of beautiful Hungarian melodies played by Berkes' inimitable band seemed to mock my anxiety.

"Mrs. Carey's maid," they told me, was having her meal in the steward's room.

I tried to prosecute my hasty inquiries as quietly as I could, but Piatti's eyes and sarcastic smile seemed to follow me everywhere, whilst he went about calmly ordering his room and seeing to the disposal of his luggage.

Almost every official at the Hungaria speaks English, and I had no difficulty in finding my way to the steward's room. To my chagrin Lady Molly was not there. Someone told me that no doubt "Mrs. Carey's maid" had gone back to her mistress's room, which they told me was No. 118 on the first floor.

A few precious moments were thus wasted whilst I ran back towards the hall; you know the long, seemingly interminable, corridors and passages of the Hungaria! Fortunately, in one of these I presently beheld my dear lady walking towards me. At sight of her all my anxieties seemed to fall from me like a discarded mantle.

She looked quite serene and placid, but with her own quick perception she at once guessed what had brought me to Budapest.

"They have found out about the coat," she said, quickly drawing me aside into one of the smaller passages, which fortunately at the moment was dark and deserted, "and, of course, he has followed you–"

I nodded affirmatively.

"That Mrs. Tadworth is a vapid, weak-kneed little fool," she said, with angry vehemence. "We ought to be at Cividale by now–and she declared herself too ill and too fatigued to continue the journey. How that poor Shuttleworth could be so blind as to trust her passes belief."

"Mary," she added more calmly, "go down into the hall at once. Watch that idiot of a woman for all you're worth. She is terrified of the Sicilians, and I firmly believe that Piatti can force her to give up the proofs of the crime to him."

"Where are they–the proofs, I mean?" I asked anxiously.

"Locked up in her trunk–she won't entrust them to me. Obstinate little fool."

I had never seen my dear lady so angry; however, she said nothing more then, and presently I took leave of her and worked my way back towards the hall. One glance round the brilliantly-lighted place assured me that neither Piatti nor Mrs. Tadworth was there. I could not tell you what it was that suddenly filled my heart with foreboding.

I ran up to the first floor and reached room No. 118. The outer door was open, and without a moment's hesitation I applied my eye to the keyhole of the inner one.

The room was brilliantly lighted from within, and exactly opposite, but with his back to me, stood Piatti, whilst squatting on a low stool beside him was Mrs. Tadworth.

A trunk stood open close to her hand, and she was obviously busy turning over its contents. My very heart stood still with horror. Was I about to witness–thus powerless to interfere–one of the most hideous acts of cowardly treachery it was possible to conceive?

Something, however, must at that moment have attracted Piatti's attention, for he suddenly turned and strode towards the door. Needless to say that I beat a hasty retreat.

My one idea was, of course, to find Lady Molly and tell her what I had seen. Unfortunately, the Hungaria is a veritable maze of corridors, stairs and passages, and I did not know the number of her room. At first I did not wish to attract further attention by again asking about "Mrs. Carey's maid" at the office, and my stupid ignorance of foreign languages precluded my talking to the female servants.

I had been up and down the stairs half a dozen times, tired, miserable, and anxious, when at last, in the far distance, I espied my dear lady's graceful silhouette. Eagerly I ran to her, and was promptly admonished for my careless impetuosity.

"Mrs. Tadworth is genuinely frightened," added Lady Molly in response to my look of painful suspense, "but so far she has been able to hoodwink Piatti by opening my trunk before him instead of hers, and telling him that the proofs were not in her own keeping. But she is too stupid to keep that deception up, and, of course, he won't allow himself to be put off a second time. We must start for Cividale as soon as possible. Unfortunately, the earliest train is not till 9.15 to-morrow morning. The danger to that unfortunate young man over at Palermo, brought about by this woman's cowardly idiocy and the father's misguided trust, is already incalculable."

It was, of course, useless for me to express fear now for my dear lady's safety. I smothered my anxiety as best I could, and, full of deadly forebodings, I bade her anon a fond good-night.

Needless to say that I scarcely slept, and at eight o'clock the next morning I was fully dressed and out of my room.

The first glance down the corridor on which gave No. 118 at once confirmed my worst fears. Unusual bustle reigned there at this early hour. Officials came and went, maids stood about gossiping, and the next moment, to my literally agonised horror, I beheld two gendarmes, with an officer, being escorted by the hotel manager to the rooms occupied by Mrs. Tadworth and Lady Molly.

Oh, how I cursed then our British ignorance of foreign tongues. The officials were too busy to bother about me, and the maids only knew that portion of the English language which refers to baths and to hot water. Finally, to my intense relief, I discovered a willing porter, ready and able to give me information in my own tongue of the events which had disturbed the serene quietude of the Hotel Hungaria.

Great heavens! Shall I ever forget what I endured when I grasped the full meaning of what he told me with a placid smile and a shrug of the shoulders!

"The affair is most mysterious," he explained, "not robbery–oh, no! no!–for it is Mrs. Carey, who has gone–disappeared! And it is Mrs. Carey's maid who was found, stunned, gagged and unconscious, tied to one of the bedposts in room No. 118."

4

WELL, why should I bore you by recounting the agonised suspense, the mortal anxiety, which I endured for all those subsequent weary days which at the time seemed like so many centuries?

My own dear lady, the woman for whom I would have gone through fire and water with a cheerful smile, had been brutally assaulted, almost murdered, so the smiling porter assured me, and my very existence was ignored by the stolid officials, who looked down upon me with a frown of impassive disapproval whilst I entreated, raged and stormed alternately, begging to be allowed to go and nurse the sick lady, who was my own dearest friend, dearer than any child could be to its mother.

Oh, that awful red tapeism that besets one at every turn, paralyses and disheartens one! What I suffered I really could not describe.

But if I was not allowed to see Lady Molly, at least I was able to wreak vengeance upon her cowardly assailants. Mrs. Tadworth, by her disappearance, had tacitly confessed her participation in the outrage, of that I had no doubt, but I was equally certain that she was both too stupid and too weak to commit such a crime unaided.

Piatti was at the bottom of it all. Without a moment's hesitation I laid information against him through the medium of an interpreter. I accused him boldly of being an accessory to the assault for purposes of robbery. Unswervingly I repeated my story of how I had seen him in close conversation the day before with Mrs. Carey, whose real name I declared to be Mrs. Tadworth.

The chief object of the robbery I suggested to be a valuable gold watch and chain, with initials "A. C.," belonging to my friend, who had travelled with Mrs. Carey to Budapest as her companion, not her maid. This was a bold move on my part, and I felt reckless, I can tell you. Fortunately, my story was corroborated by the fact that the floor valet had seen Piatti hanging about the corridor outside No. 118 at an extraordinarily early hour of the morning. My firm belief was that the wretch had been admitted into the room by that horrid Mrs. Tadworth. He had terrorised her, probably had threatened her life. She had then agreed out of sheer cowardice to deliver to him the proofs of his own guilt in the Palermo murder case, and when Lady Molly, hearing the voices, came out of her own room, Piatti knocked her down lest she should intervene. Mrs. Tadworth thereupon–weak and silly little fool!–was seized with panic, and succeeded, no doubt with his help, in leaving the hotel, and probably Budapest, before the outrage was discovered.

Why Piatti had not done likewise, I could not conjecture. He seems to have gone back quietly to his own room after that; and it was not till an hour later that the chambermaid, surprised at seeing the door of No. 118 slightly ajar, had peeped in, and there was greeted by the awful sight of "the maid," gagged, bound and unconscious.

Well, I gained my wish, and had the satisfaction presently of knowing that Piatti–although, mind you, he emphatically denied my story from beginning to end–had been placed under arrest pending further inquiries.

The British Consul was very kind to me; though I was not allowed to see my dear lady, who had been removed to the hospital. I heard that the Hungarian police were moving heaven and earth to find "Mrs. Carey" and bring her to justice.

Her disappearance told severely against her, and after three days of such intense anxiety as I never wish to live through again, I received a message from the Consulate informing me that "Mrs. Carey " had been arrested at Alsórév, on the Austro-Hungarian frontier, and was even now on her way to Budapest under escort.

You may imagine how I quivered with anxiety and with rage when, on the morning after that welcome news, I was told that "Mrs. Carey" was detained at the gendarmerie, and had asked to see Miss Mary Granard from London, at present residing at the Hotel Hungaria.

The impudent wretch! Wanting to see me, indeed! Well, I, too, wanted to see her; the woman whom I despised as a coward and a traitor; who had betrayed the fond and foolish trust of a stricken father; who had dashed the last hopes of an innocent man in danger of his life; and who, finally, had been the cause of an assault that had all but killed, perhaps, the woman I loved best in the world.

I felt like the embodiment of hate and contempt. I loathed the woman, and I hied me in a fiacre to the gendarmerie, escorted by one of the clerks from the Consulate, simply thirsting with the desire to tell an ignoble female exactly what I thought of her.

I had to wait some two or three minutes in the bare, barrack-like room of the gendarmerie; then the door opened, there was a rustle of silk, followed by the sound of measured footsteps of soldiery, and the next moment Lady Molly, serene and placid and, as usual, exquisitely dressed, stood smiling before me.

"You have got me into this plight, Mary," she said, with her merry laugh; "you'll have to get me out of it again."

"But—I don't understand," was all that I could gasp.

"It is very simple, and I'll explain it all fully when we are on our way home to Maida Vale," she said. "For the moment you and Mrs. Tadworth will have to make sundry affidavits that I did not assault my maid nor rob her of a watch and chain. The British Consul will help you, and it is only a question of days, and in the meanwhile I may tell you that Budapest prison life is quite interesting, and not so uncomfortable as one would imagine."

Of course, the moment she spoke I got an intuition of what had really occurred, and I can assure you that I was heartily ashamed that I should ever have doubted Lady Molly's cleverness in carrying through successfully so important, so vital a business as the righting of an innocent man.

Mrs. Tadworth was pusillanimous and stupid. At Budapest she cried a halt, for she really felt unstrung and ill after the hurried journey, the change of air and food, and what not. Lady Molly, however, had no difficulty in persuading her that during the enforced stay of twenty-four hours at the Hungaria their two rôles should be reversed. Lady Molly would be "Mrs. Carey," coming from England, whilst Mrs. Tadworth would be the maid.

My dear lady—not thinking at the time that my knowledge of this fact would be of any importance to her own plans—had not mentioned it to me during the brief interview which I had with her. Then, when Piatti arrived upon the scene, Mrs. Tadworth got into a real panic. Fortunately, she had the good sense, or the cowardice, then and there to entrust the coat and watch and chain to Lady Molly, and when Piatti followed her into her room she was able to show him that the proofs were not then in her possession. This was the scene which I had witnessed through the keyhole.

But, of course, the Sicilian would return to the charge, and equally, of course, Mrs. Tadworth would sacrifice the Shuttleworths, father and son, to save her own skin. Lady Molly knew that. She is strong, active and determined; she had a brief hand-to-hand struggle with Mrs. Tadworth that night, and finally succeeded in tying her, half unconscious, to the bedpost, thus assuring herself that for at least twenty-four hours that vapid little fool would be unable to either act for herself or to betray my dear, intrepid lady's plans.

When, the following morning, Piatti opened the door of No. 118, which had purposely been left on the latch, he was greeted with the sight of Mrs. Tadworth pinioned and half dead with fear, whilst the valuable proofs of his own guilt and young Shuttleworth's innocence had completely disappeared.

For remember that Lady Molly's face was not known to him or to his gang, and she had caught the first train to Cividale even whilst Piatti still believed that he held that silly Mrs. Tadworth in the hollow of his hand. I may as well tell you here that she reached the frontier safely, and was quite sharp enough to seek out Colonel Grassi and, with the necessary words of explanation, to hand over to him the proofs of young Shuttleworth's innocence.

My action in the matter helped her. At the hotel she was supposed to be the mistress and Mrs. Tadworth the maid, and everyone was told that "Mrs. Carey's maid" had been assaulted, and removed to the hospital. But I denounced Piatti then and there, thinking he had attacked my dear lady, and I got him put under lock and key so quickly that he had not the time to communicate with his associates.

Thanks to Colonel Grassi's exertions, young Shuttleworth was acquitted of the charge of murder; but I may as well tell you here that neither Piatti nor his son, nor any of that gang, were arrested for the crime. The proofs of their guilt–the Irish-tweed coat and the murdered man's watch and chain–were most mysteriously suppressed, after young Shuttleworth's advocate had obtained the verdict of "not guilty" for him.

Such is the Sicilian police. Mr. Shuttleworth, senior, evidently knew what he was talking about.

Of course, we had no difficulty in obtaining Lady Molly's release. The British Consul saw to that. But in Budapest they still call the assault on "Mrs. Carey" at the Hotel Hungaria a mystery, for she exonerated Lady Molly fully, but she refused to accuse Piatti. She was afraid of him, of course, and so they had to set him free.

I wonder where he is now, the wicked old wretch!

THE FORDWYCH CASTLE MYSTERY

CAN you wonder that, when some of the ablest of our fellows at the Yard were at their wits' ends to know what to do, the chief instinctively turned to Lady Molly?

Surely the Fordwych Castle Mystery, as it was universally called, was a case which more than any other required feminine tact, intuition, and all those qualities of which my dear lady possessed more than her usual share.

With the exception of Mr. McKinley, the lawyer, and young Jack d'Alboukirk, there were only women connected with the case.

If you have studied Debrett at all, you know as well as I do that the peerage is one of those old English ones which date back some six hundred years, and that the present Lady d'Alboukirk is a baroness in her own right, the title and estates descending to heirs-general. If you have perused that same interesting volume carefully, you will also have discovered that the late Lord d'Alboukirk had two daughters, the eldest, Clementina Cecilia—the present Baroness, who succeeded him—the other, Margaret Florence, who married in 1884 Jean Laurent Duplessis, a Frenchman whom Debrett vaguely describes as "of Pondicherry, India," and of whom she had issue two daughters, Henriette Marie, heir now to the ancient barony of d'Alboukirk of Fordwych, and Joan, born two years later.

There seems to have been some mystery or romance attached to this marriage of the Honourable Margaret Florence d'Alboukirk to the dashing young officer of the Foreign Legion. Old Lord d'Alboukirk at the time was British Ambassador in Paris, and he seems to have had grave objections to the union, but Miss Margaret, openly flouting her father's displeasure, and throwing prudence to the winds, ran away from home one fine day with Captain Duplessis, and from Pondicherry wrote a curt letter to her relatives telling them of her marriage with the man she loved best in all the world. Old Lord d'Alboukirk never got over his daughter's wilfulness. She had been his favourite, it appears, and her secret marriage and deceit practically broke his heart. He was kind to her, however, to the end, and when the first baby girl was born and the young pair seemed to be in straitened circumstances, he made them an allowance until the day of his daughter's death, which occurred three years after her elopement, on the birth of her second child.

When, on the death of her father, the Honourable Clementina Cecilia came into the title and fortune, she seemed to have thought it her duty to take some interest in her late sister's eldest child, who, failing her own marriage, and issue, was heir to the barony of d'Alboukirk. Thus it was that Miss Henriette Marie Duplessis came, with her father's consent, to live with her aunt at Fordwych Castle. Debrett will tell you, moreover, that in 1901 she assumed the name of d'Alboukirk, in lieu of her own, by royal licence. Failing her, the title and estate would devolve firstly on her sister Joan, and subsequently on a fairly distant cousin, Captain John d'Alboukirk, at present a young officer in the Guards.

According to her servants, the present Baroness d'Alboukirk is very self-willed, but otherwise neither more nor less eccentric than any north-country old maid would be who had such an exceptional position to keep up in the social world. The one soft trait in her otherwise not very lovable character is her great affection for her late sister's child. Miss Henriette Duplessis d'Alboukirk has inherited from her French father dark eyes and hair and a somewhat swarthy complexion, but no doubt it is from her English ancestry that she has derived a somewhat masculine frame and a very great fondness for all outdoor pursuits. She is very athletic, knows how to fence and to box, rides to hounds, and is a remarkably good shot.

From all accounts, the first hint of trouble in that gorgeous home was coincident with the arrival at Fordwych of a young, very pretty girl visitor, who was attended by her maid, a half-caste woman, dark-complexioned and surly of temper, but obviously of dog-like devotion towards her young mistress. This visit seems to have come as a surprise to the entire household at Fordwych Castle, her ladyship having said nothing about it until the very morning that the guests were expected. She then briefly ordered one of the housemaids to get a bedroom ready for a young lady, and to put up a small camp-bedstead in an adjoining dressing-room. Even Miss Henriette seems to have been taken by surprise at the announcement of this visit, for, according to Jane Taylor, the housemaid in question, there was a violent word-passage between the old lady and her niece, the latter winding up an excited speech with the words:

"At any rate, aunt, there won't be room for both of us in this house!" After which she flounced out of the room, banging the door behind her.

Very soon the household was made to understand that the newcomer was none other than Miss Joan Duplessis, Miss Henriette's younger sister. It appears that Captain Duplessis had recently died in Pondicherry, and that the young girl then wrote to her aunt, Lady d'Alboukirk, claiming her help and protection, which the old lady naturally considered it her duty to extend to her.

It appears that Miss Joan was very unlike her sister, as she was petite and fair, more English-looking than foreign, and had pretty, dainty ways which soon endeared her to the household. The devotion existing between her and the half-caste woman she had brought from India was, moreover, unique.

It seems, however, that from the moment these newcomers came into the house, dissensions, often degenerating into violent quarrels, became the order of the day. Henriette seemed to have taken a strong dislike to her younger sister, and most particularly to the latter's dark attendant, who was vaguely known in the house as Roonah.

That some events of serious import were looming ahead, the servants at Fordwych were pretty sure. The butler and footmen at dinner heard scraps of conversation which sounded very ominous. There was talk of "lawyers," of "proofs," of "marriage and birth certificates," quickly suppressed when the servants happened to be about. Her ladyship looked terribly anxious and worried, and she and Miss Henriette spent long hours closeted together in a small boudoir, whence proceeded ominous sounds of heartrending weeping on her ladyship's part, and angry and violent words from Miss Henriette.

Mr. McKinley, the eminent lawyer from London, came down two or three times to Fordwych, and held long conversations with her ladyship, after which the latter's eyes were very swollen and red. The household thought it more than strange that Roonah, the Indian servant, was almost invariably present at these interviews between Mr. McKinley, her ladyship, and Miss Joan. Otherwise the woman kept herself very much aloof; she spoke very little, hardly took any notice of anyone save of her ladyship and her young mistress, and the outbursts of Miss Henriette's temper seemed to leave her quite unmoved. A strange fact was that she had taken a sudden and great fancy for frequenting a small Roman Catholic convent chapel which was distant about half a mile from the Castle, and presently it was understood that Roonah, who had been a Parsee, had been converted by the attendant priest to the Roman Catholic faith.

All this happened, mind you, within the last two or three months; in fact, Miss Joan had been in the Castle exactly twelve weeks when Captain Jack d'Alboukirk came to pay his cousin one of his periodical visits. From the first he seems to have taken a great fancy to his cousin Joan, and soon everyone noticed that this fancy was rapidly ripening into love. It was equally certain that from that moment dissensions between the two sisters became more frequent and more violent; the generally accepted opinion being that Miss Henriette was jealous of Joan, whilst Lady d'Alboukirk herself, for some unexplainable reason, seems to have regarded this love-making with marked disfavour.

Then came the tragedy.

One morning Joan ran downstairs, pale, and trembling from head to foot, moaning and sobbing as she ran:

"Roonah!–my poor old Roonah!–I knew it–I knew it!"

Captain Jack happened to meet her at the foot of the stairs. He pressed her with questions, but the girl was unable to speak. She merely pointed mutely to the floor above. The young man, genuinely alarmed, ran quickly upstairs; he threw open the door leading to Roonah's room, and there, to his horror, he saw the unfortunate woman lying across the small camp-bedstead, with a handkerchief over her nose and mouth, her throat cut.

The sight was horrible.

Poor Roonah was obviously dead.

Without losing his presence of mind, Captain Jack quietly shut the door again, after urgently begging Joan to compose herself, and try to keep up, at any rate until the local doctor could be sent for and the terrible news gently broken to Lady d'Alboukirk.

The doctor, hastily summoned, arrived some twenty minutes later. He could but confirm Joan's and Captain Jack's fears. Roonah was indeed dead–in fact, she had been dead some hours.

2

FROM the very first, mind you, the public took a more than usually keen interest in this mysterious occurrence. The evening papers on the very day of the murder were ablaze with flaming headlines such as:

MYSTERIOUS MURDER OF AN IMPORTANT WITNESS

GRAVE CHARGES AGAINST PERSONS IN HIGH LIFE

and so forth.

As time went on, the mystery deepened more and more, and I suppose Lady Molly must have had an inkling that sooner or later the chief would have to rely on her help and advice, for she sent me down to attend the inquest, and gave me strict orders to keep eyes and ears open for every detail in connection with the crime—however trivial it might seem. She herself remained in town, awaiting a summons from the chief.

The inquest was held in the dining-room of Fordwych Castle, and the noble hall was crowded to its utmost when the coroner and jury finally took their seats, after having viewed the body of the poor murdered woman upstairs.

The scene was dramatic enough to please any novelist, and an awed hush descended over the crowd when, just before the proceedings began, a door was thrown open, and in walked–stiff and erect–the Baroness d'Alboukirk, escorted by her niece, Miss Henriette, and closely followed by her cousin, Captain Jack, of the Guards.

The old lady's face was as indifferent and haughty as usual, and so was that of her athletic niece. Captain Jack, on the other hand, looked troubled and flushed. Everyone noted that, directly he entered the room, his eyes sought a small, dark figure that sat silent and immovable beside the portly figure of the great lawyer, Mr. Hubert McKinley. This was Miss Joan Duplessis, in a plain black stuff gown, her young face pale and tear-stained.

Dr. Walker, the local practitioner, was, of course, the first witness called. His evidence was purely medical. He deposed to having made an examination of the body, and stated that he found that a handkerchief saturated with chloroform had been pressed to the woman's nostrils, probably while she was asleep, her throat having subsequently been cut with a sharp knife; death must have been instantaneous, as the poor thing did not appear to have struggled at all.

In answer to a question from the coroner, the doctor said that no great force or violence would be required for the gruesome deed, since the victim was undeniably unconscious when it was done. At the same time it argued unusual coolness and determination.

The handkerchief was produced, also the knife. The former was a bright-coloured one, stated to be the property of the deceased. The latter was a foreign, old-fashioned hunting-knife, one of a panoply of small arms and other weapons which adorned a corner of the hall. It had been found by Detective Elliott in a clump of gorse on the adjoining golf links. There could be no question that it had been used by the murderer for his fell purpose, since at the time it was found it still bore traces of blood.

Captain Jack was the next witness called. He had very little to say, as he merely saw the body from across the room, and immediately closed the door again and, having begged his cousin to compose herself, called his own valet and sent him off for the doctor.

Some of the staff of Fordwych Castle were called, all of whom testified to the Indian woman's curious taciturnity, which left her quite isolated among her fellow-servants. Miss Henriette's maid, however, Jane Partlett, had one or two more interesting facts to record. She seems to have been more intimate with the deceased woman than anyone else, and on one occasion, at least, had quite a confidential talk with her.

"She talked chiefly about her mistress," said Jane, in answer to a question from the coroner, "to whom she was most devoted. She told me that she loved her so, she would readily die for her. Of course, I thought that silly like, and just mad, foreign talk, but Roonah was very angry when I laughed at her, and then she undid her dress in front, and showed me some papers which were sown in the lining of her dress. 'All these papers my little missee's fortune,' she said to me. 'Roonah guard these with her life. Someone must kill Roonah before taking them from her!'

"This was about six weeks ago," continued Jane, whilst a strange feeling of awe seemed to descend upon all those present whilst the girl spoke. "Lately she became much more silent, and, on my once referring to the papers, she turned on me savage like and told me to hold my tongue."

Asked if she had mentioned the incident of the papers to anyone, Jane replied in the negative.

"Except to Miss Henriette, of course," she added, after a slight moment of hesitation.

Throughout all these preliminary examinations Lady d'Alboukirk, sitting between her cousin Captain Jack and her niece Henriette, had remained quite silent in an erect attitude expressive of haughty indifference. Henriette, on the other hand, looked distinctly bored. Once or twice she had yawned audibly, which caused quite a feeling of anger against her among the spectators. Such callousness in the midst of so mysterious a tragedy, and when her own sister was obviously in such deep sorrow, impressed everyone very unfavourably. It was well known that the young lady had had a fencing lesson just before the inquest in the room immediately below that where Roonah lay dead, and that within an hour of the discovery of the tragedy she was calmly playing golf.

Then Miss Joan Duplessis was called.

When the young girl stepped forward there was that awed hush in the room which usually falls upon an attentive audience when the curtain is about to rise on the crucial act of a dramatic play. But she was calm and self-possessed, and wonderfully pathetic-looking in her deep black and with the obvious lines of sorrow which the sad death of a faithful friend had traced on her young face.

In answer to the coroner, she gave her name as Joan Clarissa Duplessis, and briefly stated that until the day of her servant's death she had been a resident at Fordwych Castle, but that since then she had left that temporary home, and had taken up her abode at the d'Alboukirk Arms, a quiet little hostelry on the outskirts of the town.

There was a distinct feeling of astonishment on the part of those who were not aware of this fact, and then the coroner said kindly:

"You were born, I think, in Pondicherry, in India, and are the younger daughter of Captain and Mrs. Duplessis, who was own sister to her ladyship?"

"I was born in Pondicherry," replied the young girl, quietly, "and I am the only legitimate child of the late Captain and Mrs. Duplessis, own sister to her ladyship."

A wave of sensation, quickly suppressed by the coroner, went through the crowd at these words. The emphasis which the witness had put on the word "legitimate" could not be mistaken, and everyone felt that here must lie the clue to the, so far impenetrable, mystery of the Indian woman's death.

All eyes were now turned on old Lady d'Alboukirk and on her niece Henriette, but the two ladies were carrying on a whispered conversation together, and had apparently ceased to take any further interest in the proceedings.

"The deceased was your confidential maid, was she not?" asked the coroner, after a slight pause.

"Yes."

"She came over to England with you recently?"

"Yes; she had to accompany me in order to help me to make good my claim to being my late mother's only legitimate child, and therefore the heir to the barony of d'Alboukirk."

Her voice had trembled a little as she said this, but now, as breathless silence reigned in the room, she seemed to make a visible effort to control herself, and, replying to the coroner's question, she gave a clear and satisfactory account of her terrible discovery of her faithful servant's death. Her evidence had lasted about a quarter of an hour or so, when suddenly the coroner put the momentous question to her:

"Do you know anything about the papers which the deceased woman carried about her person, and reference to which has already been made?"

"Yes," she replied quietly; "they were the proofs relating to my claim. My father, Captain Duplessis, had in early youth, and before he met my mother, contracted a secret union with a half-caste woman, who was Roonah's own sister. Being tired of her, he chose to repudiate her–she had no children–but the legality of the marriage was never for a moment in question. After that, he married my mother, and his first wife subsequently died, chiefly of a broken heart; but her death only occurred two months after the birth of my sister Henriette. My father, I think, had been led to believe that his first wife had died some two years previously, and he was no doubt very much shocked when he realised what a grievous wrong he had done our mother. In order to mend matters somewhat, he and she went through a new form of marriage–a legal one this time–and my father paid a lot of money to Roonah's relatives to have the matter hushed up. Less than a year after this second–and only legal–marriage, I was born and my mother died."

"Then these papers of which so much has been said–what did they consist of?"

"There were the marriage certificates of my father's first wife–and two sworn statements as to her death, two months after the birth of my sister Henriette; one by Dr. Rénaud, who was at the time a well-known medical man in Pondicherry, and the other by Roonah herself, who had held her dying sister in her arms. Dr. Rénaud is dead, and now Roonah has been murdered, and all the proofs have gone with her–"

Her voice broke in a passion of sobs, which, with manifest self-control, she quickly suppressed. In that crowded court you could have heard a pin drop, so great was the tension of intense excitement and attention.

"Then those papers remained in your maid's possession? Why was that?" asked the coroner.

"I did not dare to carry the papers about with me," said the witness, while a curious look of terror crept into her young face as she looked across at her aunt and sister. "Roonah would not part with them. She carried them in the lining of her dress, and at night they were all under her pillow. After her–her death, and when Dr. Walker had left, I thought it my duty to take possession of the papers which meant my whole future to me, and which I desired then to place in Mr. McKinley's charge. But, though I carefully searched the bed and all the clothing by my poor Roonah's side, I did not find the papers. They were gone."

I won't attempt to describe to you the sensation caused by the deposition of this witness. All eyes wandered from her pale young face to that of her sister, who sat almost opposite to her, shrugging her athletic shoulders and gazing at the pathetic young figure before her with callous and haughty indifference.

"Now, putting aside the question of the papers for the moment," said the coroner, after a pause, "do you happen to know anything of your late servant's private life? Had she an enemy, or perhaps a lover?"

"No," replied the girl; "Roonah's whole life was centred in me and in my claim. I had often begged her to place our papers in Mr. McKinley's charge, but she would trust no one. I wish she had obeyed me," here moaned the poor girl involuntarily, "and I should not have lost what means my whole future to me, and the being who loved me best in all the world would not have been so foully murdered."

Of course, it was terrible to see this young girl thus instinctively, and surely unintentionally, proffering so awful an accusation against those who stood so near to her. That the whole case had become hopelessly involved and mysterious, nobody could deny. Can you imagine the mental picture formed in the mind of all present by the story, so pathetically told, of this girl who had come over to England in order to make good her claim which she felt to be just, and who, in one fell swoop, saw that claim rendered very difficult to prove through the dastardly murder of her principal witness?

That the claim was seriously jeopardised by the death of Roonah and the disappearance of the papers, was made very clear, mind you, through the statements of Mr. McKinley, the lawyer. He could not say very much, of course, and his statements could never have been taken as actual proof, because Roonah and Joan had never fully trusted him and had never actually placed the proofs of the claim in his hands. He certainly had seen the marriage certificate of Captain Duplessis's wife, and a copy of this, as he very properly stated, could easily be obtained. The woman seems to have died during the great cholera epidemic of 1881, when, owing to the great number of deaths which occurred, the deceit and concealment practised by the natives at Pondicherry, and the supineness of the French Government, death certificates were very casually and often incorrectly made out.

Roonah had come over to England ready to swear that her sister had died in her arms two months after the birth of Captain Duplessis's eldest child, and there was the sworn testimony of Dr. Rénaud, since dead. These affidavits Mr. McKinley had seen and read.

Against that, the only proof which now remained of the justice of Joan Duplessis's claim was the fact that her mother and father went through a second form of marriage some time after the birth of their first child, Henriette. This fact was not denied, and, of course, it could be easily proved, if necessary, but even then it would in no way be conclusive. It implied the presence of a doubt in Captain Duplessis's mind, a doubt which the second marriage ceremony may have served to set at rest; but it in no way established the illegitimacy of his eldest daughter.

In fact, the more Mr. McKinley spoke, the more convinced did everyone become that the theft of the papers had everything to do with the murder of the unfortunate Roonah. She would not part with the proofs which meant her mistress's fortune, and she paid for her devotion with her life.

Several more witnesses were called after that. The servants were closely questioned, the doctor was recalled, but, in spite of long and arduous efforts, the coroner and jury could not bring a single real fact to light beyond those already stated.

The Indian woman had been murdered!

The papers which she always carried about her body had disappeared.

Beyond that, nothing! An impenetrable wall of silence and mystery!

The butler at Fordwych Castle had certainly missed the knife with which Roonah had been killed from its accustomed place on the morning after the murder had been committed, but not before, and the mystery further gained in intensity from the fact that the only purchase of chloroform in the district had been traced to the murdered woman herself.

She had gone down to the local chemist one day some two or three weeks previously, and shown him a prescription for cleansing the hair which required some chloroform in it. He gave her a very small quantity in a tiny bottle, which was subsequently found empty on her own dressing-table. No one at Fordwych Castle could swear to having heard any unaccustomed noise during that memorable night. Even Joan, who slept in the room adjoining that where the unfortunate Roonah lay, said she had heard nothing unusual. But then, the door of communication between the two rooms was shut, and the murderer had been quick and silent.

Thus this extraordinary inquest drew to a close, leaving in its train an air of dark suspicion and of unexplainable horror.

The jury returned a verdict of "Wilful murder against some person or persons unknown," and the next moment Lady d'Alboukirk rose, and, leaning on her niece's arm, quietly walked out of the room.

3

TWO of our best men from the Yard, Pegram and Elliott, were left in charge of the case. They remained at Fordwych (the little town close by), as did Miss Joan, who had taken up her permanent abode at the d'Alboukirk Arms, whilst I returned to town immediately after the inquest. Captain Jack had rejoined his regiment, and apparently the ladies of the Castle had resumed their quiet, luxurious life just the same as heretofore. The old lady led her own somewhat isolated, semi-regal life; Miss Henriette fenced and boxed, played hockey and golf, and over the fine Castle and its haughty inmates there hovered like an ugly bird of prey the threatening presence of a nameless suspicion.

The two ladies might choose to flout public opinion, but public opinion was dead against them. No one dared formulate a charge, but everyone remembered that Miss Henriette had, on the very morning of the murder, been playing golf in the field where the knife was discovered, and that if Miss Joan Duplessis ever failed to make good her claim to the barony of d'Alboukirk, Miss Henriette would remain in undisputed possession. So now, when the ladies drove past in the village street, no one doffed a cap to salute them, and when at church the parson read out the sixth commandment, "Thou shalt do no murder," all eyes gazed with fearsome awe at the old Baroness and her niece.

Splendid isolation reigned at Fordwych Castle. The daily papers grew more and more sarcastic at the expense of the Scotland Yard authorities, and the public more and more impatient.

Then it was that the chief grew desperate and sent for Lady Molly, the result of the interview being that I once more made the journey down to Fordwych, but this time in the company of my dear lady, who had received carte blanche from headquarters to do whatever she thought right in the investigation of the mysterious crime.

She and I arrived at Fordwych at 8.0 p.m., after the usual long wait at Newcastle. We put up at the d'Alboukirk Arms, and, over a hasty and very bad supper, Lady Molly allowed me a brief insight into her plans.

"I can see every detail of that murder, Mary," she said earnestly, "just as if I had lived at the Castle all the time. I know exactly where our fellows are wrong, and why they cannot get on. But, although the chief has given me a free hand, what I am going to do is so irregular that if I fail I shall probably get my immediate congé, whilst some of the disgrace is bound to stick to you. It is not too late—you may yet draw back, and leave me to act alone."

I looked her straight in the face. Her dark eyes were gleaming; there was the power of second sight in them, or of marvelous intuition of "men and things."

"I'll follow your lead, my Lady Molly," I said quietly.

"Then go to bed now," she replied, with that strange transition of manner which to me was so attractive and to everyone else so unaccountable.

In spite of my protest, she refused to listen to any more talk or to answer any more questions, and, perforce, I had to go to my room. The next morning I saw her graceful figure, immaculately dressed in a perfect tailor-made gown, standing beside my bed at a very early hour.

"Why, what is the time?" I ejaculated, suddenly wide awake.

"Too early for you to get up," she replied quietly. "I am going to early Mass at the Roman Catholic convent close by."

"To Mass at the Roman Catholic convent?"

"Yes. Don't repeat all my words, Mary; it is silly, and wastes time. I have introduced myself in the neighbourhood as the American, Mrs. Silas A. Ogen, whose motor has broken down and is being repaired at Newcastle, while I, its owner, amuse myself by viewing the beauties of the neighbourhood. Being a Roman Catholic, I go to Mass first, and, having met Lady d'Alboukirk once in London, I go to pay her a respectful visit afterwards. When I come back we will have breakfast together. You might try in the meantime to scrape up an acquaintance with Miss Joan Duplessis, who is still staying here, and ask her to join us at breakfast."

She was gone before I could make another remark, and I could but obey her instantly to the letter.

An hour later I saw Miss Joan Duplessis strolling in the hotel garden. It was not difficult to pass the time of day with the young girl, who seemed quite to brighten up at having someone to talk to . We spoke of the weather and so forth, and I steadily avoided the topic of the Fordwych Castle tragedy until the return of Lady Molly at about ten o'clock. She came back looking just as smart, just as self-possessed, as when she had started three hours earlier. Only I, who knew her so well, noted the glitter of triumph in her eyes, and knew that she had not failed. She was accompanied by Pegram, who, however, immediately left her side and went straight into the hotel, whilst she joined us in the garden, and, after a few graceful words, introduced herself to Miss Joan Duplessis and asked her to join us in the coffee-room upstairs.

The room was empty and we sat down to table, I quivering with excitement and awaiting events. Through the open window I saw Elliott walking rapidly down the village street. Presently the waitress went off, and I being too excited to eat or speak, Lady Molly carried on a running conversation with Miss Joan, asking her about her life in India and her father, Captain Duplessis. Joan admitted that she had always been her father's favourite.

"He never liked Henriette, somehow," she explained.

Lady Molly asked her when she had first known Roonah.

"She came to the house when my mother died," replied Joan, "and she had charge of me as a baby." At Pondicherry no one had thought it strange that she came as a servant into an officer's house where her own sister had reigned as mistress. Pondicherry is a French settlement, and manners and customs there are often very peculiar.

I ventured to ask her what were her future plans.

"Well," she said, with a great touch of sadness, "I can, of course, do nothing whilst my aunt is alive. I cannot force her to let me live at Fordwych or to acknowledge me as her heir. After her death, if my sister does assume the title and fortune of d'Alboukirk," she added, whilst suddenly a strange look of vengefulness—almost of hatred and cruelty—marred the child-like expression of her face, "then I shall revive the story of the tragedy of Roonah's death, and I hope that public opinion—"

She paused here in her speech, and I, who had been gazing out of the window, turned my eyes on her. She was ashy-pale, staring straight before her; her hands dropped the knife and fork which she had held. Then I saw the Pegram had come into the room, that he had come up to the table and placed a packet of papers in Lady Molly's hand.

I saw it all as in a flash!

There was a loud cry of despair like an animal at bay, a shrill cry, followed by a deep one from Pegram of "No, you don't," and before anyone could prevent her, Joan's graceful young figure stood outlined for a short moment at the open window.

The next moment she had disappeared into the depth below, and we heard a dull thud which nearly froze the blood in my veins.

Pegram ran out of the room, but Lady Molly sat quite still.

"I have succeeded in clearing the innocent," she said quietly; "but the guilty has meted out to herself her own punishment."

"Then it was she?" I murmured, horror-struck.

"Yes. I suspected it from the first," replied Lady Molly calmly. "It was this conversion of Roonah to Roman Catholicism and her consequent change of manner which gave me the first clue."

"But why—why?" I muttered.

"A simple reason, Mary," she rejoined, tapping the packet of papers with her delicate hand; and, breaking open the string that held the letters, she laid them out upon the table. "The whole thing was a fraud from beginning to end. The woman's marriage certificate was all right, of course, but I mistrusted the genuineness of the other papers from the moment that I heard that Roonah would not part with them and would not allow Mr. McKinley to have charge of them. I am sure that the idea at first was merely one of blackmail. The papers were only to be the means of extorting money from the old lady, and there was no thought of taking them into court.

"Roonah's part was, of course, the important thing in the whole case, since she was here prepared to swear to the actual date of the first Madame Duplessis's death. The initiative, of course, may have come either from Joan or from Captain Duplessis himself, out of hatred for the family who would have nothing to do with him and his favourite younger daughter. That, of course, we shall never know. At first Roonah was a Parsee, with a dog-like devotion to the girl whom she had nursed as a baby, and who no doubt had drilled her well into the part she was to play. But presently she became a Roman Catholic—an ardent convert, remember, with all a Roman Catholic's fear of hell-fire. I went to the convent this morning. I heard the priest's sermon there, and I realised what an influence his eloquence must have had over poor, ignorant, superstitious Roonah. She was still ready to die for her young mistress, but she was no longer prepared to swear to a lie for her sake. After Mass I called at Fordwych Castle. I explained my position to old Lady d'Alboukirk, who took me into the room where Roonah had slept and died. There I found two things," continued Lady Molly, as she opened the elegant reticule which still hung upon her arm, and placed a big key and a prayer-book before me.

"The key I found in a drawer of an old cupboard in the dressing-room where Roonah slept, with all sorts of odds and ends belonging to the unfortunate woman, and going to the door which led into what had been Joan's bedroom, I found that it was locked, and that this key fitted into the lock. Roonah had locked that door herself on her own side—she was afraid of her mistress. I knew now that I was right in my surmise. The prayer-book is a Roman Catholic one. It is heavily thumbmarked there, where false oaths and lying are denounced as being deadly sins for which hell-fire would be the punishment. Roonah, terrorised by fear of the supernatural, a new convert to the faith, was afraid of committing a deadly sin.

"Who knows what passed between the two women, both of whom have come to so violent and terrible an end? Who can tell what prayers, tears, persuasions Joan Duplessis employed from the time she realised that Roonah did not mean to swear to the lie which would have brought her mistress wealth and glamour until the awful day when she finally understood that Roonah would no longer even hold her tongue, and devised a terrible means of silencing her for ever?

"With this certainty before me, I ventured on my big coup. I was so sure, you see. I kept Joan talking in here whilst I sent Pegram to her room with orders to break open the locks of her hand-bag and dressing-case. There!—I told you that if I was wrong I would probably be dismissed the force for irregularity, as of course I had no right to do that; but if Pegram found the papers there where I felt sure they would be, we could bring the murderer to justice. I know my own sex pretty well, don't I, Mary? I knew that Joan Duplessis had not destroyed—never would destroy—those papers."

Even as Lady Molly spoke we could hear heavy tramping outside the passage. I ran to the door, and there was met by Pegram.

"She is quite dead, miss," he said. "It was a drop of forty feet, and a stone pavement down below."

The guilty had indeed meted out her own punishment to herself!

Lady d'Alboukirk sent Lady Molly a cheque for £5,000 the day the whole affair was made known to the public.

I think you will say that it had been well earned. With her own dainty hands my dear lady had lifted the veil which hung over the tragedy of Fordwych Castle, and with the finding of the papers in Joan Duplessis's dressing-bag, and the unfortunate girl's suicide, the murder of the Indian woman was no longer a mystery.

A DAY'S FOLLY

I DON'T think that anyone ever knew that the real elucidation of the extraordinary mystery known to the newspaper-reading public as the "Somersetshire Outrage" was evolved in my own dear lady's quick, intuitive brain.

As a matter of fact, to this day—as far as the public is concerned—the Somersetshire outrage never was properly explained; and it is a very usual thing for those busybodies who are so fond of criticising the police to point to that case as an instance of remarkable incompetence on the part of our detective department.

A young woman named Jane Turner, a visitor at Weston-super-Mare, had been discovered one afternoon in a helpless condition, bound and gagged, and suffering from terror and inanition, in the bedroom which she occupied in a well-known apartment-house of that town. The police had been immediately sent for, and as soon as Miss Turner had recovered she gave what explanation she could of the mysterious occurrence.

She was employed in one of the large drapery shops in Bristol, and was spending her annual holiday at Weston-super-Mare. Her father was the local butcher at Banwell—a village distant about four miles from Weston—and it appears that somewhere near one o'clock in the afternoon of Friday, the 3rd of September, she was busy in her bedroom putting a few things together in a handbag, preparatory to driving out to Banwell, meaning to pay her parents a week-end visit.

There was a knock at her door, and a voice said, "It's me, Jane—may I come in?"

She did not recognise the voice, but somehow thought that it must be that of a friend, so she shouted, "Come in!"

This was all that the poor thing recollected definitely, for the next moment the door was thrown open, someone rushed at her with amazing violence, she heard the crash of a falling table and felt a blow on the side of her head, whilst a damp handkerchief was pressed to her nose and mouth.

Then she remembered nothing more.

When she gradually came to her senses she found herself in the terrible plight in which Mrs. Skeward—her landlady—discovered her twenty-four hours later.

When pressed to try and describe her assailant, she said that when the door was thrown open she thought that she saw an elderly woman in a wide mantle and wearing bonnet and veil, but that, at the same time, she was quite sure, from the strength and brutality of the onslaught, that she was attacked by a man. She had no enemies, and no possessions worth stealing; but her hand-bag, which, however, only contained a few worthless trifles, had certainly disappeared.

The people of the house, on the other hand, could throw but little light on the mystery which surrounded this very extraordinary and seemingly purposeless assault.

Mrs. Skeward only remembered that on Friday Miss Turner told her that she was just off to Banwell, and would be away for the week-end; but that she wished to keep her room on, against her return on the Monday following.

That was somewhere about half-past twelve o'clock, at the hour when luncheons were being got ready for the various lodgers; small wonder, therefore, that no one in the busy apartment-house took much count of the fact that Miss Turner was not seen to leave the house after that, and no doubt the wretched girl would have been left for several days in the pitiable condition in which she was ultimately found but for the fact that Mrs. Skeward happened to be of the usual grasping type common to those of her kind.

Weston-super-Mare was over-full that week-end, and Mrs. Skeward, beset by applicants for accommodation, did not see why she should not let her absent lodger's room for the night or two that the latter happened to be away, and thus get money twice over for it.

She conducted a visitor up to Miss Turner's room on the Saturday afternoon, and, throwing open the door–which, by the way, was not locked–was horrified to see the poor girl half-sitting, half-slipping off the chair to which she had been tied with a rope, whilst a woolen shawl was wound round the lower part of her face.

As soon as she had released the unfortunate victim, Mrs. Skeward sent for the police, and it was through the intelligent efforts of Detective Parsons–a local man–that a few scraps of very hazy evidence were then and there collected.

First, there was the question of the elderly female in the wide mantle, spoken of by Jane Turner as her assailant. It seems that someone answering to that description had called on the Friday at about one o'clock, and asked to see Miss Turner. The maid who answered the door replied that she thought Miss Turner had gone to Banwell.

"Oh!" said the old dame, "she won't have started yet. I am Miss Turner's mother, and I was to call for her so that we might drive out together."

"Then p'r'aps Miss Turner is still in her room," suggested the maid. "Shall I go and see?"

"Don't trouble," replied the woman; "I know my way. I'll go myself."

Whereupon the old dame walked past the servant, crossed the hall and went upstairs. No one saw her come down again, but one of the lodgers seems to have heard a knock at Jane Turner's door, and the female voice saying, "It's me, Jane–may I come in?"

What happened subsequently, who the mysterious old female was, and how and for what purpose she assaulted Jane Turner and robbed her of a few valueless articles, was the puzzle which faced the police then, and which–so far as the public is concerned–has never been solved. Jane Turner's mother was in bed at the time suffering from a broken ankle and unable to move. The elderly woman was, therefore, an impostor, and the search after her–though keen and hot enough at the time, I assure you–has remained, in the eyes of the public, absolutely fruitless. But of this more anon.

On the actual scene of the crime there was but little to guide subsequent investigation. The rope with which Jane Turner had been pinioned supplied no clue; the wool shawl was Miss Turner's own, snatched up by the miscreant to smother the girl's screams; on the floor was a handkerchief, without initial or laundry mark, which obviously had been saturated with chloroform; and close by a bottle which had contained the anesthetic. A small table was overturned, and the articles which had been resting upon it were lying all around—such as a vase which had held a few flowers, a box of biscuits, and several issues of the West of England Times.

And nothing more. The miscreant, having accomplished his fell purpose, succeeded evidently in walking straight out of the house unobserved; his exit being undoubtedly easily managed owing to it being the busy luncheon hour.

Various theories were, of course, put forward by some of our ablest fellows at the Yard; the most likely solution being the guilt or, at least, the complicity of the girl's sweetheart, Arthur Cutbush—a ne'er-do-well, who spent the greater part of his time on race-courses. Inspector Danvers, whom the chief had sent down to assist the local police, declared that Jane Turner herself suspected her sweetheart, and was trying to shield him by stating she possessed nothing of any value; whereas, no doubt, the young blackguard knew that she had some money, and had planned this amazing coup in order to rob her of it.

Danvers was quite chagrined when, on investigation, it was proved that Arthur Cutbush had gone to the York races three days before the assault, and never left that city until the Saturday evening, when a telegram from Miss Turner summoned him to Weston.

Moreover, the girl did not break off her engagement with young Cutbush, and thus the total absence of motive was a serious bar to the likelihood of the theory.

Then it was the Chief sent for Lady Molly. No doubt he began to feel that here, too, was a case where feminine tact and my lady's own marvellous intuition might prove more useful than the more approved methods of the sterner sex.

2

"Of course, there is a woman in the case, Mary," said Lady Molly to me, when she came home from the interview with the chief, "although they all pooh-pooh that theory at the Yard, and declare that the female voice—to which the only two witnesses we have are prepared to swear—was a disguised one."

"You think, then, that a woman assaulted Jane Turner?"

"Well," she replied somewhat evasively, "if a man assumes a feminine voice, the result is a high-pitched, unnatural treble; and that, I feel convinced, would have struck either the maid or the lodger, or both, as peculiar."

This was the train of thought which my dear lady and I were following up, when, with that sudden transition of manner so characteristic of her, she said abruptly to me:

"Mary, look out a train for Weston-super-Mare. We must try to get down there to-night."

"Chief's orders?" I asked.

"No—mine," she replied laconically. "Where's the A B C?"

Well, we got off that self-same afternoon, and in the evening we were having dinner at the Grand Hotel, Weston-super-Mare.

My dear lady had been pondering all through the journey, and even now she was singularly silent and absorbed. There was a deep frown between her eyes, and every now and then the luminous, dark orbs would suddenly narrow, and the pupils contract as if smitten with a sudden light.

I was not a little puzzled as to what was going on in that active brain of hers, but my experience was that silence on my part was the surest card to play.

Lady Molly had entered our names in the hotel book as Mrs. Walter Bell and Miss Granard from London; and the day after our arrival there came two heavy parcels for her under that name. She had them taken upstairs to our private sitting-room, and there we undid them together.

To my astonishment they contained stacks of newspapers: as far as I could see at a glance, back numbers of the West of England Times covering a whole year.

"Find and cut out the 'Personal' column of every number, Mary," said Lady Molly to me. "I'll look through them on my return. I am going for a walk, and will be home by lunch time."

I knew, of course, that she was intent on her business and on that only, and as soon as she had gone out I set myself to the wearisome task which she had allotted me. My dear lady was evidently working out a problem in her mind, the solution of which she expected to find in a back number of the West of England Times.

By the time she returned I had the "Personal" column of some three hundred numbers of the paper neatly filed and docketed for her perusal. She thanked me for my promptitude with one of her charming looks, but said little, if anything, all through luncheon. After that meal she set to work. I could see her studying each scrap of paper minutely, comparing one with the other, arranging them in sets in front of her, and making marginal notes on them all the while.

With but a brief interval for tea, she sat at her table for close on four hours, at the end of which she swept all the scraps of paper on one side, with the exception of a few which she kept in her hand. Then she looked up at me, and I sighed with relief.

My dear lady was positively beaming.

"You have found what you wanted?" I asked eagerly.

"What I expected," she replied.

"May I know?"

She spread out the bits of paper before me. There were six altogether, and each of these columns had one paragraph specially marked with a cross.

"Only look at the paragraphs which I have marked," she said.

I did what I was told. But if in my heart I had vaguely hoped that I should then and there be confronted with the solution of the mystery which surrounded the Somersetshire outrage, I was doomed to disappointment.

Each of the marked paragraphs in the "Personal" columns bore the initials H. S. H., and their purport was invariably an assignation at one of the small railway stations on the line between Bristol and Weston.

I suppose that my bewilderment must have been supremely comical, for my lady's rippling laugh went echoing through the bare, dull hotel sitting-room.

"You don't see it, Mary?" she asked gaily.

"I confess I don't," I replied. "It completely baffles me."

"And yet," she said more gravely, "those few silly paragraphs have given me the clue to the mysterious assault on Jane Turner, which has been puzzling our fellows at the Yard for over three weeks."

"But how? I don't understand."

"You will, Mary, directly we get back to town. During my morning walk I have learnt all that I want to know, and now these paragraphs have set my mind at rest."

3

THE next day we were back in town.

Already, at Bristol, we had bought a London morning paper, which contained in its centre page a short notice under the following startling headlines:

AMAZING DISCOVERY BY THE POLICE
AN UNEXPECTED CLUE

The article went on to say:

"We are officially informed that the police have recently obtained knowledge of certain facts which establish beyond a doubt the motive of the brutal assault committed on the person of Miss Jane Turner. We are not authorised to say more at present than that certain startling developments are imminent."

On the way up my dear lady had initiated me into some of her views with regard to the case itself, which at the chief's desire she had now taken entirely in hand, and also into her immediate plans, of which the above article was merely the preface.

She it was who had "officially informed" the Press Association, and, needless to say, the news duly appeared in most of the London and provincial dailies.

How unerring was her intuition, and how well thought out her scheme, was proved within the next four-and-twenty hours in our own little flat, when our Emily, looking somewhat important and awed, announced Her Serene Highness the Countess of Hohengebirg.

H. S. H.–the conspicuous initials in the "Personal" columns of the West of England Times! You may imagine how I stared at the exquisite apparition–all lace and chiffon and roses–which the next moment literally swept into our office, past poor, open-mouthed Emily.

Had my dear lady taken leave of her senses when she suggested that this beautiful young woman with the soft, fair hair, with the pleading blue eyes and childlike mouth, had anything to do with a brutal assault on a shop girl?

The young Countess shook hands with Lady Molly and with me, and then, with a deep sigh, she sank into the comfortable chair which I was offering her.

Speaking throughout with great diffidence, but always in the gentle tones of a child that knows it has been naughty, she began by explaining that she had been to Scotland Yard, where a very charming man–the chief, I presume–had been most kind and sent her hither, where he promised her she would find help and consolation in her dreadful, dreadful trouble.

Encouraged by Lady Molly, she soon plunged into her narrative: a pathetic tale of her own frivolity and foolishness.

She was originally Lady Muriel Wolfe-Strongham, daughter of the Duke of Weston, and when scarce out of the schoolroom had met the Grand Duke of

Starkburg-Nauheim, who fell in love with her and married her. The union was a morganatic one, the Grand Duke conferring on his English wife the title of the Countess of Hohengebirg and the rank of Serene Highness.

It seems that, at first, the marriage was a fairly happy one, in spite of the bitter animosity of the mother and sister of the Grand Duke: the Dowager Grand Duchess holding that all English girls were loud and unwomanly, and the Princess Amalie, seeing in her brother's marriage a serious bar to the fulfilment of her own highly ambitious matrimonial hopes.

"They can't bear me, because I don't knit socks and don't know how to bake almond cakes," said her dear little Serene Highness, looking up with tender appeal at Lady Molly's grave and beautiful face; "and they will be so happy to see a real estrangement between my husband and myself."

It appears that last year, while the Grand Duke was doing his annual cure at Marienbad, the Countess of Hohengebirg went to Folkestone for the benefit of her little boy's health. She stayed at one of the Hotels there merely as any English lady of wealth might do–with nurses and her own maid, of course, but without the paraphernalia and nuisance of her usual German retinue.

Whilst there she met an old acquaintance of her father's, a Mr. Rumboldt, who is a rich financier, it seems, and who at one time moved in the best society, but whose reputation had greatly suffered recently, owing to a much talked of divorce case which brought his name into unenviable notoriety.

Her Serene Highness, with more mopping of her blue eyes, assured Lady Molly that over at Schloss Starkburg she did not read the English papers, and was therefore quite unaware that Mr. Rumboldt, who used to be a persona grata in her father's house, was no longer a fit and proper acquaintance for her.

"It was a very fine morning," she continued with gentle pathos, "and I was deadly dull at Folkestone. Mr. Rumboldt persuaded me to go with him on a short trip on his yacht. We were to cross over to Boulogne, have luncheon there, and come home in the cool of the evening."

"And, of course, something occurred to disable the yacht," concluded Lady Molly gravely, as the lady herself had paused in her narrative.

"Of course," whispered the little Countess through her tears.

"And, of course, it was too late to get back by the ordinary afternoon mail boat?"

"That boat had gone an hour before, and the next did not leave until the middle of the night."

"So you had perforce to wait until then, and in the meanwhile you were seen by a girl named Jane Turner, who knew you by sight, and who has been blackmailing you ever since."

"How did you guess that?" ejaculated Her Highness, with a look of such comical bewilderment in her large, blue eyes that Lady Molly and I had perforce to laugh.

"Well," replied my dear lady after awhile, resuming her gravity, "we have a way in our profession of putting two and two together, haven't we? And in this case it was not very difficult. The assignations for secret meetings at out-of-the-way railway stations which were addressed to H. S. H. in the columns of the West of England Times recently, gave me one clue, shall we say? The mysterious assault on a young woman, whose home was close to those very railway stations as well as to Bristol Castle—your parents' residence, where you have frequently been staying of late, was another piece that fitted in the puzzle; whilst the number of copies of the West of England Times that were found in that same young woman's room helped to draw my thoughts to her. Then your visit to me to-day—it is very simple, you see."

"I suppose so," said H. S. H. with a sigh. "Only it is worse even than you suggest, for that horrid Jane Turner, to whom I had been ever so kind when I was a girl, took a snapshot of me and Mr. Rumboldt standing on the steps of Hôtel des Bains at Boulogne. I saw her doing it and rushed down the steps to stop her. She talked quite nicely then—hypocritical wretch!—and said that perhaps the plate would be no good when it was developed, and if it were she would destroy it. I was not to worry; she would contrive to let me know through the agony column of the West of England Times, which—as I was going home to Bristol Castle to stay with my parents—I could see every day, but she had no idea I should have minded, and all that sort of rigmarole. Oh! she is a wicked girl, isn't she, to worry me so?"

And once again the lace handkerchief found its way to the most beautiful pair of blue eyes I think I have ever seen. I could not help smiling, though I was really very sorry for the silly, emotional, dear little thing.

"And instead of reassurance in the West of England Times, you found a demand for a secret meeting at a country railway station?"

"Yes! And when I went there—terrified lest I should be seen—Jane Turner did not meet me herself. Her mother came and at once talked of selling the photograph to my husband or to my mother-in-law. She said it was worth four thousand pounds to Jane, and that she had advised her daughter not to sell it to me for less."

"What did you reply?"

"That I hadn't got four thousand pounds," said the Countess ruefully; "so after a lot of argument it was agreed that I was to pay Jane two hundred and fifty pounds a year out of my dress allowance. She would keep the negative as security, but promised never to let anyone see it so long as she got her money regularly. It was also arranged that whenever I stayed with my parents at Bristol Castle, Jane would make appointments to meet me through the columns of the West of England Times, and I was to pay up the instalments then just as she directed."

I could have laughed, if the whole thing had not been so tragic, for truly the way this silly, harmless little woman had allowed herself to be bullied and blackmailed by a pair of grasping females was beyond belief.

"And this has been going on for over a year," commented Lady Molly gravely.

"Yes, but I never met Jane Turner again: it was always her mother who came."

"You knew her mother before that, I presume?"

"Oh, no. I only knew Jane because she had been sewing-maid at the Castle some few years ago."

"I see," said Lady Molly slowly. "What was the woman like whom you used to meet at the railway stations, and to whom you paid over Miss Turner's money?"

"Oh, I couldn't tell you what she was like. I never saw her properly."

"Never saw her properly?" ejaculated Lady Molly, and it seemed to my well-trained ears as if there was a ring of exultation in my dear lady's voice.

"No," replied the little Countess ruefully. "She always appointed a late hour of the evening, and those little stations on that line are very badly lighted. I had such difficulties getting away from home without exciting comment, and used to beg her to let me meet her at a more convenient hour. But she always refused."

Lady Molly remained thoughtful for a while; then she asked abruptly:

"Why don't you prosecute Jane Turner for blackmail?"

"Oh, I dare not–I dare not!" ejaculated the little Countess, in genuine terror. "My husband would never forgive me, and his female relations would do their best afterwards to widen the breach between us. It was because of the article in the London newspaper about the assault on Jane Turner–the talk of a clue and of startling developments–that I got terrified, and went to Scotland Yard. Oh, no! no! no! Promise me that my name won't be dragged into this case. It would ruin me for ever!"

She was sobbing now; her grief and fear were very pathetic to witness, and she moaned through her sobs:

"Those wicked people know that I daren't risk an exposure, and simply prey on me like vampires because of that. The last time I saw the old woman I told her that I would confess everything to my husband–I couldn't bear to go on like this. But she only laughed; she knew I should never dare."

"When was this?" asked Lady Molly.

"About three weeks ago–just before Jane Turner was assaulted and robbed of the photographs."

"How do you know she was robbed of the photographs?"

"She wrote and told me so," replied the young Countess, who seemed strangely awed now by my dear lady's earnest question. And from a dainty reticule she took a piece of paper, which bore traces of many bitter tears on its crumpled surface. This she handed to Lady Molly, who took it from her. It was a type-written letter, which bore no signature. Lady Molly perused it in silence first, then read its contents out aloud to me:–

"To H. S. H. the Countess of Hohengebirg.

"You think I have been worrying you the past twelve months about your adventure with Mr. Rumboldt in Boulogne. But it was not me; it was one who has power over me, and who knew about the photograph. He made me act as I did. But whilst I kept the photo you were safe. Now he has assaulted me and nearly killed me, and taken the negative away. I can, and will, get it out of him again, but it will mean a large sum down. Can you manage one thousand pounds?"

"When did you get this?" asked Lady Molly.

"Only a few days ago," replied the Countess. "And oh! I have been enduring agonies of doubt and fear for the past three weeks, for I had heard nothing from Jane since the assault, and I wondered what had happened."

"You have not sent a reply, I hope."

"No. I was going to, when I saw the article in the London paper, and the fear that all had been discovered threw me into such a state of agony that I came straight up to town and saw the gentleman at Scotland Yard, who sent me on to you. Oh!" she entreated again and again, "you won't do anything that will cause a scandal! Promise me–promise me! I believe I should commit suicide rather than face it–and I could find a thousand pounds."

"I don't think you need do either," said Lady Molly. "Now, may I think over the whole matter quietly to myself," she added, "and talk it over with my friend here? I may be able to let you have some good news shortly."

She rose, intimating kindly that the interview was over. But it was by no means that yet, for there was still a good deal of entreaty and a great many tears on the one part, and reiterated kind assurances on the other. However when, some ten minutes later, the dainty clouds of lace and chiffon were finally wafted out of our office, we both felt that the poor, harmless, unutterably foolish little lady looked distinctly consoled and more happy than she had been for the past twelve months.

4

"YES! she has been an utter little goose," Lady Molly was saying to me an hour later when we were having luncheon; "but that Jane Turner is a remarkably clever girl."

"I suppose you think, as I do, that the mysterious elderly female, who seems to have impersonated the mother all through, was an accomplice of Jane Turner's, and that the assault was a put-up job between them," I said. "Inspector Danvers will be delighted--for this theory is a near approach to his own."

"H'm!" was all the comment vouchsafed on my remark.

"I am sure it was Arthur Cutbush, the girl's sweetheart, after all," I retorted hotly, "and you'll see that, put to the test of sworn evidence, his alibi at the time of the assault itself won't hold good. Moreover, now," I added triumphantly, "we have knowledge which has been lacking all along–the motive."

"Ah!" said my lady, smiling at my enthusiasm, "that's how you argue, Mary, is it?"

"Yes, and in my opinion the only question in doubt is whether Arthur Cutbush acted in collusion with Jane Turner or against her."

"Well, suppose we go and elucidate that point–and some others–at once," concluded Lady Molly as she rose from the table.

She decided to return to Bristol that same evening. We were going by the 8.50 p.m., and I was just getting ready–the cab being already at the door–when I was somewhat startled by the sudden appearance into my room of an old lady, very beautifully dressed, with snow-white hair dressed high above a severe, interesting face.

A merry, rippling laugh issuing from the wrinkled mouth, and a closer scrutiny on my part, soon revealed the identity of my dear lady, dressed up to look like an extremely dignified grande dame of the old school, whilst a pair of long, old-fashioned earrings gave a curious, foreign look to her whole appearance.

I didn't quite see why she chose to arrive at the Grand Hotel, Bristol, in that particular disguise, nor why she entered our names in the hotel book as Grand Duchess and Princess Amalie von Starkburg, from Germany; nor did she tell me anything that evening.

But by the next afternoon, when we drove out together in a fly, I was well up in the rôle which I had to play. My lady had made me dress in a very rich black silk dress of her own, and ordered me to do my hair in a somewhat frumpish fashion, with a parting, and a "bun" at the back. She herself looked more like Royalty travelling incognito than ever, and no wonder small children and tradesmen's boys stared open-mouthed when we alighted from our fly outside one of the mean-looking little houses in Bread Street.

In answer to our ring, a smutty little servant opened the door, and my lady asked her if Miss Jane Turner lived here and if she were in.

"Yes, Miss Turner lives here, and it bein' Thursday and early closin' she's home from business."

"Then please tell her," said Lady Molly in her grandest manner, "that the Dowager Grand Duchess of Starkburg-Nauheim and the Princess Amalie desire to see her."

The poor little maid nearly fell backwards with astonishment. She gasped an agitated "Lor!" and then flew down the narrow passage and up the steep staircase, closely followed by my dear lady and myself.

On the first-floor landing the girl, with nervous haste, knocked at a door, opened it and muttered half audibly:

"Ladies to see you, miss!"

Then she fled incontinently upstairs. I have never been able to decide whether that little girl thought that we were lunatics, ghosts, or criminals.

But already Lady Molly had sailed into the room, where Miss Jane Turner apparently had been sitting reading a novel. She jumped up when we entered, and stared open-eyed at the gorgeous apparitions. She was not a bad-looking girl but for the provoking, bold look in her black eyes, and the general slatternly appearance of her person.

"Pray do not disturb yourself, Miss Turner," said Lady Molly in broken English, as she sank into a chair, and beckoned me to do likewise. "Pray sit down—I vill be brief. You have a compromising photograph—is it not?—of my daughter-in-law ze Countess of Hohengebirg. I am ze Grand Duchess of Starkburg-Nauheim—zis is my daughter, ze Princess Amalie. We are here incognito. You understand? Not?"

And, with inimitable elegance of gesture, my dear lady raised a pair of "starers" to her eyes and fixed them on Jane Turner's quaking figure.

Never had I seen suspicion, nay terror, depicted so plainly on a young face, but I will do the girl the justice to state that she pulled herself together with marvellous strength of will.

She fought down her awed respect of this great lady; or rather shall I say that the British middle-class want of respect for social superiority, especially if it be foreign, now stood her in good stead?

"I don't know what you are talking about," she said with an arrogant toss of the head.

"Zat is a lie, is it not?" rejoined Lady Molly calmly, as she drew from her reticule the typewritten letter which Jane Turner had sent to the Countess of Hohengebirg. "Zis you wrote to my daughter-in-law; ze letter reached me instead of her. It interests me much. I vill give you two tousend pounds for ze photograph of her and Mr.—er—Rumboldt. You vill sell it to me for zat, is it not?"

The production of the letter had somewhat cowed Jane's bold spirit. But she was still defiant.

"I haven't got the photograph here," she said.

"Ah, no! but you vill get it—yes?" said my lady, quietly replacing the letter in her reticule. "In ze letter you offer to get it for tousend pound. I vill give you two tousend. To-day is a holiday for you. You vill get ze photograph from ze gentleman—not? And I vill vait here till you come back."

Whereupon she rearranged her skirts round her and folded her hands placidly, like one prepared to wait.

"I haven't got the photograph," said Jane Turner, doggedly, "and I can't get it to-day. The—the person who has it doesn't live in Bristol."

"No? Ah! but quite close, isn't it?" rejoined my lady, placidly. "I can vait all ze day."

"No, you shan't!" retorted Jane Turner, whose voice now shook with obvious rage or fear—I knew not which. "I can't get the photograph to-day—so there! And I won't sell it to you—I won't. I don't want your two thousand pounds. How do I know you are not an imposter?"

"From zis, my good girl," said Lady Molly, quietly; "that if I leave zis room wizout ze photograph, I go straight to ze police with zis letter, and you shall be prosecuted by ze Grand Duke, my son, for blackmailing his wife. You see, I am not like my daughter-in-law; I am not afraid of a scandal. So you vill fetch ze photograph—isn't it? I and ze Princess Amalie vill vait for it here. Zat is your bedroom—not?" she added, pointing to a door which obviously gave on an inner room. "Vill you put on your hat and go at once, please? Two tousend pound or two years in prison—you have ze choice—isn't it?"

Jane Turner tried to keep up her air of defiance, looking Lady Molly full in the face; but I who watched her could see the boldness in her eyes gradually giving place to fear, and then to terror and even despair; the girl's face seemed literally to grow old as I looked at it—pale, haggard, and drawn—whilst Lady Molly kept her stern, luminous eyes fixed steadily upon her.

Then, with a curious, wild gesture, which somehow filled me with a nameless fear, Jane Turner turned on her heel and ran into the inner room.

There followed a moment of silence. To me it was tense and agonising. I was straining my ears to hear what was going on in that inner room. That my dear lady was not as callous as she wished to appear was shown by the strange look of expectancy in her beautiful eyes.

The minutes sped on—how many I could not afterwards have said. I was conscious of a clock ticking monotonously over the shabby mantelpiece, of an errand boy outside shouting at the top of his voice, of the measured step of the cab horse which had brought us hither being walked up and down the street.

Then suddenly there was a violent crash, as of heavy furniture being thrown down. I could not suppress a scream, for my nerves by now were terribly on the jar.

"Quick, Mary—the inner room!" said Lady Molly. "I thought the girl might do that."

I dared not pause in order to ask what "that" meant, but flew to the door.

It was locked.

"Downstairs—quick!" commanded my lady. "I ordered Danvers to be on the watch outside."

You may imagine how I flew, and how I blessed my dear lady's forethought in the midst of her daring plan, when, having literally torn open the front door, I saw Inspector Danvers in plain clothes, calmly patrolling the street. I beckoned to him—

he was keeping a sharp look-out—and together we ran back into the house.

Fortunately, the landlady and the servant were busy in the basement, and had neither heard the crash nor seen me run in search of Danvers. My dear lady was still alone in the dingy parlour, stooping against the door of the inner room, her ear glued to the keyhole.

"Not too late, I think," she whispered hurriedly. "Break it open, Danvers."

Danvers, who is a great, strong man, soon put his shoulder to the rickety door, which yielded to the first blow.

The sight which greeted us filled me with horror, for I had never seen such a tragedy before. The wretched girl, Jane Turner, had tied a rope to a ring in the ceiling, which I suppose at one time held a hanging lamp; the other end of that rope she had formed into a slip-noose, and passed round her neck.

She had apparently climbed on to a table, and then used her best efforts to end her life by kicking the table away from under her. This was the crash which we had heard, and which had caused us to come to her rescue. Fortunately, her feet had caught in the back of a chair close by; the slip-noose was strangling her, and her face was awful to behold, but she was not dead.

Danvers soon got her down. He is a first-aid man, and has done these terrible jobs before. As soon as the girl had partially recovered, Lady Molly sent him and me out of the room. In the dark and dusty parlour, where but a few moments ago I had played my small part in a grim comedy, I now waited to hear what the sequel to it would be.

Danvers had been gone some time, and the shades of evening were drawing in; outside, the mean-looking street looked particularly dreary. It was close on six o'clock when at last I heard the welcome rustle of silks, the opening of a door, and at last my dear lady—looking grave but serene—came out of the inner room, and, beckoning to me, without a word led the way out of the house and into the fly, which was still waiting at the door.

"We'll send a doctor to her," were her first words as soon as we were clear of Bread Street. "But she is quite all right now, save that she wants a sleeping draught. Well, she has been punished enough, I think. She won't try her hand at blackmailing again."

"Then the photograph never existed?" I asked amazed.

"No; the plate was a failure, but Jane Turner would not thus readily give up the idea of getting money out of the poor, pusillanimous Countess. We know how she succeeded in terrorizing that silly little woman. It is wonderful how cleverly a girl like that worked out such a complicated scheme, all alone."

"All alone?"

"Yes; there was no one else. She was the elderly woman who used to meet the Countess, and who rang at the front door of the Weston apartment-house. She arranged the whole of the mise en scène of the assault on herself, all alone, and took everybody in with it—it was so perfectly done. She planned and executed it because she was afraid that the little Countess would be goaded into confessing her folly to her husband, or to her own parents, when a prosecution for blackmail would inevitably follow. So she risked everything on a big coup, and almost succeeded in getting a thousand pounds from Her Serene Highness, meaning to reassure her, as soon as she had the money, by the statement that the negative and prints had been destroyed. But the appearance of the Grand Duchess of Starkburg-Nauheim this afternoon frightened her into an act of despair. Confronted with the prosecution she dreaded and with the prison she dared not face, she, in a mad moment, attempted to take her life."

"I suppose now the whole matter will be hushed up."

"Yes," replied Lady Molly with a wistful sigh. "The public will never know who assaulted Jane Turner."

She was naturally a little regretful at that. But it was a joy to see her the day when she was able to assure Her Serene Highness the Countess of Hohengebirg that she need never again fear the consequences of that fatal day's folly.

A CASTLE IN BRITTANY

YES! we are just back from our holiday, my dear lady and I–a well-earned holiday, I can tell you that.

We went to Porhoët, you know–a dear little village in the hinterland of Brittany, not very far from the coast; an enchanting spot, hidden away in a valley, bordered by a mountain stream, wild, romantic, picturesque–Brittany, in fact.

We had discovered the little place quite accidentally last year, in the course of our wanderings, and stayed there then about three weeks, laying the foundations of that strange adventure which reached its culminating point just a month ago.

I don't know if the story will interest you, for Lady Molly's share in the adventure was purely a private one and had nothing whatever to do with her professional work. At the same time it illustrates in a very marked manner that extraordinary faculty which she possesses of divining her fellow-creatures' motives and intentions.

We had rooms and pension in the dear little convent on the outskirts of the village, close to the quaint church and the picturesque presbytery, and soon we made the acquaintance of the Curé, a simple-minded, kindly old man, whose sorrow at the thought that two such charming English ladies as Lady Molly and myself should be heretics was more than counter-balanced by his delight in having someone of the "great outside world"–as he called it–to talk to, whilst he told us quite ingenuously something of his own simple life, of this village which he loved, and also of his parishioners.

One personality among the latter occupied his thoughts and conversation a great deal, and I must say interested us keenly. It was that of Miss Angela de Genneville, who owned the magnificent château of Porhoët, one of the seven wonders of architectural France. She was an Englishwoman by birth–being of a Jersey family–and was immensely wealthy, her uncle, who was also her godfather, having bequeathed to her the largest cigar factory in St. Heliers, besides three-quarters of a million sterling.

To say that Miss de Genneville was eccentric was but to put it mildly; in the village she was generally thought to be quite mad. The Curé vaguely hinted that a tragic love story was at the bottom of all her eccentricities. Certain it is that, for no apparent reason, and when she was still a youngish woman, she had sold the Jersey business and realised the whole of her fortune. After two years of continuous travelling, she came to Brittany on a visit to her sister–the widowed Marquise de Terhoven, who owned a small property close to Porhoët, and lived there in retirement and poverty with her only son, Amédé.

Miss Angela de Genneville was agreeably taken with the beauty and quietude of this remote little village. The beautiful château of Porhoët being for sale at the time, she bought it, took out letters of naturalization, became a French subject, and from that moment never went outside the precincts of her newly acquired domain.

She never returned to England, and, with the exception of the Curé and her own sister and nephew, saw no one beyond her small retinue of servants.

But the dear old Curé thought all the world of her, for she was supremely charitable to him and to the poor, and scarcely a day passed but he told us something either of her kindness or of her eccentric ways. One day he arrived at the convent at an unaccustomed hour; we had just finished our simple déjeuner of steaming coffee and rolls when we saw him coming towards us across the garden.

That he was excited and perturbed was at once apparent by his hurried gait and by the flush on his kindly face. He bade us a very hasty "Good morning, my daughters!" and plunged abruptly into his subject. He explained with great volubility, which was intended to mask his agitation, that he was the bearer of an invitation to the charming English lady–a curious invitation, ah, yes! perhaps!– Mademoiselle de Genneville–very eccentric–but she is in great trouble–in very serious trouble–and very ill too, now–poor lady–half paralysed and feeble–yes, feeble in the brain–and then her nephew, the Marquis Amédé de Terhoven–such a misguided young man–has got into bad company in that den of wickedness called Paris–since then it has been debts–always debts–his mother is so indulgent!–too indulgent! but an only son!–the charming English ladies would understand. It was very sad–very, very sad–and no wonder Mademoiselle de Genneville was very angry. She had paid Monsieur le Marquis' debts once, twice, three times–but now she will not pay any more–but she is in great trouble and wants a friend–a female friend, one of her own country, she declares–for he himself, alas! was only a poor curé de village, and did not understand great ladies and their curious ways. It would be true Christian charity if the charming English lady would come and see Mademoiselle.

"But her own sister, the Marquise?" suggested Lady Molly, breaking in on the old man's volubility.

"Ah! her sister, of course," he replied with a sigh. "Madame la Marquise–but then she is Monsieur le Marquis' mother, and the charming English lady would understand–a mother's heart, of course–"

"But I am a complete stranger to Miss de Genneville," protested Lady Molly.

"Ah, but Mademoiselle has always remained an Englishwoman at heart," replied the Curé. "She said to me to-day: 'I seem to long for an Englishwoman's handshake, a sober-minded, sensible Englishwoman, to help me in this difficulty.

Bring your English friend to me, Monsieur le Curé, if she will come to the assistance of an old woman who has no one to turn to in her distress.'"

Of course, after that I knew that my dear lady would yield. Moreover, she was keenly interested in Miss de Genneville, and without further discussion she told Monsieur le Curé that she was quite ready to accompany him to the château of Porhoët.

2

OF course, I was not present at the interview, but Lady Molly has so often told me all that happened and how it happened, and with such a wealth of picturesque and minute detail, that sometimes I find it difficult to realise that I myself was not there in person.

It seems that Monsieur le Curé himself ushered my lady into the presence of Miss Angela de Genneville. The old lady was not alone when they entered; Madame la Marquise de Terhoven, an elderly, somewhat florid woman, whose features, though distinctly coarse, recalled those of her sister, sat on a high-backed chair close to a table, on which her fingers were nervously drumming a tattoo, whilst in the window embrasure stood a young man whose resemblance to both the ladies at once proclaimed him to Lady Molly's quick perception as the son of the one and nephew of the other—the Marquis de Terhoven, in fact.

Miss de Genneville sat erect in a huge armchair; her face was the hue of yellow wax, the flesh literally shriveled on the bones, the eyes of a curious, unnatural brilliance; one hand clutched feverishly the arm of her chair, the other, totally paralysed, lay limp and inert on her lap.

"Ah! the Englishwoman at last, thank God!" she said in a high-pitched, strident voice as soon as Lady Molly entered the room. "Come here, my dear, for I have wanted one of your kind badly. A true-hearted Englishwoman is the finest product of God's earth, after all's said and done. Pardieu! but I breathe again," she added, as my dear lady advanced somewhat diffidently to greet her, and took the trembling hand which Miss Angela extended to her.

"Sit down close to me," commanded the eccentric old lady, whilst Lady Molly, confused, and not a little angered at finding herself in the very midst of what was obviously a family conclave, was vaguely wondering how soon she could slip away again. But the trembling hand of the paralytic clutched her own slender wrist so tightly, forcing her to sink into a low chair close by, and holding her there as with a grip of steel, that it would have been useless and perhaps cruel to resist.

Satisfied now that her newly found friend, as well as Monsieur le Curé, were prepared to remain by her and to listen to what she had to say, the sick woman turned with a look of violent wrath towards the window embrasure.

"I was just telling that fine nephew of mine that he is counting his chickens before they are hatched. I am not yet dead, as Monsieur my nephew can see; and I have made a will–aye, and placed it where his thievish fingers can never reach it."

The young man, who up to now had been gazing stolidly out of the window, now suddenly turned on his heel, confronting the old woman, with a look of hate gleaming in his eyes.

"We can fight the will," here interposed Madame la Marquise, icily.

"On what grounds?" queried the other.

"That you were paralysed and imbecile when you made it," replied the Marquise, dryly.

Monsieur le Curé, who up to now had been fidgeting nervously with his hat, now raised his hands and eyes up to the ceiling to emphasise the horror which he felt at this callous suggestion. Lady Molly no longer desired to go; the half-paralysed grip on her wrist had relaxed, but she sat there quietly, interested with every fibre of her quick intelligence in the moving drama which was being unfolded before her.

There was a pause now, a silence broken only by the monotonous ticking of a monumental, curious-looking clock which stood in an angle of the room. Miss de Genneville had made no reply to her sister's cruel taunt, but a look, furtive, maniacal, almost dangerous, now crept into her eyes.

Then she addressed the Curé.

"I pray you pen, ink and paper—here, on this table," she requested. Then as he complied with alacrity, she once more turned to her nephew, and pointing to the writing materials:

"Sit down and write, Amédé," she commanded.

"Write what?" he queried.

"A confession, my nephew," said the old woman, with a shrill laugh. "A confession of those little peccadilloes of yours, which, unless I come to your rescue now, will land you for seven years in a penal settlement, if I mistake not. Eh, my fine nephew?"

"A confession?" retorted Amédé de Terhoven savagely. "Do you take me for a fool?"

"No, my nephew, I take you for a wise man—who understands that his dear aunt will not buy those interesting forgeries, perpetrated by Monsieur le Marquis Amédé de Terhoven, and offered to her by Rubinstein the money-lender, unless that confession is written and signed by you. Write Amédé, write that confession, my dear nephew, if you do not wish to see yourself in the dock on a charge of forging your aunt's name to a bill for one hundred thousand francs."

Amédé muttered a curse between his teeth. Obviously the old woman's shaft had struck home. He knew himself to be in a hopeless plight. It appears that a money-lender had threatened to send the forged bills to Monsieur le Procureur de la République unless they were paid within twenty-four hours, and no one could pay them but Miss de Genneville, who had refused to do it except at the price of this humiliating confession.

A look of intelligence passed between mother and son. Intercepted by Lady Molly and interpreted by her, it seemed to suggest the idea of humouring the old aunt, for the moment, until the forgeries were safely out of the money-lender's hands, then of mollifying her later on, when perhaps she would have forgotten, or sunk deeper into helplessness and imbecility.

As if in answer to his mother's look the young man now said curtly:

"I must know what use you mean to make of the confession if I do write it."

"That will depend on yourself," replied Mademoiselle, dryly. "You may be sure that I will not willingly send my own nephew to penal servitude."

For another moment the young man hesitated, then he sat down, sullen and wrathful, and said:

"I'll write—you may dictate—"

The old woman laughed a short, dry, sarcastic laugh. Then, at her dictation, Amédé wrote:

"I, Amédé, Marquis de Terhoven, hereby make confession to having forged Mademoiselle Angela de Genneville's name to the annexed bills, thereby obtaining the sum of one hundred thousand francs from Abraham Rubinstein, of Brest."

"Now, Monsieur le Curé, will you kindly witness le Marquis' signature?" said the irascible old lady when Amédé had finished writing; "and you, too, my dear?" she added, turning to Lady Molly.

My dear lady hesitated for a moment. Naturally she did not desire to be thus mixed up in this family feud, but a strange impulse had drawn her sympathy to this eccentric old lady, who, in the midst of her semi-regal splendour seemed so forlorn, between her nephew, who was a criminal and a blackguard, and her sister, who was but little less contemptible.

Obeying this impulse, and also a look of entreaty from the Curé, she affixed her own signature as witness to the document, and this despite the fact that both the Marquise and her son threw her a look of hate which might have made a weaker spirit tremble with foreboding.

Not so Lady Molly. Those very same threatening looks served but to decide her. Then, at Mademoiselle's command, she folded up the document, slipped it into an envelope, sealed it, and finally addressed it to M. le Procureur de la République, resident at Caen.

Amédé watched all these proceedings with eyes that were burning with impotent wrath.

"This letter," now resumed the old lady, more calmly. "will be sent under cover to my lawyer Maître Vendôme, of Paris, who drew up my will, with orders only to post it in case of certain eventualities, which I will explain later on. In the meanwhile, my dear nephew, you may apprise your friend, Abraham Rubinstein, that I will buy back those interesting forgeries of yours on the day on which I hear from Maître Vendôme that he has safely received my letter with this enclosure."

"This is infamous—" here broke in the Marquise, rising in full wrath, unable to control herself any longer. "I'll have you put under restraint as a dangerous lunatic. I—"

"Then, of course, I could not buy back the bills from Rubinstein," rejoined Mademoiselle, calmly.

Then, as the Marquise subsided—cowed, terrified, realising the hopelessness of her son's position—the old lady turned placidly to my dear lady, whilst her trembling fingers once more clutched the slender hand of her newly found English friend.

"I have asked you, my dear, and Monsieur le Curé, to come to me to-day," she said, "because I wish you both to be of assistance to me in the carrying out of my dying wishes. You must promise me most solemnly, both of you, that when I am dead you will carry out these wishes to the letter. Promise!" she added with passionate earnestness.

The promise was duly given by Lady Molly and the old Curé, then Mademoiselle resumed more calmly:

"And now I want you to look at that clock," she said abruptly, with seeming irrelevance. "It is an old heirloom which belonged to the former owners of Porhoët, and which I bought along with the house. You will notice that it is one of the most remarkable pieces of mechanism which brain of man has ever devised, for it has this great peculiarity, that it goes for three hundred and sixty-six days consecutively, keeping most perfect time. When the works have all but run down, the weights—which are enormous—release a certain spring, and the great doors of the case open of themselves, thus allowing the clock to be wound up. After that is done, and the doors pushed to again, no one can open them until another three hundred and sixty-six days have gone by—that is to say, not without breaking the case to pieces."

Lady Molly examined the curious old clock with great attention. Vaguely she guessed already what the drift of the old lady's curious explanations would be.

"Two days ago," continued Mademoiselle, "the clock was open, and Monsieur le Curé wound it up, but before I pushed the doors to again I slipped certain papers into the case—you remember, Monsieur?"

"Yes, Mademoiselle, I remember," responded the old man.

"Those papers were my last will and testament, bequeathing all I possess to the parish of Porhoët," said Miss de Genneville, dryly, "and now the doors of the massive case are closed. No one can get at my will for another three hundred and sixty-four days—no one," she added with a shrill laugh, "not even my nephew, Amédé de Terhoven."

A silence ensued, only broken by the rustle of Madame la Marquise's silk dress as she shrugged her shoulders and gave a short, sarcastic chuckle.

"My dear," resumed Mademoiselle, looking straight into Lady Molly's eager, glowing face, "you must promise me that, three hundred and sixty-four days hence, that is to say on the 20th September next year, you and Monsieur le Curé—or one of you if the other be incapacitated—will be present in this room at this hour when the door of the clock will open. You will then wind up the family heirloom, take out the papers which you will find buried beneath the weights, and hand them over to Maître Vendôme for probate at the earliest opportunity. Monseigneur the Bishop of Caen, the Mayor of this Commune, and the Souspréfet of this Department have all been informed of the contents of my will, and also that it is practically in the keeping of le Curé de Porhoët, who, no doubt, realises what the serious consequences to himself would be if he failed to produce the will at the necessary time."

The poor Curé gasped with terror.

"But—but—but—" he stammered meekly, "I may be forcibly prevented from entering the house—I might be ill or—"

He shuddered with an unavowable fear, then added more calmly:

"I might be unjustly accused then of stealing the will—of defrauding the poor of Porhoët in favour of—Mademoiselle's direct heirs."

"Have no fear, my good friend," said Mademoiselle, dryly; "though I have one foot in the grave I am not quite so imbecile as my dear sister and nephew here would suggest, and I have provided for every eventuality. If you are ill or otherwise prevented by outside causes from being present here on the day and hour named, this charming English lady will be able to replace you. But if either of you is forcibly prevented from entering this house, or if, having entered this room, the slightest violence or even pressure is put upon you, or if you should find the clock broken, damaged and–stripped of its contents, all you need do is to apprise Maître Vendôme of the fact. He will know how to act."

"What would he do?"

"Send a certain confession we all know of to Monsieur le Procureur de la République," replied the old lady, fixing the young Marquis Amédé with her irascible eye. "That same confession," she continued lightly, "Maître Vendôme is instructed to destroy if you, Monsieur, and my English friend here, and the clock, are all undamaged on the eventful day."

There was silence in the great, dark room for awhile, broken only by the sarcastic chuckle of the enfeebled invalid, tired out after this harrowing scene, wherein she had pitted her half-maniacal ingenuity against the greed and rapacity of a conscienceless roué.

That she had hemmed her nephew and sister in on every side could not be denied. Lady Molly herself felt somewhat awed at this weird revenge conceived by the outraged old lady against her grasping relatives.

She was far too interested in the whole drama to give up her own part in it, and, as she subsequently explained to me, she felt it her duty to remain the partner and co-worker of the poor Curé in this dangerous task of securing to the poor of Porhoët the fortune which otherwise would be squandered away on gaming tables and race-courses.

For this, and many reasons too complicated to analyse, she decided to accept her share in the trust imposed upon her by her newly-found friend.

Neither the Marquise nor her son took any notice of Lady Molly as she presently took leave of Mademoiselle de Genneville, who, at the last, made her take a solemn oath that she would stand by the Curé and fulfil the wishes of a dying and much-wronged woman.

Much perturbed, monsieur le Curé went away. Lady Molly went several times after that to the château of Porhoët to see the invalid, who had taken a violent fancy to her. In October we had, perforce, to return to England and to work, and the following spring we had news from the Curé that Mademoiselle de Genneville was dead.

3

LADY MOLLY had certainly been working too hard, and was in a feeble state of health when we reached Porhoët the following 19th of September, less than twenty-four hours before the eventful moment when the old clock would reveal the will and testament of Mademoiselle de Genneville.

We walked straight from the station to the presbytery, anxious to see the Curé and to make all arrangements for to-morrow's business. To our terrible sorrow and distress, we were informed by the housekeeper that the Curé was very seriously ill at the hospital at Brest, whither he had been removed by the doctor's orders.

This was the first inkling I had that things would not go as smoothly as I had anticipated. Miss de Genneville's dispositions with regard to the sensational disclosure of her will had, to my mind, been so ably taken that it had never struck me until now that the Marquise de Terhoven and her precious son would make a desperate fight before they gave up all thoughts of the coveted fortune.

I imagined the Marquis hemmed in on every side; any violence offered against the Curé or Lady Molly when they entered the château in order to accomplish the task allotted to them being visited by the sending of the confession to Monsieur le Procureur de la République, when prosecution for forgery would immediately follow. Damage to the clock itself would be punished in the same way.

But I had never thought of sudden illnesses, of–heaven help us!–poison or unaccountable accidents to either the Curé or to the woman I loved best in all the world.

No wonder Lady Molly looked pale and fragile as, having thanked the housekeeper, we found our way in silence to the convent where we had once again engaged rooms.

Somehow the hospitality shown us last year had lost something of its cordiality. Moreover, our bedrooms this time did not communicate with one another, but opened out independently on to a stone passage.

The sister who showed us upstairs explained, somewhat shamefacedly, that as the Mother Superior had not expected us, she had let the room which was between our two bedrooms to a lady visitor, who, however, was ill in bed at the present moment.

That sixth sense, of which so much has been said and written, but which I will not attempt to explain, told me plainly enough that we were no longer amidst friends in the convent.

Had bribery been at work? Was the lady visitor a spy set upon our movements by the Terhovens? It was impossible to say. I could no longer chase away the many gloomy forebodings which assailed me the rest of that day and drove away sleep during the night. I can assure you that in my heart I wished all eccentric old ladies and their hidden wills at the bottom of the sea.

My dear lady was apparently also very deeply perturbed; any attempt on my part to broach the subject of Miss de Genneville's will was promptly and authoritatively checked by her. At the same time I knew her well enough to guess that all these nameless dangers which seemed to have crept up round her only served to enhance her determination to carry out her old friend's dying wishes to the letter.

We went to bed quite early; for the first time without that delightful final gossip, when events, plans, surmises and work were freely discussed between us. The unseen lady visitor in the room which separated us acted as a wet blanket on our intimacy.

I stayed with Lady Molly until she was in bed. She hardly talked to me whilst she undressed, but when I kissed her "good-night" she whispered almost inaudibly right into my ear:

"The Terhoven faction are at work. They may waylay you and offer you a bribe to keep me out of the château to-morrow. Pretend to fall in with their views. Accept all bribes and place yourself at their disposal. I must not say more now. We are being spied upon."

That my lady was, as usual, right in her surmises was proved within the next five minutes. I had slipped out of her room, and was just going into mine, when I heard my name spoken hardly above a whisper, whilst I felt my arm gently seized from behind.

An elderly, somewhat florid, woman stood before me attired in a dingy-coloured dressing-gown. She was pointing towards my own bedroom door, implying her desire to accompany me to my room. Remembering my dear lady's parting injunctions, I nodded in acquiescence. She followed me, after having peered cautiously up and down the passage.

Then, when the door was duly closed, and she was satisfied that we were alone, she said very abruptly:

"Miss Granard, tell me! you are poor, eh?—a paid companion to your rich friend, what?"

Still thinking of Lady Molly's commands, I replied with a pathetic sigh.

"Then," said the old lady, eagerly, "would you like to earn fifty thousand francs?"

The eagerness with which I responded "Rather!" apparently pleased her, for she gave a sigh of satisfaction.

"You know the story of my sister's will—of the clock?" she asked eagerly: "of your friend's role in this shameless business?"

Once more I nodded. I knew that my lady had guessed rightly. This was the Marquise de Terhoven, planted here in the convent to gain my confidence, to spy on Lady Molly, and to offer me a bribe.

Now for some clever tactics on my part.

"Can you prevent your friend from being at the château to-morrow before one o'clock?" asked the Marquise.

"Easily," I replied calmly.

"How?"

"She is ill, as you know. The doctor has ordered her a sleeping draught. I administer it. I can arrange that she has a strong dose in the morning instead of her other medicine. She will sleep till the late afternoon."

I rattled this off glibly in my best French. Madame la Marquise heaved a deep sigh of relief.

"Ah! that is good!" she said. "Then listen to me. Do as I tell you, and to-morrow you will be richer by fifty thousand francs. Come to the château in the morning, dressed in your friend's clothes. My son will be there; together you will assist at the opening of the secret doors, and when my son has wound up the old clock himself, he will place fifty thousand francs in your hands."

"But Monsieur le Curé?" I suggested tentatively.

"He is ill," she replied curtly.

But as she spoke these three words there was such an evil sneer in her face, such a look of cruel triumph in her eyes, that all my worst suspicions were at once confirmed.

Had these people's unscrupulous rapacity indeed bribed some needy country practitioner to put the Curé temporarily out of the way? It was too awful to think of, and I can tell you that I needed all my presence of mind, all my desire to act my part bravely and intelligently to the end, not to fly from this woman in horror.

She gave me a few more instructions with regard to the services which she and her precious son would expect of me on the morrow. It seems that, some time before her death, Miss de Genneville had laid strict injunctions on two of her most trusted men-servants to remain in the château, and to be on the watch on the eventful 20th day of September of this year, lest any serious violence be done to the English lady or to the Curé. It was with a view to allay any suspicion which might arise in the minds of these two men that the Marquis desired me to impersonate Lady Molly to-morrow, and to enter with him—on seemingly friendly terms—the room where stood the monumental clock.

For these services, together with those whereby Lady Molly was to be sent into a drugged sleep whilst the theft of the will was being carried through, I–Mary Granard–was to receive from Monsieur le Marquis de Terhoven the sum of fifty thousand francs.

All these matters being settled to this wicked woman's apparent satisfaction, she presently took hold of both my hands, shook them warmly, and called me her dearest friend; assured me of everlasting gratitude, and finally, to my intense relief, slipped noiselessly out of my room.

4

I SURMISED–I think correctly–that Madame la Marquise would spend most of the night with her ear glued to the thin partition which separated her room from that of Lady Molly; so I did not dare to go and report myself and the momentous conversation which I had just had, and vaguely wondered when I should have an opportunity of talking matters over with my dear lady without feeling that a spy was at my heels.

The next morning when I went into her room, to my boundless amazement—and before I had time to utter a word–she moaned audibly, as if in great pain, and said feebly, but very distinctly:

"Oh, Mary! I'm so glad you've come. I feel terribly ill. I haven't had a wink of sleep all night, and I am too weak to attempt to get up."

Fortunately my perceptions had not been dulled by the excitement of the past few hours, and I could see that she was not so ill as she made out. Her eyes sought mine as I approached her bed, and her lips alone framed the words which I believed I interpreted correctly.

"Do as they want. I stay in bed. Will explain later."

Evidently she had reason to think that we were being closely watched; but what I could not understand was, what did she expect would happen if she herself were not present when the opening of the clock door would disclose the will? Did she want me to snatch the document: to bear the brunt of the Terhovens' wrath and disappointment? It was not like her to be afraid of fulfilling a duty, however dangerous that fulfilment might prove; and it certainly was not like her to break a promise given to a dying person.

But, of course, my business was to obey. Assuming that our movements were being watched, I poured out a dose of medicine for my dear lady, which she took and then fell back on her pillows as if exhausted.

"I think I could sleep now, Mary," she said; "but wake me later on; I must be at the château by twelve o'clock, you know."

As one of Lady Molly's boxes was in my room, I had no difficulty in arraying myself in some of her clothes. Thus equipped and closely veiled, still ignorant of my lady's plans, anxious, but determined to obey like a soldier, blindly and unquestioningly, I made my way to the château a little before noon.

An old butler opened the door in answer to my ring, and in the inner hall sat the Marquise de Terhoven, whilst her son was walking agitatedly up and down.

"Ah! here comes my lady," said the Marquise, with easy unconcern. "You have come, my lady," she added, rising and taking my hand, "to perform a duty which will rob my son of a fortune which by right should have been his. We can put no hindrance in your way, under penalty of an appalling disgrace which would then fall on my son; moreover, my late sister has filled this house with guards and spies. So, believe me, you need have no fear. You can perform your duty undisturbed. Perhaps you will not object to my son keeping you company. My precious sister had the door of her room removed before her death and a curtain put in its stead," she concluded with what was intended to be the sneer of a disappointed fortune-hunter, "so the least call from you will bring her spies to your assistance."

Without a word the Marquis and I bowed to one another, then, preceded by the old family butler, we went up the monumental staircase to what I suppose had been the eccentric old lady's room.

The butler drew the portière curtain aside and he remained in the corridor whilst we went within. There stood the massive clock exactly as my lady had often described it to me. It was ticking with slow and deep-toned majesty.

Monsieur le Marquis pointed to an armchair for me. He was obviously in a state of terrible nerve-tension. He could not sit still, and his fingers were incessantly clasped and unclasped with a curious, febrile movement, which betrayed his intense agitation.

I was about to make a remark when he abruptly seized my wrist, placed one finger to his lips, and pointed in the direction of the portière. Apparently he thought that someone was on the watch outside, but the clock itself was so placed that it could not be seen by anyone who was not actually in the room.

After that we were both silent, whilst that old piece of mechanism ticked on relentlessly, still hiding the secret which it contained.

I would have given two years' salary to know what Lady Molly would have wished me to do. Frankly, I fully expected to see her walk in at any moment. I could not bring myself to believe that she meant to shirk her duty.

But she had said to me, "Fall in with their views," So that when, presently, the Marquis beckoned to me across the room to come and examine the clock, I obeyed readily enough. I felt, by that time, as if my entire body was stuffed with needles and pins, which were pricking my nerves and skin until I could have yelled with the agony of the sensation.

I walked across the room as if in a dream, and looked at the curious clock which, in less than fifteen minutes, would reveal its hidden secret. I suppose cleverer people than poor Mary Granard could enter into long philosophical disquisitions as to this dumb piece of mechanism which held the fate of this ruined, unscrupulous gambler safely within its doors; but I was only conscious of that incessant tick, tick, tick, whilst my eyes literally ached with staring at the door.

I don't know now how it all happened, for, of course, I was taken unawares; but the next moment I found myself quite helpless, hardly able to breathe, for a woolen scarf was being wound round my mouth, whilst two strong arms encircled my body so that I could not move.

"This is only a protection for myself, my dear Miss Granard," a trembling voice whispered in my ear; "keep quite still; no harm will come to you. In ten minutes you shall have your fifty thousand francs in your pocket, and can walk unconcernedly out of the château. Neither your English lady nor Monsieur le Curé can say that they suffered any violence, nor will the clock be damaged. What happens after that I care not. The law cannot wrest the old fool's fortune from me, once I have destroyed her accursed will."

To begin to tell you what passed in my mind then were an impossibility. Did I actually guess what would happen, and what my dear lady had planned? Or was it merely the ingrafted sympathy which exists between her and me which caused me to act blindly in accordance with her wishes?

"Fall in with their views. Take their bribes," she had said, and I–like a soldier–obeyed this command to the letter.

I remained absolutely still, scarcely moving an eyelid as I watched the face of the clock, the minutes speeding on–now three–now five–now ten–

I could hear the Marquis' stertorous breathing close beside me.

Was I dreaming, or did I really see now a dark line–the width of a hair–between the massive double doors of the clock case? Oh, how my pulses throbbed!

That dark line was widening perceptibly. The doors were slowly opening! For the moment I almost felt in sympathy with the blackguard who was on the watch with me. His agitation must have been the most exquisite torture.

Now we could distinctly see the glimmer of white paper–not pressed down by the ponderous weights, but lying loosely just inside the doors; and anon, as the aperture widened, the papers fell out just at my feet.

With a smothered, gurgling exclamation which I will not attempt to describe, the Marquis literally fell on that paper, like a hungry wild beast upon its prey. He was on his knees before me, and I could see that the paper was a square envelope, which, with a trembling hand, he tore open.

It contained a short document whereon the signature "Amédé de Terhoven" was clearly visible. It was the confession of forgery made by the young Marquis just a year ago; there were also a few banknotes: some hundred thousand francs, perhaps. The young man threw them furiously aside, and once more turned to the clock. The doors were wide open, but they revealed nothing save the huge and complicated mechanism of the clock.

Mademoiselle de Genneville–eccentric and far-seeing to the last–had played this gigantic hoax on her scheming relatives. Whilst they directed all their unscrupulous energies towards trying to obtain possession of her will in one place, she had calmly put it securely somewhere else.

Meantime, Monsieur le Marquis had sufficient presence of mind, and, I must own, sufficient dignity, not only to release me from my bonds but also to offer me the fifty thousand francs which he had promised me.

"I can wind up the clock now," he said dully, "and you can walk straight out of this place. No one need know that you impersonated your friend. She, no doubt, knew of this–hoax; therefore we found the scheme to keep her out of the way so easy of accomplishment. It was a grisly joke, wasn't it? How the old witch must be chortling in her grave! "

Needless to say, I did not take his money. He escorted me downstairs silently, subdued, no doubt, by the spirit of hatred which had followed him up from the land of shadows.

He even showed no surprise when, on reaching the hall, he was met by his late aunt's lawyer, Maître Vendôme, and also by Lady Molly, who had just arrived. Madame la Marquise de Terhoven was nowhere to be seen.

My dear lady smiled at me approvingly, and when I came near her she contrived to draw me aside and to whisper hurriedly:

"You have done admirably, Mary. I came to fetch you. But now that this young blackguard is thoroughly outwitted, we may as well go, for our work here is done."

The Marquis did not even glance at her as she slightly bowed her head to him, took leave of Maître Vendôme, and finally walked out of the château with me.

As soon as we were out in the open air I begged for an explanation.

"Maître Vendôme has Mademoiselle's will," she replied. "She had enjoined him to read it in the château to-day in the presence of the three trustees appointed for the poor of Porhoët, who inherit all her wealth."

"And the Terhovens?" I asked.

"They've got his confession back," she said dryly, "and they will receive an annuity from the trustees."

"And you knew this all along?" I rejoined somewhat reproachfully.

"Yes, so did the Curé, but Mademoiselle made me swear a most solemn oath not to reveal her secret even to you; she was so afraid of the machinations of the Terhovens. You see," continued Lady Molly, smiling at my eagerness, "Miss de Genneville possessed the ancient key wherewith she could open the clock case at any time. Obviously, even so perfect a piece of mechanism might go wrong, when examination and re-adjustment of the works would be necessary. After the family conclave wherein she had announced that her will was hidden in the clock, I–at my next interview with her–begged her to modify this idea, to send her will to her solicitor, but to leave the Terhovens under the impression that it was still lying in its strange hiding place. At first she refused to listen to me or to discuss the subject, but I am happy to say that I finally succeeded in persuading her, with what result you already know."

"But poor Monsieur le Curé!" I ejaculated.

Her bright eyes gleamed with merriment.

"Oh! that was a final little hoax. He himself, poor dear, was afraid lest he might blurt out the whole thing. His illness was partly a sham, and he is quite all right again now, but the doctor at the Brest hospital is a great friend of his, and is keeping him there until all this business has blown over."

"I was the only one who was kept in the dark," I concluded ruefully.

"Yes, Mary, dear," said my dear lady, gently; "it was a promise, remember. But I never thought that we should get so much excitement outside our own professional work."

It certainly had been a non-professional experience; but here, too, as in the detection of crime, her keen intuition had proved more than a match for an unscrupulous blackguard, and certainly on the 20th day of September last I lived through the most exciting ten minutes of my life.

Baroness Orczy, C. L. Pirkis, Anna Katharine Green

A CHRISTMAS TRAGEDY

IT was a fairly merry Christmas party, although the surliness of our host somewhat marred the festivities. But imagine two such beautiful young women as my own dear lady and Margaret Ceely, and a Christmas Eve Cinderella in the beautiful ball-room at Clevere Hall, and you will understand that even Major Ceely's well-known cantankerous temper could not altogether spoil the merriment of a good, old-fashioned, festive gathering.

It is a far cry from a Christmas Eve party to a series of cattle-maiming outrages, yet I am forced to mention these now, for although they were ultimately proved to have no connection with the murder of the unfortunate Major, yet they were undoubtedly the means whereby the miscreant was enabled to accomplish the horrible deed with surety, swiftness, and—as it turned out afterwards—a very grave chance of immunity.

Everyone in the neighbourhood had been taking the keenest possible interest in those dastardly outrages against innocent animals. They were either the work of desperate ruffians who stick at nothing in order to obtain a few shillings, or else of madmen with weird propensities for purposeless crimes.

Once or twice suspicious characters had been seen lurking about in the fields, and on more than one occasion a cart was heard in the middle of the night driving away at furious speed. Whenever this occurred the discovery of a fresh outrage was sure to follow, but, so far, the miscreants had succeeded in baffling not only the police, but also the many farm hands who had formed themselves into a band of volunteer watchmen, determined to bring the cattle maimers to justice.

We had all been talking about these mysterious events during the dinner which preceded the dance at Clevere Hall; but later on, when the young people had assembled, and when the first strains of "The Merry Widow" waltz had set us aglow with prospective enjoyment, the unpleasant topic was wholly forgotten.

The guests went away early, Major Ceely, as usual, doing nothing to detain them; and by midnight all of us who were staying in the house had gone up to bed.

My dear lady and I shared a bedroom and dressing-room together, our windows giving on the front. Clevere Hall is, as you know, not very far from York, on the other side of Bishopthorpe, and is one of the finest old mansions in the neighbourhood, its only disadvantage being that, in spite of the gardens being very extensive in the rear, the front of the house lies very near the road.

It was about two hours after I had switched off the electric light and called out "Good-night" to my dear lady, that something roused me out of my first sleep. Suddenly I felt very wide-awake, and sat up in bed. Most unmistakably—though still from some considerable distance along the road—came the sound of a cart being driven at unusual speed.

Evidently my dear lady was also awake. She jumped out of bed and, drawing aside the curtains, looked out of the window. The same idea had, of course, flashed upon us both, at the very moment of waking: all the conversations anent the cattle-maimers and their cart, which we had heard since our arrival at Clevere, recurring to our minds simultaneously.

I had joined Lady Molly beside the window, and I don't know how many minutes we remained there in observation, not more than two probably, for anon the sound of the cart died away in the distance along a side road. Suddenly we were startled with a terrible cry of "Murder! Help! Help!" issuing from the other side of the house, followed by an awful, deadly silence. I stood there near the window shivering with terror, while my dear lady, having already turned on the light, was hastily slipping into some clothes.

The cry had, of course, aroused the entire household, but my dear lady was even then the first to get downstairs, and to reach the garden door at the back of the house, whence the weird and despairing cry had undoubtedly proceeded.

That door was wide open. Two steps lead from it to the terraced walk which borders the house on that side, and along these steps Major Ceely was lying, face downwards, with arms outstretched, and a terrible wound between his shoulder-blades.

A gun was lying close by—his own. It was easy to conjecture that he, too, hearing the rumble of the wheels, had run out, gun in hand, meaning, no doubt, to effect, or at least to help, in the capture of the escaping criminals. Someone had been lying in wait for him; that was obvious—someone who had perhaps waited and watched for this special opportunity for days, or even weeks, in order to catch the unfortunate man unawares.

Well, it were useless to recapitulate all the various little incidents which occurred from the moment when Lady Molly and the butler first lifted the Major's lifeless body from the terrace steps until that instant when Miss Ceely, with remarkable coolness and presence of mind, gave what details she could of the terrible event to the local police inspector and to the doctor, both hastily summoned.

These little incidents, with but slight variations, occur in every instance when a crime has been committed. The broad facts alone are of weird and paramount interest.

Major Ceely was dead. He had been stabbed with amazing sureness and terrible violence in the back. The weapon used must have been some sort of heavy, clasp knife. The murdered man was now lying in his own bedroom upstairs, even as the Christmas bells on that cold, crisp morning sent cheering echoes through the stillness of the air.

We had, of course, left the house, as had all the other guests. Everyone felt the deepest possible sympathy for the beautiful young girl who had been so full of the joy of living but a few hours ago, and was now the pivot round which revolved the weird shadow of tragedy, of curious suspicions and of an ever-growing mystery. But at such times all strangers, acquaintances, and even friends in a house, are only an additional burden to an already overwhelming load of sorrow and of trouble.

We took up our quarters at the "Black Swan," in York. The local superintendent, hearing that Lady Molly had been actually a guest at Clevere on the night of the murder, had asked her to remain in the neighbourhood.

There was no doubt that she could easily obtain the chief's consent to assist the local police in the elucidation of this extraordinary crime. At this time both her reputation and her remarkable powers were at their zenith, and there was not a single member of the entire police force in the kingdom who would not have availed himself gladly of her help when confronted with a seemingly impenetrable mystery.

That the murder of Major Ceely threatened to become such no one could deny. In cases of this sort, when no robbery of any kind has accompanied the graver crime, it is the duty of the police and also of the coroner to try to find out, first and foremost, what possible motive there could be behind so cowardly an assault; and among motives, of course, deadly hatred, revenge, and animosity stand paramount.

But here the police were at once confronted with the terrible difficulty, not of discovering whether Major Ceely had an enemy at all, but rather which, of all those people who owed him a grudge, hated him sufficiently to risk hanging for the sake of getting him out of the way.

As a matter of fact, the unfortunate Major was one of those miserable people who seem to live in a state of perpetual enmity with everything and everybody. Morning, noon and night he grumbled, and when he did not grumble he quarreled either with his own daughter or with the people of his household, or with his neighbours.

I had often heard about him and his eccentric, disagreeable ways from Lady Molly, who had known him for many years. She—like everybody in the county who otherwise would have shunned the old man—kept up a semblance of friendship with him for the sake of the daughter.

Margaret Ceely was a singularly beautiful girl, and as the Major was reputed to be very wealthy, these two facts perhaps combined to prevent the irascible gentleman from living in quite so complete an isolation as he would have wished.

Mammas of marriageable young men vied with one another in their welcome to Miss Ceely at garden parties, dances and bazaars. Indeed, Margaret had been surrounded with admirers ever since she had come out of the schoolroom. Needless to say, the cantankerous Major received these pretenders to his daughter's hand not only with insolent disdain, but at times even with violent opposition.

In spite of this the moths fluttered round the candle, and amongst this venturesome tribe none stood out more prominently than Mr. Laurence Smethick, son of the M.P. for the Pakethorpe division. Some folk there were who vowed that the young people were secretly engaged, in spite of the fact that Margaret was an outrageous flirt and openly encouraged more than one of her crowd of adorers.

Be that as it may, one thing was very certain—namely, that Major Ceely did not approve of Mr. Smethick any more than he did of the others, and there had been more than one quarrel between the young man and his prospective father-in-law.

On that memorable Christmas Eve at Clevere none of us could fail to notice his absence; whilst Margaret, on the other hand, had shown marked predilection for the society of Captain Glynne, who, since the sudden death of his cousin, Viscount Heslington, Lord Ullesthorpe's only son (who was killed in the hunting field last October, if you remember), had become heir to the earldom and its £40,000 a year.

Personally, I strongly disapproved of Margaret's behaviour the night of the dance; her attitude with regard to Mr. Smethick—whose constant attendance on her had justified the rumour that they were engaged—being more than callous.

On that morning of December 24th—Christmas Eve, in fact—the young man had called at Clevere. I remember seeing him just as he was being shown into the boudoir downstairs. A few moments later the sound of angry voices rose with appalling distinctness from that room. We all tried not to listen, yet could not fail to hear Major Ceely's overbearing words of rudeness to the visitor, who, it seems, had merely asked to see Miss Ceely, and had been most unexpectedly confronted by the irascible and extremely disagreeable Major. Of course, the young man speedily lost his temper, too, and the whole incident ended with a very unpleasant quarrel between the two men in the hall, and with the Major peremptorily forbidding Mr. Smethick ever to darken his doors again.

On that night Major Ceely was murdered.

2

OF course, at first, no one attached any importance to this weird coincidence. The very thought of connecting the idea of murder with that of the personality of a bright, good-looking young Yorkshireman like Mr. Smethick seemed, indeed, preposterous, and with one accord all of us who were practically witnesses to the quarrel between the two men, tacitly agreed to say nothing at all about it at the inquest, unless we were absolutely obliged to do so on oath.

In view of the Major's terrible temper, this quarrel, mind you, had not the importance which it otherwise would have had; and we all flattered ourselves that we had well succeeded in parrying the coroner's questions.

The verdict at the inquest was against some person or persons unknown; and I, for one, was very glad that young Smethick's name had not been mentioned in connection with this terrible crime.

Two days later the superintendent at Bishopthorpe sent an urgent telephonic message to Lady Molly, begging her to come to the police-station immediately. We had the use of a motor all the while that we stayed at the "Black Swan," and in less than ten minutes we were bowling along at express speed towards Bishopthorpe.

On arrival we were immediately shown into Superintendent Etty's private room behind the office. He was there talking with Danvers—who had recently come down from London. In a corner of the room, sitting very straight on a high-backed chair, was a youngish woman of the servant class, who, as we entered, cast a quick, and I thought suspicious, glance at us both.

She was dressed in a coat and skirt of shabby-looking black, and although her face might have been called good-looking—for she had fine, dark eyes—her entire appearance was distinctly repellent. It suggested slatternliness in an unusual degree; there were holes in her shoes and in her stockings, the sleeve of her coat was half unsewn, and the braid on her skirt hung in loops all round the bottom. She had very red and very coarse-looking hands, and undoubtedly there was a furtive expression in her eyes, which, when she began speaking, changed to one of defiance.

Etty came forward with great alacrity when my dear lady entered. He looked perturbed, and seemed greatly relieved at sight of her.

"She is the wife of one of the outdoor men at Clevere," he explained rapidly to Lady Molly, nodding in the direction of the young woman, "and she has come here with such a queer tale that I thought you would like to hear it."

"She knows something about the murder?" asked Lady Molly.

"Noa! I didn't say that!" here interposed the woman, roughly, "doan't you go and tell no lies, Master Inspector. I thought as how you might wish to know what my husband saw on the night when the Major was murdered, that's all; and I've come to tell you."

"Why didn't your husband come himself?" asked Lady Molly.

"Oh, Haggett ain't well enough—he—" she began explaining, with a careless shrug of the shoulders, "so to speak—"

"The fact of the matter is, my lady," interposed Etty, "this woman's husband is half-witted. I believe he is only kept on in the garden because he is very strong and can help with the digging. It is because his testimony is so little to be relied on that I wished to consult you as to how we should act in the matter."

"What is his testimony, then?"

"Tell this lady what you have just told us, Mrs. Haggett, will you?" said Etty, curtly.

Again that quick, suspicious glance shot into the woman's eyes. Lady Molly took the chair which Danvers had brought forward for her, and sat down opposite Mrs. Haggett, fixing her earnest, calm gaze upon her.

"There's not much to tell," said the woman, sullenly. "Haggett is certainly queer in his head sometimes—and when he is queer he goes wandering about the place of nights."

"Yes?" said my lady, for Mrs. Haggett had paused awhile and now seemed unwilling to proceed.

"Well!" she resumed with sudden determination, "he had got one of his queer fits on Christmas Eve, and didn't come in till long after midnight. He told me as how he'd seen a young gentleman prowling about the garden on the terrace side. He heard the cry of 'Murder' and 'Help' soon after that, and ran in home because he was frightened."

"Home?" asked Lady Molly, quietly, "where is home?"

"The cottage where we live. Just back of the kitchen garden."

"Why didn't you tell all this to the superintendent before?"

"Because Haggett only told me last night, when he seemed less queer-like. He is mighty silent when the fits are on him."

"Did he know who the gentleman was whom he saw?"

"No, ma'am—I don't suppose he did—leastways he wouldn't say—but—"

"Yes? But?"

"He found this in the garden yesterday," said the woman, holding out a screw of paper which apparently she had held tightly clutched up to now, "and maybe that's what brought Christmas Eve and the murder back to his mind."

Lady Molly took the thing from her, and undid the soiled bit of paper with her dainty fingers. The next moment she held up for Etty's inspection a beautiful ring composed of an exquisitely carved moonstone surrounded with diamonds of unusual brilliance.

At the moment the setting and the stones themselves were marred by scraps of sticky mud which clung to them; the ring obviously having lain on the ground, and perhaps been trampled on for some days, and then been only very partially washed.

"At any rate you can find out the ownership of the ring," commented my dear lady after awhile, in answer to Etty's silent attitude of expectancy. "There would be no harm in that."

Then she turned once more to the woman.

"I'll walk with you to your cottage, if I may," she said decisively, "and have a chat with your husband. Is he at home?"

I thought Mrs. Haggett took this suggestion with marked reluctance. I could well imagine, from her own personal appearance, that her home was most unlikely to be in a fit state for a lady's visit. However, she could, of course, do nothing but obey, and, after a few muttered words of grudging acquiescence, she rose from her chair and stalked towards the door, leaving my lady to follow as she chose.

Before going, however, she turned and shot an angry glance at Etty.

"You'll give me back the ring, Master Inspector," she said with her usual tone of sullen defiance. "'Findings is keepings' you know."

"I am afraid not," replied Etty, curtly; "but there's always the reward offered by Miss Ceely for information which would lead to the apprehension of her father's murderer. You may get that, you know. It is a hundred pounds."

"Yes! I knew that," she remarked dryly, as, without further comment, she finally went out of the room.

3

MY dear lady came back very disappointed from her interview with Haggett.

It seems that he was indeed half-witted–almost an imbecile, in fact, with but a few lucid intervals, of which this present day was one. But, of course, his testimony was practically valueless.

He reiterated the story already told by his wife, adding no details. He had seen a young gentleman roaming on the terraced walk on the night of the murder. He did not know who the young gentleman was. He was going homewards when he heard the cry of "Murder," and ran to his cottage because he was frightened. He picked up the ring yesterday in the perennial border below the terrace and gave it to his wife.

Two of these brief statements made by the imbecile were easily proved to be true, and my dear lady had ascertained this before she returned to me. One of the Clevere under-gardeners said he had seen Haggett running home in the small hours of that fateful Christmas morning. He himself had been on the watch for the cattle-maimers that night, and remembered the little circumstance quite plainly. He added that Haggett certainly looked to be in a panic.

Then Newby, another outdoor man at the Hall, saw Haggett pick up the ring in the perennial border and advised him to take it to the police.

Somehow, all of us who were so interested in that terrible Christmas tragedy felt strangely perturbed at all this. No names had been mentioned as yet, but whenever my dear lady and I looked at one another, or whenever we talked to Etty or Danvers, we all felt that a certain name, one particular personality, was lurking at the back of all our minds.

The two men, of course, had no sentimental scruples to worry them. Taking the Haggett story merely as a clue, they worked diligently on that, with the result that twenty-four hours later Etty appeared in our private room at the "Black Swan" and calmly informed us that he had just got a warrant out against Mr. Laurence Smethick on a charge of murder, and was on his way even now to effect the arrest.

"Mr. Smethick did not murder Major Ceely," was Lady Molly's firm and only comment when she heard the news.

"Well, my lady, that's as it may be!" rejoined Etty, speaking with that deference with which the entire force invariably addressed my dear lady; "but we have collected a sufficiency of evidence, at any rate, to justify the arrest, and, in my opinion, enough of it to hang any man. Mr. Smethick purchased the moonstone and diamond ring at Nicholson's in Coney Street about a week ago. He was seen abroad on Christmas Eve by several persons, loitering round the gates at Clevere Hall, somewhere about the time when the guests were leaving after the dance, and, again, some few moments after the first cry of 'Murder' had been heard. His own valet admits that his master did not get home that night until long after 2.0 a.m., whilst even Miss Granard here won't deny that there was a terrible quarrel between Mr. Smethick and Major Ceely less than twenty-four hours before the latter was murdered."

Lady Molly offered no remark to this array of facts which Etty thus pitilessly marshalled before us, but I could not refrain from exclaiming:

"Mr. Smethick is innocent, I am sure."

"I hope, for his sake, he may be," retorted Etty, gravely, "but somehow 'tis a pity that he don't seem able to give a good account of himself between midnight and two o'clock that Christmas morning."

"Oh!" I ejaculated, "what does he say about that?"

"Nothing," said the man dryly; "that's just the trouble."

Well, of course, as you who read the papers will doubtless remember, Mr. Laurence Smethick, son of Colonel Smethick, M.P., of Pakethorpe Hall, Yorks, was arrested on the charge of having murdered Major Ceely on the night of December 24th-25th, and, after the usual magisterial inquiry, was duly committed to stand his trial at the next York assizes.

I remember well that, throughout his preliminary ordeal, young Smethick bore himself like one who had given up all hope of refuting the terrible charges brought against him, and, I must say, the formidable number of witnesses which the police brought up against him more than explained that attitude.

Of course, Haggett was not called, but, as it happened, there were plenty of people to swear that Mr. Laurence Smethick was seen loitering round the gates of Clevere Hall after the guests had departed on Christmas Eve. The head gardener, who lives at the lodge actually spoke to him, and Captain Glynne, leaning out of his brougham, was heard to exclaim:

"Hello, Smethick, what are you doing here at this time of night?"

And there were others, too.

To Captain Glynne's credit, be it here recorded, he tried his best to deny having recognized his unfortunate friend in the dark. Pressed by the magistrate, he said obstinately:

"I thought at the time that it was Mr. Smethick standing by the lodge gates, but on thinking the matter over I feel sure that I was mistaken."

On the other hand, what stood dead against young Smethick was, firstly, the question of the ring, and then the fact that he was seen in the immediate neighbourhood of Clevere, both at midnight and again at about two, when some men, who had been on the watch for the cattle-maimers, saw him walking away rapidly in the direction of Pakethorpe.

What was, of course, unexplainable and very terrible to witness was Mr. Smethick's obstinate silence with regard to his own movements during those fatal hours on that night. He did not contradict those who said that they had seen him at about midnight near the gates of Clevere, nor his own valet's statements as to the hour when he returned home. All he said was that he could not account for what he did between the time when the guests left the Hall and he himself went back to Pakethorpe. He realized the danger in which he stood, and what caused him to be silent about a matter which might mean life or death to him could not easily be conjectured.

The ownership of the ring he could not and did not dispute. He had lost it in the grounds of Clevere, he said. But the jeweller in Coney Street swore that he had sold the ring to Mr. Smethick on the 8th of December, whilst it was a well-known and an admitted fact that the young man had not openly been inside the gates of Clevere for over a fortnight before that.

On this evidence Laurence Smethick was committed for trial. Though the actual weapon with which the unfortunate Major had been stabbed had not been found, nor its ownership traced, there was such a vast array of circumstantial evidence against the young man that bail was refused.

He had, on the advice of his solicitor, Mr. Grayson—one of the ablest lawyers in York—reserved his defence, and on that miserable afternoon at the close of the year, we all filed out of the crowded court, feeling terribly depressed and anxious.

4

MY dear lady and I walked back to our hotel in silence. Our hearts seemed to weigh heavily within us. We felt mortally sorry for that good-looking young Yorkshireman, who, we were convinced, was innocent, yet at the same time seemed involved in a tangled web of deadly circumstances from which he seemed quite unable to extricate himself.

We did not feel like discussing the matter in the open streets, neither did we make any comment when presently, in a block in the traffic in Coney Street, we saw Margaret Ceely driving her smart dog-cart, whilst sitting beside her, and talking with great earnestness close to her ear, sat Captain Glynne.

She was in deep mourning, and had obviously been doing some shopping, for she was surrounded with parcels; so perhaps it was hypercritical to blame her. Yet somehow it struck me that just at the moment when there hung in the balance the life and honour of a man with whose name her own had oft been linked by popular rumour, it showed more than callous contempt for his welfare to be seen driving about with another man who, since his sudden access to fortune, had undoubtedly become a rival in her favours.

When we arrived at the "Black Swan," we were surprised to hear that Mr. Grayson had called to see my dear lady, and was upstairs waiting.

Lady Molly ran up to our sitting-room and greeted him with marked cordiality. Mr. Grayson is an elderly dry-looking man, but he looked visibly affected, and it was some time before he seemed able to plunge into the subject which had brought him hither. He fidgeted in his chair, and started talking about the weather.

"I am not here in a strictly professional capacity, you know," said Lady Molly presently, with a kindly smile and with a view to helping him out of his embarrassment. "Our police, I fear me, have an exaggerated view of my capacities, and the men here asked me unofficially to remain in the neighbourhood and to give them my advice if they should require it. Our chief is very lenient to me and has allowed me to stay. Therefore, if there is anything I can do—"

"Indeed, indeed there is!" ejaculated Mr. Grayson with sudden energy. "From all I hear, there is not another soul in the kingdom but you who can save this innocent man from the gallows."

My dear lady heaved a little sigh of satisfaction. She had all along wanted to have a more important finger in that Yorkshire pie.

"Mr. Smethick?" she said.

"Yes; my unfortunate young client," replied the lawyer. "I may as well tell you," he resumed after a slight pause, during which he seemed to pull himself together, "as briefly as possible what occurred on December 24th last and on the following Christmas morning. You will then understand the terrible plight in which my client finds himself, and how impossible it is for him to explain his actions on that eventful night. You will understand, also, why I have come to ask your help and your advice. Mr. Smethick considered himself engaged to Miss Ceely. The engagement had not been made public because of Major Ceely's anticipated opposition, but the young people had been very intimate, and many letters had passed between them. On the morning of the 24th Mr. Smethick called at the Hall, his intention then being merely to present his fiancée with the ring you know of. You remember the unfortunate contretemps that occurred: I mean the unprovoked quarrel sought by Major Ceely with my poor client, ending with the irascible old man forbidding Mr. Smethick the house.

"My client walked out of Clevere feeling, as you may well imagine, very wrathful; on the doorstep, just as he was leaving, he met Miss Margaret, and told her very briefly what had occurred. She took the matter very lightly at first, but finally became more serious, and ended the brief interview with the request that, since he could not come to the dance after what had occurred, he should come and see her afterwards, meeting her in the gardens soon after midnight. She would not take the ring from him then, but talked a good deal of sentiment about Christmas morning, asking him to bring the ring to her at night, and also the letters which she had written him. Well—you can guess the rest."

Lady Molly nodded thoughtfully.

"Miss Ceely was playing a double game," continued Mr. Grayson, earnestly. "She was determined to break off all relationship with Mr. Smethick, for she had transferred her volatile affections to Captain Glynne, who had lately become heir to an earldom and £40,000 a year. Under the guise of sentimental twaddle she got my unfortunate client to meet her at night in the grounds of Clevere and to give up to her the letters which might have compromised her in the eyes of her new lover. At two o'clock a.m. Major Ceely was murdered by one of his numerous enemies; as to which I do not know, nor does Mr. Smethick. He had just parted from Miss Ceely at the very moment when the first cry of 'Murder' roused Clevere from its slumbers. This she could confirm if she only would, for the two were still in sight of each other, she inside the gates, he just a little way down the road. Mr. Smethick saw Margaret Ceely run rapidly back towards the house. He waited about a little while, half hesitating what to do; then he reflected that his presence might be embarrassing, or even compromising to her whom, in spite of all, he still loved dearly; and knowing that there were plenty of men in and about the house to render what assistance was necessary, he finally turned his steps and went home a broken-hearted man, since she had given him the go-by, taken her letters away, and flung contemptuously into the mud the ring he had bought for her."

The lawyer paused, mopping his forehead and gazing with whole-souled earnestness at my lady's beautiful, thoughtful face.

"Has Mr. Smethick spoken to Miss Ceely since?" asked Lady Molly, after a while.

"No; but I did," replied the lawyer.

"What was her attitude?"

"One of bitter and callous contempt. She denies my unfortunate client's story from beginning to end; declares that she never saw him after she bade him 'good-morning' on the doorstep of Clevere Hall, when she heard of his unfortunate quarrel with her father. Nay, more; she scornfully calls the whole tale a cowardly attempt to shield a dastardly crime behind a still more dastardly libel on a defenceless girl."

We were all silent now, buried in thought which none of us would have cared to translate into words. That the impasse seemed indeed hopeless no one could deny.

The tower of damning evidence against the unfortunate young man had indeed been built by remorseless circumstances with no faltering hand.

Margaret Ceely alone could have saved him, but with brutal indifference she preferred the sacrifice of an innocent man's life and honour to that of her own chances of a brilliant marriage. There are such women in the world; thank God I have never met any but that one!

Yet am I wrong when I say that she alone could save the unfortunate young man, who throughout was behaving with such consummate gallantry, refusing to give his own explanation of the events that occurred on that Christmas morning, unless she chose first to tell the tale. There was one present now in the dingy little room at the "Black Swan" who could disentangle that weird skein of coincidences, if any human being not gifted with miraculous powers could indeed do it at this eleventh hour.

She now said, gently:

"What would you like me to do in this matter, Mr. Grayson? And why have you come to me rather than to the police?"

"How can I go with this tale to the police?" he ejaculated in obvious despair. "Would they not also look upon it as a dastardly libel on a woman's reputation? We have no proofs, remember, and Miss Ceely denies the whole story from first to last.

No, no!" he exclaimed with wonderful fervour. "I came to you because I have heard of your marvellous gifts, your extraordinary intuition. Someone murdered Major Ceely! It was not my old friend Colonel Smethick's son. Find out who it was, then! I beg of you, find out who it was!"

He fell back in his chair broken down with grief. With inexpressible gentleness Lady Molly went up to him and placed her beautiful white hand on his shoulder.

"I will do my best, Mr. Grayson," she said simply.

5

WE remained alone and singularly quiet the whole of that evening. That my dear lady's active brain was hard at work I could guess by the brilliance of her eyes, and that sort of absolute stillness in her person through which one could almost feel the delicate nerves vibrating.

The story told her by the lawyer had moved her singularly. Mind you, she had always been morally convinced of young Smethick's innocence, but in her the professional woman always fought hard battles against the sentimentalist, and in this instance the overwhelming circumstantial evidence and the conviction of her superiors had forced her to accept the young man's guilt as something out of her ken.

By his silence, too, the young man had tacitly confessed; and if a man is perceived on the very scene of a crime, both before it has been committed and directly afterwards; if something admittedly belonging to him is found within three yards of where the murderer must have stood; if, added to this, he has had a bitter quarrel with the victim, and can give no account of his actions or whereabouts during the fatal time, it were vain to cling to optimistic beliefs in that same man's innocence.

But now matters had assumed an altogether different aspect. The story told by Mr. Smethick's lawyer had all the appearance of truth. Margaret Ceely's character, her callousness on the very day when her late fiancé stood in the dock, her quick transference of her affections to the richer man, all made the account of the events on Christmas night as told by Mr. Grayson extremely plausible.

No wonder my dear lady was buried in thought.

"I shall have to take the threads up from the beginning, Mary," she said to me the following morning, when after breakfast she appeared in her neat coat and skirt, with hat and gloves, ready to go out, "so, on the whole, I think I will begin with a visit to the Haggetts."

"I may come with you, I suppose?" I suggested meekly.

"Oh, yes!" she rejoined carelessly.

Somehow I had an inkling that the carelessness of her mood was only on the surface. It was not likely that she—my sweet, womanly, ultra-feminine, beautiful lady–should feel callously on this absorbing subject.

We motored down to Bishopthorpe. It was bitterly cold, raw, damp, and foggy. The chauffeur had some difficulty in finding the cottage, the "home" of the imbecile gardener and his wife.

There was certainly not much look of home about the place. When, after much knocking at the door, Mrs. Haggett finally opened it, we saw before us one of the most miserable, slatternly places I think I ever saw.

In reply to Lady Molly's somewhat curt inquiry, the woman said that Haggett was in bed, suffering from one of his "fits."

"That is a great pity," said my dear lady, rather unsympathetically, I thought, "for I must speak with him at once."

"What is it about?" asked the woman, sullenly. "I can take a message."

"I am afraid not," rejoined my lady. "I was asked to see Haggett personally."

"By whom, I'd like to know," she retorted, now almost insolently.

"I dare say you would. But you are wasting precious time. Hadn't you better help your husband on with his clothes? This lady and I will wait in the parlour."

After some hesitation the woman finally complied, looking very sulky the while.

We went into the miserable little room wherein not only grinding poverty but also untidiness and dirt were visible all round. We sat down on two of the cleanest-looking chairs, and waited whilst a colloquy in subdued voices went on in the room over our heads.

The colloquy, I may say, seemed to consist of agitated whispers on one part, and wailing complaints on the other. This was followed presently by some thuds and much shuffling, and presently Haggett, looking uncared-for, dirty, and unkempt, entered the parlour, followed by his wife.

He came forward, dragging his ill-shod feet and pulling nervously at his forelock.

"Ah!" said my lady, kindly; "I am glad to see you down, Haggett, though I am afraid I haven't very good news for you."

"Yes, miss!" murmured the man, obviously not quite comprehending what was said to him.

"I represent the workhouse authorities," continued Lady Molly, "and I thought we could arrange for you and your wife to come into the Union to-night, perhaps."

"The Union?" here interposed the woman, roughly. "What do you mean? We ain't going to the Union?"

"Well! but since you are not staying here," rejoined my lady, blandly, "you will find it impossible to get another situation for your husband in his present mental condition."

"Miss Ceely won't give us the go-by," she retorted defiantly.

"She might wish to carry out her late father's intentions," said Lady Molly with seeming carelessness.

"The Major was a cruel, cantankerous brute," shouted the woman with unpremeditated violence. "Haggett had served him faithfully for twelve years, and—"

She checked herself abruptly, and cast one of her quick, furtive glances at Lady Molly.

Her silence now had become as significant as her outburst of rage, and it was Lady Molly who concluded the phrase for her.

"And yet he dismissed him without warning," she said calmly.

"Who told you that?" retorted the woman.

"The same people, no doubt, who declare that you and Haggett had a grudge against the Major for this dismissal."

"That's a lie," asserted Mrs. Haggett, doggedly; "we gave information about Mr.

Smethick having killed the Major because—"

"Ah," interrupted Lady Molly, quickly, "but then Mr. Smethick did not murder Major Ceely, and your information therefore was useless!"

"Then who killed the Major, I should like to know?"

Her manner was arrogant, coarse, and extremely unpleasant. I marvelled why my dear lady put up with it, and what was going on in that busy brain of hers. She looked quite urbane and smiling, whilst I wondered what in the world she meant by this story of the workhouse and the dismissal of Haggett.

"Ah, that's what none of us know!" she now said lightly; "some folks say it was your husband."

"They lie!" she retorted quickly, whilst the imbecile, evidently not understanding the drift of the conversation, was mechanically stroking his red mop of hair and looking helplessly all round him.

"He was home before the cries of 'Murder' were heard in the house," continued Mrs. Haggett.

"How do you know?" asked Lady Molly, quickly.

"How do I know?"

"Yes; you couldn't have heard the cries all the way to this cottage—why, it's over half a mile from the Hall!"

"He was home, I say," she repeated with dogged obstinacy.

"You sent him?"

"He didn't do it—"

"No one will believe you, especially when the knife is found."

"What knife?"

"His clasp knife, with which he killed Major Ceely," said Lady Molly, quietly; "see, he has it in his hand now."

And with a sudden, wholly unexpected gesture she pointed to the imbecile, who in an aimless way had prowled round the room whilst this rapid colloquy was going on.

The purport of it all must in some sort of way have found an echo in his enfeebled brain. He wandered up to the dresser whereon lay the remnants of that morning's breakfast, together with some crockery and utensils.

In that same half-witted and irresponsible way he had picked up one of the knives and now was holding it out towards his wife, whilst a look of fear spread over his countenance.

"I can't do it, Annie, I can't—you'd better do it," he said.

There was dead silence in the little room. The woman Haggett stood as if turned to stone. Ignorant and superstitious as she was, I suppose that the situation had laid hold of her nerves, and that she felt that the finger of a relentless Fate was even now being pointed at her.

The imbecile was shuffling forward, closer and closer to his wife, still holding out the knife towards her and murmuring brokenly:

"I can't do it. You'd better, Annie—you'd better—"

He was close to her now, and all at once her rigidity and nerve-strain gave way; she gave a hoarse cry, and snatching the knife from the poor wretch, she rushed at him ready to strike.

Lady Molly and I were both young, active and strong; and there was nothing of the squeamish grande dame about my dear lady when quick action was needed. But even then we had some difficulty in dragging Annie Haggett away from her miserable husband. Blinded with fury, she was ready to kill the man who had betrayed her. Finally, we succeeded in wresting the knife from her.

You may be sure that it required some pluck after that to sit down again quietly and to remain in the same room with this woman, who already had one crime upon her conscience, and with this weird, half-witted creature who kept on murmuring pitiably:

"You'd better do it, Annie—"

Well, you've read the account of the case, so you know what followed. Lady Molly did not move from that room until she had obtained the woman's full confession. All she did for her own protection was to order me to open the window and to blow the police whistle which she handed to me. The police-station fortunately was not very far, and sound carried in the frosty air.

She admitted to me afterwards that it had been foolish, perhaps, not to have brought Etty or Danvers with her, but she was supremely anxious not to put the woman on the alert from the very start, hence her circumlocutory speeches anent the workhouse, and Haggett's probable dismissal.

That the woman had had some connection with the crime, Lady Molly, with her keen intuition, had always felt; but as there was no witness to the murder itself, and all circumstantial evidence was dead against young Smethick, there was only one chance of successful discovery, and that was the murderer's own confession.

If you think over the interview between my dear lady and the Haggetts on that memorable morning, you will realise how admirably Lady Molly had led up to the weird finish. She would not speak to the woman unless Haggett was present, and she felt sure that as soon as the subject of the murder cropped up, the imbecile would either do or say something that would reveal the truth.

Mechanically, when Major Ceely's name was mentioned, he had taken up the knife. The whole scene recurred to his tottering mind. That the Major had summarily dismissed him recently was one of those bold guesses which Lady Molly was wont to make.

That Haggett had been merely egged on by his wife, and had been too terrified at the last to do the deed himself was no surprise to her, and hardly one to me, whilst the fact that the woman ultimately wreaked her own passionate revenge upon the unfortunate Major was hardly to be wondered at, in the face of her own coarse and elemental personality.

Cowed by the quickness of events, and by the appearance of Danvers and Etty on the scene, she finally made full confession.

She was maddened by the Major's brutality, when with rough, cruel words he suddenly turned her husband adrift, refusing to give him further employment. She herself had great ascendency over the imbecile, and had drilled him into a part of hate and of revenge. At first he had seemed ready and willing to obey. It was arranged that he was to watch on the terrace every night until such time as an alarm of the recurrence of the cattle-maiming outrages should lure the Major out alone.

This effectually occurred on Christmas morning, but not before Haggett, frightened and pusillanimous, was ready to flee rather than to accomplish the villainous deed. But Annie Haggett, guessing perhaps that he would shrink from the crime at the last, had also kept watch every night. Picture the prospective murderer watching and being watched!

When Haggett came across his wife he deputed her to do the deed herself.

I suppose that either terror of discovery or merely desire for the promised reward had caused the woman to fasten the crime on another.

The finding of the ring by Haggett was the beginning of that cruel thought which, but for my dear lady's marvellous powers, would indeed have sent a brave young man to the gallows.

Ah, you wish to know if Margaret Ceely is married? No! Captain Glynne cried off. What suspicions crossed his mind I cannot say; but he never proposed to Margaret, and now she is in Australia—staying with an aunt, I think—and she has sold Clevere Hall.

THE BAG OF SAND

OF course, I knew at once by the expression of her face that morning that my dear lady had some important business on hand.

She had a bundle in her arms, consisting of a shabby-looking coat and skirt, and a very dowdy hat trimmed with bunches of cheap, calico roses.

"Put on these things at once, Mary," she said curtly, "for you are going to apply for the situation of 'good plain cook,' so mind you look the part."

"But where in the world–?" I gasped in astonishment.

"In the house of Mr. Nicholas Jones, in Eaton Terrace," she interrupted dryly, "the one occupied until recently by his sister, the late Mrs. Dunstan. Mrs. Jones is advertising for a cook, and you must get that place."

As you know, I have carried obedience to the level of a fine art. Nor was I altogether astonished that my dear lady had at last been asked to put one of her dainty fingers in that Dunstan pie, which was puzzling our fellows more completely than any other case I have ever known.

I don't know if you remember the many circumstances, the various contradictions which were cropping up at every turn, and which baffled our ablest detectives at the very moment when they thought themselves most near the solution of that strange mystery.

Mrs. Dunstan herself was a very uninteresting individual: self-righteous, self-conscious and fat, a perfect type of the moneyed middle-class woman whose balance at the local bank is invariably heavier than that of her neighbours. Her niece, Violet Frostwicke, lived with her: a smart, pretty girl, inordinately fond of dainty clothes and other luxuries which money can give. Being totally impecunious herself, she bore with the older woman's constantly varying caprices with almost angelic patience, a fact probably attributable to Mrs. Dunstan's testamentary intentions, which, as she often averred, were in favour of her niece.

In addition to these two ladies, the household consisted of three servants and Miss Cruikshank. The latter was a quiet, unassuming girl who was by way of being secretary and lady-help to Mrs. Dunstan, but who, in reality, was nothing but a willing drudge. Up betimes in the morning, she combined the work of a housekeeper with that of an upper servant. She interviewed the tradespeople, kept the servants in order, and ironed and smartened up Miss Violet's blouses. A Cinderella, in fact.

Mrs. Dunstan kept a cook and two maids, all of whom had been with her for years. In addition to these, a charwoman came very early in the morning to light fires, clean boots, and do the front steps.

On November 22nd, 1907–for the early history of this curious drama dates back to that year–the charwoman who had been employed at Mrs. Dunstan's house in Eaton Terrace for some considerable time, sent word in the morning that in future she would be unable to come. Her husband had been obliged to move to lodgings nearer to his work, and she herself could not undertake to come the greater distance at the early hour at which Mrs. Dunstan required her.

The woman had written a very nice letter explaining these facts, and sent it by hand, stating at the same time that the bearer of the note was a very respectable woman, a friend of her own, who would be very pleased to "oblige" Mrs. Dunstan by taking on the morning's work.

I must tell you that the message and its bearer arrived at Eaton Terrace somewhere about 6.0 a.m., when no one was down except the Cinderella of the house, Miss Cruikshank.

She saw the woman, liked her appearance, and there and then engaged her to do the work, subject to Mrs. Dunstan's approval.

The woman, who had given her name as Mrs. Thomas, seemed very quiet and respectable. She said that she lived close by, in St. Peter's Mews, and therefore could come as early as Mrs. Dunstan wished. In fact, from that day, she came every morning at 5.30 a.m., and by seven o'clock had finished her work, and was able to go home.

If, in addition to these details, I tell you that, at that time, pretty Miss Violet Frostwicke was engaged to a young Scotsman, Mr. David Athol, of whom her aunt totally disapproved, I shall have put before you all the personages who, directly or indirectly, were connected with that drama, the final act of which has not yet been witnessed either by the police or by the public.

2

ON the following New Year's Eve, Mrs. Dunstan, as was her invariable custom on that day, went to her married brother's house to dine and to see the New Year in.

During her absence the usual thing occurred at Eaton Terrace. Miss Violet Frostwicke took the opportunity of inviting Mr. David Athol to spend the evening with her.

Mrs. Dunstan's servants, mind you, all knew of the engagement between the young people, and with the characteristic sentimentality of their class, connived at these secret meetings and helped to hoodwink the irascible old aunt.

Mr. Athol was a good-looking young man, whose chief demerit lay in his total lack of money or prospects. Also he was by way of being an actor, another deadly sin in the eyes of the puritanically-minded old lady.

Already, on more than one occasion, there had been vigorous wordy warfare 'twixt Mr. Athol and Mrs. Dunstan, and the latter had declared that if Violet chose to take up with this mountebank, she should never see a penny of her aunt's money now or in the future.

The young man did not come very often to Eaton Terrace, but on this festive New Year's Eve, when Mrs. Dunstan was not expected to be home until long after midnight, it seemed too splendid an opportunity for an ardent lover to miss.

As ill-luck would have it, Mrs. Dunstan had not felt very well after her copious dinner, and her brother, Mr. Nicholas Jones, escorted her home soon after ten o'clock.

Jane, the parlour-maid who opened the front door, was, in her own graphic language, "knocked all of a heap" when she saw her mistress, knowing full well that Mr. Athol was still in the dining-room with Miss Violet, and that Miss Cruikshank was at that very moment busy getting him a whisky and soda.

Meanwhile the coat and hat in the hall had revealed the young man's presence in the house.

For a moment Mrs. Dunstan paused, whilst Jane stood by trembling with fright. Then the old lady turned to Mr. Nicholas Jones, who was still standing on the doorstep, and said quietly:

"Will you telephone over to Mr. Blenkinsop, Nick, the first thing in the morning, and tell him I'll be at his office by ten o'clock?"

Mr. Blenkinsop was Mrs. Dunstan's solicitor, and as Jane explained to the cook later on, what could such an appointment mean but a determination to cut Miss Violet out of the missis's will with the proverbial shilling?

After this Mrs. Dunstan took leave of her brother and went straight into the dining-room.

According to the subsequent testimony of all three servants, the mistress "went on dreadful." Words were not easily distinguishable from behind the closed door, but it seems that, immediately she entered, Mrs. Dunstan's voice was raised as if in terrible anger, and a few moments later Miss Violet fled crying from the dining-room, and ran quickly upstairs.

Whilst the door was thus momentarily opened and shut, the voice of the old lady was heard saying, in majestic wrath:

"That's what you have done. Get out of this house. As for her, she'll never see a penny of my money, and she may starve for aught I care!"

The quarrel seems to have continued for a short while after that, the servants being too deeply awed by those last vindictive words which they had heard to take much note of what went on subsequently.

Mrs. Dunstan and Mr. Athol were closeted together for some time; but apparently the old lady's wrath did not subside, for when she marched up to bed an hour later she was heard to say:

"Out of this house she shall go, and the first thing in the morning, too. I'll have no goings-on with a mountebank like you."

Miss Cruikshank was terribly upset.

"It is a frightful blow for Miss Violet," she said to cook, "but perhaps Mrs. Dunstan will feel more forgiving in the morning. I'll take her up a glass of champagne now. She is very fond of that, and it will help her to get to sleep."

Miss Cruikshank went up with the champagne, and told cook to see Mr. Athol out of the house; but the young man, who seemed very anxious and agitated, would not go away immediately. He stayed in the dining-room, smoking, for a while, and when the two younger servants went up to bed, he asked cook to let him remain until he had seen Miss Violet once more, for he was sure she would come down again—he had asked Miss Cruikshank to beg her to do so.

Mrs. Kennett, the cook, was a kind-hearted old woman. She had taken the young people under her special protection, and felt very vexed that the course of true love should not be allowed to run quite smoothly. So she told Mr. Athol to make himself happy and comfortable in the dining-room, and she would sit up by the fire in the library until he was ready to go.

The good soul thereupon made up the fire in the library, drew a chair in front of it, and went fast to sleep.

Suddenly something awoke her. She sat up and looked round in that dazed manner peculiar to people just aroused from deep sleep.

She looked at the clock; it was past three. Surely, she thought, it must have been Mr. Athol calling to her which had caused her to wake. She went into the hall, where the gas had not yet been turned off, and there she saw Miss Violet, fully dressed and wearing a hat and coat, in the very act of going out at the front door.

In the cook's own words, before she could ask a question or even utter a sound, the young girl had opened the front door, which was still on the latch, and then banged it to again, she herself having disappeared into the darkness of the street beyond.

Mrs. Kennett ran to the door and out into the street as fast as her old legs would let her; but the night was an exceptionally foggy one. Violet, no doubt, had walked rapidly away, and there came no answer to Mrs. Kennett's repeated calls.

Thoroughly upset, and not knowing what to do, the good woman went back into the house. Mr. Athol had evidently left, for there was no sign of him in the dining-room or elsewhere. She then went upstairs and knocked at Mrs. Dunstan's door. To her astonishment the gas was still burning in her mistress's room, as she could see a thin ray of light filtering through the keyhole. At her first knock there came a quick, impatient answer:

"What is it?"

"Miss Violet, 'm," said the cook, who was too agitated to speak very coherently, "she is gone—"

"The best thing she could do," came promptly from the other side of the door. "You go to bed, Mrs. Kennett, and don't worry."

Whereupon the gas was suddenly turned off inside the room, and, in spite of Mrs. Kennett's further feeble protests, no other word issued from the room save another impatient:

"Go to bed."

The cook then did as she was bid; but before going to bed she made the round of the house, turned off all the gas, and finally bolted the front door.

3

SOME three hours later the servants were called, as usual, by Miss Cruikshank, who then went down to open the area door to Mrs. Thomas, the charwoman.

At half-past six, when Mary the housemaid came down, candle in hand, she saw the charwoman a flight or two lower down, also apparently in the act of going downstairs. This astonished Mary not a little, as the woman's work lay entirely in the basement, and she was supposed never to come to the upper floors.

The woman, though walking rapidly down the stairs, seemed, moreover, to be carrying something heavy.

"Anything wrong, Mrs. Thomas?" asked Mary, in a whisper.

The woman looked up, pausing a moment immediately under the gas bracket, the by-pass of which shed a feeble light upon her and upon her burden. The latter Mary recognised as the bag containing the sand which, on frosty mornings, had to be strewn on the front steps of the house.

On the whole, though she certainly was puzzled, Mary did not think very much about the incident then. As was her custom, she went into the housemaid's closet, got the hot water for Miss Cruikshank's bath, and carried it to the latter's room, where she also pulled up the blinds and got things ready generally. For Miss Cruikshank usually ran down in her dressing-gown, and came up to tidy herself later on.

As a rule, by the time the three servants got downstairs, it was nearly seven, and Mrs. Thomas had generally gone by that time; but on this occasion Mary was earlier. Miss Cruikshank was busy in the kitchen getting Mrs. Dunstan's tea ready. Mary spoke about seeing Mrs. Thomas on the stairs with the bag of sand, and Miss Cruikshank, too, was very astonished at the occurrence.

Mrs. Kennett was not yet down, and the charwoman apparently had gone; her work had been done as usual, and the sand was strewn over the stone steps in front, as the frosty fog had rendered them very slippery.

At a quarter past seven Miss Cruikshank went up with Mrs. Dunstan's tea, and less than two minutes later a fearful scream rang through the entire house, followed by the noise of breaking crockery.

In an instant the two maids ran upstairs, straight to Mrs. Dunstan's room, the door of which stood wide open.

The first thing Mary and Jane were conscious of was a terrific smell of gas, then of Miss Cruikshank, with eyes dilated with horror, staring at the bed in front of her, whereon lay Mrs. Dunstan, with one end of a piece of india rubber piping still resting in her mouth, her jaw having dropped in death. The other end of that piece of piping was attached to the burner of a gas-bracket on the wall close by.

Every window in the room was fastened and the curtains drawn. The whole room reeked of gas.

Mrs. Dunstan had been asphyxiated by its fumes.

4

A YEAR went by after the discovery of the mysterious tragedy, and I can assure you that our fellows at the Yard had one of the toughest jobs in connection with the case that ever fell to their lot. Just think of all the contradictions which met them at every turn.

Firstly, the disappearance of Miss Violet.

No sooner had the women in the Dunstan household roused themselves sufficiently from their horror at the terrible discovery which they had just made, than they were confronted with another almost equally awful fact–awful, of course, because of its connection with the primary tragedy.

Miss Violet Frostwicke had gone. Her room was empty, her bed had not been slept in. She herself had been seen by the cook, Mrs. Kennett, stealing out of the house at dead of night.

To connect the pretty, dainty young girl even remotely with a crime so hideous, so callous, as the deliberate murder of an old woman, who had been as a mother to her, seemed absolutely out of the question, and by tacit consent the four women, who now remained in the desolate and gloom-laden house at Eaton Terrace, forbore to mention Miss Violet Frostiwicke's name either to police or doctor.

Both these, of course, had been summoned immediately; Miss Cruikshank sending Mary to the police-station and thence to Dr. Folwell, in Eaton Square, whilst Jane went off in a cab to fetch Mr. Nicholas Jones, who, fortunately, had not yet left for his place of business.

The doctor's and the police-inspector's first thought, on examining the mise en scène of the terrible tragedy, was that Mrs. Dunstan had committed suicide. It was practically impossible to imagine that a woman in full possession of health and strength would allow a piece of india rubber piping to be fixed between her teeth, and would, without a struggle, continue to inhale the poisonous fumes which would mean certain death. Yet there were no marks of injury upon the body, nothing to show how sufficient unconsciousness had been produced in the victim to permit of the miscreant completing his awesome deed.

But the theory of suicide set up by Dr. Folwell was promptly refuted by the most cursory examination of the room.

Though the drawers were found closed, they had obviously been turned over, as if the murderer had been in search either of money or papers, or the key of the safe.

The latter, on investigation, was found to be open, whilst the key lay on the floor close by. A brief examination of the safe revealed the fact that the tin boxes must have been ransacked, for they contained neither money nor important papers now, whilst the gold and platinum settings of necklaces, bracelets, and a tiara showed that the stones—which, as Mr. Nicholas Jones subsequently averred, were of considerable value—had been carefully, if somewhat clumsily, taken out by obvious inexperienced hands.

On the whole, therefore, appearances suggested deliberate, systematic, and very leisurely robbery, which wholly contradicted the theory of suicide.

Then suddenly the name of Miss Frostwicke was mentioned. Who first brought it on the tapis no one subsequently could say; but in a moment the whole story of the young girl's engagement to Mr. Athol, in defiance of her aunt's wishes, the quarrel of the night before, and the final disappearance of both young people from the house during the small hours of the morning, was dragged from the four unwilling witnesses by the able police-inspector.

Nay, more. One very unpleasant little circumstance was detailed by one of the maids and corroborated by Miss Cruikshank.

It seems that when the latter took up the champagne to Mrs. Dunstan, the old lady desired Miss Violet to come to her room. Mary, the housemaid, was on the stairs when she saw the young girl, still dressed in her evening gown of white chiffon, her eyes still swollen with tears, knocking at her aunt's door.

The police-inspector was busy taking notes, already building up in his mind a simple, if very sensational, case against Violet Frostwicke, when Mrs. Kennett promptly upset all his calculations.

Miss Violet could have had nothing to do with the murder of her aunt, seeing that Mrs. Dunstan was alive and actually spoke to the cook when the latter knocked at her bedroom door after she had seen the young girl walk out of the house.

Then came the question of Mr. Athol. But, if you remember, it was quite impossible even to begin to build up a case against the young man. His own statement that he left the house at about midnight, having totally forgotten to rouse the cook when he did so, was amply corroborated from every side.

The cabman who took him up to the corner of Eaton Terrace at 11.50 p.m. was one witness in his favour; his landlady at his rooms in Jermyn Street, who let him in, since he had mislaid his latchkey, and who took him up some tea at seven o'clock the next morning, was another; whilst, when Mary saw Miss Violet going into her aunt's room, the clock at St. Peter's, Eaton Square, was just striking twelve.

I dare say you think I ought by now to have mentioned the charwoman, Mrs. Thomas, who represented the final, most complete, most hopeless contradiction in this remarkable case.

Mrs. Thomas was seen by Mary, the housemaid, at half-past six o'clock in the morning, coming down from the upper floors, where she had no business to be, and carrying the bag of sand used for strewing over the slippery front-door steps.

The bag of sand, of course, was always kept in the area.

The moment that bag of sand was mentioned Dr. Folwell gave a curious gasp. Here, at least, was the solution to one mystery. The victim had been stunned whilst still in bed by a blow on the head dealt with that bag of sand; and whilst she was unconscious the callous miscreant had robbed her and finally asphyxiated her with the gas fumes.

Where was the woman who, at half-past six in the morning, was seen in possession of the silent instrument of death?

Mrs. Thomas had disappeared. The last that was then or ever has been seen of her was when she passed underneath the dim light of a by-pass on the landing, as if tired out with the weight which she was carrying.

Since then, as you know, the police have been unswerving in their efforts to find Mrs. Thomas. The address which she had given in St. Peter's Mews was found to be false. No one of that name or appearance had ever been seen there.

The woman who was supposed to have sent her with a letter of recommendation to Mrs. Dunstan knew nothing of her. She swore that she had never sent anyone with a letter to Mrs. Dunstan. She gave up her work there one day because she found it too hard at such an early hour in the morning; but she never heard anything more from her late employer after that.

Strange, wasn't it, that two people should have disappeared out of that house on that same memorable night?

Of course, you will remember the tremendous sensation that was caused some twenty-four hours later, when it transpired that the young person who had thrown herself into the river from Waterloo Bridge on that same eventful morning, and whose body was subsequently recovered and conveyed to the Thames Police station, was identified as Miss Violet Frostwicke, the niece of the lady who had been murdered in her own house in Eaton Terrace.

Neither money nor diamonds were found on poor Miss Violet. She had herself given the most complete proof that she, at least, had no hand in robbing or killing Mrs. Dunstan.

The public wondered why she took her aunt's wrath and her probable disinheritance so fearfully to heart, and sympathised with Mr. David Athol for the terribly sad loss which he had sustained.

But Mrs. Thomas, the charwoman, had not yet been found.

5

I THINK I looked an extremely respectable, good plain cook when I presented myself at the house in Eaton Terrace in response to the advertisement in the "Daily Telegraph."

As, in addition to my prepossessing appearance, I also asked very low wages and declared myself ready to do anything except scour the front steps and the stone area, I was immediately engaged by Mrs. Jones, and was duly installed in the house the following day under the name of Mrs. Curwen.

But few events had occurred here since the discovery of the dual tragedy, now more than a year ago, and none that had thrown any light upon the mystery which surrounded it.

The verdict at the inquest had been one of wilful murder against a person known as Mrs. Thomas, the weight of evidence, coupled with her disappearance, having been very heavy against her; and there was a warrant out for her arrest.

Mrs. Dunstan had died intestate. To the astonishment of all those in the know, she had never signed the will which Messrs. Blenkinsop and Blenkinsop had drafted for her, and wherein she bequeathed £20,000 and the lease of her house in Eaton Terrace to her beloved niece, Violet Frostwicke, £1,000 to Miss Cruikshank, and other, smaller, legacies to friends or servants.

In default of a will, Mr. Nicholas Jones, only brother of the deceased, became possessed of all her wealth.

He was a very rich man himself, and many people thought that he ought to give Miss Cruikshank the £1,000 which the poor girl had thus lost through no fault of her own.

What his ultimate intentions were with regard to this no one could know. For the present he contented himself with moving to Eaton Terrace with his family; and, as his wife was a great invalid, he asked Miss Cruikshank to continue to make her home in the house and to help in its management.

Neither the diamonds nor the money stolen from Mrs. Dunstan's safe were ever traced. It seems that Mrs. Dunstan, a day or two before her death, had sold a freehold cottage which she owned near Teddington. The money, as is customary, had been handed over to her in gold, in Mr. Blenkinsop's office, and she had been foolish enough not to bank it immediately. This money and the diamonds had been the chief spoils of her assailant. And all the while no trace of Mrs. Thomas, in spite of the most strenuous efforts on the part of the police to find. her.

Strangely enough, when I had been in Eaton Terrace about three days, and was already getting very tired of early rising and hard work, the charwoman there fell ill one day and did not come to her work as usual.

I, of course, grumbled like six, for I had to be on my hands and knees the next morning scrubbing stone steps, and my thoughts of Lady Molly, for the moment, were not quite as loyal as they usually were.

Suddenly I heard a shuffling footstep close behind me. I turned and saw a rough-looking, ill-dressed woman standing at the bottom of the steps.

"What do you want?" I asked sourly, for I was in a very bad humour.

"I saw you scrubbing them steps, miss," she replied in a raucous voice; "my 'usband is out of work, and the children hain't 'ad no breakfast this morning. I'd do them steps, miss, if you'd give me a trifle."

The woman certainly did not look very prepossessing, with her shabby, broad-brimmed hat hiding the upper part of her face, and her skirt, torn and muddy, pinned up untidily round her stooping figure.

However, I did not think that I could be doing anything very wrong by letting her do this one bit of rough work, which I hated, so I agreed to give her sixpence, and left her there with kneeling mat and scrubbing-brush, and went in, leaving, however, the front door open.

In the hall I met Miss Cruikshank, who, as usual, was down before everybody else.

"What is it, Curwen?" she asked, for through the open door she had caught sight of the woman kneeling on the step.

"A woman, miss," I replied, somewhat curtly. "She offered to do the steps. I thought Mrs. Jones wouldn't mind, as Mrs. Callaghan hasn't turned up."

Miss Cruikshank hesitated an instant, and then walked up to the front door.

At the same moment the woman looked up, rose from her knees, and boldly went up to accost Miss Cruikshank.

"You'll remember me, miss," she said, in her raucous voice. "I used to work for Mrs. Dunstan once. My name is Mrs. Thomas."

No wonder Miss Cruikshank uttered a quickly smothered cry of horror. Thinking that she would faint, I ran to her assistance; but she waved me aside and then said quite quietly:

"This poor woman's mind is deranged. She is no more Mrs. Thomas than I am. Perhaps we had better send for the police."

"Yes, miss; p'r'aps you'd better," said the woman with a sigh. "My secret has been weighin' heavy on me of late."

"But, my good woman," said Miss Cruikshank, very kindly, for I suppose that she thought, as I did, that this was one of those singular cases of madness which sometimes cause innocent people to accuse themselves of undiscovered crimes. "You are not Mrs. Thomas at all. I knew Mrs. Thomas well, of course–and–"

"Of course you knew me, miss," replied the woman. "The last conversation you and I had together was in the kitchen that morning, when Mrs. Dunstan was killed. I remember your saying to me–"

"Fetch the police, Curwen," said Miss Cruikshank, peremptorily.

Whereupon the woman broke into a harsh and loud laugh of defiance.

To tell you the truth, I was not a little puzzled. That this scene had been foreseen by my dear lady, and that she had sent me to this house on purpose that I should witness it, I was absolutely convinced. But–here was my dilemma: ought I to warn the police at once or not?

On the whole, I decided that my best plan would undoubtedly be to communicate with Lady Molly first of all, and to await her instructions. So I ran upstairs, scribbled a hasty note to my dear lady, and, in response to Miss Cruikshank's orders, flew out of the house through the area gate, noticing, as I did so, that Miss Cruikshank was still parleying with the woman on the doorstep.

I sent the note off to Maida Vale by taxicab; then I went back to Eaton Terrace. Miss Cruikshank met me at the front door, and told me that she had tried to detain the woman, pending my return; but that she felt very sorry for the unfortunate creature, who obviously was labouring under a delusion, and she had allowed her to go away.

About an hour later I received a curt note from Lady Molly ordering me to do nothing whatever without her special authorisation.

In the course of the day, Miss Cruikshank told me that she had been to the police-station, and had consulted with the inspector, who said there would be no harm in engaging the pseudo Mrs. Thomas to work at Eaton Terrace, especially as thus she would remain under observation.

Then followed a curious era in Mr. Nicholas Jones's otherwise well-ordered household. We three servants, instead of being called at six as heretofore, were allowed to sleep on until seven. When we came down we were not scolded. On the contrary, we found our work already done.

The charwoman—whoever she was—must have been a very hard-working woman. It was marvellous what she accomplished single-handed before seven a.m., by which time she had invariably gone.

The two maids, of course, were content to let this pleasant state of things go on, but I was devoured with curiosity.

One morning I crept quietly downstairs and went into the kitchen soon after six. I found the pseudo Mrs. Thomas sitting at a very copious breakfast. I noticed that she had on altogether different—though equally shabby and dirty—clothes from those she had worn when she first appeared on the doorstep of 180, Eaton Terrace. Near her plate were three or four golden sovereigns over which she had thrown her grimy hand.

Miss Cruikshank the while was on her hands and knees scrubbing the floor. At sight of me she jumped up, and with obvious confusion muttered something about "hating to be idle," etc.

That day Miss Cruikshank told me that I did not suit Mrs. Jones, who wished me to leave at the end of my month. In the afternoon I received a little note from my dear lady, telling me to be downstairs by six o'clock the following morning.

I did as I was ordered, of course, and when I came into the kitchen punctually at six a.m. I found the charwoman sitting at the table with a pile of gold in front of her, which she was counting over with a very grubby finger. She had her back to me, and was saying as I entered:

"I think if you was to give me another fifty quid I'd leave you the rest now. You'd still have the diamonds and the rest of the money."

She spoke to Miss Cruikshank, who was facing me, and who, on seeing me appear, turned as white as a ghost. But she quickly recovered herself, and, standing between me and the woman, she said vehemently:

"What do you mean by prying on me like this? Go and pack your boxes and leave the house this instant."

But before I could reply the woman had interposed.

"Don't you fret yourself, miss," she said, placing her grimy hand on Miss Cruikshank's shoulder. "There's the bag of sand in that there corner; we'll knock 'er down as we did Mrs. Dunstan—eh?"

"Hold your tongue, you lying fool!" said the girl, who now looked like a maddened fury.

"Give me that other fifty quid and I'll hold my tongue," retorted the woman, boldly.

"This creature is mad," said Miss Cruikshank, who had made a vigorous and successful effort to recover herself. "She is under the delusion that not only is she Mrs. Thomas, but that she murdered Mrs. Dunstan–"

"No–no!" interrupted the woman. "I only came back that morning because I recollected that you had left the bag of sand upstairs after you so cleverly did away with Mrs. Dunstan, robbed her of all her money and jewels, and even were sharp enough to imitate her voice when Mrs. Kennett, the cook, terrified you by speaking to Mrs. Dunstan through the door."

"It is false! You are not Mrs. Thomas. The two maids who are here now, and who were in this house at the time, can swear that you are a liar."

"Let us change clothes now, Miss Cruikshank," said a voice, which sounded almost weirdly in my ear in spite of its familiarity, for I could not locate whence it came, "and see if in a charwoman's dress those two maids would not recognise you."

"Mary," continued the same familiar voice, "help me out of these filthy clothes. Perhaps Miss Cruikshank would like to resume her own part of Mrs. Thomas, the charwoman."

"Liars and impostors–both!" shouted the girl, who was rapidly losing all presence of mind. "I'll send for the police."

"Quite unnecessary," rejoined Lady Molly coolly; "Detective-Inspector Danvers is just outside that door."

The girl made a dash for the other door, but I was too quick for her, and held her back, even whilst Lady Molly gave a short, sharp call which brought Danvers on the scene.

I must say that Miss Cruikshank made a bold fight, but Danvers had two of our fellows with him, and arrested her on the warrant for the apprehension of the person known as Mrs. Thomas.

The clothes of the charwoman who had so mysteriously disappeared had been found by Lady Molly at the back of the coal cellar, and she was still dressed in them at the present moment.

No wonder I had not recognised my own dainty lady in the grimy woman who had so successfully played the part of a blackmailer on the murderess of Mrs. Dunstan. She explained to me subsequently that the first inkling that she had had of the horrible truth–namely, that it was Miss Cruikshank who had deliberately planned to murder Mrs. Dunstan by impersonating a charwoman for a while, and thus throwing dust in the eyes of the police–was when she heard of the callous words which the old lady was supposed to have uttered when she was told of Miss Violet's flight from the house in the middle of the night.

"She may have been very angry at the girl's escapade," explained Lady Molly to me, "but she would not have allowed her to starve. Such cruelty was out of all proportion to the offence. Then I looked about me for a stronger motive for the old lady's wrath; and, remembering what she said on New Year's Eve, when Violet fled crying from the room, I came to the conclusion that her anger was not directed against her niece, but against the other girl, and against the man who had transferred his affections from Violet Frostwicke to Miss Cruikshank, and had not only irritated Mrs. Dunstan by this clandestine, double-faced love-making, but had broken the heart of his trusting fiancée.

"No doubt Miss Cruikshank did not know that the will, whereby she was to inherit £1,000, was not signed, and no doubt she and young Athol planned out that cruel murder between them. The charwoman was also a bag of sand which was literally thrown in the eyes of the police."

"But," I objected, "I can't understand how a cold-blooded creature like that Miss Cruikshank could have allowed herself to be terrorised and blackmailed. She knew that you could not be Mrs. Thomas, since Mrs. Thomas never existed."

"Yes; but one must reckon a little sometimes with that negligible quantity known as conscience. My appearance as Mrs. Thomas vaguely frightened Miss Cruikshank. She wondered who I was and what I knew. When, three days later, I found the shabby clothes in the coal-cellar and appeared dressed in them, she lost her head. She gave me money! From that moment she was done for. Confession was only a matter of time."

And Miss Cruikshank did make full confession. She was recommended to mercy on account of her sex, but she was plucky enough not to implicate David Athol in the recital of her crime.

He has since emigrated to Western Canada.

THE MAN IN THE INVERNESS CAPE

I HAVE heard many people say—people, too, mind you, who read their daily paper regularly—that it is quite impossible for anyone to "disappear" within the confines of the British Isles. At the same time these wise people invariably admit one great exception to their otherwise unimpeachable theory, and that is the case of Mr. Leonard Marvell, who, as you know, walked out one afternoon from the Scotia Hotel in Cromwell Road and has never been seen or heard of since.

Information had originally been given to the police by Mr. Marvell's sister Olive, a Scotchwoman of the usually accepted type: tall, bony, with sandy-coloured hair, and a somewhat melancholy expression in her blue-grey eyes.

Her brother, she said, had gone out on a rather foggy afternoon. I think it was the 3rd of February, just about a year ago. His intention had been to go and consult a solicitor in the City—whose address had been given him recently by a friend—about some private business of his own.

Mr. Marvell had told his sister that he would get a train at South Kensington Station to Moorgate Street, and walk thence to Finsbury Square. She was to expect him home by dinner-time.

As he was, however, very irregular in his habits, being fond of spending his evenings at restaurants and music-halls, the sister did not feel the least anxious when he did not return home at the appointed time. She had her dinner in the table d'hôte room, and went to bed soon after 10.0.

She and her brother occupied two bedrooms and a sitting-room on the second floor of the little private hotel. Miss Marvell, moreover, had a maid always with her, as she was somewhat of an invalid. This girl, Rosie Campbell, a nice-looking Scotch lassie, slept on the top floor.

It was only on the following morning, when Mr. Leonard did not put in an appearance at breakfast, that Miss Marvell began to feel anxious. According to her own account, she sent Rosie in to see if anything was the matter, and the girl, wide-eyed and not a little frightened, came back with the news that Mr. Marvell was not in his room, and that his bed had not been slept in that night.

With characteristic Scottish reserve, Miss Olive said nothing about the matter at the time to anyone, nor did she give information to the police until two days later, when she herself had exhausted every means in her power to discover her brother's whereabouts.

She had seen the lawyer to whose office Leonard Marvell had intended going that afternoon, but Mr. Statham, the solicitor in question, had seen nothing of the missing man.

With great adroitness Rosie, the maid, had made inquiries at South Kensington and Moorgate Street stations. At the former, the booking clerk, who knew Mr.

Marvell by sight, distinctly remembered selling him a first-class ticket to one of the City stations in the early part of the afternoon; but at Moorgate Street, which is a very busy station, no one recollected seeing a tall, red-haired Scotchman in an Inverness cape—such was the description given of the missing man. By that time the fog had become very thick in the City; traffic was disorganised, and everyone felt fussy, ill-tempered, and self-centred.

These, in substance, were the details which Miss Marvell gave to the police on the subject of her brother's strange disappearance.

At first she did not appear very anxious; she seemed to have great faith in Mr. Marvell's power to look after himself; moreover, she declared positively that her brother had neither valuables nor money about his person when he went out that afternoon.

But as day succeeded day and no trace of the missing man had yet been found, matters became more serious, and the search instituted by our fellows at the Yard waxed more keen.

A description of Mr. Leonard Marvell was published in the leading London and provincial dailies. Unfortunately, there was no good photograph of him extant, and descriptions are apt to prove vague.

Very little was known about the man beyond his disappearance, which had rendered him famous. He and his sister had arrived at the Scotia Hotel about a month previously, and subsequently they were joined by the maid Campbell.

Scotch people are far too reserved ever to speak of themselves or their affairs to strangers. Brother and sister spoke very little to anyone at the hotel. They had their meals in their sitting-room, waited on by the maid, who messed with the staff. But, in face of the present terrible calamity, Miss Marvell's frigidity relaxed before the police inspector, to whom she gave what information she could about her brother.

"He was like a son to me," she explained with scarcely restrained tears, "for we lost our parents early in life, and as we were left very, very badly off, our relations took but little notice of us. My brother was years younger than I am—and though he was a little wild and fond of pleasure, he was as good as gold to me, and has supported us both for years by journalistic work. We came to London from Glasgow about a month ago, because Leonard got a very good appointment on the staff of the 'Daily Post.'"

All this, of course, was soon proved to be true; and although, on minute inquiries being instituted in Glasgow, but little seemed to be known about Mr. Leonard Marvell in that city, there seemed no doubt that he had done some reporting for the "Courier," and that latterly, in response to an advertisement, he had applied for and obtained regular employment on the "Daily Post."

The latter enterprising halfpenny journal, with characteristic magnanimity, made an offer of £50 reward to any of its subscribers who gave information which would lead to the discovery of the whereabouts of Mr. Leonard Marvell.

But time went by, and that £50 remained unclaimed.

2

LADY MOLLY had not seemed as interested as she usually was in cases of this sort. With strange flippancy—wholly unlike herself—she remarked that one Scotch journalist more or less in London did not vastly matter.

I was much amused, therefore, one morning about three weeks after the mysterious disappearance of Mr. Leonard Marvell, when Jane, our little parlourmaid, brought in a card accompanied by a letter.

The card bore the name "Miss Olive Marvell." The letter was the usual formula from the chief, asking Lady Molly to have a talk with the lady in question, and to come and see him on the subject after the interview.

With a smothered yawn my dear lady told Jane to show in Miss Marvell.

"There are two of them, my lady," said Jane, as she prepared to obey.

"Two what?" asked Lady Molly with a laugh.

"Two ladies, I mean," explained Jane.

"Well! Show them both into the drawing-room," said Lady Molly, impatiently.

Then, as Jane went off on this errand, a very funny thing happened; funny, because during the entire course of my intimate association with my dear lady, I had never known her act with such marked indifference in the face of an obviously interesting case. She turned to me and said:

"Mary, you had better see these two women, whoever they may be; I feel that they would bore me to distraction. Take note of what they say, and let me know. Now, don't argue," she added with a laugh, which peremptorily put a stop to my rising protest, "but go and interview Miss Marvell and Co."

Needless to say, I promptly did as I was told, and the next few seconds saw me installed in our little drawing-room, saying polite preliminaries to the two ladies who sat opposite to me.

I had no need to ask which of them was Miss Marvell. Tall, ill-dressed in deep black, with a heavy crape veil over her face, and black cotton gloves, she looked the uncompromising Scotchwoman to the life. In strange contrast to her depressing appearance, there sat beside her an over-dressed, much behatted, peroxided young woman, who bore the stamp of the profession all over her pretty, painted face.

Miss Marvell, I was glad to note, was not long in plunging into the subject which had brought her here.

"I saw a gentleman at Scotland Yard," she explained, after a short preamble, "because Miss—er—Lulu Fay came to me at the hotel this very morning with a story which, in my opinion, should have been told to the police directly my brother's disappearance became known, and not three weeks later."

The emphasis which she laid on the last few words and the stern look with which she regarded the golden-haired young woman beside her, showed the disapproval with which the rigid Scotchwoman viewed any connection which her brother might have had with the lady, whose very name seemed unpleasant to her lips.

Miss—er—Lulu Fay blushed even through her rouge, and turned a pair of large, liquid eyes imploringly upon me.

"I—I didn't know. I was frightened," she stammered.

"There's no occasion to be frightened now," retorted Miss Marvell, "and the sooner you try and be truthful about the whole matter, the better it will be for all of us."

And the stern woman's lips closed with a snap, as she deliberately turned her back on Miss Fay and began turning over the leaves of a magazine which happened to be on a table close to her hand.

I muttered a few words of encouragement, for the little actress looked ready to cry. I spoke as kindly as I could, telling her that if indeed she could throw some light on Mr. Marvell's present whereabouts it was her duty to be quite frank on the subject.

She "hem"-ed and "ha"-ed for awhile, and her simpering ways were just beginning to tell on my nerves, when she suddenly started talking very fast.

"I am principal boy at the Grand," she explained with great volubility; "and I knew Mr. Leonard Marvell well–in fact–er–he paid me a good deal of attention and–"

"Yes–and–?" I queried, for the girl was obviously nervous.

There was a pause. Miss Fay began to cry.

"And it seems that my brother took this young–er–lady to supper on the night of February 3rd, after which no one has ever seen or heard of him again," here interposed Miss Marvell, quietly.

"Is that so?" I asked.

Lulu Fay nodded, whilst heavy tears fell upon her clasped hands.

"But why did you not tell this to the police three weeks ago?" I ejaculated, with all the sternness at my command.

"I–I was frightened," she stammered.

"Frightened? Of what?"

"I am engaged to Lord Mountnewte and–"

"And you did not wish him to know that you were accepting the attentions of Mr. Leonard Marvell–was that it? Well," I added, with involuntary impatience, "what happened after you had supper with Mr. Marvell?"

"Oh! I hope–I hope that nothing happened," she said through more tears; "we had supper at the Trocadero, and he saw me into my brougham. Suddenly, just as I was driving away, I saw Lord Mountnewte standing quite close to us in the crowd."

"Did the two men know one another?" I asked.

"No," replied Miss Fay; "at least, I didn't think so, but when I looked back through the window of my carriage I saw them standing on the kerb talking to each other for a moment, and then walk off together towards Piccadilly Circus. That is the last I have seen of either of them," continued the little actress with a fresh flood of tears. "Lord Mountnewte hasn't spoken to me since, and Mr. Marvell has disappeared with my money and my diamonds."

"Your money and your diamonds?" I gasped in amazement.

"Yes; he told me he was a jeweller, and that my diamonds wanted re-setting. He took them with him that evening, for he said that London jewellers were clumsy thieves, and that he would love to do the work for me himself. I also gave him two hundred pounds, which he said he would want for buying the gold and platinum required for the settings. And now he has disappeared–and my diamonds–and my money! Oh! I have been very–very foolish–and–"

Her voice broke down completely. Of course, one often hears of the idiocy of girls giving money and jewels unquestioningly to clever adventurers who know how to trade upon their inordinate vanity. There was, therefore, nothing very out of the way in the story just told me by Miss–er–Lulu Fay, until the moment when Miss

Marvell's quiet voice, with its marked Scotch burr, broke in upon the short silence which had followed the actress's narrative.

"As I explained to the chief detective-inspector at Scotland Yard," she said calmly, "the story which this young—er—lady tells is only partly true. She may have had supper with Mr. Leonard Marvell on the night of February 3rd, and he may have paid her certain attentions; but he never deceived her by telling her that he was a jeweller, nor did he obtain possession of her diamonds and her money through false statements. My brother was the soul of honour and loyalty. If for some reason which Miss—er—Lulu Fay chooses to keep secret, he had her jewels and money in his possession on the fatal February 3rd, then I think his disappearance is accounted for. He has been robbed and perhaps murdered."

Like a true Scotchwoman she did not give way to tears, but even her harsh voice trembled slightly when she thus bore witness to her brother's honesty, and expressed the fears which assailed her as to his fate.

Imagine my plight! I could ill forgive my dear lady for leaving me in this unpleasant position—a sort of peacemaker between two women who evidently hated one another, and each of whom was trying her best to give the other "the lie direct."

I ventured to ring for our faithful Jane and to send her with an imploring message to Lady Molly, begging her to come and disentangle the threads of this muddled skein with her clever fingers; but Jane returned with a curt note from my dear lady, telling me not to worry about such a silly case, and to bow the two women out of the flat as soon as possible and then come for a nice walk.

I wore my official manner as well as I could, trying not to betray the 'prentice hand. Of course, the interview lasted a great deal longer, and there was considerably more talk than I can tell you of in a brief narrative. But the gist of it all was just as I have said. Miss Lulu Fay stuck to every point of the story which she had originally told Miss Marvell. It was the latter uncompromising lady who had immediately marched the younger woman off to Scotland Yard in order that she might repeat her tale to the police. I did not wonder that the chief promptly referred them both to Lady Molly.

Anyway, I made excellent shorthand notes of the conflicting stories which I heard; and I finally saw, with real relief, the two women walk out of our little front door.

3

MISS—ER—LULU FAY, mind you, never contradicted in any one particular the original story which she had told me, about going out to supper with Leonard Marvell, entrusting him with £200 and the diamonds, which he said he would have reset for her, and seeing him finally in close conversation with her recognised fiancé, Lord Mountnewte. Miss Marvell, on the other hand, very commendably refused to admit that her brother acted dishonestly towards the girl. If he had her jewels and money in his possession at the time of his disappearance, then he had undoubtedly been robbed, or perhaps murdered, on his way back to the hotel, and if Lord Mountnewte had been the last to speak to him on that fatal night, then Lord Mountnewte must be able to throw some light on the mysterious occurrence.

Our fellows at the Yard were abnormally active. It seemed, on the face of it, impossible that a man, healthy, vigorous, and admittedly sober, should vanish in London between Piccadilly Circus and Cromwell Road without leaving the slightest trace of himself or of the valuables said to have been in his possession.

Of course, Lord Mountnewte was closely questioned. He was a young Guardsman of the usual pattern, and, after a great deal of vapid talk which irritated Detective-Inspector Saunders not a little, he made the following statement–

"I certainly am acquainted with Miss Lulu Fay. On the night in question I was standing outside the Troc, when I saw this young lady at her own carriage window talking to a tall man in an Inverness cape. She had, earlier in the day, refused my invitation to supper, saying that she was not feeling very well, and would go home directly after the theatre; therefore I felt, naturally, a little vexed. I was just about to hail a taxi, meaning to go on to the club, when, to my intense astonishment, the man in the Inverness cape came up to me and asked me if I could tell him the best way to get back to Cromwell Road."

"And what did you do?" asked Saunders.

"I walked a few steps with him and put him on his way," replied Lord Mountnewte, blandly.

In Saunder's own expressive words, he thought that story "fishy." He could not imagine the arm of coincidence being quite so long as to cause these two men–who presumably were both in love with the same girl, and who had just met at a moment when one of them was obviously suffering pangs of jealously–to hold merely a topographical conversation with one another. But it was equally difficult to suppose that the eldest son and heir of the Marquis of Loam should murder a successful rival and then rob him in the streets of London.

Moreover, here came the eternal and unanswerable questions: If Lord Mountnewte had murdered Leonard Marvell, where and how had he done it, and what had he done with the body?

I dare say you are wondering by this time why I have said nothing about the maid, Rosie Campbell.

Well, plenty of very clever people (I mean those who write letters to the papers and give suggestions to every official department in the kingdom) thought that the police ought to keep a very strict eye upon that pretty Scotch lassie. For she was very pretty, and had quaint, demure ways which rendered her singularly attractive, in spite of the fact that, for most masculine tastes, she would have been considered too tall. Of course, Saunders and Danvers kept an eye on her–you may be sure of that–and got a good deal of information about her from the people at the hotel. Most of it, unfortunately, was irrelevant to the case. She was maid-attendant to Miss Marvell, who was feeble in health, and who went out but little. Rosie waited on her master and mistress upstairs, carrying their meals to their private room, and doing their bedrooms. The rest of the day she was fairly free, and was quite sociable downstairs with the hotel staff.

With regard to her movements and actions on that memorable 3rd of February, Saunders--though he worked very hard–could glean but little useful information. You see, in a hotel of that kind, with an average of thirty to forty guests at one time, it is extremely difficult to state positively what any one person did or did not do on that particular day.

Most people at the Scotia remembered that Miss Marvell dined in the table d'hôte room on that 3rd of February; this she did about once a fortnight, when her maid had an evening "out."

The hotel staff also recollected fairly distinctly that Miss Rosie Campbell was not in the steward's room at supper-time that evening, but no one could remember definitely when she came in.

One of the chambermaids who occupied the bedroom adjoining hers, said she heard her moving about soon after midnight; the hall porter declared that he saw her come in just before half-past twelve when he closed the doors for the night.

But one of the ground-floor valets said that, on the morning of the 4th, he saw Miss Marvell's maid, in hat and coat, slip into the house and upstairs, very quickly and quietly, soon after the front doors were opened, namely, about 7.0 a.m.

Here, of course, was a direct contradiction between the chambermaid and hall porter on the one side, and the valet on the other, whilst Miss Marvell said that Campbell came into her room and made her some tea long before seven o'clock every morning, including that of the 4th.

I assure you our fellows at the Yard were ready to tear their hair out by the roots, from sheer aggravation at this maze of contradictions which met them at every turn.

The whole thing seemed so simple. There was nothing "to it" as it were, and but very little real suggestion of foul play, and yet Mr. Leonard Marvell had disappeared, and no trace of him could be found.

Everyone now talked freely of murder. London is a big town, and this would not have been the first instance of a stranger—for Mr. Leonard Marvell was practically a stranger in London—being enticed to a lonely part of the city on a foggy night, and there done away with and robbed, and the body hidden in an out-of-the-way cellar, where it might not be discovered for months to come.

But the newspaper-reading public is notably fickle, and Mr. Leonard Marvell was soon forgotten by everyone save the chief and the batch of our fellows who had charge of the case.

Thus I heard through Danvers one day that Rosie Campbell had left Miss Marvell's employ, and was living in rooms in Findlater Terrace, near Walham Green.

I was alone in our Maida Vale flat at the time, my dear lady having gone to spend the week-end with the Dowager Lady Loam, who was an old friend of hers; nor, when she returned, did she seem any more interested in Rosie Campbell's movements than she had been hitherto.

Yet another month went by, and I for one had absolutely ceased to think of the man in the Inverness cape, who had so mysteriously and so completely vanished in the very midst of busy London, when, one morning early in January, Lady Molly made her appearance in my room, looking more like the landlady of a disreputable gambling-house than anything else I could imagine.

"What in the world—?" I began.

"Yes! I think I look the part," she replied, surveying with obvious complacency the extraordinary figure which confronted her in the glass.

My dear lady had on a purple cloth coat and skirt of a peculiarly vivid hue, and of a singular cut, which made her matchless figure look like a sack of potatoes. Her soft brown hair was quite hidden beneath a "transformation," of that yellow-reddish tint only to be met with in very cheap dyes.

As for her hat! I won't attempt to describe it. It towered above and around her face, which was plentifully covered with brick-red and with that kind of powder which causes the cheeks to look a deep mauve.

My dear lady looked, indeed, a perfect picture of appalling vulgarity.

"Where are you going in this elegant attire?" I asked in amazement.

"I have taken rooms in Findlater Terrace," she replied lightly. "I feel that the air of Walham Green will do us both good. Our amiable, if somewhat slatternly, landlady expects us in time for luncheon. You will have to keep rigidly in the background, Mary, all the while we are there. I said that I was bringing an invalid niece with me, and, as a preliminary, you may as well tie two or three thick veils over your face. I think I may safely promise that you won't be dull."

And we certainly were not dull during our brief stay at 34, Findlater Terrace, Walham Green. Fully equipped, and arrayed in our extraordinary garments, we duly arrived there, in a rickety four-wheeler, on the top of which were perched two seedy-looking boxes.

The landlady was a toothless old creature, who apparently thought washing a quite unnecessary proceeding. In this she was evidently at one with every one of her neighbours. Findlater Terrace looked unspeakably squalid; groups of dirty children congregated in the gutters and gave forth discordant shrieks as our cab drove up.

Through my thick veils I thought that, some distance down the road, I spied a horsy-looking man in ill-fitting riding-breeches and gaiters, who vaguely reminded me of Danvers.

Within half an hour of our installation, and whilst we were eating a tough steak over a doubtful table cloth, my dear lady told me that she had been waiting a full month, until rooms in this particular house happened to be vacant. Fortunately the population in Findlater Terrace is always a shifting one, and Lady Molly had kept a sharp eye on No. 34, where, on the floor above, lived Miss Rosie Campbell. Directly the last set of lodgers walked out of the ground-floor rooms, we were ready to walk in.

My dear lady's manners and customs, whilst living at the above aristocratic address, were fully in keeping with her appearance. The shrill, rasping voice which she assumed echoed from attic to cellar.

One day I heard her giving vague hints to the landlady that her husband, Mr. Marcus Stein, had had a little trouble with the police about a small hotel which he had kept somewhere near Fitzroy Square, and where "young gentlemen used to come and play cards of a night." The landlady was also made to understand that the worthy Mr. Stein was now living temporarily at His Majesty's expense, whilst Mrs. Stein had to live a somewhat secluded life, away from her fashionable friends.

The misfortunes of the pseudo Mrs. Stein in no way marred the amiability of Mrs. Tredwen, our landlady. The inhabitants of Findlater Terrace care very little about the antecedents of their lodgers, so long as they pay their week's rent in advance, and settle their "extras" without much murmur.

This Lady Molly did, with a generosity characteristic of an ex-lady of means. She never grumbled at the quantity of jam and marmalade which we were supposed to have consumed every week, and which anon reached titanic proportions. She tolerated Mrs. Tredwen's cat, tipped Ermyntrude—the tousled lodging-house slavey—lavishly, and lent the upstairs lodger her spirit-lamp and curling-tongs when Miss Rosie Campbell's got out of order.

A certain degree of intimacy followed the loan of those curling-tongs. Miss Campbell, reserved and demure, greatly sympathised with the lady who was not on the best of terms with the police. I kept steadily in the background. The two ladies did not visit each other's rooms, but they held long and confidential conversations on the landings, and I gathered, presently, that the pseudo Mrs. Stein had succeeded in persuading Rosie Campbell that, if the police were watching No. 34, Findlater Terrace, at all, it was undoubtedly on account of the unfortunate Mr. Stein's faithful wife.

I found it a little difficult to fathom Lady Molly's intentions. We had been in the house over three weeks, and nothing whatever had happened. Once I ventured on a discreet query as to whether we were to expect the sudden re-appearance of Mr. Leonard Marvell.

"For if that's all about it," I argued, "then surely the men from the Yard could have kept the house in view, without all this inconvenience and masquerading on our part."

But to this tirade my dear lady vouchsafed no reply.

She and her newly acquired friend were, about this time, deeply interested in the case known as the "West End Shop Robberies," which no doubt you recollect, since they occurred such a very little while ago. Ladies who were shopping in the large drapers' emporiums during the crowded and busy sale time, lost reticules, purses, and valuable parcels, without any trace of the clever thief being found.

The drapers, during sale-time, invariably employ detectives in plain clothes to look after their goods, but in this case it was the customers who were robbed, and the detectives, attentive to every attempt at "shop-lifting," had had no eyes for the more subtle thief.

I had already noticed Miss Rosie Campbell's keen look of excitement whenever the pseudo Mrs. Stein discussed these cases with her. I was not a bit surprised, therefore, when, one afternoon at about teatime, my dear lady came home from her habitual walk, and, at the top of her shrill voice, called out to me from the hall:

"Mary! Mary! they've got the man of the shop robberies. He's given the silly police the slip this time, but they know who he is now, and I suppose they'll get him presently. 'Tisn't anybody I know," she added, with that harsh, common laugh which she had adopted for her part.

I had come out of the room in response to her call, and was standing just outside our own sitting-room door. Mrs. Tredwen, too, bedraggled and unkempt, as usual, had sneaked up the area steps, closely followed by Ermyntrude.

But on the half-landing just above us the trembling figure of Rosie Campbell, with scared white face and dilated eyes, looked on the verge of a sudden fall.

Still talking shrilly and volubly, Lady Molly ran up to her, but Campbell met her half-way, and the pseudo Mrs. Stein, taking vigorous hold of her wrist, dragged her into our own sitting-room.

"Pull yourself together, now," she said with rough kindness; "that owl Tredwen is listening, and you needn't let her know too much. Shut the door, Mary. Lor' bless you, m'dear, I've gone through worse scares than these. There! you just lie down on this sofa a bit. My niece'll make you a nice cup o'tea; and I'll go and get an evening paper, and see what's going on. I suppose you are very interested in the shop robbery man, or you wouldn't have took on so."

Without waiting for Campbell's contradiction to this statement, Lady Molly flounced out of the house.

Miss Campbell hardly spoke during the next ten minutes that she and I were left alone together. She lay on the sofa with eyes wide open, staring up at the ceiling, evidently still in a great state of fear.

I had just got tea ready when Lady Molly came back. She had an evening paper in her hand, but threw this down on the table directly she came in.

"I could only get an early edition," she said breathlessly, "and the silly thing hasn't got anything in it about the matter."

She drew near to the sofa, and, subduing the shrillness of her voice, she whispered rapidly, bending down towards Campbell:

"There's a man hanging about at the corner down there. No, no; it's not the police," she added quickly, in response to the girl's sudden start of alarm. "Trust me, my dear, for knowing a 'tec when I see one! Why, I'd smell one half a mile off. No; my opinion is that it's your man, my dear, and that he's in a devil of a hole."

"Oh! he oughtn't to come here," ejaculated Campbell in great alarm. "He'll get me into trouble and do himself no good. He's been a fool!" she added, with a fierceness wholly unlike her usual demure placidity, "getting himself caught like that. Now I suppose we shall have to hook it–if there's time."

"Can I do anything to help you?" asked the pseudo Mrs. Stein. "You know I've been through all this myself, when they was after Mr. Stein. Or perhaps Mary could do something."

"Well, yes," said the girl, after a slight pause, during which she seemed to be gathering her wits together; "I'll write a note, and you shall take it, if you will, to a friend of mine–a lady who lives in the Cromwell Road. But if you still see a man lurking about at the corner of the street, then, just as you pass him, say the word 'Campbell,' and if he replies 'Rosie,' then give him the note. Will you do that?"

"Of course I will, my dear. Just you leave it all to me."

And the pseudo Mrs. Stein brought ink and paper and placed them on the table. Rosie Campbell wrote a brief note, and then fastened it down with a bit of sealing-wax before she handed it over to Lady Molly. The note was addressed to Miss Marvell, Scotia Hotel, Cromwell Road.

"You understand?" she said eagerly. "Don't give the note to the man unless he says 'Rosie' in reply to the word 'Campbell.'"

"All right–all right!" said Lady Molly, slipping the note into her reticule. "And you go up to your room, Miss Campbell; it's no good giving that old fool Tredwen too much to gossip about."

Rosie Campbell went upstairs, and presently my dear lady and I were walking rapidly down the badly-lighted street.

"Where is the man?" I whispered eagerly as soon as we were out of earshot of No. 34.

"There is no man," replied Lady Molly, quickly.

"But the West End shop thief?" I asked.

"He hasn't been caught yet, and won't be either, for he is far too clever a scoundrel to fall into an ordinary trap."

She did not give me time to ask further questions, for presently, when we had reached Reporton Square, my dear lady handed me the note written by Campbell, and said:

"Go straight on to the Scotia Hotel, and ask for Miss Marvell; send up the note to her, but don't let her see you, as she knows you by sight. I must see the chief first, and will be with you as soon as possible. Having delivered the note, you must hang about outside as long as you can. Use your wits; she must not leave the hotel before I see her."

There was no hansom to be got in this elegant quarter of the town, so, having parted from my dear lady, I made for the nearest Underground station, and took a train for South Kensington.

Thus it was nearly seven o'clock before I reached the Scotia. In answer to my inquiries for Miss Marvell, I was told that she was ill in bed and could see no one. I replied that I had only brought a note for her, and would wait for a reply.

Acting on my dear lady's instructions, I was as slow in my movements as ever I could be, and was some time in finding the note and handing it to a waiter, who then took it upstairs.

Presently he returned with the message: "Miss Marvell says there is no answer."

Whereupon I asked for pen and paper at the office, and wrote the following brief note on my own responsibility, using my wits as my dear lady had bidden me to do.

"Please, madam," I wrote, "will you send just a line to Miss Rosie Campbell? She seems very upset and frightened at some news she has had."

Once more the waiter ran upstairs, and returned with a sealed envelope, which I slipped into my reticule.

Time was slipping by very slowly. I did not know how long I should have to wait outside in the cold, when, to my horror, I heard a hard voice, with a marked Scotch accent, saying:

"I am going out, waiter, and shan't be back to dinner. Tell them to lay a little cold supper upstairs in my room."

The next moment Miss Marvell, with coat, hat, and veil, was descending the stairs.

My plight was awkward. I certainly did not think it safe to present myself before the lady; she would undoubtedly recollect my face. Yet I had orders to detain her until the appearance of Lady Molly.

Miss Marvell seemed in no hurry. She was putting on her gloves as she came downstairs. In the hall she gave a few more instructions to the porter, whilst I, in a dark corner in the background, was vaguely planning an assault or an alarm of fire.

Suddenly, at the hotel entrance, where the porter was obsequiously holding open the door for Miss Marvell to pass through, I saw the latter's figure stiffen; she took one step back as if involuntarily, then, equally quickly, attempted to dart across the threshold, on which a group–composed of my dear lady, of Saunders, and of two or three people scarcely distinguishable in the gloom beyond–had suddenly made its appearance.

Miss Marvell was forced to retreat into the hall; already I had heard Saunder's hurriedly whispered words:

"Try and not make a fuss in this place, now. Everything can go off quietly, you know."

Danvers and Cotton, whom I knew well, were already standing one each side of Miss Marvell, whilst suddenly amongst this group I recognised Fanny, the wife of Danvers, who is one of our female searchers at the yard.

"Shall we go up to your own room?" suggested Saunders.

"I think that is quite unnecessary," interposed Lady Molly. "I feel convinced that Mr. Leonard Marvell will yield to the inevitable quietly, and follow you without giving any trouble."

Marvell, however, did make a bold dash for liberty. As Lady Molly had said previously, he was far too clever to allow himself to be captured easily. But my dear lady had been cleverer. As she told me subsequently, she had from the first suspected that the trio who lodged at the Scotia Hotel were really only a duo—namely, Leonard Marvell and his wife. The latter impersonated a maid most of the time; but among these two clever people the three characters were interchangeable. Of course, there was no Miss Marvell at all. Leonard was alternately dressed up as man or woman, according to the requirements of his villainies.

"As soon as I heard that Miss Marvell was very tall and bony," said Lady Molly, "I thought that there might be a possibility of her being merely a man in disguise. Then there was the fact–but little dwelt on by either the police or the public–that no one seems ever to have seen brother and sister together, nor was the entire trio ever seen at one and the same time.

"On that 3rd of February Leonard Marvell went out. No doubt he changed his attire in a lady's waiting-room at one of the railway stations; subsequently he came home, now dressed as Miss Marvell, and had dinner in the table d'hôte room so as to set up a fairly plausible alibi. But ultimately it was his wife, the pseudo Rosie Campbell, who stayed indoors that night, whilst he, Leonard Marvell, when going out after dinner, impersonated the maid until he was clear of the hotel; then he reassumed his male clothes once more, no doubt in the deserted waiting-room of some railway station, and met Miss Lulu Fay at supper, subsequently returning to the hotel in the guise of the maid.

"You see the game of criss-cross, don't you? This interchanging of characters was bound to baffle everyone. Many clever scoundrels have assumed disguises, sometimes impersonating members of the opposite sex to their own, but never before have I known two people play the part of three. Thus, endless contradictions followed as to the hour when Campbell the maid went out and when she came in, for at one time it was she herself who was seen by the valet, and at another it was Leonard Marvell dressed in her clothes."

He was also clever enough to accost Lord Mountnewte in the open street, thus bringing further complications into this strange case.

After the successful robbery of Miss Fay's diamonds, Leonard Marvell and his wife parted for awhile. They were waiting for an opportunity to get across the Channel and there turn their booty into solid cash. Whilst Mrs. Marvell, alias Rosie Campbell, led a retired life in Findlater Terrace, Leonard kept his hand in with West End shop robberies.

Then Lady Molly entered the lists. As usual, her scheme was bold and daring;

she trusted her own intuition and acted accordingly.

When she brought home the false news that the author of the shop robberies had been spotted by the police, Rosie Campbell's obvious terror confirmed her suspicions. The note written by the latter to the so-called Miss Marvell, though it contained nothing in any way incriminating, was the crowning certitude that my dear lady was right, as usual, in all her surmises.

And now Mr. Leonard Marvell will be living for a couple of years at the taxpayers' expense; he has "disappeared" temporarily from the public eye.

Rosie Campbell—i.e. Mrs. Marvell—has gone to Glasgow. I feel convinced that two years hence we shall hear of the worthy couple again.

THE WOMAN IN THE BIG HAT

LADY MOLLY always had the idea that if the finger of Fate had pointed to Mathis' in Regent Street, rather than to Lyons', as the most advisable place for us to have a cup of tea that afternoon, Mr. Culledon would be alive at the present moment.

My dear lady is quite sure—and needless to say that I share her belief in herself—that she would have anticipated the murderer's intentions, and thus prevented one of the most cruel and callous of crimes which were ever perpetrated in the heart of London.

She and I had been to a matinée of "Trilby," and were having tea at Lyons', which is exactly opposite Mathis' Vienna café in Regent Street. From where we sat we commanded a view of the street and of the café, which had been very crowded during the last hour.

We had lingered over our toasted muffin until past six, when our attention was drawn to the unusual commotion which had arisen both outside and in the brilliantly lighted place over the road.

We saw two men run out of the doorway, and return a minute or two later in company with a policeman. You know what is the inevitable result of such a proceeding in London. Within three minutes a crowd had collected outside Mathis'. Two or three more constables had already assembled, and had some difficulty in keeping the entrance clear of intruders.

But already my dear lady, keen as a pointer on the scent, had hastily paid her bill, and, without waiting to see if I followed her or not, had quickly crossed the road, and the next moment her graceful form was lost in the crowd.

I went after her, impelled by curiosity, and presently caught sight of her in close conversation with one of our own men. I have always thought that Lady Molly must have eyes at the back of her head, otherwise how could she have known that I stood behind her now? Anyway, she beckoned to me, and together we entered Mathis', much to the astonishment and anger of the less fortunate crowd.

The usually gay little place was indeed sadly transformed. In one corner the waitresses, in dainty caps and aprons, had put their heads together, and were eagerly whispering to one another whilst casting furtive looks at the small group assembled in front of one of those pretty alcoves, which, as you know, line the walls all round the big tea-room at Mathis'.

Here two of our men were busy with pencil and note-book, whilst one fair-haired waitress, dissolved in tears, was apparently giving them a great deal of irrelevant and confused information.

Chief Inspector Saunders had, I understood, been already sent for; the constables, confronted with this extraordinary tragedy, were casting anxious glances towards the main entrance, whilst putting the conventional questions to the young waitress. And in the alcove itself, raised from the floor of the room by a couple of carpeted steps, the cause of all this commotion, all this anxiety, and all these tears, sat huddled up on a chair, with arms lying straight across the marble-topped table, on which the usual paraphernalia of afternoon tea still lay scattered about. The upper part of the body, limp, backboneless, and awry, half propped up against the wall, half falling back upon the outstretched arms, told quite plainly its weird tale of death.

Before my dear lady and I had time to ask any questions, Saunders arrived in a taxicab. He was accompanied by the medical officer, Dr. Townson, who at once busied himself with the dead man, whilst Saunders went up quickly to Lady Molly.

"The chief suggested sending for you," he said quickly; "he was 'phoning you when I left. There's a woman in this case, and we shall rely on you a good deal."

"What has happened?" asked my dear lady, whose fine eyes were glowing with excitement at the mere suggestion of work.

"I have only a few stray particulars," replied Saunders, "but the chief witness is that yellow-haired girl over there. We'll find out what we can from her directly Dr. Townson has given us his opinion."

The medical officer, who had been kneeling beside the dead man, now rose and turned to Saunders. His face was very grave.

"The whole matter is simple enough, so far as I am concerned," he said. "The man has been killed by a terrific dose of morphia—administered, no doubt, in this cup of chocolate," he added, pointing to a cup in which there still lingered the cold dregs of the thick beverage.

"But when did this occur?" asked Saunders, turning to the waitress.

"I can't say," she replied, speaking with obvious nervousness. "The gentleman came in very early with a lady, somewhere about four. They made straight for this alcove. The place was just beginning to fill, and the music had begun."

"And where is the lady now?"

"She went off almost directly. She had ordered tea for herself and a cup of chocolate for the gentleman, also muffins and cakes. About five minutes afterwards, as I went past their table, I heard her say to him. 'I am afraid I must go now, or Jay's will be closed, but I'll be back in less than half an hour. You'll wait for me, won't you?'"

"Did the gentleman seem all right then?"

"Oh, yes," said the waitress. "He had just begun to sip his chocolate, and merely said 'S'long,' as she gathered up her gloves and muff and then went out of the shop."

"And she has not returned since?"

"No."

"When did you first notice there was anything wrong with this gentleman?" asked Lady Molly.

"Well," said the girl with some hesitation, "I looked at him once or twice as I went up and down, for he certainly seemed to have fallen all of a heap. Of course, I thought that he had gone to sleep, and I spoke to the manageress about him, but she thought that I ought to leave him alone for a bit. Then we got very busy, and I paid no more attention to him, until about six o'clock, when most afternoon tea customers had gone, and we were beginning to get the tables ready for dinners. Then I certainly did think there was something wrong with the man. I called to the manageress, and we sent for the police."

"And the lady who was with him at first, what was she like? Would you know her again?" queried Saunders.

"I don't know," replied the girl; "you see, I have to attend to such crowds of people of an afternoon, I can't notice each one. And she had on one of those enormous mushroom hats; no one could have seen her face—not more than her chin—unless they looked right under the hat."

"Would you know the hat again?" asked Lady Molly.

"Yes—I think I should," said the waitress. "It was black velvet and had a lot of plumes. It was enormous," she added, with a sigh of admiration and of longing for the monumental headgear.

During the girl's narrative one of the constables had searched the dead man's pockets. Among other items, he had found several letters addressed to Mark Culledon, Esq., some with an address in Lombard Street, others with one in Fitzjohn's Avenue, Hampstead. The initials M. C., which appeared both in the hat and on the silver mount of a letter-case belonging to the unfortunate gentleman, proved his identity beyond a doubt.

A house in Fitzjohn's Avenue does not, somehow, suggest a bachelor establishment. Even whilst Saunders and the other men were looking through the belongings of the deceased, Lady Molly had already thought of his family—children, perhaps a wife, a mother—who could tell?

What awful news to bring to an unsuspecting, happy family, who might even now be expecting the return of father, husband, or son, at the very moment when he lay murdered in a public place, the victim of some hideous plot or feminine revenge!

As our amiable friends in Paris would say, it jumped to the eyes that there was a woman in the case—a woman who had worn a gargantuan hat for the obvious purpose of remaining unidentifiable when the question of the unfortunate victim's companion that afternoon came up for solution. And all these facts to put before an expectant wife or an anxious mother!

As, no doubt, you have already foreseen, Lady Molly took the difficult task on her own kind shoulders. She and I drove together to Lorbury House, Fitzjohn's Avenue, and on asking of the manservant who opened the door if his mistress were at home, we were told that Lady Irene Culledon was in the drawing-room.

Mine is not a story of sentiment, so I am not going to dwell on that interview, which was one of the most painful moments I recollect having lived through.

Lady Irene was young—not five-and-twenty, I should say—petite and frail-looking, but with a quiet dignity of manner which was most impressive. She was Irish, as you know, the daughter of the Earl of Athyville, and, it seems, had married Mr. Mark Culledon in the teeth of strenuous opposition on the part of her family, which was as penniless as it was aristocratic, whilst Mr. Culledon had great prospects and a splendid business, but possessed neither ancestors nor high connections. She had only been married six months, poor little soul, and from all accounts must have idolised her husband.

Lady Molly broke the news to her with infinite tact, but there it was! It was a terrific blow—wasn't it?—to deal to a young wife—now a widow; and there was so little that a stranger could say in these circumstances. Even my dear lady's gentle voice, her persuasive eloquence, her kindly words, sounded empty and conventional in the face of such appalling grief.

2

OF course, everyone expected that the inquest would reveal something of the murdered man's inner life—would, in fact, allow the over-eager public to get a peep into Mr. Mark Culledon's secret orchard, wherein walked a lady who wore abnormally large velvet hats, and who nourished in her heart one of those terrible grudges against a man which can only find satisfaction in crime.

Equally, of course, the inquest revealed nothing that the public did not already know. The young widow was extremely reticent on the subject of her late husband's life, and the servants had all been fresh arrivals when the young couple, just home from their honeymoon, organised their new household at Lorbury House.

There was an old aunt of the deceased—a Mrs. Steinberg—who lived with the Culledons, but who at the present moment was very ill. Someone in the house—one of the younger servants, probably—very foolishly had told her every detail of the awful tragedy. With positively amazing strength, the invalid thereupon insisted on making a sworn statement, which she desired should be placed before the coroner's jury. She wished to bear solemn testimony to the integrity of her late nephew, Mark Culledon, in case the personality of the mysterious woman in the big hat suggested to evilly disposed minds any thought of scandal.

"Mark Culledon was the one nephew whom I loved," she stated with solemn emphasis. "I have shown my love for him by bequeathing to him the large fortune which I inherited from the late Mr. Steinberg. Mark was the soul of honour, or I should have cut him out of my will as I did my other nephews and nieces. I was brought up in a Scotch home, and I hate all this modern fastness and smartness, which are only other words for what I call profligacy."

Needless to say, the old lady's statement, solemn though it was, was of no use whatever for the elucidation of the mystery which surrounded the death of Mr. Mark Culledon. But as Mrs. Steinberg had talked of "other nephews," whom she had cut out of her will in favour of the murdered man, the police directed inquiries in those various quarters.

Mr. Mark Culledon certainly had several brothers and sisters, also cousins, who at different times—usually for some peccadillo or other—seemed to have incurred the wrath of the strait-laced old lady. But there did not appeal to have been any ill-feeling in the family owing to this. Mrs. Steinberg was sole mistress of her fortune. She might just as well have bequeathed it in toto to some hospital as to one particular nephew whom she favoured, and the various relations were glad, on the whole, that the money was going to remain in the family rather than be cast abroad.

The mystery surrounding the woman in the big hat deepened as the days went by. As you know, the longer the period of time which elapses between a crime and the identification of the criminal, the greater chance the latter has of remaining at large.

In spite of strenuous efforts and close questionings of every one of the employees at Mathis', no one could give a very accurate description of the lady who had tea with the deceased on that fateful afternoon.

The first glimmer of light on the mysterious occurrence was thrown, about three weeks later, by a young woman named Katherine Harris, who had been parlour-maid at Lorbury House when first Mr. and Lady Irene Culledon returned from their honeymoon.

I must tell you that Mrs. Steinberg had died a few days after the inquest. The excitement had been too much for her enfeebled heart. Just before her death she had deposited £250 with her banker, which sum was to be paid over to any person giving information which would lead to the apprehension and conviction of the murderer of Mr. Mark Culledon.

This offer had stimulated everyone's zeal, and, I presume, had aroused Katherine Harris to a realisation of what had all the while been her obvious duty.

Lady Molly saw her in the chief's private office, and had much ado to disentangle the threads of the girl's confused narrative. But the main point of Harris's story was that a foreign lady had once called at Lorbury House, about a week after the master and mistress had returned from their honeymoon. Lady Irene was out at the time, and Mr. Culledon saw the lady in his smoking-room.

"She was a very handsome lady," explained Harris, "and was beautifully dressed."

"Did she wear a large hat?" asked the chief.

"I don't remember if it was particularly large," replied the girl.

"But you remember what the lady was like?" suggested Lady Molly.

"Yes, pretty well. She was very, very tall, and very good-looking."

"Would you know her again if you saw her?" rejoined my dear lady.

"Oh, yes; I think so," was Katherine Harris's reply.

Unfortunately, beyond this assurance the girl could say nothing very definite. The foreign lady seems to have been closeted with Mr. Culledon for about an hour, at the end of which time Lady Irene came home.

The butler being out that afternoon it was Harris who let her mistress in, and as the latter asked no questions, the girl did not volunteer the information that her master had a visitor. She went back to the servants' hall, but five minutes later the smoking-room bell rang, and she had to run up again. The foreign lady was then in the hall alone, and obviously waiting to be shown out. This Harris did, after which Mr. Culledon came out of his room, and, in the girl's on graphic words, "he went on dreadful."

"I didn't know I 'ad done anything so very wrong," she explained, "but the master seemed quite furious, and said I wasn't a proper parlour-maid, or I'd have known that visitors must not be shown in straight away like that. I ought to have said that I didn't know if Mr. Culledon was in; that I would go and see. Oh, he did go on at me!" continued Katherine Harris, volubly. "And I suppose he complained to the mistress, for she give me notice the next day."

"And you have never seen the foreign lady since?" concluded Lady Molly.

"No; she never come while I was there."

"By the way, how did you know she was foreign. Did she speak like a foreigner?"

"Oh, no," replied the girl. "She did not say much—only asked for Mr. Culledon—but she looked French like."

This unanswerable bit of logic concluded Katherine's statement. She was very anxious to know whether, if the foreign lady was hanged for murder, she herself would get the £250.

On Lady Molly's assurance that she certainly would, she departed in apparent content.

3

"WELL! we are no nearer than we were before," said the chief, with an impatient sigh, when the door had closed behind Katherine Harris.

"Don't you think so?" rejoined Lady Molly, blandly.

"Do you consider that what we have heard just now has helped us to discover who was the woman in the big hat?" retorted the chief, somewhat testily.

"Perhaps not," replied my dear lady, with her sweet smile; "but it may help us to discover who murdered Mr. Culledon."

With which enigmatical statement she effectually silenced the chief, and finally walked out of his office, followed by her faithful Mary.

Following Katherine Harris's indications, a description of the lady who was wanted in connection with the murder of Mr. Culledon was very widely circulated, and within two days of the interview with the ex-parlour-maid another very momentous one took place in the same office.

Lady Molly was at work with the chief over some reports, whilst I was taking shorthand notes at a side desk, when a card was brought in by one of the men, and the next moment, without waiting either for permission to enter or to be more formally announced, a magnificent apparition literally sailed into the dust-covered little back office, filling it with an atmosphere of Parma violets and russia leather.

I don't think that I had ever seen a more beautiful woman in my life. Tall, with a splendid figure and perfect carriage, she vaguely reminded me of the portraits one sees of the late Empress of Austria. This lady was, moreover, dressed to perfection, and wore a large hat adorned with a quantity of plumes.

The chief had instinctively risen to greet her, whilst Lady Molly, still and placid, was eyeing her with a quizzical smile.

"You know who I am, sir," began the visitor as soon as she had sunk gracefully into a chair; "my name is on that card. My appearance, I understand, tallies exactly with that of a woman who is supposed to have murdered Mark Culledon."

She said this so calmly, with such perfect self-possession, that I literally gasped. The chief, too, seemed to have been metaphorically lifted off his feet. He tried to mutter a reply.

"Oh, don't trouble yourself, sir!" she interrupted him, with a smile. "My landlady, my servant, my friends have all read the description of the woman who murdered Mr. Culledon. For the past twenty-four hours I have been watched by your police, therefore I have come to you of my own accord, before they came to arrest me in my flat. I am not too soon, am I?" she asked, with that same cool indifference which was so startling, considering the subject of her conversation.

She spoke English with a scarcely perceptible foreign accent, but I quite understood what Katherine Harris had meant when she said that the lady looked "French like." She certainly did not look English, and when I caught sight of her name on the card, which the chief had handed to Lady Molly, I put her down at once as Viennese. Miss Elizabeth Löwenthal had all the charm, the grace, the elegance, which one associates with Austrian women more than with those of any other nation.

No wonder the chief found it difficult to tell her that, as a matter of fact, the police were about to apply for a warrant that very morning for her arrest on a charge of wilful murder .

"I know–I know," she said, seeming to divine his thoughts; "but let me tell you at once, sir, that I did not murder Mark Culledon. He treated me shamefully, and I would willingly have made a scandal just to spite him; he had become so respectable and strait-laced. But between scandal and murder there is a wide gulf. Don't you think so, madam," she added, turning for the first time towards Lady Molly.

"Undoubtedly," replied my dear lady, with the same quizzical smile.

"A wide gulf which, no doubt, Miss Elizabeth Löwenthal will best be able to demonstrate to the magistrate to-morrow," rejoined the chief, with official sternness of manner.

I thought that, for the space of a few seconds, the lady lost her self-assurance at this obvious suggestion–the bloom on her cheeks seemed to vanish, and two hard lines appeared between her fine eyes. But, frightened or not, she quickly recovered herself, and said quietly:

"Now, my dear sir, let us understand one another. I came here for that express purpose. I take it that you don't want your police to look ridiculous any more than I want a scandal. I don't want detectives to hang about round my flat, questioning my neighbours and my servants. They would soon find out that I did not murder Mark Culledon, of course; but the atmosphere of the police would hang round me, and I–I prefer Parma violets," she added, raising a daintily perfumed handkerchief to her nose.

"Then you have come to make a statement?" asked the chief.

"Yes," she replied; "I'll tell you all I know. Mr. Culledon was engaged to marry me; then he met the daughter of an earl, and thought he would like her better as a wife than a simple Miss Löwenthal. I suppose I should be considered an undesirable match for a young man who has a highly respectable and snobbish aunt, who would leave him all her money only on the condition that he made a suitable marriage. I have a voice, and I came over to England two years ago to study English, so that I might sing in oratorio at the Albert Hall. I met Mark on the Calais-Dover boat, when he was returning from a holiday abroad. He fell in love with me, and presently he asked me to be his wife. After some demur, I accepted him; we became engaged, but he told me that our engagement must remain a secret, for he had an old aunt from whom he had great expectations, and who might not approve of his marrying a foreign girl, who was without connections and a professional singer. From that moment I mistrusted him, nor was I very astonished when gradually his affection for me seemed to cool. Soon after, he informed me, quite callously, that he had changed his mind, and was going to marry some swell English lady. I didn't care much, but I wanted to punish him by making a scandal, you understand. I went to his house just to worry him, and finally I decided to bring an action for breach of promise against him. It would have upset him, I know; no doubt his aunt would have cut him out of her will. That is all I wanted, but I did not care enough about him to murder him."

Somehow her tale carried conviction. We were all of us obviously impressed. The chief alone looked visibly disturbed, and I could read what was going on in his mind.

"As you say, Miss Löwenthal," he rejoined, "the police would have found all this out within the next few hours. Once your connection with the murdered man was known to us, the record of your past and his becomes an easy one to peruse. No doubt, too," he added insinuatingly, "our men would soon have been placed in possession of the one indisputable proof of your complete innocence with regard to that fateful afternoon spent at Mathis' café."

"What is that?" she queried blandly.

"An alibi."

"You mean, where I was during the time that Mark was being murdered in a tea shop?"

"Yes," said the chief.

"I was out for a walk," she replied quietly.

"Shopping, perhaps?"

"No."

"You met someone who would remember the circumstance—or your servants could say at what time you came in?"

"No," she repeated dryly; 'I met no one, for I took a brisk walk on Primrose Hill. My two servants could only say that I went out at three o'clock that afternoon and returned after five."

There was silence in the little office for a moment or two. I could hear the scraping of the pen with which the chief was idly scribbling geometrical figures on his blotting pad.

Lady Molly was quite still. Her large, luminous eyes were fixed on the beautiful woman who had just told us her strange story, with its unaccountable sequel, its mystery which had deepened with the last phrase which she had uttered. Miss Löwenthal, I felt sure, was conscious of her peril. I am not sufficiently a psychologist to know whether it was guilt or merely fear which was distorting the handsome features now, hardening the face and causing the lips to tremble.

Lady Molly scribbled a few words on a scrap of paper, which she then passed over to the chief. Miss Löwenthal was making visible efforts to steady her nerves.

"That is all I have to tell you," she said, in a voice which sounded dry and harsh. "I think I will go home now."

But she did not rise from her chair, and seemed to hesitate as if fearful lest permission to go were not granted her.

To her obvious astonishment—and, I must add, to my own—the chief immediately rose and said, quite urbanely:

"I thank you very much for the helpful information which you have given me. Of course, we may rely on your presence in town for the next few days, may we not?"

She seemed greatly relieved, and all at once resumed her former charm of manner and elegance of attitude. The beautiful face was lit up by a smile.

The chief was bowing to her in quite a foreign fashion, and in spite of her visible reassurance she eyed him very intently. Then she went up to Lady Molly and held out her hand.

My dear lady took it without an instant's hesitation. I, who knew that it was the few words hastily scribbled by Lady Molly which had dictated the chief's conduct with regard to Miss Löwenthal, was left wondering whether the woman I loved best in all the world had been shaking hands with a murderess.

4

NO doubt you will remember the sensation which was caused by the arrest of Miss Löwenthal, on a charge of having murdered Mr. Mark Culledon, by administering morphia to him in a cup of chocolate at Mathis' café in Regent Street.

The beauty of the accused, her undeniable charm of manner, the hitherto blameless character of her life, all tended to make the public take violent sides either for or against her, and the usual budget of amateur correspondence, suggestions, recriminations and advice poured into the chief's office in titanic proportions.

I must say that, personally, all my sympathies went out to Miss Löwenthal. As I have said before, I am no psychologist, but I had seen her in the original interview at the office, and I could not get rid of an absolutely unreasoning certitude that the beautiful Viennese singer was innocent.

The magistrate's court was packed, as you may well imagine, on that first day of the inquiry; and, of course, sympathy with the accused went up to fever pitch when she staggered into the dock, beautiful still, despite the ravages caused by horror, anxiety, fear, in face of the deadly peril in which she stood.

The magistrate was most kind to her; her solicitor was unimpeachably assiduous; even our fellows, who had to give evidence against her, did no more than their duty, and were as lenient in their statements as possible.

Miss Löwenthal had been arrested in her flat by Danvers, accompanied by two constables. She had loudly protested her innocence all along, and did so still, pleading "Not guilty" in a firm voice.

The great points in favour of the arrest were, firstly, the undoubted motive of disappointment and revenge against a faithless sweetheart, then the total inability to prove any kind of alibi, which, under the circumstances, certainly added to the appearance of guilt.

The question of where the fatal drug was obtained was more difficult to prove. It was stated that Mr. Mark Culledon was director of several important companies, one of which carried on business as wholesale druggists.

Therefore it was argued that the accused, at different times and under some pretext or other, had obtained drugs from Mr. Culledon himself. She had admitted to having visited the deceased at his office in the City, both before and after his marriage.

Miss Löwenthal listened to all this evidence against her with a hard, set face, as she did also to Katherine Harris's statement about her calling on Mr. Culledon at Lorbury House, but she brightened up visibly when the various attendants at

Mathis' café were placed in the box.

A very large hat belonging to the accused was shown to the witnesses, but, though the police upheld the theory that that was the headgear worn by the mysterious lady at the café on that fateful afternoon, the waitresses made distinctly contradictory statements with regard to it.

Whilst one girl swore that she recognised the very hat, another was equally positive that it was distinctly smaller than the one she recollected, and when the hat was placed on the head of Miss Löwenthal, three out of the four witnesses positively refused to identify her.

Most of these young women declared that though the accused, when wearing the big hat, looked as if she might have been the lady in question, yet there was a certain something about her which was different.

With that vagueness which is a usual and highly irritating characteristic of their class, the girls finally parried every question by refusing to swear positively either for or against the identity of Miss Löwenthal.

"There's something that's different about her somehow," one of the waitresses asserted positively.

"What is it that's different?" asked the solicitor for the accused, pressing his point.

"I can't say," was the perpetual, maddening reply.

Of course the poor young widow had to be dragged into the case, and here, I think, opinions and even expressions of sympathy were quite unanimous.

The whole tragedy had been inexpressibly painful to her, of course, and now it must have seemed doubly so. The scandal which had accumulated round her late husband's name must have added the poignancy of shame to that of grief. Mark Culledon had behaved as callously to the girl whom clearly he had married from interested, family motives, as he had to the one whom he had heartlessly cast aside.

Lady Irene, however, was most moderate in her statements. There was no doubt that she had known of her husband's previous entanglement with Miss Löwenthal, but apparently had not thought fit to make him accountable for the past. She did not know that Miss Löwenthal had threatened a breach of promise action against her husband.

Throughout her evidence she spoke with absolute calm and dignity, and looked indeed a strange contrast, in her closely fitting tailor-made costume of black serge and tiny black toque, to the more brilliant woman who stood in the dock.

The two great points in favour of the accused were, firstly, the vagueness of the witnesses who were called to identify her, and, secondly, the fact that she had undoubtedly begun proceedings for breach of promise against the deceased. Judging by the latter's letters to her, she would have had a splendid case against him, which fact naturally dealt a severe blow to the theory as to motive for the murder.

On the whole, the magistrate felt that there was not a sufficiency of evidence against the accused to warrant his committing her for trial; he therefore discharged her, and, amid loud applause from the public, Miss Löwenthal left the court a free woman.

Now, I know that the public did loudly, and, to my mind, very justly, blame the police for that arrest, which was denounced as being as cruel as it was unjustifiable.

I felt as strongly as anybody on the subject, for I knew that the prosecution had been instituted in defiance of Lady Molly's express advice, and in distinct contradiction to the evidence which she had collected. When, therefore, the chief asked my dear lady to renew her efforts in that mysterious case, it was small wonder that her enthusiasm did not respond to his anxiety. That she would do her duty was beyond a doubt, but she had very naturally lost her more fervent interest in the case.

The mysterious woman in the big hat was still the chief subject of leading articles in the papers, coupled with that of the ineptitude of the police who could not discover her. There were caricatures and picture post-cards in all the shop windows of a gigantic hat covering the whole figure of its wearer, only the feet, and a very long and pointed chin, protruding from beneath the enormous brim. Below was the device, "Who is she? Ask the police?"

One day—it was the second since the discharge of Miss Löwenthal—my dear lady came into my room beaming. It was the first time I had seen her smile for more than a week, and already I had guessed what it was that had cheered her.

"Good news, Mary," she said gaily. "At last I've got the chief to let me have a free hand. Oh, dear! what a lot of argument it takes to extricate that man from the tangled meshes of red tape!"

"What are you going to do?" I asked.

"Prove that my theory is right as to who murdered Mark Culledon," she replied seriously; "and as a preliminary we'll go and ask his servants at Lorbury House a few questions."

It was then three o'clock in the afternoon. At Lady Molly's bidding, I dressed somewhat smartly, and together we went off in a taxi to Fitzjohn's Avenue.

Lady Molly had written a few words on one of her cards, urgently requesting an interview with Lady Irene Culledon. This she handed over to the man-servant who opened the door at Lorbury House. A few moments later we were sitting in the cosy boudoir. The young widow, high-bred and dignified in her tight-fitting black gown, sat opposite to us, her white hands folded demurely before her, her small head, with its very close coiffure, bent in closest attention towards Lady Molly.

"I most sincerely hope, Lady Irene," began my dear lady, in her most gentle and persuasive voice, "that you will look with all possible indulgence on my growing desire—shared, I may say, by all my superiors at Scotland Yard—to elucidate the mystery which still surrounds your late husband's death."

Lady Molly paused, as if waiting for encouragement to proceed. The subject must have been extremely painful to the young widow; nevertheless she responded quite gently:

"I can understand that the police wish to do their duty in the matter; as for me, I have done all, I think, that could be expected of me. I am not made of iron, and after that day in the police court—"

She checked herself, as if afraid of having betrayed more emotion than was consistent with good breeding, and concluded more calmly:

"I cannot do any more."

"I fully appreciate your feelings in the matter," said Lady Molly, "but you would not mind helping us—would you?—in a passive way, if you could, by some simple means, further the cause of justice."

"What is it you want me to do?" asked Lady Irene.

"Only to allow me to ring for two of your maids and to ask them a few questions. I promise you that they shall not be of such a nature as to cause you the slightest pain."

For a moment I thought that the young widow hesitated, then, without a word, she rose and rang the bell.

"Which of my servants did you wish to see?" she asked, turning to my dear lady as soon as the butler entered in answer to the bell.

"Your own maid and your parlour-maid, if I may," replied Lady Molly.

Lady Irene gave the necessary orders, and we all sat expectant and silent until, a minute or two later, two girls entered the room. One wore a cap and apron, the other, in neat black dress and dainty lace collar, was obviously the lady's maid.

"This lady," said their mistress, addressing the two girls, "wishes to ask you a few questions. She is a representative of the police, so you had better do your best to satisfy her with your answers."

"Oh!" rejoined Lady Molly pleasantly—choosing not to notice the tone of acerbity with which the young widow had spoken, nor the unmistakable barrier of hostility and reserve which her words had immediately raised between the young servants and the "representative of the police"—"what I am going to ask these two young ladies is neither very difficult nor very unpleasant. I merely want their kind help in a little comedy which will have to be played this evening, in order to test the accuracy of certain statements made by one of the waitresses at Mathis' tea shop with regard to the terrible tragedy which has darkened this house. You will do that much, will you not?" she added, speaking directly to the maids.

No one can be so winning or so persuasive as my dear lady. In a moment I saw the girls' hostility melting before the sunshine of Lady Molly's smile.

"We'll do what we can, ma'am," said the maid.

"That's a brave, good girl!" replied my lady. "You must know that the chief waitress at Mathis' has, this very morning, identified the woman in the big hat who, we all believe, murdered your late master. Yes!" she continued, in response to a gasp of astonishment which seemed to go round the room like a wave, "the girl seems quite positive, both as regards the hat and the woman who wore it. But, of course, one cannot allow a human life to be sworn away without bringing every possible proof to bear on such a statement, and I am sure that everyone in this house will understand that we don't want to introduce strangers more than we can help into this sad affair, which already has been bruited abroad too much."

She paused a moment; then, as neither Lady Irene nor the maids made any comment, she continued:

"My superiors at Scotland Yard think it their duty to try and confuse the witness as much as possible in her act of identification. They desire that a certain number of ladies wearing abnormally large hats should parade before the waitress. Among them will be, of course, the one whom the girl has already identified as being the mysterious person who had tea with Mr. Culledon at Mathis' that afternoon.

"My superiors can then satisfy themselves whether the waitress is or is not so sure of her statement that she invariably picks out again and again one particular individual amongst a number of others or not."

"Surely," interrupted Lady Irene, dryly, "you and your superiors do not expect my servants to help in such a farce?"

"We don't look upon such a proceeding as a farce, Lady Irene," rejoined Lady Molly, gently. "It is often resorted to in the interests of an accused person, and we certainly would ask the co-operation of your household."

"I don't see what they can do."

But the two girls did not seem unwilling. The idea appealed to them, I felt sure; it suggested an exciting episode, and gave promise of variety in their monotonous lives.

"I am sure both these young ladies possess fine big hats," continued Lady Molly with an encouraging smile.

"I should not allow them to wear ridiculous headgear," retorted Lady Irene, sternly.

"I have the one your ladyship wouldn't wear, and threw away," interposed the young parlour-maid. "I put it together again with the scraps I found in the dusthole."

There was just one instant of absolute silence, one of those magnetic moments when Fate seems to have dropped the spool on which she was spinning the threads of a life, and is just stooping in order to pick it up.

Lady Irene raised a black-bordered handkerchief to her lips, then said quietly:

"I don't know what you mean, Mary. I never wear big hats."

"No, my lady," here interposed the lady's maid; "but Mary means the one you ordered at Sanchia's and only wore the once—the day you went to that concert."

"Which day was that?" asked Lady Molly, blandly.

"Oh! I couldn't forget that day," ejaculated the maid; "her ladyship came home from the concert—I had undressed her, and she told me that she would never wear her big hat again—it was too heavy. That same day Mr. Culledon was murdered."

"That hat would answer our purpose very well," said Lady Molly, quite calmly. "Perhaps Mary will go and fetch it, and you had better go and help her put it on."

The two girls went out of the room without another word, and there were we three women left facing one another, with that awful secret, only half-revealed, hovering in the air like an intangible spectre.

"What are you going to do, Lady Irene?" asked Lady Molly, after a moment's pause, during which I literally could hear my own heart beating, whilst I watched the rigid figure of the widow in deep black crape, her face set and white, her eyes fixed steadily on Lady Molly.

"You can't prove it!" she said defiantly.

"I think we can," rejoined Lady Molly, simply; "at any rate, I mean to try. I have two of the waitresses from Mathis' outside in a cab, and I have already spoken to the attendant who served you at Sanchia's, an obscure milliner in a back street near Portland Road. We know that you were at great pains there to order a hat of certain dimensions and to your own minute description; it was a copy of one you had once seen Miss Löwenthal wear when you met her at your late husband's office. We can prove that meeting, too. Then we have your maid's testimony that you wore that same hat once, and once only, the day, presumably, that you went out to a concert—a statement which you will find it difficult to substantiate—and also the day on which your husband was murdered."

"Bah! the public will laugh at you!" retorted Lady Irene, still defiantly. "You would not dare to formulate so monstrous a charge!"

"It will not seem monstrous when justice has weighed in the balance the facts which we can prove. Let me tell you a few of these, the result of careful investigation. There is the fact that you knew of Mr. Culledon's entanglement with Miss Elizabeth Löwenthal, and did your best to keep it from old Mrs. Steinberg's knowledge, realising that any scandal round her favourite nephew would result in the old lady cutting him–and therefore you–out of her will. You dismissed a parlour-maid for the sole reason that she had been present when Miss Löwenthal was shown into Mr. Culledon's study. There is the fact that Mrs. Steinberg had so worded her will that, in the event of her nephew dying before her, her fortune would devolve on you; the fact that, with Miss Löwenthal's action for breach of promise against your husband, your last hope of keeping the scandal from the old lady's ears had effectually vanished. You saw the fortune eluding your grasp; you feared Mrs. Steinberg would alter her will. Had you found the means, and had you dared, would you not rather have killed the old lady? But discovery would have been certain. The other crime was bolder and surer. You have inherited the old lady's millions, for she never knew of her nephew's earlier peccadillos.

"All this we can state and prove, and the history of the hat, bought, and worn one day only, that same memorable day, and then thrown away."

A loud laugh interrupted her–a laugh that froze my very marrow.

"There is one fact you have forgotten, my lady of Scotland Yard," came in sharp, strident accents from the black-robed figure, which seemed to have become strangely spectral in the fast gathering gloom which had been enveloping the luxurious little boudoir. "Don't omit to mention the fact that the accused took the law into her own hands."

And before my dear lady and I could rush to prevent her, Lady Irene Culledon had conveyed something–we dared not think what–to her mouth.

"Find Danvers quickly, Mary!" said Lady Molly, calmly. "You'll find him outside. Bring a doctor back with you."

Even as she spoke Lady Irene, with a cry of agony, fell senseless in my dear lady's arms.

The doctor, I may tell you, came too late. The unfortunate woman evidently had a good knowledge of poisons. She had been determined not to fail; in case of discovery, she was ready and able to mete out justice to herself.

I don't think the public ever knew the real truth about the woman in the big hat. Interest in her went the way of all things. Yet my dear lady had been right from beginning to end. With unerring precision she had placed her dainty finger on the real motive and the real perpetrator of the crime–the ambitious woman who had married solely for money, and meant to have that money even at the cost of one of the most dastardly murders that have ever darkened the criminal annals of this country.

I asked Lady Molly what it was that first made her think of Lady Irene as the possible murderess. No one else for a moment had thought her guilty.

"The big hat," replied my dear lady with a smile. "Had the mysterious woman at Mathis' been tall, the waitresses would not, one and all, have been struck by the abnormal size of the hat. The wearer must have been petite, hence the reason that under a wide brim only the chin would be visible. I at once sought for a small woman. Our fellows did not think of that, because they are men."

You see how simple it all was!

SIR JEREMIAH'S WILL

MANY people have asked me whether I knew when, and in what circumstances, Lady Molly joined the detective staff at Scotland Yard, who she was, and how she managed to keep her position in Society—as she undoubtedly did—whilst exercising a profession which usually does not make for high social standing.

Well, of course, there is much that I have known all along about my dear lady—just as much, in fact, as her aristocratic friends and relations did—but I had promised her not to let the general public know anything of her private life until she gave me leave to do so.

Now things have taken a different turn, and I can tell you all I know. But I must go back some years for that, and recall to your mind that extraordinary crime known in those days as the Baddock Will Case, which sent one of the most prominent and popular young men in Society to penal servitude—a life sentence, mind you, which was considered to be remarkably lenient by a number of people who thought that Captain de Mazareen ought to have been hanged.

He was such a good-looking young soldier in those days. I specially remember him at the late Queen's funeral—one of the tallest men in the British Army, and with that peculiar charm of manner which, alas! one has ceased to associate with young Englishmen nowadays. If to these two undeniable advantages you add the one that Hubert de Mazareen was the dearly loved grandson of Sir Jeremiah Baddock, the multi-millionaire ship owner of Liverpool, you will realize how easy it was for that young Guardsman to ingratiate himself with every woman in Society, and more particularly with every mamma who had a marriageable daughter.

But Fate and Love have a proverbial knack of making a muddle of things. Captain de Mazareen, with a bevy of pretty and eligible girls from whom to select a wife, chose to fall in love with the one woman in the whole of England who, in his grandfather's opinion, should have remained a stranger, even an enemy, to him.

You remember the sad story—more than a quarter of a century old now—of Sir Jeremiah's unhappy second marriage with the pretty French actress, Mlle. Adèle Desty, who was then over thirty years younger than himself. He married her abroad, and never brought her to England. She made him supremely wretched for about three years, and finally ran away with the Earl of Flintshire, whom she had met at Monte Carlo.

Well! it was with a daughter of that same Earl of Flintshire, Lady Molly Robertson-Kirk, that Captain Hubert de Mazareen fell desperately in love. Imagine Sir Jeremiah's feelings when he heard of it.

Captain Hubert, you must know, had resigned his commission in 1902 at his grandfather's request, when the latter's health first began to fail. He had taken up his permanent abode at Appledore Castle, Sir Jeremiah's magnificent home in Cumberland, and, of course, it was generally understood that ultimately he would become possessed of the wealthy ship owner's millions as well as of the fine property, seeing that his mother had been Sir Jeremiah's only child by the latter's first marriage.

Lord Flintshire's property was quite close to Appledore; but, needless to say, old Sir Jeremiah never forgave his noble neighbour the cruel wrong he had suffered at his hands.

The second Lady Baddock, afterwards Countess of Flintshire, has been dead twenty years. Neither the county nor the more exclusive sets of London ever received her, but her daughter Molly, who inherited all her beauty and none of her faults, was the idol of her father, and the acknowledged queen of county and town Society

You see, it was the ancient, yet ever new, story of Cappelletti and Montecchi over again, and one day Captain Hubert de Mazareen had to tell Sir Jeremiah that he desired to marry the daughter of his grandfather's most cruel enemy.

What the immediate result of that announcement was no one could say. Neither Sir Jeremiah nor Captain Hubert de Mazareen would have allowed servants or dependents to hear a word of disagreement that might have passed between them, much less to suspect that an unpleasant scene had occurred.

Outwardly everything went on as usual at Appledore Castle for about a fortnight or so, after which Captain Hubert went away one day, ostensibly for a brief stay in London; but he never re-entered the doors of the Castle until after the dark veil of an appalling tragedy had begun to descend on the stately old Cumberland home.

Sir Jeremiah bore up pretty well for a time, then he had a slight paralytic stroke and became a confirmed invalid. The postmaster at Appledore declared that after that many letters came, addressed to Sir Jeremiah in Captain Hubert's well-known handwriting and bearing the London postmark; but presumably the old gentleman felt bitterly irreconcilable towards his grandson, for Captain de Mazareen was never seen at the Castle.

Soon the invalid grew more and more eccentric and morose. He ordered all the reception rooms of his magnificent home to be closed and shuttered, and he dismissed all his indoor servants, with the exception of his own male attendant and an old married couple named Bradley, who had been in his service for years, and who now did the little work that was required in what had once been one of the most richly appointed country mansions in England.

Bitter resentment against his once dearly loved grandson, and against the man who had robbed him of his young wife twenty-five years ago, seemed to have cut off the old man from contact with the outside world.

Thus matters stood until the spring of 1903, when Sir Jeremiah announced one morning to the three members of his household that Mr. Philip Baddock was coming to stay at the Castle, and that a room must be got ready immediately.

Mr. Philip Baddock came that same evening. He was a young man of quite ordinary appearance: short, rather dark, with the somewhat uncouth manners suggestive of an upbringing in a country parsonage.

His arrival created no little excitement in the neighbourhood. Who was Mr. Philip Baddock, and where did he come from? No one had ever heard of him before, and now–after a very brief time spent at the Castle–he seemed to be gradually taking up the position which originally had belonged to Captain Hubert.

He took over the command of the small household, dismissing Sir Jeremiah's personal attendant after a while and engaging another. He supervised the outdoor men, reducing the staff both in the gardens and the stables. He sold most of the horses and carriages, and presently bought a motor-car, which he at once took to driving all over the country.

But he spoke to no one in the village, and soon, in answer to inquiries by one or two of Sir Jeremiah's faithful friends and cronies, the reply came regularly from Mr. Philip Baddock that the invalid was disinclined for company. Only Doctor Thorne, the local practitioner, saw the patient. Sir Jeremiah, it was understood, was slowly sinking towards the grave; but his mind was quite clear, even if his temper was abnormal.

One day Mr. Philip Baddock made inquiries in the village for a good chauffeur. George Taylor presented himself, and was at once told off to drive the car as quickly as possible to Carlisle, to the office of Mr. Steadman, solicitor, and to bring that gentleman back to the Castle as soon as he could come.

The distance from Appledore to Carlisle is over fifty miles. It was seven o'clock in the evening before George Taylor was back, bringing Mr. Steadman with him.

The solicitor was received at the Castle door by old Bradley, and at Sir Jeremiah's door by Felkin, the new attendant, who showed him in. The interview between the invalid and Mr. Steadman lasted half an hour, after which the latter was driven back to Carlisle by George Taylor.

That same evening a telegram was sent off by Mr. Philip Baddock to Captain de Mazareen in London, containing the few words:

"Sir Jeremiah very ill. Come at once."

Twenty-four hours later Captain Hubert arrived at Appledore Castle—too late, however, to see his grandfather alive.

Sir Jeremiah Baddock had died an hour before the arrival of his once so tenderly cherished grandson, and all hopes of a reconciliation had now been mercilessly annihilated by death.

The end had come much more suddenly than Doctor Thorne had anticipated. He had seen the patient in the morning and thought that he might last some days. But when Sir Jeremiah had heard that Captain de Mazareen had been sent for he had worked himself into a state of such terrible agitation that the poor, overtaxed brain and heart finally gave way.

2

THE events of those memorable days—in the early spring of 1904—are so graven on my memory that I can recount them as if they happened yesterday.

I was maid to Lady Molly Robertson-Kirk at the time. Since then she has honoured me with her friendship.

Directly after Captain Hubert's first estrangement from his grandfather she and I came down to Cumberland and lived very quietly at Kirk Hall, which, as you know, is but a stone's throw from Appledore.

Here Captain Hubert paid my dear lady several visits. She had irrevocably made up her mind that their engagement was to be indefinitely prolonged, for she had a vague hope that, sooner or later, Sir Jeremiah would relent towards the grandson whom he had loved so dearly. At any rate there was a chance of it whilst the marriage had not actually taken place.

Captain de Mazareen, mind you, was in no sense of the word badly off. His father had left him some £25,000, and Lady Molly had a small private fortune of her own. Therefore I assure you that there was not a single mercenary thought behind this protracted engagement or Captain Hubert's desire for a reconciliation with his grandfather.

The evening that he arrived at Appledore in response to Mr. Philip Baddock's telegram Lady Molly met him at the station. He sent his luggage on to Kirk Hall, and the two young people walked together as far as the Elkhorn Woods, which divide the Earl of Flintshire's property from Appledore itself.

Here they met Mr. Steadman, the solicitor, who had motored over from Carlisle in response to an urgent summons from Sir Jeremiah Baddock, but whose car had broken down about two hundred yards up the road.

It seems that the chauffeur had suggested his walking on through the woods, it being an exceptionally fine and mild spring evening, with a glorious full moon overhead, which lit up almost every turn of the path that cuts through the pretty coppice.

Lady Molly had given me rendezvous at the edge of the wood, so that I might accompany her home after she had taken leave of Captain Hubert. It seems that the latter knew Mr. Steadman slightly, as we saw the two men shake hands with one another, then, after a few words of conversation, turn off to walk together through the wood. We then made our way back silently to Kirk Hall.

My dear lady was inexpressibly sad. She appreciated very deeply the love which Captain Hubert bore for his grandfather, and was loath to see the final annihilation of all her hopes of an ultimate reconciliation between the two men.

I had dressed Lady Molly for dinner, and she was just going downstairs when Captain de Mazareen arrived at the Hall.

He announced the sad news of his grandfather's death and looked extremely dejected and upset.

Of course, he stayed at the Hall, for Mr. Philip Baddock seemed quite to have taken command at Appledore Castle, and Captain Hubert did not care to be beholden to him for hospitality.

My dear lady asked him what had become of Mr. Steadman.

"I don't know," he replied. "He started to walk with me through the wood, then he seemed to think that the tramp would be too much for him, and that the car could be put right very quickly. He preferred to drive round, and was quite sure that he would meet me at the Castle in less than half an hour. However, he never turned up."

Lady Molly asked several more questions about Sir Jeremiah, which Captain Hubert answered in a listless way. He had been met at the door of the Castle by Mr. Philip Baddock, who told him that the old gentleman had breathed his last half an hour before.

I remember that we all went to bed that night feeling quite unaccountably depressed. It seemed that something more tragic than the natural death of a septuagenarian hovered in the air of these remote Cumberland villages.

The next morning our strange premonitions were confirmed. Lord Flintshire, my dear lady, and Captain Hubert were sitting at breakfast when the news was brought to the Hall that Mr. Steadman, the Carlisle solicitor, had been found murdered in the Elkhorn Woods earlier in the morning. Evidently he had been stunned, and then done to death by a heavily-loaded stick or some similar weapon. When he was discovered in the early hours of the morning, he had, apparently, been dead some time. The local police were at once apprised of the terrible event, which created as much excitement as the death of the eccentric old millionaire at Appledore Castle.

Everyone at Kirk Hall, of course, was keenly interested, and Captain de Mazareen went over to Appledore as soon as he could in order to place his information at the service of the police.

It is a strange fact, but nevertheless a true one, that when a deadly peril arises such as now threatened Captain de Mazareen, the person most in danger is the last to be conscious of it.

I am quite sure that Lady Molly, the moment she heard that Mr. Steadman had been murdered in the Elkhorn Woods, realized that the man she loved would be implicated in that tragedy in some sinister manner. But that is the intuition of a woman—of a woman who loves.

As for Captain Hubert, he went about during the whole of that day quite unconscious of the abyss which already was yawning at his feet. He even discussed quite equably the several valuable bits of information which the local police had already collected, and which eventually formed a portion of that damning fabric of circumstantial evidence which was to bring him within sight of the gallows.

Earlier in the day, Mr. Philip Baddock sent him a stiff little note, saying that, as Captain de Mazareen was now the owner of Appledore Castle, he (Philip Baddock) did not desire to trespass a moment longer than was necessary on his relative's hospitality, and had arranged to stay at the village inn until after the funeral, when he would leave Cumberland.

To this Captain Hubert sent an equally curt note saying that, as far as he knew, he had no say in the matter of anyone coming or going from the Castle, and that Mr. Philip Baddock must, of course, please himself as to whether he stayed there or not.

So far, of course, the old gentleman's testamentary dispositions were not known. He had made a will in 1902 bequeathing Appledore and everything he possessed unconditionally to his beloved grandson, Hubert de Mazareen, whom he also appointed his sole executor. That will was lodged with Mr. Truscott, who had been solicitor to the deceased practically until the last moment, when Mr. Steadman, a new arrival at Carlisle, had been sent for.

Whether that will had been revoked or not Mr. Truscott did not know; but, in the course of the afternoon, Lord Flintshire, whilst out driving, met the local superintendent of police, who told him that Mr. Steadman's senior partner—a Mr. Fuelling—had made a statement to the effect that Sir Jeremiah had sent for Mr. Steadman the day before his death and given instructions for the drafting of a new will whereby the old gentleman bequeathed Appledore and everything he possessed to his beloved grandson, Hubert de Mazareen, but only on the condition that the latter did not marry the daughter or any other relative of the Earl of Flintshire. In the event of Hubert de Mazareen disregarding this condition at any future time of his life, Sir Jeremiah's entire fortune was to devolve on Philip Baddock, sole issue of testator's second marriage, with Adèle Desty. The draft of this will, added Mr. Fuelling, was in Mr. Steadman's pocket ready for Sir Jeremiah's signature on that fateful night when the unfortunate young solicitor was murdered.

The draft had not been found in the murdered man's pocket. A copy of it, however, was in Mr. Fuelling's safe. But as this will had never been signed by the deceased the one of 1902 remained valid, and Captain Hubert de Mazareen remained unconditionally his grandfather's sole heir.

3

EVENTS crowded thick and fast on that day—one of the most miserable I have ever lived through.

After an early tea, which my dear lady had alone in her little boudoir, she sent me down to ask Captain Hubert to come up and speak to her. He did so at once, and I went into the next room—which was Lady Molly's bedroom—to prepare her dress for the evening.

I had, of course, discreetly closed the door of communication between the two rooms, but after the first five minutes, Lady Molly deliberately reopened it, from which I gathered that she actually wished me to know what was going on.

It was then a little after four o'clock. I could hear Captain de Mazareen's voice, low-toned and infinitely tender. He adored my dear lady, but he was a very quiet man, and it was only by the passionate tensity of his attitude when he was near her that a shrewdly observant person could guess how deeply he cared. Now, through the open door, I could see his handsome head bowed very low, so that he could better look into her upturned eyes. His arms were round her, as if he were fighting the world for the possession of her, and would never let her go again. But there were tears in her eyes.

"Hubert," she said after a while, "I want you to marry me. Will you?"

"Will I?" he whispered, with an intensity of passionate longing which seemed to me then so unutterably pathetic that I could have sat down and had a good cry.

"But," rejoined Lady Molly earnestly, "I mean as soon as possible—to-morrow, by special licence. You can wire to Mr. Hurford to-night, and he will see about it the first thing in the morning. We can travel up to town by the night train. Father and Mary will come with me. Father has promised, you know, and we can be married to-morrow . . . I think that would be the quickest way."

There was a pause. I could well imagine how astonished and perturbed Captain Hubert must be feeling. It was such a strange request for a woman to make at such a time. I could see by the expression of his eyes that he was trying to read her thoughts. But she looked up quite serenely at him, and, frankly, I do not think that he had the slightest inkling of the sublime motive at the back of her strange insistence.

"You prefer to be married in London rather than here?" he asked quite simply.

"Yes," she replied; "I desire to be married in London to-morrow."

A few moments later my dear lady quietly shut the door again, and I heard and saw no more; but half an hour later she called me. She was alone in her boudoir, bravely trying to smile through a veil of tears. Captain Hubert's footsteps could still be heard going along the hall below.

Lady Molly listened until the final echo of that tread died away in the distance;

then she buried her sweet face on my shoulder and sobbed her very heart out.

"Get ready as quickly as you can, Mary," she said to me when the paroxysm had somewhat subsided. "We go up to town by the 9.10."

"Is his lordship coming with us, my lady?" I asked.

"Oh, yes!" she said, whilst a bright smile lit up her face. "Father is simply grand . . . and yet he knows."

"Knows what, my lady?" I queried instinctively, for Lady Molly had paused, and I saw a look of acute pain once more darken her soft, grey eyes.

"My father knows," she said, slowly and almost tonelessly, "that half an hour ago the police found a weighted stick in the Elkhorn Woods not far from the spot where Mr. Steadman was murdered. The stick has the appearance of having been very vigorously cleaned and scraped recently in spite of which fact tiny traces of blood are still visible on the leaden knob. The inspector showed my father that stick. I saw it too. It is the property of Captain Hubert de Mazareen, and by tomorrow, at the latest, it will be identified as such."

There was silence in the little boudoir now: a silence broken only by the sound of dull sobs which rose from my dear lady's overburdened heart. Lady Molly at this moment had looked into the future, and with that unerring intuition which has since been of such immense service to her she had already perceived the grim web which Fate was weaving round the destiny of the man she loved.

I said nothing. What could I say? I waited for her to speak again.

The first words she uttered after the terrible pronouncement which she had just made were:

"I'll wear my white cloth gown to-morrow, Mary. It is the most becoming frock I have, and I want to look my best on my wedding day."

4

CAPTAIN HUBERT DE MAZAREEN was married to Lady Molly Robertson-Kirk by special licence on April 22nd, 1904, at the Church of St. Margaret, Westminster. No one was present to witness the ceremony except the Earl of Flintshire and myself. No one was apprised of the event at the time, nor, until recently, did anyone know that Lady Molly of Scotland Yard was the wife of De Mazareen the convict.

As you know, he was arrested at Appledore railway station the following morning and charged with the wilful murder of Alexander Steadman, solicitor, of Carlisle.

Everything was against him from the first. The draft of the will which Mr. Steadman was taking up to Sir Jeremiah for signature supplied the motive for the alleged crime, and he was the last person seen in company with the murdered man.

The chauffeur, George Taylor, who had driven to Carlisle to fetch Mr. Steadman, and brought him back that evening, explained how two of his tyres burst almost simultaneously after going over a bit of broken road close to the coppice. He had suggested to Mr. Steadman the idea of walking through the wood, and, as he had not two fresh tyres with him, he started pushing his car along, as the village was not more than half a mile away. He never saw Mr. Steadman again.

The stick with which the terrible deed had been committed was the most damning piece of evidence against the accused. It had been identified as his property by more than one witness, and was found within twenty yards of the victim, obviously cleaned and scraped, but still bearing minute traces of blood. Moreover, it had actually been seen in Captain Hubert's hand by one or two of the porters when he arrived at Appledore Station on that fatal night, was met there by Lady Molly, and subsequently walked away with her previous to meeting Mr. Steadman on the edge of the wood.

Captain de Mazareen, late of His Majesty's Household Brigade, was indicted for the wilful murder of Alexander Steadman, tried at the next assizes, found guilty, and condemned to be hanged. The jury, however, had strongly recommended him to mercy owing to his hitherto spotless reputation, and to the many services he had rendered his country during the last Boer War. A monster petition was sent up to the Home Office, and the sentence was commuted to twenty years' penal servitude.

That same year, Lady Molly applied for, and obtained, a small post on the detective staff of the police. From that small post she has worked her way upwards, analysing and studying, exercising her powers of intuition and of deduction, until at the present moment she is considered, by chiefs and men alike, the greatest authority among them on criminal investigation.

The Earl of Flintshire died some three years ago. Kirk Hall devolved on a distant cousin, but Lady Molly has kept a small home at Kirk ready for her husband when he comes back from Dartmoor.

The task of her life is to apply her gifts, and the obvious advantages at her disposal as a prominent member of the detective force, to prove the innocence of Captain Hubert de Mazareen, which she never doubted for a moment.

But it was sublime, and at the same time deeply pathetic, to see the frantic efforts at self-sacrifice which these two noble-hearted young people made for one another's sake.

Directly Captain Hubert realised that, so far as proving his innocence was concerned, he was a lost man, he used every effort to release Lady Molly from the bonds of matrimony. The marriage had been, and was still, kept a profound secret. He determined to plead guilty to murder at his trial, and then to make a declaration that he had entrapped Lady Molly into a marriage, knowing at the time that a warrant was out for his arrest, and hoping, by his connection with the Earl of Flintshire, to obtain a certain amount of leniency. When he was sufficiently convinced that such a course was out of the question, he begged Lady Molly to bring a nullity suit against him. He would not defend it. He only wished to set her free.

But the love she bore him triumphed over all. They did keep their marriage a secret, but she remained faithful to him in every thought and feeling within her, and loyal to him with her whole soul. Only I—once her maid, now her devoted friend—knew what she suffered, even whilst she threw herself heart and mind into her work.

We lived mostly in our little flat in Maida Vale, but spent some delightful days of freedom and peace in the little house at Kirk. Hither—in spite of the terrible memories the place evoked—Lady Molly loved to spend her time in wandering over the ground where that mysterious crime had been committed which had doomed an innocent man to the life of a convict.

"That mystery has got to be cleared up, Mary," she would repeat to me with unswerving loyalty, "and cleared up soon, before Captain de Mazareen loses all joy in life and all belief in me."

5

I SUSPECT you will be interested to hear something about Appledore Castle and about Mr. Philip Baddock, who had been so near getting an immense fortune, yet had it snatched from him before his very eyes.

As Sir Jeremiah Baddock never signed the will of 1904, Captain de Mazareen's solicitors, on his behalf, sought to obtain probate of the former one, dated 1902. In view of the terrible circumstances connected with the proposed last testamentary dispositions of the deceased, Mr. Philip Baddock was advised to fight that suit.

It seems that he really was the son of Sir Jeremiah by the latter's second marriage with Mlle. Desty, but the old gentleman, with heartless vengefulness, had practically repudiated the boy from the first, and absolutely refused to have anything to do with him beyond paying for his maintenance and education, and afterwards making him a goodly allowance on the express condition that Philip–soon to become a young man–never set his foot on English soil.

The condition was strictly complied with. Philip Baddock was born abroad, and lived abroad until 1903, when he suddenly appeared at Appledore Castle. Whether Sir Jeremiah, in a fit of tardy repentance, had sent for him, or whether he risked coming of his own accord, no one ever knew.

Captain de Mazareen was not, until that same year 1903, aware of the existence of Philip Baddock any more than was anybody else, and he spent his last days of freedom in stating positively that he would not accept the terms of the will of 1902, but would agree to Sir Jeremiah's fortune being divided up as it would have been if the old gentleman had died intestate. Thus Philip Baddock, the son, and Hubert de Mazareen, the grandson, received an equal share of Sir Jeremiah's immense wealth, estimated at close upon £2,000,000 sterling.

Appledore was put up for sale and bought in by Mr. Philip Baddock, who took up his residence there and gradually gained for himself a position in the county as one of the most wealthy magnates in the north of England. Thus he became acquainted with the present Lord Flintshire, and, later on, met my dear lady. She neither sought nor avoided his acquaintance, and even went once to a dinner party at Appledore Castle.

That was lately, on the occasion of our last stay at Kirk. I had gone up to the Castle in the brougham so that I might accompany Lady Molly home, and had been shown into the library, whither my dear lady came in order to put on her cloak.

While she was doing so Mr. Philip Baddock came in. He had a newspaper in his hand and seemed greatly agitated.

"Such extraordinary news, Lady Molly," he said, pointing to a head-line in the paper. "You know, of course, that the other day a convict succeeded in effecting his escape from Dartmoor?"

"Yes, I knew that," said my dear lady, quietly.

"Well, I have reason to–to suppose," continued Mr. Baddock, "that that convict was none other than my unfortunate nephew, De Mazareen."

"Yes?" rejoined Lady Molly, whose perfect calm and serene expression of face contrasted strangely with the obvious agitation of Philip Baddock.

"Heaven knows that he tried to do me an evil turn," rejoined the latter after a while; "but of course I bear him no grudge, now that the law has given me that which he tried to wrench from me—a just share of my father's possessions. Since he has thrown himself on my mercy—"

"Thrown himself on your mercy!" ejaculated my dear lady, whose face had become almost grey with a sudden fear. "What do you mean?"

"De Mazareen is in my house at the present moment," replied Mr. Baddock, quietly.

"Here?"

"Yes. It seems that he tramped here. I am afraid that his object was to try and see you. He wants money, of course. I happened to be out in the woods this afternoon, and saw him.

"No, no!" added Philip Baddock quickly, in response to an instinctive gasp of pain from Lady Molly; "you need not have the slightest fear. My nephew is as safe with me as he would be in your own house. I brought him here, for he was exhausted with fatigue and want of food. None of my servants know of his presence in the house except Felkin, whom I can trust. By to-morrow he will have rested.... We'll make a start in the very early morning in my car; we'll get to Liverpool before midday. De Mazareen shall wear Felkin's clothes—no one will know him. One of the Baddock steamers is leaving for Buenos Ayres the same afternoon, and I can arrange with the captain. You need not have the slightest fear," he repeated, with simple yet earnest emphasis; "I pledge you my word that De Mazareen will be safe."

"I should like to thank you," she murmured.

"Please don't," he rejoined with a sad smile. "It is a great happiness to me to be able to do this. . . . I know that you—you cared for him at one time. . . . I wish you had known and trusted me in those days—but I am glad of this opportunity which enables me to tell you that, even had my father signed his last will and testament, I should have shared his fortune with De Mazareen. The man whom you honoured with your love need never have resorted to crime in order to gain a fortune."

Philip Baddock paused. His eyes were fixed on Lady Molly with unmistakable love and an appeal for sympathy. I had no idea that he cared for her—nor had she, I am quite sure. Her heart belonged solely to the poor, fugitive convict, but she could not fail, I thought, to be touched by the other man's obvious sincerity and earnestness.

There was silence in the room for a few moments. Only the old clock in its Sheraton case ticked on in solemn imperturbability.

Lady Molly turned her luminous eyes on the man who had just made so simple, so touching a profession of love. Was she about to tell him that she was no longer free, that she bore the name of the man whom the law had ostracised and pronounced a criminal—who had even now, by this daring attempt at escape, added a few years to his already long term of punishment and another load to his burden of shame?

"Do you think," she asked quietly, "that I might speak to Captain de

Mazareen for a few moments without endangering his safety?"

Mr. Baddock did not reply immediately. He seemed to be pondering over the request. Then he said:

"I will see that everything is safe. I don't think there need be any danger."

He went out of the room, and my dear lady and I were left alone for a minute or two. She was so calm and serene that I marvelled at her self-control, and wondered what was going on in her mind.

"Mary," she said to me, speaking very quickly, for already we could hear two men's footsteps approaching the library door, "you must station yourself just outside the front door; you understand? If you see or hear anything suspicious come and warn me at once."

I made ready to obey, and the next moment the door opened and Mr. Philip Baddock entered, accompanied by Captain Hubert.

I smothered the involuntary sob which rose to my throat at sight of the man who had once been the most gallant, the handsomest soldier I had ever seen. I had only just time to notice that Mr. Baddock prepared to leave the room again immediately. At the door he turned back and said to Lady Molly:

"Felkin has gone down to the lodge. If he hears or sees anything that seems suspicious he will ring up on the telephone;" and he pointed to the apparatus which stood on the library table in the centre of the room.

After that he closed the door, and I was left to imagine the moments of joy, mingled with acute anguish, which my dear lady would be living through.

I walked up and down restlessly on the terrace which fronts the Castle. The house itself appeared silent and dark: I presume all the servants had gone to bed. Far away on my right I caught the glimmer of a light. It came from the lodge where Felkin was watching. From the church in Appledore village came the sound of the clock striking the hour of midnight.

How long I had been on the watch I cannot say, when suddenly I was aware of a man's figure running rapidly along the drive towards the house. The next moment the figure had skirted the Castle, apparently making for one of the back doors.

I did not hesitate a moment. Having left the big front door on the latch, I ran straight in and made for the library door.

Already Mr. Philip Baddock had forestalled me. His hand was on the latch. Without more ado he pushed open the door and I followed him in.

Lady Molly was sitting on the sofa, with Captain Hubert beside her. They both rose at our entrance.

"The police!" said Mr. Baddock, speaking very rapidly. "Felkin has just run up from the lodge. He is getting the car ready. Pray God we may yet be able to get away."

Even as he spoke the front door bell sounded with a loud clang, which to me had the sound of a death knell.

"It is too late, you see," said my dear lady, quietly.

"No, not too late," ejaculated Philip Baddock, in a rapid whisper. "Quick! De Mazareen, follow me through the hall. Felkin is at the stables getting the car ready. It will be some time before the servants are roused."

"Mary, I am sure, has failed to fasten the front door," interrupted Lady Molly, with the same strange calm. "I think the police are already in the hall."

There was no mistaking the muffled sound of feet treading the thick Turkey carpet in the hall. The library had but one exit. Captain Hubert was literally in a trap. But Mr. Baddock had not lost his presence of mind.

"The police would never dream of searching my house," he said; "they will take my word that De Mazareen is not here. Here!" he added, pointing to a tall Jacobean wardrobe which stood in an angle of the room. "In there, man, and leave the rest to me!"

"I am afraid that such a proceeding would bring useless trouble upon you, Mr. Baddock," once more interposed Lady Molly; "the police, if they do not at once find Captain de Mazareen, will surely search the house."

"Impossible! They would not dare!"

"Indeed they would. The police know that Captain de Mazareen is here."

"I swear they do not," rejoined Mr. Baddock. "Felkin is no traitor, and no one else–"

"It was I who gave information to the police," said Lady Molly, speaking loudly and clearly. "I called up the superintendent on the telephone just now, and told him that his men would find the escaped convict hiding at Appledore Castle."

"You!" ejaculated Mr. Baddock, in a tone of surprise and horror, not unmixed with a certain note of triumph. "You?"

"Yes!" she replied calmly. "I am of the police, you know. I had to do my duty. Open the door, Mary," she added, turning to me.

Captain Hubert had not spoken a word so far. Now, when the men, led by Detective-Inspector Etty, entered the room, he walked with a firm step towards them, held out his hands for the irons, and with a final look at Lady Molly, in which love, trust, and hope were clearly expressed, he passed out of the room and was soon lost to sight.

My dear lady waited until the heavy footfalls had died away; then she turned with a pleasant smile to Mr. Philip Baddock:

"I thank you for your kind thoughts of me," she said, "and for your noble efforts on behalf of your nephew. My position was a difficult one. I hope you will forgive the pain I have been obliged to bring upon you."

"I will do more than forgive, Lady Molly," he said earnestly, "I will venture to hope."

He took her hand and kissed it. Then she beckoned to me and I followed her into the hall.

Our brougham–a hired one–had been waiting in the stable-yard. We drove home in silence; but half an hour later, when my dear lady kissed me good night she whispered in my ear:

"And now, Mary, we'll prove him innocent."

THE END

ONE or two people knew that at one time Lady Molly Robertson-Kirk had been engaged to Captain Hubert de Mazareen, who was now convict No. 97, undergoing a life sentence for the murder of Mr. Steadman, a solicitor of Carlisle, in the Elkhorn woods in April, 1904. Few, on the other hand, knew of the secret marriage solemnised on that never-to-be-forgotten afternoon, when all of us present in the church, with the exception of the bridegroom himself, were fully aware that proofs of guilt–deadly and irrefutable–were even then being heaped up against the man to whom Lady Molly was plighting her troth, for better or for worse, with her mental eyes wide open, her unerring intuition keen to the fact that nothing but a miracle could save the man she loved from an ignoble condemnation, perhaps from the gallows.

The husband of my dear lady, the man whom she loved with all the strength of her romantic and passionate nature, was duly tried and convicted of murder. Condemned to be hanged, he was reprieved, and his sentence commuted to penal servitude for life.

The question of Sir Jeremiah's estate became a complicated one, for his last will and testament was never signed, and the former one, dated 1902, bequeathed everything he possessed unconditionally to his beloved grandson Hubert.

After much legal argument, which it is useless to recapitulate here, it was agreed between the parties, and ratified in court, that the deceased gentleman's vast wealth should be disposed of as if he had died intestate. One half of it, therefore, went to Captain Hubert de Mazareen, grandson, and the other half to Philip Baddock, the son. The latter bought Appledore Castle and resided there, whilst his nephew became No. 97 in Dartmoor Prison.

Captain Hubert had served two years of his sentence when he made that daring and successful escape which caused so much sensation at the time. He managed to reach Appledore, where he was discovered by Mr. Philip Baddock, who gave him food and shelter and got everything ready for the safe conveyance of his unfortunate nephew to Liverpool and thence to a port of safety in South America.

You remember how he was thwarted in this laudable attempt by Lady Molly herself, who communicated with the police and gave up convict No. 97 into the hands of the authorities once more.

Of course, public outcry was loud against my dear lady's action. Sense of duty was all very well, so people argued, but no one could forget that at one time Captain Hubert de Mazareen and Lady Molly Robertson-Kirk had actually been engaged to be married, and it seemed positively monstrous for a woman to be so pitiless towards the man whom she must at one time have loved.

You see how little people understood my dear lady's motives. Some went so far as to say that she had only contemplated marriage with Captain Hubert de Mazareen because he was then, presumably, the heir to Sir Jeremiah's fortune; now–continued the gossips–she was equally ready to marry Mr. Philip Baddock, who at any rate was the happy possessor of one half of the deceased gentleman's wealth.

Certainly Lady Molly's conduct at this time helped to foster this idea. Finding that even the chief was inclined to give her the cold shoulder, she shut up our flat in Maida Vale and took up her residence at the little house which she owned in Kirk, and from the windows of which she had a splendid view of stately Appledore Castle nestling among the trees on the hillside.

I was with her, of course, and Mr. Philip Baddock was a frequent visitor at the house. There could be no doubt that he admired her greatly, and that she accepted his attentions with a fair amount of graciousness. The county fought shy of her. Her former engagement to Captain de Mazareen was well known, and her treachery to him–so it was called–was severely censured.

Living almost in isolation m the village, her whole soul seemed wrapped in thoughts of how to unravel the mystery of the death of Mr. Steadman. Captain de Mazareen had sworn in his defence that the solicitor, after starting to walk through the Elkhorn woods with him, had feared that the tramp over rough ground would be too much for him, and had almost immediately turned back in order to regain the road. But the chauffeur, George Taylor, who was busy with the broken-down car some two hundred yards up the road, never saw Mr. Steadman again, whilst Captain de Mazareen arrived at the gates of Appledore Castle alone. Here he was met by Mr. Philip Baddock, who informed him that Sir Jeremiah had breathed his last an hour before.

No one at the Castle recollected seeing a stick in Captain Hubert's hand when he arrived, whilst there were several witnesses who swore that he carried one at Appledore Station when he started to walk with her ladyship. The stick was found close to the body of the solicitor; and the solicitor, when he met with his terrible death, had in his pocket the draft of a will which meant disinheritance to Captain de Mazareen.

Here was the awful problem which Lady Molly had to face and to solve if she persisted in believing that the man whom she loved, and whom she had married at the moment when she knew that proofs of guilt were dead against him, was indeed innocent.

2

WE had spent all the morning shopping in Carlisle, and in the afternoon we called on Mr. Fuelling, of the firm of Fuelling, Steadman and Co., solicitors.

Lady Molly had some business to arrange in connection with the purchase of an additional bit of land to round off her little garden at Kirk.

Mr. Fuelling was courteous, but distinctly stiff, in his manner towards the lady who was "connected with the police," more especially when–her business being transacted–she seemed inclined to tarry for a little while in the busy solicitor's office, and to lead conversation round to the subject of the murder of Mr. Steadman.

"Five years have gone by since then," said Mr. Fuelling, curtly, in response to a remark from Lady Molly. "I prefer not to revive unpleasant memories."

"You, of course, believed Captain de Mazareen guilty?" retorted my dear lady, imperturbably.

"There were circumstances–" rejoined the solicitor, "and–and, of course, I hardly knew the unfortunate young man. Messrs. Truscott and Truscott used to be the family solicitors."

"Yes. It seemed curious that when Sir Jeremiah wished to make his will he should have sent for you, rather than for his accustomed lawyer," mused Lady Molly.

"Sir Jeremiah did not send for me," replied Mr. Fuelling, with some acerbity, "he sent for my junior, Mr. Steadman."

"Perhaps Mr. Steadman was a personal friend of his."

"Not at all. Not at all. Mr. Steadman was a new arrival in Carlisle, and had never seen Sir Jeremiah before the day when he was sent for and, in a brief interview, drafted the will which, alas! proved to be the primary cause of my unfortunate young partner's death."

"You cannot draft a will in a brief interview, Mr. Fuelling," remarked Lady Molly, lightly.

"Mr. Steadman did so," retorted Mr. Fuelling, curtly. "Though Sir Jeremiah's mind was as clear as crystal, he was very feeble, and the interview had to take place in a darkened room. That was the only time my young partner saw Sir Jeremiah. Twenty-four hours later they were both dead."

"Oh!" commented my dear lady with sudden indifference. "Well! I won't detain you, Mr. Fuelling. Good afternoon."

A few moments later, having parted from the worthy old solicitor, we were out in the street once more.

"The darkened room is my first ray of light," quoth Lady Molly to me, with a smile at her own paradoxical remark.

When we reached home later that afternoon we were met at the garden gate by Mr. Felkin, Mr. Philip Baddock's friend and agent, who lived with him at Appledore Castle.

Mr. Felkin was a curious personality; very taciturn in manner but a man of considerable education. He was the son of a country parson, and at the time of his father's death he had been studying for the medical profession. Finding himself unable to pursue his studies for lack of means, and being left entirely destitute, he had been forced to earn his living by taking up the less exalted calling of male nurse. It seems that he had met Mr. Philip Baddock on the Continent some years ago, and the two young men had somehow drifted into close acquaintanceship. When the late Sir Jeremiah required a personal nurse-attendant Mr. Philip Baddock sent for his friend and installed him at Appledore Castle.

Here Mr. Felkin remained, even after the old gentleman's death. He was nominally called Mr. Baddock's agent, but really did very little work. He was very fond of shooting and of riding, and spent his life in the pursuit of these sports, and he always had plenty of money to spend.

But everyone voted him a disagreeable bear, and the only one who ever succeeded in making him smile was Lady Molly, who always showed an unaccountable liking for the uncouth creature. Even now, when he extended a somewhat grimy hand and murmured a clumsy apology at his intrusion, she greeted him with warm effusiveness and insisted on his coming into the house.

We all turned to walk along the little drive, when Mr. Baddock's car came whizzing round the corner of the road from the Village. He pulled up at our gate, and the next moment had joined us in the drive.

There was a very black look in his eyes, as they wandered restlessly from my dear lady's face to that of his friend. Lady Molly's little hand was even then resting on Mr. Felkin's coat-sleeve; she had been in the act of leading him herself towards the house, and did not withdraw her hand when Mr. Baddock appeared upon the scene.

"Burton has just called about those estimates, Felkin," said the latter, somewhat roughly; "he is waiting at the Castle. You had better take the car—I can walk home later on."

"Oh! how disappointing!" exclaimed Lady Molly, with what looked uncommonly like a pout. "I was going to have such a cosy chat with Mr. Felkin—all about horses and dogs. Couldn't you see that tiresome Burton, Mr. Baddock?" she added ingenuously.

I don't think that Mr. Baddock actually swore, but I am sure he was very near doing so.

"Burton can wait," said Mr. Felkin, curtly.

"No, he cannot," retorted Philip Baddock, whose face was a frowning mirror of uncontrolled jealousy; "take the car, Felkin, and go at once."

For a moment it seemed as if Felkin would refuse to obey. The two men stood looking at each other, measuring one another's power of will and strength of passion. Hate and jealousy were clearly written in each pair of glowering eyes. Philip Baddock looked defiant, and Felkin taciturn and sulky.

Close to them stood my dear lady. Her beautiful eyes literally glowed with triumph. That these two men loved her, each in his own curious, uncontrolled way, I, her friend and confidant, knew very well. I had seen, and often puzzled over, the feminine attacks which she had made on the susceptibilities of that morose lout Felkin. It had taken her nearly two years to bring him to her feet. During that time she had alternately rendered him happy with her smiles and half mad with her coquetries, whilst Philip Baddock's love for her was perpetually fanned by his ever-growing jealousy.

I remember that I often thought her game a cruel one. She was one of those women whom few men could resist; if she really desired to conquer she invariably succeeded, and her victory over Felkin seemed to me as purposeless as it was unkind. After all, she was the lawful wife of Captain de Mazareen, and to rouse hatred between two friends for the sake of her love, when that love was not hers to give, seemed unworthy of her. At this moment, when I could read deadly hatred in the faces of these two men, her cooing laugh grated unpleasantly on my ear.

"Never mind, Mr. Felkin," she said, turning her luminous eyes on him. "Since you have so hard a taskmaster, you must do your duty now. But," she added, throwing a strange, defiant look at Mr. Baddock, "I shall be at home this evening; come and have our cosy chat after dinner."

She gave him her hand, and he took it with a certain clumsy gallantry and raised it to his lips. I thought that Philip Baddock would strike his friend with his open hand. The veins on his temples were swollen like dark cords, and I don't think that I ever saw such an evil look in anyone's eyes before.

Strangely enough, the moment Mr. Felkin's back was turned my dear lady seemed to set herself the task of soothing the violent passions which she had wilfully aroused in the other man. She invited him to come into the house, and, some ten minutes later, I heard her singing to him. When, later on, I went into the boudoir to join them at tea, she was sitting on the music stool whilst he half bent over her, half knelt at her feet; her hands were clasped in her lap, and his fingers were closed over hers.

He did not attempt to leave her side when he saw me entering the room. In fact, he wore a triumphant air of possession, and paid her those little attentions which only an accepted lover would dare to offer.

He left soon after tea, and she accompanied him to the door. She gave him her hand to kiss, and I, who stood at some little distance in the shadow, thought that he would take her in his arms, so yielding and gracious did she seem. But some look or gesture on her part must have checked him, for he turned and walked quickly down the drive.

Lady Molly stood in the doorway gazing out towards the sunset. I, in my humble mind, wondered once again what was the purport of this cruel game.

3

HALF an hour later she called to me, asked for her hat, told me to put on mine and to come out for a stroll.

As so often happened, she led the way towards the Elkhorn woods, which in spite, or perhaps because, of the painful memories they evoked, was a very favourite walk of hers.

As a rule the wood, especially that portion of it where the unfortunate solicitor had been murdered, was deserted after sunset. The villagers declared that Mr. Steadman's ghost haunted the clearing, and that the cry of the murdered man, as he was being foully struck from behind, could be distinctly heard echoing through the trees.

Needless to say, these superstitious fancies never disturbed Lady Molly. She liked to wander over the ground where was committed that mysterious crime which had sent to ignominy worse than death the man she loved so passionately. It seemed as if she meant to wrench its secret from the silent ground, from the leafy undergrowth, from the furtive inhabitants of the glades.

The sun had gone down behind the hills; the wood was dark and still. We strolled up as far as the first clearing, where a plain, granite stone, put up by Mr. Philip Baddock, marked the spot where Mr. Steadman had been murdered.

We sat down on it to rest. My dear lady's mood was a silent one; I did not dare to disturb it, and, for a while, only the gentle "hush–sh–sh" of the leaves, stirred by the evening breeze, broke the peaceful stillness of the glade.

Then we heard a murmur of voices, deep-toned and low. We could not hear the words spoken, though we both strained our ears, and presently Lady Molly arose and cautiously made her way among the trees in the direction whence the voices came, I following as closely as I could.

We had not gone far when we recognised the voices, and heard the words that were said. I paused, distinctly frightened, whilst my dear lady whispered a warning "Hush!"

Never in all my life had I heard so much hatred, such vengeful malignity expressed in the intonation of the human voice as I did in the half-dozen words which now struck my ear.

"You will give her up, or—"

It was Mr. Felkin who spoke. I recognised his raucous delivery, but I could not distinguish either of the two men in the gloom.

"Or what?" queried the other, in a voice which trembled with either rage or fear—perhaps with both.

"You will give her up," repeated Felkin, sullenly. "I tell you that it is an impossibility—do you understand?—an impossibility for me to stand by and see her wedded to you, or to any other man for the matter of that. But that is neither here nor there," he added after a slight pause. "It is with you I have to deal now. You shan't have her—you shan't—I won't allow it, even if I have to—"

He paused again. I cannot describe the extraordinary effect this rough voice coming out of the darkness had upon my nerves. I had edged up to Lady Molly, and had succeeded in getting hold of her hand. It was like ice, and she herself was as rigid as that piece of granite on which we had been sitting.

"You seem bubbling over with covert threats," interposed Philip Baddock, with what was obviously a sneer; "what are the extreme measures to which you will resort if I do not give up the lady whom I love with my whole heart, and who has honoured me to-day by accepting my hand in marriage?"

"That is a lie!" ejaculated Felkin.

"What is a lie?" queried the other, quietly.

"She has not accepted you—and you know it. You are trying to keep me away from her—arrogating rights which you do not possess. Give her up, man, give her up. It will be best for you. She will listen to me—I can win her all right—but you must stand aside for me this time. Take the word of a desperate man for it, Baddock. It will be best for you to give her up."

Silence reigned in the wood for a few moments, and then we heard Philip Baddock's voice again, but he seemed to speak more calmly, almost indifferently, as I thought.

"Are you going now?" he asked. "Won't you come in to dinner? "

"No," replied Felkin, "I don't want any dinner, and I have an appointment for afterwards."

"Don't let us part ill friends, Felkin," continued Philip Baddock in conciliatory tones. "Do you know that, personally, my feeling is that no woman on earth is worth a serious quarrel between two old friends, such as we have been."

"I'm glad you think so," rejoined the other drily. "S'long."

The cracking of twigs on the moss-covered ground indicated that the two men had parted and were going their several ways.

With infinite caution, and holding my hand tightly in hers, my dear lady made her way along the narrow path which led us out of the wood.

Once in the road we walked rapidly, and soon reached our garden gate. Lady Molly had not spoken a word during all that time, and no one knew better than I did how to respect her silence.

During dinner she tried to talk of indifferent subjects, and never once alluded to the two men whom she had thus wilfully pitted one against the other. That her calm was only on the surface, however, I realised from the fact that every sound on the gravel path outside caused her to start. She was, of course, expecting the visit of Mr. Felkin.

At eight o'clock he came. It was obvious that he had spent the past hour in wandering about in the woods. He looked untidy and unkempt. My dear lady greeted him very coldly, and when he tried to kiss her hand she withdrew it abruptly.

Our drawing-room was a double one, divided by portière curtains. Lady Molly led the way into the front room, followed by Mr. Felkin. Then she drew the curtains together, leaving me standing behind them. I concluded that she wished me to stay there and to listen, conscious of the fact that Felkin, in the agitated mood in which he was, would be quite oblivious of my presence.

I almost pitied the poor man, for to me—the listener—it was at once apparent that my dear lady had only bidden him come to-night in order to torture him. For about a year she had been playing with him as a cat does with a mouse; encouraging him at times with sweet words and smiles, repelling him at others with coldness not unmixed with coquetry. But to-night her coldness was unalloyed; her voice was trenchant, her attitude almost one of contempt.

I missed the beginning of their conversation, for the curtains were thick and I did not like to go too near, but soon Mr. Felkin's voice was raised. It was harsh and uncompromising.

"I suppose that I am only good enough for a summer's flirtation?" he said sullenly, "but not to marry, eh? The owner of Appledore Castle, the millionaire, Mr. Baddock, is more in your line—"

"It certainly would be a more suitable match for me," rejoined Lady Molly, coolly.

"He told me you had formally accepted him," said the man, with enforced calm; "is that true?"

"Partly," she replied.

"But you won't marry him!"

The exclamation seemed to come straight from a heart brimful of passion, of love, of hate, and of revenge. The voice had the same intonation in it which had rung an hour ago in the dark Elkhorn woods.

"I may do," came in quiet accents from my dear lady.

"You won't marry him," repeated Felkin, roughly.

"Who shall prevent me?" retorted Lady Molly, with a low, sarcastic laugh.

"I will."

"You?" she said contemptuously.

"I told him an hour ago that he must give you up. I tell you now that you shall not be Philip Baddock's wife."

"Oh!" she interposed. And I could almost see the disdainful shrug of her shoulders, the flash of contempt in her expressive eyes.

No doubt it maddened him to see her so cool, so indifferent, when he had thought that he could win her. I do believe that the poor wretch loved her. She was always beautiful, but never more so than to-night when she had obviously determined finally to dismiss him.

"If you marry Philip Baddock," he now said, in a voice which quivered with uncontrolled passion, "then within six months of your wedding-day you will be a widow, for your husband will have ended his life on the gallows."

"You are mad!" she retorted calmly.

"That is as it may be," he replied. "I warned him to-night, and he seems inclined to heed my warning; but he won't stand aside if you beckon to him. Therefore, if you love him, take my warning. I may not be able to get you, but I swear to you that Philip Baddock shan't either. I'll see him hanged first," he added, with gruesome significance.

"And you think that you can force me to do your bidding by such paltry threats?" she retorted.

"Paltry threats? Ask Philip Baddock if my threats are paltry. He knows full well that in my room at Appledore Castle, safe from thievish fingers, lie the proofs that he killed Alexander Steadman in the Elkhorn woods. Oh! I wouldn't help him in his nefarious deeds until he placed himself in my hands. He had to take my terms or leave the thing alone altogether, for he could not work without me. My wants are few, and he has treated and paid me well. Now we are rivals, and I'll destroy him before I'll let him gloat over me.

"Do you know how we worked it? Sir Jeremiah would not disinherit his grandson—he steadily refused to make a will in Philip Baddock's favour. But when he was practically dying we sent for Alexander Steadman—a newcomer, who had never seen Sir Jeremiah before—and I impersonated the old gentleman for the occasion. Yes, I!" he repeated with a coarse laugh, "I was Sir Jeremiah for the space of half an hour, and I think that I played the part splendidly. I dictated the terms of a new will. Young Steadman never suspected the fraud for a single instant. We had darkened the room for the comedy, you see, and Mr. Steadman was destined by Baddock and myself never to set eyes on the real Sir Jeremiah.

"After the interview Baddock sent for Captain de Mazareen; this was all part of his plan and mine. We engineered it all, and we knew that Sir Jeremiah could only last a few hours. We sent for Steadman again, and I myself scattered a few dozen sharp nails among the loose stones in the road where the motorcar was intended to break down, thus forcing the solicitor to walk through the woods. Captain de Mazareen's appearance on the scene at that particular moment was an unrehearsed effect which nearly upset all our plans, for had Mr. Steadman stuck to him that night, instead of turning back, he would probably be alive now, and Baddock and I would be doing time somewhere for attempted fraud. We should have been done, at any rate.

"Well! you know what happened. Mr. Steadman was killed. Baddock killed him, and then ran straight back to the house, just in time to greet Captain de Mazareen, who evidently had loitered on his way. But it was I who thought of the stick, as an additional precaution to avert suspicion from ourselves. Captain de Mazareen was carrying one, and left it in the hall at the Castle. I cut my own hand and stained the stick with it, then polished and cleaned it up, and later, during the night, deposited it in the near neighbourhood of the murdered body. Ingenious, wasn't it? I am a clever beggar, you see. Because I was cleverer than Baddock he could not do without me, and because he could not do without me I made him write and sign a request to me to help him to manufacture a bogus will and then to murder the solicitor who had drawn it up. And I have hidden that precious document in the wing of Appledore Castle which I inhabit; the exact spot is known only to myself.

Baddock has often tried to find out, but all he knows is that these things are in that particular wing of the house. I have the document, and the draft of the will taken out of Mr. Steadman's pocket, and the short bludgeon with which he was killed–it is still stained with blood–and the rags with which I cleaned the stick. I swear that I will never make use of these things against Philip Baddock unless he drives me to it, and if you make use of what I have just told you I'll swear that I have lied. No one can find the proofs which I hold. But on the day that you marry Baddock I'll place them in the hands of the police."

There was silence in the room. I could almost hear the beating of my own heart, so horrified, so appalled was I at the horrible tale which the man had just told to my dear lady.

The villainy of the whole scheme was so terrible, and at the same time so cunning, that it seemed inconceivable that human brain could have engendered it. Vaguely in my dull mind I wondered if Lady Molly would have to commit bigamy before she could wrench from this evildoer's hands the proofs that would set her own husband free from his martyrdom.

What she said I did not hear, what he meant to retort I never knew, for at that moment my attention was attracted by the sound of running footsteps on the gravel, followed by a loud knock at our front door. Instinctively I ran to open it. Our old gardener was standing there hatless and breathless.

"Appledore Castle, miss," he stammered, "it's on fire. I thought you would like to know."

Before I had time to reply I heard a loud oath uttered close behind me, and the next moment Felkin dashed out of the drawing-room into the hall.

"Is there a bicycle here that I can take?" he shouted to the gardener.

"Yes, sir," replied the old man; "my son has one. Just in that shed, sir, on your left."

In fewer seconds than it takes to relate, Felkin had rushed to the shed, dragged out the bicycle, mounted it, and I think that within two minutes of hearing the awful news, he was bowling along the road, and was soon out of sight.

4

ONE wing of the stately mansion was ablaze when, a quarter of an hour later, my dear lady and I arrived upon the scene. We had come on our bicycles not long after Mr. Felkin.

At the very moment that the weird spectacle burst fully upon our gaze, a loud cry of horror had just risen from the hundred or so people who stood watching the terrible conflagration, whilst the local fire brigade, assisted by Mr. Baddock's men, were working with the hydrants. That cry found echo in our own throats as we saw a man clambering, with the rapidity of a monkey, up a long ladder which had been propped up against a second floor window of the flaming portion of the building. The red glow illumined the large, shaggy head of Felkin, throwing for a moment into bold relief his hooked nose and straggly beard. For the space of three seconds perhaps he stood thus, outlined against what looked like a glowing furnace behind him, and the next instant he had disappeared beyond the window embrasure.

"This is madness!" came in loud accents from out the crowd in the foreground, and before one fully realised whence that voice had come, Mr. Philip Baddock was in his turn seen clambering up that awful ladder. A dozen pairs of hands reached him just in time to drag him back from the perilous ascent. He fought to free himself, but the firemen were determined and soon succeeded in bringing him back to level ground, whilst two of them, helmeted and well-equipped, took his place upon the ladder.

The foremost had hardly reached the level of the first story when Felkin's figure once more appeared in the window embrasure above. He was staggering like a man drunk or fainting, his shaggy hair and beard were blown about his head by the terrible draught caused by the flames, and he waved his arms over his head, giving the impression to those below, who gazed horrified, that he was either possessed or dying. In one hand he held what looked like a great, long bundle.

We could see him now put one leg forward, obviously gathering strength to climb the somewhat high window ledge. With a shout of encouragement the two firemen scrambled up with squirrel-like agility, and the cry of "They're coming! they're coming! Hold on, Felkin!" rose from a hundred excited throats.

The unfortunate man made another effort. We could see his face clearly now in the almost blinding glow which surrounded him. It was distorted with fear and also with agony.

He gave one raucous cry, which I do believe will echo in my ears as long as I live, and with a superhuman effort he hurled the bundle which he held out of the window.

At that same moment there was a terrific hissing, followed by a loud crash. The floor beneath the feet of the unfortunate man must have given way, for he disappeared suddenly in a sea of flames.

The bundle which he had hurled down had struck the foremost fireman on the head. He lost his hold, and as he fell he dragged his unfortunate comrade down with him. The others ran to the rescue of their comrades. I don't think they were seriously hurt, but what happened directly after among the crowd, the firemen, or the burning building, I cannot tell you. I only know that at the moment when Felkin's figure was, for the second time, seen in the frame of the glowing window, Lady Molly seized my hand and dragged me forward through the crowd.

Her husband's life was hanging in the balance, just as much as that of the miserable wretch who was courting a horrible death for the sake of those proofs which—as it was proved afterwards—Philip Baddock tried to destroy by such drastic means.

The excitement round the ladder, the fall of the two firemen, the crashing in of the floor and the gruesome disappearance of Felkin caused so much excitement in the crowd that the bundle which the unfortunate man had thrown remained unheeded for the moment. But Philip Baddock reached the spot where it fell thirty seconds after Lady Molly did. She had already picked it up, when he said harshly:

"Give me that. It is mine. Felkin risked his life to save it for me."

Inspector Etty, however, stood close by, and before Philip Baddock realised what Lady Molly meant to do, she had turned quickly and placed the bundle in the inspector's hands.

"You know me, Etty, don't you?" she said rapidly.

"Oh, yes, my lady!" he replied.

"Then take the utmost care of this bundle. It contains proofs of one of the most dastardly crimes ever committed in this country."

No other words could have aroused the enthusiasm and caution of Etty in the same manner.

After that Philip Baddock might protest, might rage, storm, or try to bribe, but the proofs of his guilt and Captain de Mazareen's innocence were safe in the hands of the police, and bound to come to light at last.

But, as a matter of fact, Baddock neither stormed nor pleaded. When Lady Molly turned to him once more he had disappeared.

*****

You know the rest, of course. It occurred too recently to be recounted. Philip Baddock was found the next morning with a bullet through his head, lying on the granite stone which, with cruel hypocrisy, he himself had erected in memory of Mr. Steadman whom he had so foully murdered.

The unfortunate Felkin had not lied when he said that the proofs which he held of Baddock's guilt were conclusive and deadly.

Captain de Mazareen obtained His Majesty's gracious pardon after five years of martyrdom which he had borne with heroic fortitude.

I was not present when Lady Molly was once more united to the man who so ardently worshipped and trusted her, and to whose love, innocence, and cause she had remained so sublimely loyal throughout the past few years.

She has given up her connection with the police. The reason for it has gone with the return of her happiness, over which I–her ever faithful Mary Granard–will, with your permission, draw a veil.

THE END

WHO WAS BARONESS ORCZY?

AN APPRECIATION

Emma Magdolna Rozália Mária Jozefa Borbála "Emmuska" Orczy de Orczi a.k.a. Baroness Orczy (1865-1947) was a Hungarian aristocrat who emigrated to Great Britain with her family in 1868. She married a penniless artist and turned to writing after the birth of their first child. Her first novel The Emperor's Candlesticks (1899), was a failure. Next she created The Old Man in the Corner for Royal Magazine in 1901. Her anonymous armchair detective rode the popular fin de siècle interest in crime stories which Poe had kicked off with The Murders in the Rue Mourge (1841), Dickens continued in Bleak House (1853) and Conan Doyle enjoyed great success with in A Study in Scarlet. But it wasn't until the Baroness collaborated on a play with her husband Montague Barstow in 1903 that she would find true financial success. Emma and Monty managed to come up with a character whose very nature would make him proverbial. The foppish-sounding Scarlet Pimpernel was the nom de guerre of Sir Percy Blakeney, a dashing English aristocrat whose métier was rescuing doomed upper classes during the French Revolution. Although the play was not a smash, it ran for four years and the shrewd Baroness exploited the play's success by adapting it into a novel and then sitting back as the publicity from the stage success fuelled book sales. She would go on to write over a dozen sequels and related short stories between 1903 and 1940.

Today, Baroness Orczy is undoubtedly remembered for The Scarlet Pimpernell. From what she wrote in her 1947 autobiography Links in the Chain of Life it appears she would be very happy with her legacy:

"I have so often been asked the question: "But how did you come to think of The Scarlet Pimpernel?" And my answer has always been: "It was God's will that I should." And to you moderns, who perhaps do not believe as I do, I will say, "In the chain of my life, there were so many links, all of which tended towards bringing me to the fulfillment of my destiny."

— Emmuska Orczy, *Links in the Chain of Life*

THE EXPERIENCES OF LOVEDAY BROOKE, LADY DETECTIVE

BY C. L. PIRKIS

THE BLACK BAG LEFT ON A DOOR-STEP

"IT'S a big thing," said Loveday Brooke, addressing Ebenezer Dyer, chief of the well-known detective agency in Lynch Court, Fleet Street; "Lady Cathrow has lost £30,000 worth of jewellery, if the newspaper accounts are to be trusted."

"They are fairly accurate this time. The robbery differs in few respects from the usual run of country-house robberies. The time chosen, of course, was the dinner-hour, when the family and guests were at table and the servants not on duty were amusing themselves in their own quarters. The fact of its being Christmas Eve would also of necessity add to the business and consequent distraction of the household. The entry to the house, however, in this case was not effected in the usual manner by a ladder to the dressing-room window, but through the window of a room on the ground floor–a small room with one window and two doors, one of which opens into the hall, and the other into a passage that leads by the back stairs to the bedroom floor. It is used, I believe, as a sort of hat and coat room by the gentlemen of the house."

"It was, I suppose, the weak point of the house?"

"Quite so. A very weak point indeed. Craigen Court, the residence of Sir George and Lady Cathrow, is an oddly-built old place, jutting out in all directions, and as this window looked out upon a blank wall, it was filled in with stained glass, kept fastened by a strong brass catch, and never opened, day or night, ventilation being obtained by means of a glass ventilator fitted in the upper panes. It seems absurd to think that this window, being only about four feet from the ground, should have had neither iron bars nor shutters added to it; such, however, was the case. On the night of the robbery, someone within the house must have deliberately, and of intention, unfastened its only protection, the brass catch, and thus given the thieves easy entrance to the house."

"Your suspicions, I suppose, centre upon the servants?"

"Undoubtedly; and it is in the servants' hall that your services will be required. The thieves, whoever they were, were perfectly cognizant of the ways of the house. Lady Cathrow's jewellery was kept in a safe in her dressing-room, and as the dressing-room was over the dining-room, Sir George was in the habit of saying that it was the 'safest' room in the house. (Note the pun, please; Sir George is rather proud of it.) By his orders the window of the dining-room immediately under the dressing-room window was always left unshuttered and without blind during dinner, and as a full stream of light thus fell through it on to the outside terrace, it would have been impossible for anyone to have placed a ladder there unseen."

"I see from the newspapers that it was Sir George's invariable custom to fill his house and give a large dinner on Christmas Eve."

"Yes. Sir George and Lady Cathrow are elderly people, with no family and few relatives, and have consequently a large amount of time to spend on their friends."

"I suppose the key of the safe was frequently left in the possession of Lady Cathrow's maid?"

"Yes. She is a young French girl, Stephanie Delcroix by name. It was her duty to clear the dressing-room directly after her mistress left it; put away any jewellery that might be lying about, lock the safe, and keep the key till her mistress came up to bed. On the night of the robbery, however, she admits that, instead of so doing, directly her mistress left the dressing-room, she ran down to the housekeeper's room to see if any letters had come for her, and remained chatting with the other servants for some time—she could not say for how long. It was by the half-past-seven post that her letters generally arrived from St. Omer, where her home is."

"Oh, then, she was in the habit of thus running down to enquire for her letters, no doubt, and the thieves, who appear to be so thoroughly cognizant of the house, would know this also."

"Perhaps; though at the present moment I must say things look very black against the girl. Her manner, too, when questioned, is not calculated to remove suspicion. She goes from one fit of hysterics into another; contradicts herself nearly every time she opens her mouth, then lays it to the charge of her ignorance of our language; breaks into voluble French; becomes theatrical in action, and then goes off into hysterics once more."

"All that is quite Français, you know," said Loveday. "Do the authorities at Scotland Yard lay much stress on the safe being left unlocked that night?"

"They do, and they are instituting a keen enquiry as to the possible lovers the girl may have. For this purpose they have sent Bates down to stay in the village and collect all the information he can outside the house. But they want someone within the walls to hob-nob with the maids generally, and to find out if she has taken any of them into her confidence respecting her lovers. So they sent to me to know if I would send down for this purpose one of the shrewdest and most clear-headed of my female detectives. I, in my turn, Miss Brooke, have sent for you—you may take it as a compliment if you like. So please now get out your note-book, and I'll give you sailing orders."

Loveday Brooke, at this period of her career, was a little over thirty years of age, and could be best described in a series of negations.

She was not tall, she was not short; she was not dark, she was not fair; she was neither handsome nor ugly. Her features were altogether nondescript; her one noticeable trait was a habit she had, when absorbed in thought, of dropping her eyelids over her eyes till only a line of eyeball showed, and she appeared to be looking out at the world through a slit, instead of through a window.

Her dress was invariably black, and was almost Quaker-like in its neat primness.

Some five or six years previously, by a jerk of Fortune's wheel, Loveday had been thrown upon the world penniless and all but friendless. Marketable accomplishments she had found she had none, so she had forthwith defied convention, and had chosen for herself a career that had cut her off sharply from her former associates and her position in society. For five or six years she drudged away patiently in the lower walks of her profession; then chance, or, to speak more precisely, an intricate criminal case, threw her in the way of the experienced head of the flourishing detective agency in Lynch Court. He quickly enough found out the stuff she was made of, and threw her in the way of better-class work—work, indeed, that brought increase of pay and of reputation alike to him and to Loveday.

Ebenezer Dyer was not, as a rule, given to enthusiasm; but he would at times wax eloquent over Miss Brooke's qualifications for the profession she had chosen.

"Too much of a lady, do you say?" he would say to anyone who chanced to call in question those qualifications. "I don't care twopence-halfpenny whether she is or is not a lady. I only know she is the most sensible and practical woman I ever met. In the first place, she has the faculty—so rare among women—of carrying out orders to the very letter: in the second place, she has a clear, shrewd brain, unhampered by any hard-and-fast theories; thirdly, and most important item of all, she has so much common sense that it amounts to genius—positively to genius, sir."

But although Loveday and her chief as a rule, worked together upon an easy and friendly footing, there were occasions on which they were wont, so to speak, to snarl at each other.

Such an occasion was at hand now.

Loveday showed no disposition to take out her note-book and receive her "sailing orders."

"I want to know," she said, "If what I saw in one newspaper is true—that one of the thieves before leaving, took the trouble to close the safe-door, and to write across it in chalk: 'To be let, unfurnished'?"

"Perfectly true; but I do not see that stress need be laid on the fact. The scoundrels often do that sort of thing out of insolence or bravado. In that robbery at Reigate, the other day, they went to a lady's Davenport, took a sheet of her note-paper, and wrote their thanks on it for her kindness in not having had the lock of her safe repaired. Now, if you will get out your note-book—"

"Don't be in such a hurry," said Loveday calmly: "I want to know if you have seen this?" She leaned across the writing-table at which they sat, one either side, and handed to him a newspaper cutting which she took from her letter-case.

Mr. Dyer was a tall, powerfully-built man with a large head, benevolent bald forehead and a genial smile. That smile, however, often proved a trap to the unwary, for he owned a temper so irritable that a child with a chance word might ruffle it.

The genial smile vanished as he took the newspaper cutting from Loveday's hand.

"I would have you to remember, Miss Brooke," he said severely, "that although I am in the habit of using dispatch in my business, I am never known to be in a hurry; hurry in affairs I take to be the especial mark of the slovenly and unpunctual."

Then, as if still further to give contradiction to her words, he very deliberately unfolded her slip of newspaper and slowly, accentuating each word and syllable, read as follows:–

"Singular Discovery.

"A black leather bag, or portmanteau, was found early yesterday morning by one of Smith's newspaper boys on the doorstep of a house in the road running between Easterbrook and Wreford, and inhabited by an elderly spinster lady. The contents of the bag include a clerical collar and necktie, a Church Service, a book of sermons, a copy of the works of Virgil, a facsimile of Magna Charta, with translations, a pair of black kid gloves, a brush and comb, some newspapers, and several small articles suggesting clerical ownership. On the top of the bag the following extraordinary letter, written in pencil on a long slip of paper, was found:

'The fatal day has arrived. I can exist no longer. I go hence and shall be no more seen. But I would have Coroner and Jury know that I am a sane man, and a verdict of temporary insanity in my case would be an error most gross after this intimation. I care not if it is felo de se, as I shall have passed all suffering. Search diligently for my poor lifeless body in the immediate neighbourhood–on the cold heath, the rail, or the river by yonder bridge–a few moments will decide how I shall depart. If I had walked aright I might have been a power in the Church of which I am now an unworthy member and priest; but the damnable sin of gambling got hold on me, and betting has been my ruin, as it has been the ruin of thousands who have preceded me. Young man, shun the bookmaker and the race-course as you would shun the devil and hell. Farewell, chums of Magdalen. Farewell, and take warning. Though I can claim relationship with a Duke, a Marquess, and a Bishop, and though I am the son of a noble woman, yet am I a tramp and an outcast, verily and indeed. Sweet death, I greet thee. I dare not sign my name. To one and all, farewell. O, my poor Marchioness mother, a dying kiss to thee. R.I.P.'

"The police and some of the railway officials have made a 'diligent search' in the neighbourhood of the railway station, but no 'poor lifeless body' has been found. The police authorities are inclined to the belief that the letter is a hoax, though they are still investigating the matter."

In the same deliberate fashion as he had opened and read the cutting, Mr. Dyer folded and returned it to Loveday.

"May I ask," he said sarcastically, "what you see in that silly hoax to waste your and my valuable time over?"

"I wanted to know," said Loveday, in the same level tones as before, "if you saw anything in it that might in some way connect this discovery with the robbery at Craigen Court?"

Mr. Dyer stared at her in utter, blank astonishment.

"When I was a boy," he said sarcastically as before, "I used to play at a game called 'what is my thought like?' Someone would think of something absurd—say the top of the monument—and someone else would hazard a guess that his thought might be—say the toe of his left boot, and that unfortunate individual would have to show the connection between the toe of his left boot and the top of the monument. Miss Brooke, I have no wish to repeat the silly game this evening for your benefit and mine."

"Oh, very well," said Loveday, calmly; "I fancied you might like to talk it over, that was all. Give me my 'sailing orders,' as you call them, and I'll endeavour to concentrate my attention on the little French maid and her various lovers."

Mr. Dyer grew amiable again.

"That's the point on which I wish you to fix your thoughts," he said; "you had better start for Craigen Court by the first train to-morrow—it's about sixty miles down the Great Eastern line. Huxwell is the station you must land at. There one of the grooms from the Court will meet you, and drive you to the house. I have arranged with the housekeeper there—Mrs. Williams, a very worthy and discreet person—that you shall pass in the house for a niece of hers, on a visit to recruit, after severe study in order to pass board-school teachers' exams. Naturally you have injured your eyes as well as your health with overwork; and so you can wear your blue spectacles. Your name, by the way, will be Jane Smith—better write it down. All your work will be among the servants of the establishment, and there will be no necessity for you to see either Sir George or Lady Cathrow—in fact, neither of them have been apprised of your intended visit—the fewer we take into our confidence the better. I've no doubt, however, that Bates will hear from Scotland Yard that you are in the house, and will make a point of seeing you."

"Has Bates unearthed anything of importance?"

"Not as yet. He has discovered one of the girl's lovers, a young farmer of the name of Holt; but as he seems to be an honest, respectable young fellow, and entirely above suspicion, the discovery does not count for much."

"I think there's nothing else to ask," said Loveday, rising to take her departure. "Of course, I'll telegraph, should need arise, in our usual cipher."

The first train that left Bishopsgate for Huxwell on the following morning included, among its passengers, Loveday Brooke, dressed in the neat black supposed to be appropriate to servants of the upper class. The only literature with which she had provided herself in order to beguile the tedium of her journey was a small volume bound in paper boards, and entitled, "The Reciter's Treasury." It was published at the low price of one shilling, and seemed specially designed to meet the requirements of third-rate amateur reciters at penny readings.

Miss Brooke appeared to be all-absorbed in the contents of this book during the first half of her journey. During the second, she lay back in the carriage with closed eyes, and motionless as if asleep or lost in deep thought.

The stopping of the train at Huxwell aroused her, and set her collecting together her wraps.

It was easy to single out the trim groom from Craigen Court from among the country loafers on the platform. Someone else beside the trim groom at the same moment caught her eye—Bates, from Scotland Yard, got up in the style of a commercial traveler, and carrying the orthodox "commercial bag" in his hand. He was a small, wiry man, with red hair and whiskers, and an eager, hungry expression of countenance.

"I am half-frozen with cold," said Loveday, addressing Sir George's groom; "if you'll kindly take charge of my portmanteau, I'd prefer walking to driving to the Court."

The man gave her a few directions as to the road she was to follow, and then drove off with her box, leaving her free to indulge Mr. Bate's evident wish for a walk and confidential talk along the country road.

Bates seemed to be in a happy frame of mind that morning.

"Quite a simple affair, this, Miss Brooke," he said: "a walk over the course, I take it, with you working inside the castle walls and I unearthing without. No complications as yet have arisen, and if that girl does not find herself in jail before another week is over her head, my name is not Jeremiah Bates."

"You mean the French maid?"

"Why, yes, of course. I take it there's little doubt but what she performed the double duty of unlocking the safe and the window too. You see I look at it this way, Miss Brooke: all girls have lovers, I say to myself, but a pretty girl like that French maid, is bound to have double the number of lovers than the plain ones. Now, of course, the greater the number of lovers, the greater the chance there is of a criminal being found among them. That's plain as a pikestaff, isn't it?"

"Just as plain."

Bates felt encouraged to proceed.

"Well, then, arguing on the same lines, I say to myself, this girl is only a pretty, silly thing, not an accomplished criminal, or she wouldn't have admitted leaving open the safe door; give her rope enough and she'll hang herself. In a day or two, if we let her alone, she'll be bolting off to join the fellow whose nest she has helped to feather, and we shall catch the pair of them 'twixt here and Dover Straits, and also possibly get a clue that will bring us on the traces of their accomplices. Eh, Miss Brooke, that'll be a thing worth doing?"

"Undoubtedly. Who is this coming along in this buggy at such a good pace?"

The question was added as the sound of wheels behind them made her look round.

Bates turned also. "Oh, this is young Holt; his father farms land about a couple of miles from here. He is one of Stephanie's lovers, and I should imagine about the best of the lot. But he does not appear to be first favourite; from what I hear someone else must have made the running on the sly. Ever since the robbery I'm told the young woman has given him the cold shoulder."

As the young man came nearer in his buggy he slackened pace, and Loveday could not but admire his frank, honest expression of countenance,

"Room for one—can I give you a lift?" he said, as he came alongside of them.

And to the ineffable disgust of Bates, who had counted upon at least an hour's confidential talk with her, Miss Brooke accepted the young farmer's offer, and mounted beside him in his buggy.

As they went swiftly along the country road, Loveday explained to the young man that her destination was Craigen Court, and that as she was a stranger to the place, she must trust to him to put her down at the nearest point to it that he would pass.

At the mention of Craigen Court his face clouded.

"They're in trouble there, and their trouble has brought trouble on others," he said a little bitterly.

"I know," said Loveday sympathetically; "it is often so. In such circumstances as these suspicions frequently fastens on an entirely innocent person."

"That's it! that's it!" he cried excitedly; "if you go into that house you'll hear all sorts of wicked things said of her, and see everything setting in dead against her. But she's innocent. I swear to you she is as innocent as you or I are."

His voice rang out above the clatter of his horse's hoots. He seemed to forget that he had mentioned no name, and that Loveday, as a stranger, might be at a loss to know to whom he referred.

"Who is guilty Heaven only knows," he went on after a moment's pause; "it isn't for me to give an ill name to anyone in that house; but I only say she is innocent, and that I'll stake my life on."

"She is a lucky girl to have found one to believe in her, and trust her as you do," said Loveday, even more sympathetically than before.

"Is she? I wish she'd take advantage of her luck, then," he answered bitterly. "Most girls in her position would be glad to have a man to stand by them through thick and thin. But not she! Ever since the night of that accursed robbery she has refused to see me—won't answer my letters—won't even send me a message. And, great Heavens! I'd marry her to-morrow, if I had the chance, and dare the world to say a word against her."

He whipped up his pony. The hedges seemed to fly on either side of them, and before Loveday realized that half her drive was over, he had drawn rein, and was helping her to alight at the servants' entrance to Craigen Court.

"You'll tell her what I've said to you, if you get the opportunity, and beg her to see me, if only for five minutes?" he petitioned before he re-mounted his buggy. And Loveday, as she thanked the young man for his kind attention, promised to make an opportunity to give his message to the girl.

Mrs. Williams, the housekeeper, welcomed Loveday in the servants' hall, and then took her to her own room to pull off her wraps. Mrs. Williams was the widow of a London tradesman, and a little beyond the average housekeeper in speech and manner.

She was a genial, pleasant woman, and readily entered into conversation with Loveday. Tea was brought in, and each seemed to feel at home with the other. Loveday in the course of this easy, pleasant talk, elicited from her the whole history of the events of the day of the robbery, the number and names of the guests who sat down to dinner that night, together with some other apparently trivial details.

The housekeeper made no attempt to disguise the painful position in which she and every one of the servants of the house felt themselves to be at the present moment.

"We are none of us at our ease with each other now," she said, as she poured out hot tea for Loveday, and piled up a blazing fire. "Everyone fancies that everyone else is suspecting him or her, and trying to rake up past words or deeds to bring in as evidence. The whole house seems under a cloud. And at this time of year, too; just when everything as a rule is at its merriest!" and here she gave a doleful glance to the big bunch of holly and mistletoe hanging from the ceiling.

"I suppose you are generally very merry downstairs at Christmas time?" said Loveday. "Servants' balls, theatricals, and all that sort of thing?"

"I should think we were! When I think of this time last year and the fun we all had, I can scarcely believe it is the same house. Our ball always follows my lady's ball, and we have permission to ask our friends to it, and we keep it up as late as ever we please. We begin our evening with a concert and recitations in character, then we have a supper and then we dance right on till morning; but this year!"–she broke off, giving a long, melancholy shake of her head that spoke volumes.

"I suppose," said Loveday, "some of your friends are very clever as musicians or reciters?"

"Very clever indeed. Sir George and my lady are always present during the early part of the evening, and I should like you to have seen Sir George last year laughing fit to kill himself at Harry Emmett dressed in prison dress with a bit of oakum in his hand, reciting the "Noble Convict!" Sir George said if the young man had gone on the stage, he would have been bound to make his fortune."

"Half a cup, please," said Loveday, presenting her cup. "Who was this Harry Emmett then–a sweetheart of one of the maids?"

"Oh, he would flirt with them all, but he was sweetheart to none. He was footman to Colonel James, who is a great friend of Sir George's, and Harry was constantly backwards and forwards bringing messages from his master. His father, I think, drove a cab in London, and Harry for a time did so also; then he took it into his head to be a gentleman's servant, and great satisfaction he gave as such. He was always such a bright, handsome young fellow and so full of fun, that everyone liked him. But I shall tire you with all this; and you, of course, want to talk about something so different;" and the housekeeper sighed again, as the thought of the dreadful robbery entered her brain once more.

"Not at all. I am greatly interested in you and your festivities. Is Emmett still in the neighbourhood? I should amazingly like to hear him recite myself."

"I'm sorry to say he left Colonel James about six months ago. We all missed him very much at first. He was a good, kind-hearted young man, and I remember he told me he was going away to look after his dear old grandmother, who had a sweet-stuff shop somewhere or other, but where I can't remember."

Loveday was leaning back in her chair now, with eyelids drooped so low that she literally looked out through "slits" instead of eyes.

Suddenly and abruptly she changed the conversation.

"When will it be convenient for me to see Lady Cathrow's dressing-room?" she asked.

The housekeeper looked at her watch. "Now, at once," she answered: "it's a quarter to five now and my lady sometimes goes up to her room to rest for half an hour before she dresses for dinner."

"Is Stephanie still in attendance on Lady Cathrow?" Miss Brooke asked as she followed the housekeeper up the back stairs to the bedroom floor.

"Yes, Sir George and my lady have been goodness itself to us through this trying time, and they say we are all innocent till we are proved guilty, and will have it that none of our duties are to be in any way altered."

"Stephanie is scarcely fit to perform hers, I should imagine?"

"Scarcely. She was in hysterics nearly from morning till night for the first two or three days after the detectives came down, but now she has grown sullen, eats nothing and never speaks a word to any of us except when she is obliged. This is my lady's dressing-room, walk in please."

Loveday entered a large, luxuriously furnished room, and naturally made her way straight to the chief point of attraction in it—the iron safe fitted into the wall that separated the dressing-room from the bedroom.

It was a safe of the ordinary description, fitted with a strong iron door and Chubb lock. And across this door was written with chalk in characters that seemed defiant in their size and boldness, the words: "To be let, unfurnished."

Loveday spent about five minutes in front of this safe, all her attention concentrated upon the big, bold writing.

She took from her pocket-book a narrow strip of tracing-paper and compared the writing on it, letter by letter, with that on the safe door. This done she turned to Mrs. Williams and professed herself ready to follow her to the room below.

Mrs. Williams looked surprised. Her opinion of Miss Brooke's professional capabilities suffered considerable diminution.

"The gentlemen detectives," she said, "spent over an hour in this room; they paced the floor, they measured the candles, they—"

"Mrs. Williams," interrupted Loveday, "I am quite ready to look at the room below." Her manner had changed from gossiping friendliness to that of the business woman hard at work at her profession.

Without another word, Mrs. Williams led the way to the little room which had proved itself to be the "weak point" of the house.

They entered it by the door which opened into a passage leading to the backstairs of the house. Loveday found the room exactly what it had been described to her by Mr. Dyer. It needed no second glance at the window to see the ease with which anyone could open it from the outside, and swing themselves into the room, when once the brass catch had been unfastened.

Loveday wasted no time here. In fact, much to Mrs. Williams's surprise and disappointment, she merely walked across the room, in at one door and out at the opposite one, which opened into the large inner hall of the house.

Here, however, she paused to ask a question:

"Is that chair always placed exactly in that position?" she said, pointing to an oak chair that stood immediately outside the room they had just quitted.

The housekeeper answered in the affirmative. It was a warm corner. "My lady" was particular that everyone who came to the house on messages should have a comfortable place to wait in.

"I shall be glad if you will show me to my room now," said Loveday, a little abruptly; "and will you kindly send up to me a county trade directory, if, that is, you have such a thing in the house?"

Mrs. Williams, with an air of offended dignity, led the way to the bedroom quarters once more. The worthy housekeeper felt as if her own dignity had, in some sort, been injured by the want of interest Miss Brooke had evinced in the rooms which, at the present moment, she considered the "show" rooms of the house.

"Shall I send someone to help you unpack?" she asked, a little stiffly, at the door of Loveday's room.

"No, thank you; there will not be much unpacking to do. I must leave here by the first up-train to-morrow morning."

"To-morrow morning! Why, I have told everyone you will be here at least a fortnight!"

"Ah, then you must explain that I have been suddenly summoned home by telegram. I'm sure I can trust you to make excuses for me. Do not, however, make them before supper-time. I shall like to sit down to that meal with you. I suppose I shall see Stephanie then?"

The housekeeper answered in the affirmative, and went her way, wondering over the strange manners of the lady whom, at first, she had been disposed to consider "such a nice, pleasant, conversable person!"

At supper-time, however, when the upper-servants assembled at what was, to them, the pleasantest meal of the day, a great surprise was to greet them.

Stephanie did not take her usual place at table, and a fellow-servant, sent to her room to summon her returned, saying that the room was empty, and Stephanie was nowhere to be found.

Loveday and Mrs. Williams together went to the girl's bed-room. It bore its usual appearance: no packing had been done in it, and, beyond her hat and jacket, the girl appeared to have taken nothing away with her.

On enquiry, it transpired that Stephanie had, as usual, assisted Lady Cathrow to dress for dinner; but after that not a soul in the house appeared to have seen her.

Mrs. Williams thought the matter of sufficient importance to be at once reported to her master and mistress; and Sir George, in his turn, promptly dispatched a messenger to Mr. Bates, at the "King's Head," to summon him to an immediate consultation.

Loveday dispatched a messenger in another direction—to young Mr. Holt, at his farm, giving him particulars of the girl's disappearance.

Mr. Bates had a brief interview with Sir George in his study, from which he emerged radiant. He made a point of seeing Loveday before he left the Court, sending a special request to her that she would speak to him for a minute in the outside drive.

Loveday put her hat on, and went out to him. She found him almost dancing for glee.

"Told you so! told you so! Now, didn't I, Miss Brooke?" he exclaimed. "We'll come upon her traces before morning, never fear. I'm quite prepared. I knew what was in her mind all along. I said to myself, when that girl bolts it will be after she has dressed my lady for dinner—when she has two good clear hours all to herself, and her absence from the house won't be noticed, and when, without much difficulty, she can catch a train leaving Huxwell for Wreford. Well, she'll get to Wreford safe enough; but from Wreford she'll be followed every step of the way she goes. Only yesterday I set a man on there—a keen fellow at this sort of thing—and gave him full directions; and he'll hunt her down to her hole properly. Taken nothing with her, do you say? What does that matter? She thinks she'll find all she wants where she's going—'the feathered nest' I spoke to you about this morning. Ha! ha! Well, instead of stepping into it, as she fancies she will, she'll walk straight into a detective's arms, and land her pal there into the bargain. There'll be two of them netted before another forty-eight hours are over our heads, or my name's not Jeremiah Bates."

"What are you going to do now?" asked Loveday, as the man finished his long speech.

"Now! I'm back to the "King's Head" to wait for a telegram from my colleague at Wreford. Once he's got her in front of him he'll give me instructions at what point to meet him. You see, Huxwell being such an out-of-the-way place, and only one train leaving between 7.30 and 10.15, makes us really positive that Wreford must be the girl's destination and relieves my mind from all anxiety on the matter."

"Does it?" answered Loveday gravely. "I can see another possible destination for the girl–the stream that runs through the wood we drove past this morning. Good night, Mr. Bates, it's cold out here. Of course so soon as you have any news you'll send it up to Sir George."

The household sat up late that night, but no news was received of Stephanie from any quarter. Mr. Bates had impressed upon Sir George the ill-advisability of setting up a hue and cry after the girl that might possibly reach her ears and scare her from joining the person whom he was pleased to designate as her "pal."

"We want to follow her silently, Sir George, silently as, the shadow follows the man," he had said grandiloquently, "and then we shall come upon the two, and I trust upon their booty also." Sir George in his turn had impressed Mr. Bates's wishes upon his household, and if it had not been for Loveday's message, dispatched early in the evening to young Holt, not a soul outside the house would have known of Stephanie's disappearance.

Loveday was stirring early the next morning, and the eight o'clock train for Wreford numbered her among its passengers. Before starting, she dispatched a telegram to her chief in Lynch Court. It read rather oddly, as follows:–

"Cracker fired. Am just starting for Wreford. Will wire to you from there. L. B."

Oddly though it might read, Mr. Dyer did not need to refer to his cipher book to interpret it. "Cracker fired" was the easily remembered equivalent for "clue found" in the detective phraseology of the office.

"Well, she has been quick enough about it this time!" he soliquised as he speculated in his own mind over what the purport of the next telegram might be.

Half an hour later there came to him a constable from Scotland Yard to tell him of Stephanie's disappearance and the conjectures that were rife on the matter, and he then, not unnaturally, read Loveday's telegram by the light of this information, and concluded that the clue in her hands related to the discovery of Stephanie's whereabouts as well as to that of her guilt.

A telegram received a little later on, however, was to turn this theory upside down. It was, like the former one, worded in the enigmatic language current in the Lynch Court establishment, but as it was a lengthier and more intricate message, it sent Mr. Dyer at once to his cipher book.

"Wonderful! She has cut them all out this time!" was Mr. Dyer's exclamation as he read and interpreted the final word.

In another ten minutes he had given over his office to the charge of his head clerk for the day, and was rattling along the streets in a hansom in the direction of Bishopsgate Station.

There he was lucky enough to catch a train just starting for Wreford.

"The event of the day," he muttered, as he settled himself comfortably in a corner seat, "will be the return journey when she tells me, bit by bit, how she has worked it all out."

It was not until close upon three o'clock in the afternoon that he arrived at the old-fashioned market town of Wreford. It chanced to be cattle-market day, and the station was crowded with drovers and farmers. Outside the station Loveday was waiting for him, as she had told him in her telegram that she would, in a four-wheeler.

"It's all right," she said to him as he got in; "he can't get away, even if he had an idea that we were after him. Two of the local police are waiting outside the house door with a warrant for his arrest, signed by a magistrate. I did not, however, see why the Lynch Court office should not have the credit of the thing, and so telegraphed to you to conduct the arrest."

They drove through the High Street to the outskirts of the town, where the shops became intermixed with private houses let out in offices. The cab pulled up outside one of these, and two policemen in plain clothes came forward, and touched their hats to Mr. Dyer.

"He's in there now, sir, doing his office work," said one of the men pointing to a door, just within the entrance, on which was printed in black letters, "The United Kingdom Cab-drivers' Beneficent Association." "I hear however, that this is the last time he will be found there, as a week ago he gave notice to leave."

As the man finished speaking, a man, evidently of the cab-driving fraternity, came up the steps. He stared curiously at the little group just within the entrance, and then chinking his money in his hand, passed on to the office as if to pay his subscription.

"Will you be good enough to tell Mr. Emmett in there," said Mr. Dyer, addressing the man, "that a gentleman outside wishes to speak with him."

The man nodded and passed into the office. As the door opened, it disclosed to view an old gentleman seated at a desk apparently writing receipts for money. A little in his rear at his right hand, sat a young and decidedly good-looking man, at a table on which were placed various little piles of silver and pence. The get-up of this young man was gentleman-like, and his manner was affable and pleasant as he responded, with a nod and a smile, to the cab-driver's message.

"I sha'n't be a minute," he said to his colleague at the other desk, as he rose and crossed the room towards the door.

But once outside that door it was closed firmly behind him, and he found himself in the centre of three stalwart individuals, one of whom informed him that he held in his hand a warrant for the arrest of Harry Emmett on the charge of complicity in the Craigen Court robbery, and that he had "better come along quietly, for resistance would be useless."

Emmett seemed convinced of the latter fact. He grew deadly white for a moment, then recovered himself.

"Will someone have the kindness to fetch my hat and coat," he said in a lofty manner. "I don't see why I should be made to catch my death of cold because some other people have seen fit to make asses of themselves."

His hat and coat were fetched, and he was handed into the cab between the two officials.

"Let me give you a word of warning, young man," said Mr. Dyer, closing the cab door and looking in for a moment through the window at Emmett. "I don't suppose it's a punishable offence to leave a black bag on an old maid's doorstep, but let me tell you, if it had not been for that black bag you might have got clean off with your spoil."

Emmett, the irrepressible, had his answer ready. He lifted his hat ironically to Mr. Dyer; "You might have put it more neatly, guv'nor," he said; "if I had been in your place I would have said: 'Young man, you are being justly punished for your misdeeds; you have been taking off your fellow-creatures all your life long, and now they are taking off you.'"

Mr. Dyer's duty that day did not end with the depositing of Harry Emmett in the local jail. The search through Emmett's lodgings and effects had to be made, and at this he was naturally present. About a third of the lost jewellery was found there, and from this it was consequently concluded that his accomplices in the crime had considered that he had borne a third of the risk and of the danger of it.

Letters and various memoranda discovered in the rooms, eventually led to the detection of those accomplices, and although Lady Cathrow was doomed to lose the greater part of her valuable property, she had ultimately the satisfaction of knowing that each one of the thieves received a sentence proportionate to his crime.

It was not until close upon midnight that Mr. Dyer found himself seated in the train, facing Miss Brooke, and had leisure to ask for the links in the chain of reasoning that had led her in so remarkable a manner to connect the finding of a black bag, with insignificant contents, with an extensive robbery of valuable jewellery.

Loveday explained the whole thing, easily, naturally, step by step in her usual methodical manner.

"I read," she said, "as I dare say a great many other people did, the account of the two things in the same newspaper, on the same day, and I detected, as I dare say a great many other people did not, a sense of fun in the principal actor in each incident. I notice while all people are agreed as to the variety of motives that instigate crime, very few allow sufficient margin for variety of character in the criminal. We are apt to imagine that he stalks about the world with a bundle of deadly motives under his arm, and cannot picture him at his work with a twinkle in his eye and a keen sense of fun, such as honest folk have sometimes when at work at their calling."

Here Mr. Dyer gave a little grunt; it might have been either of assent or dissent.

Loveday went on:

"Of course, the ludicrousness of the diction of the letter found in the bag would be apparent to the most casual reader; to me the high falutin sentences sounded in addition strangely familiar; I had heard or read them somewhere I felt sure, although where I could not at first remember. They rang in my ears, and it was not altogether out of idle curiosity that I went to Scotland Yard to see the bag and its contents, and to copy, with a slip of tracing paper, a line or two of the letter. When I found that the handwriting of this letter was not identical with that of the translations found in the bag, I was confirmed in my impression that the owner of the bag was not the writer of the letter; that possibly the bag and its contents had been appropriated from some railway station for some distinct purpose; and, that purpose accomplished, the appropriator no longer wished to be burthened with it, and disposed of it in the readiest fashion that suggested itself. The letter, it seemed to me, had been begun with the intention of throwing the police off the scent, but the irrepressible spirit of fun that had induced the writer to deposit his clerical adjuncts upon an old maid's doorstep had proved too strong for him here, and had carried him away, and the letter that was intended to be pathetic ended in being comic."

"Very ingenious, so far," murmured Mr. Dyer: "I've no doubt when the contents of the bag are widely made known through advertisements a claimant will come forward, and your theory be found correct."

"When I returned from Scotland Yard," Loveday continued, "I found your note, asking me to go round and see you respecting the big jewel robbery. Before I did so I thought it best to read once more the newspaper account of the case, so that I might be well up in its details. When I came to the words that the thief had written across the door of the safe, 'To be Let, Unfurnished,' they at once connected themselves in my mind with the 'dying kiss to my Marchioness Mother,' and the solemn warning against the race-course and the book-maker, of the black-bag letter-writer. Then, all in a flash, the whole thing became clear to me. Some two or three years back my professional duties necessitated my frequent attendance at certain low class penny-readings, given in the South London slums. At these penny-readings young shop-assistants, and others of their class, glad of an opportunity for exhibiting their accomplishments, declaim with great vigour; and, as a rule, select pieces which their very mixed audience might be supposed to appreciate. During my attendance at these meetings, it seemed to me that one book of selected readings was a great favourite among the reciters, and I took the trouble to buy it. Here it is."

Here Loveday took from her cloak-pocket "The Reciter's Treasury," and handed it to her companion.

"Now," she said, "if you will run your eye down the index column you will find the titles of those pieces to which I wish to draw your attention. The first is 'The Suicide's Farewell;' the second, 'The Noble Convict;' the third, 'To be Let, Unfurnished.'"

"By Jove! so it is!" ejaculated Mr. Dyer.

"In the first of these pieces, 'The Suicide's Farewell,' occur the expressions with which the black-bag letter begins—'The fatal day has arrived,' etc., the warnings against gambling, and the allusions to the 'poor lifeless body.' In the second, 'The Noble Convict,' occur the allusions to the aristocratic relations and the dying kiss to the marchioness mother. The third piece, 'To be Let, Unfurnished,' is a foolish little poem enough, although I dare say it has often raised a laugh in a not too-discriminating audience. It tells how a bachelor, calling at a house to enquire after rooms to be let unfurnished, falls in love with the daughter of the house, and offers her his heart, which, he says, is to be let unfurnished. She declines his offer, and retorts that she thinks his head must be to let unfurnished, too. With these three pieces before me, it was not difficult to see a thread of connection between the writer of the black-bag letter and the thief who wrote across the empty safe at Craigen Court. Following this thread, I unearthed the story of Harry Emmett–footman, reciter, general lover and scamp. Subsequently I compared the writing on my tracing paper with that on the safe-door, and, allowing for the difference between a bit of chalk and a steel nib, came to the conclusion that there could be but little doubt but what both were written by the same hand. Before that, however, I had obtained another, and what I consider the most important, link in my chain of evidence–how Emmett brought his clerical dress into use."

"Ah, how did you find out that now?" asked Mr. Dyer, leaning forward with his elbows on his knees.

"In the course of conversation with Mrs. Williams, whom I found to be a most communicative person, I elicited the names of the guests who had sat down to dinner on Christmas Eve. They were all people of undoubted respectability in the neighbourhood. Just before dinner was announced, she said, a young clergyman had presented himself at the front door, asking to speak with the Rector of the parish. The Rector, it seems, always dines at Craigen Court on Christmas Eve. The young clergyman's story was that he had been told by a certain clergyman, whose name he mentioned, that a curate was wanted in the parish, and he had traveled down from London to offer his services. He had been, he said, to the Rectory and had been told by the servants where the Rector was dining, and fearing to lose his chance of the curacy, had followed him to the Court. Now the Rector had been wanting a curate and had filled the vacancy only the previous week; he was a little inclined to be irate at this interruption to the evening's festivities, and told the young man that he didn't want a curate. When, however, he saw how disappointed the poor young fellow looked–I believe he shed a tear or two–his heart softened; he told him to sit down and rest in the hall before he attempted the walk back to the station, and said he would ask Sir George to send him out a glass of wine. the young man sat down in a chair immediately outside the room by which the thieves entered. Now I need not tell you who that young man was, nor suggest to your mind, I am sure, the idea that while the servant went to fetch him his wine, or, indeed, so soon as he saw the coast clear, he slipped into that little room and pulled back the catch of the window that admitted his confederates, who, no doubt, at that very moment were in hiding in the grounds. The housekeeper did not know whether this meek young curate had a black bag with him. Personally I have no doubt of the fact, nor that it contained the cap, cuffs, collar, and outer garments of Harry Emmett, which were most likely redonned before he returned to his lodgings at Wreford, where I should say he repacked the bag with its clerical contents, and wrote his serio-comic letter. This bag, I suppose, he must have deposited in the very early morning, before anyone was stirring, on the door-step of the house in the Easterbrook Road."

Mr. Dyer drew a long breath. In his heart was unmitigated admiration for his colleague's skill, which seemed to him to fall little short of inspiration. By-and-by, no doubt, he would sing her praises to the first person who came along with a hearty good will; he had not, however, the slightest intention of so singing them in her own ears–excessive praise was apt to have a bad effect on the rising practitioner.

So he contented himself with saying:

"Yes, very satisfactory. Now tell me how you hunted the fellow down to his diggings?"

"Oh, that was mere ABC work," answered Loveday. "Mrs. Williams told me he had left his place at Colonel James's about six months previously, and had told her he was going to look after his dear old grandmother, who kept a sweet stuff-shop; but where she could not remember. Having heard that Emmett's father was a cab-driver, my thoughts at once flew to the cabman's vernacular–you know something of it, no doubt–in which their provident association is designated by the phase, 'the dear old grandmother,' and the office where they make and receive their payments is styled 'the sweet stuff-shop.'"

"Ha, ha, ha! And good Mrs. Williams took it all literally, no doubt?"

"She did; and thought what a dear, kind-hearted fellow the young man was. Naturally I supposed there would be a branch of the association in the nearest market town, and a local trades' directory confirmed my supposition that there was one at Wreford. Bearing in mind where the black bag was found, it was not difficult to believe that young Emmett, possibly through his father's influence and his own prepossessing manners and appearance, had attained to some position of trust in the Wreford branch. I must confess I scarcely expected to find him as I did, on reaching the place, installed as receiver of the weekly moneys. Of course, I immediately put myself in communication with the police there, and the rest I think you know."

Mr. Dyer's enthusiasm refused to be longer restrained.

"It's capital, from first to last," he cried; "you've surpassed yourself this time!"

"The only thing that saddens me," said Loveday, "is the thought of the possible fate of that poor little Stephanie."

Loveday's anxieties on Stephanie's behalf were, however, to be put to flight before another twenty-four hours had passed. The first post on the following morning brought a letter from Mrs. Williams telling how the girl had been found before the night was over, half dead with cold and fright, on the verge of the stream running through Craigen Wood–"found too"–wrote the housekeeper, "by the very person who ought to have found her, young Holt, who was, and is so desperately in love with her. Thank goodness! at the last moment her courage failed her, and instead of throwing herself into the stream, she sank down, half-fainting, beside it. Holt took her straight home to his mother, and there, at the farm, she is now, being taken care of and petted generally by everyone."

"GRIFFITHS, of the Newcastle Constabulary, has the case in hand," said Mr. Dyer; "those Newcastle men are keen-witted, shrewd fellows, and very jealous of outside interference. They only sent to me under protest, as it were, because they wanted your sharp wits at work inside the house."

"I suppose throughout I am to work with Griffiths, not with you?" said Miss Brooke.

"Yes; when I have given you in outline the facts of the case, I simply have nothing more to do with it, and you must depend on Griffiths for any assistance of any sort that you may require."

Here, with a swing, Mr. Dyer opened his big ledger and turned rapidly over its leaves till he came to the heading "Troyte's Hill" and the date "September 6th."

"I'm all attention," said Loveday, leaning back in her chair in the attitude of a listener.

"The murdered man," resumed Mr. Dyer, "is a certain Alexander Henderson—usually known as old Sandy–lodge-keeper to Mr. Craven, of Troyte's Hill, Cumberland. The lodge consists merely of two rooms on the ground floor, a bedroom and a sitting-room; these Sandy occupied alone, having neither kith nor kin of any degree. On the morning of September 6th, some children going up to the house with milk from the farm, noticed that Sandy's bed-room window stood wide open. Curiosity prompted them to peep in; and then, to their horror, they saw old Sandy, in his night-shirt, lying dead on the floor, as if he had fallen backwards from the window. They raised an alarm; and on examination, it was found that death had ensued from a heavy blow on the temple, given either by a strong fist or some blunt instrument. The room, on being entered, presented a curious appearance. It was as if a herd of monkeys had been turned into it and allowed to work their impish will. Not an article of furniture remained in its place: the bed-clothes had been rolled into a bundle and stuffed into the chimney; the bedstead–a small iron one–lay on its side; the one chair in the room stood on the top of the table; fender and fire-irons lay across the washstand, whose basin was to be found in a farther corner, holding bolster and pillow. The clock stood on its head in the middle of the mantelpiece; and the small vases and ornaments, which flanked it on either side, were walking, as it were, in a straight line towards the door. The old man's clothes had been rolled into a ball and thrown on the top of a high cupboard in which he kept his savings and whatever valuables he had. This cupboard, however, had not been meddled with, and its contents remained intact, so it was evident that robbery was not the motive for the crime. At the inquest, subsequently held, a verdict of 'willful murder' against some person or persons unknown was returned. The local police are diligently investigating the affair, but, as yet, no arrests have been made. The opinion that at present prevails in the neighbourhood is that the crime has been perpetrated by some lunatic, escaped or otherwise and enquiries are being made at the local asylums as to missing or lately released inmates. Griffiths, however, tells me that his suspicions set in another direction."

"Did anything of importance transpire at the inquest?"

"Nothing specially important. Mr. Craven broke down in giving his evidence when he alluded to the confidential relations that had always subsisted between Sandy and himself, and spoke of the last time that he had seen him alive. The evidence of the butler, and one or two of the female servants, seems clear enough, and they let fall something of a hint that Sandy was not altogether a favourite among them, on account of the overbearing manner in which he used his influence with his master. Young Mr. Craven, a youth of about nineteen, home from Oxford for the long vacation, was not present at the inquest; a doctor's certificate was put in stating that he was suffering from typhoid fever, and could not leave his bed without risk to his life. Now this young man is a thoroughly bad sort, and as much a gentleman-blackleg as it is possible for such a young fellow to be. It seems to Griffiths that there is something suspicious about this illness of his. He came back from Oxford on the verge of delirium tremens, pulled round from that, and then suddenly, on the day after the murder, Mrs. Craven rings the bell, announces that he has developed typhoid fever and orders a doctor to be sent for."

"What sort of man is Mr. Craven senior?"

"He seems to be a quiet old fellow, a scholar and learned philologist. Neither his neighbours nor his family see much of him; he almost lives in his study, writing a treatise, in seven or eight volumes, on comparative philology. He is not a rich man. Troyte's Hill, though it carries position in the county, is not a paying property, and Mr. Craven is unable to keep it up properly. I am told he has had to cut down expenses in all directions in order to send his son to college, and his daughter from first to last has been entirely educated by her mother. Mr. Craven was originally intended for the church, but for some reason or other, when his college career came to an end, he did not present himself for ordination—went out to Natal instead, where he obtained some civil appointment and where he remained for about fifteen years. Henderson was his servant during the latter portion of his Oxford career, and must have been greatly respected by him, for although the remuneration derived from his appointment at Natal was small, he paid Sandy a regular yearly allowance out of it. When, about ten years ago, he succeeded to Troyte's Hill, on the death of his elder brother, and returned home with his family, Sandy was immediately installed as lodge-keeper, and at so high a rate of pay that the butler's wages were cut down to meet it."

"Ah, that wouldn't improve the butler's feelings towards him," ejaculated Loveday.

Mr. Dyer went on: "But, in spite of his high wages, he doesn't appear to have troubled much about his duties as lodge-keeper, for they were performed, as a rule, by the gardener's boy, while he took his meals and passed his time at the house, and, speaking generally, put his finger into every pie. You know the old adage respecting the servant of twenty-one years' standing: 'Seven years my servant, seven years my equal, seven years my master.' Well, it appears to have held good in the case of Mr. Craven and Sandy. The old gentleman, absorbed in his philological studies, evidently let the reins slip through his fingers, and Sandy seems to have taken easy possession of them. The servants frequently had to go to him for orders, and he carried things, as a rule, with a high hand."

"Did Mrs. Craven never have a word to say on the matter?"

"I've not heard much about her. She seems to be a quiet sort of person. She is a Scotch missionary's daughter; perhaps she spends her time working for the Cape mission and that sort of thing."

"And young Mr. Craven: did he knock under to Sandy's rule?"

"Ah, now you're hitting the bull's eye and we come to Griffiths' theory. The young man and Sandy appear to have been at loggerheads ever since the Cravens took possession of Troyte's Hill. As a schoolboy Master Harry defied Sandy and threatened him with his hunting-crop; and subsequently, as a young man, has used strenuous endeavours to put the old servant in his place. On the day before the murder, Griffiths says, there was a terrible scene between the two, in which the young gentleman, in the presence of several witnesses, made use of strong language and threatened the old man's life. Now, Miss Brooke, I have told you all the circumstances of the case so far as I know them. For fuller particulars I must refer you to Griffiths. He, no doubt, will meet you at Grenfell—the nearest station to Troyte's Hill, and tell you in what capacity he has procured for you an entrance into the house. By-the-way, he has wired to me this morning that he hopes you will be able to save the Scotch express to-night."

Loveday expressed her readiness to comply with Mr. Griffiths' wishes.

"I shall be glad," said Mr. Dyer, as he shook hands with her at the office door, "to see you immediately on your return—that, however, I suppose, will not be yet awhile. This promises, I fancy, to be a longish affair?" This was said interrogatively.

"I haven't the least idea on the matter," answered Loveday. "I start on my work without theory of any sort—in fact, I may say, with my mind a perfect blank."

And anyone who had caught a glimpse of her blank, expressionless features, as she said this, would have taken her at her word.

Grenfell, the nearest post-town to Troyte's Hill, is a fairly busy, populous little town—looking south towards the black country, and northwards to low, barren hills. Pre-eminent among these stands Troyte's Hill, famed in the old days as a border keep, and possibly at a still earlier date as a Druid stronghold.

At a small inn at Grenfell, dignified by the title of "The Station Hotel," Mr. Griffiths, of the Newcastle constabulary, met Loveday and still further initiated her into the mysteries of the Troyte's Hill murder.

"A little of the first excitement has subsided," he said, after preliminary greetings had been exchanged; "but still the wildest rumours are flying about and repeated as solemnly as if they were Gospel truths. My chief here and my colleagues generally adhere to their first conviction, that the criminal is some suddenly crazed tramp or else an escaped lunatic, and they are confident that sooner or later we shall come upon his traces. Their theory is that Sandy, hearing some strange noise at the Park Gates, put his head out of the window to ascertain the cause and immediately had his death blow dealt him; then they suppose that the lunatic scrambled into the room through the window and exhausted his frenzy by turning things generally upside down. They refuse altogether to share my suspicions respecting young Mr. Craven."

Mr. Griffiths was a tall, thin-featured man, with iron-grey hair, but so close to his head that it refused to do anything but stand on end. This gave a somewhat comic expression to the upper portion of his face and clashed oddly with the melancholy look that his mouth habitually wore.

"I have made all smooth for you at Troyte's Hill," he presently went on. "Mr. Craven is not wealthy enough to allow himself the luxury of a family lawyer, so he occasionally employs the services of Messrs. Wells and Sugden, lawyers in this place, and who, as it happens, have, off and on, done a good deal of business for me. It was through them I heard that Mr. Craven was anxious to secure the assistance of an amanuensis. I immediately offered your services, stating that you were a friend of mine, a lady of impoverished means, who would gladly undertake the duties for the munificent sum of a guinea a month, with board and lodging. The old gentleman at once jumped at the offer, and is anxious for you to be at Troyte's Hill at once."

Loveday expressed her satisfaction with the programme that Mr. Griffiths had sketched for her, then she had a few questions to ask.

"Tell me," she said, "what led you, in the first instance, to suspect young Mr. Craven of the crime?"

"The footing on which he and Sandy stood towards each other, and the terrible scene that occurred between them only the day before the murder," answered Griffiths, promptly. "Nothing of this, however, was elicited at the inquest, where a very fair face was put on Sandy's relations with the whole of the Craven family. I have subsequently unearthed a good deal respecting the private life of Mr. Harry Craven, and, among other things, I have found out that on the night of the murder he left the house shortly after ten o'clock, and no one, so far as I have been able to ascertain, knows at what hour he returned. Now I must draw your attention, Miss Brooke, to the fact that at the inquest the medical evidence went to prove that the murder had been committed between ten and eleven at night."

"Do you surmise, then, that the murder was a planned thing on the part of this young man?"

"I do. I believe that he wandered about the grounds until Sandy shut himself in for the night, then aroused him by some outside noise, and, when the old man looked out to ascertain the cause, dealt him a blow with a bludgeon or loaded stick, that caused his death."

"A cold-blooded crime that, for a boy of nineteen?"

"Yes. He's a good-looking, gentlemanly youngster, too, with manners as mild as milk, but from all accounts is as full of wickedness as an egg is full of meat. Now, to come to another point—if, in connection with these ugly facts, you take into consideration the suddenness of his illness, I think you'll admit that it bears a suspicious appearance and might reasonably give rise to the surmise that it was a plant on his part, in order to get out of the inquest."

"Who is the doctor attending him?"

"A man called Waters; not much of a practitioner, from all accounts, and no doubt he feels himself highly honoured in being summoned to Troyte's Hill. The Cravens, it seems, have no family doctor. Mrs. Craven, with her missionary experience, is half a doctor herself, and never calls in one except in a serious emergency."

"The certificate was in order, I suppose?"

"Undoubtedly. And, as if to give colour to the gravity of the case, Mrs. Craven sent a message down to the servants, that if any of them were afraid of the infection they could at once go to their homes. Several of the maids, I believe, took advantage of her permission, and packed their boxes. Miss Craven, who is a delicate girl, was sent away with her maid to stay with friends at Newcastle, and Mrs. Craven isolated herself with her patient in one of the disused wings of the house."

"Has anyone ascertained whether Miss Craven arrived at her destination at Newcastle?"

Griffiths drew his brows together in thought.

"I did not see any necessity for such a thing," he answered. "I don't quite follow you. What do you mean to imply?"

"Oh, nothing. I don't suppose it matters much: it might have been interesting as a side-issue." She broke off for a moment, then added:

"Now tell me a little about the butler, the man whose wages were cut down to increase Sandy's pay."

"Old John Hales? He's a thoroughly worthy, respectable man; he was butler for five or six years to Mr. Craven's brother, when he was master of Troyte's Hill, and then took duty under this Mr. Craven. There's no ground for suspicion in that quarter. Hales's exclamation when he heard of the murder is quite enough to stamp him as an innocent man: 'Serve the old idiot right,' he cried: 'I couldn't pump up a tear for him if I tried for a month of Sundays!' Now I take it, Miss Brooke, a guilty man wouldn't dare make such a speech as that!"

"You think not?"

Griffiths stared at her. "I'm a little disappointed in her," he thought. "I'm afraid her powers have been slightly exaggerated if she can't see such a straight-forward thing as that."

Aloud he said, a little sharply, "Well, I don't stand alone in my thinking. No one yet has breathed a word against Hales, and if they did, I've no doubt he could prove an alibi without any trouble, for he lives in the house, and everyone has a good word for him."

"I suppose Sandy's lodge has been put into order by this time?"

"Yes; after the inquest, and when all possible evidence had been taken, everything was put straight."

"At the inquest it was stated that no marks of footsteps could be traced in any direction?"

"The long drought we've had would render such a thing impossible, let alone the fact that Sandy's lodge stands right on the graveled drive, without flower-beds or grass borders of any sort around it. But look here, Miss Brooke, don't you be wasting your time over the lodge and its surroundings. Every iota of fact on that matter has been gone through over and over again by me and my chief. What we want you to do is to go straight into the house and concentrate attention on Master Harry's sick-room, and find out what's going on there. What he did outside the house on the night of the 6th, I've no doubt I shall be able to find out for myself. Now, Miss Brooke, you've asked me no end of questions, to which I have replied as fully as it was in my power to do; will you be good enough to answer one question that I wish to put, as straightforwardly as I have answered yours? You have had fullest particulars given you of the condition of Sandy's room when the police entered it on the morning after the murder. No doubt, at the present moment, you can see it all in your mind's eye—the bedstead on its side, the clock on its head, the bed-clothes half-way up the chimney, the little vases and ornaments walking in a straight line towards the door?"

Loveday bowed her head.

"Very well, Now will you be good enough to tell me what this scene of confusion recalls to your mind before anything else?"

"The room of an unpopular Oxford freshman after a raid upon it by undergrads," answered Loveday promptly.

Mr. Griffiths rubbed his hands.

"Quite so!" he ejaculated. "I see, after all, we are one at heart in this matter, in spite of a little surface disagreement of ideas. Depend upon it, by-and-bye, like the engineers tunneling from different quarters under the Alps, we shall meet at the same point and shake hands. By-the-way, I have arranged for daily communication between us through the postboy who takes the letters to Troyte's Hill. He is trustworthy, and any letter you give him for me will find its way into my hands within the hour."

It was about three o'clock in the afternoon when Loveday drove in through the park gates of Troyte's Hill, past the lodge where old Sandy had met with his death. It was a pretty little cottage, covered with Virginia creeper and wild honeysuckle, and showing no outward sign of the tragedy that had been enacted within.

The park and pleasure-grounds of Troyte's Hill were extensive, and the house itself was a somewhat imposing red brick structure, built, possibly, at the time when Dutch William's taste had grown popular in the country. Its frontage presented a somewhat forlorn appearance, its centre windows—a square of eight—alone seeming to show signs of occupation. With the exception of two windows at the extreme end of the bedroom floor of the north wing, where, possibly, the invalid and his mother were located, and two windows at the extreme end of the ground floor of the south wing, which Loveday ascertained subsequently were those of Mr. Craven's study, not a single window in either wing owned blind or curtain. The wings were extensive, and it was easy to understand that at the extreme end of the one the fever patient would be isolated from the rest of the household, and that at the extreme end of the other Mr. Craven could secure the quiet and freedom from interruption which, no doubt, were essential to the due prosecution of his philological studies.

Alike on the house and ill-kept grounds were present the stamp of the smallness of the income of the master and owner of the place. The terrace, which ran the length of the house in front, and on to which every window on the ground floor opened, was miserably out of repair: not a lintel or door-post, window-ledge or balcony but what seemed to cry aloud for the touch of the painter. "Pity me! I have seen better days," Loveday could fancy written as a legend across the red-brick porch that gave entrance to the old house.

The butler, John Hales, admitted Loveday, shouldered her portmanteau and told her he would show her to her room. He was a tall, powerfully-built man, with a ruddy face and dogged expression of countenance. It was easy to understand that, off and on, there must have been many a sharp encounter between him and old Sandy. He treated Loveday in an easy, familiar fashion, evidently considering that an amanuensis took much the same rank as a nursery governess—that is to say, a little below a lady's maid and a little above a house-maid.

"We're short of hands, just now," he said, in broad Cumberland dialect, as he led the way up the wide stair case. "Some of the lasses downstairs took fright at the fever and went home. Cook and I are single-handed, for Moggie, the only maid left, has been told off to wait on Madam and Master Harry. I hope you're not afeared of fever?"

Loveday explained that she was not, and asked if the room at the extreme end of the north wing was the one assigned to "Madam and Master Harry."

"Yes," said the man; "it's convenient for sick nursing; there's a flight of stairs runs straight down from it to the kitchen quarters. We put all Madam wants at the foot of those stairs and Moggie herself never enters the sick-room. I take it you'll not be seeing Madam for many a day, yet awhile."

"When shall I see Mr. Craven? At dinner to-night?"

"That's what naebody could say," answered Hales. "He may not come out of his study till past midnight; sometimes he sits there till two or three in the morning. Shouldn't advise you to wait till he wants his dinner—better have a cup of tea and a chop sent up to you. Madam never waits for him at any meal."

As he finished speaking he deposited the portmanteau outside one of the many doors opening into the gallery.

"This is Miss Craven's room," he went on; "cook and me thought you'd better have it, as it would want less getting ready than the other rooms, and work is work when there are so few hands to do it. Oh, my stars! I do declare there is cook putting it straight for you now." The last sentence was added as the opened door laid bare to view, the cook, with a duster in her hand, polishing a mirror; the bed had been made, it is true, but otherwise the room must have been much as Miss Craven left it, after a hurried packing up.

To the surprise of the two servants Loveday took the matter very lightly.

"I have a special talent for arranging rooms and would prefer getting this one straight for myself," she said. "Now, if you will go and get ready that chop and cup of tea we were talking about just now, I shall think it much kinder than if you stayed here doing what I can so easily do for myself."

When, however, the cook and butler had departed in company, Loveday showed no disposition to exercise the "special talent" of which she had boasted.

She first carefully turned the key in the lock and then proceeded to make a thorough and minute investigation of every corner of the room. Not an article of furniture, not an ornament or toilet accessory, but what was lifted from its place and carefully scrutinized. Even the ashes in the grate, the debris of the last fire made there, were raked over and well looked through.

This careful investigation of Miss Craven's late surroundings occupied in all about three quarters of an hour, and Loveday, with her hat in her hand, descended the stairs to see Hales crossing the hall to the dining-room with the promised cup of tea and chop.

In silence and solitude she partook of the simple repast in a dining-hall that could with ease have banqueted a hundred and fifty guests.

"Now for the grounds before it gets dark," she said to herself, as she noted that already the outside shadows were beginning to slant.

The dining-hall was at the back of the house; and here, as in the front, the windows, reaching to the ground, presented easy means of egress. The flower-garden was on this side of the house and sloped downhill to a pretty stretch of well-wooded country.

Loveday did not linger here even to admire, but passed at once round the south corner of the house to the windows which she had ascertained, by a careless question to the butler, were those of Mr. Craven's study.

Very cautiously she drew near them, for the blinds were up, the curtains drawn back. A side glance, however, relieved her apprehensions, for it showed her the occupant of the room, seated in an easy-chair, with his back to the windows. From the length of his outstretched limbs he was evidently a tall man. His hair was silvery and curly, the lower part of his face was hidden from her view by the chair, but she could see one hand was pressed tightly across his eyes and brows. The whole attitude was that of a man absorbed in deep thought. The room was comfortably furnished, but presented an appearance of disorder from the books and manuscripts scattered in all directions. A whole pile of torn fragments of foolscap sheets, overflowing from a waste-paper basket beside the writing-table, seemed to proclaim the fact that the scholar had of late grown weary of, or else dissatisfied with his work, and had condemned it freely.

Although Loveday stood looking in at this window for over five minutes, not the faintest sign of life did that tall, reclining figure give, and it would have been as easy to believe him locked in sleep as in thought.

From here she turned her steps in the direction of Sandy's lodge. As Griffiths had said, it was graveled up to its doorstep. The blinds were closely drawn, and it presented the ordinary appearance of a disused cottage.

A narrow path beneath over-arching boughs of cherry-laurel and arbutus, immediately facing the lodge, caught her eye, and down this she at once turned her footsteps.

This path led, with many a wind and turn, through a belt of shrubbery that skirted the frontage of Mr. Craven's grounds, and eventually, after much zig-zagging, ended in close proximity to the stables. As Loveday entered it, she seemed literally to leave daylight behind her.

"I feel as if I were following the course of a circuitous mind," she said to herself as the shadows closed around her. "I could not fancy Sir Isaac Newton or Bacon planning or delighting in such a wind-about-alley as this!"

The path showed greyly in front of her out of the dimness. On and on she followed it; here and there the roots of the old laurels, struggling out of the ground, threatened to trip her up. Her eyes, however, had now grown accustomed to the half-gloom, and not a detail of her surroundings escaped her as she went along.

A bird flew from out the thicket on her right hand with a startled cry. A dainty little frog leaped out of her way into the shriveled leaves lying below the laurels. Following the movements of this frog, her eye was caught by something black and solid among those leaves. What was it? A bundle—a shiny black coat? Loveday knelt down, and using her hands to assist her eyes, found that they came into contact with the dead, stiffened body of a beautiful black retriever. She parted, as well as she was able, the lower boughs of the evergreens, and minutely examined the poor animal. Its eyes were still open, though glazed and bleared, and its death had, undoubtedly, been caused by the blow of some blunt, heavy instrument, for on one side its skull was almost battered in.

"Exactly the death that was dealt to Sandy," she thought, as she groped hither and thither beneath the trees in hopes of lighting upon the weapon of destruction.

She searched until increasing darkness warned her that search was useless. Then, still following the zig-zagging path, she made her way out by the stables and thence back to the house.

She went to bed that night without having spoken to a soul beyond the cook and butler. The next morning, however, Mr. Craven introduced himself to her across the breakfast-table. He was a man of really handsome personal appearance, with a fine carriage of the head and shoulders, and eyes that had a forlorn, appealing look in them. He entered the room with an air of great energy, apologized to Loveday for the absence of his wife, and for his own remissness in not being in the way to receive her on the previous day. Then he bade her make herself at home at the breakfast-table, and expressed his delight in having found a coadjutor in his work.

"I hope you understand what a great–a stupendous work it is?" he added, as he sank into a chair. "It is a work that will leave its impress upon thought in all the ages to come. Only a man who has studied comparative philology as I have for the past thirty years, could gauge the magnitude of the task I have set myself."

With the last remark, his energy seemed spent, and he sank back in his chair, covering his eyes with his hand in precisely the same attitude as that in which Loveday had seen him over-night, and utterly oblivious of the fact that breakfast was before him and a stranger-guest seated at table. The butler entered with another dish. "Better go on with your breakfast," he whispered to Loveday, "he may sit like that for another hour."

He placed his dish in front of his master.

"Captain hasn't come back yet, sir," he said, making an effort to arouse him from his reverie.

"Eh, what?" said Mr. Craven, for a moment lifting his hand from his eyes.

"Captain, sir–the black retriever," repeated the man.

The pathetic look in Mr. Craven's eyes deepened.

"Ah, poor Captain!" he murmured; "the best dog I ever had."

Then he again sank back in his chair, putting his hand to his forehead.

The butler made one more effort to arouse him.

"Madam sent you down a newspaper, sir, that she thought you would like to see," he shouted almost into his master's ear, and at the same time laid the morning's paper on the table beside his plate.

"Confound you! leave it there," said Mr. Craven irritably. "Fools! dolts that you all are! With your trivialities and interruptions you are sending me out of the world with my work undone!"

And again he sank back in his chair, closed his eyes and became lost to his surroundings.

Loveday went on with her breakfast. She changed her place at table to one on Mr. Craven's right hand, so that the newspaper sent down for his perusal lay between his plate and hers. It was folded into an oblong shape, as if it were wished to direct attention to a certain portion of a certain column.

A clock in a corner of the room struck the hour with a loud, resonant stroke. Mr. Craven gave a start and rubbed his eyes.

"Eh, what's this?" he said. "What meal are we at?" He looked around with a bewildered air. "Eh!–who are you?" he went on, staring hard at Loveday. "What are you doing here? Where's Nina?–Where's Harry?"

Loveday began to explain, and gradually recollection seemed to come back to him.

"Ah, yes, yes," he said. "I remember; you've come to assist me with my great work. You promised, you know, to help me out of the hole I've got into. Very enthusiastic, I remember they said you were, on certain abstruse points in comparative philology. Now, Miss–Miss–I've forgotten your name–tell me a little of what you know about the elemental sounds of speech that are common to all languages. Now, to how many would you reduce those elemental sounds–to six, eight, nine? No, we won't discuss the matter here, the cups and saucers distract me. Come into my den at the other end of the house; we'll have perfect quiet there."

And utterly ignoring the fact that he had not as yet broken his fast, he rose from the table, seized Loveday by the wrist, and led her out of the room and down the long corridor that led through the south wing to his study.

But seated in that study his energy once more speedily exhausted itself.

He placed Loveday in a comfortable chair at his writing-table, consulted her taste as to pens, and spread a sheet of foolscap before her. Then he settled himself in his easy-chair, with his back to the light, as if he were about to dictate folios to her.

In a loud, distinct voice he repeated the title of his learned work, then its sub-division, then the number and heading of the chapter that was at present engaging his attention. Then he put his hand to his head. "It's the elemental sounds that are my stumbling-block," he said. "Now, how on earth is it possible to get a notion of a sound of agony that is not in part a sound of terror? or a sound of surprise that is not in part a sound of either joy or sorrow?"

With this his energies were spent, and although Loveday remained seated in that study from early morning till daylight began to fade, she had not ten sentences to show for her day's work as amanuensis.

Loveday in all spent only two clear days at Troyte's Hill.

On the evening of the first of those days Detective Griffiths received, through the trustworthy post-boy, the following brief note from her:

"I have found out that Hales owed Sandy close upon a hundred pounds, which he had borrowed at various times. I don't know whether you will think this fact of any importance.–L. B."

Mr. Griffiths repeated the last sentence blankly. "If Harry Craven were put upon his defence, his counsel, I take it, would consider the fact of first importance," he muttered. And for the remainder of that day Mr. Griffiths went about his work in a perturbed state of mind, doubtful whether to hold or to let go his theory concerning Harry Craven's guilt.

The next morning there came another brief note from Loveday which ran thus:

"As a matter of collateral interest, find out if a person, calling himself Harold Cousins, sailed two days ago from London Docks for Natal in the Bonnie Dundee?"

To this missive Loveday received, in reply, the following somewhat lengthy dispatch:

"I do not quite see the drift of your last note, but have wired to our agents in London to carry out its suggestion. On my part, I have important news to communicate. I have found out what Harry Craven's business out of doors was on the night of the murder, and at my instance a warrant has been issued for his arrest. This warrant it will be my duty to serve on him in the course of to-day. Things are beginning to look very black against him, and I am convinced his illness is all a sham. I have seen Waters, the man who is supposed to be attending him, and have driven him into a corner and made him admit that he has only seen young Craven once–on the first day of his illness–and that he gave his certificate entirely on the strength of what Mrs. Craven told him of her son's condition. On the occasion of this, his first and only visit, the lady, it seems, also told him that it would not be necessary for him to continue his attendance, as she quite felt herself competent to treat the case, having had so much experience in fever cases among the blacks at Natal.

"As I left Waters's house, after eliciting this important information, I was accosted by a man who keeps a low-class inn in the place, McQueen by name. He said that he wished to speak to me on a matter of importance. To make a long story short, this McQueen stated that on the night of the sixth, shortly after eleven o'clock, Harry Craven came to his house, bringing with him a valuable piece of plate–a handsome epergne–and requested him to lend him a hundred pounds on it, as he hadn't a penny in his pocket. McQueen complied with his request to the extent of ten sovereigns, and now, in a fit of nervous terror, comes to me to confess himself a receiver of stolen goods and play the honest man! He says he noticed that the young gentleman was very much agitated as he made the request, and he also begged him to mention his visit to no one. Now, I am curious to learn how Master Harry will get over the fact that he passed the lodge at the hour at which the murder was most probably committed; or how he will get out of the dilemma of having repassed the lodge on his way back to the house, and not noticed the wide-open window with the full moon shining down on it?

"Another word! Keep out of the way when I arrive at the house, somewhere between two and three in the afternoon, to serve the warrant. I do not wish your professional capacity to get wind, for you will most likely yet be of some use to us in the house.

"S.G."

Loveday read this note, seated at Mr. Craven's writing-table, with the old gentleman himself reclining motionless beside her in his easy-chair. A little smile played about the corners of her mouth as she read over again the words–"for you will most likely yet be of some use to us in the house."

Loveday's second day in Mr. Craven's study promised to be as unfruitful as the first. For fully an hour after she had received Griffiths' note, she sat at the writing-table with her pen in her hand, ready to transcribe Mr. Craven's inspirations. Beyond, however, the phrase, muttered with closed eyes–"It's all here, in my brain, but I can't put it into words"–not a half-syllable escaped his lips.

At the end of that hour the sound of footsteps on the outside gravel made her turn her head towards the window. It was Griffiths approaching with two constables. She heard the hall door opened to admit them, but, beyond that, not a sound reached her ear, and she realized how fully she was cut off from communication with the rest of the household at the farther end of this unoccupied wing.

Mr. Craven, still reclining in his semi-trance, evidently had not the faintest suspicion that so important an event as the arrest of his only son on a charge of murder was about to be enacted in the house.

Meantime, Griffiths and his constables had mounted the stairs leading to the north wing, and were being guided through the corridors to the sick-room by the flying figure of Moggie, the maid.

"Hoot, mistress!" cried the girl, "here are three men coming up the stairs–policemen, every one of them–will ye come and ask them what they be wanting?"

Outside the door of the sick-room stood Mrs. Craven–a tall, sharp-featured woman with sandy hair going rapidly grey.

"What is the meaning of this? What is your business here?" she said haughtily, addressing Griffiths, who headed the party.

Griffiths respectfully explained what his business was, and requested her to stand on one side that he might enter her son's room.

"This is my daughter's room; satisfy yourself of the fact," said the lady, throwing back the door as she spoke.

And Griffiths and his confrères entered, to find pretty Miss Craven, looking very white and scared, seated beside a fire in a long flowing robe de chambre.

Griffiths departed in haste and confusion, without the chance of a professional talk with Loveday. That afternoon saw him telegraphing wildly in all directions, and dispatching messengers in all quarters. Finally he spent over an hour drawing up an elaborate report to his chief at Newcastle, assuring him of the identity of one, Harold Cousins, who had sailed in the Bonnie Dundee for Natal, with Harry Craven, of Troyte's Hill, and advising that the police authorities in that far-away district should be immediately communicated with.

The ink had not dried on the pen with which this report was written before a note, in Loveday's writing, was put into his hand.

Loveday evidently had had some difficulty in finding a messenger for this note, for it was brought by a gardener's boy, who informed Griffiths that the lady had said he would receive a gold sovereign if he delivered the letter all right.

Griffiths paid the boy and dismissed him, and then proceeded to read Loveday's communication.

It was written hurriedly in pencil, and ran as follows:

"Things are getting critical here. Directly you receive this, come up to the house with two of your men, and post yourselves anywhere in the grounds where you can see and not be seen. There will be no difficulty in this, for it will be dark by the time you are able to get there. I am not sure whether I shall want your aid to-night, but you had better keep in the grounds until morning, in case of need; and above all, never once lose sight of the study windows." (This was underscored.) "If I put a lamp with a green shade in one of those windows, do not lose a moment in entering by that window, which I will contrive to keep unlocked."

Detective Griffiths rubbed his forehead–rubbed his eyes, as he finished reading this.

"Well, I daresay it's all right," he said, "but I'm bothered, that's all, and for the life of me I can't see one step of the way she is going."

He looked at his watch: the hands pointed to a quarter past six. The short September day was drawing rapidly to a close. A good five miles lay between him and Troyte's Hill–there was evidently not a moment to lose.

At the very moment that Griffiths, with his two constables, were once more starting along the Grenfell High Road behind the best horse they could procure, Mr. Craven was rousing himself from his long slumber, and beginning to look around him. That slumber, however, though long, had not been a peaceful one, and it was sundry of the old gentleman's muttered exclamations, as he had started uneasily in his sleep, that had caused Loveday to open, and then to creep out of the room to dispatch, her hurried note.

What effect the occurrence of the morning had had upon the household generally, Loveday, in her isolated corner of the house, had no means of ascertaining. She only noted that when Hales brought in her tea, as he did precisely at five o'clock, he wore a particularly ill-tempered expression of countenance, and she heard him mutter, as he set down the tea-tray with a clatter, something about being a respectable man, and not used to such "goings on."

It was not until nearly an hour and a half after this that Mr. Craven had awakened with a sudden start, and, looking wildly around him, had questioned Loveday who had entered the room.

Loveday explained that the butler had brought in lunch at one, and tea at five, but that since then no one had come in.

"Now that's false," said Mr. Craven, in a sharp, unnatural sort of voice; "I saw him sneaking round the room, the whining, canting hypocrite, and you must have seen him, too! Didn't you hear him say, in his squeaky old voice: 'Master, I knows your secret—'" He broke off abruptly, looking wildly round. "Eh, what's this?" he cried. "No, no, I'm all wrong—Sandy is dead and buried—they held an inquest on him, and we all praised him up as if he were a saint."

"He must have been a bad man, that old Sandy," said Loveday sympathetically.

"You're right! you're right!" cried Mr. Craven, springing up excitedly from his chair and seizing her by the hand. "If ever a man deserved his death, he did. For thirty years he held that rod over my head, and then—ah where was I?"

He put his hand to his head and again sank, as if exhausted, into his chair.

"I suppose it was some early indiscretion of yours at college that he knew of?" said Loveday, eager to get at as much of the truth as possible while the mood for confidence held sway in the feeble brain.

"That was it! I was fool enough to marry a disreputable girl—a barmaid in the town—and Sandy was present at the wedding, and then—" Here his eyes closed again and his mutterings became incoherent.

For ten minutes he lay back in his chair, muttering thus; "A yelp—a groan," were the only words Loveday could distinguish among those mutterings, then suddenly, slowly and distinctly, he said, as if answering some plainly-put question: "A good blow with the hammer and the thing was done."

"I should like amazingly to see that hammer," said Loveday; "do you keep it anywhere at hand?"

His eyes opened with a wild, cunning look in them.

"Who's talking about a hammer? I did not say I had one. If anyone says I did it with a hammer, they're telling a lie."

"Oh, you've spoken to me about the hammer two or three times," said Loveday calmly; "the one that killed your dog, Captain, and I should like to see it, that's all."

The look of cunning died out of the old man's eye—"Ah, poor Captain! splendid dog that! Well, now, where were we? Where did we leave off? Ah, I remember, it was the elemental sounds of speech that bothered me so that night. Were you here then? Ah, no! I remember. I had been trying all day to assimilate a dog's yelp of pain to a human groan, and I couldn't do it. The idea haunted me—followed me about wherever I went. If they were both elemental sounds, they must have something in common, but the link between them I could not find; then it occurred to me, would a well-bred, well-trained dog like my Captain in the stables, there, at the moment of death give an unmitigated currish yelp; would there not be something of a human note in his death-cry? The thing was worth putting to the test. If I could hand down in my treatise a fragment of fact on the matter, it would be worth a dozen dogs' lives. so I went out into the moonlight—ah, but you know all about it—now, don't you?"

"Yes. Poor Captain! did he yelp or groan?"

"Why, he gave one loud, long, hideous yelp, just as if he had been a common cur. I might just as well have let him alone; it only set that other brute opening his window and spying out on me, and saying in his cracked old voice: 'Master, what are you doing out here at this time of night?'"

Again he sank back in his chair, muttering incoherently with half-closed eyes.

Loveday let him alone for a minute or so; then she had another question to ask.

"And that other brute—did he yelp or groan when you dealt him your blow?"

"What, old Sandy—the brute? he fell back—Ah, I remember, you said you would like to see the hammer that stopped his babbling old tongue—now didn't you?"

He rose a little unsteadily from his chair, and seemed to drag his long limbs with an effort across the room to a cabinet at the farther end. Opening a drawer in this cabinet, he produced, from amidst some specimens of strata and fossils, a large-sized geological hammer.

He brandished it for a moment over his head, then paused with his finger on his lip.

"Hush!" he said, "we shall have the fools creeping in to peep at us if we don't take care." And to Loveday's horror he suddenly made for the door, turned the key in the lock, withdrew it and put it into his pocket.

She looked at the clock; the hands pointed to half-past seven. Had Griffiths received her note at the proper time, and were the men now in the grounds? She could only pray that they were.

"The light is too strong for my eyes," she said, and rising from her chair, she lifted the green-shaded lamp and placed it on a table that stood at the window.

"No, no, that won't do," said Mr. Craven; "that would show everyone outside what we're doing in here." He crossed to the window as he spoke and removed the lamp thence to the mantelpiece.

Loveday could only hope that in the few seconds it had remained in the window it had caught the eye of the outside watchers.

The old man beckoned to Loveday to come near and examine his deadly weapon. "Give it a good swing round," he said, suiting the action to the word, "and down it comes with a splendid crash." He brought the hammer round within an inch of Loveday's forehead.

She started back.

"Ha, ha," he laughed harshly and unnaturally, with the light of madness dancing in his eyes now; "did I frighten you? I wonder what sort of sound you would make if I were to give you a little tap just there." Here he lightly touched her forehead with the hammer. "Elemental, of course, it would be, and—"

Loveday steadied her nerves with difficulty. Locked in with this lunatic, her only chance lay in gaining time for the detectives to reach the house and enter through the window.

"Wait a minute," she said, striving to divert his attention; "you have not yet told me what sort of an elemental sound old Sandy made when he fell. If you'll give me pen and ink, I'll write down a full account of it all, and you can incorporate it afterwards in your treatise."

For a moment a look of real pleasure flitted across the old man's face, then it faded. "The brute fell back dead without a sound," he answered; "it was all for nothing, that night's work; yet not altogether for nothing. No, I don't mind owning I would do it all over again to get the wild thrill of joy at my heart that I had when I looked down into that old man's dead face and felt myself free at last! Free at last!" his voice rang out excitedly—once more he brought his hammer round with an ugly swing.

"For a moment I was a young man again; I leaped into his room—the moon was shining full in through the window—I thought of my old college days, and the fun we used to have at Pembroke—topsy turvey I turned everything—" He broke off abruptly, and drew a step nearer to Loveday. "The pity of it all was," he said, suddenly dropping from his high, excited tone to a low, pathetic one, "that he fell without a sound of any sort." Here he drew another step nearer. "I wonder–" he said, then broke off again, and came close to Loveday's side. "It has only this moment occurred to me," he said, now with his lips close to Loveday's ear, "that a woman, in her death agony, would be much more likely to give utterance to an elemental sound than a man."

He raised his hammer, and Loveday fled to the window, and was lifted from the outside by three pairs of strong arms.

"I thought I was conducting my very last case–I never had such a narrow escape before!" said Loveday, as she stood talking with Mr. Griffiths on the Grenfell platform, awaiting the train to carry her back to London. "It seems strange that no one before suspected the old gentleman's sanity–I suppose, however, people were so used to his eccentricities that they did not notice how they had deepened into positive lunacy. His cunning evidently stood him in good stead at the inquest."

"It is possible" said Griffiths thoughtfully, "that he did not absolutely cross the very slender line that divided eccentricity from madness until after the murder. The excitement consequent upon the discovery of the crime may just have pushed him over the border. Now, Miss Brooke, we have exactly ten minutes before your train comes in. I should feel greatly obliged to you if you would explain one or two things that have a professional interest for me."

"With pleasure," said Loveday. "Put your questions in categorical order and I will answer them."

"Well, then, in the first place, what suggested to your mind the old man's guilt?"

"The relations that subsisted between him and Sandy seemed to me to savour too much of fear on the one side and power on the other. Also the income paid to Sandy during Mr. Craven's absence in Natal bore, to my mind, an unpleasant resemblance to hush-money."

"Poor wretched being! And I hear that, after all, the woman he married in his wild young days died soon afterwards of drink. I have no doubt, however, that

Sandy sedulously kept up the fiction of her existence, even after his master's second marriage. Now for another question: how was it you knew that Miss Craven had taken her brother's place in the sick-room?"

"On the evening of my arrival I discovered a rather long lock of fair hair in the unswept fireplace of my room, which, as it happened, was usually occupied by Miss Craven. It at once occurred to me that the young lady had been cutting off her hair and that there must be some powerful motive to induce such a sacrifice. The suspicious circumstances attending her brother's illness soon supplied me with such a motive."

"Ah! that typhoid fever business was very cleverly done. Not a servant in the house, I verily believe, but who thought Master Harry was upstairs, ill in bed, and Miss Craven away at her friends' in Newcastle. The young fellow must have got a clear start off within an hour of the murder. His sister, sent away the next day to Newcastle, dismissed her maid there, I hear, on the plea of no accommodation at her friends' house—sent the girl to her own home for a holiday and herself returned to Troyte's Hill in the middle of the night, having walked the five miles from Grenfell. No doubt her mother admitted her through one of those easily-opened front windows, cut her hair and put her to bed to personate her brother without delay. With Miss Craven's strong likeness to Master Harry, and in a darkened room, it is easy to understand that the eyes of a doctor, personally unacquainted with the family, might easily be deceived. Now, Miss Brooke, you must admit that with all this elaborate chicanery and double dealing going on, it was only natural that my suspicions should set in strongly in that quarter."

"I read it all in another light, you see," said Loveday. "It seemed to me that the mother, knowing her son's evil proclivities, believed in his guilt, in spite, possibly, of his assertions of innocence. The son, most likely, on his way back to the house after pledging the family plate, had met old Mr. Craven with the hammer in his hand. Seeing, no doubt, how impossible it would be for him to clear himself without incriminating his father, he preferred flight to Natal to giving evidence at the inquest."

"Now about his alias?" said Mr. Griffiths briskly, for the train was at that moment steaming into the station. "How did you know that Harold Cousins was identical with Harry Craven, and had sailed in the Bonnie Dundee?"

"Oh, that was easy enough," said Loveday, as she stepped into the train; "a newspaper sent down to Mr. Craven by his wife, was folded so as to direct his attention to the shipping list. In it I saw that the Bonnie Dundee had sailed two days previously for Natal. Now it was only natural to connect Natal with Mrs. Craven, who had passed the greater part of her life there; and it was easy to understand her wish to get her scapegrace son among her early friends. The alias under which he sailed came readily enough to light. I found it scribbled all over one of Mr. Craven's writing pads in his study; evidently it had been drummed into his ears by his wife as his son's alias, and the old gentleman had taken this method of fixing it in his memory. We'll hope that the young fellow, under his new name, will make a new reputation for himself—at any rate, he'll have a better chance of doing so with the ocean between him and his evil companions. Now it's good-bye, I think."

"No," said Mr. Griffiths; "it's au revoir, for you'll have to come back again for the assizes, and give the evidence that will shut old Mr. Craven in an asylum for the rest of his life."

THE REDHILL SISTERHOOD

"THEY want you at Redhill, now," said Mr. Dyer, taking a packet of papers from one of his pigeon-holes. "The idea seems gaining ground in manly quarters that in cases of mere suspicion, women detectives are more satisfactory than men, for they are less likely to attract attention. And this Redhill affair, so far as I can make out, is one of suspicion only."

It was a dreary November morning; every gas jet in the Lynch Court office was alight, and a yellow curtain of outside fog draped its narrow windows.

"Nevertheless, I suppose one can't afford to leave it uninvestigated at this season of the year, with country-house robberies beginning in so many quarters," said Miss Brooke.

"No; and the circumstances in this case certainly seem to point in the direction of the country-house burglar. Two days ago a somewhat curious application was made privately, by a man giving the name of John Murray, to Inspector Gunning, of the Reigate police—Redhill, I must tell you is in the Reigate police district. Murray stated that he had been a greengrocer somewhere in South London, had sold his business there, and had, with the proceeds of the sale, bought two small houses in Redhill, intending to let the one and live in the other. These houses are situated in a blind alley, known as Paved Court, a narrow turning leading off the London and Brighton coach road. Paved Court has been known to the sanitary authorities for the past ten years as a regular fever nest, and as the houses which Murray bought—numbers 7 and 8—stand at the very end of the blind alley, with no chance of thorough ventilation, I dare say the man got them for next to nothing. He told the Inspector that he had had great difficulty in procuring a tenant for the house he wished to let, number 8, and that consequently when, about three weeks back, a lady, dressed as a nun, made him an offer for it, he immediately closed with her. The lady gave her name simply as 'Sister Monica,' and stated that she was a member of an undenominational Sisterhood that had recently been founded by a wealthy lady, who wished her name kept a secret. Sister Monica gave no references, but, instead, paid a quarter's rent in advance, saying that she wished to take possession of the house immediately, and open it as a home for crippled orphans."

"Gave no references—home for cripples," murmured Loveday, scribbling hard and fast in her note-book.

"Murray made no objection to this," continued Mr. Dyer, "and, accordingly, the next day, Sister Monica, accompanied by three other Sisters and some sickly children, took possession of the house, which they furnished with the barest possible necessaries from cheap shops in the neighbourhood. For a time, Murray said, he thought he had secured most desirable tenants, but during the last ten days suspicions as to their real character have entered his mind, and these suspicions he thought it his duty to communicate to the police. Among their possessions, it seems, these Sisters number an old donkey and a tiny cart, and this they start daily on a sort of begging tour through the adjoining villages, bringing back every evening a perfect hoard of broken victuals and bundles of old garments. Now comes the extraordinary fact on which Murray bases his suspicions. He says, and Gunning verifies his statement, that in whatever direction those Sisters turn the wheels of their donkey-cart, burglaries, or attempts at burglaries, are sure to follow. A week ago they went along towards Horley, where, at an outlying house, they received much kindness from a wealthy gentleman. That very night an attempt was made to break into that gentleman's house—an attempt, however, that was happily frustrated by the barking of the house-dog. And so on in other instances that I need not go into. Murray suggests that it might be as well to have the daily movements of these sisters closely watched, and that extra vigilance should be exercised by the police in the districts that have had the honour of a morning call from them. Gunning coincides with this idea, and so has sent to me to secure your services."

Loveday closed her note-book. "I suppose Gunning will meet me somewhere and tell me where I'm to take up my quarters?" she said.

"Yes; he will get into your carriage at Merstham—the station before Redhill—if you will put your hand out of window, with the morning paper in it. By-the-way, he takes it for granted that you will save the 11.5 train from Victoria. Murray, it seems has been good enough to place his little house at the disposal of the police, but Gunning does not think espionage could be so well carried on there as from other quarters. The presence of a stranger in an alley of that sort is bound to attract attention. So he has hired a room for you in a draper's shop that immediately faces the head of the court. There is a private door to this shop of which you will have the key, and can let yourself in and out as you please. You are supposed to be a nursery governess on the lookout for a situation, and Gunning will keep you supplied with letters to give colour to the idea. He suggests that you need only occupy the room during the day, at night you will find far more comfortable quarters at Laker's Hotel, just outside the town."

This was about the sum total of the instructions that Mr. Dyer had to give.

The 11.5 train from Victoria, that carried Loveday to her work among the Surrey Hills, did not get clear of the London fog till well away on the other side of Purley. When the train halted at Merstham, in response to her signal a tall, soldier-like individual made for her carriage, and, jumping in, took the seat facing her. He introduced himself to her as Inspector Gunning, recalled to her memory a former occasion on which they had met, and then, naturally enough, turned the talk upon the present suspicious circumstances they were bent upon investigating.

"It won't do for you and me to be seen together," he said; "of course I am known for miles round, and anyone seen in my company will be at once set down as my coadjutor, and spied upon accordingly. I walked from Redhill to Merstham on purpose to avoid recognition on the platform at Redhill, and half-way here, to my great annoyance, found that I was being followed by a man in a workman's dress and carrying a basket of tools. I doubled, however, and gave him the slip, taking a short cut down a lane which, if he had been living in the place, he would have known as well as I did. By Jove!" this was added with a sudden start, "there is the fellow, I declare; he has weathered me after all, and has no doubt taken good stock of us both, with the train going at this snail's pace. It was unfortunate that your face should have been turned towards that window, Miss Brooke."

"My veil is something of a disguise, and I will put on another cloak before he has a chance of seeing me again," said Loveday.

All she had seen in the brief glimpse that the train had allowed, was a tall, powerfully-built man walking along a siding of the line. His cap was drawn low over his eyes, and in his hand he carried a workman's basket.

Gunning seemed much annoyed at the circumstance. "Instead of landing at Redhill," he said, "we'll go on to Three Bridges and wait there for a Brighton train to bring us back, that will enable you to get to your room somewhere between the lights; I don't want to have you spotted before you've so much as started your work."

Then they went back to their discussion of the Redhill Sisterhood.

"They call themselves 'undenominational,' whatever that means," said Gunning "they say they are connected with no religious sect whatever, they attend sometimes one place of worship, sometimes another, sometimes none at all. They refuse to give up the name of the founder of their order, and really no one has any right to demand it of them, for, as no doubt you see, up to the present moment the case is one of mere suspicion, and it may be a pure coincidence that attempts at burglary have followed their footsteps in this neighbourhood. By-the-way, I have heard of a man's face being enough to hang him, but until I saw Sister Monica's, I never saw a woman's face that could perform the same kind office for her. Of all the lowest criminal types of faces I have ever seen, I think hers is about the lowest and most repulsive."

After the Sisters, they passed in review the chief families resident in the neighbourhood.

."This," said Gunning, unfolding a paper, "is a map I have specially drawn up for you–it takes in the district for ten miles round Redhill, and every country house of any importance is marked with it in red ink. Here, in addition, is an index to those houses, with special notes of my own to every house."

Loveday studied the map for a minute or so, then turned her attention to the index.

"Those four houses you've marked, I see, are those that have been already attempted. I don't think I'll run them through, but I'll mark them 'doubtful;' you see the gang–for, of course, it is a gang–might follow our reasoning on the matter, and look upon those houses as our weak point. Here's one I'll run through, 'house empty during winter months,' that means plate and jewellery sent to the bankers. Oh! and this one may as well be crossed off, 'father and four sons all athletes and sportsmen,' that means firearms always handy–I don't think burglars will be likely to trouble them. Ah! now we come to something! Here's a house to be marked 'tempting' in a burglar's list. 'Wootton Hall, lately changed hands and re-built, with complicated passages and corridors. Splendid family plate in daily use and left entirely to the care of the butler.' I wonder, does the master of that house trust to his 'complicated passages' to preserve his plate for him? A dismissed dishonest servant would supply a dozen maps of the place for half-a-sovereign. What do these initials, 'E.L.,' against the next house in the list, North Cape, stand for?"

"Electric lighted. I think you might almost cross that house off also. I consider electric lighting one of the greatest safeguards against burglars that a man can give his house."

"Yes, if he doesn't rely exclusively upon it; it might be a nasty trap under certain circumstances. I see this gentleman also has magnificent presentation and other plate."

"Yes. Mr. Jameson is a wealthy man and very popular in the neighbourhood; his cups and epergnes are worth looking at."

"Is it the only house in the district that is lighted with electricity?"

"Yes; and, begging your pardon, Miss Brooke, I only wish it were not so. If electric lighting were generally in vogue it would save the police a lot of trouble on these dark winter nights."

"The burglars would find some way of meeting such a condition of things, depend upon it; they have reached a very high development in these days. They no longer stalk about as they did fifty years ago with blunderbuss and bludgeon; they plot, plan, contrive and bring imagination and artistic resource to their aid. By-the-way, it often occurs to me that the popular detective stories, for which there seems to large a demand at the present day, must be, at times, uncommonly useful to the criminal classes."

At Three Bridges they had to wait so long for a return train that it was nearly dark when Loveday got back to Redhill. Mr. Gunning did not accompany her thither, having alighted at a previous station. Loveday had directed her portmanteau to be sent direct to Laker's Hotel, where she had engaged a room by telegram from Victoria Station. So, unburthened by luggage, she slipped quietly out of the Redhill Station and made her way straight for the draper's shop in the London Road. She had no difficulty in finding it, thanks to the minute directions given her by the Inspector.

Street lamps were being lighted in the sleepy little town as she went along, and as she turned into the London Road, shopkeepers were lighting up their windows on both sides of the way. A few yards down this road, a dark patch between the lighted shops showed her where Paved Court led off from the thoroughfare. A side-door of one of the shops that stood at the corner of the court seemed to offer a post of observation whence she could see without being seen, and here Loveday, shrinking into the shadows, ensconced herself in order to take stock of the little alley and its inhabitants. She found it much as it had been described to her—a collection of four-roomed houses of which more than half were unlet. Numbers 7 and 8 at the head of the court presented a slightly less neglected appearance than the other tenements. Number 7 stood in total darkness, but in the upper window of number 8 there showed what seemed to be a night-light burning, so Loveday conjectured that this possibly was the room set apart as a dormitory for the little cripples.

While she stood thus surveying the home of the suspected Sisterhood, the Sisters themselves—two, at least, of them—came into view, with their donkey-cart and their cripples, in the main road. It was an odd little cortège. One Sister, habited in a nun's dress of dark blue serge, led the donkey by the bridle; another Sister, similarly attired, walked alongside the low cart, in which were seated two sickly-looking children. They were evidently returning from one of their long country circuits, and unless they had lost their way and been belated—it certainly seemed a late hour for the sickly little cripples to be abroad.

As they passed under the gas lamp at the corner of the court, Loveday caught a glimpse of the faces of the Sisters. It was easy, with Inspector Gunning's description before her mind, to identify the older and taller woman as Sister Monica, and a more coarse-featured and generally repellant face Loveday admitted to herself she had never before seen. In striking contrast to this forbidding countenance, was that of the younger Sister. Loveday could only catch a brief passing view of it, but that one brief view was enough to impress it on her memory as of unusual sadness and beauty. As the donkey stopped at the corner of the court, Loveday heard this sad-looking young woman addressed as "Sister Anna" by one of the cripples, who asked plaintively when they were going to have something to eat.

"Now, at once," said Sister Anna, lifting the little one, as it seemed to Loveday, tenderly out of the cart, and carrying him on her shoulder down the court to the door of number 8, which opened to them at their approach. The other Sister did the same with the other child; then both Sisters returned, unloaded the cart of sundry bundles and baskets, and, this done, led off the old donkey and trap down the road, possibly to a neighbouring costermonger's stables.

A man, coming along on a bicycle, exchanged a word of greeting with the Sisters as they passed, then swung himself off his machine at the corner of the court, and walked it along the paved way to the door of number 7. This he opened with a key, and then, pushing the machine before him, entered the house.

Loveday took it for granted that this man must be the John Murray of whom she had heard. She had closely scrutinized him as he had passed her, and had seen that he was a dark, well-featured man of about fifty years of age.

She congratulated herself on her good fortune in having seen so much in such a brief space of time, and coming forth from her sheltered corner turned her steps in the direction of the draper's shop on the other side of the road.

It was easy to find it. "Golightly" was the singular name that figured above the shop-front, in which were displayed a variety of goods calculated to meet the wants of servants and the poorer classes generally. A tall, powerfully-built man appeared to be looking in at this window. Loveday's foot was on the doorstep of the draper's private entrance, her hand on the door-knocker, when this individual, suddenly turning, convinced her of his identity with the journeyman workman who had so disturbed Mr. Gunning's equanimity. It was true he wore a bowler instead of a journeyman's cap, and he no longer carried a basket of tools, but there was no possibility for anyone, with so good an eye for an outline as Loveday possessed, not to recognize the carriage of the head and shoulders as that of the man she had seen walking along the railway siding. He gave her no time to make minute observation of his appearance, but turned quickly away, and disappeared down a by-street.

Loveday's work seemed to bristle with difficulties now. Here was she, as it were, unearthed in her own ambush; for there could be but little doubt that during the whole time she had stood watching those Sisters, that man, from a safe vantage point, had been watching her.

She found Mrs. Golightly a civil and obliging person. She showed Loveday to her room above the shop, brought her the letters which Inspector Gunning had been careful to have posted to her during the day. Then she supplied her with pen and ink and, in response to Loveday's request, with some strong coffee that she said, with a little attempt at a joke, would "keep a dormouse awake all through the winter without winking."

While the obliging landlady busied herself about the room, Loveday had a few questions to ask about the Sisterhood who lived down the court opposite. On this head, however, Mrs. Golightly could tell her no more than she already knew, beyond the fact that they started every morning on their rounds at eleven o'clock punctually, and that before that hour they were never to be seen outside their door.

Loveday's watch that night was to be a fruitless one. Although she sat, with her lamp turned out and safely screened from observation, until close upon midnight, with eyes fixed upon numbers 7 and 8 Paved Court, not so much as a door opening or shutting at either house rewarded her vigil. The lights flitted from the lower to the upper floors in both houses, and then disappeared somewhere between nine and ten in the evening; and after that, not a sign of life did either tenement show.

And all through the long hours of that watch, backwards and forwards there seemed to flit before her mind's eye, as if in some sort it were fixed upon its retina, the sweet, sad face of Sister Anna.

Why it was this face should so haunt her, she found it hard to say.

"It has a mournful past and a mournful future written upon it as a hopeless whole," she said to herself. "It is the face of an Andromeda! 'here am I,' it seems to say, 'tied to my stake, helpless and hopeless.'"

The church clocks were sounding the midnight hour as Loveday made her way through the dark streets to her hotel outside the town. As she passed under the railway arch that ended in the open country road, the echo of not very distant footsteps caught her ear. When she stopped they stopped, when she went on they went on, and she knew that once more she was being followed and watched, although the darkness of the arch prevented her seeing even the shadow of the man who was thus dogging her steps.

The next morning broke keen and frosty. Loveday studied her map and her country-house index over a seven o'clock breakfast, and then set off for a brisk walk along the country road. No doubt in London the streets were walled in and roofed with yellow fog; here, however, bright sunshine played in and out of the bare tree-boughs and leafless hedges on to a thousand frost spangles, turning the prosaic macadamized road into a gangway fit for Queen Titania herself and her fairy train.

Loveday turned her back on the town and set herself to follow the road as it wound away over the hill in the direction of a village called Northfield. Early as she was, she was not to have that road to herself. A team of strong horses trudged by on their way to their work in the fuller's-earth pits. A young fellow on a bicycle flashed past at a tremendous pace, considering the upward slant of the road. He looked hard at her as he passed, then slackened pace, dismounted, and awaited her coming on the brow of the hill.

"Good morning, Miss Brooke," he said, lifting his cap as she came alongside of him. "May I have five minutes' talk with you?"

The young man who thus accosted her had not the appearance of a gentleman. He was a handsome, bright-faced young fellow of about two-and-twenty, and was dressed in ordinary cyclists' dress; his cap was pushed back from his brow over thick, curly, fair hair, and Loveday, as she looked at him, could not repress the thought how well he would look at the head of a troop of cavalry, giving the order to charge the enemy.

He led his machine to the side of the footpath.

"You have the advantage of me," said Loveday; "I haven't the remotest notion who you are."

"No," he said; "although I know you, you cannot possibly know me. I am a north country man, and I was present, about a month ago, at the trial of old Mr. Craven, of Troyte's Hill–in fact, I acted as reporter for one of the local papers. I watched your face so closely as you gave your evidence that I should know it anywhere, among a thousand."

"And your name is—?"

"George White, of Grenfell. My father is part proprietor of one of the Newcastle papers. I am a bit of a literary man myself, and sometimes figure as a reporter, sometimes as leader-writer, to that paper." Here he gave a glance towards his side pocket, from which protruded a small volume of Tennyson's poems.

The facts he had stated did not seem to invite comment, and Loveday ejaculated merely:

"Indeed!"

The young man went back to the subject that was evidently filling his thoughts. "I have special reasons for being glad to have met you this morning, Miss Brooke," he want on, making his footsteps keep pace with hers. "I am in great trouble, and I believe you are the only person in the whole world who can help me out of that trouble."

"I am rather doubtful as to my power of helping anyone out of trouble," said Loveday; "so far as my experience goes, our troubles are as much a part of ourselves as our skins are of our bodies."

"Ah, but not such trouble as mine," said White eagerly. He broke off for a moment, then, with a sudden rush of words, told her what that trouble was. For the past year he had been engaged to be married to a young girl, who, until quite recently had been fulfilling the duties of a nursery governess in a large house in the neighbourhood of Redhill.

"Will you kindly give me the name of that house?" interrupted Loveday.

"Certainly; Wootton Hall, the place is called, and Annie Lee is my sweetheart's name. I don't care who knows it!" He threw his head back as he said this, as if he would be delighted to announce the fact to the whole world. "Annie's mother," he went on, "died when she was a baby, and we both thought her father was dead also, when suddenly, about a fortnight ago, it came to her knowledge that instead of being dead, he was serving his time at Portland for some offence committed years ago."

"Do you know how this came to Annie's knowledge?"

"Not the least in the world; I only know that I suddenly got a letter from her announcing the fact, and at the same time, breaking off her engagement with me. I tore the letter into a thousand pieces, and wrote back saying I would not allow the engagement to be broken off, but would marry her to-morrow if she would have me. To this letter she did not reply; there came instead a few lines from Mrs. Copeland, the lady at Wootton Hall, saying that Annie had thrown up her engagement and joined some Sisterhood, and that she, Mrs. Copeland, had pledged her word to Annie to reveal to no one the name and whereabouts of that

Sisterhood."

"And I suppose you imagine I am able to do what Mrs. Copeland is pledged not to do?"

"That's just it, Miss Brooke," cried the young man enthusiastically. "You do such wonderful things; everyone knows you do. It seems as if, when anything is wanted to be found out, you just walk into a place, look round you and, in a moment, everything becomes clear as noonday."

"I can't quite lay claim to such wonderful powers as that. As it happens, however, in the present instance, no particular skill is needed to find out what you wish to know, for I fancy I have already come upon the traces of Miss Annie Lee."

"Miss Brooke!"

"Of course, I cannot say for certain, but is a matter you can easily settle for yourself–settle, too, in a way that will confer a great obligation on me."

"I shall be only too delighted to be of any–the slightest service to you," cried White, enthusiastically as before.

"Thank you. I will explain. I came down here specially to watch the movements of a certain Sisterhood who have somehow aroused the suspicions of the police. Well, I find that instead of being able to do this, I am myself so closely watched–possibly by confederates of these Sisters–that unless I can do my work by deputy I may as well go back to town at once."

"Ah! I see–you want me to be that deputy."

"Precisely. I want you to go to the room in Redhill that I have hired, take your place at the window–screened, of course, from observation–at which I ought to be seated–watch as closely as possible the movements of these Sisters and report them to me at the hotel, where I shall remain shut in from morning till night–it is the only way in which I can throw my persistent spies off the scent. Now, in doing this for me, you will be also doing yourself a good turn, for I have little doubt but what under the blue serge hood of one of the sisters you will discover the pretty face of Miss Annie Lee."

As they had talked they had walked, and now stood on the top of the hill at the head of the one little street that constituted the whole of the village of Northfield.

On their left hand stood the village schools and the master's house; nearly facing these, on the opposite side of the road, beneath a clump of elms, stood the village pound. Beyond this pound, on either side of the way, were two rows of small cottages with tiny squares of garden in front, and in the midst of these small cottages a swinging sign beneath a lamp announced a "Postal and Telegraph Office."

"Now that we have come into the land of habitations again," said Loveday, "it will be best for us to part. It will not do for you and me to be seen together, or my spies will be transferring their attentions from me to you, and I shall have to find another deputy. You had better start on your bicycle for Redhill at once, and I will walk back at leisurely speed. Come to me at my hotel without fail at one o'clock and report proceedings. I do not say anything definite about remuneration, but I assure you, if you carry out my instructions to the letter, your services will be amply rewarded by me and by my employers."

There were yet a few more details to arrange. White had been, he said, only a day and night in the neighbourhood, and special directions as to the locality had to be given to him. Loveday advised him not to attract attention by going to the draper's private door, but to enter the shop as if he were a customer, and then explain matters to Mrs. Golightly, who, no doubt, would be in her place behind the counter; tell her he was the brother of the Miss Smith who had hired her room, and ask permission to go through the shop to that room, as he had been commissioned by his sister to read and answer any letters that might have arrived there for her.

"Show her the key of the side door—here it is," said Loveday; "it will be your credentials, and tell her you did not like to make use of it without acquainting her with the fact."

The young man took the key, endeavoured to put it in his waistcoat pocket, found the space there occupied and so transferred it to the keeping of a side pocket in his tunic.

All this time Loveday stood watching him.

"You have a capital machine there," she said, as the young man mounted his bicycle once more, "and I hope you will turn it to account in following the movements of these Sisters about the neighbourood. I feel confident you will have something definite to tell me when you bring me your first report at one o'clock."

White once more broke into a profusion of thanks, and then, lifting his cap to the lady, started his machine at a fairly good pace.

Loveday watched him out of sight down the slope of the hill, then, instead of following him as she had said she would "at a leisurely pace," she turned her steps in the opposite direction along the village street.

It was an altogether ideal country village. Neatly-dressed chubby-faced children, now on their way to the schools, dropped quaint little curtsies, or tugged at curly locks as Loveday passed; every cottage looked the picture of cleanliness and trimness, and although so late in the year, the gardens were full of late flowering chrysanthemums and early flowering Christmas roses.

At the end of the village, Loveday came suddenly into view of a large, handsome, red-brick mansion. It presented a wide frontage to the road, from which it lay back amid extensive pleasure grounds. On the right hand, and a little in the rear of the house, stood what seemed to be large and commodious stables, and immediately adjoining these stables was a low-built, red-brick shed, that had evidently been recently erected.

That low-build, red-brick shed excited Loveday's curiosity.

"Is this house called North Cape?" she asked of a man, who chanced at that moment to be passing with a pickaxe and shovel.

The man answered in the affirmative, and Loveday then asked another question: could he tell her what was that small shed so close to the house—it looked like a glorified cowhouse—now what could be its use?

The man's face lighted up as if it were a subject on which he liked to be questioned. He explained that that small shed was the engine-house where the electricity that lighted North Cape was made and stored. Then he dwelt with pride upon the fact, as if he held a personal interest in it, that North Cape was the only house, far or near, that was thus lighted.

"I suppose the wires are carried underground to the house," said Loveday, looking in vain for signs of them anywhere.

The man was delighted to go into details on the matter. He had helped to lay those wires, he said: they were two in number, one for supply and one for return, and were laid three feet below ground, in boxes filled with pitch. These wires were switched on to jars in the engine-house, where the electricity was stored, and, after passing underground, entered the family mansion under its flooring at its western end.

Loveday listened attentively to these details, and then took a minute and leisurely survey of the house and its surroundings. This done, she retraced her steps through the village, pausing, however, at the "Postal and Telegraph Office" to dispatch a telegram to Inspector Gunning.

It was one to send the Inspector to his cipher-book. It ran as follows:

"Rely solely on chemist and coal-merchant throughout the day.–L. B."

After this, she quickened her pace, and in something over three-quarters of an hour was back again at her hotel.

There she found more of life stirring than when she had quitted it in the early morning. There was to be a meeting of the "Surrey Stags," about a couple of miles off, and a good many hunting men were hanging about the entrance to the house, discussing the chances of sport after last night's frost. Loveday made her way through the throng in leisurely fashion, and not a man but what had keen scrutiny from her sharp eyes. No, there was no cause for suspicion there: they were evidently one and all just what they seemed to be–loud-voiced, hard-riding men, bent on a day's sport; but–and here Loveday's eyes traveled beyond the hotel court-yard to the other side of the road–who was that man with a bill-hook hacking at the hedge there–a thin-featured, round-shouldered old fellow, with a bent-about hat? It might be as well not to take it too rashly for granted that her spies had withdrawn, and had left her free to do her work in her own fashion.

She went upstairs to her room. It was situated on the first floor in the front of the house, and consequently commanded a good view of the high road. She stood well back from the window, and at an angle whence she could see and not be seen, took a long, steady survey of the hedger. And the longer she looked the more convinced she was that the man's real work was something other than the bill-hook seemed to imply. He worked, so to speak, with his head over his shoulder, and when Loveday supplemented her eyesight with a strong field-glass, she could see more than one stealthy glance shot from beneath his bent-about hat in the direction of her window.

There could be little doubt about it: her movements were to be as closely watched to-day as they had been yesterday. Now it was of first importance that she should communicate with Inspector Gunning in the course of the afternoon: the question to solve was how it was to be done?

To all appearance Loveday answered the question in extraordinary fashion. She pulled up her blind, she drew back her curtain, and seated herself, in full view, at a small table in the window recess. Then she took a pocket inkstand from her pocket, a packet or correspondence cards from her letter-case, and with rapid pen, set to work on them.

About an hour and a half afterwards, White, coming in, according to his promise, to report proceedings, found her still seated at the window, not, however, with writing materials before her, but with needle and thread in her hand with which she was mending her gloves.

"I return to town by the first train to-morrow morning," she said as he entered, "and I find these wretched things want no end of stitches. Now for your report."

White appeared to be in an elated frame of mind. "I've seen her!" he cried, "my Annie–they've got her, those confounded Sisters; but they sha'n't keep her–no, not if I have to pull the house down about their ears to get her out."

"Well, now you know where she is, you can take your time about getting her out," said Loveday. "I hope, however, you haven't broken faith with me, and betrayed yourself by trying to speak with her, because, if so, I shall have to look out for another deputy."

"Honour, Miss Brooke!" answered White indignantly. "I stuck to my duty, though it cost me something to see her hanging over those kids and tucking them into the cart, and never say a word to her, never so much as wave my hand."

"Did she go out with the donkey-cart to-day?"

"No, she only tucked the kids into the cart with a blanket, and then went back to the house. Two old Sisters, ugly as sin, went out with them. I watched them from the window, jolt, jolt, jolt, round the corner, out of sight, and then I whipped down the stairs, and on to my machine, and was after them in a trice and managed to keep them well in sight for over an hour and a half."

"And their destination to-day was?"

"Wootton Hall."

"Ah, just as I expected."

"Just as you expected?" echoed White.

"I forgot. You do not know the nature of the suspicions that are attached to this Sisterhood, and the reasons I have for thinking that Wootton Hall, at this season of the year, might have an especial attraction for them."

White continued staring at her. "Miss Brooke," he said presently, in an altered tone, "whatever suspicions may attach to the Sisterhood, I'll stake my life on it, my Annie has had no share in any wickedness of any sort."

"Oh, quite so; it is most likely that your Annie has, in some way, been inveigled into joining these Sisters–has been taken possession of by them, in fact, just as they have taken possession of the little cripples."

"That's it!" he cried excitedly; "that was the idea that occurred to me when you spoke to me on the hill about them, otherwise you may be sure—"

"Did they get relief of any sort at the Hall?" interrupted Loveday..

"Yes; one of the two ugly old women stopped outside the lodge gates with the donkey-cart, and the other beauty went up to the house alone. She stayed there, I should think, about a quarter of an hour, and when she came back, was followed by a servant, carrying a bundle and a basket."

"Ah! I've no doubt they brought away with them something else beside old garments and broken victuals."

White stood in front of her, fixing a hard, steady gaze upon her.

"Miss Brooke," he said presently, in a voice that matched the look on his face, "what do you suppose was the real object of these women in going to Wootton Hall this morning?"

"Mr. White, if I wished to help a gang of thieves break into Wootton Hall tonight, don't you think I should be greatly interested in procuring from them the information that the master of the house was away from home; that two of the men servants, who slept in the house, had recently been dismissed and their places had not yet been filled; also that the dogs were never unchained at night, and that their kennels were at the side of the house at which the butler's pantry is not situated? These are particulars I have gathered in this house without stirring from my chair, and I am satisfied that they are likely to be true. A the same time, if I were a professed burglar, I should not be content with information that was likely to be true, but would be careful to procure such that was certain to be true, and so would set accomplices to work at the fountain head. Now do you understand?"

White folded his arms and looked down on her.

"What are you going to do?" he asked, in short, brusque tones.

Loveday looked him full in the face. "Communicate with the police immediately," she answered; "and I should feel greatly obliged if you will at once take a note from me to Inspector Gunning at Reigate."

"And what becomes of Annie?"

"I don't think you need have any anxiety on that head. I've no doubt that when the circumstances of her admission to the Sisterhood are investigated, it will be proved that she has been as much deceived and imposed upon as the man, John Murray, who so foolishly let his house to these women. Remember, Annie has Mrs. Copeland's good word to support her integrity."

White stood silent for awhile.

"What sort of a note do you wish me to take to the Inspector?" he presently asked.

"You shall read it as I write it, if you like," answered Loveday. She took a correspondence card from her letter case, and, with an indelible pencil, wrote as follows–

"Wooton Hall is threatened to-night–concentrate attention there.

"L. B."

White read the words as she wrote them with a curious expression passing over his handsome features.

"Yes," he said, curtly as before. "I'll deliver that, I give you my word, but I'll bring back no answer to you. I'll do no more spying for you–it's a trade that doesn't suit me. There's a straight-forward way of doing straight-forward work, and I'll take that way–no other–to get my Annie out of that den."

He took the note, which she sealed and handed to him, and strode out of the room.

Loveday, from the window, watched him mount his bicycle. Was it her fancy, or did there pass a swift, furtive glance of recognition between him and the hedger on the other side of the way as he rode out of the court-yard?

Loveday seemed determined to make that hedger's work easy for him. The short winter's day was closing in now, and her room must consequently have been growing dim to outside observation. She lighted the gas chandelier which hung from the ceiling and, still with blinds and curtains undrawn, took her old place at the window, spread writing materials before her and commenced a long and elaborate report to her chief at Lynch Court.

About half-an-hour afterwards, as she threw a casual glance across the road, she saw that the hedger had disappeared, but that two ill-looking tramps sat munching bread and cheese under the hedge to which his bill-hook had done so little service. Evidently the intention was, one way or another, not to lose sight of her so long as she remained in Redhill.

Meantime, White had delivered Loveday's note to the Inspector at Reigate, and had disappeared on his bicycle once more.

Gunning read it without a change of expression. Then he crossed the room to the fire-place and held the card as close to the bars as he could without scorching it.

"I had a telegram from her this morning," he explained to his confidential man, "telling me to rely upon chemicals and coals throughout the day, and that, of course, meant that she would write to me in invisible ink. No doubt this message about Wootton Hall means nothing—"

He broke off abruptly, exclaiming: "Eh! what's this!" as, having withdrawn the card from the fire, Loveday's real message stood out in bold, clear characters between the lines of the false one.

Thus it ran:

"North Cape will be attacked to-night–a desperate gang–be prepared for a struggle. Above all, guard the electrical engine-house. On no account attempt to communicate with me; I am so closely watched that any endeavour to do so may frustrate your chance of trapping the scoundrels. L. B."

That night when the moon went down behind Reigate Hill an exciting scene was enacted at "North Cape." The Surrey Gazette, in its issue the following day, gave the subjoined account of it under the heading, "Desperate encounter with burglars."

"Last night, 'North Cape,' the residence of Mr. Jameson, was the scene of an affray between the police and a desperate gang of burglars. 'North Cape' is lighted throughout with electricity, and the burglars, four in number, divided in half–two being told off to enter and rob the house, and two to remain at the engine-shed, where the electricity is stored, so that, at a given signal, should need arise, the wires might be unswitched, the inmates of the house thrown into sudden darkness and confusion, and the escape of the marauders thereby facilitated. Mr. Jameson, however, had received timely warning from the police of the intended attack, and he, with his two sons, all well armed, sat in darkness in the inner hall awaiting the coming of the thieves. The police were stationed, some in the stables, some in out-buildings nearer to the house, and others in more distant parts of the grounds. The burglars effected their entrance by means of a ladder placed to a window of the servants' stair case which leads straight down to the butler's pantry and to the safe where the silver is kept. The fellows, however, had no sooner got into the house than the police issuing from their hiding-place outside, mounted the ladder after them and thus cut off their retreat. Mr. Jameson and his two sons, at the same moment, attacked them in front, and thus overwhelmed by numbers, the scoundrels were easily secured. It was at the engine-house outside that the sharpest struggle took place. The thieves had forced open the door of this engine-shed with their jimmies immediately on their arrival, under the very eyes of the police, who lay in ambush in the stables, and when one of the men, captured in the house, contrived to sound an alarm on his whistle, these outside watchers made a rush for the electrical jars, in order to unswitch the wires. Upon this the police closed upon them, and a hand-to-hand struggle followed, and if it had not been for the timely assistance of Mr. Jameson and his sons, who had fortunately conjectured that their presence here might be useful, it is more than likely that one of the burglars, a powerfully-built man, would have escaped.

"The names of the captured men are John Murray, Arthur and George Lee (father and son), and a man with so many aliases that it is difficult to know which is his real name. The whole thing had been most cunningly and carefully planned. The elder Lee, lately released from penal servitude for a similar offence, appears to have been prime mover in the affair. This man had, it seems, a son and a daughter, who, through the kindness of friends, had been fairly well placed in life: the son at an electrical engineers' in London, the daughter as nursery governess at Wootton Hall. Directly this man was released from Portland, he seems to have found out his children and done his best to ruin them both. He was constantly at Wootton Hall endeavouring to induce his daughter to act as an accomplice to a robbery of the house. This so worried the girl that she threw up her situation and joined a Sisterhood that had recently been established in the neighbourhood. Upon this, Lee's thoughts turned in another direction. He induced his son, who had saved a little money, to throw up his work in London, and join him in his disreputable career. The boy is a handsome young fellow, but appears to have in him the makings of a first-class criminal. In his work as an electrical engineer he had made the acquaintance of the man John Murray, who, it is said, has been rapidly going downhill of late. Murray was the owner of the house rented by the Sisterhood that Miss Lee had joined, and the idea evidently struck the brains of these three scoundrels that this Sisterhood, whose antecedents were a little mysterious, might be utilized to draw off the attention of the police from themselves and from the especial house in the neighbourhood that they had planned to attack. With this end in view, Murray made an application to the police to have the Sisters watched, and still further to give colour to the suspicions he had endeavoured to set afloat concerning them, he and his confederates made feeble attempts at burglary upon the houses at which the Sisters had called, begging for scraps. It is a matter for congratulation that the plot, from beginning to end, has been thus successfully unearthed, and it is felt on all sides that great credit is due to Inspector Gunning and his skilled coadjutors for the vigilance and promptitude they have displayed throughout the affair."

Loveday read aloud this report, with her feet on the fender of the Lynch Court office.

"Accurate, as far as it goes," she said, as she laid down the paper.

"But we want to know a little more," said Mr. Dyer. "In the first place, I would like to know what it was that diverted your suspicions from the unfortunate Sisters?"

"The way in which they handled the children," answered Loveday promptly. "I have seen female criminals of all kinds handling children, and I have noticed that although they may occasionally—even this is rare—treat them with a certain rough sort of kindness, of tenderness they are utterly incapable. Now Sister Monica, I must admit, is not pleasant to look at; at the same time, there was something absolutely beautiful in the way in which she lifted the little cripple out of the cart, put his tiny thin hand round her neck, and carried him into the house. By-the-way I would like to ask some rapid physiognolmist how he would account for Sister Monica's repulsiveness of feature as contrasted with young Lee's undoubted good looks—heredity, in this case, throws no light on the matter."

"Another question," said Mr. Dyer, not paying much heed to Loveday's digression: "how was it you transferred your suspicions to John Murray?"

"I did not do so immediately, although at the very first it had struck me as odd that he should be so anxious to do the work of the police for them. The chief thing I noticed concerning Murray, on the first and only occasion on which I saw him, was that he had had an accident with his bicycle, for in the right-hand corner of his lamp-glass there was a tiny star, and the lamp itself had a dent on the same side, had also lost its hook, and was fastened to the machine by a bit of electric fuse. The next morning as I was walking up the hill towards Northfield, I was accosted by a young man mounted on that self-same bicycle—not a doubt of it—star in glass, dent, fuse, all three."

"Ah, that sounded an important keynote, and led you to connect Murray and the younger Lee immediately."

"It did, and, of course, also at once gave the lie to his statement that he was a stranger in the place, and confirmed my opinion that there was nothing of the north-countryman in his accent. Other details in his manner and appearance gave rise to other suspicions. For instance, he called himself a press reporter by profession, and his hands were coarse and grimy as only a mechanic's could be. He said he was a bit of a literary man, but the Tennyson that showed so obtrusively from his pocket was new, and in parts uncut, and totally unlike the well-thumbed volume of the literary student. Finally, when he tried and failed to put my latch-key into his waistcoat pocket, I saw the reason lay in the fact that the pocket was already occupied by a soft coil of electric fuse, the end of which protruded. Now, an electric fuse is what an electrical engineer might almost unconsciously carry about with him, it is so essential a part of his working tools, but it is a thing that a literary man or a press reporter could have no possible use for."

"Exactly, exactly. And it was no doubt, that bit of electric fuse that turned your thoughts to the one house in the neighbourhood lighted by electricity, and suggested to your mind the possibility of electrical engineers turning their talents to account in that direction. Now, will you tell me, what, at that stage of your day's work, induced you to wire to Gunning that you would bring your invisible-ink bottle into use?"

"That was simply a matter or precaution; it did not compel me to the use of invisible ink, if I saw other safe methods of communication. I felt myself being hemmed in on all sides with spies, and I could not tell what emergency might arise. I don't think I have ever had a more difficult game to play. As I walked and talked with the young fellow up the hill, it became clear to me that if I wished to do my work I must lull the suspicions of the gang, and seem to walk into their trap. I saw by the persistent way in which Wootton Hall was forced on my notice that it was wished to fix my suspicions there. I accordingly, to all appearance, did so, and allowed the fellows to think they were making a fool of me."

"Ha! ha! Capital that—the biter bit, with a vengeance! Splendid idea to make that young rascal himself deliver the letter that was to land him and his pals in jail.

And he all the time laughing in his sleeve and thinking what a fool he was making of you! Ha, ha, ha!" And Mr. Dyer made the office ring again with his merriment.

"The only person one is at all sorry for in this affair is poor little Sister Anna," said Loveday pityingly; "and yet, perhaps, all things considered, after her sorry experience of life, she may not be so badly placed in a Sisterhood where practical Christianity–not religious hysterics–is the one and only rule of the order."

A PRINCESS'S VENGEANCE

"THE girl is young, pretty, friendless and a foreigner, you say, and has disappeared as completely as if the earth had opened to receive her," said Miss Brooke, making a résumé of the facts that Mr. Dyer had been relating to her. "Now, will you tell me why two days were allowed to elapse before the police were communicated with?"

"Mrs. Druce, the lady to whom Lucie Cunier acted as amanuensis," answered Mr. Dyer, "took the matter very calmly at first and said she felt sure that the girl would write to her in a day or so, explaining her extraordinary conduct. Major Druce, her son, the gentleman who came to me this morning, was away from home, on a visit, when the girl took flight. Immediately on his return, however, he communicated the fullest particulars to the police."

"They do not seem to have taken up the case very heartily at Scotland Yard."

"No, they have as good as dropped it. They advised Major Druce to place the matter in my hands, saying that they considered it a case for private rather than police investigation."

"I wonder what made them come to that conclusion."

"I think I can tell you, although the Major seemed quite at a loss on the matter. It seems he had a photograph of the missing girl, which he kept in a drawer of his writing-table. (By-the-way, I think the young man is a good deal 'gone' on this Mdlle. Cunier, in spite of his engagement to another lady.) Well, this portrait he naturally thought would be most useful in helping to trace the girl, and he went to his drawer for it, intending to take it with him to Scotland Yard. To his astonishment, however, it was nowhere to be seen, and, although he at once instituted a rigorous search, and questioned his mother and the servants, one and all, on the matter, it was all to no purpose."

Loveday thought for a moment.

"Well, of course," she said presently "that photograph must have been stolen by someone in the house, and, equally of course, that someone must know more on the matter than he or she cares to avow, and, most probably, has some interest in throwing obstacles in the way of tracing the girl. At the same time, however, the fact in no way disproves the possibility that a crime, and a very black one, may underlie the girl's disappearance."

"The Major himself appears confident that a crime of some sort has been committed, and he grew very excited and a little mixed in his statements more than once just now."

"What sort of woman is the Major's mother?"

"Mrs. Druce? She is rather a well-known personage in certain sets. Her husband died about ten years ago, and since his death she has posed as promoter and propagandist of all sorts of benevolent, though occasionally somewhat visionary ideas; theatrical missions, magic-lantern and playing cards missions, societies for providing perpetual music for the sick poor, for supplying cabmen with comforters, and a hundred other similar schemes have in turn occupied her attention. Her house is a rendezvous for faddists of every description. The latest fad, however, seems to have put all others to flight; it is a scheme for alleviating the condition of 'our sisters in the East,' so she puts it in her prospectus; in other words a Harem Mission on somewhat similar, but I suppose broader lines than the old-fashioned Zenana Mission. This Harem Mission has gathered about her a number of Turkish and Egyptian potentates resident in or visiting London, and has thus incidentally brought about the engagement of her son, Major Druce, with the Princess Dullah-Veih. This Princess is a beauty and an heiress, and although of Turkish parentage, has been brought up under European influence in Cairo."

"Is anything known of the antecedents of Mdlle. Cunier?"

"Very little. She came to Mrs. Druce from a certain Lady Gwynne, who had brought her to England from an orphanage for the daughters of jewellers and watchmakers at Echallets, in Geneva. Lady Gwynne intended to make her governess to her young children, but when she saw that the girl's good looks had attracted her husband's attention, she thought better of it, and suggested to Mrs. Druce that Mademoiselle might be useful to her in conducting her foreign correspondence. Mrs. Druce accordingly engaged the young lady to act as her secretary and amanuensis, and appears, on the whole, to have taken to the girl, and to have been on a pleasant, friendly footing with her. I wonder if the Princess Dullah-Veih was on an equally pleasant footing with her when she saw, as no doubt she did, the attention she received at the Major's hands." (Mr. Dyer shrugged his shoulders.) "The Major's suspicions do not point in that direction, in spite of the fact which I elicited from him by judicious questioning, that the Princess has a violent and jealous temper, and has at times made his life a burden to him. His suspicions centre solely upon a certain Hafiz Cassimi, son of the Turkish-Egyptian banker of that name. It was at the house of these Cassimis that the Major first met the Princess, and he states that she and young Cassimi are like brother and sister to each other. He says that this young man has had the run of his mother's house and made himself very much at home in it for the past three weeks, ever since, in fact, the Princess came to stay with Mrs. Druce, in order to be initiated into the mysteries of English family life. Hafiz Cassimi, according to the Major's account, fell desperately in love with the little Swiss girl almost at first sight and pestered her with his attentions, and off and on there appear to have passed hot words between the two young men."

"One could scarcely expect a princess with Eastern blood in her veins to be a quiet and passive spectator to such a drama of cross-purposes."

"Scarcely. The Major, perhaps, hardly takes the Princess sufficiently into his reckoning. According to him, young Cassimi is a thorough-going Iago, and he begs me to concentrate attention entirely on him. Cassimi, he says, has stolen the photograph. Cassimi has inveigled the girl out of the house on some pretext—perhaps out of the country also, and he suggests that it might be as well to communicate with the police at Cairo, with as little delay as possible."

"And it hasn't so much as entered his mind that his Princess might have a hand in such a plot as that!"

"Apparently not. I think I told you that Mademoiselle had taken no luggage—not so much as a hand-bag—with her. Nothing, beyond her coat and hat, has disappeared from her wardrobe. Her writing-desk, and, in fact, all her boxes and drawers, have been opened and searched, but no letters or papers of any sort have been found that throw any light upon her movements."

"At what hour in the day is the girl supposed to have left the house?"

"No one can say for certain. It is conjectured that it was some time in the afternoon of the second of this month–a week ago to-day. It was one of Mrs. Druce's big reception days, and with a stream of people going and coming, a young lady, more or less, leaving the house would scarcely be noticed."

"I suppose," said Loveday, after a moment's pause, "this Princess Dullah-Veih has something of a history. One does not often get a Turkish princess in London."

"Yes, she has a history. She is only remotely connected with the present reigning dynasty in Turkey, and I dare say her princess-ship has been made the most of. All the same, however, she has had an altogether exceptional career for an Oriental lady. She was left an orphan at an early age, and was consigned to the guardianship of the elder Cassimi by her relatives. The Cassimis, both father and son, seem to be very advanced and European in their ideas, and by them she was taken to Cairo for her education. About a year ago they 'brought her out' in London, where she made the acquaintance of Major Druce. The young man, by-the-way, appears to be rather hot-headed in his love-making, for within six weeks of his introduction to her their engagement was announced. No doubt it had Mrs. Druce's fullest approval, for knowing her son's extravagant habits and his numerous debts, it must have been patent to her that a rich wife was a necessity to him. The marriage, I believe, was to have taken place this season; but taking into consideration the young man's ill-advised attentions to the little Swiss girl, and the fervour he is throwing into the search for her, I should say it was exceedingly doubtful whether—"

"Major Druce, sir, wishes to see you," said a clerk at that moment, opening the door leading from the outer office.

"MAJOR DRUCE, SIR!"

"Very good; show him in," said Mr. Dyer. Then he turned to Loveday.

"Of course I have spoken to him about you, and he is very anxious to take you to his mother's reception this afternoon, so that you may have a look round and—"

He broke off, having to rise and greet Major Druce, who at that moment entered the room.

He was a tall, handsome young fellow of about seven or eight and twenty, "well turned out" from head to foot, moustache waxed, orchid in button-hole, light kid gloves, and patent leather boots. There was assuredly nothing in his appearance to substantiate his statement to Mr. Dyer that he "hadn't slept a wink all night, that in fact another twenty-four hours of this terrible suspense would send him into his grave."

Mr. Dyer introduced Miss Brooke, and she expressed her sympathy with him on the painful matter that was filling his thoughts.

"It is very good of you, I'm sure," he replied, in a slow, soft drawl, not unpleasant to listen to. "My mother receives this afternoon from half past four to half past six, and I shall be very glad if you will allow me to introduce you to the inside of our house, and to the very ill-looking set that we have somehow managed to gather about us."

"The ill-looking set?"

"Yes; Jews, Turks, heretics and infidels—all there. And they're on the increase too, that's the worst of it. Every week a fresh importation from Cairo."

"Ah, Mrs. Druce is a large-hearted, benevolent woman," interposed Mr. Dyer; "all nationalities gather within her walls."

"Was your mother a large-hearted, benevolent woman?" said the young man, turning upon him. "No! well then, thank Providence that she wasn't; and admit that you know nothing at all on the matter. Miss Brooke," he continued, turning to Loveday, "I've brought round my hansom for you; it's nearly half past four now, and it's a good twenty minutes' drive from here to Portland Place. If you're ready, I'm at your service."

Major Druce's hansom was, like himself, in all respects "well turned out," and the India rubber tires round its wheels allowed an easy flow of conversation to be kept up during the twenty minutes' drive from Lynch Court to Portland Place.

The Major led off the talk in frank and easy fashion.

"My mother," he said, "prides herself on being cosmopolitan in her tastes, and just now we are very cosmopolitan indeed. Even our servants represent divers nationalities; the butler is French, the two footmen Italians, the maids, I believe, are some of them German, some Irish; and I've no doubt if you penetrated to the kitchen-quarters, you'd find the staff there composed in part of Scandinavians, in part of South Sea Islanders. The other quarters of the globe you will find fully represented in the drawing-room."

Loveday had a direct question to ask.

"Are you certain that Mdlle. Cunier had no friends in England?" she said.

"Positive. She hadn't a friend in the world outside my mother's four walls, poor child! She told me more than once that she was 'seule sur la terre.'" He broke off for a moment, as if overcome by a sad memory, then added: "But I'll put a bullet into him, take my word for it, if she isn't found within another twenty-four hours. Personally I should prefer settling the brute in that fashion to handing him over to the police."

His face flushed a deep red, there came a sudden flash to his eye, but for all that, his voice was as soft and slow and unemotional, as though he were talking of nothing more serious than bringing down a partridge.

There fell a brief pause; then Loveday asked another question.

"Is Mademoiselle Catholic or Protestant, can you tell me?"

The Major thought for a moment, then replied:

"'Pon my word, I don't know. She used sometimes to attend a little charge in South Savile Street—I've walked with her occasionally to the church door—but I couldn't for the life of me say whether it was a Catholic, Protestant, or Pagan place of worship. But—but you don't think those confounded priests have—"

"Here, we are in Portland place," interrupted Loveday. "Mrs. Druce's rooms are already full, to judge from that long line of carriages!"

"Miss Brooke," said the Major suddenly, bethinking himself of his responsibilities, "how am I to introduce you? what rôle will you take up this afternoon? Pose as a faddist of some sort, if you want to win my mother's heart. What do you say to having started a grand scheme for supplying Hottentots and Kaffirs with eye-glasses? My mother would swear eternal friendship with you at once."

"Don't introduce me at all at first," answered Loveday. "Get me into some quiet corner, where I can see without being seen. Later on in the afternoon, when I have had time to look round a little, I'll tell you whether it will be necessary to introduce me or not."

"It will be a mob this afternoon, and no mistake," said Major Druce, as side by side, they entered the house. "Do you hear that fizzing and clucking just behind us? That's Arabic; you'll get it in whiffs between gusts of French and German all the afternoon. The Egyptian contingent seems to be in full force to-day. I don't see any Choctaw Indians, but no doubt they'll send their representatives later on. Come in at this side door, and we'll work our way round to that big palm. My mother is sure to be at the principal doorway."

The drawing rooms were packed from end to end, and Major Druce's progress, as he headed Loveday through the crowd, was impeded by hand-shaking and the interchange of civilities with his mother's guests.

Eventually the big palm standing in a Chinese cistern was reached, and there, half screened from view by its graceful branches, he placed a chair for Miss Brooke.

From this quiet nook, as now and again the crowd parted, Loveday could command a fair view of both drawing-rooms.

"Don't attract attention to me by standing at my elbow," she whispered to the Major.

He answered her whisper with another.

"There's the Beast—Iago, I mean," he said; "do you see him? He's standing talking to that fair, handsome woman in pale green, with a picture hat. She's Lady Gwynne. And there's my mother, and there's Dolly—the Princess I mean—alone on the sofa. Ah! you can't see her now for the crowd. Yes, I'll go, but if you want me, just nod to me and I shall understand."

If was easy to see what had brought such a fashionable crowd to Mrs. Druce's rooms that afternoon. Every caller, as soon as she had shaken hands with the hostess, passed on to the Princess's sofa, and there waited patiently till opportunity presented itself for an introduction to her Eastern Highness.

Loveday found it impossible to get more than the merest glimpse of her, and so transferred her attention to Mr. Hafiz Cassimi, who had been referred to in such unceremonious language by Major Druce.

He was a swarthy, well-featured man, with bold, black eyes, and lips that had the habit of parting now and again, not to smile, but as if for no other purpose than to show a double row of gleaming white teeth. The European dress he wore seemed to accord ill with the man; and Loveday could fancy that those black eyes and that double row of white teeth would have shown to better advantage beneath a turban or a fez cap. From Cassimi, her eye wandered to Mrs. Druce—a tall, stout woman, dressed in black velvet, and with hair mounted high on her head, that had the appearance of being either bleached or powdered. She gave Loveday the impression of being that essentially modern product of modern society—the woman who combines in one person the hard-working philanthropist with the hard-working woman of fashion. As arrivals began to slacken, she left her post near the door and began to make the round of the room. From snatches of talk that came to her where she sat, Loveday could gather that with one hand, as it were, this energetic lady was organizing a grand charity concert, and with the other pushing the interests of a big ball that was shortly to be given by the officers of her son's regiment.

It was a hot June day. In spite of closed blinds and open windows, the rooms were stifling to a degree. The butler, a small dark, slight Frenchman, made his way through the throng to a window at Loveday's right hand, to see if a little more air could be admitted.

Major Druce followed on his heels to Loveday's side.

"Will you come into the next room and have some tea?" he asked; "I'm sure you must feel nearly suffocated here." He broke off, then added in a lower tone: "I hope you have kept your eyes on the Beast. Did you ever in your life see a more repulsive-looking animal?"

Loveday took his questions in their order.

"No tea, thank you," she said, "but I shall be glad if you will tell your butler to bring me a glass of water—there he is, at your elbow. Yes, off and on I have been studying Mr. Cassimi, and I must admit I do not like his smileless smile."

The butler brought the water. The Major, much to his annoyance, was seized upon simultaneously by two ladies, one eager to know if any tidings had been received of Mdlle. Cunier, the other anxious to learn if a distinguished president to the Harem Mission had been decided upon.

Soon after six the rooms began to thin somewhat, and presentations to the Princess ceasing, Loveday was able to get a full view of her.

She presented a striking picture, seated, half-reclining, on a sofa, with two white-robed, dark-skinned Egyptian maidens standing behind it. A more unfortunate sobriquet than "Dolly" could scarcely have been found by the Major for this Oriental beauty, with her olive complexion, her flashing eyes and extravagant richness of attire.

"'Queen of Sheba' would be far more appropriate," thought Loveday. "She turns the commonplace sofa into a throne, and, I should say, makes every one of those ladies feel as if she ought to have donned court dress and plumes for the occasion."

It was difficult for her, from where she sat, to follow the details of the Princess's dress. She could only see that a quantity of soft orange-tinted silk was wound about the upper part of her arms and fell from her shoulders like drooping wings, and that here and there jewels flashed out from its folds. Her thick black hair was loosely knotted, and kept in its place by jeweled pins and a bandeau of pearls; and similar bandeaus adored her slender throat and wrists.

"Are you lost in admiration?" said the Major, once more at her elbow, in a slightly sarcastic tone. "That sort of thing is very taking and effective at first, but after a time—"

He did not finish his sentence, shrugged his shoulders and walked away. Half-past six chimed from a small clock on a bracket. Carriage after carriage was rolling away from the door now, and progress on the stairs was rendered difficult by a descending crowd.

A quarter to seven struck, the last hand-shaking had been gone through, and Mrs. Druce, looking hot and tired, had sunk into a chair at the Princess's right hand, bending slightly forward to render conversation with her easy.

On the Princess's left hand, Lady Gwynne had taken a chair, and sat in converse with Hafiz Cassimi, who stood beside her.

Evidently these four were on very easy and intimate terms with each other. Lady Gwynne had tossed her big picture hat on a chair at her left hand, and was fanning herself with a palm-leaf. Mrs. Druce, beckoning to the butler, desired him to bring them some claret-cup from the refreshment-room.

No one seemed to observe Loveday seated still in her nook beside the big palm.

She signaled to the Major, who stood looking discontentedly from one of the windows.

"That is a most interesting group," she said; "now, if you like, you may introduce me to your mother."

"Oh, with pleasure—under what name?" he asked.

"Under my own," she answered, "and please be very distinct in pronouncing it, raise your voice slightly so that every one of those persons may hear it. And then, please add my profession, and say I am here at your request to investigate the circumstances connected with Mdlle. Cunier's disappearance."

Major Druce looked astounded.

"But—but," he stammered, "have you seen anything—found out anything? If not, don't you think it will be better to preserve your incognita a little longer."

"Don't stop to ask questions," said Loveday sharply; "now, this very minute, do what I ask you, or the opportunity will be gone."

The Major without further demur, escorted Loveday across the room. The conversation between the four intimate friends had now become general and animated, and he had to wait for a minute or so before he could get an opportunity to speak to his mother.

During that minute Loveday stood a little in his rear, with Lady Gwynne and Cassimi at her right hand.

"I want to introduce this lady to you," said the Major, when a pause in the talk gave him his opportunity. "This is Miss Loveday Brooke, a lady detective, and she is here at my request to investigate the circumstances connected with the disappearance of Mdlle. Cunier."

He said the words slowly and distinctly.

"There!" he said to himself complacently, as he ended; "if I had been reading the lessons in church, I couldn't have been more emphatic."

A blank silence for a moment fell upon the group, and even the butler, just then entering with the claret-cup, came to a standstill at the door.

Then, simultaneously, a glance flashed from Mrs. Druce to Lady Gwynne, from Lady Gwynne to Mrs. Druce, and then, also simultaneously, the eyes of both ladies rested, though only for an instant, on the big picture hat lying on the chair.

Lady Gwynne started to her feet and seized her hat, adjusting it without so much as a glance at a mirror.

"I must go at once; this very minute," she said. "I promised Charlie I would back soon after six, and now it is past seven. Mr. Cassimi, will you take me down to my carriage?" And with the most hurried of leave-takings to the Princess and her hostess, the lady swept out of the room, followed by Mr. Cassimi.

The butler still standing at the door, drew back to allow the lady to pass, and then, claret-cup and all, followed her out of the room.

Mrs. Druce drew a long breath and bowed formally to Loveday.

"I was a little taken by surprise," she began—

But here the Princess rose suddenly from the sofa.

"Moi, je suis fatiguée," she said in excellent French to Mrs. Druce, and she too swept out of the room, throwing, as she passed, what seemed to Loveday a slightly scornful glance towards the Major.

Her two attendants, one carrying her fan, and the other her reclining cushions, followed.

Mrs. Druce again turned to Loveday.

"Yes, I confess I was taken a little by surprise," she said, her manner thawing slightly. "I am not accustomed to the presence of detectives in my house; but now tell me what do you propose doing: how do you mean to begin your investigations— by going over the house and looking in all the corners, or by cross-questioning the servants? Forgive my asking, but really I am quite at a loss; I haven't the remotest idea how such investigations are generally conducted."

"I do not propose to do much in the way of investigation to-night," answered Loveday as formally as she had been addressed, "for I have very important business to transact before eight o'clock this evening. I shall ask you to allow me to see Mdlle. Cunier's room—ten minutes there will be sufficient—after that, I do not think I need further trouble you."

"Certainly; by all means," answered Mrs. Druce; "you'll find the room exactly as Lucie left it, nothing has been disturbed."

She turned to the butler, who had by this time returned and stood presenting the claret-cup, and, in French, desired him to summon her maid, and tell her to show Miss Brooke to Mdlle. Cunier's room.

The ten minutes that Loveday had said would suffice for her survey of this room extended themselves to fifteen, but the extra five minutes assuredly were not expended by her in the investigation of drawers and boxes. The maid, a pleasant, well-spoken young woman, jingled her keys, and opened every lock, and seemed not at all disinclined to enter into the light gossip that Loveday contrived to set going.

She answered freely a variety of questions that Loveday put to her respecting Mademoiselle and her general habits, and from Mademoiselle, the talk drifted to other members of Mrs. Druce's household.

If Loveday had, as she had stated, important business to transact that evening, she certainly set about it in a strange fashion.

After she quitted Mademoiselle's room, she went straight out of the house, without leaving a message of any sort for either Mrs. or Major Druce. She walked the length of Portland Place in leisurely fashion, and then, having first ascertained that her movements were not being watched, she called a hansom, and desired the man to drive her to Madame Celine's, a fashionable milliner's in Old Bond Street.

At Madame Celine's she spent close upon half-an-hour, giving many and minute directions for the making of a hat, which assuredly, when finished, would compare with nothing in the way of millinery that she had ever before put upon her head.

From Madame Celine's the hansom conveyed her to an undertaker's shop, at the corner of South Savile Street, and here she spent a brief ten minutes in conversation with the undertaker himself in his little back parlour.

From the undertaker's she drove home to her rooms in Gower Street, and then, before she divested herself of hat and coat, she wrote a brief note to Major Druce, requesting him to meet her on the following morning at Eglacé's, the confectioner's, in South Savile Street, at nine o'clock punctually.

This note she committed to the charge of the cab-driver, desiring him to deliver it at Portland Place on his way back to his stand.

"They've queer ways of doing things—these people!" said the Major, as he opened and read the note. "Suppose I must keep the appointment though, confound it. I can't see that she can possibly have found out anything by just sitting still in a corner for a couple of hours! And I'm confident she didn't give that beast Cassimi one quarter the attention she bestowed on other people."

In spite of his grumbling, however, the Major kept his appointment, and nine o'clock the next morning saw him shaking hands with Miss Brooke on Eglacé's doorstep.

"Dismiss your hansom," she said to him. "I only want you to come a few doors down the street, to the French Protestant church, to which you have sometimes escorted Mdlle. Cunier."

At the church door Loveday paused a moment.

"Before we enter," she said, "I want you to promise that whatever you may see going on there—however greatly you may be surprised—you will make no disturbance, not so much as open your lips till we come out."

The Major, not a little bewildered, gave the required promise; and, side by side, the two entered the church.

It was little more than a big room; at the farther end, in the middle of the nave, stood the pulpit, and immediately behind this was a low platform, enclosed by a brass rail.

Behind this brass rail, in black Geneva gown, stood the pastor of the church, and before him, on cushions, kneeled two persons, a man and a woman.

These two persons and an old man, the verger, formed the whole of the congregation. The position of the church, amid shops and narrow back-yards, had necessitated the filling in of every one of its windows with stained glass; it was, consequently, so dim that, coming in from the outside glare of sunlight, the Major found it difficult to make out what was going on at the farther end.

The verger came forward and offered to show them to a seat. Loveday shook her head—they would be leaving in a minute, she said, and would prefer standing where they were.

The Major began to take in the situation.

"Why they're being married!" he said in a loud whisper. "What on earth have you brought me in here for?"

Loveday laid her finger on her lips and frowned severely at him.

The marriage service came to an end, the pastor extended his black-gowned arms like the wings of a bat and pronounced the benediction; the man and woman rose from their knees and proceeded to follow him into the vestry.

The woman was neatly dressed in a long dove-coloured travelling cloak. She wore a large hat, from which fell a white gossamer veil that completely hid her face from view. The man was small, dark and slight, and as he passed on to the vestry beside his bride, the Major at once identified him as his mother's butler.

"Why, that's Lebrun!" he said in a still louder whisper than before. "Why, in the name of all that's wonderful, have you brought me here to see that fellow married?"

"You'd better come outside if you can't keep quiet," said Loveday severely, and leading the way out of the church as she spoke.

Outside, South Savile Street was busy with early morning traffic.

"Let us go back to Eglacé's" said Loveday, "and have some coffee. I will explain to you there all you are wishing to know."

But before the coffee could be brought to them, the Major had asked at least a dozen questions.

Loveday put them all on one side.

"All in good time" she said. "You are leaving out the most important question of all. Have you no curiosity to know who was the bride that Lebrun has chosen?"

"I don't suppose it concerns me in the slightest degree," he answered indifferently; "but since you wish me to ask the question—Who was she?"

"Lucie Cunier, lately your mother's amanuensis."

"The —!" cried the Major, jumping to his feet and uttering an exclamation that must be indicated by a blank.

"Take it calmly," said Loveday; "don't rave. Sit down and I'll tell you all about it. No, it is not the doing of your friend Cassimi, so you need not threaten to put a bullet into him; the girl has married Lebrun of her own free will—no one has forced her into it."

"Lucie has married Lebrun of her own free will!" he echoed, growing very white and taking the chair which faced Loveday at the little table.

"Will you have sugar?" asked Loveday, stirring the coffee, which the waiter at that moment brought.

"Yes, I repeat," she presently resumed, "Lucie has married Lebrun of her own free will, although I conjecture she might not perhaps have been quite so willing to crown his happiness if the Princess Dullah-Veih had not made it greatly to her interest to do so."

"Dolly made it to her interest to do so?" again echoed the Major.

"Do not interrupt me with exclamations; let me tell the story my own fashion, and then you may ask as many questions as you please. Now, to begin at the beginning, Lucie became engaged to Lebrun within a month of her coming to your mother's house, but she carefully kept the secret from everyone, even from the servants, until about a month ago, when she mentioned the fact in confidence to Mrs. Druce in order to defend herself from the charge of having sought to attract your attention. There was nothing surprising in this engagement; they were both lonely and in a foreign land, spoke the same language, and no doubt had many things in common; and, although chance has lifted Lucie somewhat out of her station, she really belongs to the same class in life as Lebrun. Their love-making appears to have run along smoothly enough until you came home on leave, and the girl's pretty face attracted your attention. Your evident admiration for her disturbed the equanimity of the Princess, who saw your devotion to herself waning; of Lebrun, who fancied Lucie's manner to him had changed; of your mother, who was anxious that you should make a suitable marriage. Also additional complications arose from the fact that your attentions to the little Swiss girl had drawn Mr. Cassimi's notice to her numerous attractions, and there was the danger of you two young men posing as rivals. At this juncture Lady Gwynne, as an intimate friend, and one who had herself suffered a twinge of heartache on Mademoiselle's account, was taken into your mother's confidence, and the three ladies in council decided that Lucie, in some fashion, must be got out of the way before you, and Mr. Cassimi came to an open breach, or you had spoilt your matrimonial prospects."

Here the Major made a slightly impatient movement.

Loveday went on: "It was the Princess who solved the question how this was to be done. Fair Rosamonds are no longer put out of the way by 'a cup of cold poison'–golden guineas do the thing far more easily and innocently. The Princess expressed her willingness to bestow a thousand pounds on Lucie on the day that she married Lebrun, and to set her up afterwards as a fashionable milliner in Paris. After this munificent offer, everything else became mere matter of detail. The main thing was to get the damsel out of the way without your being able to trace her–perhaps work on her feelings, and induce her, at the last moment, to throw over Lebrun. Your absence from home, on a three days' visit, gave them the wished-for opportunity. Lady Gwynne took her milliner into her confidence. Madame Celine consented to receive Lucie into her house, seclude her in a room on the upper floor, and at the same time give her an insight into the profession of a fashionable milliner. The rest I think you know. Lucie quietly walks out of the house one afternoon, taking no luggage, calling no cab, and thereby cutting off one very obvious means of being traced. Madame Celine receives and hides her–not a difficult feat to accomplish in London, more especially if the one to be hidden is a foreign amanuensis, who is seldom seen out of doors, and who leaves no photograph behind her."

"I suppose it was Lebrun who had the confounded cheek to go to my drawer and appropriate that photograph. I wish it had been Cassimi–I could have kicked him, but–but it makes one feel rather small to have posed as rival to one's mother's butler."

"I think you may congratulate yourself that Lebrun did nothing worse than go to your drawer and appropriate that photograph. I never saw a man bestow a more deadly look of hatred than he threw at you yesterday afternoon in your mother's drawing-room; it was that look of hatred that first drew my attention to the man and set me on the track that has ended in the Swiss Protestant church this morning."

"Ah! let me hear about that–let me have the links in the chain, one by one, as you came upon them," said the Major.

He was still pale–almost as the marble table at which they sat, but his voice had gone back to its normal slow, soft drawl.

"With pleasure. The look that Lebrun threw at you, as he crossed the room to open the window, was link number one. As I saw that look, I said to myself there is someone in that corner whom that man hates with a deadly hatred. Then you came forward to speak to me, and I saw that it was you that the man was ready to murder, if opportunity offered. After this, I scrutinized him closely–not a detail of his features or his dress escaped me, and I noticed, among other things, that on the fourth finger of his left hand, half hidden by a more pretentious ring, was an old fashioned curious looking silver one. That silver ring was link number two in the chain."

"Ah, I suppose you asked for that glass of water on purpose to get a closer view of the ring?"

"I did, I found it was a Genevese ring of ancient make, the like of which I had not seen since I was a child and played with one, that my old Swiss bonne used to wear. Now I must tell you a little bit of Genevese history before I can make you understand how important a link that silver ring was to me. Echallets, the town in which Lucie was born, and her father had kept a watchmaker's shop, has long been famous for its jewellery and watchmaking. The two trades, however, were not combined in one until about a hundred years ago, when the corporation of the town passed a law decreeing that they should unite in one guild for their common good. To celebrate this amalgamation of interests, the jewellers fabricated a certain number of silver rings, consisting of a plain band of silver, on which two hands, in relief, clasped each other. These rings were distributed among the members of the guild, and as time has gone on they have become scarce and valuable as relics of the past. In certain families, they have been handed down as heirlooms, and have frequently done duty as betrothal rings–the clasped hands no doubt suggesting their suitability for this purpose. Now, when I saw such a ring on Lebrun's finger, I naturally guessed from whom he had received it, and at once classed his interests with those of your mother and the Princess, and looked upon him as their possible coadjutor."

"What made you throw the brute Cassimi altogether out of your reckoning?"

"I did not do so at this stage of events; only, so to speak, marked him as 'doubtful' and kept my eye on him. I determined to try an experiment that I have never before attempted in my work. You know what that experiment was. I saw five persons, Mrs. Druce, the Princess, Lady Gwynne, Mr. Cassimi and Lebrun all in the room within a few yards of each other, and I asked you to take them by surprise and announce my name and profession, so that every one of those five persons could hear you."

"You did. I could not, for the life of me, make out what was your motive for so doing."

"My motive for so doing was simply, as it were, to raise the sudden cry, 'The enemy is upon you,' and to set every one of those five persons guarding their weak point–that is, if they had one. I'll draw your attention to what followed. Mr. Cassimi remained nonchalant and impassive; your mother and Lady Gwynne exchanged glances, and they both simultaneously threw a nervous look at Lady Gwynne's hat lying on the chair. Now as I had stood waiting to be introduced to Mrs. Druce, I had casually read the name of Madame Céline on the lining of the hat and I at once concluded that Madame Céline must be a very weak point indeed; a conclusion that was confirmed when Lady Gwynne hurriedly seized her hat and as hurriedly departed. Then the Princess scarcely less abruptly rose and left the room, and Lebrun on the point of entering, quitted it also. When he returned five minutes later, with the claret-cup, he had removed the ring from his finger, so I had now little doubt where his weak point lay."

"It's wonderful; it's like a fairy tale!," drawled the Major. "Pray, go on."

"After this," continued Loveday, "my work became very simple. I did not care two straws for seeing Mademoiselle's room, but I cared very much to have a talk with Mrs. Druce's maid. From her I elicited the important fact that Lebrun was leaving very unexpectedly on the following day, and that his boxes were packed and labeled for Paris. After I left your house, I drove to Madame Céline's, and there, as a sort of entrance fee, ordered an elaborate hat. I praised freely the hats they had on view, and while giving minute directions as to the one I required, I extracted the information that Madame Céline had recently taken on a new milliner who had very great artistic skill. Upon this, I asked permission to see this new milliner and give her special instructions concerning my hat. My request was referred to Madame Céline, who appeared much ruffled by it, and informed me that it would be quite useless for me to see this new milliner; she could execute no more orders, as she was leaving the next day for Paris, where she intended opening an establishment on her own account.

"Now you see the point at which I had arrived. There was Lebrun and there was this new milliner each leaving for Paris on the same day; it was not unreasonable to suppose that they might start in company, and that before so doing, a little ceremony might be gone through in the Swiss Protestant church that Mademoiselle occasionally attended. This conjecture sent me to the undertaker in South Savile Street, who combines with his undertaking the office of verger to the little church. From him I learned that a marriage was to take place at the church at a quarter to nine the next morning and that the names of the contracting parties were Pierre Lebrun and Lucie Cuénin."

"Cuénin!"

"Yes, that is the girl's real name; it seems Lady Gwynne re-christened her Cunier, because she said the English pronunciation of Cuénin grated on her ear—people would insist upon adding a g after the n. She introduced her to Mrs. Druce under the name of Cunier, forgetting, perhaps, the girl's real name, or else thinking it a matter of no importance. This fact, no doubt, considerably lessened Lebrun's fear of detection in procuring his licence and transmitting it to the Swiss pastor. Perhaps you are a little surprised at my knowledge of the facts I related to you at the beginning of our conversation. I got at them through Lebrun this morning. At half-past eight I went down to the church and found him there, waiting for his bride. He grew terribly excited at seeing me, and thought I was going to bring you down on him and upset his wedding arrangements at the last moment. I assured him to the contrary, and his version of the facts I have handed on to you. Should, however, any details of the story seem to you to be lacking, I have no doubt that Mrs. Druce or the Princess will supply them, now that all necessity for secrecy has come to an end."

The Major drew on his gloves; his colour had come back to him; he had resumed his easy suavity of manner.

"I don't think," he said slowly, "I'll trouble my mother or the Princess; and I shall be glad, if you have the opportunity, if you will make people understand that I only moved in the matter at all out of—of mere kindness to a young and friendless foreigner."

DRAWN DAGGERS

"I ADMIT that the dagger business is something of a puzzle to me, but as for the lost necklace–well, I should have thought a child would have understood that," said Mr. Dyer irritably. "When a young lady loses a valuable article of jewellery and wishes to hush the matter up, the explanation is obvious."

"Sometimes," answered Miss Brooke calmly, "the explanation that is obvious is the one to be rejected, not accepted."

Off and on these two had been, so to speak, "jangling" a good deal that morning. Perhaps the fact was in part to be attributed to the biting east wind which had set Loveday's eyes watering with the gritty dust, as she had made her way to Lynch Court, and which was, at the present moment, sending the smoke, in aggravating gusts, down the chimney into Mr. Dyer's face. Thus it was, however. On the various topics that had chanced to come up for discussion that morning between Mr. Dyer and his colleague, they had each taken up, as if by design, diametrically opposite points of view.

His temper altogether gave way now.

"If," he said, bringing his hand down with emphasis on his writing table, "you lay it down as a principle that the obvious is to be rejected in favour of the abstruse, you'll soon find yourself launched in the predicament of having to prove that two apples added to two other apples do not make four. But there, if you don't choose to see things from my point of view, that is no reason why you should lose your temper!"

"Mr. Hawke wishes to see you, sir," said a clerk, at that moment entering the room.

It was a fortunate diversion. Whatever might be the differences of opinion in which these two might indulge in private, they were careful never to parade those differences before their clients.

Mr. Dyer's irritability vanished in a moment.

"Show the gentleman in," he said to the clerk. Then he turned to Loveday. "This is the Rev. Anthony Hawke, the gentleman at whose house I told you that Miss Monroe is staying temporarily. He is a clergyman of the Church of England, but gave up his living some twenty years ago when he married a wealthy lady. Miss Monroe has been sent over to his guardianship from Pekin by her father, Sir George Monroe, in order to get her out of the way of a troublesome and undesirable suitor."

The last sentence was added in a low and hurried tone, for Mr. Hawke was at that moment entering the room.

He was a man close upon sixty years of age, white-haired, clean shaven, with a full, round face, to which a small nose imparted a somewhat infantine expression. His manner of greeting was urbane but slightly flurried and nervous. He gave Loveday the impression of being an easy-going, happy-tempered man who, for the moment, was unusually disturbed and perplexed.

He glanced uneasily at Loveday. Mr. Dyer hastened to explain that this was the lady by whose aid he hoped to get to the bottom of the matter now under consideration.

"In that case there can be no objection to my showing you this," said Mr. Hawke; "it came by post this morning. You see my enemy still pursues me."

As he spoke he took from his pocket a big, square envelope, from which he drew a large-sized sheet of paper.

On this sheet of paper were roughly drawn, in ink, two daggers, about six inches in length, with remarkably pointed blades.

Mr. Dyer looked at the sketch with interest.

"We will compare this drawing and its envelope with those you previously received," he said, opening a drawer of his writing-table and taking thence a precisely similar envelope. On the sheet of paper, however, that this envelope enclosed, there was drawn one dagger only.

He placed both envelopes and their enclosures side by side, and in silence compared them. Then, without a word, he handed them to Miss Brooke, who, taking a glass from her pocket, subjected them to a similar careful and minute scrutiny.

Both envelopes were of precisely the same make, and were each addressed to Mr. Hawke's London address in a round, school-boyish, copy-book sort of hand– the hand so easy to write and so difficult to being home to any writer on account of its want of individuality. Each envelope likewise bore a Cork and a London postmark.

The sheet of paper, however, that the first envelope enclosed bore the sketch of one dagger only.

Loveday laid down her glass.

"The envelopes," she said, "have, undoubtedly, been addressed by the same person, but these last two daggers have not been drawn by the hand that drew the first. Dagger number one was, evidently, drawn by a timid, uncertain and inartistic hand–see how the lines wave and how they have been patched here and there. The person who drew the other daggers, I should say, could do better work; the outline, though rugged, is bold and free. I should like to take these sketches home with me and compare them again at my leisure."

"Ah, I felt sure what your opinion would be!" said Mr. Dyer complacently.

Mr. Hawke seemed much disturbed.

"Good gracious!" he ejaculated; "you don't mean to say I have two enemies pursuing me in this fashion! What does it mean? Can it be–is it possible, do you think, that these things have been sent to me by the members of some Secret Society in Ireland–under error, of course–mistaking me for someone else? They can't be meant for me; I have never, in my whole life, been mixed up with any political agitation of any sort."

Mr. Dyer shook his head. "Members of secret societies generally make pretty sure of their ground before they send out missives of this kind," he said. "I have never heard of such an error being made. I think, too, we mustn't build any theories on the Irish post-mark; the letters may have been posted in Cork for the whole and sole purpose of drawing off attention from some other quarter."

"Will you mind telling me a little about the loss of the necklace?" here said Loveday, bringing the conversation suddenly round from the daggers to the diamonds.

"I think," interposed Mr. Dyers, turning towards her, "that the episode of the drawn daggers—drawn in a double sense—should be treated entirely on its own merits, considered as a thing apart from the loss of the necklace. I am inclined to believe that when we have gone a little further into the matter we shall find that each circumstance belongs to a different group of facts. After all, it is possible that these daggers may have been sent by way of a joke—a rather foolish one, I admit—by some harum-scarum fellow bent on causing a sensation."

Mr. Hawke's face brightened.

"Ah! now, do you think so—really think so?" he ejaculated. "It would lift such a load from my mind if you could bring the thing home, in this way, to some practical joker. There are a lot of such fellows knocking about the world. Why, now I come to think of it, my nephew, Jack, who is a good deal with us just now, and is not quite so steady a fellow as I should like him to be, must have a good many such scamps among his acquaintances."

"A good many such scamps among his acquaintances," echoed Loveday; "that certainly gives plausibility to Mr. Dyer's supposition. At the same time, I think we are bound to look at the other side of the case, and admit the possibility of these daggers being sent in right-down sober earnest by persons concerned in the robbery, with the intention of intimidating you and preventing full investigation of the matter. If this be so, it will not signify which thread we take up and follow. If we find the sender of the daggers we are safe to come upon the thief; or, if we follow up and find the thief, the sender of the daggers will not be far off."

Mr. Hawke's face fell once more.

"It's an uncomfortable position to be in," he said slowly. "I suppose, whoever they are, they will do the regulation thing, and next time will send an instalment of three daggers, in which case I may consider myself a doomed man. It did not occur to me before, but I remember now that I did not receive the first dagger until after I had spoken very strongly to Mrs. Hawke, before the servants, about my wish to set the police to work. I told her I felt bound, in honour to Sir George, to do so, as the necklace had been lost under my roof."

"Did Mrs. Hawke object to your calling in the aid of the police?" asked Loveday.

"Yes, most strongly. She entirely supported Miss Monroe in her wish to take no steps in the matter. Indeed, I should not have come round as I did last night to Mr. Dyer, if my wife had not been suddenly summoned from home by the serious illness of her sister. At least," he corrected himself with a little attempt at self-assertion, "my coming to him might have been a little delayed. I hope you understand, Mr. Dyer; I do not mean to imply that I am not master in my own house."

"Oh, quite so, quite so," responded Mr. Dyer. "Did Mrs. Hawke or Miss Monroe give any reasons for not wishing you to move in the matter?"

"All told, I should think they gave about a hundred reasons—I can't remember them all. For one thing, Miss Monroe said it might necessitate her appearing in the police courts, a thing she would not consent to do; and she certainly did not consider the necklace was worth the fuss I was making over it. And that necklace, sir, has been valued at over nine hundred pounds, and has come down to the young lady from her mother."

"And Mrs. Hawke?"

"Mrs. Hawke supported Miss Monroe in her views in her presence. But privately to me afterwards, she gave other reasons for not wishing the police called in. Girls, she said, were always careless with their jewellery, she might have lost the necklace in Pekin, and never have brought it to England at all."

"Quite so," said Mr. Dyer. "I think I understood you to say that no one had seen the necklace since Miss Monroe's arrival in England. Also, I believe it was she who first discovered it to be missing?"

"Yes. Sir George, when he wrote apprising me of his daughter's visit, added a postscript to his letter, saying that his daughter was bringing her necklace with her and that he would feel greatly obliged if I would have it deposited with as little delay as possible at my bankers', where it could be easily got at if required. I spoke to Miss Monroe about doing this two or three times, but she did not seem at all inclined to comply with her father's wishes. Then my wife took the matter in hand—Mrs. Hawke, I must tell you, has a very firm, resolute manner—she told Miss Monroe plainly that she would not have the responsibility of those diamonds in the house, and insisted that there and then they should be sent off to the bankers. Upon this Miss Monroe went up to her room, and presently returned, saying that her necklace had disappeared. She herself, she said, had placed it in her jewel-case and the jewel-case in her wardrobe, when her boxes were unpacked. The jewel-case was in the wardrobe right enough, and no other article of jewellery appeared to have been disturbed, but the little padded niche in which the necklace had been deposited was empty. My wife and her maid went upstairs immediately, and searched every corner of the room, but, I'm sorry to say, without any result."

"Miss Monroe, I suppose, has her own maid?"

"No, she has not. The maid—an elderly native woman—who left Pekin with her, suffered so terribly from sea-sickness that, when they reached Malta, Miss Monroe allowed her to land and remain there in charge of an agent of the P. and O. Company till an outward bound packet could take her back to China. It seems the poor woman thought she was going to die, and was in a terrible state of mind because she hadn't brought her coffin with her. I dare say you know the terror these Chinese have of being buried in foreign soil. After her departure, Miss Monroe engaged one of the steerage passengers to act as her maid for the remainder of the voyage."

"Did Miss Monroe make the long journey from Pekin accompanied only by this native woman?"

"No; friends escorted her to Hong King—by far the roughest part of the journey. From Hong Kong she came on in The Colombo, accompanied only by her maid. I wrote and told her father I would meet her at the docks in London; the young lady, however, preferred landing at Plymouth, and telegraphed to me from there that she was coming on by rail to Waterloo, where, if I liked, I might meet her."

"She seems to be a young lady of independent habits. Was she brought up and educated in China?"

"Yes; by a succession of French and American governesses. After her mother's death, when she was little more than a baby, Sir George could not make up his mind to part with her, as she was his only child."

"I suppose you and Sir George Monroe are old friends?"

"Yes; he and I were great chums before he went out to China—now about twenty years ago—and it was only natural, when he wished to get his daughter out of the way of young Danvers's impertinent attentions, that he should ask me to take charge of her till he could claim his retiring pension and set up his tent in England."

"What was the chief objection to Mr. Danvers's attentions?"

"Well, he is only a boy of one-and-twenty, and has no money into the bargain. He has been sent out to Pekin by his father to study the language, in order to qualify for a billet in the customs, and it may be a dozen years before he is in a position to keep a wife. Now, Miss Monroe is an heiress—will come into her mother's large fortune when she is of age—and Sir George, naturally, would like her to make a good match."

"I suppose Miss Monroe came to England very reluctantly?"

"I imagine so. No doubt it was a great wrench for her to leave her home and friends in that sudden fashion and come to us, who are, one and all, utter strangers to her. She is very quiet, very shy and reserved. She goes nowhere, sees no one. When some old China friends of her father's called to see her the other day, she immediately found she had a headache, and went to bed. I think, on the whole, she gets on better with my nephew than with anyone else."

"Will you kindly tell me of how many persons your household consists at the present moment?

"At the present moment we are one more than usual, for my nephew, Jack, is home with his regiment from India, and is staying with us. As a rule, my household consists of my wife and myself, butler, cook, housemaid and my wife's maid, who just now is doing double duty as Miss Monroe's maid also."

Mr. Dyer looked at his watch.

"I have an important engagement in ten minutes' time," he said, "so I must leave you and Miss Brooke to arrange details as to how and when she is to begin her work inside your house, for, of course, in a case of this sort we must, in the first instance at any rate, concentrate attention within your four walls."

"The less delay the better," said Loveday. "I should like to attack the mystery at once—this afternoon."

Mr. Hawke thought for a moment.

"According to present arrangements," he said, with a little hesitation, "Mrs. Hawke will return next Friday, that is the day after to-morrow, so I can only ask you to remain in the house till the morning of that day. I'm sure you will understand that there might be some—some little awkwardness in—"

"Oh, quite so," interrupted Loveday. "I don't see at present that there will be any necessity for me to sleep in the house at all. How would it be for me to assume the part of a lady house decorator in the employment of a West-end firm, and sent by them to survey your house and advise upon its re-decoration? All I should have to do, would be to walk about your rooms with my head on one side, and a pencil and note-book in my hand. I should interfere with no one, your family life would go on as usual, and I could make my work as short or as long as necessity might dictate."

Mr. Hawke had no objection to offer to this. He had, however, a request to make as he rose to depart, and he made it a little nervously.

"If," he said, "by any chance there should come a telegram from Mrs. Hawke, saying she will return by an earlier train, I suppose—I hope, that is, you will make some excuse, and—and not get me into hot water, I mean."

To this, Loveday answered a little evasively that she trusted no such telegram would be forthcoming, but that, in any case, he might rely upon her discretion.

Four o'clock was striking from a neighbouring church clock as Loveday lifted the old-fashioned brass knocker of Mr. Hawke's house in Tavistock Square. An elderly butler admitted her and showed her into the drawing-room on the first floor. A single glance round showed Loveday that if her rôle had been real instead of assumed, she would have found plenty of scope for her talents. Although the house was in all respects comfortably furnished, it bore unmistakably the impress of those early Victorian days when aesthetic surroundings were not deemed a necessity of existence; an impress which people past middle age, and growing increasingly indifferent to the accessories of life, are frequently careless to remove.

"Young life here is evidently an excrescence, not part of the home; a troop of daughters turned into this room would speedily set going a different condition of things," thought Loveday, taking stock of the faded white and gold wall paper, the chairs covered with lilies and roses in cross-stitch, and the knick-knacks of a past generation that were scattered about on tables and mantelpiece.

A yellow damask curtain, half-festooned, divided the back drawing-room from the front in which she was seated. From the other side of this curtain there came to her the sound of voices—those of a man and a girl.

"Cut the cards again, please," said the man's voice. "Thank you. There you are again—the queen of hearts, surrounded with diamonds, and turning her back on a knave. Miss Monroe, you can't do better than make that fortune come true. Turn your back on the man who let you go without a word and—"

"Hush!" interrupted the girl with a little laugh: "I heard the next room door open—I'm sure someone came in."

The girl's laugh seemed to Loveday utterly destitute of that echo of heart-ache that in the circumstances might have been expected.

At this moment Mr. Hawke entered the room, and almost simultaneously the two young people came from the other side of the yellow curtain and crossed towards the door.

Loveday took a survey of them as they passed.

The young man—evidently "my nephew, Jack"—was a good-looking young fellow, with dark eyes and hair. The girl was small, slight and fair. She was perceptibly less at home with Jack's uncle than she was with Jack, for her manner changed and grew formal and reserved as she came face to face with him.

"We're going downstairs to have a game of billiards," said Jack, addressing Mr. Hawke, and throwing a look of curiosity at Loveday.

"Jack," said the old gentleman, "what would you say if I told you I was going to have the house re-decorated from top to bottom, and that this lady had come to advise on the matter."

This was the nearest (and most Anglicé) approach to a fabrication that Mr. Hawke would allow to pass his lips.

"Well," answered Jack promptly, "I should say, 'not before its time.' That would cover a good deal."

Then the two young people departed in company.

Loveday went straight to her work.

"I'll begin my surveying at the top of the house, and at once, if you please," she said. "Will you kindly tell one of your maids to show me through the bedrooms? If it is possible, let that maid be the one who waits on Miss Monroe and Mrs. Hawke."

The maid who responded to Mr. Hawke's summons was in perfect harmony with the general appearance of the house. In addition, however, to being elderly and faded, she was also remarkably sour-visaged, and carried herself as if she thought that Mr. Hawke had taken a great liberty in thus commanding her attendance.

In dignified silence she showed Loveday over the topmost story, where the servants' bed-rooms were situated, and with a somewhat supercilious expression of countenance, watched her making various entries in her note-book.

In dignified silence, also, she led the way down to the second floor, where were the principal bed-rooms of the house.

"This is Miss Monroe's room," she said, as she threw back a door of one of these rooms, and then shut her lips with a snap, as if they were never going to open again.

The room that Loveday entered was, like the rest of the house, furnished in the style that prevailed in the early Victorian period. The bedstead was elaborately curtained with pink lined upholstery; the toilet-table was befrilled with muslin and tarlatan out of all likeness to a table. The one point, however, that chiefly attracted Loveday's attention was the extreme neatness that prevailed throughout the apartment–a neatness, however, that was carried out with so strict an eye to comfort and convenience that it seemed to proclaim the hand of a first-class maid. Everything in the room was, so to speak, squared to the quarter of an inch, and yet everything that a lady could require in dressing lay ready to hand. The dressing-gown lying on the back of a chair had footstool and slippers beside it. A chair stood in front of the toilet table, and on a small Japanese table to the right of the chair were placed hair-pin box, comb and brush, and hand mirror.

"This room will want money spent upon it," said Loveday, letting her eyes roam critically in all directions. "Nothing but Moorish wood-work will take off the squareness of those corners. But what a maid Miss Monroe must have. I never before saw a room so orderly and, at the same time, so comfortable."

This was so direct an appeal to conversation that the sour-visaged maid felt compelled to open her lips.

"I wait on Miss Monroe, for the present," she said snappishly; "but, to speak the truth, she scarcely requires a maid. I never before in my life had dealings with such a young lady."

"She does so much for herself, you mean–declines much assistance."

"She's like no one else I ever had to do with." (This was said even more snappishly than before.) "She not only won't be helped in dressing, but she arranges her room every day before leaving it, even to placing the chair in front of the looking glass."

"And to opening the lid of the hair-pin box, so that she may have the pins ready to her hand," added Loveday, for a moment bending over the Japanese table, with its toilet accessories.

Another five minutes were all that Loveday accorded to the inspection of this room. Then, a little to the surprise of the dignified maid, she announced her intention of completing her survey of the bed-rooms some other time, and dismissed her at the drawing-room door, to tell Mr. Hawke that she wished to see him before leaving.

Mr. Hawke, looking much disturbed and with a telegram in his hand, quickly made his appearance.

"From my wife, to say she'll be back to-night. She'll be at Waterloo in about half an hour from now," he said, holding up the brown envelope. "Now, Miss Brooke, what are we to do? I told you how much Mrs. Hawke objected to the investigation of this matter, and she is very—well—firm when she once says a thing, and—and—"

"Set your mind at rest," interrupted Loveday; "I have done all I wished to do within your walls, and the remainder of my investigation can be carried on just as well at Lynch Court or at my own private rooms."

"Done all you wished to do!" echoed Mr. Hawke in amazement; "why, you've not been an hour in the house, and do you mean to tell me you've found out anything about the necklace or the daggers?"

"Don't ask me any questions just yet; I want you to answer one or two instead. Now, can you tell me anything about any letters Miss Monroe may have written or received since she has been in your house?"

"Yes, certainly, Sir George wrote to me very strongly about her correspondence, and begged me to keep a sharp eye on it, so as to nip in the bud any attempt to communicate with Danvers. So far, however, she does not appear to have made any such attempt. She is frankness itself over her correspondence. Every letter that has come addressed to her, she has shown either to me or to my wife, and they have one and all been letters from old friends of her father's, wishing to make her acquaintance now that she is in England. With regard to letter-writing, I am sorry to say she has a marked and most peculiar objection to it. Every one of the letters she has received, my wife tells, me, remain unanswered still. She has never once been seen, since she came to the house, with a pen in her hand. And if she wrote on the sly, I don't know how she would get her letters posted—she never goes outside the door by herself, and she would have no opportunity of giving them to any of the servants to post except Mrs. Hawke's maid, and she is beyond suspicion in such a matter. She has been well cautioned, and, in addition, is not the sort of person who would assist a young lady in carrying on a clandestine correspondence."

"I should imagine not! I suppose Miss Monroe has been present at the breakfast table each time that you have received your daggers through the post—you told me, I think, that they had come by the first post in the morning?"

"Yes; Miss Monroe is very punctual at meals, and has been present each time. Naturally, when I received such unpleasant missives, I made some sort of exclamation and then handed the thing round the table for inspection, and Miss Monroe was very much concerned to know who my secret enemy could be."

"No doubt. Now, Mr. Hawke, I have a very special request to make to you, and I hope you will be most exact in carrying it out."

"You may rely upon my doing so to the very letter."

"Thank you. If, then, you should receive by post to-morrow morning one of those big envelopes you already know the look of, and find that it contains a sketch of three, not two, drawn daggers—"

"Good gracious! what makes you think such a thing likely?" exclaimed Mr. Hawke, greatly disturbed. "Why am I to be persecuted in this way? Am I to take it for granted that I am a doomed man?"

He began to pace the room in a state of great excitement.

"I don't think I would if I were you," answered Loveday calmly. "Pray let me finish. I want you to open the big envelope that may come to you by post to-morrow morning just you have opened the others–in full view of your family at the breakfast-table–and to hand round the sketch it may contain for inspection to your wife, your nephew and to Miss Monroe. Now, will you promise me to do this?"

"Oh, certainly; I should most likely have done so without any promising. But–but–I'm sure you'll understand that I feel myself to be in a peculiarly uncomfortable position, and I shall feel so very much obliged to you if you'll tell me–that is if you'll enter a little more fully into an explanation."

Loveday looked at her watch. "I should think Mrs. Hawke would be just at this moment arriving at Waterloo; I'm sure you'll be glad to see the last of me. Please come to me at my rooms in Gower Street to-morrow at twelve–here is my card. I shall then be able to enter into fuller explanations I hope. Good-bye."

The old gentleman showed her politely downstairs, and, as he shook hands with her at the front door, again asked, in a most emphatic manner, if she did not consider him to be placed in a "peculiarly unpleasant position."

Those last words at parting were to be the first with which he greeted her on the following morning when he presented himself at her rooms in Gower Street. They were, however, repeated in considerably more agitated a manner.

"Was there ever a man in a more miserable position!" he exclaimed, as he took the chair that Loveday indicated. "I not only received the three daggers for which you prepared me, but I got an additional worry, for which I was totally unprepared. This morning, immediately after breakfast, Miss Monroe walked out of the house all by herself, and no one knows where she has gone. And the girl has never before been outside the door alone. It seems the servants saw her go out, but did not think it necessary to tell either me or Mrs. Hawke, feeling sure we must have been aware of the fact."

"So Mrs. Hawke has returned," said Loveday. "Well, I suppose you will be greatly surprised if I inform you that the young lady, who has so unceremoniously left your house, is at the present moment to be found at the Charing Cross Hotel, where she has engaged a private room in her real name of Miss Mary O'Grady."

"Eh! What! Private room! Real name O'Grady! I'm all bewildered!"

"It is a little bewildering; let me explain. The young lady whom you received into your house as the daughter of your old friend, was in reality the person engaged by Miss Monroe to fulfill the duties of her maid on board ship, after her native attendant had been landed at Malta. Her real name, as I have told you, is Mary O'Grady, and she has proved herself a valuable coadjutor to Miss Monroe in assisting her to carry out a programme, which she must have arranged with her lover, Mr. Danvers, before she left Pekin."

"Eh! what!" again ejaculated Mr. Hawke; "how do you know all this? Tell me the whole story."

"I will tell you the whole story first, and then explain to you how I came to know it. From what has followed, it seems to me that Miss Monroe must have arranged with Mr. Danvers that he was to leave Pekin within ten days of her so doing, travel by the route by which she came, and land at Plymouth, where he was to receive a note from her, apprising him of her whereabouts. So soon as she was on board ship, Miss Monroe appears to have set her wits to work with great energy; every obstacle to the carrying-out of her programme she appears to have met and conquered. Step number one was to get rid of her native maid, who, perhaps, might have been faithful to her master's interests and have proved troublesome. I have no doubt the poor woman suffered terribly from sea-sickness, as it was her first voyage, and I have equally no doubt that Miss Monroe worked on her fears, and persuaded her to land at Malta, and return to China by the next packet. Step number two was to find a suitable person, who for a consideration, would be willing to play the part of the Pekin heiress among the heiress's friends in England, while the young lady herself arranged her private affairs to her own liking. That person was quickly found among the steerage passengers of the Colombo in Miss Mary O'Grady, who had come on board with her mother at Ceylon, and who, from the glimpse I had of her, must, I should conjecture, have been absent many years from the land of her birth. You know how cleverly this young lady has played her part in your house—how, without attracting attention to the matter, she has shunned the society of her father's old Chinese friends, who might be likely to involve her in embarrassing conversations; how she has avoided the use of pen and ink lest—"

"Yes, yes," interrupted Mr. Hawke; "but, my dear Miss Brooke, wouldn't it be as well for you and me to go at once to the Charing Cross Hotel, and get all the information we can out of her respecting Miss Monroe and her movements—she may be bolting, you know?"

"I do not think she will. She is waiting there patiently for an answer to a telegram she dispatched more than two hours ago to her mother, Mrs. O'Grady, at 14, Woburn Place, Cork."

"Dear me! dear me! How is it possible for you to know all this."

"Oh, that last little fact was simply a matter of astuteness on the part of the man whom I have deputed to watch the young lady's movements to-day. Other details, I assure you, in this somewhat intricate case, have been infinitely more difficult to get at. I think I have to thank those 'drawn daggers,' that caused you so much consternation, for having, in the first instance, put me on the right track."

"Ah-h," said Mr. Hawke, drawing a long breath; "now we come to the daggers! I feel sure you are going to set my mind at rest on that score."

"I hope so. Would it surprise you very much to be told that it was I who sent to you those three daggers this morning?"

"You! Is it possible?"

"Yes, they were sent by me, and for a reason that I will presently explain to you. But let me begin at the beginning. Those roughly-drawn sketches, that to you suggested terrifying ideas of blood-shedding and violence, to my mind were open to a more peaceful and commonplace explanation. They appeared to me to suggest the herald's office rather than the armoury; the cross fitchée of the knight's shield rather than the poniard with which the members of secret societies are supposed to render their recalcitrant brethren familiar. Now, if you will look at these sketches again, you will see what I mean." Here Loveday produced from her writing-table the missives which had so greatly disturbed Mr. Hawke's peace of mind. "To begin with, the blade of the dagger of common life is, as a rule, at least two-thirds of the weapon in length; in this sketch, what you would call the blade, does not exceed the hilt in length. Secondly, please note the absence of guard for the hand. Thirdly, let me draw your attention to the squareness of what you considered the hilt of the weapon, and what, to my mind, suggested the upper portion of a crusader's cross. No hand could grip such a hilt as the one outlined here. After your departure yesterday, I drove to the British Museum, and there consulted a certain valuable work on heraldry, which has more than once done me good service. There I found my surmise substantiated in a surprising manner. Among the illustrations of the various crosses borne on armorial shields, I found one that had been taken by Henri d'Anvers from his own armorial bearings, for his crest when he joined the Crusaders under Edward I., and which has since been handed down as the crest of the Danvers family. This was an important item of information to me. Here was someone in Cork sending to your house, on two several occasions, the crest of the Danvers family; with what object it would be difficult to say, unless it were in some sort a communication to someone in your house. With my mind full of this idea, I left the Museum and drove next to the office of the P. and O. Company, and requested to have given me the list of the passengers who arrived by the Colombo. I found this list to be a remarkably small one; I suppose people, if possible, avoid crossing the Bay of Biscay during the Equinoxes. The only passengers who landed at Plymouth besides Miss Monroe, I found, were a certain Mrs. and Miss O'Grady, steerage passengers who had gone on board at Ceylon on their way home from Australia. Their name, together with their landing at Plymouth, suggested the possibility that Cork might be their destination. After this I asked to see the list of the passengers who arrived by the packet following the Colombo, telling the clerk who attended to me that I was on the look-out for the arrival of a friend. In that second list of arrivals I quickly found my friend—William Wentworth Danvers by name."

"No! The effrontery! How dared he! In his own name, too!"

"Well, you see, a plausible pretext for leaving Pekin could easily be invented by him—the death of a relative, the illness of a father or mother. And Sir George, though he might dislike the idea of the young man going to England so soon after his daughter's departure, and may, perhaps, write to you by the next mail on the matter, was utterly powerless to prevent his so doing. This young man, like Miss Monroe and the O'Gradys, also landed at Plymouth. I had only arrived so far in my investigation when I went to your house yesterday afternoon. By chance, as I waited a few minutes in your drawing-room, another important item of information was acquired. A fragment of conversation between your nephew and the supposed Miss Monroe fell upon my ear, and one word spoken by the young lady convinced me of her nationality. That one word was the monosyllable 'Hush.'"

"No! You surprise me!"

"Have you never noted the difference between the 'hush' of an Englishman and that of an Irishman? The former begins his 'hush' with a distinct aspirate, the latter with as distinct a W. That W is a mark of his nationality which he never loses. The unmitigated 'whist' may lapse into a 'whish' when he is is transplanted to another soil, and the 'whish' may in course of time pass into a 'whush,' but to the distinct aspirate of the English 'hush,' he never attains. Now Miss O'Grady's was as pronounced a 'whush' as it was possible for the lips of a Hibernian to utter."

"And from that you concluded that Mary O'Grady was playing the part of Miss Monroe in my house?"

"Not immediately. My suspicions were excited, certainly; and when I went up to her room, in company with Mrs. Hawke's maid, those suspicions were confirmed. The orderliness of that room was something remarkable. Now, there is the orderliness of a lady in the arrangement of her room, and the orderliness of a maid, and the two things, believe me, are widely different. A lady, who has no maid, and who has the gift of orderliness, will put things away when done with, and so leave her room a picture of neatness. I don't think, however, it would for a moment occur to her to pull things so as to be conveniently ready for her to use the next time she dresses in that room. This would be what a maid, accustomed to arrange a room for her mistress's use, would do mechanically. Miss Monroe's room was the neatness of a maid–not of a lady, and I was assured by Mrs. Hawke's maid that it was a neatness accomplished by her own hands. As I stood there, looking at that room, the whole conspiracy–if I may so call it–little by little pieced itself together, and became plain to me. Possibilities quickly grew into probabilities, and these probabilities once admitted, brought other suppositions in their train. Now, supposing that Miss Monroe and Mary O'Grady had agreed to change places, the Pekin heiress, for the time being, occupying Mary O'Grady's place in the humble home at Cork and vice versa, what means of communicating with each other had they arranged? How was Mary O'Grady to know when she might lay aside her assumed rôle and go back to her mother's house. There was no denying the necessity for such communication; the difficulties in its way must have been equally obvious to the two girls. Now, I think we must admit that we must credit these young women with having hit upon a very clever way of meeting those difficulties. An anonymous and startling missive sent to you would be bound to be mentioned in the house, and in this way a code of signals might be set up between them that could not direct suspicion to them. In this connection, the Danvers crest, which it is possible that they mistook for a dagger, suggested itself naturally, for no doubt Miss Monroe had many impressions of it on her lover's letters. As I thought over these things, it occurred to me that possibly dagger (or cross) number one was sent to notify the safe arrival of Miss Monroe and Mrs. O'Grady at Cork. The two daggers or crosses you subsequently received were sent on the day of Mr. Danvers's arrival at Plymouth, and were, I should say, sketched by his hand. Now, was it not within the bounds of likelihood that Miss Monroe's marriage to this young man, and the consequent release of Mary O'Grady from the onerous part she was playing, might be notified to her by the sending of three such crosses or daggers to you. The idea no sooner occurred to me than I determined to act upon it, forestall the sending of this latest communication, and watch the result. Accordingly, after I left your house yesterday, I had a sketch made of three daggers of crosses exactly similar to those you had already received, and had it posted to you so that you would get it by the first post. I told off one of our staff at Lynch Court to watch your house, and gave him special directions to follow and report on Miss O'Grady's movements throughout the day. The results I anticipated quickly came to pass. About half-past nine this morning the man sent a telegram to me from your house to the Charing Cross Hotel, and furthermore had ascertained that she had since despatched a telegram, which (possibly by following the hotel servant who carried it to the telegraph office), he had overheard was addressed to Mrs. O'Grady, at Woburn Place, Cork. Since I received this information an altogether remarkable cross-firing of telegrams has been going backwards and forwards along the wires to Cork."

A CROSS-FIRING OF TELEGRAMS.
"A cross-firing of telegrams! I do not understand."
"In this way. So soon as I knew Mrs. O'Grady's address I telegraphed to her, in her daughter's name, desiring her to address her reply to 1154 Gower Street, not to Charing Cross Hotel. About three-quarters of an hour afterwards I received in reply this telegram, which I am sure you will read with interest."

Here Loveday handed a telegram—one of several that lay on her writing-table—to Mr. Hawke.

He opened it and read aloud as follows:
"Am puzzled. Why such hurry? Wedding took place this morning. You will receive signal as agreed to-morrow. Better return to Tavistock Square for the night."

"The wedding took place this morning," repeated Mr. Hawke blankly. "My poor old friend! It will break his heart."

"Now that the thing is done past recall we must hope he will make the best of it," said Loveday. "In reply to this telegram," she went on, "I sent another, asking as to the movements of the bride and bridegroom, and got in reply this:"

Here she read aloud as follows:
"They will be at Plymouth to-morrow night; at Charing Cross Hotel and next day, as agreed."

"So, Mr. Hawke," she added, "if you wish to see your old friend's daughter and tell her what you think of the part she has played, all you will have to do will be to watch the arrival of the Plymouth trains."

"Miss O'Grady has called to see a lady and gentleman," said a maid at that moment entering.

"Miss O'Grady!" repeated Mr. Hawke in astonishment.

"Ah, yes, I telegraphed to her, just before you came in, to come here to meet a lady and gentlemen, and she, no doubt thinking that she would find here the newly-married pair, has, you see, lost no time in complying with my request. Show the lady in."

"It's all so intricate—so bewildering," said Mr. Hawke, as he lay back in his chair. "I can scarcely get it all into my head."

His bewilderment, however, was nothing compared with that of Miss O'Grady, when she entered the room and found herself face to face with her late guardian, instead of the radiant bride and bridegroom whom she had expected to meet.

She stood silent in the middle of the room, looking the picture of astonishment and distress.

Mr. Hawke also seemed a little at a loss for words, so Loveday took the initiative.

"Please sit down," she said, placing a chair for the girl. "Mr. Hawke and I have sent to you in order to ask you a few questions. Before doing so, however, let me tell you that the whole of your conspiracy with Miss Monroe has been brought to light, and the best thing you can do, if you want your share in it treated leniently, will be to answer our questions as fully and truthfully as possible."

The girl burst into tears. "It was all Miss Monroe's fault from beginning to end," she sobbed. "Mother didn't want to do it—I didn't want to—to go into a gentleman's house and pretend to be what I was not. And we didn't want her hundred pounds—"

Here sobs checked her speech.

"Oh," said Loveday contemptuously, "so you were to have a hundred pounds for your share in this fraud, were you?"

"We didn't want to take it," said the girl, between hysterical bursts of tears; "but Miss Monroe said if we didn't help her someone else would, and so I agreed to—"

"I think," interrupted Loveday, "that you can tell us very little that we do not already know about what you agreed to do. What we want you to tell us is what has been done with Miss Monroe's diamond necklace—who has possession of it now?"

The girl's sobs and tears redoubled. "I've had nothing to do with the necklace—it has never been in my possession," she sobbed. "Miss Monroe gave it to Mr. Danvers two or three months before she left Pekin, and he sent it on to some people he knew in Hong Kong, diamond merchants, who lent him money on it. Decastro, Miss Monroe said, was the name of these people."

"Decastro, diamond merchant, Hong Kong. I should think that would be sufficient address," said Loveday, entering it in a ledger; "and I suppose Mr. Danvers retained part of that money for his own use and travelling expenses, and handed the remainder to Miss Monroe to enable her to bribe such creatures as you and your mother, to practice a fraud that ought to land both of you in jail."

The girl grew deadly white. "Oh, don't do that—don't send us to prison!" she implored, clasping her hands together. "We haven't touched a penny of Miss Monroe's money yet, and we don't want to touch a penny, if you'll only let us off! Oh, pray, pray, pray be merciful!"

Loveday looked at Mr. Hawke.

He rose from his chair. "I think the best thing you can do," he said, "will be to get back home to your mother at Cork as quickly as possible, and advise her never to play such a risky game again. Have you any money in your purse? No—well then here's some for you, and lose no time in getting home. It will be best for Miss Monroe—Mrs. Danvers I mean—to come to my house and claim her own property there. At any rate, there it will remain until she does so."

As the girl, with incoherent expressions of gratitude, left the room, he turned to Loveday.

"I should like to have consulted Mrs. Hawke before arranging matters in this way," he said a little hesitatingly; "but still, I don't see that I could have done otherwise."

"I feel sure Mrs. Hawke will approve what you have done when she hears all the circumstance of the case," said Loveday.

"And," continued the old clergyman, "when I write to Sir George, as, of course, I must immediately, I shall advise him to make the best of a bad bargain, now that the thing is done. 'Past cure should be past care;' eh, Miss Brooke? And, think! what a narrow escape my nephew, Jack, has had!"

THE GHOST OF FOUNTAIN LANE

"WILL you be good enough to tell me how you procured my address?" said Miss Brooke, a little irritably. "I left strict orders that it was to be given to no one."

"I only obtained it with great difficulty from Mr. Dyer; had, in fact, to telegraph three times before I could get it," answered Mr. Clampe, the individual thus addressed. "I'm sure I'm awfully sorry to break into your holiday in this fashion, but—but pardon me if I say that it seems to be one in little more than name." Here he glanced meaningly at the newspapers, memoranda and books of reference with which the table at which Loveday sat was strewn.

She gave a little sigh.

"I suppose you are right," she answered; "it is a holiday in little more than name. I verily believe that we hard workers, after a time, lose our capacity for holiday-keeping. I thought I was pining for a week of perfect laziness and sea-breezes, and so I locked up my desk and fled. No sooner, however, do I find myself in full view of that magnificent sea-and-sky picture than I shut my eyes to it, fasten them instead on the daily papers and set my brains to work, con amore, on a ridiculous case that is never likely to come into my hands."

That "magnificent sea-and-sky picture" was one framed by the windows of a room on the fifth floor of the Métropole, at Brighton, whither Loveday, overtaxed in mind and body, had fled for a brief respite from hard work. Here Inspector Clampe, of the Local District Constabulary, had found her out, in order to press the claims of what seemed to him an important case upon her. He was a neat, dapper-looking man, of about fifty, with a manner less brusque and business-like than that of most men in his profession.

"Oh pray drop the ridiculous case," he said earnestly, "and set to work, 'con amore,' upon another far from ridiculous, and most interesting."

"I'm not sure that it would interest me one quarter so much as the ridiculous one."

"Don't be sure till you've heard the particulars. Listen to this." Here the inspector took a newspaper-cutting from his pocket-book and read aloud as follows:

"'A cheque, the property of the Rev. Charles Turner, Vicar of East Downes, has been stolen under somewhat peculiar circumstances. It appears that the Rev. gentleman was suddenly called from home by the death of a relative, and thinking he might possibly be away some little time, he left with his wife four blank cheques, signed, for her to fill in as required. They were made payable to self or bearer, and were drawn on the West Sussex Bank. Mrs. Turner, when first questioned on the matter, stated that as soon as her husband had departed, she locked up these cheques in her writing desk. She subsequently, however, corrected this statement, and admitted having left them on the table while she went into the garden to cut some flowers. In all, she was absent, she says, about ten minutes. When she came in from cutting her flowers, she immediately put the cheques away. She had not counted them on receiving them from her husband, and when, as she put them into her Davenport, she saw there were only three, she concluded that that was the number he had left with her. The loss of the cheque was not discovered until her husband's return, about a week later on. As soon as he was aware of the fact, he telegraphed to the West Sussex Bank to stop payment, only, however, to make the unpleasant discovery that the cheque, filled in to the amount of six hundred pounds, had been presented and cashed (in gold) two days previously. The clerk who cashed it took no particular notice of the person presenting it, except that he was of gentlemanly appearance, and declares himself to be quite incapable of identifying him. The largeness of the amount raised no suspicion in the mind of the clerk, as Mr. Turner is a man of good means, and since his marriage, about six months back, has been refurnishing the Vicarage, and paying away large sums for old oak furniture and for pictures.'"

"There, Miss Brooke," said the inspector as he finished reading, "if, in addition to these particulars, I tell you that one or two circumstances that have arisen seem to point suspicion in the direction of the young wife, I feel sure you will admit that a more interesting case, and one more worthy of your talents, is not to be found."

Loveday's answer was to take up a newspaper that lay beside her on the table. "So much for your interesting case," she said; "now listen to my ridiculous one." Then she read aloud as follows:–

"'Authentic Ghost Story.–The inhabitants of Fountain Lane, a small turning leading off Ship Street, have been greatly disturbed by the sudden appearance of a ghost in their midst. Last Tuesday night, between ten and eleven o'clock, a little girl named Martha Watts, who lives as a help to a shoemaker and his wife at No. 5 in the lane, ran out into the streets in her night-clothes in a great state of terror, saying that a ghost had come to her bedside. The child refused to return to the house to sleep, and was accordingly taken in by some neighbours. The shoemaker and his wife, Freer by name, when questioned by the neighbours on the matter, admitted, with great reluctance, that they, too, had seen the apparition, which they described as being a soldier-like individual, with a broad, white forehead and having his arms folded on his breast. This description is, in all respects confirmed by the child, Martha Watts, who asserts that the ghost she saw reminded her of pictures she had seen of the great Napoleon. The Freers state that it first appeared in the course of a prayer-meeting held at their house on the previous night, when it was distinctly seen by Mr. Freer. Subsequently, the wife, awakening suddenly in the middle of the night, saw the apparition standing at the foot of the bed. They are quite at a loss for an explanation of the matter. The affair has caused quite a sensation in the district, and at the time of going to press, the lane is so thronged and crowded by would-be ghost-seers that the inhabitants have great difficulty in going to and from their houses.'"

"A scare–a vulgar scare, nothing more," said the inspector as Loveday laid aside the paper. "Now, Miss Brooke, I ask you seriously, supposing you get to the bottom of such a stupid, commonplace fraud as that, will you in any way add to your reputation?"

"And supposing I get to the bottom of such a stupid, commonplace fraud as a stolen cheque, how much, I should like to know, do I add to my reputation?"

"Well, put it on other grounds and allow Christian charity to have some claims. Think of the misery in that gentleman's house unless suspicion can be lifted from the young wife and directed to the proper quarter."

"Think of the misery of the landlord of the Fountain Lane houses if all his tenants decamp in a body, as they no doubt will, unless the ghost mystery is solved."

The inspector sighed. "Well, I suppose I must take it for granted that you will have nothing to do with the case," he said. "I brought the cheque with me, thinking you might like to see it."

"I suppose it's very much like other cheques?" said Loveday indifferently, and turning over her memoranda as if she meant to go back to her ghost again.

"Ye--es," said Mr. Clampe, taking the cheque from his pocket-book and glancing down at it. "I suppose the cheque is very much like other cheques. This little scribble of figures in pencil at the back–144,000–can scarcely be called a distinguishing mark."

"What's that, Mr. Clampe?" asked Loveday, pushing her memoranda on one side. "144,000 did you say?"

Her whole manner had suddenly changed from apathy to that of keenest interest.

Mr. Clampe, delighted, rose and spread the cheque before her on the table.

"The writing of the words "six hundred pounds," he said, "bears so close a resemblance to Mr. Turner's signature, that the gentleman himself told me he would have thought it was his own writing if he had not known that he had not drawn a cheque for that amount on the given date. You see it is that round, schoolboy's hand, so easy to imitate, I could write it myself with half-an-hour's practice; no flourishes, nothing distinctive about it."

Loveday made no reply. She had turned the cheque, and was now closely scrutinizing the pencilled figures at the back.

"Of course," continued the inspector, "those figures were not written by the person who wrote the figures on the face of the cheque. That, however, matters but little. I really do not think they are of the slightest importance in the case. They might have been scribbled by some one making a calculation as to the number of pennies in six hundred pounds–there are, as no doubt you know, exactly 144,000."

"Who has engaged your services in this case, the Bank or Mr. Turner?"

"Mr. Turner. When the loss of the cheque was first discovered, he was very excited and irate, and when he came to me the day before yesterday, I had much difficulty in persuading him that there was no need to telegraph to London for half-a-dozen detectives, as we could do the work quite as well as the London men. When, however, I went over to East Downes yesterday to look round and ask a few questions; I found things had altogether changed. He was exceedingly reluctant to answer any questions, lost his temper when I pressed them, and as good as told me that he wished he had not moved in the matter at all. It was this sudden change of demeanour that turned my thoughts in the direction of Mrs. Turner. A man must have a very strong reason for wishing to sit idle under a loss of six hundred pounds, for, of course, under the circumstances, the Bank will not bear the brunt of it."

"Some other motives may be at work in his mind, consideration for old servants, the wish to avoid a scandal in the house."

"Quite so. The fact, taken by itself, would give no ground for suspicion, but certainly looks ugly if taken in connection with another fact which I have since ascertained, namely, that during her husband's absence from home, Mrs. Turner paid off certain debts contracted by her in Brighton before the marriage, and amounting to nearly £500. Paid them off, too, in gold. I think I mentioned to you that the gentleman who presented the stolen cheque at the Bank preferred payment in gold."

"You are supposing not only a confederate, but also a vast amount of cunning as well as of simplicity on the lady's part."

"Quite so. Three parts cunning to one of simplicity is precisely what lady criminals are composed of. And it is, as a rule, that one part of simplicity that betrays them and leads to their detection."

"What sort of woman is Mrs. Turner in other respects?"

"She is young, handsome and of good birth, but is scarcely suited for the position of vicar's wife in a country parish. She has lived a good deal in society and is fond of gaiety, and, in addition, is a Roman Catholic, and, I am told, utterly ignores her husband's church and drives every Sunday to Brighton to attend mass."

"What about the servants in the house? Do they seem steady-going and respectable?"

"There was nothing on the surface to excite suspicion against any one of them. But it is precisely in that quarter than your services would be invaluable. It will, however, be impossible to get you inside the vicarage walls. Mr. Turner, I am confident, would never open his doors to you."

"What do you suggest?"

"I can suggest nothing better than the house of the village schoolmistress, or, rather, of the village schoolmistress's mother, Mrs. Brown. It is only a stone's throw from the vicarage; in fact, its windows overlook the vicarage grounds. It is a four-roomed cottage, and Mrs. Brown, who is a very respectable person, turns over a little money in the summer by receiving lady lodgers desirous of a breath of country air. There would be no difficulty in getting you in there; her spare bedroom is empty now."

"I should have preferred being at the vicarage, but if it cannot be, I must make the most of my stay at Mrs. Brown's. How do we get there?'"

"I drove from East Downes here in a trap I hired at the village inn where I put up last night, and where I shall stay to-night. I will drive you, if you will allow me; it is only seven miles off. It's a lovely day for a drive; breezy and not too much dust. Could you be ready in about half an hour's time, say?"

But this, Loveday said, would be an impossibility. She had a special engagement that afternoon; there was a religious service in the town that she particularly wished to attend. It would not be over until three o'clock, and, consequently, not until half-past three would she be ready for the drive to East Downes.

Although Mr. Clampe looked unutterable astonishment at the claims of a religious service being set before those of professional duty, he made no demur to the arrangement, and accordingly half-past three saw Loveday and the inspector in a high-wheeled dog-cart rattling along the Marina in the direction of East Downes.

Loveday made no further allusion to her ghost story, so Mr. Clampe, out of politeness, felt compelled to refer to it.

"I heard all about the Fountain Lane ghost yesterday, before I started for East

Downes," he said; "and it seemed to me, with all deference to you, Miss Brooke, an every-day sort of affair, the sort of thing to be explained by a heavy supper or an extra glass of beer."

"There are a few points in this ghost story that separate it from the every-day ghost story," answered Loveday. "For instance, you would expect that such emotionally religious people, as I have since found the Freers to be, would have seen a vision of angels, or at least a solitary saint. Instead, they see a soldier! A soldier, too, in the likeness of a man who is anathema maranatha to every religious mind—the great Napoleon."

"To what denomination do the Freers belong?"

"To the Wesleyan. Their fathers and mothers before them were Wesleyans; their relatives and friends are Wesleyans, one and all, they say; and, most important item of all, the man's boot and shoe connection lies exclusively among Wesleyan ministers. This, he told me, is the most paying connection that a small boot-maker can have. Half-a-dozen Wesleyan ministers pay better than three times the number of Church clergy, for whereas the Wesleyan minister is always on the tramp among his people, the clergyman generally contrives in the country to keep a horse, or else turns student, and shuts himself up in his study."

"Ha, ha! Capital," laughed Mr. Clampe; "tell that to the Church Defence Society in Wales. Isn't this a first-rate little horse? In another ten minutes we shall be in sight of East Downes."

The long, dusty road down which they had driven, was ending now in a narrow, sloping lane, hedged in on either side with hawthorns and wild plum trees. Through these, the August sunshine was beginning to slant now, and from a distant wood there came a faint sound of fluting and piping, as if the blackbirds were thinking of tuning up for their evening carols.

A sudden, sharp curve in this lane brought them in sight of East Downes, a tiny hamlet of about thirty cottages, dominated by the steeple of a church of early English architecture. Adjoining the church was the vicarage, a goodly-sized house, with extensive grounds, and in a lane running alongside these grounds were situated the village schools and the schoolmistress's house. The latter was simply a four-roomed cottage, standing in a pretty garden, with cluster roses and honeysuckle, now in the fullness of their August glory, climbing upwards to its very roof.

Outside this cottage Mr. Clampe drew rein.

"If you'll give me five minutes' grace," he said, "I'll go in and tell the good woman that I have brought her, as a lodger, a friend of mine, who is anxious to get away for a time from the noise and glare of Brighton. Of course, the story of the stolen cheque is all over the place, but I don't think anyone has, at present, connected me with the affair. I am supposed to be a gentleman from Brighton, who is anxious to buy a horse the Vicar wishes to sell, and who can't quite arrange terms with him."

While Loveday waited outside in the cart, an open carriage drove past and then in through the vicarage gates. In the carriage were seated a gentleman and lady whom, from the respectful greetings they received from the village children, she conjectured to be the Rev. Charles and Mrs. Turner. Mr. Turner was sanguine-complexioned, red-haired, and wore a distinctly troubled expression of countenance. With Mrs. Turner's appearance Loveday was not favourably impressed. Although a decidedly handsome woman, she was hard-featured and had a scornful curl to her upper lip. She was dressed in the extreme of London fashion.

They threw a look of enquiry at Loveday as they passed, and she felt sure that enquiries as to the latest addition to Mrs. Brown's ménage would soon be afloat in the village.

Mr. Clampe speedily returned, saying that Mrs. Brown was only too delighted to get her spare-room occupied. He whispered a hint as they made their way up to the cottage door between borders thickly planted with stocks and mignonette.

It was:

"Don't ask her any questions, or she'll draw herself up as straight as a ramrod, and say she never listens to gossip of any sort. But just let her alone, and she'll run on like a mill-stream, and tell you as much as you'll want to know about everyone and everything. She and the village postmistress are great friends, and between them they contrive to know pretty much what goes on inside every house in the place."

Mrs. Brown was a stout, rosy-cheeked woman of about fifty, neatly dressed in a dark stuff gown with a big white cap and apron. She welcomed Loveday respectfully, and introduced, evidently with a little pride, her daughter, the village schoolmistress, a well-spoken young woman of about eight-and-twenty.

Mr. Clampe departed with his dog-cart to the village inn, announcing his intention of calling on Loveday at the cottage on the following morning before he returned to Brighton.

Miss Brown also departed, saying she would prepare tea. Left alone with Loveday, Mrs. Brown speedily unloosed her tongue. She had a dozen questions to ask respecting Mr. Clampe and his business in the village. Now, was it true that he had come to East Downes for the whole and sole purpose of buying one of the Vicar's horses? She had heard it whispered that he had been sent by the police to watch the servants at the vicarage. She hoped it was not true, for a more respectable set of servants were not to be met with in any house, far or near. Had Miss Brooke heard about that lost cheque? Such a terrible affair! She had been told that the story of it had reached London. Now, had Miss Brooke seen an account of it in any of the London papers?

Here a reply from Loveday in the negative formed a sufficient excuse for relating with elaborate detail the story of the stolen cheque. Except in its elaborateness of detail, it differed but little from the one Loveday had already heard.

She listened patiently, bearing in mind Mr. Clampe's hint, and asking no questions. And when, in about a quarter of an hour's time, Miss Brown came in with the tea-tray in her hand, Loveday could have passed an examination in the events of the daily family life at the vicarage. She could have answered questions as to the ill-assortedness of the newly-married couple; she knew that they wrangled from morning till night; that the chief subjects of their disagreement were religion and money matters; that the Vicar was hot-tempered, and said whatever came to the tip of his tongue; that the beautiful young wife, though slower of speech, was scathing and sarcastic, and that, in addition, she was wildly extravagant and threw money away in all directions.

In addition to these interesting facts, Loveday could have undertaken to supply information respecting the number of servants at the vicarage, together with their names, ages and respective duties.

During tea, conversation flagged somewhat; Miss Brown's presence evidently acted repressively on her mother, and it was not until the meal was over and Loveday was being shown to her room by Mrs. Brown that opportunity to continue the talk was found.

Loveday opened the ball by remarking on the fact that no Dissenting chapel was to be found in the village.

"Generally, wherever there is a handful of cottages, we find a church at one end and a chapel at the other," she said; "but here, willy-nilly, one must go to church."

"Do you belong to chapel, ma'am?" was Mrs. Brown's reply. "Old Mrs. Turner, the Vicar's mother, who died over a year ago, was so 'low' she was almost chapel, and used often to drive over to Brighton to attend the Countess of Huntingdon's church. People used to say that was bad enough in the Vicar's mother; but what was it compared with what goes on now—the Vicar's wife driving regularly every Sunday into Brighton to a Catholic Church to say her prayers to candles and images? I'm glad you like the room, ma'am. Feather bolster, feather pillows, do you see, ma'am? I've nothing in the way of flock or wool on either of my beds to make people's head ache." Here Mrs. Brown, by way of emphasis, patted and pinched the fat pillows and bolster showing above the spotless white counterpane.

Loveday stood at the cottage window drinking in the sweetness of the country air, laden now with the heavy evening scents of carnation and essamine. Across the road, from the vicarage, came the loud clanging of a dinner-gong, and almost simultaneously the church clock chimed the hour—seven o'clock.

"Who is that person coming up the lane?" asked Loveday, her attention suddenly attracted by a tall, thin figure, dressed in shabby black, with a large, dowdyish bonnet, and carrying a basket in her hand as if she were returning from some errand. Mrs. Brown peeped over Loveday's shoulder.

"Ah, that's the peculiar young woman I was telling you about, ma'am—Maria Lisle, who used to be old Mrs. Turner's maid. Not that she is over young now; she's five-and-thirty if she's a day. The Vicar kept her on to be his wife's maid after the old lady died, but young Mrs. Turner will have nothing to do with her, she's not good enough for her; so Mr. Turner is just paying her £30 a year for doing nothing. And what Maria does with all that money it would be hard to say. She doesn't spend it on dress, that's certain, and she hasn't kith nor kin, not a soul belonging to her to give a penny to."

"Perhaps she gives it to charities in Brighton. There are plenty of outlets for money there."

"She may," said Mrs. Brown dubiously; "she is always going to Brighton whenever she gets a chance. She used to be a Wesleyan in old Mrs. Turner's time, and went regularly to all the revival meetings for miles round; what she is now, it would be hard to say. Where she goes to church in Brighton, no one knows. She drives over with Mrs. Turner every Sunday, but everyone knows nothing would induce her to go near the candles and images. Thomas—that's the coachman—says he puts her down at the corner of a dirty little street in mid-Brighton, and there he picks her up again after he has fetched Mrs. Turner from her church. No, there's something very queer in her ways."

Maria passed in through the lodge gates of the vicarage. She walked with her head bent, her eyes cast down to the ground.

"Something very queer in her ways," repeated Mrs. Brown. "She never speaks to a soul unless they speak first to her, and gets by herself on every possible opportunity. Do you see that old summer-house over there in the vicarage grounds—it stands between the orchard and kitchen garden—well, every evening at sunset, out comes Maria and disappears into it, and there she stays for over an hour at a time. And what she does there goodness only knows!"

"Perhaps she keeps books there, and studies."

"Studies! My daughter showed her some new books that had come down for the fifth standard the other day, and Maria turned upon her and said quite sharply that there was only one book in the whole world that people ought to study, and that book was the Bible."

"How pretty those vicarage gardens are," said Loveday, a little abruptly. "Does the Vicar ever allow people to see them?"

"Oh, yes, miss; he doesn't at all mind people taking a walk round them. Only yesterday he said to me, 'Mrs. Brown, if ever you feel yourself circumscribed'—yes, 'circumscribed' was the word—'just walk out of your garden-gate and in at mine and enjoy yourself at your leisure among my fruit-trees.' Not that I would like to take advantage of his kindness and make too free; but if you'd care, ma'am, to go for a walk through the grounds, I'll go with you with pleasure. There's a wonderful old cedar hard by the pond people have come ever so far to see."

"It's that old summer-house and little bit of orchard that fascinate me," said Loveday, putting on her hat.

"We shall frighten Maria to death if she sees us so near her haunt," said Mrs. Brown as she led the way downstairs. "This way, if you please, ma'am, the kitchen-garden leads straight into the orchard."

Twilight was deepening rapidly into night now. Bird notes had ceased, the whirr of insects, the croaking of a distant frog were the only sounds that broke the evening stillness.

As Mrs. Brown swung back the gate that divided the kitchen-garden from the orchard, the gaunt, black figure of Maria Lisle was seen approaching in an opposite direction.

"Well, really, I don't see why she should expect to have the orchard all to herself every evening," said Mrs. Brown, with a little toss of her head. "Mind the gooseberry bushes, ma'am, they do catch at your clothes so. My word! what a fine show of fruit the Vicar has this year! I never saw pear trees more laden!"

They were now in the "bit of orchard" to be seen from the cottage windows. As they rounded the corner of the path in which the old summer-house stood, Maria Lisle turned its corner at the farther end, and suddenly found herself almost face to face with them. If her eyes and not been so persistently fastened on the ground, she would have noted the approach of the intruders as quickly as they had noted hers. Now, as she saw them for the first time, she gave a sudden start, paused for a moment irresolutely, and then turned sharply and walked rapidly away in an opposite direction.

"Maria, Maria!" called Mrs. Brown, "don't run away; we sha'n't stay here for more than a minute or so."

Her words met with no response. The woman did not so much as turn her head.

Loveday stood at the entrance of the old summer-house. It was considerably out of repair, and most probably was never entered by anyone save Maria Lisle, its unswept, undusted condition suggesting colonies of spiders and other creeping things within.

Loveday braved them all and took her seat on the bench that ran round the little place in a semi-circle.

"Do try and overtake the girl, and tell her we shall be gone in a minute," she said, addressing Mrs. Brown. "I will wait here meanwhile. I am so sorry to have frightened her away in that fashion."

Mrs. Brown, under protest, and with a little grumble at the ridiculousness of "people who couldn't look other people in the face," set off in pursuit of Maria.

It was getting dim inside the summer-house now. There was, however, sufficient light to enable Loveday to discover a small packet of books lying in a corner of the bench on which she sat.

One by one she took them in her hand and closely scrutinized them. The first was a much read and pencil-marked Bible; the others were respectively, a "congregational hymn-book," a book in a paper cover, on which was printed a flaming picture of a red and yellow angel, pouring blood and fire from out a big black bottle, and entitled "The End of the Age," and a smaller book, also in a paper cover, on which was depicted a huge black horse, snorting fire and brimstone into ochre-coloured clouds. This book was entitled "The Year Book of the Saints," and was simply a ruled diary with sensational mottoes for every day in the year. In parts, this diary was filled in with large and very untidy handwriting.

THE FIRST WAS A PENCIL-MARKED BIBLE.

In these books seemed to lie the explanation of Maria Lisle's love of evening solitude and the lonely old summer-house.

Mrs. Brown pursued Maria to the servants' entrance to the house, but could not overtake her, the girl making good her retreat there.

She returned to Loveday a little hot, a little breathless and a little out of temper. It was all so absurd, she said; why couldn't the woman have stayed and had a chat with them? It wasn't as if she would get any harm out of the talk; she knew as well as everyone else in the village that she (Mrs. Brown) was no idle gossip, tittle-tattling over other people's affairs.

But here Loveday, a little sharply, cut short her meanderings.

"Mrs. Brown," she said, and to Mrs. Brown's fancy her voice and manner had entirely changed from that of the pleasant, chatty lady of half-an-hour ago, "I'm sorry to say it will be impossible for me to stay even one night in your pleasant home, I have just recollected some important business that I must transact in Brighton to-night. I haven't unpacked my portmanteau, so if you'll kindly have it taken to your garden-gate, I'll call for it as we drive past—I am going now, at once, to the inn, to see if Mr. Clampe can drive me back into Brighton to-night."

Mrs. Brown had no words ready wherewith to express her astonishment, and

Loveday assuredly gave her no time to hunt for them. Ten minutes later saw her rousing Mr. Clampe from a comfortable supper, to which he had just settled himself, with the surprising announcement that she must get back to Brighton with as little delay as possible; now, would he be good enough to drive her there?

"We'll have a pair if they are to be had," she added. "The road is good; it will be moonlight in a quarter of an hour; we ought to do it in less than half the time we took coming."

While a phaeton and pair were being got ready, Loveday had time for a few words of explanation.

Maria Lisle's diary in the old summer-house had given her the last of the links in her chain of evidence that was to bring the theft of the cheque home to the criminal.

"It will be best to drive straight to the police station," she said; "they must take out three warrants, one for Maria Lisle, and two others respectively for Richard Steele, late Wesleyan minister of a chapel in Gordon Street, Brighton, and John Rogers, formerly elder of the same chapel. And let me tell you," she added with a little smile, "that these three worthies would most likely have been left at large to carry on their depredations for some little time to come if it had not been for that ridiculous ghost in Fountain Lane."

More than this there was not time to add, and when, a few minutes later, the two were rattling along the road to Brighton, the presence of the man, whom they were forced to take with them in order to bring back the horses to East Downes, prevented any but the most jerky and fragmentary of additions to this brief explanation.

"I very much fear that John Rogers has bolted," once Loveday whispered under her breath.

And again, a little later, when a smooth bit of road admitted of low-voiced talk, she said:

"We can't wait for the warrant for Steele; they must follow us with it to 15, Draycott Street."

"But I want to know about the ghost," said Mr. Clampe; "I am deeply interested in that 'ridiculous ghost.'"

"Wait till we get to 15, Draycott Street," was Loveday's reply; "when you've been there, I feel sure you will understand everything."

Church clocks were chiming a quarter to nine as they drove through Kemp Town at a pace that made the passers-by imagine they must be bound on an errand of life and death.

Loveday did not alight at the police station, and five minutes' talk with the inspector in charge there was all that Mr. Clampe required to put things en train for the arrest of the three criminals.

It had evidently been an "excursionists' day" at Brighton. The streets leading to the railway station were thronged, and their progress along the bye streets was impeded by the overflow of traffic from the main road.

"We shall get along better on foot; Draycott Street is only a stone's throw from here," said Loveday; "there's a turning on the north side of Western Road that will bring us straight into it."

So they dismissed their trap, and Loveday, acting as cicerone still, led the way through narrow turnings into the district, half town, half country, that skirts the road leading to the Dyke.

Draycott Street was not difficult to find. It consisted of two rows of newly-built houses of the eight-roomed, lodging-letting order. A dim light shone from the first-floor windows of number fifteen, but the lower window was dark and uncurtained, and a board hanging from its balcony rails proclaimed that it was "to let unfurnished." The door of the house stood slightly ajar, and pushing it open, Loveday led the way up a flight of stairs–lighted halfway up with a paraffin lamp–to the first floor.

"I know the way. I was here this afternoon," she whispered to her companion. "This is the last lecture he will give before he starts for Judaea; or, in other words, bolts with the money he has managed to conjure from other people's purses into his own."

The door of the room for which they were making, on the first floor, stood open, possibly on account of the heat. It laid bare to view a double row of forms, on which were seated some eight or ten persons in the attitude of all-absorbed listeners. Their faces were upturned, as if fixed on a preacher at the farther end of the room, and wore that expression of rapt, painful interest that is sometimes seen on the faces of a congregation of revivalists before the smouldering excitement bursts into flame.

As Loveday and her companion mounted the last of the flight of stairs, the voice of the preacher–full, arrestive, resonant–fell upon their ear; and, standing on the small outside landing, it was possible to catch a glimpse of that preacher through the crack of the half-opened door.

He was a tall, dignified-looking man, of about five-and-forty, with a close crop of white hair, black eye-brows and remarkably luminous and expressive eyes. Altogether his appearance matched his voice: it was emphatically that of a man born to sway, lead, govern the multitude.

A MAN BORN TO SWAY.

A boy came out of an adjoining room and asked Loveday respectfully if she would not like to go in and hear the lecture. She shook her head.

"I could not stand the heat," she said. "Kindly bring us chairs here."

The lecture was evidently drawing to a close now, and Loveday and Mr. Clampe, as they sat outside listening, could not resist an occasional thrill of admiration at the skilful manner in which the preacher led his hearers from one figure of rhetoric to another, until the oratorical climax was reached.

"That man is a born orator," whispered Loveday; "and in addition to the power of the voice has the power of the eye. That audience is as completely hypnotized by him as if they had surrendered themselves to a professional mesmerist."

To judge from the portion of the discourse that fell upon their ear, the preacher was a member of one of the many sects known under the generic name, "Millenarian." His topic was Apollyon and the great battle of Armageddon. This he described as vividly as if it were being fought out under his very eye, and it would scarcely be an exaggeration to say that he made the cannon roar in the ears of his listeners and the tortured cries of the wounded wail in them. He drew an appalling picture of the carnage of that battlefield, of the blood flowing like a river across the plain, of the mangled men and horses, with the birds of prey swooping down from all quarters, and the stealthy tigers and leopards creeping out from their mountain lairs. "And all this time," he said, suddenly raising his voice from a whisper to a full, thrilling tone, "gazing calmly down upon the field of slaughter, with bent brows and folded arms, stands the imperial Apollyon. Apollyon did I say? No, I will give him his right name, the name in which he will stand revealed in that dread day, Napoleon! A Napoleon it will be who, in that day, will stand as the embodiment of Satanic majesty. Out of the mists suddenly he will walk, a tall, dark figure, with frowning brows and firm-set lips. A man to rule, a man to drive, a man to kill! Apollyon the mighty, Napoleon the imperial, they are one and the same—"

Here a sob and a choking cry from one of the women in the front seats interrupted the discourse and sent the small boy who acted as verger into the room with a glass of water.

"That sermon has been preached before," said Loveday. "Now can you not understand the origin of the ghost in Fountain Lane?"

"Hysterics are catching, there's another woman off now," said Mr. Clampe; "it's high time this sort of thing was put a stop to. Pearson ought to be here in another minute with his warrant."

The words had scarcely passed his lips before heavy steps mounting the stairs announced that Pearson and his warrant were at hand.

"I don't think I can be of any further use," said Loveday, rising to depart. "If you like to come to me to-morrow morning at my hotel at ten o'clock I will tell you, step by step, how I came to connect a stolen cheque with a 'ridiculous ghost.'"

"We had a tussle–he showed fight at first," said Mr. Clampe, when, precisely at ten o'clock the next morning, he called upon Miss Brooke at the Métropole. "If he had had time to get his wits together and had called some of the men in that room to the rescue, I verily believe we should have been roughly handled and he might have slipped through our fingers after all. It's wonderful what power these 'born orators,' as you call them, have over minds of a certain order."

"Ah, yes," answered Loveday thoughtfully; "we talk glibly enough about 'magnetic influence,' but scarcely realize how literally true the phrase is. It is my firm opinion that the 'leaders of men,' as they are called, have as absolute and genuine hypnotic power as any modern French expert, although perhaps it may be less consciously exercised. Now tell me about Rogers and Maria Lisle."

"Rogers had bolted, as you expected he would have done, with the six hundred pounds he had been good enough to cash for his reverend colleague. Ostensibly he had started for Judea to collect the elect, as he phrased it, under one banner. In reality, he has sailed for New York, where, thanks to the cable, he will be arrested on his arrival and sent back by return packet. Maria Lisle was arrested this morning on a charge of having stolen the cheque from Mrs. Turner. By the way, Miss Brooke, I think it is almost a pity you didn't take possession of her diary when you had the chance. It would have been invaluable evidence against her and her rascally colleagues."

"I did not see the slightest necessity for so doing. Remember, she is not one of the criminal classes, but a religious enthusiast, and when put upon her defence will at once confess and plead religious conviction as an extenuating circumstance—at least, if she is well advised she will do so. I never read anything that laid bare more frankly than did this diary the mischief that the sensational teaching of these millenarians is doing at the present moment. But I must not take up your time with moralizing. I know you are anxious to learn what, in the first instance, led me to identify a millenarian preacher with a receiver of stolen property."

"Yes, that's it; I want to know about the ghost; that's the point that interests me."

"I WANT TO KNOW ABOUT THE GHOST."

"Very well. As I told you yesterday afternoon, the first thing that struck me as remarkable in this ghost story was the soldierly character of the ghost. One expects emotionally religious people like Freer and his wife to see visions, but one also expects those visions to partake of the nature of those emotions, and to be somewhat shadowy and ecstatic. It seemed to me certain that this Napoleonic ghost must have some sort of religious significance to these people. This conviction it was that set my thoughts running in the direction of the millenarians, who have attached a religious significance (although not a polite one) to the name of Napoleon by embodying the evil Apollyon in the person of a descendant of the great Emperor, and endowing him with all the qualities of his illustrious ancestor. I called upon the Freers, ordered a pair of boots, and while the man was taking my measure, I asked him a few very pointed questions on these millenarian notions. The man prevaricated a good deal at first, but at length was driven to admit that he and his wife were millenarians at heart, that, in fact, the prayer meeting at which the Napoleonic ghost had made its first appearance was a millenarian one, held by a man who had at one time been a Wesleyan preacher in the chapel in Gordon Street, but who had been dismissed from his charge there because his teaching had been held to be unsound. Freer further stated that this man had been so much liked that many members of the congregation seized every opportunity that presented itself of attending his ministrations, some openly, others, like himself and his wife, secretly, lest they might give offence to the elders and ministers of their chapel."

"And the bootmaking connection suffer proportionately," laughed Mr. Clampe.

"Precisely. A visit to the Wesleyan chapel in Gordon Street and a talk with the chapel attendant enabled me to complete the history of this inhibited preacher, the Rev. Richard Steele. From this attendant I ascertained that a certain elder of their chapel, John Rogers by name, had seceded from their communion, thrown in his lot with Richard Steele, and that the two together were now going about the country preaching that the world would come to an end on Thursday, April 11th, 1901, and that five years before this event, viz., on the 5th of March, 1896 one hundred and forty-four thousand living saints would be caught up to heaven. They furthermore announced that this translation would take place in the land of Judaea, that, shortly, saints from all parts of the world would be hastening thither, and that in view of this event a society had been formed to provide homes—a series, I suppose—for the multitudes who would otherwise be homeless. Also (a very vital point this), that subscriptions for this society would be gladly received by either gentleman. I had arrived so far in my ghost enquiry when you came to me, bringing the stolen cheque with its pencilled figures, 144,000."

"Ah, I begin to see!" murmured Mr. Clampe.

"It immediately occurred to me that the man who could make persons see an embodiment of his thought at will, would have very little difficulty in influencing other equally receptive minds to a breach of the ten commandments. The world, it seems to me, abounds in people who are little more than blank sheets of paper, on which a strong hand may transcribe what it will—hysteric subjects, the doctors would call them; hypnotic subjects others would say; really the line that divides the hysteric condition from the hypnotic is a very hazy one. So now, when I saw your stolen cheque, I said to myself, 'there is a sheet of blank paper somewhere in that country vicarage, the thing is to find it out.'"

"Ah, good Mrs. Brown's gossip made your work easy to you there."

"It did. She not only gave me a complete summary of the history of the people within the vicarage walls, but she put so many graphic touches to that history that they lived and moved before me. For instance, she told me that Maria Lisle was in the habit of speaking of Mrs. Turner as a 'Child of the Scarlet Woman,' a 'Daughter of Babylon,' and gave me various other minute particulars, which enabled me, so to speak, to see Maria Lisle going about her daily duties, rendering her mistress reluctant service, hating her in her heart as a member of a corrupt faith, and thinking she was doing God service by despoiling her of some of her wealth, in order to devote it to what seemed to her a holy cause. I would like here to read to you two entries which I copied from her diary under dates respectively, August 3rd (the day the cheque was lost), and August 7th (the following Sunday), when Maria no doubt found opportunity to meet Steele at some prayer-meeting in Brighton."

Here Loveday produced her note-book and read from it as follows:

"'To-day I have spoiled the Egyptians! Taken from a Daughter of Babylon that which would go to increase the power of the Beast!'

"And again, under date August 7th, she writes:

"'I have handed to-day to my beloved pastor that of which I despoiled at Daughter of Babylon. It was blank, but he told me he would fill it in so that 144,000 of the elect would be each the richer by one penny. Blessed thought! this is the doing of my most unworthy hand.'

"A wonderful farrago, that diary of distorted Scriptural phraseology—wild eulogies on the beloved pastor, and morbid ecstatics, such as one would think could be the outcome only of a diseased brain. It seems to me that Portland or Broadmoor, and the ministrations of a sober-minded chaplain, may be about the happiest thing that could befall Maria Lisle at this period of her career. I think I ought to mention in this connection that when at the religious service yesterday afternoon (to attend which I slightly postponed my drive to East Downes), I heard Steele pronounce a fervid eulogy on those who had strengthened his hands for the fight which he knew it would shortly fall to his lot to wage against Apollyon, I did not wonder at weak-minded persons like Maria Lisle, swayed by such eloquence, setting up new standards of right and wrong for themselves."

"Miss Brooke, another question or two. Can you in any way account for the sudden payment of Mrs. Turner's debts—a circumstance that led me a little astray in the first instance?"

"Mrs. Brown explained the matter easily enough. She said that a day or two back, when she was walking on the other side of the vicarage hedge, and the husband and wife in the garden were squabbling as usual over money-matters, she heard Mr. Turner say indignantly, 'only a week or two ago I gave you nearly £500 to pay your debts in Brighton, and now there comes another bill.'"

"Ah, that makes it plain enough. One more question and I have done. I have no doubt there's something in your theory of the hypnotic power (unconsciously exercised) of such men as Richard Steele, although, at the same time, it seems to me a trifle far-fetched and fanciful. But even admitting it, I don't see how you account for the girl, Martha Watts, seeing the ghost. She was not present at the prayer-meeting which called the ghost into being, nor does she appear in any way to have come into contact with the Rev. Richard Steele."

"Don't you think that ghost-seeing is quite as catching as scarlet-fever or measles?" answered Loveday, with a little smile. "Let one member of a family see a much individualized and easily described ghost, such as the one these good people saw, and ten to one others in the same house will see it before the week is over. We are all in the habit of asserting that 'seeing is believing.' Don't you think the converse of the saying is true also, and that 'believing is seeing?'Insert chapter one text here. Insert chapter one text here.

MISSING!

"NOW, Miss Brooke, if this doesn't inspire you I don't know what will," said Mr. Dyer. And, taking up a handbill that lay upon his writing-table, he read aloud as follows:

"Five hundred pounds reward.—Missing, since Monday, September 20th, Irené, only daughter of Richard Golding, of Langford Hall, Langford Cross, Leicestershire. Age 18, height five feet seven; dark hair and eyes, olive complexion, small features; was dressed when she left home in dark blue serge walking costume, with white straw sailor hat trimmed with cream ribbon. Jewellery worn; plain gold brooch, leather strap bracelet holding small watch, and on the third finger of left hand a marquise ring consisting of one large diamond, surrounded with twelve rubies. Was last seen about ten o'clock on the morning of the 20th leaving Langford Hall Park for the high road leading to Langford Cross. The above reward will be paid to any one giving such information as will lead to the young lady's restoration to her home; or portions of the reward, according to the value of the information received. All communications to be addressed to the Chief Inspector, Police Station, Langford Cross."

"Was last seen on the 20th of September!" exclaimed Loveday, as Mr. Dyer finished reading. "Why, that is ten days ago! Do you mean to say that reward has not stimulated the energies of the local police and long ago put them on the traces of the missing girl?"

"It has stimulated their energies, not a doubt, for the local papers teem with accounts of the way in which the whole country about Langford has been turned upside down generally. Every river, far and near has been dragged; every wood scoured; every railway official at every station for miles round has been driven nearly mad with persistent cross-questioning. But all to no purpose. The affair remains as great a mystery as ever. The girl, as the handbill says, was seen leaving the Park for the high road by some children who chanced to be passing, but after that she seems to have disappeared as completely as if the earth had opened to receive her."

"Cannot her own people suggest any possible motive for her thus suddenly leaving home?"

"It appears not; they seem absolutely incapable of assigning any reason whatever for her extraordinary conduct. This morning I received a letter from Inspector Ramsay, asking me to get you to take up the case. Mr. Golding will not have the slightest objection to your staying at the Hall and thoroughly investigating the matter. Ramsay says it is just possible that they have concentrated too much attention on the search outside the house, and that a promising field for investigation may lie within."

"They should have thought of that before," said Loveday sharply. "I hope you declined the case. Here's the country inspector to the backbone! He'll keep a case in his own hands so long as there's a chance of success; then, when it becomes practically hopeless, hand it over to you just to keep his own failure in countenance by yours."

"Ye-es," said Mr. Dyer, slowly. "I suppose that's about it. But still, business has been slack of late—expenses are heavy—if you thought there was a ghost of a chance—"

"After ten days!" interrupted Miss Brooke, "when the house has settled down into routine, and every one has his story cut and dried, and all sorts of small details have been falsified or smudged over! Criminal cases are like fevers; they should be taken in hand within twenty-four hours."

"Yes, I know," said Mr. Dyer irritably, "but still, as I said before, business is slack—"

"Oh, well, if I'm to go, I'm to go, and there's an end of it," said Loveday resignedly. "I only say it would have been better, for the credit of the office, if you had declined such a hopeless affair. Tell me a little about this Mr. Richard Golding, who and what he is."

Mr. Dyer's temper grew serene again.

"He is a very wealthy man," he answered, "an Australian merchant; came over to England about a dozen years ago, and settled down at Langford Hall. He had, however, been living in Italy for some six or seven years previously. On his way home from Australia he did Italy, as so many Australians do, fell in love with a pretty girl, whom he met at Naples, and married her, and by her had this one child, Irené, who is causing such a sensation at the present moment."

"Is this Italian wife living?"

"No, she died just before Mr. Golding came to England. He has not yet married again, but I hear is on the point of so doing. The lady he contemplates making the second Mrs. Golding is a certain Mrs. Greenhow, a widow, who for the past year or so has acted as chaperon to his daughter and housekeeper to himself."

"It is possible that Miss Irené was not too well pleased at the idea of having a stepmother."

"Such is the fact. From all accounts she and her future stepmother did not get on at all well together. Miss Irené has a very hasty, imperious temper, and Mrs. Greenhow seems to have been quite incapable of holding her own with her. She was to have left the hall this month to make her preparations for the approaching wedding; the young lady's disappearance, however, has naturally brought matters to a standstill."

"Did Miss Golding take any money away with her, do you know?"

"Ah, nobody seems sure on that head. Mr. Golding gave her a liberal allowance and exacted no accounts. Sometimes she had her purse full at the end of the quarter, sometimes it was empty before her quarterly cheque had been cashed a week. I fear you will have to do without exact information on that most important point."

"She had lovers, of course?"

"Yes; in spite of her quick temper she seems to have been a lovable and most attractive young woman, with her half-Australian half-Italian parentage, and to have turned the heads of all the men in the neighbourhood. Only two, however, appear to have found the slightest favour in her eyes—a certain Lord Guilleroy, who owns nearly all the land for miles round Langford, and a young fellow called Gordon Cleeve, the only son of Sir Gordon Cleeve, a wealthy baronet. The girl seems to have coquetted pretty equally with these two; then suddenly, for some reason or other, she gives Mr. Cleeve to understand that his attentions are distasteful to her, and gives unequivocal encouragement to Lord Guilleroy. Gordon Cleeve does not sit down quietly under this treatment. He threatens to shoot first his rival, then himself, then Miss Golding; finally, does none of these three things, but starts off on a three years' journey round the world."

"Threatens to shoot her; starts off on a journey round the world," summed up Loveday. "Do you know the date of the day on which he left Langford?"

"Yes, it was on the 19th; the day before Miss Golding disappeared. But Ramsay has already traced him down to Brindisi; ascertained that he went on board the Buckingham, en route for Alexandria, and has beaten out the theory that he can, by any possibility, be connected with the affair. So I wouldn't advise you to look in that quarter for your clue."

"I am not at all sanguine about finding a clue in any quarter," said Loveday, as she rose to take leave.

She did not feel in the best of tempers, and was a little disposed to resent having a case, so to speak, forced upon her under such disadvantageous conditions.

Her last words to Mr. Dyer were almost the first she addressed to Inspector Ramsay when, towards the close of the day, she was met by him at Langford Cross Station. Ramsay was a lanky, bony Scotchman, sandy-haired and slow of speech.

"Our hopes centre on you; we trust you'll not disappoint us," he said, by way of a greeting.

His use of the plural number made Loveday turn in the direction of a tall, good-looking man, with a remarkably frank expression of countenance, who stood at the inspector's elbow.

"I am Lord Guilleroy," said this gentleman, coming forward. "Will you allow me to drive you to Langford Hall? My cab is waiting outside."

"Thank you; one moment," answered Loveday, again turning to Ramsay. "Now, do you wish," she said, addressing him, "to tell me anything beyond the facts you have already communicated to Mr. Dyer?"

"No-o," answered the inspector, slowly and sententiously. "I would rather not bias your mind in any direction by any theory of mine." ("It would be rather a waste of time to attempt such a thing," thought Loveday.) "The only additional fact I have to mention is one you would see for yourself so soon as you arrived at the Hall, namely, that Mr. Golding is keeping up with great difficulty–in fact, is on the verge of a break-down. He has not had half an hour's sleep since his daughter left home,–a serious thing that for a man at his age."

Loveday was favourably impressed with Lord Guilleroy. He gave her the idea of being a man of strong common-sense and great energy. His conversation was marked by a certain reserve. Although, however, he evidently declined to wear his heart upon his sleeve, it was easy to see, from a few words that escaped him, that if the search for Miss Golding proved fruitless his whole life would be wrecked.

He did not share Inspector Ramsay's wish not to bias Loveday's mind by any theory of his own.

"If I had a theory you should have it in a minute," he said, as he whipped up his horse and drove rapidly along the country road; "but I confess at the present moment my mind is a perfect blank on the matter. I have had a dozen theories, and have been compelled, one by one, to let them all go. I have suspected every one in turn, Cleeve, her own father (God forgive me!), her intended step-mother, the very servants in the house, and, one by one, circumstances have seemed to exonerate them all. It's bewildering–it's maddening! And most maddening of all it is to have to sit here with idle hands, when I would scour the earth from end to end to find her!"

The country around Langford Hall, like most of the hunting districts in Leicestershire, was as flat as if a gigantic stream-roller had passed over it. The Hall itself was a somewhat imposing Gothic structure, of rough grey stone. Very grey and drear it showed in the autumn landscape as Loveday drove in through the park gates and caught her first glimpse of it between the all but leafless elms that flanked the drive. The equinoctial gales had set in early this year, and heavy rains had helped forward their work of wreckage and destruction. The green sward of the park was near akin to a swamp; and the trout stream that flowed across it at an angle showed swollen to its very banks. The sky was leaden with gathering masses of clouds; a flight of rooks, wheeling low and flapping their black wings, with their mournful cawing, completed the dreariness of the scene.

"A companion picture, this," Loveday thought, "to the desolation that must reign within the house with the fate of its only daughter unknown–unguessed at even."

As she alighted at the hall door, a magnificent Newfoundland dog came bounding forth. Lord Guilleroy caressed it heartily.

"It was her dog," he explained. "We have tried in vain to make him track down his mistress–these dogs haven't the scent of hounds."

He excused himself from entering the house with Loveday.

"It's like a vault–a catacomb; I can't stand it," he said. "No, I'll take back my horse;" this was said to the man who stood waiting. "Tell Mr. Golding he'll see me round in the morning without fail."

Loveday was shown into the library, where Mr. Golding was waiting to receive her. In the circumstances no disguise as to her name and profession had been deemed necessary, and she was announced simply as Miss Brooke from Lynch Court.

Mr. Golding greeted her warmly. One glance at him convinced her that Inspector Ramsay had given no exaggerated account of the bereaved father. His face was wan and haggard; his head was bowed; his voice sounded strained and weak. He seemed incapable of speaking on any save the one topic that filled his thoughts.

"We pin our faith on you, Miss Brooke," he said; "you are our last hope. Now, tell me you do not despair of being able to end this awful suspense one way or another. A day or two more of it will put me into my coffin!"

"Miss Brooke will perhaps like to have some tea, and to rest a little, after her long journey before she begins to talk?" said a lady, at that moment entering the room and advancing towards her. Loveday could only conjecture that this was Mrs. Greenhow, for Mr. Golding was too preoccupied to make any attempt to an introduction.

Mrs. Greenhow was a small, slight woman, with fluffy hair and green-grey eyes. Her voice suggested a purr; her eyes, a scratch.

"Cat-tribe!" thought Loveday; "the velvet paw and the hidden claw—the exact antithesis, I should say, to one of Miss Golding's temperament."

Mr. Golding went back to the one subject he had at heart.

"You have had my daughter's photograph given to you, I've no doubt," he said; "but this I consider a far better likeness." Here he pointed to a portrait in pastels that hung above his writing-table. It was that of a large-eyed, handsome girl of eighteen, with a remarkably sweet expression about the mouth.

Mrs. Greenhow again interposed. "I think, if you don't mind my saying so," she said, "you would slightly mislead Miss Brooke if you led her to think that that was a perfect likeness of dear René. Much as I love the dear girl," here she turned to Loveday, "I'm bound to admit that one seldom or never saw her wearing such a sweet expression of countenance."

Mr. Golding frowned, and sharply changed the subject.

"Tell me, Miss Brooke," he said, "what was your first impression when the facts of the case were submitted to you? I have been told that first impressions with you are generally infallible."

Loveday parried the question.

"I am not at present sure that I am in possession of all the facts," she answered. "There are one or two questions I particularly want to ask—you must forgive me if they seem to you a little irrelevant to the matter in hand. First and foremost, I want to know if any formal good-bye took place between your daughter and Mr. Gordon Cleeve?"

"I think not. A sudden coolness arose between them, and the young fellow went away without so much as shaking hands with me."

"I fear an irreparable breach has occurred between the Cleeves and yourself on account of dear René's extraordinary treatment of Gordon," said Mrs. Greenhow sweetly.

"There was no extraordinary treatment," said Mr. Golding, now almost in anger. "My daughter and Mr. Cleeve were good friends—nothing more, I assure you—until one day René saw him cruelly thrashing one of his setters, and after that she cut him dead—would have nothing whatever to do with him."

"Maddalena told Inspector Ramsay," said Mrs. Greenhow, sweetly still, "that on the evening before Gordon Cleeve left Langford dear René received a note from him—"

"Which she tossed unopened into the fire," finished Mr. Golding.

"Who is Maddalena?" interrupted Loveday.

"My daughter's maid. I brought her over from Naples twelve years ago as nurse, and as René grew older she naturally enough fell into her duties as René's maid. She is a dear, faithful creature; her aunt was nurse to René's mother."

"Is it possible for Maddalena to be told off to wait upon me while I am in the house?" asked Loveday, turning to Mrs. Greenhow.

"Certainly, if you wish it. At the same time, I warn you that she is not in a particularly amiable frame of mind just now, and will be very likely to be sullen and disobliging," answered the lady.

"Maddalena is not generally either one or the other," said Mr. Golding deprecatingly; "but just now she is a little unlike herself. The truth is, all the servants have been a little too rigorously cross-examined by the police on matters of which they could have absolutely no knowledge, and Ramsay made such a dead set at Lena that the girl felt herself insulted, grew sullen, and refused to open her lips."

"She must be handled judiciously. I suppose she was broken-hearted when Miss Golding did not return from her morning's walk?"

A reply was prevented by the entrance of a servant with a telegram in his hand.

Mr. Golding tore it open, and, in a trembling voice, read aloud as follows:

"Some one answering to the description of your daughter was seen yesterday in the Champs Elysées, but disappeared before she could be detained. Watch arrivals at Folkestone and Dover."

The telegram was dated from Paris, and was from M. Dulau, of the Paris police. Mr. Golding's agitation was pitiable.

"Great heavens! is it possible?" he cried, putting his hand to his forehead as if stunned. "I'll start for Dover–no, Paris, I think, at once." He staggered to his feet, looking around him in a dazed and bewildered fashion. He might as well have talked of starting for the moon or the north star.

"Pardon me," said Loveday, "Inspector Ramsay is the right person to deal with that telegram. It should be sent to him at once."

Mr. Golding sank back in his chair, trembling from head to foot.

"I think you are right," he said faintly. "I might break down and lose a possible chance."

Then he turned once more to the man, who stood waiting for orders, and desired him to take the fastest horse to the stables and ride at once with the telegram to the Inspector.

"And," he added, "on your way back call at the Castle, see Lord Guilleroy, and give him the news." He turned a pleading face towards Loveday. "This is good news–you consider it good news, do you not?" he asked piteously.

"It won't do to depend too much on it, will it?" said Mrs. Greenhow. "You see, there have been so many false alarms–if I may use the word."–This was said to Loveday.--"Three times last week we had telegrams from different parts of the country saying dear René had been seen–now here, now there, I think there must be a good many girls like her wandering about the world."

"The dress has something to do with it, no doubt," answered Loveday; "it is not a very distinctive one. Still, we must hope for the best. It is possible, of course, that at this very moment the young lady may be on her way home with a full explanation of what has seemed extraordinary conduct on her part. Now, if you will allow me, I will go to my room. And will you please give the order that Maddalena shall follow me there as quickly as possible?"

Loveday's thoughts were very busy when, in the quietude of her own room, she sank into an easy chair beside the fire. The case to which she had so unwillingly devoted her attention was beginning to present some interesting intricacies. She passed in view the dramatis personae of the little drama which she could only hope might not end in a tragedy. The broken-hearted father; the would-be-step-mother, with her feline affinities; the faithful maid; the cruel-tempered lover; the open-faced, energetic one; each in turn received their meed of attention.

"That man would be one to depend on in an emergency," she said to herself, allowing her thoughts to dwell a little longer upon Lord Guilleroy than upon the others. "He has, I should say, a good head on his shoulders and–"

But here a tap-tap at the door brought her thinking to a standstill, and in response to her "come in" the door opened and the maid Lena entered.

She was a tall, black-eyed, dark-skinned woman of about thirty, dressed in a neat black stuff gown. Twelve years of English domestic life had considerably modified the outer tokens of her nationality; a gold dagger that kept a thick coil of hair in its place, and a massive Roman-cut cameo ring on the third finger of her right hand, were about the only things that differentiated her appearance from that of the ordinary English lady's maid. Possibly as a rule she wore a pleasant, smiling expression of countenance. For the moment, however, her face was shadowed by a sullen scowl, that said plainly as words could: "I am here very much against my will, and intend to render you the most unwilling of services."

Loveday felt that she must be taken in hand at once.

"You are Miss Golding's maid, I believe?" she said in a short, sharp tone.

"Yes, madame." This in a slow, sullen one.

"Very well, Kindly unstrap that portmanteau and open my dressing-bag. I am glad you are to wait upon me while I am here. I don't suppose you ever before in your life acted maid to a lady detective?"

"Never, madame." This in a still more sullen tone than before.

"Ah, it will be a new experience to you, and I hope that it may be made a profitable one also. Tell me, are you saving up money to get married?"

Lena, on her knees unstrapping the portmanteau, started and looked up.

"How does madame know that?" she asked, Loveday pointed to the cameo ring on her third finger. "I only guessed at such a possibility," she answered. "Well, now, Lena, I am going to make you an offer. I will give you fifty pounds–fifty, remember, in English gold–if you will procure for me certain information that I require in the prosecution of my work here."

The sullen look on Lena's face deepened.

"I am a servant of the house," she answered, bending lower over the portmanteau; "I do not sell its secrets even for English gold."

"But it is not the secrets of your master's house I am wanting to buy–no, nor anybody else's secrets; I only want you to procure for me certain information that I could easily have procured for myself if I had been a little sooner on the scene. And the information I want relates to no one inside the house, but some one outside of it–Mr. Gordon Cleeve."

The sullen look on Lena's face gave place to one of intense, unutterable relief.

"Mr. Gordon Cleeve!" she repeated. "Oh-h, for fifty pounds, I will undertake to bring madame a good deal of information about him; I know some of the servants in Sir Gordon's house. I know, too, the mother of Mr. Cleeve's valet who has started with him on his journey round the world."

"Good. So, then, it is a bargain. Now, Lena, tell me truly, is this Mr. Cleeve a great favourite with you?"

"With me! Ah, the good God forbid, madame! I never liked him; I used to say to Miss René when I brought her his flowers and his notes: 'Have nothing to do with him, he is cruel–bad at heart.'"

"Ah, yes; I read all that in your face when I mentioned his name. Now what I want you first and foremost to do for me is to find out how this young man spent the last day that he was at Langford. I want you to bring me a report of his doings—as exact a report as possible—on the 18th of this month."

"I will do my best, madame."

"Very good. Now, there is something else. Would you be greatly surprised if I told you that the young man did not sail in the Buckingham from Brindisi as is generally supposed?"

"Madame! Inspector Ramsay said he had ascertained beyond a doubt that Mr. Cleeve went on board the Buckingham at Brindisi!"

"Ah, to go on board is one thing; to sail is another! Now, listen, Lena, very carefully to what I am going to say. I am expecting daily to receive some most important information respecting this gentleman's movements, and I may want some one to set off at a minute's notice for Paris, perhaps; or, perhaps, Florence or Naples, to verify that information: would you do this for me?—of course, I would supply you with money and full details as to your journey."

A flush of pleasure passed over Lena's face.

"Yes, madame," she answered; "if you could get my master's permission for me to go."

"I will undertake to do so." She pondered a moment, then added a little tentatively, and closely watching Lena's face as she asked the question, "I suppose Miss Golding resembled her mother in appearance—I do not see any likeness between her portrait and her father."

Lena's sullenness and stateliness had vanished together now, and once upon the topic of her nursling she was the warm-hearted, enthusiastic Italian woman once more. She became voluble in her description of her dear Miss René, her beauty, her fascinating ways, which she traced entirely to the Italian blood that flowed in her veins; and anecdote after anecdote she related of the happy time when they lived among the lakes and mountains of her native land.

The room grew dark and darker, while she gossiped apace, and presently the dressing-bell clanged through the house.

"Light the candles now," said Loveday, rising from her seat beside the fire; "draw down the blinds and shut out that dreary autumn scene, it sets me shivering!"

It might well do so. The black clouds had fulfilled their threat, and rain was now dashing in torrents against the panes. A tall sycamore, immediately outside the window, creaked and groaned dismally in response to the wind that came whistling round the corner of the house, and between the swaying and all but leafless elms Loveday could catch a glimpse of the grey, winding trout stream, swollen now to its limits and threatening to overflow its banks.

Dinner that night was in keeping with the gloom that overhung the house within and without; although the telegram from Paris had seemed to let in a ray of hope, Mr. Golding was evidently afraid to put much trust in it.

"As Mrs. Greenhow says, 'we have had so many disappointments,'" he said sadly, as he took his place at table. "So many false clues—false scents started. Ramsay has at once put himself in communication with the police at Boulogne and Calais, as well as at Dover and Folkestone. We can only pray that something may come of it!"

"And dear Lord Guilleroy," chimed in Mrs. Greenhow, in her soft, purring voice, "has started for Paris immediately. The young man has such a vast amount of energy, and thinks he can do the work of the police better than they can do it for themselves."

"That's hardly a fair way of putting it, Clare," interrupted Mr. Golding irritably; "he is working heart and soul with the police, and thinks it advisable that some one representing me should be in Paris, in case an emergency should arise; also he wants himself to question Dulau respecting my daughter's sudden appearance and disappearance in the Paris streets. Guilleroy," here he turned to Loveday, "is devotedly attached to my daughter, and—why, Dryad, what's the matter, old man? down, down! Don't growl and whine in that miserable fashion."

He had broken off to address these words to the Newfoundland, who, until that moment, had been comfortably stretched on the hearth-rug before the fire, but who now had suddenly started to his feet with ears erect, and given a prolonged growl, that ended in something akin to a whine.

"It may be a fox trotting past the window," said Mrs. Greenhow, whipping at the dog with her lace handkerchief. But Dryad was not to be so easily subdued. With his nose to the ground now he was sniffing uneasily at and around the heavy curtains that half draped the long French windows of the room.

"Something has evidently disturbed him. Why not let him out into the garden?" said Loveday. And Mr. Golding, with a "Hey, Dryad, go find!" unfastened the window and let the dog out into the windy darkness.

Dinner was a short meal that night. It was easy to see that it was only by a strong effort of will that Mr. Golding kept his place at table, and made even a pretence of eating.

At the close of the meal Loveday asked for a quiet corner, in which to write some business letters, and was shown into the library by Mr. Golding.

"You'll find all you require here, I think," he said, with something of a sigh, as he placed a chair for her at a lady's davenport. "This was René's favourite corner, and here are the last flowers she gathered—dead, all dead, but I will not have them touched!" He broke off abruptly, set down the vase of dead asters which he had taken in his hand, and quitted the room, leaving Loveday to the use of René's pen, ink, paper, and blotting-pad.

Loveday soon became absorbed in her business letters. Time flew swiftly, and it was not until a clock on the mantelpiece chimed the hour—ten o'clock—that she gave a thought as to what might be the hour for retiring at the Hall.

Something else beside the striking of the clock almost simultaneously caught her ear—the whining and scratching of a dog at one of the windows. These, like those of the dining-room, opened as doors into an outside verandah. They were, however, closely shuttered, and Loveday had to ring for a servant to undo the patent fastener.

So soon as the window was opened Dryad rushed into the room, plastered with mud, and dripping with water from every hair.

"He must have been in the stream," said the footman, trying to collar the dog and lead him out of the room.

"Stop! one moment!" cried Loveday, for her eye had caught sight of something hanging in shreds between the dog's teeth. She bent over him, patting and soothing him, and contrived to disentangle those shreds, which a closer examination proved to be a few tattered fragments of dark blue serge.

"Is your letter-writing nearly ended, Miss Brooke?" asked Mr. Golding, at that moment entering the room.

For reply, Loveday held up the shreds of blue serge. His face grew ashen white; he needed no explanation; those shreds and the dripping dog seemed to tell their own tale.

"Great heavens!" he cried, "why did I not follow the dog out! There must be a search at once. Get men, lanterns, ropes, a ladder—the dog, too, will be of use."

A terrible energy took possession of him. "Find, Dryad, find!" he shouted to the dog, and then, hatless and thin-shoed as he was, he rushed out into the darkness with Dryad at his heels.

In less than five minutes afterwards the whole of the men-servants of the house, with lanterns, ropes, and a ladder long enough to span the stream, had followed him. The wind had fallen, the rain had ceased now, and a watery half-moon was struggling through the thin, flying clouds. Loveday and Mrs. Greenhow, standing beneath the verandah, watched the men disappear in the direction of the trout stream, whither Dryad had led the way. From time to time shouts came to them, through the night stillness, of "This way!" "No, here!" together with Dryad's sharp bark and the occasional distant flash of a bull's-eye lantern. It was not until nearly half an hour afterwards that one of the men came running back to the house with a solemn white face and a pitiful tale. He wanted something that would serve for a stretcher, he said in a subdued tone—the two-fold oak screen in the hall would do—and please, into which room was "it" to be brought?—

On the following evening Mr. Dyer received a lengthy dispatch from Miss Brooke, which ran as follows:—

"LANGFORD HALL.

"This is to supplement my telegram of an hour back, telling you of the finding of Miss Golding's body in the stream that runs through her father's grounds. Mr. Golding has himself identified the body, and has now utterly collapsed. At the present moment it seems rather doubtful whether he will be in a fit state to give evidence at the inquest, which will be held to-morrow. Miss Golding appears to be dressed as she was when she left home, with this notable exception—the marquise ring has disappeared from the third finger of her left hand, and in its stead she wears a plain gold wedding-ring. Now this is a remarkable circumstance, and strikes a strange keynote to my mind. I am writing hurriedly, and can only give you the most important points in this very singular case. The maid, Lena, a reserved, self-contained woman, gave way to a passion of grief when the young lady's body was brought in and laid upon her own bed. She insisted on performing all the last sad offices for the dead, however, in spite of her grief, and is now, I am glad to say, calmer and capable of a little quiet conversation with me. I keep her continually in attendance on me, as I am rather anxious to keep my eye on her just now. I have telegraphed to Lord Guilleroy, asking him, in spite of the terrible news which will in due course reach him, to be good enough to remain in Paris awaiting directions from me, which may have to be carried out at a minute's notice. I hope to have further news to send a little later on."

Mr. Dyer laid aside the letter with a grunt of dissatisfaction.

"Well," he said to himself, "I suppose she expects me to be able to read between the lines, but I'm bothered if I can make head or tail of it all. She seems to me to be going a little wide of the mark just now; it might be as well to give her a hint." So he dashed off a few brief lines as follows:–

"I suppose you are concentrating now on finding out what were Miss Golding's movements while absent from her home. It seems to me this could be better done in Paris than at Langford Hall. The ring on her finger necessarily implies that she has gone through a marriage service somewhere, and as she was seen in Paris a day or two ago, it is as likely as not that the ceremony took place there. The Paris police could give you 'yea or nay' on this matter within twenty-four hours. As to the maid, Lena, I think you are laying too much stress upon her possible knowledge of her mistress's movements.

"If she had been tied down to secrecy by promise of reward, she would naturally, now that all such promises are rendered futile, reveal all she knows on the matter–she has nothing to gain by keeping the secrets of the dead."

This letter crossed on its road a telegram from Loveday running thus:–

"Inquest over. Verdict, 'Found drowned, but how deceased got into the water there is no evidence to show.' Funeral takes place to-morrow; Mr. Golding delirious with brain fever."

On the day following Mr. Dyer received a second letter from Loveday. Thus it ran:–

"The funeral is over; Mr. Golding is much worse, I have dispatched Lena to Paris, telling her I require her services there to follow up a clue I hold respecting Mr. Gordon Cleeve, and promising her rewards commensurate with the manner in which she carries out my orders. I have also written to Lord Guilleroy, telling him the sort of assistance I require from him. If he is the man I take him for he will be more useful to me than all the Paris police put together. I will answer your letter in detail in a day or two. The neighbourhood is still in a state of great excitement, and all sorts of wild reports are flying about. Ramsay and Dulau have traced a lady, dressed in dark blue serge, and answering in other respects to Miss Golding's description, from the Gare du Midi, Paris, step by step to her arrival at Langford Cross, whence, poor thing, she must have walked through the pouring rain to the Hall. I do not see, however, that this information helps us forward one step towards the solution of the mystery of the girl's disappearance. Ramsay is a little inclined to criticize what he calls my 'leisurely handling' of the case. Mrs. Greenhow, who is a terribly empty-headed, but at the same time essentially hard-natured little woman, appears disposed to follow suit, and has more than once thrown out hints that my stay in the house is being unnecessarily prolonged. As there is practically no further necessity for my remaining at the Hall, I have told her that I shall to-day take up my quarters at the Roebuck Inn (by courtesy hotel), at Langford Cross. I believe she is unfeignedly glad at what she considers the ending of the affair. The imperious yet fascinating young lady no doubt ruled her and the household generally with a rod of iron, and the little woman, I feel sure, if she had dared, would have ordered bonfires and a general rejoicing on the day of the funeral. Well, I have not much sympathy with her, and am preparing for her a shock to her not too-sensitive nerves which she little suspects. My chief anxiety at the present moment is Mr. Golding, who still remains unconscious. I have requested the doctors to send me two bulletins daily of his condition, which I fear is a most serious one."

There could be little doubt on this head. The doctors' verdict on the day that Loveday left Langford Hall for "The Roebuck" was: "Absolutely no hope." The bulletin brought to her on the following morning was "Condition remains unchanged." On the third day, however, the report was "Slight improvement." Then followed the welcome bulletins of "Improvement maintained," and "Out of danger," to be followed by the most welcome report of all: "Is making steady progress towards recovery."

"It is Mr. Golding's illness that has kept me here so long," said Loveday to Inspector Ramsay, as if by way of apology for her continued presence on the scene. "I think, however, I can see my way to departure now. Going to Paris? Oh, dear me, no. I have telegraphed to Mr. Dyer to expect me back the day after to-morrow; if you will like to come to me here, or will meet me at Langford Cross Station, I will give you a full report of all I have done since I took the case in hand. Now I am going to the Hall to ascertain at what hour to-morrow it will be convenient for me to say good-bye to Mr. Golding."

More than this Ramsay was unable to extract from Miss Brooke. His open strictures upon what he called her "leisurely handling of the case" had put her upon her mettle, and she had decided that Ramsay and his colleagues should be taught that Lynch Court had a special way of doing things, and could hold its own with the best.

On her way to the Hall Loveday called at the post-office, and there had a letter with a London postmark handed to her. This she at once opened and read, and then dispatched a reply to it by telegram. The reply was an enigmatic one to the village post-master, for Loveday, after a few casual questions as to his knowledge of Continental languages, chose German as her medium of communication. The address, however, "to Lord Guilleroy, at Charing Cross Hotel," was plain reading enough.

At the Hall Loveday found Mrs. Greenhow in an active state of mind. Mr. Golding, she informed her with a sweet effusiveness, would come downstairs for a short time on the following day, and she was doing all that lay in her power to put out of sight anything that might awaken painful recollections. "I have had dear René's harp removed to a lumber room, her portrait taken down from the library wall," she said, in her usual purring tones; "and her davenport is being wheeled into my own sitting-room. Poor dear René! If only she could have been taught to govern her willful temper a happier fate might have befallen her. What that fate was I suppose we shall never know now."

Loveday's only reply to this was to ask for an exact report of the doctor's opinion of Mr. Golding's condition. Mrs. Greenhow put her handkerchief to her eyes as she answered that Doctor Godwin's opinion was that, so far as bodily strength was concerned, he was considerably better, but that his mental condition was a serious one. His brain appeared to be in a state of semi-stupefaction, which it was possible might be indicative of the softening of its tissues.

Loveday expressed a wish to see this doctor—to time her farewell visit to Mr. Golding on the following day with Dr. Godwin's daily call. In fact, she would like a little private talk with him before she went in to see his patient.

To all this Mrs. Greenhow offered no objection. Lady detectives, she said to herself, were a race apart, and had a curious way of doing things; but, thank Heaven, she would soon see the last of this one!

The stormy autumnal weather had given place now to a brief spell of late summer sunshine, and on the last day of her visit to Langford, Miss Brooke had a cheerier view of the Hall and its surroundings than she had had on the day of her arrival there. The trout stream had retreated to its natural proportions, and showed like a streak of molten silver–not a grey, turbid flood–in the bright sunlight that played at hide-and-seek between the branches of the stript elms. Even the old rooks seemed to have a cheery undernote to their "caw, caw" as they wheeled about the old house; and Dryad himself, as he once more came bounding forth to greet her, appeared to her fancy to have a less dolorous ring in his noisy bark.

"That dog is a perfect nuisance–has been utterly spoilt. I must have him chained up," said Mrs. Greenhow, as she led the way into a room where Dr. Godwin sat awaiting Loveday. She introduced them one to the other. "Shall I remain, or do you wish to converse alone?" she asked.

And as Loveday answered with decision "Alone," the little woman had no choice but to withdraw, wondering once more over the vagaries of lady detectives.

Half an hour afterwards the doctor, a clever-looking, active little man, led the way into the library where Mr. Golding was seated.

Loveday was greatly shocked at the change which a few days' illness had wrought in him. His chair was drawn close to the window, and the autumn sunshine that filled the room threw into pitiful relief his shrunken frame and pallid face, aged now by about a dozen years. His eyes were closed, his head was bent low on his breast, and he did not lift it as the door opened.

"You need not remain," said Dr. Godwin to the nurse, who rose as they entered; and Loveday and the doctor were left alone with the patient.

Loveday drew near softly. "I am going back to town this evening, and have come to say good-bye," she said, extending her hand.

Mr. Golding opened his eyes, staring vaguely at the extended hand. "To say good-bye!" he repeated, in a dreamy, far-away tone.

"I am Miss Brooke," Loveday explained. "I came down from London to investigate the strange circumstances connected with your daughter's disappearance."

"My daughter's disappearance!" He started and began to tremble violently.

The doctor had his hand on his patient's pulse now.

"I have conducted my investigations under somewhat disadvantageous circumstances," Loveday went on quietly, "and, for a time, with but little result. A few days back, however, I received important information from Lord Guilleroy, and to-day I have seen and communicated with him. In fact, it was his carriage that brought me to your house this afternoon."

"Lord Guilleroy!" repeated Mr. Golding slowly. His voice had a more natural ring in it; recollection, although, perhaps, a painful one, seemed to sound in it.

"Yes. He said he would wander about the park until I had seen and prepared you for his visit. Ah! there he is coming up the drive."

Here she drew back the curtain that half draped the open window.

This window commanded a good view of the drive, with its overarching elms, that led from the lodge gates to the house. Along that drive two persons were advancing at that moment in leisurely fashion; one of those two was undoubtedly Lord Guilleroy, the other was a tall, graceful girl, dressed in deep mourning.

Mr. Golding's eyes followed Loveday's at first with a blank, expressionless stare. Then, little by little, that stare changed into a look of intelligence and recognition. His face grew ashen white, then a wave of colour swept over it.

"Lord Guilleroy, yes," he said, panting and struggling for breath. "But—but who is that walking with him? Tell me, tell me quickly, for the love of Heaven!"

He tried to rise to his feet, but his limbs failed him. The doctor poured out a cordial, and put it to his lips.

"Drink this, please," he said. "Now tell him quickly," he whispered to Loveday.

"That young lady," she resumed calmly, "is your daughter René. She drove up with me and Lord Guilleroy from Langford Cross. Shall I ask her to come in and see you? She is only waiting for Dr. Godwin's permission to do so."

Time to grant or refuse that permission, however, was not accorded to Dr. Godwin. René—a sadder, sweeter-faced René than the one who had so impetuously discarded home and father—now stood outside in the "half-sun, half-shade" of the verandah, and had caught the sound of Loveday's last words.

She swept impetuously past her into the room.

"Father, father!" she said, as she knelt down beside his chair, "I have come back at last! Are you not glad to see me?"

"I daresay it all seems very mysterious to you," said Loveday to Inspector Ramsay, as together they paced the platform of Langford Cross Station, waiting for the incoming of the London train, "but, I assure you, it all admits of the easiest and simplest of explanations—Who on earth was it that the inquest was held over, and who was buried about a week ago, do you say? Oh, that was Mr. Golding's wife, Irené, daughter of Count Mascagni, of Alguida, in South Italy, whom every one believed to be dead. It is her history that holds the key to the whole affair from first to last. I will begin at the beginning, and tell you her story as nearly as possible as it was told to me. To be quite frank with you, I would have admitted you long ago into my confidence, and told you, step by step, how things were working themselves out, if you had not offended me by criticizing my method of doing my work."

"I'm sure I'm very sorry," here broke in Ramsay in a deprecating tone.

"Oh, pray don't mention it. Let me see, where was I? Ah, I must go back some nineteen or twenty years in Mr. Golding's life in order to make things clear to you. The particulars which I had from Mr. Dyer, and which I fancy you supplied him with, respecting Mr. Golding's early life were so meager that directly I arrived at the Hall I set to work to supplement them; this I contrived to do in a before-dinner chat with Lena, Miss Golding's maid. I found out through her that Irené Mascagni was a typical Italian woman of the half-educated, passionate, beautiful, animal kind, and that Mr. Golding's early married life was anything but a happy one. Irené was motherless, and had been so spoilt from babyhood upwards by her old nurse, Lena's aunt, that she could not brook the slightest opposition to her whims and wishes. She was a great coquette also; lovers were an absolute necessity to her. Remonstrance on Mr. Golding's part was useless; Irené met it by appeals to her father for protection against what she considered her husband's brutality; in consequence, a serious quarrel ensued between the Count and Mr. Golding, and when the latter announced his intention of breaking up his Italian home and buying an estate in England, Irené, accompanied by her nurse, Antonia, left her husband and little daughter and went back to her father's house, vowing that nothing would induce her to leave her beloved Italy. At this crisis in his affairs, Mr. Golding was suddenly compelled to undertake a journey to Australia to adjust certain complicated matters of business. He took with him on this voyage his little girl, René, and her nurse–now her maid, Lena. The visit to Australia in all occupied about six months. During that time no communication of any sort passed between him and his wife or her father. He resolved, however, to make one more effort to induce Irené to return to her home and her duty; and, with this object, he went to Naples on his return to Europe and wrote to his wife from there, asking her to appoint a day for a meeting. In reply to this letter he received a visit from Antonia, who, with a great show of sorrow, informed him that Irené had caught a fever during his absence, and had died, and now lay buried in the family vault at Alguida. Mr. Golding's grief at the tidings was no doubt mitigated by the recollection of the unfortunate married life he had led. He made no attempt to communicate with Count Mascagni, started at once for England, and set up his establishment at Langford Hall. All this, with the exception of the name of Irené's father and that of his estate, was told me by Lena, who, I may mention in passing, laid great stress upon the wonderful likeness that existed between Miss Golding and her mother. She was, she said, the exact counterpart of what her mother had been at her age."

"It is marvelous to me how you contrived to get anything out of that woman Lena," said Ramsay; "she was most obstinately taciturn with me."

"Pardon me if I say that was because she had been most injudiciously handled. In the circumstances it would never have occurred to me to put a single direct question to her, although I like you, felt convinced that she was the one and only person likely to be in her young mistress's confidence. So fully imbued was I with this idea that I felt certain that, if she could be sent out of the house on any pretext, by closely following her movements we should, sooner or later, come upon the traces of Miss Golding. To attain this end, I feigned suspicion of Mr. Gordon Cleeve, and promised her rewards if she would bring me tidings of his doings. This was to pave the way to dismissing her on a journey to Italy. It also had the most welcome effect of calming her mind and convincing her of my belief in her innocence. With her fears thus allayed, I found her no longer sullen but communicative to a degree."

"Pardon my interrupting you at this point, but will you kindly tell me what, in the first instance, aroused your suspicious as to the identity of the person 'found drowned' by the coroner's jury?"

"Lena's conduct when the body was brought into the house. I should, however, tell you that a keynote of suspicion as to the possibility of Mrs. Golding being still alive had been struck when, as I sat writing at Miss Golding's davenport, I found the words "Mia Madre" scribbled here and there on her blotting-pad. Now what, I said to myself, could, after all these years, have turned her thoughts to her mother and her early Italian home? The wedding-ring on the lady's finger, coupled with Lena's statement as to Miss Golding's marvelous likeness to her mother, together with an exclamation of Mr. Golding's, after identifying the body, that his daughter had 'aged by a dozen years,' made these suspicions grow stronger. It was, however, Lena's own conduct that resolved them into positive certainty. I watched her narrowly after the body had been brought into the house. At first her grief was passionate and intense, and in it she let fall—in Italian—the extraordinary exclamation that a woman should break her heart for her lover, not for her mother. Then she, too, went into the room where the body lay—went in weeping, came out dry-eyed, and in the most methodical manner set to work to perform the last sad offices for the dead."

"Ah, yes, I see. Pray go on."

"It was on the day of the funeral, if you remember, that I dispatched Lena to Paris. I had previously written to Lord Guilleroy, hinting my suspicions, and begging him, in spite of everything, to remain at Paris, and to carry out any directions I might send him to the very letter. On dispatching Lena, I again wrote to him, telling him when she would arrive, where she would put up, and bidding him keep his eye on her, and follow her movements step by step. From Paris, I sent Lena on to Naples, bidding her await further orders there, and, all unknown to her, the train that carried her thither, carried also Lord Guilleroy. Naples had been the only place she had mentioned to me by name in her gossip about her life in Italy, but I felt confident, from some casual remarks she had let fall, that Irené Mascagni's early home, as well, also, as the home of her own lover, was within easy reach of the city. It was only natural to conjecture that if I kept her waiting there for orders she would utilize the opportunity for paying a visit to her friends and relatives, and also to her young mistress, if she were, as I supposed, in that neighbourhood. The result proved my conjecture correct."

"And Lord Guilleroy, thus following her movements, step by step, came upon her and Miss Golding in company?"

"He did. I think Lord Guilleroy deserves high encomium for the way in which he performed his share in this somewhat intricate case. No trained detective could have done better. He tracked Lena home to Alguida, a small hamlet within fifteen miles of Naples, and came upon her talking to Miss Golding, who stood at the gate of her grandfather's chateau dressed in her mother's Neapolitan dress. Miss Golding was unfeignedly glad to be taken possession of, so to speak, by one of her father's English friends, for she was becoming nervous and distressed at the position in which she found herself. Her mother was dead; her grandfather, a man of a violent temper, refused to allow her to leave his chateau, as he alleged he required, in his old age, the attendance of one who was his own kith and kin. Also there was in her mind a natural shrinking from the story she would have to tell her father, and the fear lest he might not be willing to forgive her for the part she had played. Nothing could have been more opportune than Lord Guilleroy's arrival. Miss Golding accorded to him her full confidence, and from this point the story ceases to be mine and becomes Lord Guilleroy's as communicated to him by Miss Golding."

"It is, in fact, the other half of the story that was told you by Lena?"

"It is; it starts from the period, twelve years back, when Mrs. Golding was supposed by her husband and child to be dead. Instead of dying, however, she had, after a month's stay at her father's lonely country house, joined a company of actors, then passing through Alguida. Her great personal beauty ensured her ready admission to the corps; and in her new life, no doubt, her vanity and innate love of coquetry found ample gratification. The faithful old nurse had followed her in her new career; the dramatic corps was actually in Naples when Mr. Golding arrived there, and the two women, neither of whom was disposed to enter upon the dull routine of English domestic life, had fabricated the lie in order the more effectually to retain their liberty. It is most probable that Count Mascagni knew nothing whatever of his daughter's movements at this period of her career. It is possible that, after a time, he may have believed her to be dead, for eleven years passed without his receiving any communication from her."

"Eleven years! Was she on the stage the whole of that time?"

"I have not been able to ascertain—in fact, I have not been very keen in making inquiries on this point, for it really is of little or no importance to the case. So far as we are concerned, her career is of importance only after her return to her father's house, now about a year ago. She came back one day, attended by Antonia, evidently out of health and in great poverty. Her father received her back conditionally; she had disgraced him and his ancient name, he said; dead she was supposed to be by her friends, dead she must remain—she must go nowhere, she must see no one."

"Ah, a sad story! And I suppose after a time the poor woman's thoughts flew to her husband and little daughter?"

"Yes. Antonia wrote to Lena that the mother was dying for the sight of her child, and implored her to tell René that her mother lived—a mother who had been cruelly treated alike by husband and father—and beg her, at all hazards, to come to her, that she might clasp her in her arms before the shadows of death closed in around her. This part of the story I had from René herself as we drove together to the Hall. The girl told me that when she read that letter all her blood was stirred within her. She was seized with a burning desire there and then to kiss that mother and to right her wrongs. For the moment she hated her father, felt that she must at once confront him and denounce him for his cruelty. Second thoughts suggested another course. Her father might forbid her all intercourse with her mother; she had plenty of money, why not start for Italy at once, and from her mother's lips dictate to her father the terms on which she would return to her English home? So the journey was planned, and Lena was promised by the young lady a pair of her handsome diamond earrings if she kept her secret till she herself gave her permission to speak. Not so much as a hand-bag was packed, for fear of exciting attention in the house; the undistinctive blue serge and sailor hat—supplemented subsequently by a thick veil—were selected as a travelling dress. Market-day at Langford, with a crowded railway station, was chosen for the day of departure, and the young lady walked the two miles that lay between it and her father's house in easy, leisurely fashion, as if she contemplated nothing more serious than a morning walk."

"Of course, so soon as she reached London all was plain sailing to her?"

"Yes. Lena, no doubt, supplied her with all necessary details respecting her journey. When she arrived at the Chateau Mascagni, she appears to have at once thoroughly succumbed to her mother's influence. Out of health although that mother was, René described her to me as the most fascinating woman she had ever met. I suppose the likeness between the two must have been something remarkable, for René said, after she had been a few days in the house and the mother had rallied a little in strength, the servants declared it was only by their dress that they could distinguish one from the other. On the fourth day after Miss Golding's arrival at the Chateau, her mother met her with a plan which, for fear of the effect that a refusal might have upon her health, she at once fell in with. It was to the effect that, instead of attempting negotiations with Mr. Golding through lawyers or by letter, she should herself go to him at his country house, throw herself upon his generosity, plead for forgiveness, and beg to be taken back to his heart once more."

"But why did not Miss René accompany her mother on this journey?"

"René was a force to be held in reserve. If her father refused her mother's request, she in her turn would refuse to return to her home, but would live on with her mother and grandfather at Alguida. The girl appears to have entertained bitter feelings against her father at this juncture—feelings possibly intensified by the thought of the sort of step-mother he intended to bestow upon her."

"Well, anyhow, so far as I can make out, Miss René's own mother hadn't much to boast of—in the way of common sense, at any rate. In fact, the two together appear to me to have acted more like a couple of school-girls than anything else. What made Mrs. Golding dress up in her daughter's clothes?"

"That, I believe, was a matter of convenience merely. Mrs. Golding had no money, and her father was not over-burdened with riches, and what little he had he held tightly. She had, for some reason or other, returned home with next to no wardrobe; René's dress was suitable for travelling, and not likely to attract attention. They neither of them seem to have given a thought to the possibility of rewards being offered for tidings of René; and thus, no doubt, while waiting for her train in Paris, Mrs. Golding did not hesitate to show herself in Paris streets. I need not go into the details of her journey to Langford; they are already known to you. The poor woman, not seeing any conveyance at the country station, must have walked in the drenching rain to the Hall. At the hall door, possibly, her courage suddenly failed her, and, instead of ringing for admission, she creeps to a window to get a glimpse of the home-life within. That glimpse is fatal. She sees her husband and the woman he intends to marry seated together at table. She takes in at a glance the refinement of the home, together with the rigid conventionality of English domestic life. A wave of memory, perhaps, brings before her episodes in her past career altogether out of tune with this home picture. She feels the impracticability of the mission on which she is bent; a fit of her old impetuosity seizes her; she rushes away in the darkness, takes a wrong turning, perhaps—who knows—?"

"Ah, yes; and the stream was there waiting for her, and she thought she would end it all. Poor soul!"

"Or it may be," said Loveday pityingly, "that some sweet story of sainthood and martyrdom that she had heard in her childish days came floating dimly into her brain as she made her way through the darkness, and she thought she would do her best to make atonement to the one whom she had so deeply injured by not standing in the way of his future happiness. Here is my train! Ah, yes; it is a sad, sad story!"

"Yes; for the present things are a trifle gloomy for the family at the Hall, I'll admit," said Ramsay, as he shut the carriage-door on Loveday; "but they'll turn over a new leaf there before long. There'll be a couple of weddings in the house before the year comes to an end, I'll be bound."

"No," said Loveday, as she steeled herself comfortably in a corner; "Mrs. Greenhow has shown herself in her true colours at this time of distress, and, from what I hear, will stand but little chance of becoming the second Mrs. Golding. Lord Guilleroy and the runaway René are the only two who will have to be congratulated as bride and bridegroom."

THE END

THE AMELIA BUTTERWORTH MYSTERIES

BY
ANNA KATHARINE GREEN

THAT AFFAIR NEXT DOOR

BOOK I   MISS BUTTERWORTH'S WINDOW

I   A DISCOVERY

I am not an inquisitive woman, but when, in the middle of a certain warm night in September, I heard a carriage draw up at the adjoining house and stop, I could not resist the temptation of leaving my bed and taking a peep through the curtains of my window.

First: because the house was empty, or supposed to be so, the family still being, as I had every reason to believe, in Europe; and secondly: because, not being inquisitive, I often miss in my lonely and single life much that it would be both interesting and profitable for me to know.

Luckily I made no such mistake this evening. I rose and looked out, and though I was far from realizing it at the time, took, by so doing, my first step in a course of inquiry which has ended——

But it is too soon to speak of the end. Rather let me tell you what I saw when I parted the curtains of my window in Gramercy Park, on the night of September 17, 1895.

Not much at first glance, only a common hack drawn up at the neighboring curbstone. The lamp which is supposed to light our part of the block is some rods away on the opposite side of the street, so that I obtained but a shadowy glimpse of a young man and woman standing below me on the pavement. I could see, however, that the woman—and not the man—was putting money into the driver's hand. The next moment they were on the stoop of this long-closed house, and the coach rolled off.

It was dark, as I have said, and I did not recognize the young people,—at least their figures were not familiar to me; but when, in another instant, I heard the click of a night-key, and saw them, after a rather tedious fumbling at the lock, disappear from the stoop, I took it for granted that the gentleman was Mr. Van Burnam's eldest son Franklin, and the lady some relative of the family; though why this, its most punctilious member, should bring a guest at so late an hour into a house devoid of everything necessary to make the least exacting visitor comfortable, was a mystery that I retired to bed to meditate upon.

I did not succeed in solving it, however, and after some ten minutes had elapsed, I was settling myself again to sleep when I was re-aroused by a fresh sound from the quarter mentioned. The door I had so lately heard shut, opened again, and though I had to rush for it, I succeeded in getting to my window in time to catch a glimpse of the departing figure of the young man hurrying away towards Broadway. The young woman was not with him, and as I realized that he had left her behind him in the great, empty house, without apparent light and certainly without any companion, I began to question if this was like Franklin Van Burnam. Was it not more in keeping with the recklessness of his more easy-natured and less reliable brother, Howard, who, some two or three years back, had married a young wife of no very satisfactory antecedents, and who, as I had heard, had been ostracized by the family in consequence?

Whichever of the two it was, he had certainly shown but little consideration for his companion, and thus thinking, I fell off to sleep just as the clock struck the half hour after midnight.

Next morning as soon as modesty would permit me to approach the window, I surveyed the neighboring house minutely. Not a blind was open, nor a shutter displaced. As I am an early riser, this did not disturb me at the time, but when after breakfast I looked again and still failed to detect any evidences of life in the great barren front beside me, I began to feel uneasy. But I did nothing till noon, when going into my rear garden and observing that the back windows of the Van Burnam house were as closely shuttered as the front, I became so anxious that I stopped the next policeman I saw going by, and telling him my suspicions, urged him to ring the bell.

No answer followed the summons.

"There is no one here," said he.

"Ring again!" I begged.

And he rang again but with no better result.

"Don't you see that the house is shut up?" he grumbled. "We have had orders to watch the place, but none to take the watch off."

"There is a young woman inside," I insisted. "The more I think over last night's occurrence, the more I am convinced that the matter should be looked into."

He shrugged his shoulders and was moving away when we both observed a common-looking woman standing in front looking at us. She had a bundle in her hand, and her face, unnaturally ruddy though it was, had a scared look which was all the more remarkable from the fact that it was one of those wooden-like countenances which under ordinary circumstances are capable of but little expression. She was not a stranger to me; that is, I had seen her before in or about the house in which we were at that moment so interested; and not stopping to put any curb on my excitement, I rushed down to the pavement and accosted her.

"Who are you?" I asked. "Do you work for the Van Burnams, and do you know who the lady was who came here last night?"

The poor woman, either startled by my sudden address or by my manner which may have been a little sharp, gave a quick bound backward, and was only deterred by the near presence of the policeman from attempting flight. As it was, she stood her ground, though the fiery flush, which made her face so noticeable, deepened till her cheeks and brow were scarlet.

"I am the scrub-woman," she protested. "I have come to open the windows and air the house,"—ignoring my last question.

"Is the family coming home?" the policeman asked.

"I don't know; I think so," was her weak reply.

"Have you the keys?" I now demanded, seeing her fumbling in her pocket.

She did not answer; a sly look displaced the anxious one she had hitherto displayed, and she turned away.

"I don't see what business it is of the neighbors," she muttered, throwing me a dissatisfied scowl over her shoulder.

"If you've got the keys, we will go in and see that things are all right," said the policeman, stopping her with a light touch.

She trembled; I saw that she trembled, and naturally became excited. Something was wrong in the Van Burnam mansion, and I was going to be present at its discovery. But her next words cut my hopes short.

"I have no objection to your going in," she said to the policeman, "but I will not give up my keys to her. What right has she in our house any way." And I thought I heard her murmur something about a meddlesome old maid.

The look which I received from the policeman convinced me that my ears had not played me false.

"The lady's right," he declared; and pushing by me quite disrespectfully, he led the way to the basement door, into which he and the so-called cleaner presently disappeared.

I waited in front. I felt it to be my duty to do so. The various passers-by stopped an instant to stare at me before proceeding on their way, but I did not flinch from my post. Not till I had heard that the young woman whom I had seen enter these doors at midnight was well, and that her delay in opening the windows was entirely due to fashionable laziness, would I feel justified in returning to my own home and its affairs. But it took patience and some courage to remain there. Several minutes elapsed before I perceived the shutters in the third story open, and a still longer time before a window on the second floor flew up and the policeman looked out, only to meet my inquiring gaze and rapidly disappear again.

Meantime three or four persons had stopped on the walk near me, the nucleus of a crowd which would not be long in collecting, and I was beginning to feel I was paying dearly for my virtuous resolution, when the front door burst violently open and we caught sight of the trembling form and shocked face of the scrub-woman.

"She's dead!" she cried, "she's dead! Murder!" and would have said more had not the policeman pulled her back, with a growl which sounded very much like a suppressed oath.

He would have shut the door upon me had I not been quicker than lightning. As it was, I got in before it slammed, and happily too; for just at that moment the house-cleaner, who had grown paler every instant, fell in a heap in the entry, and the policeman, who was not the man I would want about me in any trouble, seemed somewhat embarrassed by this new emergency, and let me lift the poor thing up and drag her farther into the hall.

She had fainted, and should have had something done for her, but anxious though I always am to be of help where help is needed, I had no sooner got within range of the parlor door with my burden, than I beheld a sight so terrifying that I involuntarily let the poor woman slip from my arms to the floor.

In the darkness of a dim corner (for the room had no light save that which came through the doorway where I stood) lay the form of a woman under a fallen piece of furniture. Her skirts and distended arms alone were visible; but no one who saw the rigid outlines of her limbs could doubt for a moment that she was dead.

At a sight so dreadful, and, in spite of all my apprehensions, so unexpected, I felt a sensation of sickness which in another moment might have ended in my fainting also, if I had not realized that it would never do for me to lose my wits in the presence of a man who had none too many of his own. So I shook off my momentary weakness, and turning to the policeman, who was hesitating between the unconscious figure of the woman outside the door and the dead form of the one within I cried sharply:

"Come, man, to business! The woman inside there is dead, but this one is living. Fetch me a pitcher of water from below if you can, and then go for whatever assistance you need. I'll wait here and bring this woman to. She is a strong one, and it won't take long."

"You'll stay here alone with that——" he began.

But I stopped him with a look of disdain.

"Of course I will stay here; why not? Is there anything in the dead to be afraid of? Save me from the living, and I undertake to save myself from the dead."

But his face had grown very suspicious.

"You go for the water," he cried. "And see here! Just call out for some one to telephone to Police Headquarters for the Coroner and a detective. I don't quit this room till one or the other of them comes."

Smiling at a caution so very ill-timed, but abiding by my invariable rule of never arguing with a man unless I see some way of getting the better of him, I did what he bade me, though I hated dreadfully to leave the spot and its woeful mystery, even for so short a time as was required.

"Run up to the second story," he called out, as I passed by the prostrate figure of the cleaner. "Tell them what you want from the window, or we will have the whole street in here."

So I ran up-stairs,—I had always wished to visit this house, but had never been encouraged to do so by the Misses Van Burnam,—and making my way into the front room, the door of which stood wide open, I rushed to the window and hailed the crowd, which by this time extended far out beyond the curb-stone.

"An officer!" I called out, "a police officer! An accident has occurred and the man in charge here wants the Coroner and a detective from Police Headquarters."

"Who's hurt?" "Is it a man?" "Is it a woman?" shouted up one or two; and "Let us in!" shouted others; but the sight of a boy rushing off to meet an advancing policeman satisfied me that help would soon be forthcoming, so I drew in my head and looked about me for the next necessity—water.

I was in a lady's bed-chamber, probably that of the eldest Miss Van Burnam; but it was a bed-chamber which had not been occupied for some months, and naturally it lacked the very articles which would have been of assistance to me in the present emergency. No eau de Cologne on the bureau, no camphor on the mantel-shelf. But there was water in the pipes (something I had hardly hoped for), and a mug on the wash-stand; so I filled the mug and ran with it to the door, stumbling, as I did so, over some small object which I presently perceived to be a little round pin-cushion. Picking it up, for I hate anything like disorder, I placed it on a table near by, and continued on my way.

The woman was still lying at the foot of the stairs. I dashed the water in her face and she immediately came to.

Sitting up, she was about to open her lips when she checked herself; a fact which struck me as odd, though I did not allow my surprise to become apparent.

Meantime I stole a glance into the parlor. The officer was standing where I had left him, looking down on the prostrate figure before him.

There was no sign of feeling in his heavy countenance, and he had not opened a shutter, nor, so far as I could see, disarranged an object in the room.

The mysterious character of the whole affair fascinated me in spite of myself, and leaving the now fully aroused woman in the hall, I was half-way across the parlor floor when the latter stopped me with a shrill cry:

"Don't leave me! I have never seen anything before so horrible. The poor dear! The poor dear! Why don't he take those dreadful things off her?"

She alluded not only to the piece of furniture which had fallen upon the prostrate woman, and which can best be described as a cabinet with closets below and shelves above, but to the various articles of bric-à-brac which had tumbled from the shelves, and which now lay in broken pieces about her.

"He will do so; they will do so very soon," I replied. "He is waiting for some one with more authority than himself; for the Coroner, if you know what that means."

"But what if she's alive! Those things will crush her. Let us take them off. I'll help. I'm not too weak to help."

"Do you know who this person is?" I asked, for her voice had more feeling in it than I thought natural to the occasion, dreadful as it was.

"I?" she repeated, her weak eyelids quivering for a moment as she tried to sustain my scrutiny. "How should I know? I came in with the policeman and haven't been any nearer than I now be. What makes you think I know anything about her? I'm only the scrubwoman, and don't even know the names of the family."

"I thought you seemed so very anxious," I explained, suspicious of her suspiciousness, which was of so sly and emphatic a character that it changed her whole bearing from one of fear to one of cunning in a moment.

"And who wouldn't feel the like of that for a poor creature lying crushed under a heap of broken crockery!"

Crockery! those Japanese vases worth hundreds of dollars! that ormulu clock and those Dresden figures which must have been more than a couple of centuries old!

"It's a poor sense of duty that keeps a man standing dumb and staring like that, when with a lift of his hand he could show us the like of her pretty face, and if it's dead she be or alive."

As this burst of indignation was natural enough and not altogether uncalled for from the standpoint of humanity, I gave the woman a nod of approval, and wished I were a man myself that I might lift the heavy cabinet or whatever it was that lay upon the poor creature before us. But not being a man, and not judging it wise to irritate the one representative of that sex then present, I made no remark, but only took a few steps farther into the room, followed, as it afterwards appeared, by the scrub-woman.

The Van Burnam parlors are separated by an open arch. It was to the right of this arch and in the corner opposite the doorway that the dead woman lay. Using my eyes, now that I was somewhat accustomed to the semi-darkness enveloping us, I noticed two or three facts which had hitherto escaped me. One was, that she lay on her back with her feet pointing towards the hall door, and another, that nowhere in the room, save in her immediate vicinity, were there to be seen any signs of struggle or disorder. All was as set and proper as in my own parlor when it has been undisturbed for any length of time by guests; and though I could not see far into the rooms beyond, they were to all appearance in an equally orderly condition.

Meanwhile the cleaner was trying to account for the overturned cabinet.

"Poor dear! poor dear! she must have pulled it over on herself! But however did she get into the house? And what was she doing in this great empty place?"

The policeman, to whom these remarks had evidently been addressed, growled out some unintelligible reply, and in her perplexity the woman turned towards me.

But what could I say to her? I had my own private knowledge of the matter, but she was not one to confide in, so I stoically shook my head. Doubly disappointed, the poor thing shrank back, after looking first at the policeman and then at me in an odd, appealing way, difficult to understand. Then her eyes fell again on the dead girl at her feet, and being nearer now than before, she evidently saw something that startled her, for she sank on her knees with a little cry and began examining the girl's skirts.

"What are you looking at there?" growled the policeman. "Get up, can't you! No one but the Coroner has right to lay hand on anything here."

"I'm doing no harm," the woman protested, in an odd, shaking voice. "I only wanted to see what the poor thing had on. Some blue stuff, isn't it?" she asked me.

"Blue serge," I answered; "store-made, but very good; must have come from Altman's or Stern's."

"I—I'm not used to sights like this," stammered the scrub-woman, stumbling awkwardly to her feet, and looking as if her few remaining wits had followed the rest on an endless vacation. "I—I think I shall have to go home." But she did not move.

"The poor dear's young, isn't she?" she presently insinuated, with an odd catch in her voice that gave to the question an air of hesitation and doubt.

"I think she is younger than either you or myself," I deigned to reply. "Her narrow pointed shoes show she has not reached the years of discretion."

"Yes, yes, so they do!" ejaculated the cleaner, eagerly—too eagerly for perfect ingenuousness. "That's why I said 'Poor dear!' and spoke of her pretty face. I am sorry for young folks when they get into trouble, aint you? You and me might lie here and no one be much the worse for it, but a sweet lady like this——"

This was not very flattering to me, but I was prevented from rebuking her by a prolonged shout from the stoop without, as a rush was made against the front door, followed by a shrill peal of the bell.

"Man from Headquarters," stolidly announced the policeman. "Open the door, ma'am; or step back into the further hall if you want me to do it."

Such rudeness was uncalled for; but considering myself too important a witness to show feeling, I swallowed my indignation and proceeded with all my native dignity to the front door.

II   QUESTIONS

As I did so, I could catch the murmur of the crowd outside as it seethed forward at the first intimation of the door being opened; but my attention was not so distracted by it, loud as it sounded after the quiet of the shut-up house, that I failed to notice that the door had not been locked by the gentleman leaving the night before, and that, consequently, only the night latch was on. With a turn of the knob it opened, showing me the mob of shouting boys and the forms of two gentlemen awaiting admittance on the door-step. I frowned at the mob and smiled on the gentlemen, one of whom was portly and easy-going in appearance, and the other spare, with a touch of severity in his aspect. But for some reason these gentlemen did not seem to appreciate the honor I had done them, for they both gave me a displeased glance, which was so odd and unsympathetic in its character that I bridled a little, though I soon returned to my natural manner. Did they realize at the first glance that I was destined to prove a thorn in the sides of every one connected with this matter, for days to come?

"Are you the woman who called from the window?" asked the larger of the two, whose business here I found it difficult at first to determine.

"I am," was my perfectly self-possessed reply. "I live next door and my presence here is due to the anxious interest I always take in my neighbors. I had reason to think that all was not as it should be in this house, and I was right. Look in the parlor, sirs."

They were already as far as the threshold of that room and needed no further encouragement to enter. The heavier man went first and the other followed, and you may be sure I was not far behind. The sight meeting our eyes was ghastly enough, as you know; but these men were evidently accustomed to ghastly sights, for they showed but little emotion.

"I thought this house was empty," observed the second gentleman, who was evidently a doctor.

"So it was till last night," I put in; and was about to tell my story, when I felt my skirts jerked.

Turning, I found that this warning had come from the cleaner who stood close beside me.

"What do you want?" I asked, not understanding her and having nothing to conceal.

"I?" she faltered, with a frightened air. "Nothing, ma'am, nothing."

"Then don't interrupt me," I harshly admonished her, annoyed at an interference that tended to throw suspicion upon my candor. "This woman came here to scrub and clean," I now explained; "it was by means of the key she carried that we were enabled to get into the house. I never spoke to her till a half hour ago."

At which, with a display of subtlety I was far from expecting in one of her appearance, she let her emotions take a fresh direction, and pointing towards the dead woman, she impetuously cried:

"But the poor child there! Aint you going to take those things off of her? It's wicked to leave her under all that stuff. Suppose there was life in her!"

"Oh! there's no hope of that," muttered the doctor, lifting one of the hands, and letting it fall again.

"Still—" he cast a side look at his companion, who gave him a meaning nod—"it might be well enough to lift this cabinet sufficiently for me to lay my hand on her heart."

They accordingly did this; and the doctor, leaning down, placed his hand over the poor bruised breast.

"No life," he murmured. "She has been dead some hours. Do you think we had better release the head?" he went on, glancing up at the portly man at his side.

But the latter, who was rapidly growing serious, made a slight protest with his finger, and turning to me, inquired, with sudden authority:

"What did you mean when you said that the house had been empty till last night?"

"Just what I said, sir. It was empty till about midnight, when two persons——" Again I felt my dress twitched, this time very cautiously. What did the woman want? Not daring to give her a look, for these men were only too ready to detect harm in everything I did, I gently drew my skirt away and took a step aside, going on as if no interruption had occurred. "Did I say persons? I should have said a man and a woman drove up to the house and entered. I saw them from my window."

"You did?" murmured my interlocutor, whom I had by this time decided to be a detective. "And this is the woman, I suppose?" he proceeded, pointing to the poor creature lying before us.

"Why, yes, of course. Who else can she be? I did not see the lady's face last night, but she was young and light on her feet, and ran up the stoop gaily."

"And the man? Where is the man? I don't see him here."

"I am not surprised at that. He went very soon after he came, not ten minutes after, I should say. That is what alarmed me and caused me to have the house investigated. It did not seem natural or like any of the Van Burnams to leave a woman to spend the night in so large a house alone."

"You know the Van Burnams?"

"Not well. But that don't signify. I know what report says of them; they are gentlemen."

"But Mr. Van Burnam is in Europe."

"He has two sons."

"Living here?"

"No; the unmarried one spends his nights at Long Branch, and the other is with his wife somewhere in Connecticut."

"How did the young couple you saw get in last night? Was there any one here to admit them?"

"No; the gentleman had a key."

"Ah, he had a key."

The tone in which this was said recurred to me afterwards, but at the moment I was much more impressed by a peculiar sound I heard behind me, something between a gasp and a click in the throat, which came I knew from the scrub-woman, and which, odd and contradictory as it may appear, struck me as an expression of satisfaction, though what there was in my admission to give satisfaction to this poor creature I could not conjecture. Moving so as to get a glimpse of her face, I went on with the grim self-possession natural to my character:

"And when he came out he walked briskly away. The carriage had not waited for him."

"Ah!" again muttered the gentleman, picking up one of the broken pieces of china which lay haphazard about the floor, while I studied the cleaner's face, which, to my amazement, gave evidences of a confusion of emotions most unaccountable to me.

Mr. Gryce may have noticed this too, for he immediately addressed her, though he continued to look at the broken piece of china in his hand.

"And how come you to be cleaning the house?" he asked. "Is the family coming home?"

"They are, sir," she answered, hiding her emotion with great skill the moment she perceived attention directed to herself, and speaking with a sudden volubility that made us all stare. "They are expected any day. I didn't know it till yesterday—was it yesterday? No, the day before—when young Mr. Franklin—he is the oldest son, sir, and a very nice man, a very nice man—sent me word by letter that I was to get the house ready. It isn't the first time I have done it for them, sir, and as soon as I could get the basement key from the agent, I came here, and worked all day yesterday, washing up the floors and dusting. I should have been at them again this morning if my husband hadn't been sick. But I had to go to the infirmary for medicine, and it was noon when I got here, and then I found this lady standing outside with a policeman, a very nice lady, a very nice lady indeed, sir, I pay my respects to her"—and she actually dropped me a curtsey like a peasant woman in a play—"and they took my key from me, and the policeman opens the door, and he and me go upstairs and into all the rooms, and when we come to this one——"

She was getting so excited as to be hardly intelligible. Stopping herself with a jerk, she fumbled nervously with her apron, while I asked myself how she could have been at work in this house the day before without my knowing it. Suddenly I remembered that I was ill in the morning and busy in the afternoon at the Orphan Asylum, and somewhat relieved at finding so excellent an excuse for my ignorance, I looked up to see if the detective had noticed anything odd in this woman's behavior. Presumably he had, but having more experience than myself with the susceptibility of ignorant persons in the presence of danger and distress, he attached less importance to it than I did, for which I was secretly glad, without exactly knowing my reasons for being so.

"You will be wanted as a witness by the Coroner's jury," he now remarked to her, looking as if he were addressing the piece of china he was turning over in his hand. "Now, no nonsense!" he protested, as she commenced to tremble and plead. "You were the first one to see this dead woman, and you must be on hand to say so. As I cannot tell you when the inquest will be held, you had better stay around till the Coroner comes. He'll be here soon. You, and this other woman too."

By other woman he meant me, Miss Butterworth, of Colonial ancestry and no inconsiderable importance in the social world. But though I did not relish this careless association of myself with this poor scrub-woman, I was careful to show no displeasure, for I reasoned that as witnesses we were equal before the law, and that it was solely in this light he regarded us.

There was something in the manner of both these gentlemen which convinced me that while my presence was considered desirable in the house, it was not especially wanted in the room. I was therefore moving reluctantly away, when I felt a slight but peremptory touch on the arm, and turning, saw the detective at my side, still studying his piece of china.

He was, as I have said, of portly build and benevolent aspect; a fatherly-looking man, and not at all the person one would be likely to associate with the police. Yet he could take the lead very naturally, and when he spoke, I felt bound to answer him.

"Will you be so good, madam, as to relate over again, what you saw from your window last night? I am likely to have charge of this matter, and would be pleased to hear all you may have to say concerning it."

"My name is Butterworth," I politely intimated.

"And my name is Gryce."

"A detective?"

"The same."

"You must think this matter very serious," I ventured.

"Death by violence is always serious."

"You must regard this death as something more than an accident, I mean."

His smile seemed to say: "You will not know to-day how I regard it."

"And you will not know to-day what I think of it either," was my inward rejoinder, but I said nothing aloud, for the man was seventy-five if he was a day, and I have been taught respect for age, and have practised the same for fifty years and more.

I must have shown what was passing in my mind, and he must have seen it reflected on the polished surface of the porcelain he was contemplating, for his lips showed the shadow of a smile sufficiently sarcastic for me to see that he was far from being as easy-natured as his countenance indicated.

"Come, come," said he, "there is the Coroner now. Say what you have to say, like the straightforward, honest woman you appear."

"I don't like compliments," I snapped out. Indeed, they have always been obnoxious to me. As if there was any merit in being honest and straightforward, or any distinction in being told so!

"I am Miss Butterworth, and not in the habit of being spoken to as if I were a simple countrywoman," I objected. "But I will repeat what I saw last night, as it is no secret, and the telling of it won't hurt me and may help you."

Accordingly I went over the whole story, and was much more loquacious than I had intended to be, his manner was so insinuating and his inquiries so pertinent. But one topic we both failed to broach, and that was the peculiar manner of the scrub-woman. Perhaps it had not struck him as peculiar and perhaps it should not have struck me so, but in the silence which was preserved on the subject I felt I had acquired an advantage over him, which might lead to consequences of no small importance. Would I have felt thus or congratulated myself quite so much upon my fancied superiority, if I had known he was the man who managed the Leavenworth case, and who in his early years had experienced that very wonderful adventure on the staircase of the Heart's Delight? Perhaps I would; for though I have had no adventures, I feel capable of them, and as for any peculiar acumen he may have shown in his long and eventful career, why that is a quality which others may share with him, as I hope to be able to prove before finishing these pages.

III   AMELIA DISCOVERS HERSELF

There is a small room at the extremity of the Van Burnam mansion. In this I took refuge after my interview with Mr. Gryce. As I picked out the chair which best suited me and settled myself for a comfortable communion with my own thoughts, I was astonished to find how much I was enjoying myself, notwithstanding the thousand and one duties awaiting me on the other side of the party-wall.

Even this very solitude was welcome, for it gave me an opportunity to consider matters. I had not known up to this very hour that I had any special gifts. My father, who was a shrewd man of the old New England type, said more times than I am years old (which was not saying it as often as some may think) that Araminta (the name I was christened by, and the name you will find in the Bible record, though I sign myself Amelia, and insist upon being addressed as Amelia, being, as I hope, a sensible woman and not the piece of antiquated sentimentality suggested by the former cognomen)—that Araminta would live to make her mark; though in what capacity he never informed me, being, as I have observed, a shrewd man, and thus not likely to thoughtlessly commit himself.

I now know he was right; my pretensions dating from the moment I found that this affair, at first glance so simple, and at the next so complicated, had aroused in me a fever of investigation which no reasoning could allay. Though I had other and more personal matters on my mind, my thoughts would rest nowhere but on the details of this tragedy; and having, as I thought, noticed some few facts in connection with it, from which conclusions might be drawn, I amused myself with jotting them down on the back of a disputed grocer's bill I happened to find in my pocket.

Valueless as explaining this tragedy, being founded upon insufficient evidence, they may be interesting as showing the workings of my mind even at this early stage of the matter. They were drawn up under three heads.

First, was the death of this young woman an accident?

Second, was it a suicide?

Third, was it a murder?

Under the first head I wrote:

My reasons for not thinking it an accident.

1. If it had been an accident and she had pulled the cabinet over upon herself, she would have been found with her feet pointing towards the wall where the cabinet had stood.

(But her feet were towards the door and her head under the cabinet.)

2. The decent, even precise, arrangement of the clothing about her feet, which precludes any theory involving accident.

Under the second:

Reason for not thinking it suicide.

She could not have been found in the position observed without having lain down on the floor while living and then pulled the shelves down upon herself.

(A theory obviously too improbable to be considered.)

Under the third:

Reason for not thinking it murder.

She would need to have been held down on the floor while the cabinet was being pulled over on her; something which the quiet aspect of the hands and feet made appear impossible.

To this I added:

Reasons for accepting the theory of murder.

1. The fact that she did not go into the house alone; that a man entered with her, remained ten minutes, and then came out again and disappeared up the street with every appearance of haste and an anxious desire to leave the spot.

2. The front door, which he had unlocked on entering, was not locked by him on his departure, the catch doing the locking. Yet, though he could have re-entered so easily, he had shown no disposition to return.

3. The arrangement of the skirts, which show the touch of a careful hand after death.

Nothing clear, you see. I was doubtful of all; and yet my suspicions tended most toward murder.

I had eaten my luncheon before interfering in this matter, which was fortunate for me, as it was three o'clock before I was summoned to meet the Coroner, of whose arrival I had been conscious some time before.

He was in the front parlor where the dead girl lay, and as I took my way thither I felt the same sensations of faintness which had so nearly overcome me on the previous occasion. But I mastered them, and was quite myself before I crossed the threshold.

There were several gentlemen present, but of them all I only noticed two, one of whom I took to be the Coroner, while the other was my late interlocutor, Mr. Gryce. From the animation observable in the latter, I gathered that the case was growing in interest from the detective standpoint.

"Ah, and is this the witness?" asked the Coroner, as I stepped into the room.

"I am Miss Butterworth," was my calm reply. "Amelia Butterworth. Living next door and present at the discovery of this poor murdered body."

"Murdered," he repeated. "Why do you say murdered?"

For reply I drew from my pocket the bill on which I had scribbled my conclusions in regard to this matter.

"Read this," said I.

Evidently astonished, he took the paper from my hand, and, after some curious glances in my direction, condescended to do as I requested. The result was an odd but grudging look of admiration directed towards myself and a quick passing over of the paper to the detective.

The latter, who had exchanged his bit of broken china for a very much used and tooth-marked lead-pencil, frowned with a whimsical air at the latter before he put it in his pocket. Then he read my hurried scrawl.

"Two Richmonds in the field!" commented the Coroner, with a sly chuckle. "I am afraid I shall have to yield to their allied forces. Miss Butterworth, the cabinet is about to be raised; do you feel as if you could endure the sight?"

"I can stand anything where the cause of justice is involved," I replied.

"Very well, then, sit down, if you please. When the whole body is visible I will call you."

And stepping forward he gave orders to have the clock and broken china removed from about the body.

As the former was laid away on one end of the mantel some one observed:

"What a valuable witness that clock might have been had it been running when the shelves fell!"

But the fact was so patent that it had not been in motion for months that no one even answered; and Mr. Gryce did not so much as look towards it. But then we had all seen that the hands stood at three minutes to five.

I had been asked to sit down, but I found this impossible. Side by side with the detective, I viewed the replacing of that heavy piece of furniture against the wall, and the slow disclosure of the upper part of the body which had so long lain hidden.

That I did not give way is a proof that my father's prophecy was not without some reasonable foundation; for the sight was one to try the stoutest nerves, as well as to awaken the compassion of the hardest heart.

The Coroner, meeting my eye, pointed at the poor creature inquiringly.

"Is this the woman you saw enter here last night?"

I glanced down at her dress, noted the short summer cape tied to the neck with an elaborate bow of ribbon, and nodded my head.

"I remember the cape," said I. "But where is her hat? She wore one. Let me see if I can describe it." Closing my eyes I endeavored to recall the dim silhouette of her figure as she stood passing up the change to the driver; and was so far successful that I was ready to announce at the next moment that her hat presented the effect of a soft felt with one feather or one bow of ribbon standing upright from the side of the crown.

"Then the identity of this woman with the one you saw enter here last night is established," remarked the detective, stooping down and drawing from under the poor girl's body a hat, sufficiently like the one I had just described, to satisfy everybody that it was the same.

"As if there could be any doubt," I began.

But the Coroner, explaining that it was a mere formality, motioned me to stand aside in favor of the doctor, who seemed anxious to approach nearer the spot where the dead woman lay. This I was about to do when a sudden thought struck me, and I reached out my hand for the hat.

"Let me look at it for a moment," said I.

Mr. Gryce at once handed it over, and I took a good look at it inside and out.

"It is pretty badly crushed," I observed, "and does not present a very fresh appearance, but for all that it has been worn but once."

"How do you know?" questioned the Coroner.

"Let the other Richmond inform you," was my grimly uttered reply, as I gave it again into the detective's hand.

There was a murmur about me, whether of amusement or displeasure, I made no effort to decide. I was finding out something for myself, and I did not care what they thought of me.

"Neither has she worn this dress long," I continued; "but that is not true of the shoes. They are not old, but they have been acquainted with the pavement, and that is more than can be said of the hem of this gown. There are no gloves on her hands; a few minutes elapsed then before the assault; long enough for her to take them off."

"Smart woman!" whispered a voice in my ear; a half-admiring, half-sarcastic voice that I had no difficulty in ascribing to

Mr. Gryce. "But are you sure she wore any? Did you notice that her hand was gloved when she came into the house?"

"No," I answered, frankly; "but so well-dressed a woman would not enter a house like this, without gloves."

"It was a warm night," some one suggested.

"I don't care. You will find her gloves as you have her hat; and you will find them with the fingers turned inside out, just as she drew them from her hand. So much I will concede to the warmth of the weather."

"Like these, for instance," broke in a quiet voice.

Startled, for a hand had appeared over my shoulder dangling a pair of gloves before my eyes, I cried out, somewhat too triumphantly I own:

"Yes, yes, just like those! Did you pick them up here? Are they hers?"

"You say that this is the way hers should look."

"And I repeat it."

"Then allow me to pay you my compliments. These were picked up here."

"But where?" I cried. "I thought I had looked this carpet well over."

He smiled, not at me but at the gloves, and the thought crossed me that he felt as if something more than the gloves was being turned inside out. I therefore pursed my mouth, and determined to stand more on my guard.

"It is of no consequence," I assured him; "all such matters will come out at the inquest."

Mr. Gryce nodded, and put the gloves back in his pocket. With them he seemed to pocket some of his geniality and patience.

"All these facts have been gone over before you came in," said he, which statement I beg to consider as open to doubt.

The doctor, who had hardly moved a muscle during all this colloquy, now rose from his kneeling position beside the girl's head.

"I shall have to ask the presence of another physician," said he. "Will you send for one from your office, Coroner Dahl?"

At which I stepped back and the Coroner stepped forward, saying, however, as he passed me:

"The inquest will be held day after to-morrow in my office. Hold yourself in readiness to be present. I regard you as one of my chief witnesses."

I assured him I would be on hand, and, obeying a gesture of his finger, retreated from the room; but I did not yet leave the house. A straight, slim man, with a very small head but a very bright eye, was leaning on the newel-post in the front hall, and when he saw me, started up so alertly I perceived that he had business with me, and so waited for him to speak.

"You are Miss Butterworth?" he inquired.

"I am, sir."

"And I am a reporter from the New York World. Will you allow me——"

Why did he stop? I had merely looked at him. But he did stop, and that is saying considerable for a reporter from the New York World.

"I certainly am willing to tell you what I have told every one else," I interposed, considering it better not to make an enemy of so judicious a young man; and seeing him brighten up at this, I thereupon related all I considered desirable for the general public to know.

I was about passing on, when, reflecting that one good turn deserves another, I paused and asked him if he thought they would leave the dead girl in that house all night.

He answered that he did not think they would. That a telegram had been sent some time before to young Mr. Van Burnam, and that they were only awaiting his arrival to remove her.

"Do you mean Howard?" I asked.

"Is he the elder one?"

"No."

"It is the elder one they have summoned; the one who has been staying at Long Branch."

"How can they expect him then so soon?"

"Because he is in the city. It seems the old gentleman is going to return on the New York, and as she is due here to-day, Franklin Van Burnam has come to New York to meet him."

"Humph!" thought I, "lively times are in prospect," and for the first time I remembered my dinner and the orders which had not been given about some curtains which were to have been hung that day, and all the other reasons I had for being at home.

I must have shown my feelings, much as I pride myself upon my impassibility upon all occasions, for he immediately held out his arm, with an offer to pilot me through the crowd to my own house; and I was about to accept it when the door-bell rang so sharply that we involuntarily stopped.

"A fresh witness or a telegram for the Coroner," whispered the reporter in my ear.

I tried to look indifferent, and doubtless made out pretty well, for he added, after a sly look in my face:

"You do not care to stay any longer?"

I made no reply, but I think he was impressed by my dignity. Could he not see that it would be the height of ill-manners for me to rush out in the face of any one coming in?

An officer opened the door, and when we saw who stood there, I am sure that the reporter, as well as myself, was grateful that we listened to the dictates of politeness. It was young Mr. Van Burnam—Franklin; I mean the older and more respectable of the two sons.

He was flushed and agitated, and looked as if he would like to annihilate the crowd pushing him about on his own stoop. He gave an angry glance backward as he stepped in, and then I saw that a carriage covered with baggage stood on the other side of the street, and gathered that he had not returned to his father's house alone.

"What has happened? What does all this mean?" were the words he hurled at us as the door closed behind him and he found himself face to face with a half dozen strangers, among whom the reporter and myself stood conspicuous.

Mr. Gryce, coming suddenly from somewhere, was the one to answer him.

"A painful occurrence, sir. A young girl has been found here, dead, crushed under one of your parlor cabinets."

"A young girl!" he repeated. (Oh, how glad I was that I had been brought up never to transgress the principles of politeness.) "Here! in this shut-up house? What young girl? You mean old woman, do you not? the house-cleaner or some one———"

"No, Mr. Van Burnam, we mean what we say, though possibly I should call her a young lady. She is dressed quite fashionably."

"The ———" Really I cannot repeat in this public manner the word which Mr. Van Burnam used. I excused him at the time, but I will not perpetuate his forgetfulness in these pages.

"She is still lying as we found her," Mr. Gryce now proceeded in his quiet, almost fatherly way. "Will you not take a look at her? Perhaps you can tell us who she is?"

"I?" Mr. Van Burnam seemed quite shocked. "How should I know her! Some thief probably, killed while meddling with other people's property."

"Perhaps," quoth Mr. Gryce, laconically; at which I felt so angry, as tending to mislead my handsome young neighbor, that I irresistibly did what I had fully made up my mind not to do, that is, stepped into view and took a part in this conversation.

"How can you say that," I cried, "when her admittance here was due to a young man who let her in at midnight with a key, and then left her to eat out her heart in this great house all alone."

I have made sensations in my life, but never quite so marked a one as this. In an instant every eye was on me, with the exception of the detective's. His was on the figure crowning the newel-post, and bitterly severe his gaze was too, though it immediately grew wary as the young man started towards me and impetuously demanded:

"Who talks like that? Why, it's Miss Butterworth. Madam, I fear I did not fully understand what you said."

Whereupon I repeated my words, this time very quietly but clearly, while Mr. Gryce continued to frown at the bronze figure he had taken into his confidence. When I had finished, Mr. Van Burnam's countenance had changed, so had his manner. He held himself as erect as before, but not with as much bravado. He showed haste and impatience also, but not the same kind of haste and not quite the same kind of impatience. The corners of Mr. Gryce's mouth betrayed that he noted this change, but he did not turn away from the newel-post.

"This is a remarkable circumstance which you have just told me," observed Mr. Van Burnam, with the first bow I had ever received from him. "I don't know what to think of it. But I still hold that it's some thief. Killed, did you say? Really dead? Well, I'd have given five hundred dollars not to have had it happen in this house."

He had been moving towards the parlor door, and he now entered it. Instantly Mr. Gryce was by his side.

"Are they going to close the door?" I whispered to the reporter, who was taking this all in equally with myself.

"I'm afraid so," he muttered.

And they did. Mr. Gryce had evidently had enough of my interference, and was resolved to shut me out, but I heard one word and caught one glimpse of Mr. Van Burnam's face before the heavy door fell to. The word was: "Oh, so bad as that! How can any one recognize her———" And the glimpse—well, the glimpse proved to me that he was much more profoundly agitated than he wished to appear, and any extraordinary agitation on his part was certainly in direct contradiction to the very sentence he was at that moment uttering.

IV   SILAS VAN BURNAM

"However much I may be needed at home, I cannot reconcile it with my sense of duty to leave just yet," I confided to the reporter, with what I meant to be a proper show of reason and self-restraint; "Mr. Van Burnam may wish to ask me some questions."

"Of course, of course," acquiesced the other. "You are very right; always are very right, I should judge."

As I did not know what he meant by this, I frowned, always a wise thing to do in an uncertainty; that is,—if one wishes to maintain an air of independence and aversion to flattery.

"Will you not sit down?" he suggested. "There is a chair at the end of the hall."

But I had no need to sit. The front door-bell again rang, and simultaneously with its opening, the parlor door unclosed and Mr. Franklin Van Burnam appeared in the hall, just as Mr. Silas Van Burnam, his father, stepped into the vestibule.

"Father!" he remonstrated, with a troubled air; "could you not wait?"

The elder gentleman, who had evidently just been driven up from the steamer, wiped his forehead with an irascible air, that I will say I had noticed in him before and on much less provocation.

"Wait, with a yelling crowd screaming murder in my ear, and Isabella on one side of me calling for salts, and Caroline on the opposite seat getting that blue look about the mouth we have learned to dread so in a hot day like this? No, sir, when there is anything wrong going on I want to know it, and evidently there is something wrong going on here. What is it? Some of Howard's——"

But the son, seizing me by the hand and drawing me forward, put a quick stop to the old gentleman's sentence. "Miss Butterworth, father! Our next-door neighbor, you know."

"Ah! hum! ha! Miss Butterworth. How do you do, ma'am? What the —— is she doing here?" he grumbled, not so low but that I heard both the profanity and the none too complimentary allusion to myself.

"If you will come into the parlor, I will tell you," urged the son. "But what have you done with Isabella and Caroline? Left them in the carriage with that hooting mob about them?"

"I told the coachman to drive on. They are probably half-way around the block by this time."

"Then come in here. But don't allow yourself to be too much affected by what you will see. A sad accident has occurred here, and you must expect the sight of blood."

"Blood! Oh, I can stand that, if Howard——"

The rest was lost in the sound of the closing door.

And now, you will say, I ought to have gone. And you are right, but would you have gone yourself, especially as the hall was full of people who did not belong there?

If you would, then condemn me for lingering just a few minutes longer.

The voices in the parlor were loud, but they presently subsided; and when the owner of the house came out again, he had a subdued look which was as great a contrast to his angry aspect on entering, as was the change I had observed in his son. He was so absorbed indeed that he did not notice me, though I stood directly in his way.

"Don't let Howard come," he was saying in a thick, low voice to his son. "Keep Howard away till we are sure——"

I am confident that his son pressed his arm at this point, for he stopped short and looked about him in a blind and dazed way.

"Oh!" he ejaculated, in a tone of great displeasure. "This is the woman who saw——"

"Miss Butterworth, father," the anxious voice of his son broke in. "Don't try to talk; such a sight is enough to unnerve any man."

"Yes, yes," blustered the old gentleman, evidently taking some hint from the other's tone or manner. "But where are the girls? They will be dead with terror, if we don't relieve their minds. They got the idea it was their brother Howard who was hurt; and so did I, but it's only some wandering waif—some——"

It seemed as if he was not to be allowed to finish any of his sentences, for Franklin interrupted him at this point to ask him what he was going to do with the girls. Certainly he could not bring them in here.

"No," answered the father, but in the dreamy, inconsequential way of one whose thoughts were elsewhere. "I suppose I shall have to take them to some hotel."

Ah, an idea! I flushed as I realized the opportunity which had come to me and had to wait a moment not to speak with too much eagerness.

"Let me play the part of a neighbor," I prayed, "and accommodate the young ladies for the night. My house is near and quiet."

"But the trouble it will involve," protested Mr. Franklin.

"Is just what I need to allay my excitement," I responded. "I shall be glad to offer them rooms for the night. If they are equally glad to accept them——"

"They must be!" the old gentleman declared. "I can't go running round with them hunting up rooms to-night. Miss Butterworth is very good; go find the girls, Franklin; let me have them off my mind, at least."

The young man bowed. I bowed, and was slipping at last from my place by the stairs when, for the third time, I felt my dress twitched.

"Are you going to keep to that story?" a voice whispered in my ear. "About the young man and woman coming in the night, you know."

"Keep to it!" I whispered back, recognizing the scrub-woman, who had sidled up to me from some unknown quarter in the semi-darkness. "Why, it's true. Why shouldn't I keep to it."

A chuckle, difficult to describe but full of meaning, shook the arm of the woman as she pressed close to my side.

"Oh, you are a good one," she said. "I didn't know they made 'em so good!" And with another chuckle full of satisfaction and an odd sort of admiration I had certainly not earned, she slid away again into the darkness.

Certainly there was something in this woman's attitude towards this affair which merited attention.

V   "THIS IS NO ONE I KNOW."

I welcomed the Misses Van Burnam with just enough good-will to show that I had not been influenced by any unworthy motives in asking them to my house.

I gave them my guest-chamber, but I invited them to sit in my front room as long as there was anything interesting going on in the street. I knew they would like to look out, and as this chamber boasts of a bay with two windows, we could all be accommodated. From where I sat I could now and then hear what they said, and I considered this but just, for if the young woman who had suffered so untimely an end was in any way connected with them, it was certainly best that the fact should not lie concealed; and one of them, that is Isabella, is such a chatterbox.

Mr. Van Burnam and his son had returned next door, and so far as we could observe from our vantage-point, preparations were being made for the body's removal. As the crowd below, driven away by the policemen one minute, only to collect again in another, swayed and grumbled in a continual expectation that was as continually disappointed, I heard Caroline's voice rise in two or three short sentences.

"They can't find Howard, or he would have been here before now. Did you see her that time when we were coming out of Clark's? Fanny Preston did, and said she was pretty."

"No, I didn't get a glimpse——" A shout from the street below.

"I can't believe it," were the next words I heard, "but Franklin is awfully afraid——"

"Hush! or the ogress——" I am sure I heard her say ogress; but what followed was drowned in another loud murmur, and I caught nothing further till these sentences were uttered by the trembling and over-excited Caroline: "If it is she, pa will never be the same man again. To have her die in our house! O, there's Howard now!"

The interruption came quick and sharp, and it was followed by a double cry and an anxious rustle, as the two girls sprang to their feet in their anxiety to attract their brother's attention or possibly to convey him some warning.

But I did not give much heed to them. My eyes were on the carriage in which Howard had arrived, and which, owing to the ambulance in front, had stopped on the other side of the way. I was anxious to see him descend that I might judge if his figure recalled that of the man I had seen cross the pavement the night before. But he did not descend. Just as his hand was on the carriage door, a half dozen men appeared on the adjoining stoop carrying a burden which they hastened to deposit in the ambulance. He sank back when he saw it, and when his face became visible again, it was so white it seemed to be the only face in the street, though fifty people stood about staring at the house, at the ambulance, and at him.

Franklin Van Burnam had evidently come to the door with the rest; for Howard no sooner showed his face the second time than we saw the former dash down the steps and try to part the crowd in a vain attempt to reach his brother's side. Mr. Gryce was more successful. He had no difficulty in winning his way across the street, and presently I perceived him standing near the carriage exchanging a few words with its occupant. A moment later he drew back, and addressing the driver, jumped into the carriage with Howard, and was speedily driven off. The ambulance followed and some of the crowd, and as soon as a hack could be obtained, Mr. Van Burnam and his son took the same road, leaving us three women in a state of suspense, which as far as one of us was concerned, ended in a nervous attack that was not unlike heart failure. I allude, of course, to Caroline, and it took Isabella and myself a good half hour to bring her back to a normal condition, and when this was done, Isabella thought it incumbent upon her to go off into hysterics, which, being but a weak simulation of the other's state, I met with severity and cured with a frown. When both were in trim again I allowed myself one remark.

"One would think," said I, "that you knew the young woman who has fallen victim to her folly next door."

At which Isabella violently shook her head and Caroline observed:

"It is the excitement which has been too much for me. I am never strong, and this is such a dreadful home-welcoming. When will father and Franklin come back? It was very unkind of them to go off without one word of encouragement."

"They probably did not consider the fate of this unknown woman a matter of any importance to you."

The Van Burnam girls were unlike in appearance and character, but they showed an equal embarrassment at this, casting down their eyes and behaving so strangely that I was driven to wonder, without any show of hysterics I am happy to say, what would be the upshot of this matter, and how far I would become involved in it before the truth came to light.

At dinner they displayed what I should call their best society manner. Seeing this, I assumed my society manner also. It is formed on a different pattern from theirs, but is fully as impressive, I judge.

A most formal meal was the result. My best china was in use, but I had added nothing to my usual course of viands. Indeed, I had abstracted something. An entrée, upon which my cook prides herself, was omitted. Was I going to allow these proud young misses to think I had exerted myself to please them? No; rather would I have them consider me niggardly and an enemy to good living; so the entrée was, as the French say, suppressed.

In the evening their father came in. He was looking very dejected, and half his bluster was gone. He held a telegram crushed in his hand, and he talked very rapidly. But he confided none of his secrets to me, and I was obliged to say good-night to these young ladies without knowing much more about the matter engrossing us than when I left their house in the afternoon.

But others were not as ignorant as myself. A dramatic and highly exciting scene had taken place that evening at the undertaker's to which the unknown's body had been removed, and as I have more than once heard it minutely described, I will endeavor to transcribe it here with all the impartiality of an outsider.

When Mr. Gryce entered the carriage in which Howard sat, he noted first, that the young man was frightened; and secondly, that he made no effort to hide it. He had heard almost nothing from the detective. He knew that there had been a hue and cry for him ever since noon, and that he was wanted to identify a young woman who had been found dead in his father's house, but beyond these facts he had been told little, and yet he seemed to have no curiosity nor did he venture to express any surprise. He merely accepted the situation and was troubled by it, showing no inclination to talk till very near the end of his destination, when he suddenly pulled himself together and ventured this question:

"How did she—the young woman as you call her—kill herself?"

The detective, who in his long career among criminals and suspected persons, had seen many men and encountered many conditions, roused at this query with much of his old spirit. Turning from the man rather than toward him, he allowed himself a slight shrug of the shoulders as he calmly replied:

"She was found under a heavy piece of furniture; the cabinet with the vases on it, which you must remember stood at the left of the mantel-piece. It had crushed her head and breast. Quite a remarkable means of death, don't you think? There has been but one occurrence like it in my long experience."

"I don't believe what you tell me," was the young man's astonishing reply. "You are trying to frighten me or to make game of me. No lady would make use of any such means of death as that."

"I did not say she was a lady," returned Mr. Gryce, scoring one in his mind against his unwary companion.

A quiver passed down the young man's side where he came in contact with the detective.

"No," he muttered; "but I gathered from what you said, she was no common person; or why," he flashed out in sudden heat, "do you require me to go with you to see her? Have I the name of associating with any persons of the sex who are not ladies?"

"Pardon me," said Mr. Gryce, in grim delight at the prospect he saw slowly unfolding before him of one of those complicated affairs in which minds like his unconsciously revel; "I meant no insinuations. We have requested you, as we have requested your father and brother, to accompany us to the undertaker's, because the identification of the corpse is a most important point, and every formality likely to insure it must be observed."

"And did not they—my father and brother, I mean—recognize her?"

"It would be difficult for any one to recognize her who was not well acquainted with her."

A horrified look crossed the features of Howard Van Burnam, which, if a part of his acting, showed him to have genius for his rôle. His head sank back on the cushions of the carriage, and for a moment he closed his eyes. When he opened them again, the carriage had stopped, and Mr. Gryce, who had not noticed his emotion, of course, was looking out of the window with his hand on the handle of the door.

"Are we there already?" asked the young man, with a shudder. "I wish you had not considered it necessary for me to see her. I shall detect nothing familiar in her, I know."

Mr. Gryce bowed, repeated that it was a mere formality, and followed the young gentleman into the building and afterwards into the room where the dead body lay. A couple of doctors and one or two officials stood about, in whose faces the young man sought for something like encouragement before casting his eyes in the direction indicated by the detective. But there was little in any of these faces to calm him, and turning shortly away, he walked manfully across the room and took his stand by the detective.

"I am positive," he began, "that it is not my wife——" At this moment the cloth that covered the body was removed, and he gave a great start of relief. "I said so," he remarked, coldly. "This is no one I know."

His sigh was echoed in double chorus from the doorway. Glancing that way he encountered the faces of his father and elder brother, and moved towards them with a relieved air that made quite another man of him in appearance.

"I have had my say," he remarked. "Shall I wait outside till you have had yours?"

"We have already said all that we had to," Franklin returned. "We declared that we did not recognize this person."

"Of course, of course," assented the other. "I don't see why they should have expected us to know her. Some common suicide who thought the house empty—But how did she get in?"

"Don't you know?" said Mr. Gryce. "Can it be that I forgot to tell you? Why, she was let in at night by a young man of medium height"—his eye ran up and down the graceful figure of the young élégant before him as he spoke—"who left her inside and then went away. A young man who had a key——"

"A key? Franklin, I——"

Was it a look from Franklin which made him stop? It is possible, for he turned on his heel as he reached this point, and tossing his head with quite a gay air, exclaimed: "But it is of no consequence! The girl is a stranger, and we have satisfied, I believe, all the requirements of the law in saying so, and may now drop the matter. Are you going to the club, Franklin?"

"Yes, but——" Here the elder brother drew nearer and whispered something into the other's ear, who at that whisper turned again towards the place where the dead woman lay. Seeing this movement, his anxious father wiped the moisture from his forehead. Silas Van Burnam had been silent up to this moment and seemed inclined to continue so, but he watched his younger son with painful intentness.

"Nonsense!" broke from Howard's lips as his brother ceased his communication; but he took a step nearer the body, notwithstanding, and then another and another till he was at its side again.

The hands had not been injured, as we have said, and upon these his eyes now fell.

"They are like hers! O God! they are like hers!" he muttered, growing gloomy at once. "But where are the rings? There are no rings to be seen on these fingers, and she wore five, including her wedding-ring."

"Is it of your wife you are speaking?" inquired Mr. Gryce, who had edged up close to his side.

The young man was caught unawares.

He flushed deeply, but answered up boldly and with great appearance of candor:

"Yes; my wife left Haddam yesterday to come to New York, and I have not seen her since. Naturally I have felt some doubts lest this unhappy victim should be she. But I do not recognize her clothing; I do not recognize her form; only the hands look familiar."

"And the hair?"

"Is of the same color as hers, but it's a very ordinary color. I do not dare to say from anything I see that this is my wife."

"We will call you again after the doctor has finished his autopsy," said Mr. Gryce. "Perhaps you will hear from Mrs. Van Burnam before then."

But this intimation did not seem to bring comfort with it. Mr. Van Burnam walked away, white and sick, for which display of emotion there was certainly some cause, and rejoining his father tried to carry off the moment with the aplomb of a man of the world.

But that father's eye was fixed too steadily upon him; he faltered as he sat down, and finally spoke up, with feverish energy:

"If it is she, so help me, God, her death is a mystery to me! We have quarrelled more than once lately, and I have sometimes lost my patience with her, but she had no reason to wish for death, and I am ready to swear in defiance of those hands, which are certainly like hers, and the nameless something which Franklin calls a likeness, that it is a stranger who lies there, and that her death in our house is a coincidence."

"Well, well, we will wait," was the detective's soothing reply. "Sit down in the room opposite there, and give me your orders for supper, and I will see that a good meal is served you."

The three gentlemen, seeing no way of refusing, followed the discreet official who preceded them, and the door of the doctor's room closed upon him and the inquiries he was about to make.

VI   NEW FACTS

Mr. Van Burnam and his sons had gone through the formality of a supper and were conversing in the haphazard way natural to men filled with a subject they dare not discuss, when the door opened and Mr. Gryce came in.

Advancing very calmly, he addressed himself to the father:

"I am sorry," said he, "to be obliged to inform you that this affair is much more serious than we anticipated. This young woman was dead before the shelves laden with bric-à-brac fell upon her. It is a case of murder; obviously so, or I should not presume to forestall the Coroner's jury in their verdict."

Murder! it is a word to shake the stoutest heart!

The older gentleman reeled as he half rose, and Franklin, his son, betrayed in his own way an almost equal amount of emotion. But Howard, shrugging his shoulders as if relieved of an immense weight, looked about with a cheerful air, and briskly cried:

"Then it is not the body of my wife you have there. No one would murder Louise. I shall go away and prove the truth of my words by hunting her up at once."

The detective opened the door, beckoned in the doctor, who whispered two or three words into Howard's ear.

They failed to awake the emotion he evidently expected. Howard looked surprised, but answered without any change of voice:

"Yes, Louise had such a scar; and if it is true that this woman is similarly marked, then it is a mere coincidence. Nothing will convince me that my wife has been the victim of murder."

"Had you not better take a look at the scar just mentioned?"

"No. I am so sure of what I say that I will not even consider the possibility of my being mistaken. I have examined the clothing on this body you have shown me, and not one article of it came from my wife's wardrobe; nor would my wife go, as you have informed me this woman did, into a dark house at night with any other man than her husband."

"And so you absolutely refuse to acknowledge her."

"Most certainly."

The detective paused, glanced at the troubled faces of the other two gentlemen, faces that had not perceptibly altered during these declarations, and suggestively remarked:

"You have not asked by what means she was killed."

"And I don't care," shouted Howard.

"It was by very peculiar means, also new in my experience."

"It does not interest me," the other retorted.

Mr. Gryce turned to his father and brother.

"Does it interest you?" he asked.

The old gentleman, ordinarily so testy and so peremptory, silently nodded his head, while Franklin cried:

"Speak up quick. You detectives hesitate so over the disagreeables. Was she throttled or stabbed with a knife?"

"I have said the means were peculiar. She was stabbed, but not—with a knife."

I know Mr. Gryce well enough now to be sure that he did not glance towards Howard while saying this, and yet at the same time that he did not miss the quiver of a muscle on his part or the motion of an eyelash. But Howard's assumed sang froid remained undisturbed and his countenance imperturbable.

"The wound was so small," the detective went on, "that it is a miracle it did not escape notice. It was made by the thrust of some very slender instrument through——"

"The heart?" put in Franklin.

"Of course, of course," assented the detective; "what other spot is vulnerable enough to cause death?"

"Is there any reason why we should not go?" demanded Howard, ignoring the extreme interest manifested by the other two, with a determination that showed great doggedness of character.

The detective ignored him.

"A quick stroke, a sure stroke, a fatal stroke. The girl never breathed after."

"But what of those things under which she lay crushed?"

"Ah, in them lies the mystery! Her assailant must have been as subtle as he was sure."

And still Howard showed no interest.

"I wish to telegraph to Haddam," he declared, as no one answered the last remark. Haddam was the place where he and his wife had been spending the summer.

"We have already telegraphed there," observed Mr. Gryce. "Your wife has not yet returned."

"There are other places," defiantly insisted the other. "I can find her if you give me the opportunity."

Mr. Gryce bowed.

"I am to give orders, then, for this body to be removed to the Morgue."

It was an unexpected suggestion, and for an instant Howard showed that he had feelings with the best. But he quickly recovered himself, and avoiding the anxious glances of his father and brother, answered with offensive lightness:

"I have nothing to do with that. You must do as you think proper."

And Mr. Gryce felt that he had received a check, and did not know whether to admire the young man for his nerve or to execrate him for his brutality. That the woman whom he had thus carelessly dismissed to the ignominy of the public gaze was his wife, the detective did not doubt.

VII   MR. GRYCE DISCOVERS MISS AMELIA

To return to my own observations. I was almost as ignorant of what I wanted to know at ten o'clock on that memorable night as I was at five, but I was determined not to remain so. When the two Misses Van Burnam had retired to their room, I slipped away to the neighboring house and boldly rang the bell. I had observed Mr. Gryce enter it a few minutes before, and I was resolved to have some talk with him.

The hall-lamp was lit, and we could discern each other's faces as he opened the door. Mine may have been a study, but I am sure his was. He had not expected to be confronted by an elderly lady at that hour of night.

"Well!" he dryly ejaculated, "I am sensible of the honor, Miss Butterworth." But he did not ask me in.

"I expected no less," said I. "I saw you come in, and I followed as soon after as I could. I have something to say to you."

He admitted me then and carefully closed the door. Feeling free to be myself, I threw off the veil I had tied under my chin and confronted him with what I call the true spirit.

"Mr. Gryce," I began, "let us make an exchange of civilities. Tell me what you have done with Howard Van Burnam, and I will tell you what I have observed in the course of this afternoon's investigation."

This aged detective is used to women, I have no doubt, but he is not used to me. I saw it by the way he turned over and over the spectacles he held in his hand. I made an effort to help him out.

"I have noted something to-day which I think has escaped you. It is so slight a clue that most women would not speak of it. But being interested in the case, I will mention it, if in return you will acquaint me with what will appear in the papers to-morrow."

He seemed to like it. He peered through his glasses and at them with the smile of a discoverer. "I am your very humble servant," he declared; and I felt as if my father's daughter had received her first recognition.

But he did not overwhelm me with confidences. O, no, he is very sly, this old and well-seasoned detective; and while appearing to be very communicative, really parted with but little information. He said enough, however, for me to gather that matters looked grim for Howard, and if this was so, it must have become apparent that the death they were investigating was neither an accident nor a suicide.

I hinted as much, and he, for his own ends no doubt, admitted at last that a wound had been found on the young woman which could not have been inflicted by herself; at which I felt such increased interest in this remarkable murder that I must have made some foolish display of it, for the wary old gentleman chuckled and ogled his spectacles quite lovingly before shutting them up and putting them into his pocket.

"And now what have you to tell me?" he inquired, sliding softly between me and the parlor door.

"Nothing but this. Question that queer-acting house-cleaner closely. She has something to tell which it is your business to know."

I think he was disappointed. He looked as if he regretted the spectacles he had pocketed, and when he spoke there was an edge to his tone I had not noticed in it before.

"Do you know what that something is?" he asked.

"No, or I should tell you myself."

"And what makes you think she is hiding anything from us?"

"Her manner. Did you not notice her manner?"

He shrugged his shoulders.

"It conveyed much to me," I insisted. "If I were a detective I would have the secret out of that woman or die in the attempt."

He laughed; this sly, old, almost decrepit man laughed outright. Then he looked severely at his old friend on the newel-post, and drawing himself up with some show of dignity, made this remark:

"It is my very good fortune to have made your acquaintance, Miss Butterworth. You and I ought to be able to work out this case in a way that will be satisfactory to all parties."

He meant it for sarcasm, but I took it quite seriously, that is to all appearance. I am as sly as he, and though not quite as old—now I am sarcastic—have some of his wits, if but little of his experience.

"Then let us to work," said I. "You have your theories about this murder, and I have mine; let us see how they compare."

If the image he had under his eye had not been made of bronze, I am sure it would have become petrified by the look he now gave it. What to me seemed but the natural proposition of an energetic woman with a special genius for his particular calling, evidently struck him as audacity of the grossest kind. But he confined his display of astonishment to the figure he was eying, and returned me nothing but this most gentlemanly retort:

"I am sure I am obliged to you, madam, and possibly I may be willing to consider your very thoughtful proposition later, but now I am busy, very busy, and if you will await my presence in your house for a half hour——"

"Why not let me wait here," I interposed. "The atmosphere of the place may sharpen my faculties. I already feel that another sharp look into that parlor would lead to the forming of some valuable theory."

"You—" Well, he did not say what I was, or rather, what the image he was apostrophizing, was. But he must have meant to utter a compliment of no common order.

The prim courtesy I made in acknowledgment of his good intention satisfied him that I had understood him fully; and changing his whole manner to one more in accordance with business, he observed after a moment's reflection:

"You came to a conclusion this afternoon, Miss Butterworth, for which I should like some explanation. In investigating the hat which had been drawn from under the murdered girl's remains, you made the remark that it had been worn but once. I had already come to the same conclusion, but by other means, doubtless. Will you tell me what it was that gave point to your assertion?"

"There was but one prick of a hat-pin in it," I observed. "If you have been in the habit of looking into young women's hats, you will appreciate the force of my remark."

"The deuce!" was his certainly uncalled for exclamation. "Women's eyes for women's matters! I am greatly indebted to you, ma'am. You have solved a very important problem for us. A hat-pin! humph!" he muttered to himself. "The devil in a man is not easily balked; even such an innocent article as that can be made to serve, when all other means are lacking."

It is perhaps a proof that Mr. Gryce is getting old, that he allowed these words to escape him. But having once given vent to them, he made no effort to retract them, but proceeded to take me into his confidence so far as to explain:

"The woman who was killed in that room owed her death to the stab of a thin, long pin. We had not thought of a hat-pin, but upon your mentioning it, I am ready to accept it as the instrument of death. There was no pin to be seen in the hat when you looked at it?"

"None. I examined it most carefully."

He shook his head and seemed to be meditating. As I had plenty of time I waited, expecting him to speak again. My patience seemed to impress him. Alternately raising and lowering his hands like one in the act of weighing something, he soon addressed me again, this time in a tone of banter:

"This pin—if pin it was—was found broken in the wound. We have been searching for the end that was left in the murderer's hand, and we have not found it. It is not on the floors of the parlors nor in this hallway. What do you think the ingenious user of such an instrument would do with it?"

This was said, I am now sure, out of a spirit of sarcasm. He was amusing himself with me, but I did not realize it then. I was too full of my subject.

"He would not have carried it away," I reasoned shortly, "at least not far. He did not throw it aside on reaching the street, for I watched his movements so closely that I would have observed him had he done this. It is in the house then, and presumably in the parlor, even if you do not find it on the floor."

"Would you like to look for it?" he impressively asked. I had no means of knowing at that time that when he was impressive he was his least candid and trustworthy self.

"Would I," I repeated; and being spare in figure and much more active in my movements that one would suppose from my age and dignified deportment, I ducked under his arms and was in Mr. Van Burnam's parlor before he had recovered from his surprise.

That a man like him could look foolish I would not have you for a moment suppose. But he did not look very well satisfied, and I had a chance to throw more than one glance around me before he found his tongue again.

"An unfair advantage, ma'am; an unfair advantage! I am old and I am rheumatic; you are young and sound as a nut. I acknowledge my folly in endeavoring to compete with you and must make the best of the situation. And now, madam, where is that pin?"

It was lightly said, but for all that I saw that my opportunity had come. If I could find this instrument of murder, what might I not expect from his gratitude. Nerving myself for the task thus set me, I peered hither and thither, taking in every article in the room before I made a step forward. There had been some attempt to rectify its disorder. The broken pieces of china had been lifted and laid carefully away on newspapers upon the shelves from which they had fallen. The cabinet stood upright in its place, and the clock which had tumbled face upward, had been placed upon the mantel shelf in the same position. The carpet was therefore free, save for the stains which told such a woeful story of past tragedy and crime.

"You have moved the tables and searched behind the sofas," I suggested.

"Not an inch of the floor has escaped our attention, madam."

My eyes fell on the register, which my skirts half covered. It was closed; I stooped and opened it. A square box of tin was visible below, at the bottom of which I perceived the round head of a broken hat-pin.

Never in my life had I felt as I did at that minute. Rising up, I pointed at the register and let some of my triumph become apparent; but not all, for I was by no means sure at that moment, nor am I by any means sure now, that he had not made the discovery before I did and was simply testing my pretensions.

However that may be, he came forward quickly and after some little effort drew out the broken pin and examined it curiously.

"I should say that this is what we want," he declared, and from that moment on showed me a suitable deference.

"I account for its being there in this way," I argued. "The room was dark; for whether he lighted it or not to commit his crime, he certainly did not leave it lighted long. Coming out, his foot came in contact with the iron of the register and he was struck by a sudden thought. He had not dared to leave the head of the pin lying on the floor, for he hoped that he had covered up his crime by pulling the heavy cabinet over upon his victim; nor did he wish to carry away such a memento of his cruel deed. So he dropped it down the register, where he doubtless expected it would fall into the furnace pipes out of sight. But the tin box retained it. Is not that plausible, sir?"

"I could not have reasoned better myself, madam. We shall have you on the force, yet."

But at the familiarity shown by this suggestion, I bridled angrily. "I am Miss Butterworth," was my sharp retort, "and any interest I may take in this matter is due to my sense of justice."

Seeing that he had offended me, the astute detective turned the conversation back to business.

"By the way," said he, "your woman's knowledge can help me out at another point. If you are not afraid to remain in this room alone for a moment, I will bring an article in regard to which I should like your opinion."

I assured him I was not in the least bit afraid, at which he made me another of his anomalous bows and passed into the adjoining parlor. He did not stop there. Opening the sliding-doors communicating with the dining-room beyond, he disappeared in the latter room, shutting the doors behind him. Being now alone for a moment on the scene of crime, I crossed over to the mantel-shelf, and lifted the clock that lay there.

Why I did this I scarcely know. I am naturally very orderly (some people call me precise) and it probably fretted me to see so valuable an object out of its natural position. However that was, I lifted it up and set it upright, when to my amazement it began to tick. Had the hands not stood as they did when my eyes first fell on the clock lying face up on the floor at the dead girl's side, I should have thought the works had been started since that time by Mr. Gryce or some other officious person. But they pointed now as then to a few minutes before five and the only conclusion I could arrive at was, that the clock had been in running order when it fell, startling as this fact appeared in a house which had not been inhabited for months.

But if it had been in running order and was only stopped by its fall upon the floor, why did the hands point at five instead of twelve which was the hour at which the accident was supposed to have happened? Here was matter for thought, and that I might be undisturbed in my use of it, I hastened to lay the clock down again, even taking the precaution to restore the hands to the exact position they had occupied before I had started up the works. If Mr. Gryce did not know their secret, why so much the worse for Mr. Gryce.

I was back in my old place by the register before the folding-doors unclosed again. I was conscious of a slight flush on my cheek, so I took from my pocket that perplexing grocer-bill and was laboriously going down its long line of figures, when Mr. Gryce reappeared.

He had to my surprise a woman's hat in his hand.

"Well!" thought I, "what does this mean!"

It was an elegant specimen of millinery, and was in the latest style. It had ribbons and flowers and bird wings upon it, and presented, as it was turned about by Mr. Gryce's deft hand, an appearance which some might have called charming, but to me was simply grotesque and absurd.

"Is that a last spring's hat?" he inquired.

"I don't know, but I should say it had come fresh from the milliner's."

"I found it lying with a pair of gloves tucked inside it on an otherwise empty shelf in the dining-room closet. It struck me as looking too new for a discarded hat of either of the Misses Van Burnam. What do you think?"

"Let me take it," said I.

"O, it's been worn," he smiled, "several times. And the hat-pin is in it, too."

"There is something else I wish to see."

He handed it over.

"I think it belongs to one of them," I declared. "It was made by La Mole of Fifth Avenue, whose prices are simply—wicked."

"But the young ladies have been gone—let me see—five months. Could this have been bought before then?"

"Possibly, for this is an imported hat. But why should it have been left lying about in that careless way? It cost twenty dollars, if not thirty, and if for any reason its owner decided not to take it with her, why didn't she pack it away properly? I have no patience with the modern girl; she is made up of recklessness and extravagance."

"I hear that the young ladies are staying with you," was his suggestive remark.

"They are."

"Then you can make some inquiries about this hat; also about the gloves, which are an ordinary street pair."

"Of what color?"

"Grey; they are quite fresh, size six."

"Very well; I will ask the young ladies about them."

"This third room is used as a dining-room, and the closet where I found them is one in which glass is kept. The presence of this hat there is a mystery, but I presume the Misses Van Burnam can solve it. At all events, it is very improbable that it has anything to do with the crime which has been committed here."

"Very," I coincided.

"So improbable," he went on, "that on second thoughts I advise you not to disturb the young ladies with questions concerning it unless further reasons for doing so become apparent."

"Very well," I returned. But I was not deceived by his second thoughts.

As he was holding open the parlor door before me in a very significant way, I tied my veil under my chin, and was about to leave when he stopped me.

"I have another favor to ask," said he, and this time with his most benignant smile.

"Miss Butterworth, do you object to sitting up for a few nights till twelve o'clock?"

"Not at all," I returned, "if there is any good reason for it."

"At twelve o'clock to-night a gentleman will enter this house. If you will note him from your window I will be obliged."

"To see whether he is the same one I saw last night? Certainly I will take a look, but——"

"To-morrow night," he went on, imperturbably, "the test will be repeated, and I should like to have you take another look; without prejudice, madam; remember, without prejudice."

"I have no prejudices——" I began.

"The test may not be concluded in two nights," he proceeded, without any notice of my words. "So do not be in haste to spot your man, as the vulgar expression is. And now good-night—we shall meet again to-morrow."

"Wait!" I called peremptorily, for he was on the point of closing the door. "I saw the man but faintly; it is an impression only that I received. I would not wish a man to hang through any identification I could make."

"No man hangs on simple identification. We shall have to prove the crime, madam, but identification is important; even such as you can make."

There was no more to be said; I uttered a calm good-night and hastened away. By a judicious use of my opportunities I had become much less ignorant on the all-important topic than when I entered the house.

It was half past eleven when I returned home, a late hour for me to enter my respectable front door alone. But circumstances had warranted my escapade, and it was with quite an easy conscience and a cheerful sense of accomplishment that I went up to my room and prepared to sit out the half hour before midnight.

I am a comfortable sort of person when alone, and found no difficulty in passing this time profitably. Being very orderly, as you must have remarked, I have everything at hand for making myself a cup of tea at any time of day or night; so feeling some need of refreshment, I set out the little table I reserve for such purposes and made the tea and sat down to sip it.

While doing so, I turned over the subject occupying my mind, and endeavored to reconcile the story told by the clock with my preconceived theory of this murder; but no reconcilement was possible. The woman had been killed at twelve, and the clock had fallen at five. How could the two be made to agree, and which, since agreement was impossible, should be made to give way, the theory or the testimony of the clock? Both seemed incontrovertible, and yet one must be false. Which?

I was inclined to think that the trouble lay with the clock; that I had been deceived in my conclusions, and that it was not running at the time of the crime. Mr. Gryce may have ordered it wound, and then have had it laid on its back to prevent the hands from shifting past the point where they had stood at the time of the crime's discovery. It was an unexplainable act, but a possible one; while to suppose that it was going when the shelves fell, stretched improbability to the utmost, there having been, so far as we could learn, no one in the house for months sufficiently dexterous to set so valuable a timepiece; for who could imagine the scrub-woman engaging in a task requiring such delicate manipulation.

No! some meddlesome official had amused himself by starting up the works, and the clue I had thought so important would probably prove valueless.

There was humiliation in the thought, and it was a relief to me to hear an approaching carriage just as the clock on my mantel struck twelve. Springing from my chair, I put out my light and flew to the window.

The coach drew up and stopped next door. I saw a gentleman descend and step briskly across the pavement to the neighboring stoop. The figure he presented was not that of the man I had seen enter the night before.

VIII   THE MISSES VAN BURNAM

Late as it was when I retired, I was up betimes in the morning—as soon, in fact, as the papers were distributed. The Tribune lay on the stoop. Eagerly I seized it; eagerly I read it. From its headlines you may judge what it had to say about this murder:

A STARTLING DISCOVERY IN THE VAN BURNAM MANSION IN GRAMERCY PARK.

A YOUNG GIRL FOUND THERE, LYING DEAD UNDER AN OVERTURNED CABINET.

EVIDENCES THAT SHE WAS MURDERED BEFORE IT WAS PULLED DOWN UPON HER.

THOUGHT BY SOME TO BE MRS. HOWARD VAN BURNAM.

A FEARFUL CRIME INVOLVED IN AN IMPENETRABLE MYSTERY.

WHAT MR. VAN BURNAM SAYS ABOUT IT: HE DOES NOT RECOGNIZE THE WOMAN AS HIS WIFE.

So, so, it was his wife they were talking about. I had not expected that. Well! well! no wonder the girls looked startled and concerned. And I paused to recall what I had heard about Howard Van Burnam's marriage.

It had not been a fortunate one. His chosen bride was pretty enough, but she had not been bred in the ways of fashionable society, and the other members of the family had never recognized her. The father, especially, had cut his son dead since his marriage, and had even gone so far as to threaten to dissolve the partnership in which they were all involved. Worse than this, there had been rumors of a disagreement between Howard and his wife. They were not always on good terms, and opinions differed as to which was most in fault. So much for what I knew of these two mentioned parties.

Reading the article at length, I learned that Mrs. Van Burnam was missing; that she had left Haddam for New York the day before her husband, and had not since been heard from. Howard was confident, however, that the publicity given to her disappearance by the papers would bring immediate news of her.

The effect of the whole article was to raise grave doubts as to the candor of Mr. Van Burnam's assertions, and I am told that in some of the less scrupulous papers these doubts were not only expressed, but actual surmises ventured upon as to the identity between the person whom I had seen enter the house with the young girl. As for my own name, it was blazoned forth in anything but a gratifying manner. I was spoken of in one paper—a kind friend told me this—as the prying Miss Amelia. As if my prying had not given the police their only clue to the identification of the criminal.

The New York World was the only paper that treated me with any consideration. That young man with the small head and beady eyes was not awed by me for nothing. He mentioned me as the clever Miss Butterworth whose testimony is likely to be of so much value in this very interesting case.

It was the World I handed the Misses Van Burnam when they came down-stairs to breakfast. It did justice to me and not too much injustice to him. They read it together, their two heads plunged deeply into the paper so that I could not watch their faces. But I could see the sheet shake, and I noticed that their social veneer was not as yet laid on so thickly that they could hide their real terror and heart-ache when they finally confronted me again.

"Did you read—have you seen this horrible account?" quavered Caroline, as she met my eye.

"Yes, and I now understand why you felt such anxiety yesterday. Did you know your sister-in-law, and do you think she could have been beguiled into your father's house in that way?"

It was Isabella who answered.

"We never have seen her and know little of her, but there is no telling what such an uncultivated person as she might do. But that our good brother Howard ever went in there with her is a lie, isn't it, Caroline?—a base and malicious lie?"

"Of course it is, of course, of course. You don't think the man you saw was Howard, do you, dear Miss Butterworth?"

Dear? O dear!

"I am not acquainted with your brother," I returned. "I have never seen him but a few times in my life. You know he has not been a very frequent visitor at your father's house lately."

They looked at me wistfully, so wistfully.

"Say it was not Howard," whispered Caroline, stealing up a little nearer to my side.

"And we will never forget it," murmured Isabella, in what I am obliged to say was not her society manner.

"I hope to be able to say it," was my short rejoinder, made difficult by the prejudices I had formed. "When I see your brother, I may be able to decide at a glance that the person I saw entering your house was not he."

"Yes, oh, yes. Do you hear that, Isabella? Miss Butterworth will save Howard yet. O you dear old soul. I could almost love you!"

This was not agreeable to me. I a dear old soul! A term to be applied to a butter-woman not to a Butterworth. I drew back and their sentimentalities came to an end. I hope their brother Howard is not the guilty man the papers make him out to be, but if he is, the Misses Van Burnam's fine phrase, We could almost love you, will not deter me from being honest in the matter.

Mr. Gryce called early, and I was glad to be able to tell him that the gentleman who visited him the night before did not recall the impression made upon me by the other. He received the communication quietly, and from his manner I judged that it was more or less expected. But who can be a correct judge of a detective's manner, especially one so foxy and imperturbable as this one? I longed to ask who his visitor was, but I did not dare, or rather—to be candid in little things that you may believe me in great—I was confident he would not tell me, so I would not compromise my dignity by a useless question.

He went after a five minutes' stay, and I was about to turn my attention to household affairs, when Franklin came in.

His sisters jumped like puppets to meet him.

"O," they cried, for once thinking and speaking alike, "have you found her?"

His silence was so eloquent that he did not need to shake his head.

"But you will before the day is out?" protested Caroline.

"It is too early yet," added Isabella.

"I never thought I would be glad to see that woman under any circumstances," continued the former, "but I believe now that if I saw her coming up the street on Howard's arm, I should be happy enough to rush out and—and——"

"Give her a hug," finished the more impetuous Isabella.

It was not what Caroline meant to say, but she accepted the emendation, with just the slightest air of deprecation. They were both evidently much attached to Howard, and ready in his trouble to forget and forgive everything. I began to like them again.

"Have you read the horrid papers?" and "How is papa this morning?" and "What shall we do to save Howard?" now flew in rapid questions from their lips; and feeling that it was but natural they should have their little say, I sat down in my most uncomfortable chair and waited for these first ebullitions to exhaust themselves.

Instantly Mr. Van Burnam took them by the arm, and led them away to a distant sofa.

"Are you happy here?" he asked, in what he meant for a very confidential tone. But I can hear as readily as a deaf person anything which is not meant for my ears.

"O she's kind enough," whispered Caroline, "but so stingy. Do take us where we can get something to eat."

"She puts all her money into china! Such plates!—and so little on them!"

At these expressions, uttered with all the emphasis a whisper will allow, I just hugged myself in my quiet corner. The dear, giddy things! But they should see, they should see.

"I fear"—it was Mr. Van Burnam who now spoke—"I shall have to take my sisters from under your kind care to-day. Their father needs them, and has, I believe, already engaged rooms for them at the Plaza."

"I am sorry," I replied, "but surely they will not leave till they have had another meal with me. Postpone your departure, young ladies, till after luncheon, and you will greatly oblige me. We may never meet so agreeably again."

They fidgeted (which I had expected), and cast secret looks of almost comic appeal at their brother, but he pretended not to see them, being disposed for some reason to grant my request. Taking advantage of the momentary hesitation that ensued, I made them all three my most conciliatory bow, and said as I retreated behind the portière:

"I shall give my orders for luncheon now. Meanwhile, I hope the young ladies will feel perfectly free in my house. All that I have is at their command." And was gone before they could protest.

When I next saw them, they were upstairs in my front room. They were seated together in the window and looked miserable enough to have a little diversion. Going to my closet, I brought out a band-box. It contained my best bonnet.

"Young ladies, what do you think of this?" I inquired, taking the bonnet out and carefully placing it on my head.

I myself consider it a very becoming article of headgear, but their eyebrows went up in a scarcely complimentary fashion.

"You don't like it?" I remarked. "Well, I think a great deal of young girls' taste; I shall send it back to Madame More's to-morrow."

"I don't think much of Madame More," observed Isabella, "and after Paris——"

"Do you like La Mole better?" I inquired, bobbing my head to and fro before the mirror, the better to conceal my interest in the venture I was making.

"I don't like any of them but D'Aubigny," returned Isabella. "She charges twice what La Mole does——"

Twice! What are these girls' purses made of, or rather their father's!

"But she has the chic we are accustomed to see in French millinery. I shall never go anywhere else."

"We were recommended to her in Paris," put in Caroline, more languidly. Her interest was only half engaged by this frivolous topic.

"But did you never have one of La Mole's hats?" I pursued, taking down a hand-mirror, ostensibly to get the effect of my bonnet in the back, but really to hide my interest in their unconscious faces.

"Never!" retorted Isabella. "I would not patronize the thing."

"Nor you?" I urged, carelessly, turning towards Caroline.

"No; I have never been inside her shop."

"Then whose is——" I began and stopped. A detective doing the work I was, would not give away the object of his questions so recklessly.

"Then who is," I corrected, "the best person after D'Aubigny? I never can pay her prices. I should think it wicked."

"O don't ask us," protested Isabella. "We have never made a study of the best bonnet-maker. At present we wear hats."

And having thus thrown their youth in my face, they turned away to the window again, not realizing that the middle-aged lady they regarded with such disdain had just succeeded in making them dance to her music most successfully.

The luncheon I ordered was elaborate, for I was determined that the Misses Van Burnam should see that I knew how to serve a fine meal, and that my plates were not always better than my viands.

I had invited in a couple of other guests so that I should not seem to have put myself out for two young girls, and as they were quiet people like myself, the meal passed most decorously. When it was finished, the Misses Caroline and Isabella had lost some of their consequential airs, and I really think the deference they have since showed me is due more to the surprise they felt at the perfection of this dainty luncheon, than to any considerate appreciation of my character and abilities.

They left at three o'clock, still without news of Mrs. Van Burnam; and being positive by this time that the shadows were thickening about this family, I saw them depart with some regret and a positive feeling of commiseration. Had they been reared to a proper reverence for their elders, how much more easy it would have been to see earnestness in Caroline and affectionate impulses in Isabella.

The evening papers added but little to my knowledge. Great disclosures were promised, but no hint given of their nature. The body at the Morgue had not been identified by any of the hundreds who had viewed it, and Howard still refused to acknowledge it as that of his wife. The morrow was awaited with anxiety.

So much for the public press!

At twelve o'clock at night, I was again seated in my window. The house next door had been lighted since ten, and I was in momentary expectation of its nocturnal visitor. He came promptly at the hour set, alighted from the carriage with a bound, shut the carriage-door with a slam, and crossed the pavement with cheerful celerity. His figure was not so positively like, nor yet so positively unlike, that of the supposed murderer that I could definitely say, "This is he," or, "This is not he," and I went to bed puzzled, and not a little burdened by a sense of the responsibility imposed upon me in this matter.

And so passed the day between the murder and the inquest.

IX DEVELOPMENTS

Mr. Gryce called about nine o'clock next morning.

"Well," said he, "what about the visitor who came to see me last night?"

"Like and unlike," I answered. "Nothing could induce me to say he is the man we want, and yet I would not dare to swear he was not."

"You are in doubt, then, concerning him?"

"I am."

Mr. Gryce bowed, reminded me of the inquest, and left. Nothing was said about the hat.

At ten o'clock I prepared to go to the place designated by him. I had never attended an inquest in my life, and felt a little flurried in consequence, but by the time I had tied the strings of my bonnet (the despised bonnet, which, by the way, I did not return to More's), I had conquered this weakness, and acquired a demeanor more in keeping with my very important position as chief witness in a serious police investigation.

I had sent for a carriage to take me, and I rode away from my house amid the shouts of some half dozen boys collected on the curb-stone. But I did not allow myself to feel dashed by this publicity. On the contrary, I held my head as erect as nature intended, and my back kept the line my good health warrants. The path of duty has its thorny passages, but it is for strong minds like mine to ignore them.

Promptly at ten o'clock I entered the room reserved for the inquest, and was ushered to the seat appointed me. Though never a self-conscious woman, I could not but be aware of the many eyes that followed me, and endeavored so to demean myself that there should be no question as to my respectable standing in the community. This I considered due to the memory of my father, who was very much in my thoughts that day.

The Coroner was already in his seat when I entered, and though I did not perceive the good face of Mr. Gryce anywhere in his vicinity, I had no doubt he was within ear-shot. Of the other people I took small note, save of the honest scrub-woman, of whose red face and anxious eyes under a preposterous bonnet (which did not come from La Mole's), I caught vague glimpses as the crowd between us surged to and fro.

None of the Van Burnams were visible, but this did not necessarily mean that they were absent. Indeed, I was very sure, from certain indications, that more than one member of the family could be seen in the small room connecting with the large one in which we witnesses sat with the jury.

The policeman, Carroll, was the first man to talk. He told of my stopping him on his beat and of his entrance into Mr. Van Burnam's house with the scrub-woman. He gave the details of his discovery of the dead woman's body on the parlor floor, and insisted that no one—here he looked very hard at me—had been allowed to touch the body till relief had come to him from Headquarters.

Mrs. Boppert, the scrub-woman, followed him; and if she was watched by no one else in that room, she was watched by me. Her manner before the Coroner was no more satisfactory, according to my notion, than it had been in Mr. Van Burnam's parlor. She gave a very perceptible start when they spoke her name, and looked quite scared when the Bible was held out towards her. But she took the oath notwithstanding, and with her testimony the inquiry began in earnest.

"What is your name?" asked the Coroner.

As this was something she could not help knowing, she uttered the necessary words glibly, though in a way that showed she resented his impertinence in asking her what he already knew.

"Where do you live? And what do you do for a living?" rapidly followed.

She replied that she was a scrub-woman and cleaned people's houses, and having said this, she assumed a very dogged air, which I thought strange enough to raise a question in the minds of those who watched her. But no one else seemed to regard it as anything but the embarrassment of ignorance.

"How long have you known the Van Burnam family?" the Coroner went on.

"Two years, sir, come next Christmas."

"Have you often done work for them?"

"I clean the house twice a year, fall and spring."

"Why were you at this house two days ago?"

"To scrub the kitchen floors, sir, and put the pantries in order."

"Had you received notice to do so?"

"Yes, sir, through Mr. Franklin Van Burnam."

"And was that the first day of your work there?"

"No, sir; I had been there all the day before."

"You don't speak loud enough," objected the Coroner; "remember that every one in this room wants to hear you."

She looked up, and with a frightened air surveyed the crowd about her. Publicity evidently made her most uncomfortable, and her voice sank rather than rose.

"Where did you get the key of the house, and by what door did you enter?"

"I went in at the basement, sir, and I got the key at Mr. Van Burnam's agent in Dey Street. I had to go for it; sometimes they send it to me; but not this time."

"And now relate your meeting with the policeman on Wednesday morning, in front of Mr. Van Burnam's house."

She tried to tell her story, but she made awkward work of it, and they had to ply her with questions to get at the smallest fact. But finally she managed to repeat what we already knew, how she went with the policeman into the house, and how they stumbled upon the dead woman in the parlor.

Further than this they did not question her, and I, Amelia Butterworth, had to sit in silence and see her go back to her seat, redder than before, but with a strangely satisfied air that told me she had escaped more easily than she had expected. And yet Mr. Gryce had been warned that she knew more than appeared, and by one in whom he seemed to have placed some confidence!

The doctor was called next. His testimony was most important, and contained a surprise for me and more than one surprise for the others. After a short preliminary examination, he was requested to state how long the woman had been dead when he was called in to examine her.

"More than twelve and less than eighteen hours," was his quiet reply.

"Had the rigor mortis set in?"

"No; but it began very soon after."

"Did you examine the wounds made by the falling shelves and the vases that tumbled with them?"

"I did."

"Will you describe them?"

He did so.

"And now"—there was a pause in the Coroner's question which roused us all to its importance, "which of these many serious wounds was in your opinion the cause of her death?"

The witness was accustomed to such scenes, and was perfectly at home in them. Surveying the Coroner with a respectful air, he turned slowly towards the jury and answered in a slow and impressive manner:

"I feel ready to declare, sirs, that none of them did. She was not killed by the falling of the cabinet upon her."

"Not killed by the falling shelves! Why not? Were they not sufficiently heavy, or did they not strike her in a vital place?"

"They were heavy enough, and they struck her in a way to kill her if she had not been already dead when they fell upon her. As it was, they simply bruised a body from which life had already departed."

As this was putting it very plainly, many of the crowd who had not been acquainted with these facts previously, showed their interest in a very unmistakable manner; but the Coroner, ignoring these symptoms of growing excitement, hastened to say:

"This is a very serious statement you are making, doctor. If she did not die from the wounds inflicted by the objects which fell upon her, from what cause did she die? Can you say that her death was a natural one, and that the falling of the shelves was merely an unhappy accident following it?"

"No, sir; her death was not natural. She was killed, but not by the falling cabinet."

"Killed, and not by the cabinet? How then? Was there any other wound upon her which you regard as mortal?"

"Yes, sir. Suspecting that she had perished from other means than appeared, I made a most rigid examination of her body, when I discovered under the hair in the nape of the neck, a minute spot, which, upon probing, I found to be the end of a small, thin point of steel. It had been thrust by a careful hand into the most vulnerable part of the body, and death must have ensued at once."

This was too much for certain excitable persons present, and a momentary disturbance arose, which, however, was nothing to that in my own breast.

So! so! it was her neck that had been pierced, and not her heart. Mr. Gryce had allowed us to think it was the latter, but it was not this fact which stupefied me, but the skill and diabolical coolness of the man who had inflicted this death-thrust.

After order had been restored, which I will say was very soon, the Coroner, with an added gravity of tone, went on with his questions:

"Did you recognize this bit of steel as belonging to any instrument in the medical profession?"

"No; it was of too untempered steel to have been manufactured for any thrusting or cutting purposes. It was of the commonest kind, and had broken short off in the wound. It was the end only that I found."

"Have you this end with you,—the point, I mean, which you found imbedded at the base of the dead woman's brain?"

"I have, sir"; and he handed it over to the jury. As they passed it along, the Coroner remarked:

"Later we will show you the remaining portion of this instrument of death," which did not tend to allay the general excitement. Seeing this, the Coroner humored the growing interest by pushing on his inquiries.

"Doctor," he asked, "are you prepared to say how long a time elapsed between the infliction of this fatal wound and those which disfigured her?"

"No, sir, not exactly; but some little time."

Some little time, when the murderer was in the house only ten minutes! All looked their surprise, and, as if the Coroner had divined this feeling of general curiosity, he leaned forward and emphatically repeated:

"More than ten minutes?"

The doctor, who had every appearance of realizing the importance of his reply, did not hesitate. Evidently his mind was quite made up.

"Yes; more than ten minutes."

This was the shock I received from his testimony.

I remembered what the clock had revealed to me, but I did not move a muscle of my face. I was learning self-control under these repeated surprises.

"This is an unexpected statement," remarked the Coroner. "What reasons have you to urge in explanation of it?"

"Very simple and very well known ones; at least, among the profession. There was too little blood seen, for the wounds to have been inflicted before death or within a few minutes after it. Had the woman been living when they were made, or even had she been but a short time dead, the floor would have been deluged with the blood gushing from so many and such serious injuries. But the effusion was slight, so slight that I noticed it at once, and came to the conclusions mentioned before I found the mark of the stab that occasioned death."

"I see, I see! And was that the reason you called in two neighboring physicians to view the body before it was removed from the house?"

"Yes, sir; in so important a matter, I wished to have my judgment confirmed."

"And these physicians were———"

"Dr. Campbell, of 110 East ——— Street, and Dr. Jacobs, of ——— Lexington Avenue."

"Are these gentlemen here?" inquired the Coroner of an officer who stood near.

"They are, sir."

"Very good; we will now proceed to ask one or two more questions of this witness. You told us that even had the woman been but a few minutes dead when she received these contusions, the floor would have been more or less deluged by her blood. What reason have you for this statement?"

"This; that in a few minutes, let us say ten, since that number has been used, the body has not had time to cool, nor have the blood-vessels had sufficient opportunity to stiffen so as to prevent the free effusion of blood."

"Is a body still warm at ten minutes after death?"

"It is."

"So that your conclusions are logical deductions from well-known facts?"

"Certainly, sir."

A pause of some duration followed.

When the Coroner again proceeded, it was to remark:

"The case is complicated by these discoveries; but we must not allow ourselves to be daunted by them. Let me ask you, if you found any marks upon this body which might aid in its identification?"

"One; a slight scar on the left ankle."

"What kind of a scar? Describe it."

"It was such as a burn might leave. In shape it was long and narrow, and it ran up the limb from the ankle-bone."

"Was it on the right foot?"

"No; on the left."

"Did you call the attention of any one to this mark during or after your examination?"

"Yes; I showed it to Mr. Gryce the detective, and to my two coadjutors; and I spoke of it to Mr. Howard Van Burnam, son of the gentleman in whose house the body was found."

It was the first time this young gentleman's name had been mentioned, and it made my blood run cold to see how many side-long looks and expressive shrugs it caused in the motley assemblage. But I had no time for sentiment; the inquiry was growing too interesting.

"And why," asked the Coroner, "did you mention it to this young man in preference to others?"

"Because Mr. Gryce requested me to. Because the family as well as the young man himself had evinced some apprehension lest the deceased might prove to be his missing wife, and this seemed a likely way to settle the question."

"And did it? Did he acknowledge it to be a mark he remembered to have seen on his wife?"

"He said she had such a scar, but he would not acknowledge the deceased to be his wife."

"Did he see the scar?"

"No; he would not look at it."

"Did you invite him to?"

"I did; but he showed no curiosity."

Doubtless thinking that silence would best emphasize this fact, which certainly was an astonishing one, the Coroner waited a minute. But there was no silence. An indescribable murmur from a great many lips filled up the gap. I felt a movement of pity for the proud family whose good name was thus threatened in the person of this young gentleman.

"Doctor," continued the Coroner, as soon as the murmur had subsided, "did you notice the color of the woman's hair?"

"It was a light brown."

"Did you sever a lock? Have you a sample of this hair here to show us?"

"I have, sir. At Mr. Gryce's suggestion I cut off two small locks. One I gave him and the other I brought here."

"Let me see it."

The doctor passed it up, and in sight of every one present the Coroner tied a string around it and attached a ticket to it.

"That is to prevent all mistake," explained this very methodical functionary, laying the lock aside on the table in front of him. Then he turned again to the witness.

"Doctor, we are indebted to you for your valuable testimony, and as you are a busy man, we will now excuse you. Let Dr. Jacobs be called."

As this gentleman, as well as the witness who followed him, merely corroborated the statements of the other, and made it an accepted fact that the shelves had fallen upon the body of the girl some time after the first wound had been inflicted, I will not attempt to repeat their testimony. The question now agitating me was whether they would endeavor to fix the time at which the shelves fell by the evidence furnished by the clock.

X IMPORTANT EVIDENCE

Evidently not; for the next words I heard were: "Miss Amelia Butterworth!"

I had not expected to be called so soon, and was somewhat flustered by the suddenness of the summons, for I am only human. But I rose with suitable composure, and passed to the place indicated by the Coroner, in my usual straightforward manner, heightened only by a sense of the importance of my position, both as a witness and a woman whom the once famous Mr. Gryce had taken more or less into his confidence.

My appearance seemed to awaken an interest for which I was not prepared. I was just thinking how well my name had sounded uttered in the sonorous tones of the Coroner, and how grateful I ought to be for the courage I had displayed in substituting the genteel name of Amelia for the weak and sentimental one of Araminta, when I became conscious that the eyes directed towards me were filled with an expression not easy to understand. I should not like to call it admiration and will not call it amusement, and yet it seemed to be made up of both. While I was puzzling myself over it, the first question came.

As my examination before the Coroner only brought out the facts already related, I will not burden you with a detailed account of it. One portion alone may be of interest. I was being questioned in regard to the appearance of the couple I had seen entering the Van Burnam mansion, when the Coroner asked if the young woman's step was light, or if it betrayed hesitation.

I replied: "No hesitation; she moved quickly, almost gaily."

"And he?"

"Was more moderate; but there is no signification in that; he may have been older."

"No theories, Miss Butterworth; it is facts we are after. Now, do you know that he was older?"

"No, sir."

"Did you get any idea as to his age?"

"The impression he made was that of being a young man."

"And his height?"

"Was medium, and his figure slight and elegant. He moved as a gentleman moves; of this I can speak with great positiveness."

"Do you think you could identify him, Miss Butterworth, if you should see him?"

I hesitated, as I perceived that the whole swaying mass eagerly awaited my reply. I even turned my head because I saw others doing so; but I regretted this when I found that I, as well as others, was glancing towards the door beyond which the Van Burnams were supposed to sit. To cover up the false move I had made—for I had no wish as yet to centre suspicion upon anybody—I turned my face quickly back to the crowd and declared in as emphatic a tone as I could command:

"I have thought I could do so if I saw him under the same circumstances as those in which my first impression was made. But lately I have begun to doubt even that. I should never dare trust to my memory in this regard."

The Coroner looked disappointed, and so did the people around me.

"It is a pity," remarked the Coroner, "that you did not see more plainly. And, now, how did these persons gain an entrance into the house?"

I answered in the most succinct way possible.

I told them how he had used a door-key in entering, of the length of time the man stayed inside, and of his appearance on going away. I also related how I came to call a policeman to investigate the matter next day, and corroborated the statements of this official as to the appearance of the deceased at time of discovery.

And there my examination stopped. I was not asked any questions tending to bring out the cause of the suspicion I entertained against the scrub-woman, nor were the discoveries I had made in conjunction with Mr. Gryce inquired into. It was just as well, perhaps, but I would never approve of a piece of work done for me in this slipshod fashion.

A recess now followed. Why it was thought necessary, I cannot imagine, unless the gentlemen wished to smoke. Had they felt as much interest in this murder as I did, they would not have wanted bite or sup till the dreadful question was settled. There being a recess, I improved the opportunity by going into a restaurant near by where one can get very good buns and coffee at a reasonable price. But I could have done without them.

The next witness, to my astonishment, was Mr. Gryce. As he stepped forward, heads were craned and many women rose in their seats to get a glimpse of the noted detective. I showed no curiosity myself, for by this time I knew his features well, but I did feel a great satisfaction in seeing him before the Coroner, for now, thought I, we shall hear something worth our attention.

But his examination, though interesting, was not complete. The Coroner, remembering his promise to show us the other end of the steel point which had been broken off in the dead girl's brain, limited himself to such inquiries as brought out the discovery of the broken hat-pin in Mr. Van Burnam's parlor register. No mention was made by the witness of any assistance which he may have received in making this discovery; a fact which caused me to smile: men are so jealous of any interference in their affairs.

The end found in the register and the end which the Coroner's physician had drawn from the poor woman's head were both handed to the jury, and it was interesting to note how each man made his little effort to fit the two ends together, and the looks they interchanged as they found themselves successful. Without doubt, and in the eyes of all, the instrument of death had been found. But what an instrument!

The felt hat which had been discovered under the body was now produced and the one hole made by a similar pin examined. Then Mr. Gryce was asked if any other pin had been picked up from the floor of the room, and he replied, no; and the fact was established in the minds of all present that the young woman had been killed by a pin taken from her own hat.

"A subtle and cruel crime; the work of a calculating intellect," was the Coroner's comment as he allowed the detective to sit down. Which expression of opinion I thought reprehensible, as tending to prejudice the jury against the only person at present suspected.

The inquiry now took a turn. The name of Miss Ferguson was called. Who was Miss Ferguson? It was a new name to most of us, and her face when she rose only added to the general curiosity. It was the plainest face imaginable, yet it was neither a bad nor unintelligent one. As I studied it and noted the nervous contraction that disfigured her lip, I could not but be sensible of my blessings. I am not handsome myself, though there have been persons who have called me so, but neither am I ugly, and in contrast to this woman—well, I will say nothing. I only know that, after seeing her, I felt profoundly grateful to a kind Providence.

As for the poor woman herself, she knew she was no beauty, but she had become so accustomed to seeing the eyes of other people turn away from her face, that beyond the nervous twitching of which I have spoken, she showed no feeling.

"What is your full name, and where do you live?" asked the Coroner.

"My name is Susan Ferguson, and I live in Haddam, Connecticut," was her reply, uttered in such soft and beautiful tones that every one was astonished. It was like a stream of limpid water flowing from a most unsightly-looking rock. Excuse the metaphor; I do not often indulge.

"Do you keep boarders?"

"I do; a few, sir; such as my house will accommodate."

"Whom have you had with you this summer?"

I knew what her answer would be before she uttered it; so did a hundred others, but they showed their knowledge in different ways. I did not show mine at all.

"I have had with me," said she, "a Mr. and Mrs. Van Burnam from New York. Mr. Howard Van Burnam is his full name, if you wish me to be explicit."

"Any one else?"

"A Mr. Hull, also from New York, and a young couple from Hartford. My house accommodates no more."

"How long have the first mentioned couple been with you?"

"Three months. They came in June."

"Are they with you still?"

"Virtually, sir. They have not moved their trunks; but neither of them is in Haddam at present. Mrs. Van Burnam came to New York last Monday morning, and in the afternoon her husband also left, presumably for New York. I have seen nothing of either of them since."

(It was on Tuesday night the murder occurred.)

"Did either of them take a trunk?"

"No, sir."

"A hand-bag?"

"Yes; Mrs. Van Burnam carried a bag, but it was a very small one."

"Large enough to hold a dress?"

"O no, sir."

"And Mr. Van Burnam?"

"He carried an umbrella; I saw nothing else."

"Why did they not leave together? Did you hear any one say?"

"Yes; I heard them say Mrs. Van Burnam came against her husband's wishes. He did not want her to leave Haddam, but she would, and he was none too pleased at it. Indeed they had words about it, and as both our rooms overlook the same veranda, I could not help hearing some of their talk."

"Will you tell us what you heard?"

"It does not seem right" (thus this honest woman spoke), "but if it's the law, I must not go against it. I heard him say these words: 'I have changed my mind, Louise. The more I think of it, the more disinclined I am to have you meddle in the matter. Besides, it will do no good. You will only add to the prejudice against you, and our life will become more unbearable than it is now.'"

"Of what were they speaking?"

"I do not know."

"And what did she reply?"

"O, she uttered a torrent of words that had less sense in them than feeling. She wanted to go, she would go, she had not changed her mind, and considered that her impulses were as well worth following as his cool judgment. She was not happy, had never been happy, and meant there should be a change, even if it were for the worse. But she did not believe it would be for the worse. Was she not pretty? Was she not very pretty when in distress and looking up thus? And I heard her fall on her knees, a movement which called out a grunt from her husband, but whether this was an expression of approval or disapproval I cannot say. A silence followed, during which I caught the sound of his steady tramping up and down the room. Then she spoke again in a petulant way. 'It may seem foolish to you' she cried, 'knowing me as you do, and being used to seeing me in all my moods. But to him it will be a surprise, and I will so manage it that it will effect all we want, and more, too, perhaps. I—I have a genius for some things, Howard; and my better angel tells me I shall succeed.'"

"And what did he reply to that?"

"That the name of her better angel was Vanity; that his father would see through her blandishments; that he forbade her to prosecute her schemes; and much more to the same effect. To all of which she answered by a vigorous stamp of her foot, and the declaration that she was going to do what she thought best in spite of all opposition; that it was a lover, and not a tyrant that she had married, and that if he did not know what was good for himself, she did, and that when he received an intimation from his father that the breach in the family was closed, then he would acknowledge that if she had no fortune and no connections, she had at least a plentiful supply of wit. Upon which he remarked: 'A poor qualification when it verges upon folly!' which seemed to close the conversation, for I heard no more till the sound of her skirts rustling past my door assured me she had carried her point and was leaving the house. But this was not done without great discomfiture to her husband, if one may judge from the few brief but emphatic words that escaped him before he closed his own door and followed her down the hall."

"Do you remember those words?"

"They were swear words, sir; I am sorry to say it, but he certainly cursed her and his own folly. Yet I always thought he loved her."

"Did you see her after she passed your door?"

"Yes, sir, on the walk outside."

"Was she then on the way to the train?"

"Yes, sir."

"Carrying the bag of which you have spoken?"

"Yes, sir; another proof of the state of feeling between them, for he was very considerate in his treatment of ladies, and I never saw him do anything ungallant before."

"You say you watched her as she went down the walk?"

"Yes, sir; it is human nature, sir; I have no other excuse to offer."

It was an apology I myself might have made. I conceived a liking for this homely matter-of-fact woman.

"Did you note her dress?"

"Yes, sir; that is human nature also, or, rather, woman's nature."

"Particularly, madam; so that you can describe it to the jury before you?"

"I think so."

"Will you, then, be good enough to tell us what sort of a dress Mrs. Van Burnam wore when she left your house for the city?"

"It was a black and white plaid silk, very rich——"

Why, what did this mean? We had all expected a very different description.

"It was made fashionably, and the sleeves—well, it is impossible to describe the sleeves. She wore no wrap, which seemed foolish to me, for we have very sudden changes sometimes in September."

"A plaid dress! And did you notice her hat?"

"O, I have seen the hat often. It was of every conceivable color. It would have been called bad taste at one time, but now-a-days——"

The pause was significant. More than one man in the room chuckled, but the women kept a discreet silence.

"Would you know that hat if you saw it?"

"I should think I would!"

The emphasis was that of a countrywoman, and amused some people notwithstanding the melodious tone in which it was uttered. But it did not amuse me; my thoughts had flown to the hat which Mr. Gryce had found in the third room of Mr. Van Burnam's house, and which was of every color of the rainbow.

The Coroner asked two other questions, one in regard to the gloves worn by Mrs. Van Burnam, and the other in regard to her shoes. To the first, Miss Ferguson replied that she did not notice her gloves, and to the other, that Mrs. Van Burnam was very fashionable, and as pointed shoes were the fashion, in cities at least, she probably wore pointed shoes.

The discovery that Mrs. Van Burnam had been differently dressed on that day from the young woman found dead in the Van Burnam parlors, had acted as a shock upon most of the spectators. They were just beginning to recover from it when Miss Ferguson sat down. The Coroner was the only one who had not seemed at a loss. Why, we were soon destined to know.

XI THE ORDER CLERK

A lady well known in New York society was the next person summoned. She was a friend of the Van Burnam family, and had known Howard from childhood. She had not liked his marriage; indeed, she rather participated in the family feeling against it, but when young Mrs. Van Burnam came to her house on the preceding Monday, and begged the privilege of remaining with her for one night, she had not had the heart to refuse her. Mrs. Van Burnam had therefore slept in her house on Monday night.

Questioned in regard to that lady's appearance and manner, she answered that her guest was unnaturally cheerful, laughing much and showing a great vivacity; that she gave no reason for her good spirits, nor did she mention her own affairs in any way,—rather took pains not to do so.

"How long did she stay?"

"Till the next morning."

"And how was she dressed?"

"Just as Miss Ferguson has described."

"Did she bring her hand-bag to your house?"

"Yes, and left it there. We found it in her room after she was gone."

"Indeed! And how do you account for that?"

"She was preoccupied. I saw it in her cheerfulness, which was forced and not always well timed."

"And where is that bag now?"

"Mr. Van Burnam has it. We kept it for a day and as she did not call for it, sent it down to the office on Wednesday morning."

"Before you had heard of the murder?"

"O yes, before I had heard anything about the murder."

"As she was your guest, you probably accompanied her to the door?"

"I did, sir."

"Did you notice her hands? Can you say what was the color of her gloves?"

"I do not think she wore any gloves on leaving; it was very warm, and she held them in her hand. I remembered this, for I noticed the sparkle of her rings as she turned to say good-bye."

"Ah, you saw her rings!"

"Distinctly."

"So that when she left you she was dressed in a black and white plaid silk, had a large hat covered with flowers on her head, and wore rings?"

"Yes, sir."

And with these words ringing in the ears of the jury, the witness sat down.

What was coming? Something important, or the Coroner would not look so satisfied, or the faces of the officials about him so expectant. I waited with great but subdued eagerness for the testimony of the next witness, who was a young man by the name of Callahan.

I don't like young men in general. They are either over-suave and polite, as if they condescended to remember that you are elderly and that it is their duty to make you forget it, or else they are pert and shallow and disgust you with their egotism. But this young man looked sensible and business-like, and I took to him at once, though what connection he could have with this affair I could not imagine.

His first words, however, settled all questions as to his personality: He was the order clerk at Altman's.

As he acknowledged this, I seemed to have some faint premonition of what was coming. Perhaps I had not been without some vague idea of the truth ever since I had put my mind to work on this matter; perhaps my wits only received their real spur then; but certainly I knew what he was going to say as soon as he opened his lips, which gave me quite a good opinion of myself, whether rightfully or not, I leave you to judge.

His evidence was short, but very much to the point. On the seventeenth of

September, as could be verified by the books, the firm had received an order for a woman's complete outfit, to be sent, C.O.D., to Mrs. James Pope at the Hotel D——, on Broadway. Sizes and measures and some particulars were stated, and as the order bore the words In haste underlined upon it, several clerks had assisted him in filling this order, which when filled had been sent by special messenger to the place designated.

Had he this order with him?

He had.

And could he identify the articles sent to fill it?

He could.

At which the Coroner motioned to an officer and a pile of clothing was brought forward from some mysterious corner and laid before the witness.

Immediately expectation rose to a high pitch, for every one recognized, or thought he did, the apparel which had been taken from the victim.

The young man, who was of the alert, nervous type, took up the articles one by one and examined them closely.

As he did so, the whole assembled crowd surged forward and lightning-like glances from a hundred eyes followed his every movement and expression.

"Are they the same?" inquired the Coroner.

The witness did not hesitate. With one quick glance at the blue serge dress, black cape, and battered hat, he answered in a firm tone:

"They are."

And a clue was given at last to the dreadful mystery absorbing us.

The deep-drawn sigh which swept through the room testified to the universal satisfaction; then our attention became fixed again, for the Coroner, pointing to the undergarments accompanying the articles already mentioned, demanded if they had been included in the order.

There was as little hesitation in the reply given to this question as to the former. He recognized each piece as having come from his establishment. "You will note," said he, "that they have never been washed, and that the pencil marks are still on them."

"Very good," observed the Coroner, "and you will note that one article there is torn down the back. Was it in that condition when sent?"

"It was not, sir."

"All were in perfect order?"

"Most assuredly, sir."

"Very good, again. The jury will take cognizance of this fact, which may be useful to them in their future conclusions. And now, Mr. Callahan, do you notice anything lacking here from the list of articles forwarded by you?"

"No, sir."

"Yet there is one very necessary adjunct to a woman's outfit which is not to be found here."

"Yes, sir, the shoes; but I am not surprised at that. We sent shoes, but they were not satisfactory, and they were returned."

"Ah, I see. Officer, show the witness the shoes that were taken from the deceased."

This was done, and when Mr. Callahan had examined them, the Coroner inquired if they came from his store. He replied no.

Whereupon they were held up to the jury, and attention called to the fact that, while rather new than old, they gave signs of having been worn more than once; which was not true of anything else taken from the victim.

This matter settled, the Coroner proceeded with his questions.

"Who carried the articles ordered, to the address given?"

"A man in our employ, named Clapp."

"Did he bring back the amount of the bill?"

"Yes, sir; less the five dollars charged for the shoes."

"What was the amount, may I ask?"

"Here is our cash-book, sir. The amount received from Mrs. James Pope, Hotel D——, on the seventeenth of September, is, as you see, seventy-five dollars and fifty-eight cents."

"Let the jury see the book; also the order."

They were both handed to the jury, and if ever I wished myself in any one's shoes, save my own very substantial ones, it was at that moment. I did so want a peep at that order.

It seemed to interest the jury also, for their heads drew together very eagerly over it, and some whispers and a few knowing looks passed between them. Finally one of them spoke:

"It is written in a very odd hand. Do you call this a woman's writing or a man's?"

"I have no opinion to give on the subject," rejoined the witness. "It is intelligible writing, and that is all that comes within my province."

The twelve men shifted on their seats and surveyed the Coroner eagerly. Why did he not proceed? Evidently he was not quick enough to suit them.

"Have you any further questions for this witness?" asked that gentleman after a short delay.

Their nervousness increased, but no one ventured to follow the Coroner's suggestion. A poor lot, I call them, a very poor lot! I would have found plenty of questions to put to him.

I expected to see the man Clapp called next, but I was disappointed in this. The name uttered was Henshaw, and the person who rose in answer to it was a tall, burly man with a shock of curly black hair. He was the clerk of the Hotel D——, and we all forgot Clapp in our eagerness to hear what this man had to say.

His testimony amounted to this:

That a person by the name of Pope was registered on his books. That she came to his house on the seventeenth of September, some time near noon. That she was not alone; that a person she called her husband accompanied her, and that they had been given a room, at her request, on the second floor overlooking Broadway.

"Did you see the husband? Was it his handwriting we see in your register?"

"No, sir. He came into the office, but he did not approach the desk. It was she who registered for them both, and who did all the business in fact. I thought it queer, but took it for granted he was ill, for he held his head very much down, and acted as if he felt disturbed or anxious."

"Did you notice him closely? Would you be able to identify him on sight?"

"No, sir, I should not. He looked like a hundred other men I see every day: medium in height and build, with brown hair and brown moustache. Not noticeable in any way, sir, except for his hang-dog air and evident desire not to be noticed."

"But you saw him later?"

"No, sir. After he went to his room he stayed there, and no one saw him. I did not even see him when he left the house. His wife paid the bill and he did not come into the office."

"But you saw her well; you would know her again?"

"Perhaps, sir; but I doubt it. She wore a thick veil when she came in, and though I might remember her voice, I have no recollection of her features for I did not see them."

"You can give a description of her dress, though; surely you must have looked long enough at a woman who wrote her own and her husband's name in your register, for you to remember her clothes."

"Yes, for they were very simple. She had on what is called a gossamer, which covered her from neck to toe, and on her head a hat wrapped all about with a blue veil."

"So that she might have worn any dress under that gossamer?"

"Yes, sir."

"And any hat under that veil?"

"Any one that was large enough, sir."

"Very good. Now, did you see her hands?"

"Not to remember them."

"Did she have gloves on?"

"I cannot say. I did not stand and watch her, sir."

"That is a pity. But you say you heard her voice."

"Yes, sir."

"Was it a lady's voice? Was her tone refined and her language good?"

"They were, sir."

"When did they leave? How long did they remain in your house?"

"They left in the evening; after tea, I should say."

"How? On foot or in a carriage?"

"In a carriage; one of the hacks that stand in front of the door."

"Did they bring any baggage with them?"

"No, sir."

"Did they take any away?"

"The lady carried a parcel."

"What kind of a parcel?"

"A brown-paper parcel, like clothing done up."

"And the gentleman?"

"I did not see him."

"Was she dressed the same in going as in coming?"

"To all appearance, except her hat. That was smaller."

"She had the gossamer on still, then?"

"Yes, sir."

"And a veil?"

"Yes, sir."

"Only that the hat it covered was smaller?"

"Yes, sir."

"And now, how did you account to yourself for the parcel and the change of hat?"

"I didn't account for them. I didn't think anything about them at the time; but, since I have had the subject brought to my mind, I find it easy enough. She had a package delivered to her while she was in our house, or rather packages; they were quite numerous, I believe."

"Can you recall the circumstances of their delivery?"

"Yes, sir; the man who brought the packages said that they had not been paid for, so I allowed him to carry them to Mrs. James Pope's room. When he went away, he had but one small parcel with him; the rest he had left."

"And this is all you can tell us about this singular couple? Had they no meals in your house?"

"No, sir; the gentleman—or I suppose I should say the lady, sir, for the order was given in her voice—sent for two dozen oysters and a bottle of ale, which were furnished to them in their rooms; but they didn't come to the dining-room."

"Is the boy here who carried up those articles?"

"He is, sir."

"And the chambermaid who attended to their rooms?"

"Yes, sir."

"Then you may answer this question, and we will excuse you. How was the gentleman dressed when you saw him?"

"In a linen duster and a felt hat."

"Let the jury remember that. And now let us hear from Richard Clapp. Is Richard Clapp in the room?"

"I am, sir," answered a cheery voice; and a lively young man with a shrewd eye and a wide-awake manner popped up from behind a portly woman on a side seat and rapidly came forward.

He was asked several questions before the leading one which we all expected; but I will not record them here. The question which brought the reply most eagerly anticipated was this:

"Do you remember being sent to the Hotel D——with several packages for a Mrs. James Pope?"

"I do, sir."

"Did you deliver them in person? Did you see the lady?"

A peculiar look crossed his face and we all leaned forward. But his answer brought a shock of disappointment with it.

"No, I didn't, sir. She wouldn't let me in. She bade me lay the things down by the door and wait in the rear hall till she called me."

"And you did this?"

"Yes, sir."

"But you kept your eye on the door, of course?"

"Naturally, sir."

"And saw——"

"A hand steal out and take in the things."

"A woman's hand?"

"No; a man's. I saw the white cuff."

"And how long was it before they called you?"

"Fifteen minutes, I should say. I heard a voice cry 'Here!' and seeing their door open, I went toward it. But by the time I reached it, it was shut again, and I only heard the lady say that all the articles but the shoes were satisfactory, and would I thrust the bill in under the door. I did so, and they were some minutes counting out the change, but presently the door opened slightly, and I saw a man's hand holding out the money, which was correct to the cent. 'You need not receipt the bill,' cried the lady from somewhere in the room. 'Give him the shoes and let him go.' So I received the shoes in the same mysterious way I had the money, and seeing no reason for waiting longer, pocketed the bills and returned to the store."

"Has the jury any further questions to ask the witness?"

Of course not. They were ninnies, all of them, and——But, contrary to my expectation, one of them did perk up courage, and, wriggling very much on his seat, ventured to ask if the cuff he had seen on the man's hand when it was thrust through the doorway had a button in it.

The answer was disappointing. The witness had not noticed any.

The juror, somewhat abashed, sank into silence, at which another of the precious twelve, inspired no doubt by the other's example, blurted out:

"Then what was the color of the coat sleeve? You surely can remember that."

But another disappointment awaited us.

"He did not wear any coat. It was a shirt sleeve I saw."

A shirt sleeve! There was no clue in that. A visible look of dejection spread through the room, which was not dissipated till another witness stood up.

This time it was the bell-boy of the hotel who had been on duty that day. His testimony was brief, and added but little to the general knowledge. He had been summoned more than once by these mysterious parties, but only to receive his orders through a closed door. He had not entered the room at all.

He was followed by the chambermaid, who testified that she was in the room once while they were there; that she saw them both then, but did not catch a glimpse of their faces; Mr. Pope was standing in the window almost entirely shielded by the curtains, and Mrs. Pope was busy hanging up something in the wardrobe. The gentleman had on his duster and the lady her gossamer; it was but a few minutes after their arrival.

Questioned in regard to the state of the room after they left it, she said that there was a lot of brown paper lying about, marked B. Altman, but nothing else that did not belong there.

"Not a tag, nor a hat-pin, nor a bit of memorandum, lying on bureau or table?"

"Nothing, sir, so far as I mind. I wasn't on the look-out for anything, sir. They were a queer couple, but we have lots of queer couples at our house, and the most I notices, sir, is those what remember the chambermaid and those what don't. This couple was of the kind what don't."

"Did you sweep the room after their departure?"

"I always does. They went late, so I swept the room the next morning."

"And threw the sweepings away, of course?"

"Of course; would you have me keep them for treasures?"

"It might have been well if you had," muttered the Coroner. "The combings from the lady's hair might have been very useful in establishing her identity."

The porter who has charge of the lady's entrance was the last witness from this house. He had been on duty on the evening in question and had noticed this couple leaving. They both carried packages, and had attracted his attention first, by the long, old-fashioned duster which the gentleman wore, and secondly, by the pains they both took not to be observed by any one. The woman was veiled, as had already been said, and the man held his package in such a way as to shield his face entirely from observation.

"So that you would not know him if you saw him again?" asked the Coroner.

"Exactly, sir," was the uncompromising answer.

As he sat down, the Coroner observed: "You will note from this testimony, gentlemen, that this couple, signing themselves Mr. and Mrs. James Pope of Philadelphia, left this house dressed each in a long garment eminently fitted for purposes of concealment,—he in a linen duster, and she in a gossamer. Let us now follow this couple a little farther and see what became of these disguising articles of apparel. Is Seth Brown here?"

A man, who was so evidently a hackman that it seemed superfluous to ask him what his occupation was, shuffled forward at this.

It was in his hack that this couple had left the D——. He remembered them very well as he had good reason to. First, because the man paid him before entering the carriage, saying that he was to let them out at the northwest corner of Madison Square, and secondly——But here the Coroner interrupted him to ask if he had seen the gentleman's face when he paid him. The answer was, as might have been expected, No. It was dark, and he had not turned his head.

"Didn't you think it queer to be paid before you reached your destination?"

"Yes, but the rest was queerer. After I had taken the money—I never refuses money, sir—and was expecting him to get into the hack, he steps up to me again and says in a lower tone than before: 'My wife is very nervous. Drive slow, if you please, and when you reach the place I have named, watch your horses carefully, for if they should move while she is getting out, the shock would throw her into a spasm.' As she had looked very pert and lively, I thought this mighty queer, and I tried to get a peep at his face, but he was too smart for me, and was in the carriage before I could clap my eye on him."

"But you were more fortunate when they got out? You surely saw one or both of them then?"

"No, sir, I didn't. I had to watch the horses' heads, you know. I shouldn't like to be the cause of a young lady having a spasm."

"Do you know in what direction they went?"

"East, I should say. I heard them laughing long after I had whipped up my horses. A queer couple, sir, that puzzled me some, though I should not have thought of them twice if I had not found next day——"

"Well?"

"The gentleman's linen duster and the neat brown gossamer which the lady had worn, lying folded under the two back cushions of my hack; a present for which I was very much obliged to them, but which I was not long allowed to enjoy, for yesterday the police——"

"Well, well, no matter about that. Here is a duster and here is a brown gossamer. Are these the articles you found under your cushions?"

"If you will examine the neck of the lady's gossamer, you can soon tell, sir. There was a small hole in the one I found, as if something had been snipped out of it; the owner's name, most likely."

"Or the name of the place where it was bought," suggested the Coroner, holding the garment up to view so as to reveal a square hole under the collar.

"That's it!" cried the hackman. "That's the very one. Shame, I say, to spoil a new garment that way."

"Why do you call it new?" asked the Coroner.

"Because it hasn't a mud spot or even a mark of dust upon it. We looked it all over, my wife and I, and decided it had not been long off the shelf. A pretty good haul for a poor man like me, and if the police——"

But here he was cut short again by an important question:

"There is a clock but a short distance from the place where you stopped. Did you notice what time it was when you drove away?"

"Yes, sir. I don't know why I remember it, but I do. As I turned to go back to the hotel, I looked up at this clock. It was half-past eleven."

XII THE KEYS

We were all by this time greatly interested in the proceedings; and when another hackman was called we recognized at once that an effort was about to be made to connect this couple with the one who had alighted at Mr. Van Burnam's door.

The witness, who was a melancholy chap, kept his stand on the east side of the Square. At about twenty minutes to twelve, he was awakened from a nap he had been taking on the top of his coach, by a sharp rap on his whip arm, and looking down, he saw a lady and gentleman standing at the door of his vehicle.

"We want to go to Gramercy Park," said the lady. "Drive us there at once."

"I nodded, for what is the use of wasting words when it can be avoided; and they stepped at once into the coach."

"Can you describe them—tell us how they looked?"

"I never notice people; besides, it was dark; but he had a swell air, and she was pert and merry, for she laughed as she closed the door."

"Can't you remember how they were dressed?"

"No, sir; she had on something that flapped about her shoulders, and he had a dark hat on his head, but that was all I saw."

"Didn't you see his face?"

"Not a bit of it; he kept it turned away. He didn't want nobody looking at him. She did all the business."

"Then you saw her face?"

"Yes, for a minute. But I wouldn't know it again. She was young and purty, and her hand which dropped the money into mine was small, but I couldn't say no more, not if you was to give me the town."

"Did you know that the house you stopped at was Mr. Van Burnam's, and that it was supposed to be empty?"

"No, sir, I'm not one of the swell ones. My acquaintances live in another part of the town."

"But you noticed that the house was dark?"

"I may have. I don't know."

"And that is all you have to tell us about them?"

"No, sir; the next morning, which was yesterday, sir, as I was a-dusting out the coach I found under the cushions a large blue veil, folded and lying very flat. But it had been slit with a knife and could not be worn."

This was strange too, and while more than one person about me ventured an opinion, I muttered to myself, "James Pope, his mark!" astonished at a coincidence which so completely connected the occupants of the two coaches.

But the Coroner was able to produce a witness whose evidence carried the matter on still farther. A policeman in full uniform testified next, and after explaining that his beat led him from Madison Avenue to Third on Twenty-seventh Street, went on to say that as he was coming up this street on Tuesday evening some few minutes before midnight, he encountered, somewhere between Lexington Avenue and Third, a man and woman walking rapidly towards the latter avenue, each carrying a parcel of some dimensions; that he noted them because they seemed so merry, but would have thought nothing of it, if he had not presently perceived them coming back without the parcels. They were chatting more gaily than ever. The lady wore a short cape, and the gentleman a dark coat, but he could give no other description of their appearance, for they went by rapidly, and he was more interested in wondering what they had done with such large parcels in such a short time at that hour of night, than in noting how they looked or whither they were going. He did observe, however, that they proceeded towards Madison Square, and remembers now that he heard a carriage suddenly drive away from that direction.

The Coroner asked him but one question:
"Had the lady no parcel when you saw her last?"
"I saw none."
"Could she not have carried one under her cape?"
"Perhaps, if it was small enough."
"As small as a lady's hat, say?"
"Well, it would have to be smaller than some of them are now, sir."
And so terminated this portion of the inquiry.

A short delay followed the withdrawal of this witness. The Coroner, who was a somewhat portly man, and who had felt the heat of the day very much, leaned back and looked anxious, while the jury, always restless, moved in their seats like a set of school-boys, and seemed to long for the hour of adjournment, notwithstanding the interest which everybody but themselves seemed to take in this exciting investigation.

Finally an officer, who had been sent into the adjoining room, came back with a gentleman, who was no sooner recognized as Mr. Franklin Van Burnam than a great change took place in the countenances of all present. The Coroner sat forward and dropped the large palm-leaf fan he had been industriously using for the last few minutes, the jury settled down, and the whispering of the many curious ones about me grew less audible and finally ceased altogether. A gentleman of the family was about to be interrogated, and such a gentleman!

I have purposely refrained from describing this best known and best reputed member of the Van Burnam family, foreseeing this hour when he would attract the attention of a hundred eyes and when his appearance would require our special notice. I will therefore endeavor to picture him to you as he looked on this memorable morning, with just the simple warning that you must not expect me to see with the eyes of a young girl or even with those of a fashionable society woman. I know a man when I see him, and I had always regarded Mr. Franklin as an exceptionally fine-looking and prepossessing gentleman, but I shall not go into raptures, as I heard a girl behind me doing, nor do I feel like acknowledging him as a paragon of all the virtues—as Mrs. Cunningham did that evening in my parlor.

He is a medium-sized man, with a shape not unlike his brother's. His hair is dark and so are his eyes, but his moustache is brown and his complexion quite fair. He carries himself with distinction, and though his countenance in repose has a precise air that is not perfectly agreeable, it has, when he speaks or smiles, an expression at once keen and amiable.

On this occasion he failed to smile, and though his elegance was sufficiently apparent, his worth was not so much so. Yet the impression generally made was favorable, as one could perceive from the air of respect with which his testimony was received.

He was asked many questions. Some were germane to the matter in hand and some seemed to strike wide of all mark. He answered them all courteously, showing a manly composure in doing so, that served to calm the fever-heat into which many had been thrown by the stories of the two hackmen. But as his evidence up to this point related merely to minor concerns, this was neither strange nor conclusive. The real test began when the Coroner, with a certain bluster, which may have been meant to attract the attention of the jury, now visibly waning, or, as was more likely, may have been the unconscious expression of a secret if hitherto well concealed embarrassment, asked the witness whether the keys to his father's front door had any duplicates.

The answer came in a decidedly changed tone. "No. The key used by our agent opens the basement door only."

The Coroner showed his satisfaction. "No duplicates," he repeated; "then you will have no difficulty in telling us where the keys to your father's front door were kept during the family's absence."

Did the young man hesitate, or was it but imagination on my part—"They were usually in my possession."

"Usually!" There was irony in the tone; evidently the Coroner was getting the better of his embarrassment, if he had felt any. "And where were they on the seventeenth of this month? Were they in your possession then?"

"No, sir." The young man tried to look calm and at his ease, but the difficulty he felt in doing so was apparent. "On the morning of that day," he continued, "I passed them over to my brother."

Ah! here was something tangible as well as important. I began to fear the police understood themselves only too well; and so did the whole crowd of persons there assembled. A groan in one direction was answered by a sigh in another, and it needed all the Coroner's authority to prevent an outbreak.

Meanwhile Mr. Van Burnam stood erect and unwavering, though his eye showed the suffering which these demonstrations awakened. He did not turn in the direction of the room where we felt sure his family was gathered, but it was evident that his thoughts did, and that most painfully. The Coroner, on the contrary, showed little or no feeling; he had brought the investigation up to this critical point and felt fully competent to carry it farther.

"May I ask," said he, "where the transference of these keys took place?"

"I gave them to him in our office last Tuesday morning. He said he might want to go into the house before his father came home."

"Did he say why he wanted to go into the house?"

"No."

"Was he in the habit of going into it alone and during the family's absence?"

"No."

"Had he any clothes there? or any articles belonging to himself or his wife which he would be likely to wish to carry away?"

"No."

"Yet he wanted to go in?"

"He said so."

"And you gave him the keys without question?"

"Certainly, sir."

"Was that not opposed to your usual principles—to your way of doing things, I should say?"

"Perhaps; but principles, by which I suppose you mean my usual business methods, do not govern me in my relations with my brother. He asked me a favor, and I granted it. It would have to have been a much larger one for me to have asked an explanation from him before doing so."

"Yet you are not on good terms with your brother; at least you have not had the name of being, for some time?"

"We have had no quarrel."

"Did he return the keys you lent him?"

"No."

"Have you seen them since?"

"No."

"Would you know them if they were shown you?"

"I would know them if they unlocked our front door."

"But you would not know them on sight?"

"I don't think so."

"Mr. Van Burnam, it is disagreeable for me to go into family matters, but if you have had no quarrel with your brother, how comes it that you and he have had so little intercourse of late?"

"He has been in Connecticut and I at Long Branch. Is not that a good answer, sir?"

"Good, but not good enough. You have a common office in New York, have you not?"

"Certainly, the firm's office."

"And you sometimes meet there, even while residing in different localities?"

"Yes, our business calls us in at times and then we meet, of course."

"Do you talk when you meet?"

"Talk?"

"Of other matters besides business, I mean. Are your relations friendly? Do you show the same spirit towards each other as you did three years ago, say?"

"We are older; perhaps we are not quite so voluble."

"But do you feel the same?"

"No. I see you will have it, and so I will no longer hold back the truth. We are not as brotherly in our intercourse as we used to be; but there is no animosity between us. I have a decided regard for my brother."

This was said quite nobly, and I liked him for it, but I began to feel that perhaps it had been for the best after all that I had never been intimate with the family. But I must not forestall either events or my opinions.

"Is there any reason"—it is the Coroner, of course, who is speaking—"why there should be any falling off in your mutual confidence? Has your brother done anything to displease you?"

"We did not like his marriage."

"Was it an unhappy one?"

"It was not a suitable one."

"Did you know Mrs. Van Burnam well, that you say this?"

"Yes, I knew her, but the rest of the family did not."

"Yet they shared in your disapprobation?"

"They felt the marriage more than I did. The lady—excuse me, I never like to speak ill of the sex—was not lacking in good sense or virtue, but she was not the person we had a right to expect Howard to marry."

"And you let him see that you thought so?"

"How could we do otherwise?"

"Even after she had been his wife for some months?"

"We could not like her."

"Did your brother—I am sorry to press this matter—ever show that he felt your change of conduct towards him?"

"I find it equally hard to answer," was the quick reply. "My brother is of an affectionate nature, and he has some, if not all, of the family's pride. I think he did feel it, though he never said so. He is not without loyalty to his wife."

"Mr. Van Burnam, of whom does the firm doing business under the name of Van Burnam & Sons consist?"

"Of the three persons mentioned."

"No others?"

"No."

"Has there ever been in your hearing any threat made by the senior partner of dissolving this firm as it stands?"

"I have heard"—I felt sorry for this strong but far from heartless man, but I would not have stopped the inquiry at this point if I could; I was far too curious—"I have heard my father say that he would withdraw if Howard did not. Whether he would have done so, I consider open to doubt. My father is a just man and never fails to do the right thing, though he sometimes speaks with unnecessary harshness."

"He made the threat, however?"

"Yes."

"And Howard heard it?"

"Or of it; I cannot say which."

"Mr. Van Burnam, have you noticed any change in your brother since this threat was uttered?"

"How, sir; what change?"

"In his treatment of his wife, or in his attitude towards yourself?"

"I have not seen him in the company of his wife since they went to Haddam. As for his conduct towards myself, I can say no more than I have already. We have never forgotten that we are children of one mother."

"Mr. Van Burnam, how many times have you seen Mrs. Howard Van Burnam?"

"Several. More frequently before they were married than since."

"You were in your brother's confidence, then, at that time; knew he was contemplating marriage?"

"It was in my endeavors to prevent the match that I saw so much of Miss Louise Stapleton."

"Ah! I am glad of the explanation! I was just going to inquire why you, of all members of the family, were the only one to know your brother's wife by sight."

The witness, considering this question answered, made no reply. But the next suggestion could not be passed over.

"If you saw Mrs. Van Burnam so often, you are acquainted with her personal appearance?"

"Sufficiently so; as well as I know that of my ordinary calling-acquaintance."

"Was she light or dark?"

"She had brown hair."

"Similar to this?"

The lock held up was the one which had been cut from the head of the dead girl.

"Yes, somewhat similar to that." The tone was cold; but he could not hide his distress.

"Mr. Van Burnam, have you looked well at the woman who was found murdered in your father's house?"

"I have, sir."

"Is there anything in her general outline or in such features as have escaped disfigurement to remind you of Mrs. Howard Van Burnam?"

"I may have thought so—at first glance," he replied, with decided effort.

"And did you change your mind at the second?"

He looked troubled, but answered firmly: "No, I cannot say that I did. But you must not regard my opinion as conclusive," he hastily added. "My knowledge of the lady was comparatively slight."

"The jury will take that into account. All we want to know now is whether you can assert from any knowledge you have or from anything to be noted in the body itself, that it is not Mrs. Howard Van Burnam?"

"I cannot."

And with this solemn assertion his examination closed.

The remainder of the day was taken up in trying to prove a similarity between Mrs. Van Burnam's handwriting and that of Mrs. James Pope as seen in the register of the Hotel D—— and on the order sent to Altman's. But the only conclusion reached was that the latter might be the former disguised, and even on this point the experts differed.

XIII HOWARD VAN BURNAM

The gentleman who stepped from the carriage and entered Mr. Van Burnam's house at twelve o'clock that night produced so little impression upon me that I went to bed satisfied that no result would follow these efforts at identification.

And so I told Mr. Gryce when he arrived next morning. But he seemed by no means disconcerted, and merely requested that I would submit to one more trial. To which I gave my consent, and he departed.

I could have asked him a string of questions, but his manner did not invite them, and for some reason I was too wary to show an interest in this tragedy superior to that felt by every right-thinking person connected with it.

At ten o'clock I was in my old seat in the court-room. The same crowd with different faces confronted me, amid which the twelve stolid countenances of the jury looked like old friends. Howard Van Burnam was the witness called, and as he came forward and stood in full view of us all, the interest of the occasion reached its climax.

His countenance wore a reckless look that did not serve to prepossess him with the people at whose mercy he stood. But he did not seem to care, and waited for the Coroner's questions with an air of ease which was in direct contrast to the drawn and troubled faces of his father and brother just visible in the background.

Coroner Dahl surveyed him a few minutes before speaking, then he quietly asked if he had seen the dead body of the woman who had been found lying under a fallen piece of furniture in his father's house.

He replied that he had.

"Before she was removed from the house or after it?"

"After."

"Did you recognize it? Was it the body of any one you know?"

"I do not think so."

"Has your wife, who was missing yesterday, been heard from yet, Mr. Van Burnam?"

"Not to my knowledge, sir."

"Had she not—that is, your wife—a complexion similar to that of the dead woman just alluded to?"

"She had a fair skin and brown hair, if that is what you mean. But these attributes are common to too many women for me to give them any weight in an attempted identification of this importance."

"Had they no other similar points of a less general character? Was not your wife of a slight and graceful build, such as is attributed to the subject of this inquiry?"

"My wife was slight and she was graceful, common attributes also."

"And your wife had a scar?"

"Yes."

"On the left ankle?"

"Yes."

"Which the deceased also has?"

"That I do not know. They say so, but I had no interest in looking."

"Why, may I ask? Did you not think it a remarkable coincidence?"

The young man frowned. It was the first token of feeling he had given.

"I was not on the look-out for coincidences," was his cold reply. "I had no reason to think this unhappy victim of an unknown man's brutality my wife, and so did not allow myself to be moved by even such a fact as this."

"You had no reason," repeated the Coroner, "to think this woman your wife. Had you any reason to think she was not?"

"Yes."

"Will you give us that reason?"

"I had more than one. First, my wife would never wear the clothes I saw on the girl whose dead body was shown to me. Secondly, she would never go to any house alone with a man at the hour testified to by one of your witnesses."

"Not with any man?"

"I did not mean to include her husband in my remark, of course. But as I did not take her to Gramercy Park, the fact that the deceased woman entered an empty house accompanied by a man, is proof enough to me that she was not Louise Van Burnam."

"When did you part with your wife?"

"On Monday morning at the depot in Haddam."

"Did you know where she was going?"

"I knew where she said she was going."

"And where was that, may I ask?"

"To New York, to interview my father."

"But your father was not in New York?"

"He was daily expected here. The steamer on which he had sailed from Southampton was due on Tuesday."

"Had she an interest in seeing your father? Was there any special reason why she should leave you for doing so?"

"She thought so; she thought he would become reconciled to her entrance into our family if he should see her suddenly and without prejudiced persons standing by."

"And did you fear to mar the effect of this meeting if you accompanied her?"

"No, for I doubted if the meeting would ever take place. I had no sympathy with her schemes, and did not wish to give her the sanction of my presence."

"Was that the reason you let her go to New York alone?"

"Yes."

"Had you no other?"

"No."

"Why did you follow her, then, in less than five hours?"

"Because I was uneasy; because I also wanted to see my father; because I am a man accustomed to carry out every impulse; and impulse led me that day in the direction of my somewhat headstrong wife."

"Did you know where your wife intended to spend the night?"

"I did not. She has many friends, or at least I have, in the city, and I concluded she would go to one of them—as she did."

"When did you arrive in the city? before ten o'clock?"

"Yes, a few minutes before."

"Did you try to find your wife?"

"No. I went directly to the club."

"Did you try to find her the next morning?"

"No; I had heard that the steamer had not yet been sighted off Fire Island, so considered the effort unnecessary."

"Why? What connection is there between this fact and an endeavor on your part to find your wife?"

"A very close one. She had come to New York to throw herself at my father's feet.

Now she could only do this at the steamer or in——"

"Why do you not proceed, Mr. Van Burnam?"

"I will. I do not know why I stopped,—or in his own house."

"In his own house? In the house in Gramercy Park, do you mean?"

"Yes, he has no other."

"The house in which this dead girl was found?"

"Yes,"—impatiently.

"Did you think she might throw herself at his feet there?"

"She said she might; and as she is romantic, foolishly romantic, I thought her fully capable of doing so."

"And so you did not seek her in the morning?"

"No, sir."

"How about the afternoon?"

This was a close question; we saw that he was affected by it though he tried to carry it off bravely.

"I did not see her in the afternoon. I was in a restless frame of mind, and did not remain in the city."

"Ah! indeed! and where did you go?"

"Unless necessary, I prefer not to say."

"It is necessary."

"I went to Coney Island."

"Alone?"

"Yes."

"Did you see anybody there you know?"

"No."

"And when did you return?"

"At midnight."

"When did you reach your rooms?"

"Later."

"How much later?"

"Two or three hours."

"And where were you during those hours?"

"I was walking the streets."

The ease, the quietness with which he made these acknowledgments were remarkable. The jury to a man honored him with a prolonged stare, and the awe-struck crowd scarcely breathed during their utterance. At the last sentence a murmur broke out, at which he raised his head and with an air of surprise surveyed the people before him. Though he must have known what their astonishment meant, he neither quailed nor blanched, and while not in reality a handsome man, he certainly looked handsome at this moment.

I did not know what to think; so forbore to think anything. Meanwhile the examination went on.

"Mr. Van Burnam, I have been told that the locket I see there dangling from your watch-chain contains a lock of your wife's hair. Is it so?"

"I have a lock of her hair in this; yes."

"Here is a lock clipped from the head of the unknown woman whose identity we seek. Have you any objection to comparing the two?"

"It is not an agreeable task you have set me," was the imperturbable response; "but I have no objection to doing what you ask." And calmly lifting the chain, he took off the locket, opened it, and held it out courteously toward the Coroner. "May I ask you to make the first comparison," he said.

The Coroner, taking the locket, laid the two locks of brown hair together, and after a moment's contemplation of them both, surveyed the young man seriously, and remarked:

"They are of the same shade. Shall I pass them down to the jury?"

Howard bowed. You would have thought he was in a drawing-room, and in the act of bestowing a favor. But his brother Franklin showed a very different countenance, and as for their father, one could not even see his face, he so persistently held up his hand before it.

The jury, wide-awake now, passed the locket along, with many sly nods and a few whispered words. When it came back to the Coroner, he took it and handed it to Mr. Van Burnam, saying:

"I wish you would observe the similarity for yourself. I can hardly detect any difference between them."

"Thank you! I am willing to take your word for it," replied the young man, with most astonishing aplomb. And Coroner and jury for a moment looked baffled, and even Mr. Gryce, of whose face I caught a passing glimpse at this instant, stared at the head of his cane, as if it were of thicker wood than he expected and had more knotty points on it than even his accustomed hand liked to encounter.

Another effort was not out of place, however; and the Coroner, summoning up some of the pompous severity he found useful at times, asked the witness if his attention had been drawn to the dead woman's hands.

He acknowledged that it had. "The physician who made the autopsy urged me to look at them, and I did; they were certainly very like my wife's."

"Only like."

"I cannot say that they were my wife's. Do you wish me to perjure myself?"

"A man should know his wife's hands as well as he knows her face."

"Very likely."

"And you are ready to swear these were not the hands of your wife?"

"I am ready to swear I did not so consider them."

"And that is all?"

"That is all."

The Coroner frowned and cast a glance at the jury. They needed prodding now and then, and this is the way he prodded them. As soon as they gave signs of recognizing the hint he gave them, he turned back, and renewed his examination in these words:

"Mr. Van Burnam, did your brother at your request hand you the keys of your father's house on the morning of the day on which this tragedy occurred?"

"He did."

"Have you those keys now?"

"I have not."

"What have you done with them? Did you return them to your brother?"

"No; I see where your inquiries are tending, and I do not suppose you will believe my simple word; but I lost the keys on the day I received them; that is why———"

"Well, you may continue, Mr. Van Burnam."

"I have no more to say; my sentence was not worth completing."

The murmur which rose about him seemed to show dissatisfaction; but he remained imperturbable, or rather like a man who did not hear. I began to feel a most painful interest in the inquiry, and dreaded, while I anxiously anticipated, his further examination.

"You lost the keys; may I ask when and where?"

"That I do not know; they were missing when I searched for them; missing from my pocket, I mean."

"Ah! and when did you search for them?"

"The next day—after I had heard—of—of what had taken place in my father's house."

The hesitations were those of a man weighing his reply. They told on the jury, as all such hesitations do; and made the Coroner lose an atom of the respect he had hitherto shown this easy-going witness.

"And you do not know what became of them?"

"No."

"Or into whose hands they fell?"

"No, but probably into the hands of the wretch——"

To the astonishment of everybody he was on the verge of vehemence; but becoming sensible of it, he controlled himself with a suddenness that was almost shocking.

"Find the murderer of this poor girl," said he, with a quiet air that was more thrilling than any display of passion, "and ask him where he got the keys with which he opened the door of my father's house at midnight."

Was this a challenge, or just the natural outburst of an innocent man. Neither the jury nor the Coroner seemed to know, the former looking startled and the latter nonplussed. But Mr. Gryce, who had moved now into view, smoothed the head of his cane with quite a loving touch, and did not seem at this moment to feel its inequalities objectionable.

"We will certainly try to follow your advice," the Coroner assured him. "Meanwhile we must ask how many rings your wife is in the habit of wearing?"

"Five. Two on the left hand and three on the right."

"Do you know these rings?"

"I do."

"Better than you know her hands?"

"As well, sir."

"Were they on her hands when you parted from her in Haddam?"

"They were."

"Did she always wear them?"

"Almost always. Indeed I do not ever remember seeing her take off more than one of them."

"Which one?"

"The ruby with the diamond setting."

"Had the dead girl any rings on when you saw her?"

"No, sir."

"Did you look to see?"

"I think I did in the first shock of the discovery."

"And you saw none?"

"No, sir."

"And from this you concluded she was not your wife?"

"From this and other things."

"Yet you must have seen that the woman was in the habit of wearing rings, even if they were not on her hands at that moment?"

"Why, sir? What should I know about her habits?"

"Is not that a ring I see now on your little finger?"

"It is; my seal ring which I always wear."

"Will you pull it off?"

"Pull it off!"

"If you please; it is a simple test I am requiring of you, sir."

The witness looked astonished, but pulled off the ring at once.

"Here it is," said he.

"Thank you, but I do not want it. I merely want you to look at your finger."

The witness complied, evidently more nonplussed than disturbed by this command.

"Do you see any difference between that finger and the one next it?"

"Yes; there is a mark about my little finger showing where the ring has pressed."

"Very good; there were such marks on the fingers of the dead girl, who, as you say, had no rings on. I saw them, and perhaps you did yourself?"

"I did not; I did not look closely enough."

"They were on the little finger of the right hand, on the marriage finger of the left, and on the forefinger of the same. On which fingers did your wife wear rings?"

"On those same fingers, sir, but I will not accept this fact as proving her identity with the deceased. Most women do wear rings, and on those very fingers."

The Coroner was nettled, but he was not discouraged. He exchanged looks with Mr. Gryce, but nothing further passed between them and we were left to conjecture what this interchange of glances meant.

The witness, who did not seem to be affected either by the character of this examination or by the conjectures to which it gave rise, preserved his sang-froid, and eyed the Coroner as he might any other questioner, with suitable respect, but with no fear and but little impatience. And yet he must have known the horrible suspicion darkening the minds of many people present, and suspected, even if against his will, that this examination, significant as it was, was but the forerunner of another and yet more serious one.

"You are very determined," remarked the Coroner in beginning again, "not to accept the very substantial proofs presented you of the identity between the object of this inquiry and your missing wife. But we are not yet ready to give up the struggle, and so I must ask if you heard the description given by Miss Ferguson of the manner in which your wife was dressed on leaving Haddam?"

"I have."

"Was it a correct account? Did she wear a black and white plaid silk and a hat trimmed with various colored ribbons and flowers?"

"She did."

"Do you remember the hat? Were you with her when she bought it, or did you ever have your attention drawn to it in any particular way?"

"I remember the hat."

"Is this it, Mr. Van Burnam?"

I was watching Howard, and the start he gave was so pronounced and the emotion he displayed was in such violent contrast to the self-possession he had maintained up to this point, that I was held spell-bound by the shock I received, and forebore to look at the object which the Coroner had suddenly held up for inspection. But when I did turn my head towards it, I recognized at once the multi-colored hat which Mr. Gryce had brought in from the third room of Mr. Van Burnam's house on the evening I was there, and realized almost in the same breath that great as this mystery had hitherto seemed it was likely to prove yet greater before its proper elucidation was arrived at.

"Was that found in my father's house? Where—where was that hat found?" stammered the witness, so far forgetting himself as to point towards the object in question.

"It was found by Mr. Gryce in a closet off your father's dining-room, a short time after the dead girl was carried out."

"I don't believe it," vociferated the young man, paling with something more than anger, and shaking from head to foot.

"Shall I put Mr. Gryce on his oath again?" asked the Coroner, mildly.

The young man stared; evidently these words failed to reach his understanding.

"Is it your wife's hat?" persisted the Coroner with very little mercy. "Do you recognize it for the one in which she left Haddam?"

"Would to God I did not!" burst in vehement distress from the witness, who at the next moment broke down altogether and looked about for the support of his brother's arm.

Franklin came forward, and the two brothers stood for a moment in the face of the whole surging mass of curiosity-mongers before them, arm in arm, but with very different expressions on their two proud faces. Howard was the first to speak.

"If that was found in the parlors of my father's house," he cried, "then the woman who was killed there was my wife." And he started away with a wild air towards the door.

"Where are you going?" asked the Coroner, quietly, while an officer stepped softly before him, and his brother compassionately drew him back by the arm.

"I am going to take her from that horrible place; she is my wife. Father, you would not wish her to remain in that spot for another moment, would you, while we have a house we call our own?"

Mr. Van Burnam the senior, who had shrunk as far from sight as possible through these painful demonstrations, rose up at these words from his agonized son, and making him an encouraging gesture, walked hastily out of the room; seeing which, the young man became calmer, and though he did not cease to shudder, tried to restrain his first grief, which to those who looked closely at him was evidently very sincere.

"I would not believe it was she," he cried, in total disregard of the presence he was in, "I would not believe it; but now——" A certain pitiful gesture finished the sentence, and neither Coroner nor jury seemed to know just how to proceed, the conduct of the young man being so markedly different from what they had expected. After a short pause, painful enough to all concerned, the Coroner, perceiving that very little could be done with the witness under the circumstances, adjourned the sitting till afternoon.

FOOTNOTES:
Why could he not have said Miss Butterworth? These Van Burnams are proud, most vilely proud as the poet has it.—A. B.

XIV A SERIOUS ADMISSION

I went at once to a restaurant. I ate because it was time to eat, and because any occupation was welcome that would pass away the hours of waiting. I was troubled; and I did not know what to make of myself. I was no friend to the Van Burnams; I did not like them, and certainly had never approved of any of them but Mr. Franklin, and yet I found myself altogether disturbed over the morning's developments, Howard's emotion having appealed to me in spite of my prejudices. I could not but think ill of him, his conduct not being such as I could honestly commend. But I found myself more ready to listen to the involuntary pleadings of my own heart in his behalf than I had been prior to his testimony and its somewhat startling termination.

But they were not through with him yet, and after the longest three hours I ever passed, we were again convened before the Coroner.

I saw Howard as soon as anybody did. He came in, arm in arm as before, with his faithful brother, and sat down in a retired corner behind the Coroner. But he was soon called forward.

His face when the light fell on it was startling to most of us. It was as much changed as if years, instead of hours, had elapsed since last we saw it. No longer reckless in its expression, nor easy, nor politely patient, it showed in its every lineament that he had not only passed through a hurricane of passion, but that the bitterness, which had been its worst feature, had not passed with the storm, but had settled into the core of his nature, disturbing its equilibrium forever. My emotions were not allayed by the sight; but I kept all expression of them out of view. I must be sure of his integrity before giving rein to my sympathies.

The jury moved and sat up quite alert when they saw him. I think that if these especial twelve men could have a murder case to investigate every day, they would grow quite wide-awake in time. Mr. Van Burnam made no demonstration. Evidently there was not likely to be a repetition of the morning's display of passion. He had been iron in his impassibility at that time, but he was steel now, and steel which had been through the fiercest of fires.

The opening question of the Coroner showed by what experience these fires had been kindled.

"Mr. Van Burnam, I have been told that you have visited the Morgue in the interim which has elapsed since I last questioned you. Is that true?"

"It is."

"Did you, in the opportunity thus afforded, examine the remains of the woman whose death we are investigating, attentively enough to enable you to say now whether they are those of your missing wife?"

"I have. The body is that of Louise Van Burnam; I crave your pardon and that of the jury for my former obstinacy in refusing to recognize it. I thought myself fully justified in the stand I took. I see now that I was not."

The Coroner made no answer. There was no sympathy between him and this young man. Yet he did not fail in a decent show of respect; perhaps because he did feel some sympathy for the witness's unhappy father and brother.

"You then acknowledge the victim to have been your wife?"

"I do."

"It is a point gained, and I compliment the jury upon it. We can now proceed to settle, if possible, the identity of the person who accompanied Mrs. Van Burnam into your father's house."

"Wait," cried Mr. Van Burnam, with a strange air, "I acknowledge I was that person."

It was coolly, almost fiercely said, but it was an admission that wellnigh created a hubbub. Even the Coroner seemed moved, and cast a glance at Mr. Gryce which showed his surprise to be greater than his discretion.

"You acknowledge," he began—but the witness did not let him finish.

"I acknowledge that I was the person who accompanied her into that empty house; but I do not acknowledge that I killed her. She was alive and well when I left her, difficult as it is for me to prove it. It was the realization of this difficulty which made me perjure myself this morning."

"So," murmured the Coroner, with another glance at Mr. Gryce, "you acknowledge that you perjured yourself. Will the room be quiet!"

But the lull came slowly. The contrast between the appearance of this elegant young man and the significant admissions he had just made (admissions which to three quarters of the persons there meant more, much more, than he acknowledged), was certainly such as to provoke interest of the deepest kind. I felt like giving rein to my own feelings, and was not surprised at the patience shown by the Coroner. But order was restored at last, and the inquiry proceeded.

"We are then to consider the testimony given by you this morning as null and void?"

"Yes, so far as it contradicts what I have just stated."

"Ah, then you will no doubt be willing to give us your evidence again?"

"Certainly, if you will be so kind as to question me."

"Very well; where did your wife and yourself first meet after your arrival in New York?"

"In the street near my office. She was coming to see me, but I prevailed upon her to go uptown."

"What time was this?"

"After ten and before noon. I cannot give the exact hour."

"And where did you go?"

"To a hotel on Broadway; you have already heard of our visit there."

"You are, then, the Mr. James Pope, whose wife registered in the books of the Hotel D—— on the seventeenth of this month?"

"I have said so."

"And may I ask for what purpose you used this disguise, and allowed your wife to sign a wrong name?"

"To satisfy a freak. She considered it the best way of covering up a scheme she had formed; which was to awaken the interest of my father under the name and appearance of a stranger, and not to inform him who she was till he had given some evidence of partiality for her."

"Ah, but for such an end was it necessary for her to assume a strange name before she saw your father, and for you both to conduct yourselves in the mysterious way you did all that day and evening?"

"I do not know. She thought so, and I humored her. I was tired of working against her, and was willing she should have her own way for a time."

"And for this reason you let her fit herself out with clothes down to her very undergarments?"

"Yes; strange as it may seem, I was just such a fool. I had entered into her scheme, and the means she took to change her personality only amused me. She wished to present herself to my father as a girl obliged to work for her living, and was too shrewd to excite suspicion in the minds of any of the family by any undue luxury in her apparel. At least that was the excuse she gave me for the precautions she took, though I think the delight she experienced in anything romantic and unusual had as much to do with it as anything else. She enjoyed the game she was playing, and wished to make as much of it as possible."

"Were her own garments much richer than those she ordered from Altman's?"

"Undoubtedly. Mrs. Van Burnam wore nothing made by American seamstresses. Fine clothes were her weakness."

"I see, I see; but why such an attempt on your part to keep yourself in the background? Why let your wife write your assumed names in the hotel register, for instance, instead of doing it yourself?"

"It was easier for her; I know no other reason. She did not mind putting down the name Pope. I did."

It was an ungracious reflection upon his wife, and he seemed to feel it so; for he almost immediately added: "A man will sometimes lend himself to a scheme of which the details are obnoxious. It was so in this case; but she was too interested in her plans to be affected by so small a matter as this."

This explained more than one mysterious action on the part of this pair while they were at the Hotel D——. The Coroner evidently considered it in this light, for he dwelt but little longer on this phase of the case, passing at once to a fact concerning which curiosity had hitherto been roused without receiving any satisfaction.

"In leaving the hotel," said he, "you and your wife were seen carrying certain packages, which were missing from your arms when you alighted at Mr. Van Burnam's house. What was in those packages, and where did you dispose of them before you entered the second carriage?"

Howard made no demur in answering.

"My wife's clothes were in them," said he, "and we dropped them somewhere on Twenty-seventh Street near Third Avenue, just as we saw an old woman coming along the sidewalk. We knew that she would stop and pick them up, and she did, for we slid into a dark shadow made by a projecting stoop and watched her. Is that too simple a method for disposing of certain encumbering bundles, to be believed, sir?"

"That is for the jury to decide," answered the Coroner, stiffly. "But why were you so anxious to dispose of these articles? Were they not worth some money, and would it not have been simpler and much more natural to have left them at the hotel till you chose to send for them? That is, if you were simply engaged in playing, as you say, a game upon your father, and not upon the whole community?"

"Yes," Mr. Van Burnam acknowledged, "that would have been the natural thing, no doubt; but we were not following natural instincts at the time, but a woman's bizarre caprices. We did as I said; and laughed long, I assure you, over its unqualified success; for the old woman not only grabbed the packages with avidity, but turned and fled away with them, just as if she had expected this opportunity and had prepared herself to make the most of it."

"It was very laughable, certainly," observed the Coroner, in a hard voice. "You must have found it very ridiculous"; and after giving the witness a look full of something deeper than sarcasm, he turned towards the jury as if to ask them what they thought of these very forced and suspicious explanations.

But they evidently did not know what to think, and the Coroner's looks flew back to the witness who of all the persons present seemed the least impressed by the position in which he stood.

"Mr. Van Burnam," said he, "you showed a great deal of feeling this morning at being confronted with your wife's hat. Why was this, and why did you wait till you saw this evidence of her presence on the scene of death to acknowledge the facts you have been good enough to give us this afternoon?"

"If I had a lawyer by my side, you would not ask me that question, or if you did, I would not be allowed to answer it. But I have no lawyer here, and so I will say that I was greatly shocked by the catastrophe which had happened to my wife, and under the stress of my first overpowering emotions had the impulse to hide the fact that the victim of so dreadful a mischance was my wife. I thought that if no connection was found between myself and this dead woman, I would stand in no danger of the suspicion which must cling to the man who came into the house with her. But like most first impulses, it was a foolish one and gave way under the strain of investigation. I, however, persisted in it as long as possible, partially because my disposition is an obstinate one, and partially because I hated to acknowledge myself a fool; but when I saw the hat, and recognized it as an indisputable proof of her presence in the Van Burnam house that night, my confidence in the attempt I was making broke down all at once. I could deny her shape, her hands, and even the scar, which she might have had in common with other women, but I could not deny her hat. Too many persons had seen her wear it."

But the Coroner was not to be so readily imposed upon.

"I see, I see," he repeated with great dryness, "and I hope the jury will be satisfied. And they probably will, unless they remember the anxiety which, according to your story, was displayed by your wife to have her whole outfit in keeping with her appearance as a working girl. If she was so particular as to think it necessary to dress herself in store-made undergarments, why make all these precautions void by carrying into the house a hat with the name of an expensive milliner inside it?"

"Women are inconsistent, sir. She liked the hat and hated to part with it. She thought she could hide it somewhere in the great house, at least that was what she said to me when she tucked it under her cape."

The Coroner, who evidently did not believe one word of this, stared at the witness as if curiosity was fast taking the place of indignation. And I did not wonder. Howard Van Burnam, as thus presented to our notice by his own testimony, was an anomaly, whether we were to believe what he was saying at the present time or what he had said during the morning session. But I wished I had had the questioning of him.

His next answer, however, opened up one dark place into which I had been peering for some time without any enlightenment. It was in reply to the following query:

"All this," said the Coroner, "is very interesting; but what explanation have you to give for taking your wife into your father's empty house at an hour so late, and then leaving her to spend the best part of the dark night alone?"

"None," said he, "that will strike you as sensible and judicious. But we were not sensible that night, neither were we judicious, or I would not be standing here trying to explain what is not explainable by any of the ordinary rules of conduct. She was set upon being the first to greet my father on his entrance into his own home, and her first plan had been to do so in her own proper character as my wife, but afterwards the freak took her, as I have said, to personify the housekeeper whom my father had cabled us to have in waiting at his house,—a cablegram which had reached us too late for any practical use, and which we had therefore ignored,—and fearing he might come early in the morning, before she could be on hand to make the favorable impression she intended, she wished to be left in the house that night; and I humored her. I did not foresee the suffering that my departure might cause her, or the fears that were likely to spring from her lonely position in so large and empty a dwelling. Or rather, I should say, she did not foresee them; for she begged me not to stay with her, when I hinted at the darkness and dreariness of the place, saying that she was too jolly to feel fear or think of anything but the surprise my father and sisters would experience in discovering that their very agreeable young housekeeper was the woman they had so long despised."

"And why," persisted the Coroner, edging forward in his interest and so allowing me to catch a glimpse of Mr. Gryce's face as he too leaned forward in his anxiety to hear every word that fell from this remarkable witness,—"why do you speak of her fear? What reason have you to think she suffered apprehension after your departure?"

"Why?" echoed the witness, as if astounded by the other's lack of perspicacity. "Did she not kill herself in a moment of terror and discouragement? Leaving her, as I did, in a condition of health and good spirits, can you expect me to attribute her death to any other cause than a sudden attack of frenzy caused by terror?"

"Ah!" exclaimed the Coroner in a suspicious tone, which no doubt voiced the feelings of most people present; "then you think your wife committed suicide?"

"Most certainly," replied the witness, avoiding but two pairs of eyes in the whole crowd, those of his father and brother.

"With a hat-pin," continued the Coroner, letting his hitherto scarcely suppressed irony become fully visible in voice and manner, "thrust into the back of her neck at a spot young ladies surely would have but little reason to know is peculiarly fatal! Suicide! when she was found crushed under a pile of bric-à-brac, which was thrown down or fell upon her hours after she received the fatal thrust!"

"I do not know how else she could have died," persisted the witness, calmly, "unless she opened the door to some burglar. And what burglar would kill a woman in that way, when he could pound her with his fists? No; she was frenzied and stabbed herself in desperation; or the thing was done by accident, God knows how! And as for the testimony of the experts—we all know how easily the wisest of them can be mistaken even in matters of as serious import as these. If all the experts in the world"—here his voice rose and his nostrils dilated till his aspect was actually commanding and impressed us all like a sudden transformation—"If all the experts in the world were to swear that those shelves were thrown upon her after she had lain therefor four hours dead, I would not believe them. Appearances or no appearances, blood or no blood, I here declare that she pulled that cabinet over in her death-struggle; and upon the truth of this fact I am ready to rest my honor as a man and my integrity as her husband."

An uproar immediately followed, amid which could be heard cries of "He lies!" "He's a fool!" The attitude taken by the witness was so unexpected that the most callous person present could not fail to be affected by it. But curiosity is as potent a passion as surprise, and in a few minutes all was still again and everybody intent to hear how the Coroner would answer these asseverations.

"I have heard of a blind man denying the existence of light," said that gentleman, "but never before of a sensible being like yourself urging the most untenable theories in face of such evidence as has been brought before us during this inquiry. If your wife committed suicide, or if the entrance of the point of a hat-pin into her spine was effected by accident, how comes the head of the pin to have been found so many feet away from her and in such a place as the parlor register?"

"It may have flown there when it broke, or, what is much more probable, been kicked there by some of the many people who passed in and out of the room between the time of her death and that of its discovery."

"But the register was found closed," urged the Coroner. "Was it not, Mr. Gryce?"

That person thus appealed to, rose for an instant.

"It was," said he, and deliberately sat down again.

The face of the witness, which had been singularly free from expression since his last vehement outbreak, clouded over for an instant and his eye fell as if he felt himself engaged in an unequal struggle. But he recovered his courage speedily, and quietly observed:

"The register may have been closed by a passing foot. I have known of stranger coincidences than that."

"Mr. Van Burnam," asked the Coroner, as if weary of subterfuges and argument, "have you considered the effect which this highly contradictory evidence of yours is likely to have on your reputation?"

"I have."

"And are you ready to accept the consequences?"

"If any especial consequences follow, I must accept them, sir."

"When did you lose the keys which you say you have not now in your possession? This morning you asserted that you did not know; but perhaps this afternoon you may like to modify that statement."

"I lost them after I left my wife shut up in my father's house."

"Soon?"

"Very soon."

"How soon?"

"Within an hour, I should judge."

"How do you know it was so soon?"

"I missed them at once."

"Where were you when you missed them?"

"I don't know; somewhere. I was walking the streets, as I have said. I don't remember just where I was when I thrust my hands into my pocket and found the keys gone."

"You do not?"

"No."

"But it was within an hour after leaving the house?"

"Yes."

"Very good; the keys have been found."

The witness started, started so violently that his teeth came together with a click loud enough to be heard over the whole room.

"Have they?" said he, with an effort at nonchalance which, however, failed to deceive any one who noticed his change of color. "You can tell me, then, where I lost them."

"They were found," said the Coroner, "in their usual place above your brother's desk in Duane Street."

"Oh!" murmured the witness, utterly taken aback or appearing so. "I cannot account for their being found in the office. I was so sure I dropped them in the street."

"I did not think you could account for it," quietly observed the Coroner. And without another word he dismissed the witness, who staggered to a seat as remote as possible from the one where he had previously been sitting between his father and brother.

XV A RELUCTANT WITNESS

A pause of decided duration now followed; an exasperating pause which tried even me, much as I pride myself upon my patience. There seemed to be some hitch in regard to the next witness. The Coroner sent Mr. Gryce into the neighboring room more than once, and finally, when the general uneasiness seemed on the point of expressing itself by a loud murmur, a gentleman stepped forth, whose appearance, instead of allaying the excitement, renewed it in quite an unprecedented and remarkable way.

I did not know the person thus introduced.

He was a handsome man, a very handsome man, if the truth must be told, but it did not seem to be this fact which made half the people there crane their heads to catch a glimpse of him. Something else, something entirely disconnected with his appearance there as a witness, appeared to hold the people enthralled and waken a subdued enthusiasm which showed itself not only in smiles, but in whispers and significant nudges, chiefly among the women, though I noticed that the jurymen stared when somebody obliged them with the name of this new witness. At last it reached my ears, and though it awakened in me also a decided curiosity, I restrained all expression of it, being unwilling to add one jot to this ridiculous display of human weakness.

Randolph Stone, as the intended husband of the rich Miss Althorpe, was a figure of some importance in the city, and while I was very glad of this opportunity of seeing him, I did not propose to lose my head or forget, in the marked interest his person invoked, the very serious cause which had brought him before us. And yet I suppose no one in the room observed his figure more minutely.

He was elegantly made and possessed, as I have said, a face of peculiar beauty. But these were not his only claims to admiration. He was a man of undoubted intelligence and great distinction of manner. The intelligence did not surprise me, knowing, as I did, how he had raised himself to his present enviable position in society in the short space of five years. But the perfection of his manner astonished me, though how I could have expected anything less in a man honored by Miss Althorpe's regard, I cannot say. He had that clear pallor of complexion which in a smooth-shaven face is so impressive, and his voice when he spoke had that music in it which only comes from great cultivation and a deliberate intent to please.

He was a friend of Howard's, that I saw by the short look that passed between them when he first entered the room; but that it was not as a friend he stood there was apparent from the state of amazement with which the former recognized him, as well as from the regret to be seen underlying the polished manner of the witness himself. Though perfectly self-possessed and perfectly respectful, he showed by every means possible the pain he felt in adding one feather-weight to the evidence against a man with whom he was on terms of more or less intimacy.

But let me give his testimony. Having acknowledged that he knew the Van Burnam family well, and Howard in particular, he went on to state that on the night of the seventeenth he had been detained at his office by business of a more than usual pressing nature, and finding that he could expect no rest for that night, humored himself by getting off the cars at Twenty-first Street instead of proceeding on to Thirty-third Street, where his apartments were.

The smile which these words caused (Miss Althorpe lives in Twenty-first Street) woke no corresponding light on his face. Indeed, he frowned at it, as if he felt that the gravity of the situation admitted of nothing frivolous or humorsome. And this feeling was shared by Howard, for he started when the witness mentioned Twenty-first Street, and cast him a haggard look of dismay which happily no one saw but myself, for every one else was concerned with the witness. Or should I except Mr. Gryce?

"I had of course no intentions beyond a short stroll through this street previous to returning to my home," continued the witness, gravely; "and am sorry to be obliged to mention this freak of mine, but find it necessary in order to account for my presence there at so unusual an hour."

"You need make no apologies," returned the Coroner. "Will you state on what line of cars you came from your office?"

"I came up Third Avenue."

"Ah! and walked towards Broadway?"

"Yes."

"So that you necessarily passed very near the Van Burnam mansion?"

"Yes."

"At what time was this, can you say?"

"At four, or nearly four. It was half-past three when I left my office."

"Was it light at that hour? Could you distinguish objects readily?"

"I had no difficulty in seeing."

"And what did you see? Anything amiss at the Van Burnam mansion?"

"No, sir, nothing amiss. I merely saw Howard Van Burnam coming down the stoop as I went by the corner."

"You made no mistake. It was the gentleman you name, and no other whom you saw on this stoop at this hour?"

"I am very sure that it was he. I am sorry——"

But the Coroner gave him no opportunity to finish.

"You and Mr. Van Burnam are friends, you say, and it was light enough for you to recognize each other; then you probably spoke?"

"No, we did not. I was thinking—well of other, things," and here he allowed the ghost of a smile to flit suggestively across his firm-set lips. "And Mr. Van Burnam seemed preoccupied also, for, as far as I know, he did not even look my way."

"And you did not stop?"

"No, he did not look like a man to be disturbed."

"And this was at four on the morning of the eighteenth?"

"At four."

"You are certain of the hour and of the day?"

"I am certain. I should not be standing here if I were not very sure of my memory. I am sorry," he began again, but he was stopped as peremptorily as before by the Coroner.

"Feeling has no place in an inquiry like this." And the witness was dismissed.

Mr. Stone, who had manifestly given his evidence under compulsion, looked relieved at its termination. As he passed back to the room from which he had come, many only noticed the extreme elegance of his form and the proud cast of his head, but I saw more than these. I saw the look of regret he cast at his friend Howard.

A painful silence followed his withdrawal, then the Coroner spoke to the jury:

"Gentlemen, I leave you to judge of the importance of this testimony. Mr. Stone is a well-known man of unquestionable integrity, but perhaps Mr. Van Burnam can explain how he came to visit his father's house at four o'clock in the morning on that memorable night, when according to his latest testimony he left his wife there at twelve. We will give him the opportunity."

"There is no use," began the young man from the place where he sat. But gathering courage even while speaking, he came rapidly forward, and facing Coroner and jury once more, said with a false kind of energy that imposed upon no one:

"I can explain this fact, but I doubt if you will accept my explanation. I was at my father's house at that hour, but not in it. My restlessness drove me back to my wife, but not finding the keys in my pocket, I came down the stoop again and went away."

"Ah, I see now why you prevaricated this morning in regard to the time when you missed those keys."

"I know that my testimony is full of contradictions."

"You feared to have it known that you were on the stoop of your father's house for the second time that night?"

"Naturally, in face of the suspicion I perceived everywhere about me."

"And this time you did not go in?"

"No."

"Nor ring the bell?"

"No."

"Why not, if you left your wife within, alive and well?"

"I did not wish to disturb her. My purpose was not strong enough to surmount the least difficulty. I was easily deterred from going where I had little wish to be."

"So that you merely went up the stoop and down again at the time Mr. Stone saw you?"

"Yes, and if he had passed a minute sooner he would have seen this: seen me go up, I mean, as well as seen me come down. I did not linger long in the doorway."

"But you did linger there a moment?"

"Yes; long enough to hunt for the keys and get over my astonishment at not finding them."

"Did you notice Mr. Stone going by on Twenty-first Street?"

"No."

"Was it as light as Mr. Stone has said?"

"Yes, it was light."

"And you did not notice him?"

"No."

"Yet you must have followed very closely behind him?"

"Not necessarily. I went by the way of Twentieth Street, sir. Why, I do not know, for my rooms are uptown. I do not know why I did half the things I did that night."

"I can readily believe it," remarked the Coroner.

Mr. Van Burnam's indignation rose.

"You are trying," said he, "to connect me with the fearful death of my wife in my father's lonely house. You cannot do it, for I am as innocent of that death as you are, or any other person in this assemblage. Nor did I pull those shelves down upon her as you would have this jury think, in my last thoughtless visit to my father's door. She died according to God's will by her own hand or by means of some strange and unaccountable accident known only to Him. And so you will find, if justice has any place in these investigations and a manly intelligence be allowed to take the place of prejudice in the breasts of the twelve men now sitting before me."

And bowing to the Coroner, he waited for his dismissal, and receiving it, walked back not to his lonely corner, but to his former place between his father and brother, who received him with a wistful air and strange looks of mingled hope and disbelief.

"The jury will render their verdict on Monday morning," announced the Coroner, and adjourned the inquiry.

BOOK II THE WINDINGS OF A LABYRINTH

XVI COGITATIONS

My cook had prepared for me a most excellent dinner, thinking that I needed all the comfort possible after a day of such trying experiences. But I ate little of it; my thoughts were too busy, my mind too much exercised. What would be the verdict of the jury, and could this especial jury be relied upon to give a just verdict?

At seven I had left the table and was shut up in my own room. I could not rest till I had fathomed my own mind in regard to the events of the day.

The question—the great question, of course, now—was how much of Howard's testimony was to be believed, and whether he was, notwithstanding his asseverations to the contrary, the murderer of his wife. To most persons the answer seemed easy. From the expression of such people as I had jostled in leaving the court-room, I judged that his sentence had already been passed in the minds of most there present. But these hasty judgments did not influence me. I hope I look deeper than the surface, and my mind would not subscribe to his guilt, notwithstanding the bad impression made upon me by his falsehoods and contradictions.

Now why would not my mind subscribe to it? Had sentiment got the better of me, Amelia Butterworth, and was I no longer capable of looking a thing squarely in the face? Had the Van Burnams, of all people in the world, awakened my sympathies at the cost of my good sense, and was I disposed to see virtue in a man in whom every circumstance as it came to light revealed little but folly and weakness? The lies he had told—for there is no other word to describe his contradictions—would have been sufficient under most circumstances to condemn a man in my estimation. Why, then, did I secretly look for excuses to his conduct?

Probing the matter to the bottom, I reasoned in this way: The latter half of his evidence was a complete contradiction of the first, purposely so. In the first, he made himself out a cold-hearted egotist with not enough interest in his wife to make an effort to determine whether she and the murdered woman were identical; in the latter, he showed himself in the light of a man influenced to the point of folly by a woman to whom he had been utterly unyielding a few hours before.

Now, knowing human nature to be full of contradictions, I could not satisfy myself that I should be justified in accepting either half of his testimony as absolutely true. The man who is all firmness one minute may be all weakness the next, and in face of the calm assertions made by this one when driven to bay by the unexpected discoveries of the police, I dared not decide that his final assurances were altogether false, and that he was not the man I had seen enter the adjoining house with his wife.

Why, then, not carry the conclusion farther and admit, as reason and probability suggested, that he was also her murderer; that he had killed her during his first visit and drawn the shelves down upon her in the second? Would not this account for all the phenomena to be observed in connection with this otherwise unexplainable affair? Certainly, all but one—one that was perhaps known to nobody but myself, and that was the testimony given by the clock. It said that the shelves fell at five, whereas, according to Mr. Stone's evidence, it was four, or thereabouts, when Mr. Van Burnam left his father's house. But the clock might not have been a reliable witness. It might have been set wrong, or it might not have been running at all at the time of the accident. No, it would not do for me to rely too much upon anything so doubtful, nor did I; yet I could not rid myself of the conviction that Howard spoke the truth when he declared in face of Coroner and jury that they could not connect him with this crime; and whether this conclusion sprang from sentimentality or intuition, I was resolved to stick to it for the present night at least. The morrow might show its futility, but the morrow had not come.

Meanwhile, with this theory accepted, what explanation could be given of the very peculiar facts surrounding this woman's death? Could the supposition of suicide advanced by Howard before the Coroner be entertained for a moment, or that equally improbable suggestion of accident?

Going to my bureau drawer, I drew out the old grocer-bill which has already figured in these pages, and re-read the notes I had scribbled on its back early in the history of this affair. They related, if you will remember, to this very question, and seemed even now to answer it in a more or less convincing way. Will you pardon me if I transcribe these notes again, as I cannot imagine my first deliberations on this subject to have made a deep enough impression for you to recall them without help from me.

The question raised in these notes was threefold, and the answers, as you will recollect, were transcribed before the cause of death had been determined by the discovery of the broken pin in the dead woman's brain.

These are the queries:

First: was her death due to accident?

Second: was it effected by her own hand?

Third: was it a murder?

The replies given are in the form of reasons, as witness:

My reasons for not thinking it an accident.

1. If it had been an accident, and she had pulled the cabinet over upon herself, she would have been found with her feet pointing towards the wall where the cabinet had stood. But her feet were towards the door and her head under the cabinet.

2. The precise arrangement of the clothing about her feet, which precluded any theory involving accident.

My reason for not thinking it a suicide.

She could not have been found in the position observed without having lain down on the floor while living, and then pulled the shelves down upon herself. (A theory obviously too improbable to be considered.)

My reason for not thinking it murder.

She would need to have been held down on the floor while the cabinet was being pulled over on her, a thing which the quiet aspect of the hands and feet make appear impossible. (Very good, but we know now that she was dead when the shelves fell over, so that my one excuse for not thinking it a murder is rendered null.)

My reasons for thinking it a murder.

----But I will not repeat these. My reasons for not thinking it an accident or a suicide remained as good as when they were written, and if her death had not been due to either of these causes, then it must have been due to some murderous hand. Was that hand the hand of her husband? I have already given it as my opinion that it was not.

Now, how to make that opinion good, and reconcile me again to myself; for I am not accustomed to have my instincts at war with my judgment. Is there any reason for my thinking as I do? Yes, the manliness of man. He only looked well when he was repelling the suspicion he saw in the surrounding faces. But that might have been assumed, just as his careless manner was assumed during the early part of the inquiry. I must have some stronger reason than this for my belief. The two hats? Well, he had explained how there came to be two hats on the scene of crime, but his explanation had not been very satisfactory. I had seen no hat in her hand when she crossed the pavement to her father's house. But then she might have carried it under her cape without my seeing it—perhaps. The discovery of two hats and of two pairs of gloves in Mr. Van Burnam's parlors was a fact worth further investigation, and mentally I made a note of it, though at the moment I saw no prospect of engaging in this matter further than my duties as a witness required.

And now what other clue was offered me, save the one I have already mentioned as being given by the clock? None that I could seize upon; and feeling the weakness of the cause I had so obstinately embraced, I rose from my seat at the tea-table and began making such alterations in my toilet as would prepare me for the evening and my inevitable callers.

"Amelia," said I to myself, as I encountered my anything but satisfied reflection in the glass, "can it be that you ought, after all, to have been called Araminta? Is a momentary display of spirit on the part of a young man of doubtful principles, enough to make you forget the dictates of good sense which have always governed you up to this time?"

The stern image which confronted me from the mirror made me no reply, and smitten with sudden disgust, I left the glass and went below to greet some friends who had just ridden up in their carriage.

They remained one hour, and they discussed one subject: Howard Van Burnam and his probable connection with the crime which had taken place next door. But though I talked some and listened more, as is proper for a woman in her own house, I said nothing and heard nothing which had not been already said and heard in numberless homes that night. Whatever thoughts I had which in any way differed from those generally expressed, I kept to myself,—whether guided by discretion or pride, I cannot say; probably by both, for I am not deficient in either quality.

Arrangements had already been made for the burial of Mrs. Van Burnam that night, and as the funeral ceremony was to take place next door, many of my guests came just to sit in my windows and watch the coming and going of the few people invited to the ceremony.

But I discouraged this. I have no patience with idle curiosity. Consequently by nine I was left alone to give the affair such real attention as it demanded; something which, of course, I could not have done with a half dozen gossiping friends leaning over my shoulder.

FOOTNOTES:

As was asserted by her husband in his sworn examination.

XVII   BUTTERWORTH VERSUS GRYCE

The result of this attention can be best learned from the conversation I held with Mr. Gryce the next morning.

He came earlier than usual, but he found me up and stirring.

"Well," he cried, accosting me with a smile as I entered the parlor where he was seated, "it is all right this time, is it not? No trouble in identifying the gentleman who entered your neighbor's house last night at a quarter to twelve?"

Resolved to probe this man's mind to the bottom, I put on my sternest air.

"I had not expected any one to enter there so late last night," said I. "Mr. Van Burnam declared so positively at the inquest that he was the person we have been endeavoring to identify, that I did not suppose you would consider it necessary to bring him to the house for me to see."

"And so you were not in the window?"

"I did not say that; I am always where I have promised to be, Mr. Gryce."

"Well, then?" he inquired sharply.

I was purposely slow in answering him—I had all the longer time to search his face. But its calmness was impenetrable, and finally I declared:

"The man you brought with you last night—you were the person who accompanied him, were you not—was not the man I saw alight there four nights ago."

He may have expected it; it may have been the very assertion he desired from me, but his manner showed displeasure, and the quick "How?" he uttered was sharp and peremptory.

"I do not ask who it was," I went on, with a quiet wave of my hand that immediately restored him to himself, "for I know you will not tell me. But what I do hope to know is the name of the man who entered that same house at just ten minutes after nine. He was one of the funeral guests, and he arrived in a carriage that was immediately preceded by a coach from which four persons alighted, two ladies and two gentlemen."

"I do not know the gentleman, ma'am," was the detective's half-surprised and half-amused retort. "I did not keep track of every guest that attended the funeral."

"Then you didn't do your work as well as I did mine," was my rather dry reply. "For I noted every one who went in; and that gentleman, whoever he was, was more like the person I have been trying to identify than any one I have seen enter there during my four midnight vigils."

Mr. Gryce smiled, uttered a short "Indeed!" and looked more than ever like a sphinx. I began quietly to hate him, under my calm exterior.

"Was Howard at his wife's funeral?" I asked.

"He was, ma'am."

"And did he come in a carriage?"

"He did, ma'am."

"Alone?"

"He thought he was alone; yes, ma'am."

"Then may it not have been he?"

"I can't say, ma'am."

Mr. Gryce was so obviously out of his element under this cross-examination that I could not suppress a smile even while I experienced a very lively indignation at his reticence. He may have seen me smile and he may not, for his eyes, as I have intimated, were always busy with some object entirely removed from the person he addressed; but at all events he rose, leaving me no alternative but to do the same.

"And so you didn't recognize the gentleman I brought to the neighboring house just before twelve o'clock," he quietly remarked, with a calm ignoring of my last question which was a trifle exasperating.

"No."

"Then, ma'am," he declared, with a quick change of manner, meant, I should judge, to put me in my proper place, "I do not think we can depend upon the accuracy of your memory;" and he made a motion as if to leave.

As I did not know whether his apparent disappointment was real or not, I let him move to the door without a reply. But once there I stopped him.

"Mr. Gryce," said I, "I don't know what you think about this matter, nor whether you even wish my opinion upon it. But I am going to express it, for all that. I do not believe that Howard killed his wife with a hat-pin."

"No?" retorted the old gentleman, peering into his hat, with an ironical smile which that inoffensive article of attire had certainly not merited. "And why, Miss Butterworth, why? You must have substantial reasons for any opinion you would form."

"I have an intuition," I responded, "backed by certain reasons. The intuition won't impress you very deeply, but the reasons may not be without some weight, and I am going to confide them to you."

"Do," he entreated in a jocose manner which struck me as inappropriate, but which I was willing to overlook on account of his age and very fatherly manner.

"Well, then," said I, "this is one. If the crime was a premeditated one, if he hated his wife and felt it for his interest to have her out of the way, a man of Mr. Van Burnam's good sense would have chosen any other spot than his father's house to kill her in, knowing that her identity could not be hidden if once she was associated with the Van Burnam name. If, on the contrary, he took her there in good faith, and her death was the unexpected result of a quarrel between them, then the means employed would have been simpler. An angry man does not stop to perform a delicate surgical operation when moved to the point of murder, but uses his hands or his fists, just as Mr. Van Burnam himself suggested."

"Humph!" grunted the detective, staring very hard indeed into his hat.

"You must not think me this young man's friend," I went on, with a well meant desire to impress him with the impartiality of my attitude. "I never have spoken to him nor he to me, but I am the friend of justice, and I must declare that there was a note of surprise in the emotion he showed at sight of his wife's hat, that was far too natural to be assumed."

The detective failed to be impressed. I might have expected this, knowing his sex and the reliance such a man is apt to place upon his own powers.

"Acting, ma'am, acting!" was his laconic comment. "A very uncommon character, that of Mr. Howard Van Burnam. I do not think you do it full justice."

"Perhaps not, but see that you don't slight mine. I do not expect you to heed these suggestions any more than you did those I offered you in connection with Mrs. Boppert, the scrub-woman; but my conscience is eased by my communication, and that is much to a solitary woman like myself who is obliged to spend many a long hour alone with no other companion."

"Something has been accomplished, then, by this delay," he observed. Then, as if ashamed of this momentary display of irritation, he added in the genial tones more natural to him: "I don't blame you for your good opinion of this interesting, but by no means reliable, young man, Miss Butterworth. A woman's kind heart stands in the way of her proper judgment of criminals."

"You will not find its instincts fail even if you do its judgment."

His bow was as full of politeness as it was lacking in conviction.

"I hope you won't let your instincts lead you into any unnecessary detective work," he quietly suggested.

"That I cannot promise. If you arrest Howard Van Burnam for murder, I may be tempted to meddle with matters which don't concern me."

An amused smile broke through his simulated seriousness.

"Pray accept my congratulations, then, in advance, ma'am. My health has been such that I have long anticipated giving up my profession; but if I am to have such assistants as you in my work, I shall be inclined to remain in it some time longer."

"When a man as busy as you stops to indulge in sarcasm, he is in more or less good spirits. Such a condition, I am told, only prevails with detectives when they have come to a positive conclusion concerning the case they are engaged upon."

"I see you already understand the members of your future profession."

"As much as is necessary at this juncture," I retorted. Then seeing him about to repeat his bow, I added sharply: "You need not trouble yourself to show me too much politeness. If I meddle in this matter at all it will not be as your coadjutor, but as your rival."

"My rival?"

"Yes, your rival; and rivals are never good friends until one of them is hopelessly defeated."

"Miss Butterworth, I see myself already at your feet."

And with this sally and a short chuckle which did more than anything he had said towards settling me in my half-formed determination to do as I had threatened, he opened the door and quietly disappeared.

XVIII THE LITTLE PINCUSHION

The verdict rendered by the Coroner's jury showed it to be a more discriminating set of men than I had calculated upon. It was murder inflicted by a hand unknown.

I was so gratified by this that I left the court-room in quite an agitated frame of mind, so agitated, indeed, that I walked through one door instead of another, and thus came unexpectedly upon a group formed almost exclusively of the Van Burnam family.

Starting back, for I dislike anything that looks like intrusion, especially when no great end is to be gained by it, I was about to retrace my steps when I felt two soft arms about my neck.

"Oh, Miss Butterworth, isn't it a mercy that this dreadful thing is over! I don't know when I have ever felt anything so keenly."

It was Isabella Van Burnam.

Startled, for the embraces bestowed on me are few, I gave a subdued sort of grunt, which nevertheless did not displease this young lady, for her arms tightened, and she murmured in my ear: "You dear old soul! I like you so much."

"We are going to be very good neighbors," cooed a still sweeter voice in my other ear. "Papa says we must call on you soon." And Caroline's demure face looked around into mine in a manner some would have thought exceedingly bewitching.

"Thank you, pretty poppets!" I returned, freeing myself as speedily as possible from embraces the sincerity of which I felt open to question. "My house is always open to you." And with little ceremony, I walked steadily out and betook myself to the carriage awaiting me.

I looked upon this display of feeling as the mere gush of two over-excited young women, and was therefore somewhat astonished when I was interrupted in my afternoon nap by an announcement that the two Misses Van Burnam awaited me in the parlor.

Going down, I saw them standing there hand in hand and both as white as a sheet.

"O Miss Butterworth!" they cried, springing towards me, "Howard has been arrested, and we have no one to say a word of comfort to us."

"Arrested!" I repeated, greatly surprised, for I had not expected it to happen so soon, if it happened at all.

"Yes, and father is just about prostrated. Franklin, too, but he keeps up, while father has shut himself into his room and won't see anybody, not even us. O, I don't know how we are to bear it! Such a disgrace, and such a wicked, wicked shame! For Howard never had anything to do with his wife's death, had he, Miss Butterworth?"

"No," I returned, taking my ground at once, and vigorously, for I really believed what I said. "He is innocent of her death, and I would like the chance of proving it."

They evidently had not expected such an unqualified assertion from me, for they almost smothered me with kisses, and called me their only friend! and indeed showed so much real feeling this time that I neither pushed them away nor tried to withdraw myself from their embraces.

When their emotions were a little exhausted I led them to a sofa and sat down before them. They were motherless girls, and my heart, if hard, is not made of adamant or entirely unsusceptible to the calls of pity and friendship.

"Girls," said I, "if you will be calm, I should like to ask you a few questions."

"Ask us anything," returned Isabella; "nobody has more right to our confidence than you."

This was another of their exaggerated expressions, but I was so anxious to hear what they had to tell, I let it pass. So instead of rebuking them, I asked where their brother had been arrested, and found it had been at his rooms and in presence of themselves and Franklin. So I inquired further and learned that, so far as they knew, nothing had been discovered beyond what had come out at the inquest except that Howard's trunks had been found packed, as if he had been making preparations for a journey when interrupted by the dreadful event which had put him into the hands of the police. As there was a certain significance in this, the girls seemed almost as much impressed by it as I was, but we did not discuss it long, for I suddenly changed my manner, and taking them both by the hand, asked if they could keep a secret.

"Secret?" they gasped.

"Yes, a secret. You are not the girls I should confide in ordinarily; but this trouble has sobered you."

"O, we can do anything," began Isabella; and "Only try us," murmured Caroline.

But knowing the volubility of the one and the weakness of the other, I shook my head at their promises, and merely tried to impress them with the fact that their brother's safety depended upon their discretion. At which they looked very determined for poppets, and squeezed my hands so tightly that I wished I had left off some of my rings before engaging in this interview.

When they were quiet again and ready to listen I told them my plans. They were surprised, of course, and wondered how I could do anything towards finding out the real murderer of their sister-in-law; but seeing how resolved I looked, changed their tone and avowed with much feeling their perfect confidence in me and in the success of anything I might undertake.

This was encouraging, and ignoring their momentary distrust, I proceeded to say:

"But for me to be successful in this matter, no one must know my interest in it. You must pay me no visits, give me no confidences, nor, if you can help it, mention my name before any one, not even before your father and brother. So much for precautionary measures, my dears; and now for the active ones. I have no curiosity, as I think you must see, but I shall have to ask you a few questions which under other circumstances would savor more or less of impertinence. Had your sister-in-law any special admirers among the other sex?"

"Oh," protested Caroline, shrinking back, while Isabella's eyes grew round as a frightened child's. "None that we ever heard of. She wasn't that kind of a woman, was she, Belle? It wasn't for any such reason papa didn't like her."

"No, no, that would have been too dreadful. It was her family we objected to, that's all."

"Well, well," I apologized, tapping their hands reassuringly, "I only asked—let me now say—from curiosity, though I have not a particle of that quality, I assure you."

"Did you think—did you have any idea—" faltered Caroline, "that———"

"Never mind," I interrupted. "You must let my words go in one ear and out of the other after you have answered them. I wish"—here I assumed a brisk air—"that I could go through your parlors again before every trace of the crime perpetrated there has been removed."

"Why, you can," replied Isabella.

"There is no one in them now," added Caroline, "Franklin went out just before we left."

At which I blandly rose, and following their leadership, soon found myself once again in the Van Burnam mansion.

My first glance upon re-entering the parlors was naturally directed towards the spot where the tragedy had taken place. The cabinet had been replaced and the shelves set back upon it; but the latter were empty, and neither on them nor on the adjacent mantel-piece did I see the clock. This set me thinking, and I made up my mind to have another look at that clock. By dint of judicious questions I found that it had been carried into the third room, where we soon found it lying on a shelf of the same closet where the hat had been discovered by Mr. Gryce. Franklin had put it there, fearing that the sight of it might affect Howard, and from the fact that the hands stood as I had left them, I gathered that neither he nor any of the family had discovered that it was in running condition.

Assured of this, I astonished them by requesting to have it taken down and set up on the table, which they had no sooner done than it started to tick just as it had done under my hand a few nights before.

The girls, greatly startled, surveyed each other wonderingly.

"Why, it's going!" cried Caroline.

"Who could have wound it!" marvelled Isabella.

"Hark!" I cried. The clock had begun to strike.

It gave forth five clear notes.

"Well, it's a mystery!" Isabella exclaimed. Then seeing no astonishment in my face, she added: "Did you know about this, Miss Butterworth?"

"My dear girls," I hastened to say, with all the impressiveness characteristic of me in my more serious moments. "I do not expect you to ask me for any information I do not volunteer. This is hard, I know; but some day I will be perfectly frank with you. Are you willing to accept my aid on these terms?"

"O yes," they gasped, but they looked not a little disappointed.

"And now," said I, "leave the clock where it is, and when your brother comes home, show it to him, and say that having the curiosity to examine it you were surprised to find it going, and that you had left it there for him to see. He will be surprised also, and as a consequence will question first you and then the police to find out who wound it. If they acknowledge having done it, you must notify me at once, for that's what I want to know. Do you understand, Caroline? And, Isabella, do you feel that you can go through all this without dropping a word concerning me and my interest in this matter?"

Of course they answered yes, and of course it was with so much effusiveness that I was obliged to remind them that they must keep a check on their enthusiasm, and also to suggest that they should not come to my house or send me any notes, but simply a blank card, signifying: "No one knows who wound the clock."

"How delightfully mysterious!" cried Isabella. And with this girlish exclamation our talk in regard to the clock closed.

The next object that attracted our attention was a paper-covered novel I discovered on a side-table in the same room.

"Whose is this?" I asked.

"Not mine."

"Yet it was published this summer," I remarked.

They stared at me astonished, and Isabella caught up the book. It was one of those summer publications intended mainly for railroad distribution, and while neither ragged nor soiled, bore evidence of having been read.

"Let me take it," said I.

Isabella at once passed it into my hands.

"Does your brother smoke?" I asked.

"Which brother?"

"Either of them."

"Franklin sometimes, but Howard, never. It disagrees with him, I believe."

"There is a faint odor of tobacco about these pages. Can it have been brought here by Franklin?"

"O no, he never reads novels, not such novels as this, at all events. He loses a lot of pleasure, we think."

I turned the pages over. The latter ones were so fresh I could almost put my finger on the spot where the reader had left off. Feeling like a bloodhound who has just run upon a trail, I returned the book to Caroline, with the injunction to put it away; adding, as I saw her air of hesitation: "If your brother Franklin misses it, it will show that he brought it here, and then I shall have no further interest in it." Which seemed to satisfy her, for she put it away at once on a high shelf.

Perceiving nothing else in these rooms of a suggestive character, I led the way into the hall. There I had a new idea.

"Which of you was the first to go through the rooms upstairs?" I inquired.

"Both of us," answered Isabella. "We came together. Why do you ask, Miss Butterworth?"

"I was wondering if you found everything in order there?"

"We did not notice anything wrong, did we, Caroline? Do you think that the—the person who committed that awful crime went up-stairs? I couldn't sleep a wink if I thought so."

"Nor I," Caroline put in. "O, don't say that he went up-stairs, Miss Butterworth!"

"I do not know it," I rejoined.

"But you asked——"

"And I ask again. Wasn't there some little thing out of its usual place? I was up in your front chamber after water for a minute, but I didn't touch anything but the mug."

"We missed the mug, but—O Caroline, the pin-cushion! Do you suppose Miss Butterworth means the pin-cushion?"

I started. Did she refer to the one I had picked up from the floor and placed on a side-table?

"What about the pin-cushion?" I asked.

"O nothing, but we did not know what to make of its being on the table. You see, we had a little pin-cushion shaped like a tomato which always hung at the side of our bureau. It was tied to one of the brackets and was never taken off; Caroline having a fancy for it because it kept her favorite black pins out of the reach of the neighbor's children when they came here. Well, this cushion, this sacred cushion which none of us dared touch, was found by us on a little table by the door, with the ribbon hanging from it by which it had been tied to the bureau. Some one had pulled it off, and very roughly too, for the ribbon was all ragged and torn. But there is nothing in a little thing like that to interest you, is there, Miss Butterworth?"

"No," said I, not relating my part in the affair; "not if our neighbor's children were the marauders."

"But none of them came in for days before we left."

"Are there pins in the cushion?"

"When we found it, do you mean? No."

I did not remember seeing any, but one cannot always trust to one's memory.

"But you had left pins in it?"

"Possibly, I don't remember. Why should I remember such a thing as that?"

I thought to myself, "I would know whether I left pins on my pin-cushion or not," but every one is not as methodical as I am, more's the pity.

"Have you anywhere about you a pin like those you keep on that cushion?" I inquired of Caroline.

She felt at her belt and neck and shook her head.

"I may have upstairs," she replied.

"Then get me one." But before she could start, I pulled her back. "Did either of you sleep in that room last night?"

"No, we were going to," answered Isabella, "but afterwards Caroline took a freak to sleep in one of the rooms on the third floor. She said she wanted to get away from the parlors as far as possible."

"Then I should like a peep at the one overhead."

The wrenching of the pin-cushion from its place had given me an idea.

They looked at me wistfully as they turned to mount the stairs, but I did not enlighten them further. What would an idea be worth shared by them!

Their father undoubtedly lay in the back room, for they moved very softly around the head of the stairs, but once in front they let their tongues run loose again. I, who cared nothing for their babble when it contained no information, walked slowly about the room and finally stopped before the bed.

It had a fresh look, and I at once asked them if it had been lately made up. They assured me that it had not, saying that they always kept their beds spread during their absence, as they did so hate to enter a room disfigured by bare mattresses.

I could have read them a lecture on the niceties of housekeeping, but I refrained; instead of that I pointed to a little dent in the smooth surface of the bed nearest the door.

"Did either of you two make that?" I asked.

They shook their heads in amazement.

"What is there in that?" began Caroline; but I motioned her to bring me the little cushion, which she no sooner did than I laid it in the little dent, which it fitted to a nicety.

"You wonderful old thing!" exclaimed Caroline. "How ever did you think———"

But I stopped her enthusiasm with a look. I may be wonderful, but I am not old, and it is time they knew it.

"Mr. Gryce is old," said I; and lifting the cushion, I placed it on a perfectly smooth portion of the bed. "Now take it up," said I, when, lo! a second dent similar to the first.

"You see where that cushion has lain before being placed on the table," I remarked, and reminding Caroline of the pin I wanted, I took my leave and returned to my own house, leaving behind me two girls as much filled with astonishment as the giddiness of their pates would allow.

XIX   A DECIDED STEP FORWARD

I felt that I had made an advance. It was a small one, no doubt, but it was an advance. It would not do to rest there, however, or to draw definite conclusions from what I had seen without further facts to guide me. Mrs. Boppert could supply these facts, or so I believed. Accordingly I decided to visit Mrs. Boppert.

Not knowing whether Mr. Gryce had thought it best to put a watch over my movements, but taking it for granted that it would be like him to do so, I made a couple of formal calls on the avenue before I started eastward. I had learned Mrs. Boppert's address before leaving home, but I did not ride directly to the tenement where she lived. I chose, instead, to get out at a little fancy store I saw in the neighborhood.

It was a curious place. I never saw so many or such variety of things in one small spot in my life, but I did not waste any time upon this quaint interior, but stepped immediately up to the good woman I saw leaning over the counter.

"Do you know a Mrs. Boppert who lives at 803?" I asked.

The woman's look was too quick and suspicious for denial; but she was about to attempt it, when I cut her short by saying:

"I wish to see Mrs. Boppert very much, but not in her own rooms. I will pay any one well who will assist me to five minutes' conversation with her in such a place, say, as that I see behind the glass door at the end of this very shop."

The woman, startled by so unexpected a proposition, drew back a step, and was about to shake her head, when I laid on the counter before her (shall I say how much? Yes, for it was not thrown away) a five-dollar bill, which she no sooner saw than she gave a gasp of delight.

"Will you give me that?" she cried.

For answer I pushed it towards her, but before her fingers could clutch it, I resolutely said:

"Mrs. Boppert must not know there is anybody waiting here to see her, or she will not come. I have no ill-will towards her, and mean her only good, but she's a timid sort of person, and———"

"I know she's timid," broke in the good woman, eagerly. "And she's had enough to make her so! What with policemen drumming her up at night, and innocent-looking girls and boys luring her into corners to tell them what she saw in that grand house where the murder took place, she's grown that feared of her shadow you can hardly get her out after sundown. But I think I can get her here; and if you mean her no harm, why, ma'am———" Her fingers were on the bill, and charmed with the feel of it, she forgot to finish her sentence.

"Is there any one in the room back there?" I asked, anxious to recall her to herself.

"No, ma'am, no one at all. I am a poor widder, and not used to such company as you; but if you will sit down, I will make myself look more fit and have Mrs. Boppert over here in a minute." And calling to some one of the name of Susie to look after the shop, she led the way towards the glass door I have mentioned.

Relieved to find everything working so smoothly and determined to get the worth of my money out of Mrs. Boppert when I saw her, I followed the woman into the most crowded room I ever entered. The shop was nothing to it; there you could move without hitting anything; here you could not. There were tables against every wall, and chairs where there were no tables. Opposite me was a window-ledge filled with flowering plants, and at my right a grate and mantel-piece covered, that is the latter, with innumerable small articles which had evidently passed a long and forlorn probation on the shop shelves before being brought in here. While I was looking at them and marvelling at the small quantity of dust I found, the woman herself disappeared behind a stack of boxes, for which there was undoubtedly no room in the shop. Could she have gone for Mrs. Boppert already, or had she slipped into another room to hide the money which had come so unexpectedly into her hands?

I was not long left in doubt, for in another moment she returned with a flower-bedecked cap on her smooth gray head, that transformed her into a figure at once so complacent and so ridiculous that, had my nerves not been made of iron, I should certainly have betrayed my amusement. With it she had also put on her company manner, and what with the smiles she bestowed upon me and her perfect satisfaction with her own appearance, I had all I could do to hold my own and keep her to the matter in hand. Finally she managed to take in my anxiety and her own duty, and saying that Mrs. Boppert could never refuse a cup of tea, offered to send her an invitation to supper. As this struck me favorably, I nodded, at which she cocked her head on one side and insinuatingly whispered:

"And would you pay for the tea, ma'am?"

I uttered an indignant "No!" which seemed to surprise her. Immediately becoming humble again, she replied it was no matter, that she had tea enough and that the shop would supply cakes and crackers; to all of which I responded with a look which awed her so completely that she almost dropped the dishes with which she was endeavoring to set one of the tables.

"She does so hate to talk about the murder that it will be a perfect godsend to her to drop into good company like this with no prying neighbors about. Shall I set a chair for you, ma'am?"

I declined the honor, saying that I would remain seated where I was, adding, as I saw her about to go:

"Let her walk straight in, and she will be in the middle of the room before she sees me. That will suit her and me too; for after she has once seen me, she won't be frightened. But you are not to listen at the door."

This I said with great severity, for I saw the woman was becoming very curious, and having said it, I waved her peremptorily away.

She didn't like it, but a thought of the five dollars comforted her. Casting one final look at the table, which was far from uninvitingly set, she slipped out and I was left to contemplate the dozen or so photographs that covered the walls. I found them so atrocious and their arrangement so distracting to my bump of order, which is of a pronounced character, that I finally shut my eyes on the whole scene, and in this attitude began to piece my thoughts together. But before I had proceeded far, steps were heard in the shop, and the next moment the door flew open and in popped Mrs. Boppert, with a face like a peony in full blossom. She stopped when she saw me and stared.

"Why, if it isn't the lady——"

"Hush! Shut the door. I have something very particular to say to you."

"O," she began, looking as if she wanted to back out. But I was too quick for her. I shut the door myself and, taking her by the arm, seated her in the corner.

"You don't show much gratitude," I remarked.

I did not know what she had to be grateful to me for, but she had so plainly intimated at our first interview that she regarded me as having done her some favor, that I was disposed to make what use of it I could, to gain her confidence.

"I know, ma'am, but if you could see how I've been harried, ma'am. It's the murder, and nothing but the murder all the time; and it was to get away from the talk about it that I came here, ma'am, and now it's you I see, and you'll be talking about it too, or why be in such a place as this, ma'am?"

"And what if I do talk about it? You know I'm your friend, or I never would have done you that good turn the morning we came upon the poor girl's body."

"I know, ma'am, and grateful I am for it, too; but I've never understood it, ma'am. Was it to save me from being blamed by the wicked police, or was it a dream you had, and the gentleman had, for I've heard what he said at the inquest, and it's muddled my head till I don't know where I'm standing."

What I had said and what the gentleman had said! What did the poor thing mean? As I did not dare to show my ignorance, I merely shook my head.

"Never mind what caused us to speak as we did, as long as we helped you. And we did help you? The police never found out what you had to do with this woman's death, did they?"

"No, ma'am, O no, ma'am. When such a respectable lady as you said that you saw the young lady come into the house in the middle of the night, how was they to disbelieve it. They never asked me if I knew any different."

"No," said I, almost struck dumb by my success, but letting no hint of my complacency escape me. "And I did not mean they should. You are a decent woman, Mrs. Boppert, and should not be troubled."

"Thank you, ma'am. But how did you know she had come to the house before I left. Did you see her?"

I hate a lie as I do poison, but I had to exercise all my Christian principles not to tell one then.

"No," said I, "I didn't see her, but I don't always have to use my eyes to know what is going on in my neighbor's houses." Which is true enough, if it is somewhat humiliating to confess it.

"O ma'am, how smart you are, ma'am! I wish I had some smartness in me. But my husband had all that. He was a man—O what's that?"

"Nothing but the tea-caddy; I knocked it over with my elbow."

"How I do jump at everything! I'm afraid of my own shadow ever since I saw that poor thing lying under that heap of crockery."

"I don't wonder."

"She must have pulled those things over herself, don't you think so, ma'am? No one went in there to murder her. But how came she to have those clothes on. She was dressed quite different when I let her in. I say it's all a muddle, ma'am, and it will be a smart man as can explain it."

"Or a smart woman," I thought.

"Did I do wrong, ma'am? That's what plagues me. She begged so hard to come in, I didn't know how to shut the door on her. Besides her name was Van Burnam, or so she told me."

Here was a coil. Subduing my surprise, I remarked:

"If she asked you to let her in, I do not see how you could refuse her. Was it in the morning or late in the afternoon she came?"

"Don't you know, ma'am? I thought you knew all about it from the way you talked."

Had I been indiscreet? Could she not bear questioning? Eying her with some severity, I declared in a less familiar tone than any I had yet used:

"Nobody knows more about it than I do, but I do not know just the hour at which this lady came to the house. But I do not ask you to tell me if you do not want to."

"O ma'am," she humbly remonstrated, "I am sure I am willing to tell you everything. It was in the afternoon while I was doing the front basement floor."

"And she came to the basement door?"

"Yes, ma'am."

"And asked to be let in?"

"Yes, ma'am."

"Young Mrs. Van Burnam?"

"Yes, ma'am."

"Dressed in a black and white plaid silk, and wearing a hat covered with flowers?"

"Yes, ma'am, or something like that. I know it was very bright and becoming."

"And why did she come to the basement door—a lady dressed like that?"

"Because she knew I couldn't open the front door; that I hadn't the key. O she talked beautiful, ma'am, and wasn't proud with me a bit. She made me let her stay in the house, and when I said it would be dark after a while and that I hadn't done nothing to the rooms upstairs, she laughed and said she didn't care, that she wasn't afraid of the dark and had just as lieve as not stay in the big house alone all night, for she had a book—Did you say anything, ma'am?"

"No, no, go on, she had a book."

"Which she could read till she got sleepy. I never thought anything would happen to her."

"Of course not, why should you? And so you let her into the house and left her there when you went out of it? Well, I don't wonder you were shocked to see her lying dead on the floor next morning."

"Awful, ma'am. I was afraid they would blame me for what had happened. But I didn't do nothing to make her die. I only let her stay in the house. Do you think they will do anything to me if they know it?"

"No," said I, trying to understand this woman's ignorant fears, "they don't punish such things. More's the pity!"—this in confidence to myself. "How could you know that a piece of furniture would fall on her before morning. Did you lock her in when you left the house?"

"Yes, ma'am. She told me to."

Then she was a prisoner.

Confounded by the mystery of the whole affair, I sat so still the woman looked up in wonder, and I saw I had better continue my questions.

"What reason did she give for wanting to stay in the house all night?"

"What reason, ma'am? I don't know. Something about her having to be there when

Mr. Van Burnam came home. I didn't make it out, and I didn't try to. I was too busy wondering what she would have to eat."

"And what did she have?"

"I don't know, ma'am. She said she had something, but I didn't see it."

"Perhaps you were blinded by the money she gave you. She gave you some, of course?"

"O, not much, ma'am, not much. And I wouldn't have taken a cent if it had not seemed to make her so happy to give it. The pretty, pretty thing! A real lady, whatever they say about her!"

"And happy? You said she was happy, cheerful-looking, and pretty."

"O yes, ma'am; she didn't know what was going to happen. I even heard her sing after she went up-stairs."

I wished that my ears had been attending to their duty that day, and I might have heard her sing too. But the walls between my house and that of the Van Burnams are very thick, as I have had occasion to observe more than once.

"Then she went up-stairs before you left?"

"To be sure, ma'am; what would she do in the kitchen?"

"And you didn't see her again?"

"No, ma'am; but I heard her walking around."

"In the parlors, you mean?"

"Yes, ma'am, in the parlors."

"You did not go up yourself?"

"No, ma'am, I had enough to do below."

"Didn't you go up when you went away?"

"No, ma'am; I didn't like to."

"When did you go?"

"At five, ma'am; I always go at five."

"How did you know it was five?"

"The kitchen clock told me; I wound it, ma'am and set it when the whistles blew at twelve."

"Was that the only clock you wound?"

"Only clock? Do you think I'd be going around the house winding any others?"

Her face showed such surprise, and her eyes met mine so frankly, that I was convinced she spoke the truth. Gratified—I don't know why,—I bestowed upon her my first smile, which seemed to affect her, for her face softened, and she looked at me quite eagerly for a minute before she said:

"You don't think so very bad of me, do you, ma'am?"

But I had been struck by a thought which made me for the moment oblivious to her question. She had wound the clock in the kitchen for her own uses, and why may not the lady above have wound the one in the parlor for hers? Filled with this startling idea, I remarked:

"The young lady wore a watch, of course?"

But the suggestion passed unheeded. Mrs. Boppert was as much absorbed in her own thoughts as I was.

"Did young Mrs. Van Burnam wear a watch?" I persisted.

Mrs. Boppert's face remained a blank.

Provoked at her impassibility, I shook her with an angry hand, imperatively demanding:

"What are you thinking of? Why don't you answer my questions?"

She was herself again in an instant.

"O ma'am, I beg your pardon. I was wondering if you meant the parlor clock."

I calmed myself, looked severe to hide my more than eager interest, and sharply cried:

"Of course I mean the parlor clock. Did you wind it?"

"O no, no, no, I would as soon think of touching gold or silver. But the young lady did, I'm sure, ma'am, for I heard it strike when she was setting of it."

Ah! If my nature had not been an undemonstrative one, and if I had not been bred to a strong sense of social distinctions, I might have betrayed my satisfaction at this announcement in a way that would have made this homely German woman start. As it was I sat stock-still, and even made her think I had not heard her. Venturing to rouse me a bit, she spoke again after a minute's silence.

"She might have been lonely, you know, ma'am; and the ticking of a clock is such company."

"Yes," I answered with more than my accustomed vivacity, for she jumped as if I had struck her. "You have hit the nail on the head, Mrs. Boppert, and are a much smarter woman than I thought. But when did she wind the clock?"

"At five o'clock, ma'am; just before I left the house."

"O, and did she know you were going?"

"I think so, ma'am, for I called up, just before I put on my bonnet, that it was five o'clock and that I was going."

"O, you did. And did she answer back?"

"Yes, ma'am. I heard her step in the hall and then her voice. She asked if I was sure it was five, and I told her yes, because I had set the kitchen clock at twelve. She didn't say any more, but just after that I heard the parlor clock begin to strike."

O, thought I, what cannot be got out of the most stupid and unwilling witness by patience and a judicious use of questions. To know that this clock was started after five o'clock, that is, after the hour at which the hands pointed when it fell, and that it was set correctly in starting, and so would give indisputable testimony of the hour when the shelves fell, were points of the greatest importance. I was so pleased I gave the woman another smile.

Instantly she cried:

"But you won't say anything about it, will you, ma'am? They might make me pay for all the things that were broke."

My smile this time was not one of encouragement simply. But it might have been anything for all effect it had on her. The intricacies of the affair had disturbed her poor brain again, and all her powers of mind were given up to lament.

"O," she bemoaned, "I wish I had never seen her! My head wouldn't ache so with the muddle of it. Why, ma'am, her husband said he came to the house at midnight with his wife! How could he when she was inside of it all the time. But then perhaps he said that, just as you did, to save me blame. But why should a gentleman like him do that?"

"It isn't worth while for you to bother your head about it," I expostulated. "It is enough that my head aches over it."

I don't suppose she understood me or tried to. Her wits had been sorely tried and my rather severe questioning had not tended to clear them. At all events she went on in another moment as if I had not spoken:

"But what became of her pretty dress? I was never so astonished in my life as when I saw that dark skirt on her."

"She might have left her fine gown upstairs," I ventured, not wishing to go into the niceties of evidence with this woman.

"So she might, so she might, and that may have been her petticoat we saw." But in another moment she saw the impossibility of this, for she added: "But I saw her petticoat, and it was a brown silk one. She showed it when she lifted her skirt to get at her purse. I don't understand it, ma'am."

As her face by this time was almost purple, I thought it a mercy to close the interview; so I uttered some few words of a soothing and encouraging nature, and then seeing that something more tangible was necessary to restore her to any proper condition of spirits, I took out my pocket-book and bestowed on her some of my loose silver.

This was something she could understand. She brightened immediately, and before she was well through her expressions of delight, I had quitted the room and in a few minutes later the shop.

I hope the two women had their cup of tea after that.

XX   MISS BUTTERWORTH'S THEORY

I was so excited when I entered my carriage that I rode all the way home with my bonnet askew and never knew it. When I reached my room and saw myself in the glass, I was shocked, and stole a glance at Lena, who was setting out my little tea-table, to see if she noticed what a ridiculous figure I cut. But she is discretion itself, and for a girl with two undeniable dimples in her cheeks, smiles seldom—at least when I am looking at her. She was not smiling now, and though, for the reason given above, this was not as comforting as it may appear, I chose not to worry myself any longer about such a trifle when I had matters of so much importance on my mind.

Taking off my bonnet, whose rakish appearance had given me such a shock, I sat down, and for half an hour neither moved nor spoke. I was thinking. A theory which had faintly suggested itself to me at the inquest was taking on body with these later developments. Two hats had been found on the scene of the tragedy, and two pairs of gloves, and now I had learned that there had been two women there, the one whom Mrs. Boppert had locked into the house on leaving it, and the one whom I had seen enter at midnight with Mr. Van Burnam. Which of the two had perished? We had been led to think, and Mr. Van Burnam had himself acknowledged, that it was his wife; but his wife had been dressed quite differently from the murdered woman, and was, as I soon began to see, much more likely to have been the assassin than the victim. Would you like to know my reasons for this extraordinary statement? If so, they are these:

I had always seen a woman's hand in this work, but having no reason to believe in the presence of any other woman on the scene of crime than the victim, I had put this suspicion aside as untenable. But now that I had found the second woman, I returned to it.

But how connect her with the murder? It seemed easy enough to do so if this other woman was her rival. We have heard of no rival, but she may have known of one, and this knowledge may have been at the bottom of her disagreement with her husband and the half-crazy determination she evinced to win his family over to her side. Let us say, then, that the second woman was Mrs. Van Burnam's rival. That he brought her there not knowing that his wife had effected an entrance into the house; brought her there after an afternoon spent at the Hotel D——, during which he had furnished her with a new outfit of less pronounced type, perhaps, than that she had previously worn. The use of the two carriages and the care they took to throw suspicion off their track, may have been part of a scheme of future elopement, for I had no idea they meant to remain in Mr. Van Burnam's house. For what purpose, then, did they go there? To meet Mrs. Van Burnam and kill her, that their way might be clearer for flight? No; I had rather think that they went to the house without a thought of whom they would encounter, and that only after they had entered the parlors did he realize that the two women he least wished to see together had been brought by his folly face to face.

The presence in the third room of Mrs. Van Burnam's hat, gloves, and novel seemed to argue that she had spent the evening in reading by the dining-room table, but whether this was so or not, the stopping of a carriage in front and the opening of the door by an accustomed hand undoubtedly assured her that either the old gentleman or some other member of the family had unexpectedly arrived. She was, therefore, in or near the parlor-door when they entered, and the shock of meeting her hated rival in company with her husband, under the very roof where she had hoped to lay the foundations of her future happiness, must have been great, if not maddening. Accusations, recriminations even, did not satisfy her. She wanted to kill; but she had no weapon. Suddenly her eyes fell on the hat-pin which her more self-possessed rival had drawn from her hat, possibly before their encounter, and she conceived a plan which seemed to promise her the very revenge she sought. How she carried it out; by what means she was enabled to approach her victim and inflict with such certainty the fatal stab which laid her enemy at her feet, can be left to the imagination. But that she, a woman, and not Howard, a man, drove this woman's weapon into the stranger's spine, I will yet prove, or lose all faith in my own intuitions.

But if this theory is true, how about the shelves that fell at daybreak, and how about her escape from the house without detection? A little thought will explain all that. The man, horrified, no doubt, at the result of his imprudence, and execrating the crime to which it had led, left the house almost immediately. But the woman remained there, possibly because she had fainted, possibly because he would have nothing to do with her; and coming to herself, saw her victim's face staring up at her with an accusing beauty she found it impossible to meet. What should she do to escape it? Where should she go? She hated it so she could have trampled on it, but she restrained her passions till daybreak, when in one wild burst of fury and hatred she drew down the cabinet upon it, and then fled the scene of horror she had herself caused. This was at five, or, to be exact, three minutes before that hour, as shown by the clock she had carelessly set in her lighter moments.

She escaped by the front door, which her husband had mercifully forborne to lock; and she had not been discovered by the police, because her appearance did not tally with the description which had been given them. How did I know this? Remember the discoveries I had made in Miss Van Burnam's room, and allow them to assist you in understanding my conclusions.

Some one had gone into that room; some one who wanted pins; and keeping this fact before my eyes, I saw through the motive and actions of the escaping woman. She had on a dress separated at the waist, and finding, perhaps, a spot of blood on the skirt, she conceived the plan of covering it with her petticoat, which was also of silk and undoubtedly as well made as many women's dresses. But the skirt of the gown was longer than the petticoat and she was obliged to pin it up. Having no pins herself, and finding none on the parlor floor, she went up-stairs to get some. The door at the head of the stairs was locked, but the front room was open, so she entered there. Groping her way to the bureau, for the place was very dark, she found a pin-cushion hanging from a bracket. Feeling it to be full of pins, and knowing that she could see nothing where she was, she tore it away and carried it towards the door. Here there was some light from the skylight over the stairs, so setting the cushion down on the bed, she pinned up the skirt of her gown.

When this was done she started away, brushing the cushion off the bed in her excitement, and fearing to be traced by her many-colored hat, or having no courage remaining for facing again the horror in the parlor, she slid out without one and went, God knows whither, in her terror and remorse.

So much for my theory; now for the facts standing in the way of its complete acceptance. They were two: the scar on the ankle of the dead girl, which was a peculiarity of Louise Van Burnam, and the mark of the rings on her fingers. But who had identified the scar? Her husband. No one else. And if the other woman had, by some strange freak of chance, a scar also on her left foot, then the otherwise unaccountable apathy he had shown at being told of this distinctive mark, as well as his temerity in afterwards taking it as a basis for his false identification, becomes equally consistent and natural; and as for the marks of the rings, it would be strange if such a woman did not wear rings and plenty of them.

Howard's conduct under examination and the contradiction between his first assertions and those that followed, all become clear in the light of this new theory. He had seen his wife kill a defenceless woman before his eyes, and whether influenced by his old affection for her or by his pride in her good name, he could not but be anxious to conceal her guilt even at the cost of his own truthfulness. As long then as circumstances permitted, he preserved his indifferent attitude, and denied that the dead woman was his wife. But when driven to the wall by the indisputable proof which was brought forth of his wife having been in the place of murder, he saw, or thought he did, that a continued denial on his part of Louise Van Burnam being the victim might lead sooner or later to the suspicion of her being the murderer, and influenced by this fear, took the sudden resolution of profiting by all the points which the two women had in common by acknowledging, what everybody had expected him to acknowledge from the first, that the woman at the Morgue was his wife. This would exonerate her, rid him of any apprehension he may have entertained of her ever returning to be a disgrace to him, and would (and perhaps this thought influenced him most, for who can understand such men or the passions that sway them) insure the object of his late devotion a decent burial in a Christian cemetery. To be sure, the risk he ran was great, but the emergency was great, and he may not have stopped to count the cost. At all events, the fact is certain that he perjured himself when he said that it was his wife he brought to the house from the Hotel D——, and if he perjured himself in this regard, he probably perjured himself in others, and his testimony is not at all to be relied upon.

Convinced though I was in my own mind that I had struck a truth which would bear the closest investigation, I was not satisfied to act upon it till I had put it to the test. The means I took to do this were daring, and quite in keeping with the whole desperate affair. They promised, however, a result important enough to make Mr. Gryce blush for the disdain with which he had met my threats of interference.

XXI   A SHREWD CONJECTURE

The test of which I speak was as follows:

I would advertise for a person dressed as I believed Mrs. Van Burnam to have been when she left the scene of crime. If I received news of such a person, I might safely consider my theory established.

I accordingly wrote the following advertisement:

"Information wanted of a woman who applied for lodgings on the morning of the eighteenth inst., dressed in a brown silk skirt and a black and white plaid blouse of fashionable cut. She was without a hat, or if a person so dressed wore a hat, then it was bought early in the morning at some store, in which case let shopkeepers take notice. The person answering this description is eagerly sought for by her relatives, and to any one giving positive information of the same, a liberal reward will be paid. Please address, T. W. Alvord, —— Liberty Street."

I purposely did not mention her personal appearance, for fear of attracting the attention of the police.

This done, I wrote the following letter:

"DEAR MISS FERGUSON:

"One clever woman recognizes another. I am clever and am not ashamed to own it. You are clever and should not be ashamed to be told so. I was a witness at the inquest in which you so notably distinguished yourself, and I said then, 'There is a woman after my own heart!' But a truce to compliments! What I want and ask of you to procure for me is a photograph of Mrs. Van Burnam. I am a friend of the family, and consider them to be in more trouble than they deserve. If I had her picture I would show it to the Misses Van Burnam, who feel great remorse at their treatment of her, and who want to see how she looked. Cannot you find one in their rooms? The one in Mr. Howard's room here has been confiscated by the police.

"Hoping that you will feel disposed to oblige me in this—and I assure you that my motives in making this request are most excellent—I remain,

"Cordially yours,

"AMELIA BUTTERWORTH.

"P. S.—Address me, if you please, at 564 —— Avenue. Care of J. H. Denham."

This was my grocer, with whom I left word the next morning to deliver this package in the next bushel of potatoes he sent me.

My smart little maid, Lena, carried these two communications to the east side, where she posted the letter herself and entrusted the advertisement to a lover of hers who carried it to the Herald office. While she was gone I tried to rest by exercising my mind in other directions. But I could not. I kept going over Howard's testimony in the light of my own theory, and remarking how the difficulty he experienced in maintaining the position he had taken, forced him into inconsistencies and far-fetched explanations. With his wife for a companion at the Hotel D——, his conduct both there and on the road to his father's house was that of a much weaker man than his words and appearance led one to believe; but if, on the contrary, he had with him a woman with whom he was about to elope (and what did the packing up of all his effects mean, if not that?), all the precautions they took seemed reasonable.

Later, my mind fixed itself on one point. If it was his wife who was with him, as he said, then the bundle they dropped at the old woman's feet contained the much-talked of plaid silk. If it was not, then it was a gown of some different material. Now, could this bundle be found? If it could, then why had not Mr. Gryce produced it? The sight of Mrs. Van Burnam's plaid silk spread out on the Coroner's table would have had a great effect in clinching the suspicion against her husband. But no plaid silk had been found (because it was not dropped in the bundle, but worn away on the murderess's back), and no old woman. I thought I knew the reason of this too. There was no old woman to be found, and the bundle they carried had been got rid of some other way. What way? I would take a walk down that same block and see, and I would take it at the midnight hour too, for only so could I judge of the possibilities there offered for concealing or destroying such an article.

Having made this decision, I cast about to see how I could carry it into effect. I am not a coward, but I have a respectability to maintain, and what errand could Miss Butterworth be supposed to have in the streets at twelve o'clock at night! Fortunately, I remembered that my cook had complained of toothache when I gave her my orders for breakfast, and going down at once into the kitchen, where she sat with her cheek propped up in her hand waiting for Lena, I said with an asperity which admitted of no reply:

"You have a dreadful tooth, Sarah, and you must have something done for it at once. When Lena comes home, send her to me. I am going to the drug-store for some drops, and I want Lena to accompany me."

She looked astounded, of course, but I would not let her answer me. "Don't speak a word," I cried, "it will only make your toothache worse; and don't look as if some hobgoblin had jumped up on the kitchen table. I guess I know my duty, and just what kind of a breakfast I will have in the morning, if you sit up all night groaning with the toothache." And I was out of the room before she had more than begun to say that it was not so bad, and that I needn't trouble, and all that, which was true enough, no doubt, but not what I wanted to hear at that moment.

When Lena came in, I saw by the brightness of her face that she had accomplished her double errand. I therefore signified to her that I was satisfied, and asked if she was too tired to go out again, saying quite peremptorily that Sarah was ill, and that I was going to the drug-store for some medicine, and did not wish to go alone.

Lena's round-eyed wonder was amusing; but she is very discreet, as I have said before, and she ventured nothing save a meek, "It's very late, Miss Butterworth," which was an unnecessary remark, as she soon saw.

I do not like to obtrude my aristocratic tendencies too much into this narrative, but when I found myself in the streets alone with Lena, I could not help feeling some secret qualms lest my conduct savored of impropriety. But the thought that I was working in the cause of truth and justice came to sustain me, and before I had gone two blocks, I felt as much at home under the midnight skies as if I were walking home from church on a Sunday afternoon.

There is a certain drug-store on Third Avenue where I like to deal, and towards this I ostensibly directed my steps. But I took pains to go by the way of Lexington Avenue and Twenty-seventh Street, and upon reaching the block where this mysterious couple were seen, gave all my attention to the possible hiding-places it offered.

Lena, who had followed me like my shadow, and who was evidently too dumfounded at my freak to speak, drew up to my side as we were half-way down it and seized me tremblingly by the arm.

"Two men are coming," said she.

"I am not afraid of men," was my sharp rejoinder. But I told a most abominable lie; for I am afraid of them in such places and under such circumstances, though not under ordinary conditions, and never where the tongue is likely to be the only weapon employed.

The couple who were approaching us now seemed to be in a merry mood. But when they saw us keep to our own side of the way, they stopped their chaffing and allowed us to go by, with just a mocking word or two.

"Sarah ought to be very much obliged to you," whispered Lena.

At the corner of Third Avenue I paused. I had seen nothing so far but bare stoops and dark area-ways. Nothing to suggest a place for the disposal of such cumbersome articles as these persons had made way with. Had the avenue anything better to offer? I stopped under the gas-lamp at the corner to consider, notwithstanding Lena's gentle pull towards the drugstore. Looking to left and right and over the muddy crossings, I sought for inspiration. An almost obstinate belief in my own theory led me to insist in my own mind that they had encountered no old woman, and consequently had not dropped their bundles in the open street. I even entered into an argument about it, standing there with the cable cars whistling by me and Lena tugging away at my arm. "If," said I to myself, "the woman with him had been his wife and the whole thing nothing more than a foolish escapade, they might have done this; but she was not his wife, and the game they were playing was serious, if they did laugh over it, and so their disposal of these tell-tale articles would be serious and such as would protect their secret. Where, then, could they have thrust them?"

My eyes, as I muttered this, were on the one shop in my line of vision that was still open and lighted. It was the den of a Chinese laundryman, and through the windows in front I could see him still at work, ironing.

"Ah!" thought I, and made such a start across the street that Lena gasped in dismay and almost fell to the ground in her frightened attempt to follow me.

"Not that way!" she called. "Miss Butterworth, you are going wrong."

But I kept right on, and only stopped when I reached the laundry.

"I have an errand here," I explained. "Wait in the doorway, Lena, and don't act as if you thought me crazy, for I was never saner in my life."

I don't think this reassured her much, lunatics not being supposed to be very good judges of their own mental condition, but she was so accustomed to obey, that she drew back as I opened the door before me and entered. The surprise on the face of the poor Chinaman when he turned and saw before him a lady of years and no ordinary appearance, daunted me for an instant. But another look only showed me that his very surprise was inoffensive, and gathering courage from the unexpectedness of my own position, I inquired with all the politeness I could show one of his abominable nationality:

"Didn't a gentleman and a heavily veiled lady leave a package with you a few days ago at about the same hour of night as this?"

"Some lalee clo' washee? Yes, ma'am. No done. She tellee me no callee for one week."

"Then that's all right; the lady has died very suddenly, and the gentleman gone away; you will have to keep the clothes a long time."

"Me wantee money, no wantee clo'!"

"I'll pay you for them; I don't care about them being ironed."

"Givee tickee, givee clo'! No givee tickee, no givee clo'!"

This was a poser! But as I did not want the clothes so much as a look at them, I soon got the better of this difficulty.

"I don't want them to-night," said I. "I only wanted to make sure you had them. What night were these people here?"

"Tuesday night, velly late; nicee man, nicee lalee. She wantee talk. Nicee man he pullee she; I no hear if muchee stasch. All washee, see!" he went on, dragging a basket out of the corner, "him no ilon."

I was in such a quiver; so struck with amazement at my own perspicacity in surmising that here was a place where a bundle of underclothing could be lost indefinitely, that I just stared while he turned over the clothes in the basket. For by means of the quality of the articles he was preparing to show me, the question which had been agitating me for hours could be definitely decided. If they proved to be fine and of foreign manufacture, then Howard's story was true and all my fine-spun theories must fall to the ground. But if, on the contrary, they were such as are usually worn by American women, then my own idea as to the identity of the woman who left them here was established, and I could safely consider her as the victim and Louise Van Burnam as the murderess, unless further facts came to prove that he was the guilty one, after all.

The sight of Lena's eyes staring at me with great anxiety through the panes of the door distracted my attention for a moment, and when I looked again, he was holding up two or three garments before me. The articles thus revealed told their story in a moment. They were far from fine, and had even less embroidery on them than I expected.

"Are there any marks on them?" I asked.

He showed me two letters stamped in indelible ink on the band of a skirt. I did not have my glasses with me, but the ink was black, and I read O. R. "The minx's initials," thought I.

When I left the place my complacency was such that Lena did not know what to make of me. She has since informed me that I looked as if I wanted to shout Hurrah! but I cannot believe I so far forgot myself as that. But pleased as I was, I had only discovered how one bundle had been disposed of. The dress and outside fixings still had to be accounted for, and I was the woman to do it.

We had mechanically moved in the direction of the drug-store and were near the curb-stone when I reached this point in my meditations. It had rained a little while before, and a small stream was running down the gutter and emptying itself into the sewer opening. The sight of it sharpened my wits.

If I wanted to get rid of anything of a damaging character, I would drop it at the mouth of one of these holes and gently thrust it into the sewer with my foot, thought I. And never doubting that I had found an explanation of the disappearance of the second bundle, I walked on, deciding that if I had the police at my command I would have the sewer searched at those four corners.

We rode home after visiting the drug-store. I was not going to subject Lena or myself to another midnight walk through Twenty-seventh Street.

FOOTNOTES:

This was so probable, it cannot be considered an untruth.—A. B.

XXII   A BLANK CARD

The next day at noon Lena brought me up a card on her tray. It was a perfectly blank one.

"Miss Van Burnam's maid said you sent for this," was her demure announcement.

"Miss Van Burnam's maid is right," said I, taking the card and with it a fresh installment of courage.

Nothing happened for two days, then there came word from the kitchen that a bushel of potatoes had arrived. Going down to see them, I drew from their midst a large square envelope, which I immediately carried to my room. It failed to contain a photograph; but there was a letter in it couched in these terms:

"DEAR MISS BUTTERWORTH:

"The esteem which you are good enough to express for me is returned. I regret that I cannot oblige you. There are no photographs to be found in Mrs. Van Burnam's rooms. Perhaps this fact may be accounted for by the curiosity shown in those apartments by a very spruce new boarder we have had from New York. His taste for that particular quarter of the house was such that I could not keep him away from it except by lock and key. If there was a picture there of Mrs. Van Burnam, he took it, for he departed very suddenly one night. I am glad he took nothing more with him. The talks he had with my servant-girl have almost led to my dismissing her.

"Praying your pardon for the disappointment I am forced to give you, I remain,

"Yours sincerely,

"SUSAN FERGUSON."

So! so! balked by an emissary of Mr. Gryce. Well, well, we would do without the photograph! Mr. Gryce might need it, but not Amelia Butterworth.

This was on a Thursday, and on the evening of Saturday the long-desired clue was given me. It came in the shape of a letter brought me by Mr. Alvord.

Our interview was not an agreeable one. Mr. Alvord is a clever man and an adroit one, or I should not persist in employing him as my lawyer; but he never understood me. At this time, and with this letter in his hand, he understood me less than ever, which naturally called out my powers of self-assertion and led to some lively conversation between us. But that is neither here nor there. He had brought me an answer to my advertisement and I was presently engrossed by it. It was an uneducated woman's epistle and its chirography and spelling were dreadful; so I will just mention its contents, which were highly interesting in themselves, as I think you will acknowledge.

She, that is, the writer, whose name, as nearly as I could make out, was Bertha Desberger, knew such a person as I described, and could give me news of her if I would come to her house in West Ninth Street at four o'clock Sunday afternoon.

If I would! I think my face must have shown my satisfaction, for Mr. Alvord, who was watching me, sarcastically remarked:

"You don't seem to find any difficulties in that communication. Now, what do you think of this one?"

He held out another letter which had been directed to him, and which he had opened. Its contents called up a shade of color to my cheek, for I did not want to go through the annoyance of explaining myself again:

"DEAR SIR:

"From a strange advertisement which has lately appeared in the Herald, I gather that information is wanted of a young woman who on the morning of the eighteenth inst.

entered my store without any bonnet on her head, and saying she had met with an accident, bought a hat which she immediately put on. She was pale as a girl could be and looked so ill that I asked her if she was well enough to be out alone; but she gave me no reply and left the store as soon as possible. That is all I can tell you about her."

With this was enclosed his card:

PHINEAS COX, Millinery,
Trimmed and Untrimmed Hats,
—— Sixth Avenue.

"Now, what does this mean?" asked Mr. Alvord. "The morning of the eighteenth was the morning when the murder was discovered in which you have shown such interest."

"It means," I retorted with some spirit, for simple dignity was thrown away on this man, "that I made a mistake in choosing your office as a medium for my business communications."

This was to the point and he said no more, though he eyed the letter in my hand very curiously, and seemed more than tempted to renew the hostilities with which we had opened our interview.

Had it not been Saturday, and late in the day at that, I would have visited Mr. Cox's store before I slept, but as it was I felt obliged to wait till Monday. Meanwhile I had before me the still more important interview with Mrs. Desberger.

As I had no reason to think that my visiting any number in Ninth Street would arouse suspicion in the police, I rode there quite boldly the next day, and with Lena at my side, entered the house of Mrs. Bertha Desberger.

For this trip I had dressed myself plainly, and drawn over my eyes—and the puffs which I still think it becoming in a woman of my age to wear—a dotted veil, thick enough to conceal my features, without robbing me of that aspect of benignity necessary to the success of my mission. Lena wore her usual neat gray dress, and looked the picture of all the virtues.

A large brass door-plate, well rubbed, was the first sign vouchsafed us of the respectability of the house we were about to enter; and the parlor, when we were ushered into it, fully carried out the promise thus held forth on the door-step. It was respectable, but in wretched taste as regards colors. I, who have the nicest taste in such matters, looked about me in dismay as I encountered the greens and blues, the crimsons and the purples which everywhere surrounded me.

But I was not on a visit to a temple of art, and resolutely shutting my eyes to the offending splendor about me—worsted splendor, you understand,—I waited with subdued expectation for the lady of the house.

She came in presently, bedecked in a flowered gown that was an epitome of the blaze of colors everywhere surrounding us; but her face was a good one, and I saw that I had neither guile nor over-much shrewdness to contend with.

She had seen the coach at the door, and she was all smiles and flutter.

"You have come for the poor girl who stopped here a few days ago," she began, glancing from my face to Lena's with an equally inquiring air, which in itself would have shown her utter ignorance of social distinctions if I had not bidden Lena to keep at my side and hold her head up as if she had business there as well as myself.

"Yes," returned I, "we have. Lena here, has lost a relative (which was true), and knowing no other way of finding her, I suggested the insertion of an advertisement in the paper. You read the description given, of course. Has the person answering it been in this house?"

"Yes; she came on the morning of the eighteenth. I remember it because that was the very day my cook left, and I have not got another one yet." She sighed and went on. "I took a great interest in that unhappy young woman—Was she your sister?" This, somewhat doubtfully, to Lena, who perhaps had too few colors on to suit her.

"No," answered Lena, "she wasn't my sister, but———"

I immediately took the words out of her mouth.

"At what time did she come here, and how long did she stay? We want to find her very much. Did she give you any name, or tell where she was going?"

"She said her name was Oliver." (I thought of the O. R. on the clothes at the laundry.) "But I knew this wasn't so; and if she had not looked so very modest, I might have hesitated to take her in. But, lor! I can't resist a girl in trouble, and she was in trouble, if ever a girl was. And then she had money—Do you know what her trouble was?" This again to Lena, and with an air at once suspicious and curious. But Lena has a good face, too, and her frank eyes at once disarmed the weak and good-natured woman before us.

"I thought"—she went on before Lena could answer—"that whatever it was, you had nothing to do with it, nor this lady either."

"No," answered Lena, seeing that I wished her to do the talking. "And we don't know" (which was true enough so far as Lena went) "just what her trouble was. Didn't she tell you?"

"She told nothing. When she came she said she wanted to stay with me a little while. I sometimes take boarders———" She had twenty in the house at that minute, if she had one. Did she think I couldn't see the length of her dining-room table through the crack of the parlor door? "'I can pay,' she said, which I had not doubted, for her blouse was a very expensive one; though I thought her skirt looked queer, and her hat—Did I say she had a hat on? You seemed to doubt that fact in your advertisement. Goodness me! if she had had no hat on, she wouldn't have got as far as my parlor mat. But her blouse showed her to be a lady—and then her face—it was as white as your handkerchief there, madam, but so sweet—I thought of the Madonna faces I had seen in Catholic churches."

I started; inwardly commenting: "Madonna-like, that woman!" But a glance at the room about me reassured me. The owner of such hideous sofas and chairs and of the many pictures effacing or rather defacing the paper on the walls, could not be a judge of Madonna faces.

"You admire everything that is good and lovely," I suggested, for Mrs. Desberger had paused at the movement I made.

"Yes, it is my nature to do so, ma'am. I love the beautiful," and she cast a half-apologetic, half-proud look about her. "So I listened to the girl and let her sit down in my parlor. She had had nothing to eat that morning, and though she didn't ask for it, I went to order her a cup of tea, for I knew she couldn't get up-stairs without it. Her eyes followed me when I went out of the room in a way that haunted me, and when I came back—I shall never forget it, ma'am—there she lay stretched out on the floor with her face on the ground and her hands thrown out. Wasn't it horrible, ma'am? I don't wonder you shudder."

Did I shudder? If I did, it was because I was thinking of that other woman, the victim of this one, whom I had seen, with her face turned upward and her arms outstretched, in the gloom of Mr. Van Burnam's half-closed parlor.

"She looked as if she was dead," the good woman continued, "but just as I was about to call for help, her fingers moved and I rushed to lift her. She was neither dead nor had she fainted; she was simply dumb with misery. What could have happened to her? I have asked myself a hundred times."

My mouth was shut very tight, but I shut it still tighter, for the temptation was great to cry: "She had just committed murder!" As it was, no sound whatever left my lips, and the good woman doubtless thought me no better than a stone, for she turned with a shrug to Lena, repeating still more wistfully than before:

"Don't you know what her trouble was?"

But, of course, poor Lena had nothing to say, and the woman went on with a sigh:

"Well, I suppose I shall never know what had used that poor creature up so completely. But whatever it was, it gave me enough trouble, though I do not want to complain of it, for why are we here, if not to help and comfort the miserable. It was an hour, ma'am; it was an hour, miss, before I could get that poor girl to speak; but when I did succeed, and had got her to drink the tea and eat a bit of toast, then I felt quite repaid by the look of gratitude she gave me and the way she clung to my sleeve when I tried to leave her for a minute. It was this sleeve, ma'am," she explained, lifting a cluster of rainbow flounces and ribbons which but a minute before had looked little short of ridiculous in my eyes, but which in the light of the wearer's kind-heartedness had lost some of their offensive appearance.

"Poor Mary!" murmured Lena, with what I considered most admirable presence of mind.

"What name did you say?" cried Mrs. Desberger, eager enough to learn all she could of her late mysterious lodger.

"I had rather not tell her name," protested Lena, with a timid air that admirably fitted her rather doll-like prettiness. "She didn't tell you what it was, and I don't think I ought to."

Good for little Lena! And she did not even know for whom or what she was playing the rôle I had set her.

"I thought you said Mary. But I won't be inquisitive with you. I wasn't so with her. But where was I in my story? Oh, I got her so she could speak, and afterwards I helped her upstairs; but she didn't stay there long. When I came back at lunch time—I have to do my marketing no matter what happens—I found her sitting before a table with her head on her hands. She had been weeping, but her face was quite composed now and almost hard.

"'O you good woman!' she cried as I came in. 'I want to thank you.' But I wouldn't let her go on wasting words like that, and presently she was saying quite wildly: 'I want to begin a new life. I want to act as if I had never had a yesterday. I have had trouble, overwhelming trouble, but I will get something out of existence yet. I will live, and in order to do so, I will work. Have you a paper, Mrs. Desberger, I want to look at the advertisements?' I brought her a Herald and went to preside at my lunch table. When I saw her again she looked almost cheerful. 'I have found just what I want,' she cried, 'a companion's place. But I cannot apply in this dress,' and she looked at the great puffs of her silk blouse as if they gave her the horrors, though why, I cannot imagine, for they were in the latest style and rich enough for a millionaire's daughter, though as to colors I like brighter ones myself. 'Would you'—she was very timid about it—'buy me some things if I gave you the money?'

"If there is one thing more than another that I like, it is to shop, so I expressed my willingness to oblige her, and that afternoon I set out with a nice little sum of money to buy her some clothes. I should have enjoyed it more if she had let me do my own choosing—I saw the loveliest pink and green blouse—but she was very set about what she wanted, and so I just got her some plain things which I think even you, ma'am, would have approved of. I brought them home myself, for she wanted to apply immediately for the place she had seen advertised, but, O dear, when I went up to her room——"

"Was she gone?" burst in Lena.

"O no, but there was such a smudge in it, and—and I could cry when I think of it—there in the grate were the remains of her beautiful silk blouse, all smoking and ruined. She had tried to burn it, and she had succeeded too. I could not get a piece out as big as my hand."

"But you got some of it!" blurted out Lena, guided by a look which I gave her.

"Yes, scraps, it was so handsome. I think I have a bit in my work-basket now."

"O get it for me," urged Lena. "I want it to remember her by."

"My work-basket is here." And going to a sort of etagère covered with a thousand knick-knacks picked up at bargain counters, she opened a little cupboard and brought out a basket, from which she presently pulled a small square of silk. It was, as she said, of the richest weaving, and was, as I had not the least doubt, a portion of the dress worn by Mrs. Van Burnam from Haddam.

"Yes, it was hers," said Lena, reading the expression of my face, and putting the scrap away very carefully in her pocket.

"Well, I would have given her five dollars for that blouse," murmured Mrs. Desberger, regretfully. "But girls like her are so improvident."

"And did she leave that day?" I asked, seeing that it was hard for this woman to tear her thoughts away from this coveted article.

"Yes, ma'am. It was late, and I had but little hopes of her getting the situation she was after. But she promised to come back if she didn't; and as she did not come back I decided that she was more successful than I had anticipated."

"And don't you know where she went? Didn't she confide in you at all?"

"No; but as there were but three advertisements for a lady-companion in the Herald that day, it will be easy to find her. Would you like to see those advertisements? I saved them out of curiosity."

I assented, as you may believe, and she brought us the clippings at once. Two of them I read without emotion, but the third almost took my breath away. It was an advertisement for a lady-companion accustomed to the typewriter and of some taste in dressmaking, and the address given was that of Miss Althorpe.

If this woman, steeped in misery and darkened by crime, should be there!

As I shall not mention Mrs. Desberger again for some time, I will here say that at the first opportunity which presented itself I sent Lena to the shops with orders to buy and have sent to Mrs. Desberger the ugliest and most flaunting of silk blouses that could be found on Sixth Avenue; and as Lena's dimples were more than usually pronounced on her return, I have no doubt she chose one to suit the taste and warm the body of the estimable woman, whose kindly nature had made such a favorable impression upon me.

XXIII   RUTH OLIVER

From Mrs. Desberger's I rode immediately to Miss Althorpe's, for the purpose of satisfying myself at once as to the presence there of the unhappy fugitive I was tracing.

Six o'clock Sunday night is not a favorable hour for calling at a young lady's house, especially when that lady has a lover who is in the habit of taking tea with the family. But I was in a mood to transgress all rules and even to forget the rights of lovers. Besides, much is forgiven a woman of my stamp, especially by a person of the good sense and amiability of Miss Althorpe.

That I was not mistaken in my calculations was evident from the greeting I received. Miss Althorpe came forward as graciously and with as little surprise in her manner as any one could expect under the circumstances, and for a moment I was so touched by her beauty and the unaffected charm of her manners that I forgot my errand and only thought of the pleasure of meeting a lady who fairly comes up to the standard one has secretly set for one's self. Of course she is much younger than I—some say she is only twenty-three; but a lady is a lady at any age, and Ella Althorpe might be a model for a much older woman than myself.

The room in which we were seated was a large one, and though I could hear Mr. Stone's voice in the adjoining apartment, I did not fear to broach the subject I had come to discuss.

"You may think this intrusion an odd one," I began, "but I believe you advertised a few days ago for a young lady-companion. Have you been suited, Miss Althorpe?"

"O yes; I have a young person with me whom I like very much."

"Ah, you are supplied! Is she any one you know?"

"No, she is a stranger, and what is more, she brought no recommendations with her. But her appearance is so attractive and her desire for the place was so great, that I consented to try her. And she is very satisfactory, poor girl! very satisfactory indeed!"

Ah, here was an opportunity for questions. Without showing too much eagerness and yet with a proper show of interest, I smilingly remarked:

"No one can be called poor long who remains under your roof, Miss Althorpe. But perhaps she has lost friends; so many nice girls are thrown upon their own resources by the death of relatives?"

"She does not wear mourning; but she is in some great trouble for all that. But this cannot interest you, Miss Butterworth; have you some protégé whom you wished to recommend for the position?"

I heard her, but did not answer at once. In fact, I was thinking how to proceed. Should I take her into my confidence, or should I continue in the ambiguous manner in which I had begun. Seeing her smile, I became conscious of the awkward silence.

"Pardon me," said I, resuming my best manner, "but there is something I want to say which may strike you as peculiar."

"O no," said she.

"I am interested in the girl you have befriended, and for very different reasons from those you suppose. I fear—I have great reason to fear—that she is not just the person you would like to harbor under your roof."

"Indeed! Why, what do you know about her? Anything bad, Miss Butterworth?"

I shook my head, and prayed her first to tell me how the girl looked and under what circumstances she came to her; for I was desirous of making no mistake concerning her identity with the person of whom I was in search.

"She is a sweet-looking girl," was the answer I received; "not beautiful, but interesting in expression and manner. She has brown hair,"—I shuddered,—"brown eyes, and a mouth that would be lovely if it ever smiled. In fact, she is very attractive and so lady-like that I have desired to make a companion of her. But while attentive to all her duties, and manifestly grateful to me for the home I have given her, she shows so little desire for company or conversation that I have desisted for the last day or so from urging her to speak at all. But you asked me under what circumstances she came to me?"

"Yes, on what day, and at what time of day? Was she dressed well, or did her clothes look shabby?"

"She came on the very day I advertised; the eighteenth—yes, it was the eighteenth of this month; and she was dressed, so far as I noticed, very neatly. Indeed, her clothes appeared to be new. They needed to have been, for she brought nothing with her save what was contained in a small hand-bag."

"Also new?" I suggested.

"Very likely; I did not observe."

"O Miss Althorpe!" I exclaimed, this time with considerable vehemence, "I fear, or rather I hope, she is the woman I want."

"You want!"

"Yes, I; but I cannot tell you for what just yet. I must be sure, for I would not subject an innocent person to suspicion any more than you would."

"Suspicion! She is not honest, then? That would worry me, Miss Butterworth, for the house is full now, as you know, of wedding presents, and—But I cannot believe such a thing of her. It is some other fault she has, less despicable and degrading."

"I do not say she has any faults; I only said I feared. What name does she go by?"

"Oliver; Ruth Oliver."

Again I thought of the O. R. on the clothes at the laundry.

"I wish I could see her," I ventured. "I would give anything for a peep at her face unobserved."

"I don't know how I can manage that; she is very shy, and never shows herself in the front of the house. She even dines in her own room, having begged for that privilege till after I was married and the household settled on a new basis. But you can go to her room with me. If she is all right, she can have no objection to a visitor; and if she is not, it would be well for me to know it at once."

"Certainly," said I, and rose to follow her, turning over in my mind how I should account to this young woman for my intrusion. I had just arrived at what I considered a sensible conclusion, when Miss Althorpe, leaning towards me, said with a whole-souled impetuosity for which I could not but admire her:

"The girl is very nervous, she looks and acts like a person who has had some frightful shock. Don't alarm her, Miss Butterworth, and don't accuse her of anything wrong too suddenly. Perhaps she is innocent, and perhaps if she is not innocent, she has been driven into evil by very great temptations. I am sorry for her, whether she is simply unhappy or deeply remorseful. For I never saw a sweeter face, or eyes with such boundless depths of misery in them."

Just what Mrs. Desberger had said! Strange, but I began to feel a certain sort of sympathy for the wretched being I was hunting down.

"I will be careful," said I. "I merely want to satisfy myself that she is the same girl I heard of last from a Mrs. Desberger."

Miss Althorpe, who was now half-way up the rich staircase which makes her house one of the most remarkable in the city, turned and gave me a quick look over her shoulder.

"I don't know Mrs. Desberger," she remarked.

At which I smiled. Did she think Mrs. Desberger in society?

At the end of an upper passage-way we paused.

"This is the door," whispered Miss Althorpe. "Perhaps I had better go in first and see if she is at all prepared for company."

I was glad to have her do so, for I felt as if I needed to prepare myself for encountering this young girl, over whom, in my mind, hung the dreadful suspicion of murder.

But the time between Miss Althorpe's knock and her entrance, short as it was, was longer than that which elapsed between her going in and her hasty reappearance.

"You can have your wish," said she. "She is lying on her bed asleep, and you can see her without being observed. But," she entreated, with a passionate grip of my arm, which proclaimed her warm nature, "doesn't it seem a little like taking advantage of her?"

"Circumstances justify it in this case," I replied, admiring the consideration of my hostess, but not thinking it worth while to emulate it. And with very little ceremony I pushed open the door and entered the room of the so-called Ruth Oliver.

The hush and quiet which met me, though nothing more than I had reason to expect, gave me my first shock, and the young figure outstretched on a bed of dainty whiteness, my second. Everything about me was so peaceful, and the delicate blue and white of the room so expressive of innocence and repose, that my feet instinctively moved more softly over the polished floor and paused, when they did pause, before that dimly shrouded bed, with something like hesitation in their usually emphatic tread.

The face of that bed's occupant, which I could now plainly see, may have had an influence in producing this effect. It was so rounded with health, and yet so haggard with trouble. Not knowing whether Miss Althorpe was behind me or not, but too intent upon the sleeping girl to care, I bent over the half-averted features and studied them carefully.

They were indeed Madonna-like, something which I had not expected, notwithstanding the assurances I had received to that effect, and while distorted with suffering, amply accounted for the interest shown in her by the good-hearted Mrs. Desberger and the cultured Miss Althorpe.

Resenting this beauty, which so poorly accommodated itself to the character of the woman who possessed it, I leaned nearer, searching for some defect in her loveliness, when I saw that the struggle and anguish visible in her expression were due to some dream she was having.

Moved, even against my will, by the touching sight of her trembling eyelids and working mouth, I was about to wake her when I was stopped by the gentle touch of Miss Althorpe on my shoulder.

"Is she the girl you are looking for?"

I gave one quick glance around the room, and my eyes lighted on the little blue pin-cushion on the satin-wood bureau.

"Did you put those pins there?" I asked, pointing to a dozen or more black pins grouped in one corner.

"I did not, no; and I doubt if Crescenze did. Why?"

I drew a small black pin from my belt where I had securely fastened it, and carrying it over to the cushion, compared it with those I saw. They were identical.

"A small matter," I inwardly decided, "but it points in the right direction"; then, in answer to Miss Althorpe, added aloud: "I fear she is. At least I have seen no reason yet for doubting it. But I must make sure. Will you allow me to wake her?"

"O it seems cruel! She is suffering enough already. See how she twists and turns!"

"It will be a mercy, it seems to me, to rouse her from dreams so full of pain and trouble."

"Perhaps, but I will leave you alone to do it. What will you say to her? How account for your intrusion?"

"O I will find means, and they won't be too cruel either. You had better stand back by the bureau and listen. I think I had rather not have the responsibility of doing this thing alone."

Miss Althorpe, not understanding my hesitation, and only half comprehending my errand, gave me a doubtful look but retreated to the spot I had mentioned, and whether it was the rustle of her silk dress or whether the dream of the girl we were watching had reached its climax, a momentary stir took place in the outstretched form before me, and next moment she was flinging up her hands with a cry.

"O how can I touch her! She is dead, and I have never touched a dead body."

I fell back breathing hard, and Miss Althorpe's eyes, meeting mine, grew dark with horror. Indeed she was about to utter a cry herself, but I made an imperative motion, and she merely shrank farther away towards the door.

Meantime I had bent forward and laid my hand on the trembling figure before me.

"Miss Oliver," I said, "rouse yourself, I pray. I have a message for you from Mrs. Desberger."

She turned her head, looked at me like a person in a daze, then slowly moved and sat up.

"Who are you?" she asked, surveying me and the space about her with eyes which seemed to take in nothing till they lit upon Miss Althorpe's figure standing in an attitude of mingled shame and sympathy by the half-open door.

"Oh, Miss Althorpe!" she entreated, "I pray you to excuse me. I did not know you wanted me. I have been asleep."

"It is this lady who wants you," answered Miss Althorpe. "She is a friend of mine and one in whom you can confide."

"Confide!" This was a word to rouse her. She turned livid, and in her eyes as she looked my way both terror and surprise were visible. "Why should you think I had anything to confide? If I had, I should not pass by you, Miss Althorpe, for another."

There were tears in her voice, and I had to remember the victim just laid away in Woodlawn, not to bestow much more compassion on this woman than she rightfully deserved. She had a magnetic voice and a magnetic presence, but that was no reason why I should forget what she had done.

"No one asks for your confidence," I protested, "though it might not hurt you to accept a friend whenever you can get one. I merely wish, as I said before, to give you a message from Mrs. Desberger, under whose roof you stayed before coming here."

"I am obliged to you," she responded, rising to her feet, and trembling very much. "Mrs. Desberger is a kind woman; what does she want of me?"

So I was on the right track; she acknowledged Mrs. Desberger.

"Nothing but to return you this. It fell out of your pocket while you were dressing." And I handed her the little red pin-cushion I had taken from the Van Burnams' front room.

She looked at it, shrunk violently back, and with difficulty prevented herself from showing the full depth of her feelings.

"I don't know anything about it. It is not mine, I don't know it!" And her hair stirred on her forehead as she gazed at the small object lying in the palm of my hand, proving to me that she saw again before her all the horrors of the house from which it had been taken.

"Who are you?" she suddenly demanded, tearing her eyes from this simple little cushion and fixing them wildly on my face. "Mrs. Desberger never sent me this. I——"

"You are right to stop there," I interposed, and then paused, feeling that I had forced a situation which I hardly knew how to handle.

The instant's pause she had given herself seemed to restore her self-possession. Leaving me, she moved towards Miss Althorpe.

"I don't know who this lady is," said she, "or what her errand here with me may mean. But I hope that it is nothing that will force me to leave this house which is my only refuge."

Miss Althorpe, too greatly prejudiced in favor of this girl to hear this appeal unmoved, notwithstanding the show of guilt with which she had met my attack, smiled faintly as she answered:

"Nothing short of the best reasons would make me part from you now. If there are such reasons, you will spare me the pain of making use of them. I think I can so far trust you, Miss Oliver."

No answer; the young girl looked as if she could not speak.

"Are there any reasons why I should not retain you in my house, Miss Oliver?" the gentle mistress of many millions went on. "If there are, you will not wish to stay, I know, when you consider how near my marriage day is, and how undisturbed my mind should be by any cares unattending my wedding."

And still the girl was silent, though her lips moved slightly as if she would have spoken if she could.

"But perhaps you are only unfortunate," suggested Miss Althorpe, with an almost angelic look of pity—I don't often see angels in women. "If that is so, God forbid that you should leave my protection or my house. What do you say, Miss Oliver?"

"That you are God's messenger to me," burst from the other, as if her tongue had been suddenly loosed. "That misfortune, and not wickedness, has driven me to your doors; and that there is no reason why I should leave you unless my secret sufferings make my presence unwelcome to you."

Was this the talk of a frivolous woman caught unawares in the meshes of a fearful crime? If so, she was a more accomplished actress than we had been led to expect even from her own words to her disgusted husband.

"You look like one accustomed to tell the truth," proceeded Miss Althorpe. "Do you not think you have made some mistake, Miss Butterworth?" she asked, approaching me with an ingenuous smile.

I had forgotten to caution her not to make use of my name, and when it fell from her lips I looked to see her unhappy companion recoil from me with a scream.

But strange to say she evinced no emotion, and seeing this, I became more distrustful of her than ever; for, for her to hear without apparent interest the name of the chief witness in the inquest which had been held over the remains of the woman with whose death she had been more or less intimately concerned, argued powers of duplicity such as are only associated with guilt or an extreme simplicity of character. And she was not simple, as the least glance from her deep eyes amply showed.

Recognizing, therefore, that open measures would not do with this woman, I changed my manner at once, and responding to Miss Althorpe, with a gracious smile, remarked with an air of sudden conviction:

"Perhaps I have made some mistake. Miss Oliver's words sound very ingenuous, and I am disposed, if you are, to take her at her word. It is so easy to draw false conclusions in this world." And I put back the pin-cushion into my pocket with an air of being through with the matter, which seemed to impose upon the young woman, for she smiled faintly, showing a row of splendid teeth as she did so.

"Let me apologize," I went on, "if I have intruded upon Miss Oliver against her wishes." And with one comprehensive look about the room which took in all that was visible of her simple wardrobe and humble belongings, I led the way out. Miss Althorpe immediately followed.

"This is a much more serious affair than I have led you to suppose," I confided to her as soon as we were at a suitable distance from Miss Oliver's door. "If she is the person I think her, she is amenable to law, and the police will have to be notified of her whereabouts."

"She has stolen, then?"

"Her fault is a very grave one," I returned.

Miss Althorpe, deeply troubled, looked about her as if for guidance. I, who could have given it to her, made no movement to attract her attention to myself, but waited calmly for her own decision in this matter.

"I wish you would let me consult Mr. Stone," she ventured at last. "I think his judgment might help us."

"I had rather take no one into our confidence,—especially no man. He would consider your welfare only and not hers."

I did not consider myself obliged to acknowledge that the work upon which I was engaged could not be shared by one of the male sex without lessening my triumph over Mr. Gryce.

"Mr. Stone is very just," she remarked, "but he might be biased in a matter of this kind. What way do you see out of the difficulty?"

"Only this. To settle at once and unmistakably, whether she is the person who carried certain articles from the house of a friend of mine. If she is, there will be some evidence of the fact visible in her room or on her person. She has not been out, I believe?"

"Not since she came into the house."

"And has remained for the most part in her own apartment?"

"Always, except when I have summoned her to my assistance."

"Then what I want to know I can learn there. But how can I make my investigations without offence?"

"What do you want to know, Miss Butterworth?"

"Whether she has in her keeping some half dozen rings of considerable value."

"Oh! she could conceal rings so easily."

"She does conceal them; I have no more doubt of it than I have of my standing here; but I must know it before I shall feel ready to call the attention of the police to her."

"Yes, we should both know it. Poor girl! poor girl! to be suspected of a crime! How great must have been her temptation!"

"I can manage this matter, Miss Althorpe, if you will entrust it to me."

"How, Miss Butterworth?"

"The girl is ill; let me take care of her."

"Really ill?"

"Yes, or will be so before morning. There is fever in her veins; she has worried herself ill. Oh, I will be good to her."

This in answer to a doubtful look from Miss Althorpe.

"This is a difficult problem you have set me," that lady remarked after a moment's thought. "But anything seems better than sending her away, or sending for the police. But do you suppose she will allow you in her room?"

"I think so; if her fever increases she will not notice much that goes on about her, and I think it will increase; I have seen enough of sickness to be something of a judge."

"And you will search her while she is unconscious?"

"Don't look so horrified, Miss Althorpe. I have promised you I will not worry her. She may need assistance in getting to bed. While I am giving it to her I can judge if there is anything concealed upon her person."

"Yes, perhaps."

"At all events, we shall know more than we do now. Shall I venture, Miss Althorpe?"

"I cannot say no," was the hesitating answer; "you seem so very much in earnest."

"And I am in earnest. I have reasons for being; consideration for you is one of them."

"I do not doubt it. And now will you come down to supper, Miss Butterworth?"

"No," I replied. "My duty is here. Only send word to Lena that she is to drive home and take care of my house in my absence. I shall want nothing, so do not worry about me. Join your lover now, dear; and do not bestow another thought upon this self-styled Miss Oliver or what I am about to do in her room."

XXIV   A HOUSE OF CARDS

I did not return immediately to my patient. I waited till her supper came up. Then I took the tray, and assured by the face of the girl who brought it that Miss Althorpe had explained my presence in her house sufficiently for me to feel at my ease before her servants, I carried in the dainty repast she had provided and set it down on the table.

The poor woman was standing where we had left her; but her whole figure showed languor, and she more than leaned against the bedpost behind her. As I looked up from the tray and met her eyes, she shuddered and seemed to be endeavoring to understand who I was and what I was doing in her room. My premonitions in regard to her were well based. She was in a raging fever, and was already more than half oblivious to her surroundings.

Approaching her, I spoke as gently as I could, for her hapless condition appealed to me in spite of my well founded prejudices against her; and seeing she was growing incapable of response, I drew her up on the bed and began to undress her.

I half expected her to recoil at this, or at least to make some show of alarm, but she submitted to my ministrations almost gratefully, and neither shrank nor questioned me till I laid my hands upon her shoes. Then indeed she quivered, and drew her feet away with such an appearance of terror that I was forced to desist from my efforts or drive her into violent delirium.

This satisfied me that Louise Van Burnam lay before me. The scar concerning which so much had been said in the papers would be ever present in the thoughts of this woman as the tell-tale mark by which she might be known, and though at this moment she was on the borders of unconsciousness, the instinct of self-preservation still remained in sufficient force to prompt her to make this effort to protect herself from discovery.

I had told Miss Althorpe that my chief reason for intruding upon Miss Oliver, was to determine if she had in her possession certain rings supposed to have been taken from a friend of mine; and while this was in a measure true—the rings being an important factor in the proof I was accumulating against her,—I was not so anxious to search for them at this time as to find the scar which would settle at once the question of her identity.

When she drew her foot away from me then, so violently, I saw that I needed to search no farther for the evidence required, and could give myself up to making her comfortable. So I bathed her temples, now throbbing with heat, and soon had the satisfaction of seeing her fall into a deep and uneasy slumber. Then I tried again to draw off her shoes, but the start she gave and the smothered cry which escaped her warned me that I must wait yet longer before satisfying my curiosity; so I desisted at once, and out of pure compassion left her to get what good she might from the lethargy into which she had fallen.

Being hungry, or at least feeling the necessity of some slight aliment to help me sustain the fatigues of the night, I sat down now at the table and partook of some of the dainties with which Miss Althorpe had kindly provided me. After which I made out a list of such articles as were necessary to my proper care of the patient who had so strangely fallen into my hands, and then, feeling that I had a right at last to indulge in pure curiosity, I turned my attention to the clothing I had taken from the self-styled Miss Oliver.

The dress was a simple gray one, and the skirts and underclothing all white. But the latter was of the finest texture, and convinced me, before I had given them more than a glance, that they were the property of Howard Van Burnam's wife. For, besides the exquisite quality of the material, there were to be seen, on the edges of the bands and sleeves, the marks of stitches and clinging threads of lace, where the trimming had been torn off, and in one article especially, there were tucks such as you see come from the hands of French needlewomen only.

This, taken with what had gone before, was proof enough to satisfy me that I was on the right track, and after Crescenze had come and gone with the tray and all was quiet in this remote part of the house, I ventured to open a closet door at the foot of the bed. A brown silk skirt was hanging within, and in the pocket of that skirt I found a purse so gay and costly that all doubt vanished as to its being the property of Howard's luxurious wife.

There were several bills in this purse, amounting to about fifteen dollars in money, but no change and no memoranda, which latter seemed a pity. Restoring the purse to its place and the skirt to its peg, I came softly back to the bedside and examined my patient still more carefully than I had done before. She was asleep and breathing heavily, but even with this disadvantage her face had its own attraction, an attraction which evidently had more or less influenced men, and which, for the reason perhaps that I have something masculine in my nature, I discovered to be more or less influencing me, notwithstanding my hatred of an intriguing character.

However, it was not her beauty I came to study, but her hair, her complexion, and her hands. The former was brown, the brown of that same lock I remembered to have seen in the jury's hands at the inquest; and her skin, where fever had not flushed it, was white and smooth. So were her hands, and yet they were not a lady's hands. That I noticed when I first saw her. The marks of the rings she no longer wore, were not enough to blind me to the fact that her fingers lacked the distinctive shape and nicety of Miss Althorpe's, say, or even of the Misses Van Burnam's; and though I do not object to this, for I like strong-looking, capable hands myself, they served to help me understand the face, which otherwise would have looked too spiritual for a woman of the peevish and self-satisfied character of Louise Van Burnam. On this innocent and appealing expression she had traded in her short and none too happy career. And as I noted it, I recalled a sentence in Miss Ferguson's testimony, in which she alluded to Mrs. Van Burnam's confidential remark to her husband upon the power she exercised over people when she raised her eyes in entreaty towards them. "Am I not pretty," she had said, "when I am in distress and looking up in this way?" It was the suggestion of a scheming woman, but from what I had seen and was seeing of the woman before me, I could imagine the picture she would thus make, and I do not think she overrated its effects.

Withdrawing from her side once more, I made a tour of the room. Nothing escaped my eyes; nothing was too small to engage my attention. But while I failed to see anything calculated to shake my confidence in the conclusions I had come to, I saw but little to confirm them. This was not strange; for, apart from a few toilet articles and some knitting-work on a shelf, she appeared to have no belongings; everything else in sight being manifestly the property of Miss Althorpe. Even the bureau drawers were empty, and her bag, found under a small table, had not so much in it as a hair-pin, though I searched it inside and out for her rings, which I was positive she had with her, even if she dared not wear them.

When every spot was exhausted I sat down and began to brood over what lay before this poor being, whose flight and the great efforts she made at concealment proved only too conclusively the fatal part she had played in the crime for which her husband had been arrested. I had reached her arraignment before a magistrate, and was already imagining her face with the appeal in it which such an occasion would call forth, when there came a low knock at the door, and Miss Althorpe re-entered.

She had just said good-night to her lover, and her face recalled to me a time when my own cheek was round and my eye was bright and—Well! what is the use of dwelling on matters so long buried in oblivion! A maiden-woman, as independent as myself, need not envy any girl the doubtful blessing of a husband. I chose to be independent, and I am, and what more is there to be said about it? Pardon the digression.

"Is Miss Oliver any better?" asked Miss Althorpe; "and have you found——"

I put up my finger in warning. Of all things, it was most necessary that the sick woman should not know my real reason for being there.

"She is asleep," I answered quietly, "and I think I have found out what is the matter with her."

Miss Althorpe seemed to understand. She cast a look of solicitude towards the bed and then turned towards me.

"I cannot rest," said she, "and will sit with you for a little while, if you don't mind."

I felt the implied compliment keenly.

"You can do me no greater favor," I returned.

She drew up an easy-chair. "That is for you," she smiled, and sat down in a little low rocker at my side.

But she did not talk. Her thoughts seemed to have recurred to some very near and sweet memory, for she smiled softly to herself and looked so deeply happy that I could not resist saying:

"These are delightful days for you, Miss Althorpe."

She sighed softly—how much a sigh can reveal!—and looked up at me brightly. I think she was glad I spoke. Even such reserved natures as hers have their moments of weakness, and she had no mother or sister to appeal to.

"Yes," she replied, "I am very happy; happier than most girls are, I think, just before marriage. It is such a revelation to me—this devotion and admiration from one I love. I have had so little of it in my life. My father——"

She stopped; I knew why she stopped. I gave her a look of encouragement.

"People have always been anxious for my happiness, and have warned me against matrimony since I was old enough to know the difference between poverty and wealth. Before I was out of short dresses I was warned against fortune-seekers. It was not good advice; it has stood in the way of my happiness all my life, made me distrustful and unnaturally reserved. But now—ah, Miss Butterworth, Mr. Stone is so estimable a man, so brilliant and so universally admired, that all my doubts of manly worth and disinterestedness have disappeared as if by magic. I trust him implicitly, and—Do I talk too freely? Do you object to such confidences as these?"

"On the contrary," I answered. I liked Miss Althorpe so much and agreed with her so thoroughly in her opinion of this man, that it was a real pleasure to me to hear her speak so unreservedly.

"We are not a foolish couple," she went on, warming with the charm of her topic till she looked beautiful in the half light thrown upon her by the shaded lamp. "We are interested in people and things, and get half our delight from the perfect congeniality of our natures. Mr. Stone has given up his club and all his bachelor pursuits since he knew me, and——"

O love, if at any time in my life I have despised thee, I did not despise thee then! The look with which she finished this sentence would have moved a cynic.

"Forgive me," she prayed. "It is the first time I have poured out my heart to any one of my own sex. It must sound strange to you, but it seemed natural while I was doing it, for you looked as if you could understand."

This to me, to me, Amelia Butterworth, of whom men have said I had no more sentiment than a wooden image. I looked my appreciation, and she, blushing slightly, whispered in a delicious tone of mingled shyness and pride:

"Only two weeks now, and I shall have some one to stand between me and the world. You have never needed any one, Miss Butterworth, for you do not fear the world, but it awes and troubles me, and my whole heart glows with the thought that I shall be no longer alone in my sorrows or my joys, my perplexities or my doubts. Am I to blame for anticipating this with so much happiness?"

I sighed. It was a less eloquent sigh than hers, but it was a distinct one and it had a distinct echo. Lifting my eyes, for I sat so as to face the bed, I was startled to observe my patient leaning towards us from her pillows, and staring upon us with eyes too hollow for tears but filled with unfathomable grief and yearning.

She had heard this talk of love, she, the forsaken and crime-stained one. I shuddered and laid my hand on Miss Althorpe's.

But I did not seek to stop the conversation, for as our looks met, the sick woman fell back and lapsed, or seemed to lapse, into immediate insensibility again.

"Is Miss Oliver worse?" inquired Miss Althorpe.

I rose and went to the bedside, renewed the bandages on my patient's head, and forced a drop or two of medicine between her half-shut lips.

"No," I returned, "I think her fever is abating." And it was, though the suffering on her face was yet heart-rendingly apparent.

"Is she asleep?"

"She seems to be."

Miss Althorpe made an effort.

"I am not going to talk any more about myself." Then as I came back and sat down by her side, she quietly asked:

"What do you think of the Van Burnam murder?"

Dismayed at the introduction of this topic, I was about to put my hand over her mouth, when I noticed that her words had made no evident impression upon my patient, who lay quietly and with a more composed expression than when I left her bedside. This assured me, as nothing else could have done, that she was really asleep, or in that lethargic state which closes the eyes and ears to what is going on.

"I think," said I, "that the young man Howard stands in a very unfortunate position. Circumstances certainly do look very black against him."

"It is dreadful, unprecedently dreadful. I do not know what to think of it all. The Van Burnams have borne so good a name, and Franklin especially is held in such high esteem. I don't think anything more shocking has ever happened in this city, do you, Miss Butterworth? You saw it all, and should know. Poor, poor Mrs. Van Burnam!"

"She is to be pitied!" I remarked, my eyes fixed on the immovable face of my patient.

"When I heard that a young woman had been found dead in the Van Burnam mansion," Miss Althorpe pursued with such evident interest in this new theme that I did not care to interrupt her unless driven to it by some token of consciousness on the part of my patient, "my thoughts flew instinctively to Howard's wife. Though why, I cannot say, for I never had any reason to expect so tragic a termination to their marriage relations. And I cannot believe now that he killed her, can you, Miss Butterworth? Howard has too much of the gentleman in him to do a brutal thing, and there was brutality as well as adroitness in the perpetration of this crime. Have you thought of that, Miss Butterworth?"

"Yes," I nodded, "I have looked at the crime on all sides."

"Mr. Stone," said she, "feels dreadfully over the part he was forced to play at the inquest. But he had no choice, the police would have his testimony."

"That was right," I declared.

"It has made us doubly anxious to have Howard free himself. But he does not seem able to do so. If his wife had only known——"

Was there a quiver in the lids I was watching? I half raised my hand and then I let it drop again, convinced that I had been mistaken. Miss Althorpe at once continued:

"She was not a bad-hearted woman, only vain and frivolous. She had set her heart on ruling in the great leather-merchant's house, and she did not know how to bear her disappointment. I have sympathy for her myself. When I saw her——"

Saw her! I started, upsetting a small work-basket at my side which for once I did not stop to pick up.

"You have seen her!" I repeated, dropping my eyes from the patient to fix them in my unbounded astonishment on Miss Althorpe's face.

"Yes, more than once. She was—if she were living I would not repeat this—a nursery governess in a family where I once visited. That was before her marriage; before she had met either Howard or Franklin Van Burnam."

I was so overwhelmed, that for once I found difficulty in speaking. I glanced from her to the white form in the shrouded bed, and back again in ever-growing astonishment and dismay.

"You have seen her!" I at last reiterated in what I meant to be a whisper, but which fell little short of being a cry, "and you took in this girl?"

Her surprise at this burst was almost equal to mine.

"Yes, why not; what have they in common?"

I sank back, my house of cards was trembling to its foundations.

"Do they—do they not look alike?" I gasped. "I thought—I imagined——"

"Louise Van Burnam look like that girl! O no, they were very different sort of women. What made you think there was any resemblance between them?"

I did not answer her; the structure I had reared with such care and circumspection had fallen about my ears and I lay gasping under the ruins.

XXV   "THE RINGS! WHERE ARE THE RINGS?"

Had Mr. Gryce been present, I would have instantly triumphed over my disappointment, bottled up my chagrin, and been the inscrutable Amelia Butterworth before he could say, "Something has gone wrong with this woman!" But Mr. Gryce was not present, and though I did not betray the half I felt, I yet showed enough emotion for Miss Althorpe to remark:

"You seemed surprised by what I have told you. Has any one said that these two women were alike?"

Having to speak, I became myself again in a trice, and nodded vigorously.

"Some one was so foolish," I remarked.

Miss Althorpe looked thoughtful. While she was interested she was not so interested as to take the subject in fully. Her own concerns made her abstracted, and I was very glad of it.

"Louise Van Burnam had a sharp chin and a very cold blue eye. Yet her face was a fascinating one to some."

"Well, it was a dreadful tragedy!" I observed, and tried to turn the subject aside, which fortunately I was able to do after a short effort.

Then I picked the basket up, and perceiving the sick woman's lips faintly moving, I went over to her and found her murmuring to herself.

As Miss Althorpe had risen when I did, I did not dare to listen to these murmurs, but when my charming hostess had bidden me good-night, with many injunctions not to tire myself, and to be sure and remember that a decanter and a plate of biscuits stood on a table outside, I hastened back to the bedside, and leaning over my patient, endeavored to catch the words as they fell from her lips.

As they were simple and but the echo of those running at that very moment through my own brain, I had no difficulty in distinguishing them.

"Van Burnam!" she was saying, "Van Burnam!" varied by a short "Howard!" and once by a doubtful "Franklin!"

"Ah," thought I, with a sudden reaction, "she is the woman I seek, if she is not Louise Van Burnam." And unheeding the start she gave, I pulled off the blanket I had spread over her, and willy-nilly drew off her left shoe and stocking.

Her bare ankle showed no scar, and covering it quickly up I took up her shoe. Immediately the trepidation she had shown at the approach of a stranger's hand towards that article of clothing was explained. In the lining around the top were sewn bills of no ordinary amount, and as the other shoe was probably used as a like depository, she naturally felt concern at any approach which might lead to a discovery of her little fortune.

Amazed at a mystery possessing so many points of interest, I tucked the shoe in under the bedclothes and sat down to review the situation.

The mistake I had made was in concluding that because the fugitive whose traces I had followed had worn the clothes of Louise Van Burnam, she must necessarily be that unfortunate lady. Now I saw that the murdered woman was Howard's wife after all, and this patient of mine her probable rival.

But this necessitated an entire change in my whole line of reasoning. If the rival and not the wife lay before me, then which of the two accompanied him to the scene of tragedy? He had said it was his wife; I had proven to myself that it was the rival; was he right, or was I right, or were neither of us right?

Not being able to decide, I fixed my mind upon another query. When did the two women exchange clothes, or rather, when did this woman procure the silk habiliments and elaborate adornments of her more opulent rival? Was it before either of them entered Mr. Van Burnam's house? Or was it after their encounter there?

Running over in my mind certain little facts of which I had hitherto attempted no explanation, I grouped them together and sought amongst them for inspiration.

These are the facts:

1. One of the garments found on the murdered woman had been torn down the back. As it was a new one, it had evidently been subjected to some quick strain, not explainable by any appearance of struggle.

2. The shoes and stockings found on the victim were the only articles she wore which could not be traced back to Altman's. In the re-dressing of the so-called Mrs. James Pope, these articles had not been changed. Could not that fact be explained by the presence of a considerable sum of money in her shoes?

3. The going out bareheaded of a fugitive, anxious to avoid observation, leaving hat and gloves behind her in a dining-room closet.

I had endeavored to explain this last anomalous action by her fear of being traced by so conspicuous an article as this hat; but it was not a satisfactory explanation to me then and much less so now.

4. And last, and most vital of all, the words which I had heard fall from this half-conscious girl: "O how can I touch her! She is dead, and I have never touched a dead body!"

Could inspiration fail me before such a list? Was it not evident that the change had been made after death, and by this seemingly sensitive girl's own hands?

It was a horrible thought and led to others more horrible. For the very commission of such a revolting act argued a desire for concealment only to be explained by great guilt. She had been the offender and the wife the victim; and Howard—Well, his actions continued to be a mystery, but I would not admit his guilt even now. On the contrary, I saw his innocence in a still stronger light. For if he had openly or even covertly connived at his wife's death, would he have so immediately forsaken the accomplice of his guilt, to say nothing of leaving to her the dreadful task of concealing the crime? No, I would rather think that the tragedy took place after his departure, and that his action in denying his wife's identity, as long as it was possible to do so, was to be explained by the fact of his ignorance in regard to his wife's presence in the house where he had supposed himself to have simply left her rival. As the exchange made in the clothing worn by the two women could only have taken place later, and as he naturally judged the victim by her clothing, perhaps he was really deceived himself as to her identity. It was certainly not an improbable supposition, and accounted for much that was otherwise inexplicable in Mr. Van Burnam's conduct.

But the rings? Why could I not find the rings? If my present reasoning were correct, this woman should have those evidences of guilt about her. But had I not searched for them in every available place without success? Annoyed at my failure to fix this one irrefutable proof of guilt upon her, I took up the knitting-work I saw in Miss Oliver's basket, and began to ply the needles by way of relief to my thoughts. But I had no sooner got well under way than some movement on the part of my patient drew my attention again to the bed, and I was startled by beholding her sitting up again, but this time with a look of fear rather than of suffering on her features.

"Don't!" she gasped, pointing with an unsteady hand at the work in my hand. "The click, click of the needles is more than I can stand. Put them down, pray; put them down!"

Her agitation was so great and her nervousness so apparent that I complied at once. However much I might be affected by her guilt, I was not willing to do the slightest thing to worry her nerves even at the expense of my own. As the needles fell from my hand, she sank back and a quick, short sigh escaped her lips. Then she was again quiet, and I allowed my thoughts to return to the old theme. The rings! the rings! Where were the rings, and was it impossible for me to find them?

XXVI   A TILT WITH MR. GRYCE

At seven o'clock the next morning my patient was resting so quietly that I considered it safe to leave her for a short time. So I informed Miss Althorpe that I was obliged to go down-town on an important errand, and requested Crescence to watch over the sick girl in my absence. As she agreed to this, I left the house as soon as breakfast was over and went immediately in search of Mr. Gryce. I wished to make sure that he knew nothing about the rings.

It was eleven o'clock before I succeeded in finding him. As I was certain that a direct question would bring no answer, I dissembled my real intention as much as my principles would allow, and accosted him with the eager look of one who has great news to impart.

"O, Mr. Gryce!" I impetuously cried, just as if I were really the weak woman he thought me, "I have found something; something in connection with the Van Burnam murder. You know I promised to busy myself about it if you arrested Howard Van Burnam."

His smile was tantalizing in the extreme. "Found something?" he repeated. "And may I ask if you have been so good as to trouble it with you?"

He was playing with me, this aged and reputable detective. I subdued my anger, subdued my indignation even, and smiling much in his own way, answered briefly:

"I never carry valuables on my person. A half-dozen expensive rings stand for too much money for me to run any undue risk with them."

He was caressing his watch-chain as I spoke, and I noticed that he paused in this action for just an infinitesimal length of time as I said the word rings. Then he went on as before, but I knew I had caught his attention.

"Of what rings do you speak, madam? Of those missing from Mrs. Van Burnam's hands?"

I took a leaf from his book, and allowed myself to indulge in a little banter.

"O, no," I remonstrated, "not those rings, of course. The Queen of Siam's rings, any rings but those in which we are specially interested."

This meeting him on his own ground evidently puzzled him.

"You are facetious, madam. What am I to gather from such levity? That success has crowned your efforts, and that you have found a guiltier party than the one now in custody?"

"Possibly," I returned, limiting my advance by his. "But it would be going too fast to mention that yet. What I want to know is whether you have found the rings belonging to Mrs. Van Burnam?"

My triumphant tone, the almost mocking accent I purposely gave to the word you, accomplished its purpose. He never dreamed I was playing with him; he thought I was bursting with pride; and casting me a sharp glance (the first, by the way, I had received from him), he inquired with perceptible interest:

"Have you?"

Instantly convinced that the whereabouts of these jewels was as little known to him as to me, I rose and prepared to leave. But seeing that he was not satisfied, and that he expected an answer, I assumed a mysterious air and quietly remarked:

"If you will come to my house to-morrow I will explain myself. I am not prepared to more than intimate my discoveries to-day."

But he was not the man to let one off so easily.

"Excuse me," said he, "but matters of this kind do not admit of delay. The grand jury sits within the week, and any evidence worth presenting them must be collected at once. I must ask you to be frank with me, Miss Butterworth."

"And I will be, to-morrow."

"To-day," he insisted, "to-day."

Seeing that I should gain nothing by my present course, I reseated myself, bestowing upon him a decidedly ambiguous smile as I did so.

"You acknowledge then," said I, "that the old maid can tell you something after all. I thought you regarded all my efforts in the light of a jest. What has made you change your mind?"

"Madam, I decline to bandy words. Have you found those rings, or have you not?"

"I have not," said I, "but neither have you, and as that is what I wanted to make sure of, I will now take my leave without further ceremony."

Mr. Gryce is not a profane man, but he allowed a word to slip from him which was not entirely one of blessing. He made amends for it next moment, however, by remarking:

"Madam, I once said, as you will doubtless remember, that the day would come when I should find myself at your feet. That day has arrived. And now is there any other little cherished fact known to the police which you would like to have imparted to you?"

I took his humiliation seriously.

"You are very good," I rejoined, "but I will not trouble you for any facts,—those I am enabled to glean for myself; but what I should like you to tell me is this: Whether if you came upon those rings in the possession of a person known to have been on the scene of crime at the time of its perpetration, you would not consider them as an incontrovertible proof of guilt?"

"Undoubtedly," said he, with a sudden alteration in his manner which warned me that I must muster up all my strength if I would keep my secret till I was quite ready to part with it.

"Then," said I, with a resolute movement towards the door, "that's the whole of my business for to-day. Good-morning, Mr. Gryce; to-morrow I shall expect you."

He made me stop though my foot had crossed the threshold; not by word or look but simply by his fatherly manner.

"Miss Butterworth," he observed, "the suspicions which you have entertained from the first have within the last few days assumed a definite form. In what direction do they point?—tell me."

Some men and most women would have yielded to that imperative tell me! But there was no yielding in Amelia Butterworth. Instead of that I treated him to a touch of irony.

"Is it possible," I asked, "that you think it worth while to consult me? I thought your eyes were too keen to seek assistance from mine. You are as confident as I am that Howard Van Burnam is innocent of the crime for which you have arrested him."

A look that was dangerously insinuating crossed his face at this. He came forward rapidly and, joining me where I stood, said smilingly:

"Let us join forces, Miss Butterworth. You have from the first refused to consider the younger son of Silas Van Burnam as guilty. Your reasons then were slight and hardly worth communicating. Have you any better ones to advance now? It is not too late to mention them, if you have."

"It will not be too late to-morrow," I retorted.

Convinced that I was not to be moved from my position, he gave me one of his low bows.

"I forgot," said he, "that it was as a rival and not as a coadjutor you meddled in this matter." And he bowed again, this time with a sarcastic air I felt too self-satisfied to resent.

"To-morrow, then?" said I.

"To-morrow."

At that I left him.

I did not return immediately to Miss Althorpe. I visited Cox's millinery store, Mrs. Desberger's house, and the offices of the various city railways. But I got no clue to the rings; and finally satisfied that Miss Oliver, as I must now call her, had not lost or disposed of them on her way from Gramercy Park to her present place of refuge, I returned to Miss Althorpe's with even a greater determination than before to search that luxurious home till I found them.

But a decided surprise awaited me. As the door opened I caught a glimpse of the butler's face, and noticing its embarrassed expression, I at once asked what had happened.

His answer showed a strange mixture of hesitation and bravado.

"Not much, ma'am; only Miss Althorpe is afraid you may not be pleased. Miss Oliver is gone, ma'am; she ran away while Crescenze was out of the room."

XXVII   FOUND

I gave a low cry and rushed down the steps.

"Don't go!" I called out to the driver. "I shall want you in ten minutes." And hurrying back, I ran up-stairs in a condition of mind such as I have no reason to be proud of. Happily Mr. Gryce was not there to see me.

"Gone? Miss Oliver gone?" I cried to the maid whom I found trembling in a corner of the hall.

"Yes, ma'am; it was my fault, ma'am. She was in bed so quiet, I thought I might step out for a minute, but when I came back her clothes were missing and she was gone. She must have slipped out at the front door while Dan was in the back hall. I don't see how ever she had the strength to do it."

Nor did I. But I did not stop to reason about it; there was too much to be done. Rushing on, I entered the room I had left in such high hopes a few hours before. Emptiness was before me, and I realized what it was to be baffled at the moment of success. But I did not waste an instant in inactivity. I searched the closets and pulled open the drawers; found her coat and hat gone, but not Mrs. Van Burnam's brown skirt, though the purse had been taken out of the pocket.

"Is her bag here?" I asked.

Yes, it was in its old place under the table; and on the wash-stand and bureau were the simple toilet articles I had been told she had brought there. In what haste she must have fled to leave these necessities behind her!

But the greatest shock I received was the sight of the knitting-work, with which I had so inconsiderately meddled the evening before, lying in ravelled heaps on the table, as if torn to bits in a frenzy. This was a proof that the fever was yet on her; and as I contemplated this fact I took courage, thinking that one in her condition would not be allowed to run the streets long, but would be picked up and put in some hospital.

In this hope I began my search. Miss Althorpe, who came in just as I was about to leave the house, consented to telephone to Police Headquarters a description of the girl, with a request to be notified if such a person should be found in the streets or on the docks or at any of the station-houses that night. "Not," I assured her, as we left the telephone and I prepared to say good-bye for the day, "that you need expect her to be brought back to this house, for I do not mean that she shall ever darken your doors again. So let me know if they find her, and I will relieve you of all further responsibility in the matter."

Then I started out.

To name the streets I traversed or the places I visited that day, would take more space than I would like to devote to the subject. Dusk came, and I had failed in obtaining the least clue to her whereabouts; evening followed, and still no trace of the fugitive. What was I to do? Take Mr. Gryce into my confidence after all? That would be galling to my pride, but I began to fear I should have to submit to this humiliation when I happened to think of the Chinaman. To think of him once was to think of him twice, and to think of him twice was to be conscious of an irresistible desire to visit his place and find out if any one but myself had been there to inquire after the lost one's clothes.

Accompanied by Lena, I hurried away to Third Avenue. The laundry was near Twenty-seventh Street. As we approached I grew troubled and unaccountably expectant. When we reached it I understood my excitement and instantly became calm. For there stood Miss Oliver, gazing like one under a spell through the lighted window-panes into the narrow shop where the owner bent over his ironing. She had evidently stood there some time, for a small group of half-grown lads were watching her with every symptom of being about to break into a mischievous display of curiosity. Her hands, which were without gloves, were pressed against the glass, and her whole attitude showed an intensity of fatigue which would have laid her on the ground had she not been sustained by an equal intensity of purpose.

Sending Lena for a carriage, I approached the poor creature and drew her forcibly from the window.

"Do you want anything here?" I asked. "I will go in with you if you do."

She surveyed me with strange apathy, and yet with a certain sort of relief too. Then she slowly shook her head.

"I don't know anything about it. My head swims and everything looks queer, but some one or something sent me to this place."

"Come in," I urged, "come in for a minute." And half supporting her, half dragging her, I managed to get her across the threshold and into the Chinaman's shop.

Immediately a dozen faces were pressed where hers had been.

The Chinaman, a stolid being, turned as he heard the little bell tinkle which announced a customer.

"Is this the lady who left the clothes here a few nights ago?" I asked.

He stopped and stared, recognizing me slowly, and remembering by degrees what had passed between us at our last interview.

"You tellee me lalee die; how him lalee when lalee die?"

"The lady is not dead; I made a mistake. Is this the lady?"

"Lalee talk; I no see face, I hear speak."

"Have you seen this man before?" I inquired of my nearly insensible companion.

"I think so in a dream," she murmured, trying to recall her poor wandering wits back from some region into which they had strayed.

"Him lalee!" cried the Chinaman, overjoyed at the prospect of getting his money. "Pletty speak, I knowee him. Lalee want clo?"

"Not to-night. The lady is sick; see, she can hardly stand." And overjoyed at this seeming evidence that the police had failed to get wind of my interest in this place, I slipped a coin into the Chinaman's hand, and drew Miss Oliver away towards the carriage I now saw drawing up before the shop.

Lena's eyes when she came up to help me were a sight to see. They seemed to ask who this girl was and what I was going to do with her. I answered the look by a very brief and evidently wholly unexpected explanation.

"This is your cousin who ran away," I remarked. "Don't you recognize her?"

Lena gave me up then and there; but she accepted my explanation, and even lied in her desire to carry out my whim.

"Yes, ma'am," said she, "and glad I am to see her again." And with a deft push here and a gentle pull there, she succeeded in getting the sick woman into the carriage.

The crowd, which had considerably increased by this time, was beginning to flock about us with shouts of no little derision. Escaping it as best I could, I took my seat by the poor girl's side, and bade Lena give the order for home. When we left the curb-stone behind, I felt that the last page in my adventures as an amateur detective had closed.

But I counted without my cost. Miss Oliver, who was in an advanced stage of fever, lay like a dead weight on my shoulder during the drive down the avenue, but when we entered the Park and drew near my house, she began to show such signs of violent agitation that it was with difficulty that the united efforts of Lena and myself could prevent her from throwing herself out of the carriage door which she had somehow managed to open.

As the carriage stopped she grew worse, and though she made no further efforts to leave it, I found her present impulses even harder to contend with than the former. For now she would not be pushed out or dragged out, but crouched back moaning and struggling, her eyes fixed on the stoop, which is not unlike that of the adjoining house; till with a sudden realization that the cause of her terror lay in her fear of re-entering the scene of her late terrifying experiences, I bade the coachman drive on, and reluctantly, I own, carried her back to the house she had left in the morning.

And this is how I came to spend a second night in Miss Althorpe's hospitable mansion.

XXVIII   TAKEN ABACK

One incident more and this portion of my story is at an end. My poor patient, sicker than she had been the night before, left me but little leisure for thought or action disconnected with my care for her. But towards morning she grew quieter, and finding in an open drawer those tangled threads of yarn of which I have spoken, I began to rewind them, out of a natural desire to see everything neat and orderly about me. I had nearly finished my task when I heard a strange noise from the bed. It was a sort of gurgling cry which I found hard to interpret, but which only stopped when I laid my work down again. Manifestly this sick girl had very nervous fancies.

When I went down to breakfast the next morning, I was in that complacent state of mind natural to a woman who feels that her abilities have asserted themselves and that she would soon receive a recognition of the same at the hands of the one person for whose commendation she had chiefly been working. The identification of Miss Oliver by the Chinaman was the last link in the chain connecting her with the Mrs. James Pope who had accompanied Mr. Van Burnam to his father's house in Gramercy Park, and though I would fain have had the murdered woman's rings to show, I was contented enough with the discoveries I had made to wish for the hour which would bring me face to face with the detective.

But a surprise awaited me at the breakfast table in the shape of a communication from that gentleman. It had just been brought from my house by Lena, and it ran thus:

"DEAR MISS BUTTERWORTH:

"Pardon our interference. We have found the rings which you think so conclusive an evidence of guilt against the person secreting them; and, with your permission [this was basely underlined], Mr. Franklin Van Burnam will be in custody to-day.

"I will wait upon you at ten.

"Respectfully yours,

"EBENEZAR GRYCE."

Franklin Van Burnam! Was I dreaming? Franklin Van Burnam accused of this crime and in custody! What did it mean? I had found no evidence against Franklin Van Burnam.

BOOK III   THE GIRL IN GRAY

XXIX   AMELIA BECOMES PEREMPTORY

"Madam, I hope I see you satisfied?"

This was Mr. Gryce's greeting as he entered my parlor on that memorable morning.

"Satisfied?" I repeated, rising and facing him with what he afterwards described as a stony glare.

"Pardon me! I suppose you would have been still more satisfied if we had waited for you to point out the guilty man to us. But you must make some allowances for professional egotism, Miss Butterworth. We really could not allow you to take the initiatory step in a matter of such importance."

"Oh!" was my sole response; but he has since told me that there was a great deal in that oh; so much, that even he was startled by it.

"You set to-day for a talk with me," he went on; "probably relying upon what you intended to assure yourself of yesterday. But our discovery at the same time as yourself of the rings in Mr. Van Burnam's office, need not interfere with your giving us your full confidence. The work you have done has been excellent, and we are disposed to give you considerable credit for it."

"Indeed!"

I had no choice but to thus indulge in ejaculations. The communication he had just made was so startling, and his assumption of my complete understanding of and participation in the discovery he professed to have made, so puzzling, that I dared not venture beyond these simple exclamations, lest he should see the state of mind into which he had thrown me, and shut up like an oyster.

"We have kept counsel over what we have found," the wary old detective continued, with a smile, which I wish I could imitate, but which unhappily belongs to him alone. "I hope that you, or your maid, I should say, have been equally discreet."

My maid!

"I see you are touched; but women find it so hard to keep a secret. But it does not matter. To-night the whole town will know that the older and not the younger brother has had these rings in his keeping."

"It will be nuts for the papers," I commented; then making an effort, I remarked: "You are a most judicious man, Mr. Gryce, and must have other reasons than the discovery of these rings for your threatened arrest of a man of such excellent repute as Silas Van Burnam's eldest son. I should like to hear them, Mr. Gryce. I should like to hear them very much."

My attempt to seem at ease under these embarrassing conditions must have given a certain sharpness to my tone; for, instead of replying, he remarked, with well simulated concern and a fatherly humoring of my folly peculiarly exasperating to one of my temperament: "You are displeased, Miss Butterworth, because we did not let you find the rings."

"Perhaps; but we were engaged in an open field. I could not expect the police to stand aside for me."

"Exactly! Especially when you have the secret satisfaction of having put the police on the track of these jewels."

"How?"

"We were simply fortunate in laying our hands on them first. You, or your maid rather, showed us where to look for them."

Lena again.

I was so dumfounded by this last assertion, I did not attempt to reply. Fortunately, he misinterpreted my silence and the "stony glare" with which it was accompanied.

"I know that it must seem to you altogether too bad, to be tripped up at the moment of your anticipated triumph. But if apologies will suffice to express our sense of presumption, then I pray you to accept them, Miss Butterworth, both on my own part and on that of the Superintendent of Police."

I did not understand in the least what he was talking about, but I recognized the sarcasm of his final expression, and had spirit enough to reply:

"The subject is too important for any more nonsense. Whereabouts in Franklin Van Burnam's desk were these rings found, and how do you know that his brother did not put them there?"

"Your ignorance is refreshing, Miss Butterworth. If you will ask a certain young girl dressed in gray, upon what object connected with Mr. Van Burnam's desk she laid her hands yesterday morning, you will have an answer to your first question. The second one is still more easily answered. Mr. Howard Van Burnam did not conceal the rings in the Duane Street office for the reason that he has not been in that office since his wife was killed. Regarding this fact we are as well advised as yourself. Now you change color, Miss Butterworth. But there is no necessity. For an amateur you have made less trouble and fewer mistakes than were to be expected."

Worse and worse! He was patronizing me now, and for results I had done nothing to bring about. I surveyed him in absolute amazement. Was he amusing himself with me, or was he himself deceived as to the nature and trend of my late investigations. This was a question to settle, and at once; and as duplicity had hitherto proved my best weapon in dealing with Mr. Gryce, I concluded to resort to it in this emergency. Clearing my brow, I regarded with a more amenable air the little Hungarian vase he had taken up on entering the room, and into which he had been talking ever since he thought it worth while to compliment its owner.

"I do not wish," said I, "to be published to the world as the discoverer of Franklin Van Burnam's guilt. But I do want credit with the police, if only because one of their number has chosen to look upon my efforts with disdain. I mean you, Mr. Gryce; so, if you are in earnest"—he smiled at the vase most genially—"I will accept your apologies just so far as you honor me with your confidence. I know you are anxious to hear what evidence I have collected, or you would not be wasting time on me this busy morning."

"Shrewd!" was the short ejaculation he shot into the mouth of the vase he was handling.

"If that term of admiration is intended for me," I remarked, "I am sure I am only too sensible of the honor. But flattery has never succeeded in making me talk against my better judgment. I may be shrewd, but a fool could see what you are after this morning. Compliment me when I have deserved it. I can wait."

"I begin to think that what you withhold so resolutely has more than common value, Miss Butterworth. If this is so, I must not be the only one to listen to your explanations. Is not that a carriage I hear stopping? I am expecting Inspector Z———. If that is he you have been wise to delay your communications till he came."

A carriage was stopping, and it was the Inspector who alighted from it. I began to feel my importance in a way that was truly gratifying, and cast my eyes up at the portrait of my father with a secret longing that its original stood by to witness the verification of his prophecy.

But I was not so distracted by these thoughts as not to make one attempt to get something from Mr. Gryce before the Inspector joined us.

"Why do you speak to me of my maid in one breath and of a girl in gray in another?

Did you think Lena———"

"Hush!" he enjoined, "we will have ample opportunities to discuss this subject later."

"Will we?" thought I. "We will discuss nothing till I know more positively what you are aiming at."

But I showed nothing of this determination in my face. On the contrary, I became all affability as the Inspector entered, and I did the honors of the house in a way I hope my father would have approved of, had he been alive and present.

Mr. Gryce continued to stare into the vase.

"Miss Butterworth,"—it was the Inspector who was speaking,—"I have been told that you take great interest in the Van Burnam murder, and that you have even gone so far as to collect some facts in connection with it which you have not as yet given to the police."

"You have heard correctly," I returned. "I have taken a deep interest in this tragedy, and have come into possession of some facts in reference to it which as yet I have imparted to no living soul."

Mr. Gryce's interest in my poor little vase increased marvellously. Seeing this, I complacently continued:

"I could not have accomplished so much had I indulged in a confidant. Such work as I have attempted depends for its success upon the secrecy with which it is carried on. That is why amateur work is sometimes more effective than professional. No one suspected me of making inquiries, unless it was this gentleman, and he was forewarned of my possible interference. I told him that in case Howard Van Burnam was put under arrest, I should take it upon myself to stir up matters; and I have."

"Then you do not believe in Mr. Van Burnam's guilt? Not even in his complicity, I suppose?" ventured the Inspector.

"I do not know anything about his complicity; but I do not believe the stroke given to his wife came from his hand."

"I see, I see. You believe it the work of his brother."

I stole a look at Mr. Gryce before replying. He had turned the vase upside down, and was intently studying its label; but he could not conceal his expectation of an affirmative answer. Greatly relieved, I immediately took the position I had resolved upon, and calmly but vigorously observed:

"What I believe, and what I have learned in support of my belief, will sound as well in your ears ten minutes hence as now. Before I give you the result of such inquiries as I have been enabled to make, I require to know what evidence you have yourself collected against the gentleman you have just named, and in what respect it is as criminating as that against his brother?"

"Is not that peremptory, Miss Butterworth? And do you think us called upon to part with all or any of the secrets of our office? We have informed you that we have new and startling evidence against the older brother; should not that be sufficient for you?"

"Perhaps so if I were an assistant of yours, or even in your employ. But I am neither; I stand alone, and although I am a woman and unused to this business, I have earned, as I think you will acknowledge later, the right to some consideration on your part. I cannot present the facts I have to relate in a proper manner till I know just how the case stands."

"It is not curiosity that troubles Miss Butterworth—Madam, I said it was not curiosity—but a laudable desire to have the whole matter arranged with precision," dropped now in his dryest tones from the detective's lips.

"Mr. Gryce has a most excellent understanding of my character," I gravely observed.

The Inspector looked nonplussed. He glanced at Mr. Gryce and he glanced at me, but the smile of the former was inscrutable, and my expression, if I showed any, must have betrayed but little relenting.

"If called as a witness, Miss Butterworth,"—this was how he sought to manage me,—"you will have no choice in the matter. You will be compelled to speak or show contempt of court."

"That is true," I acknowledged. "But it is not what I might feel myself called upon to say then, but what I can say now, that is of interest to you at this present moment. So be generous, gentlemen, and satisfy my curiosity, for such Mr. Gryce considers it, in spite of his assertions to the contrary. Will it not all come out in the papers a few hours hence, and have I not earned as much at your hands as the reporters?"

"The reporters are our bane. Do not liken yourself to the reporters."

"Yet they sometimes give you a valuable clue."

Mr. Gryce looked as if he would like to disclaim this, but he was a judicious soul, and merely gave a twist to the vase which I thought would cost me that small article of vertu.

"Shall we humor Miss Butterworth?" asked the Inspector.

"We will do better," answered Mr. Gryce, setting the vase down with a precision that made me jump; for I am a worshipper of bric-à-brac, and prize the few articles I own, possibly beyond their real value. "We will treat her as a coadjutor, which, by the way, she says she is not, and by the trust we place in her, secure that discretionary use of our confidence which she shows with so much spirit in regard to her own."

"Begin then," said I.

"I will," said he, "but first allow me to acknowledge that you are the person who first put us on the track of Franklin Van Burnam."

XXX   THE MATTER AS STATED BY MR. GRYCE

I had exhausted my wonder, so I accepted this statement with no more display of surprise than a grim smile.

"When you failed to identify Howard Van Burnam as the man who accompanied his wife into the adjacent house, I realized that I must look elsewhere for the murderer of Louise Van Burnam. You see I had more confidence in the excellence of your memory than you had yourself, so much indeed that I gave you more than one chance to exercise it, having, by certain little methods I sometimes employ, induced different moods in Mr. Van Burnam at the time of his several visits, so that his bearing might vary, and you have every opportunity to recognize him for the man you had seen on that fatal night."

"Then it was he you brought here each time?" I broke in.

"It was he."

"Well!" I ejaculated.

"The Superintendent and some others whom I need not mention,"—here Mr. Gryce took up another small object from the table,—"believed implicitly in his guilt; conjugal murder is so common and the causes which lead to it so frequently puerile. Therefore I had to work alone. But this did not cause me any concern. Your doubts emphasized mine, and when you confided to me that you had seen a figure similar to the one we were trying to identify, enter the adjoining house on the evening of the funeral, I made immediate inquiries and discovered that the gentleman who had entered the house right after the four persons described by you was Franklin Van Burnam. This gave me a definite clue, and this is why I say that it was you who gave me my first start in this matter."

"Humph!" thought I to myself, as with a sudden shock I remembered that one of the words which had fallen from Miss Oliver's lips during her delirium had been this very name of Franklin.

"I had had my doubts of this gentleman before," continued the detective, warming gradually with his subject. "A man of my experience doubts every one in a case of this kind, and I had formed at odd times a sort of side theory, so to speak, into which some little matters which came up during the inquest seemed to fit with more or less nicety; but I had no real justification for suspicion till the event of which I speak. That you had evidently formed the same theory as myself and were bound to enter into the lists with me, put me on my mettle, madam, and with your knowledge or without it, the struggle between us began."

"So your disdain of me," I here put in with a triumphant air I could not subdue, "was only simulated? I shall know what to think of you hereafter. But don't stop, go on, this is all deeply interesting to me."

"I can understand that. To proceed then; my first duty, of course, was to watch you. You had reasons of your own for suspecting this man, so by watching you I hoped to surprise them."

"Good!" I cried, unable to entirely conceal the astonishment and grim amusement into which his continued misconception of the trend of my suspicions threw me.

"But you led us a chase, madam; I must acknowledge that you led us a chase. Your being an amateur led me to anticipate your using an amateur's methods, but you showed skill, madam, and the man I sent to keep watch over Mrs. Boppert against your looked-for visit there, was foiled by the very simple strategy you used in meeting her at a neighboring shop."

"Good!" I again cried, in my relief that the discovery made at that meeting had not been shared by him.

"We had sounded Mrs. Boppert ourselves, but she had seemed a very hopeless job, and I do not yet see how you got any water out of that stone—if you did."

"No?" I retorted ambiguously, enjoying the Inspector's manifest delight in this scene as much as I did my own secret thoughts and the prospect of the surprise I was holding in store for them.

"But your interference with the clock and the discovery you made that it had been going at the time the shelves fell, was not unknown to us, and we have made use of it, good use as you will hereafter see."

"So! those girls could not keep a secret after all," I muttered; and waited with some anxiety to hear him mention the pin-cushion; but he did not, greatly to my relief.

"Don't blame the girls!" he put in (his ears evidently are as sharp as mine); "the inquiries having proceeded from Franklin, it was only natural for me to suspect that he was trying to mislead us by some hocus-pocus story. So I visited the girls. That I had difficulty in getting to the root of the matter is to their credit, Miss Butterworth, seeing that you had made them promise secrecy."

"You are right," I nodded, and forgave them on the spot. If I could not withstand Mr. Gryce's eloquence—and it affected me at times—how could I expect these girls to. Besides, they had not revealed the more important secret I had confided to them, and in consideration of this I was ready to pardon them most anything.

"That the clock was going at the time the shelves fell, and that he should be the one to draw our attention to it would seem to the superficial mind proof positive that he was innocent of the deed with which it was so closely associated," the detective proceeded. "But to one skilled in the subterfuges of criminals, this seemingly conclusive fact in his favor was capable of an explanation so in keeping with the subtlety shown in every other feature of this remarkable crime, that I began to regard it as a point against him rather than in his favor. Of which more hereafter.

"Not allowing myself to be deterred, then, by this momentary set-back, and rejoicing in an affair considered as settled by my superiors, I proceeded to establish Franklin Van Burnam's connection with the crime which had been laid with so much apparent reason at his brother's door.

"The first fact to be settled was, of course, whether your identification of him as the gentleman who accompanied his victim into Mr. Van Burnam's house could be corroborated by any of the many persons who had seen the so-called Mr. James Pope at the Hotel D——.

"As none of the witnesses who attended the inquest had presumed to recognize in either of these sleek and haughty gentlemen the shrinking person just mentioned, I knew that any open attempt on my part to bring about an identification would result disastrously. So I employed strategy—like my betters, Miss Butterworth" (here his bow was overpowering in its mock humility); "and rightly considering that for a person to be satisfactorily identified with another, he must be seen under the same circumstances and in nearly the same place, I sought out Franklin Van Burnam, and with specious promises of some great benefit to be done his brother, induced him to accompany me to the Hotel D——.

"Whether he saw through my plans and thought that a brave front and an assumption of candor would best serve him in this unexpected dilemma, or whether he felt so entrenched behind the precautions he had taken as not to fear discovery under any circumstances, he made but one demur before preparing to accompany me. This demur was significant, however, for it was occasioned by my advice to change his dress for one less conspicuously fashionable, or to hide it under an ulster or mackintosh. And as a proof of his hardihood—remember, madam, that his connection with this crime has been established—he actually did put on the ulster, though he must have known what a difference it would make in his appearance.

"The result was all I could desire. As we entered the hotel, I saw a certain hackman start and lean forward to look after him. It was the one who had driven Mr. and Mrs. Pope away from the hotel. And when we passed the porter, the wink which I gave him was met by a lift of his eyelids which he afterwards interpreted into 'Like! very like!'

"But it was from the clerk I received the most unequivocal proof of his identity. On entering the office I had left Mr. Van Burnam as near as possible to the spot where Mr. Pope had stood while his so-called wife was inscribing their names in the register, and bidding him to remain in the background while I had a few words at the desk, all in his brother's interests of course, I succeeded in secretly directing Mr. Henshaw's attention towards him. The start which he gave and the exclamation he uttered were unequivocal. 'Why, there's the man now!' he cried, happily in a whisper. 'Anxious look, drooping head, brown moustache, everything but the duster.' 'Bah!' said I; 'that's Mr.Franklin Van Burnam you are looking at! What are you thinking of?' 'Can't help it,' said he; 'I saw both of the brothers at the inquest, and saw nothing in them then to remind us of our late mysterious guest. But as he stands there, he's a ---- sight more like James Pope than the other one is, and don't you forget it.' I shrugged my shoulders, told him he was a fool, and that fools had better keep their follies to themselves, and came away with my man, outwardly disgusted but inwardly in most excellent trim for pursuing an investigation which had opened so auspiciously.

"Whether this man possessed any motive for a crime so seemingly out of accordance with his life and disposition was, of course, the next point to settle. His conduct at the inquest certainly showed no decided animosity toward his brother's wife, nor was there on the surface of affairs any token of the mortal hatred which alone could account for a crime at once so deliberate and so brutal. But we detectives plunge below the surface, and after settling the question of Franklin's identity with the so-called Mr. Pope of the Hotel D——, I left New York and its interests—among which I reckoned your efforts at detective work, Miss Butterworth—to a young man in my office, who, I am afraid, did not quite understand the persistence of your character; for he had nothing to tell me concerning you on my return, save that you had been cultivating Miss Althorpe, which, of course, was such a natural thing for you to do, I wonder he thought it necessary to mention it.

"My destination was Four Corners, the place where Howard first met his future wife. In relating what I learned there, I shall doubtless repeat facts with which you are acquainted, Miss Butterworth."

"That is of no consequence," I returned, with almost brazen duplicity; for I not only was ignorant of what he was going to say, but had every reason to believe that it would bear as remote a connection as possible to the secret then laboring in my breast. "A statement of the case from your lips," I pursued, "will emphasize what I know. Do not stint any of your disclosures, then, I beg. I have an ear for all." This was truer than my rather sarcastic tone would convey, for might not his story after all prove to have some unexpected relation with the facts I had myself gathered together.

"It is a pleasure," said he, "to think I am capable of giving any information to Miss Butterworth, and as I did not run across you or your very nimble and pert little maid during my stay at Four Corners, I shall take it for granted that you confined your inquiries to the city and the society of which you are such a shining light."

This in reference to my double visit at Miss Althorpe's, no doubt.

"Four Corners is a charming town in Southern Vermont, and here, three years ago, Howard Van Burnam first met Miss Stapleton. She was living in a gentleman's family at that time as travelling companion to his invalid daughter."

Ah, now I could see what explanation this wary old detective gave himself of my visits to Miss Althorpe, and began to hug myself in anticipation of my coming triumph over him.

"The place did not fit her, for Miss Stapleton only shone in the society of men; but Mr. Harrison had not yet discovered this special idiosyncrasy of hers, and as his daughter was able to see a few friends, and in fact needed some diversion, the way was open to her companion for that acquaintance with Mr. Van Burnam which has led to such disastrous results.

"The house at which their meeting took place was a private one, and I soon found out many facts not widely known in this city. First, that she was not so much in love with Howard as he was with her. He succumbed to her fascinations at once, and proposed, I believe, within two weeks after seeing her; but though she accepted him, few of those who saw them together thought her affections very much engaged till Franklin suddenly appeared in town, when her whole manner underwent a change, and she became so sparklingly and irresistibly beautiful that her avowed lover became doubly enslaved, and Franklin—Well, there is evidence to prove that he was not insensible to her charms either; that, in spite of her engagement to his brother and the attitude which honor bade him hold towards his prospective sister-in-law, he lost his head for a short time at least, and under her seductions I do not doubt, for she was a double-faced woman according to general repute, went so far as to express his passion in a letter of which I heard much before I was so fortunate as to obtain a sight of it. This was three years ago, and I think Miss Stapleton would have been willing to have broken with Howard and married Franklin if the latter had had the courage to meet his brother's reproaches. But he evidently was deficient in this quality. His very letter, which is a warm one, but which holds out no hope to her of any closer bond between them than that offered by her prospective union with his brother, shows that he still retained some sense of honor, and as he presently left Four Corners and did not appear again where they were till just before their marriage, it is probable that all would have gone well if the woman had shared this sentiment with him. But she was made up of mean materials, and while willing to marry Howard for what he could give her or what she thought he could give her, she yet cherished an implacable grudge against Franklin for his weakness, as she called it, in not following the dictates of his heart. Being sly as well as passionate, she hid her feelings from every one but a venial, though apparently devoted confidante, a young girl named——"

"Oliver," I finished in my own mind.

But the name he mentioned was quite different.

"Pigot," he said, looking at the filigree basket he held in his hand as if he picked this word out from one of its many interstices. "She was French, and after once finding her, I had but little difficulty in learning all she had to tell. She had been Miss Harrison's maid, but she was not above serving Miss Stapleton in many secret and dishonorable ways. As a consequence, she could give me the details of an interview which that lady had held with Franklin Van Burnam on the evening of her wedding. It took place in Mr. Harrison's garden, and was supposed to be a secret one, but the woman who arranged the meeting was not the person to keep away from it when it occurred, and consequently I have been enabled to learn with more or less accuracy what took place between them. It was not to Miss Stapleton's credit. Mr. Van Burnam merely wanted his letter back, but she refused to return it unless he would promise her a complete recognition by his family of her marriage and ensure her a reception in his father's house as Howard's wife. This was more than he could engage himself to perform. He had already, according to his own story, made every effort possible to influence the old gentleman in her favor, but had only succeeded in irritating him against himself. It was an acknowledgment which would have satisfied most women, but it did not satisfy her. She declared her intention of keeping the letter for fear he would cease his exertions; and heedless of the effect produced upon him by the barefaced threat, proceeded to inveigh against his brother for the very love which made her union with him possible; and as if this was not bad enough, showed at the same time such a disposition to profit by whatever worldly good the match promised, that Franklin lost all regard for her, and began to hate her.

"As he made no effort to conceal his feelings, she must have become immediately aware of the change which had taken place in them. But however affected by this, she gave no sign of relenting in her purpose. On the contrary, she persisted in her determination to retain his letter, and when he remonstrated with her and threatened to leave town before her marriage, she retorted by saying that, if he did so, she would show his letter to his brother as soon as the minister had made them one. This threat seemed to affect Franklin deeply, and while it intensified his feeling of animosity towards her, subjected him for the moment to her whim. He stayed in Four Corners till the ceremony was performed, but was such a gloomy guest that all united in saying that he did the occasion no credit.

"So much for my work in Four Corners."

I had by this time become aware that Mr. Gryce was addressing himself chiefly to the Inspector, being gratified no doubt at this opportunity of presenting his case at length before that gentleman. But true to his special habits, he looked at neither of us, but rather at the fretted basket, upon the handle of which he tapped out his arguments as he quickly proceeded:

"The young couple spent the first months of their married life in Yonkers; so to Yonkers I went next. There I learned that Franklin had visited the place twice; both times, as I judge, upon a peremptory summons from her. The result was mutual fret and heartburning, for she had made no progress in her endeavors to win recognition from the Van Burnams; and even had had occasion to perceive that her husband's love, based as it was upon her physical attributes, had begun to feel the stress of her uneasiness and dissatisfaction. She became more anxious than ever for social recognition and distinction, and when the family went to Europe, consented to accompany her husband into the quiet retreat he thought best calculated to win the approbation of his father, only upon the assurance of better times in the fall and a possible visit to Washington in the winter. But the quiet to which she was subjected had a bad effect upon her. Under it she grew more and more restless, and as the time approached for the family's return, conceived so many plans for conciliating them that her husband could not restrain his disgust. But the worst plan of all and the one which undoubtedly led to her death, he never knew. This was to surprise Franklin at his office and, by renewed threats of showing this old love-letter to his brother, win an absolute promise from him to support her in a fresh endeavor to win his father's favor. You see she did not understand Silas Van Burnam's real character, and persisted in holding the most extravagant views concerning Franklin's ascendancy over him as well as over the rest of the family. She even went so far as to insist in the interview, which Jane Pigot overheard, that it was Franklin himself who stood in the way of her desires, and that if he chose he could obtain for her an invitation to take up her abode with the rest of them in Gramercy Park. To Duane Street she therefore went before making her appearance at Mrs. Parker's; a fact which was not brought out at the inquest; Franklin not disclosing it of course, and the clerk not recognizing her under the false name she chose to give. Of the details of this interview I am ignorant, but as she was closeted with him some time, it is only natural to suppose that conversation of some importance took place between them. The clerk who works in the outer office did not, as I have said, know who she was at the time, but he noticed her face when she came out, and he declares that it was insolent with triumph, while Mr. Franklin, who was polite enough or calculating enough to bow her out of the room, was pale with rage, and acted so unlike himself that everybody observed it. She held his letter in her hand, a letter easily distinguishable by the violet-colored seal on the back, and she filliped with it in a most aggravating way as she crossed the floor, pretending to lay it down on Howard's desk as she went by and then taking it up again with an arch look at Franklin, pretty enough to see but hateful in its effect on him. As he went back to his own room his face was full of anger, and such was the effect of this visit on him that he declined to see any one else that day. She had probably shown such determination to reveal his past perfidy to her husband, that his fears were fully aroused at last, and he saw he was not only likely to lose his good name but the esteem with which he was accustomed to be regarded by this younger and evidently much-loved brother.

"And now, considering his intense pride, as well as his affection for Howard, do you not see the motive which this seemingly good man had for putting his troublesome sister-in-law out of existence? He wanted that letter back, and to obtain it had to resort to crime. Or such is my present theory of this murder, Miss Butterworth. Does it correspond with yours?"

XXXI   SOME FINE WORK

"O perfectly!" I assented, with just the shade of irony necessary to rob the assertion of its mendacity. "But go on, go on. You have not begun to satisfy me yet. You did not stop with finding a motive for the crime I am sure."

"Madam, you are a female Shylock; you will have the whole of the bond or none."

"We are not here to draw comparisons," I retorted. "Keep to the subject, Mr. Gryce; keep to the subject."

He laughed; laid down the little basket he held, took it up again, and finally resumed:

"Madam, you are right; we did not stop at finding a motive. Our next step was to collect evidence directly connecting him with the crime."

"And you succeeded in this?"

My tone was unnecessarily eager, this was all so unaccountable to me; but he did not appear to notice it.

"We did. Indeed the evidence against him is stronger than that against his brother. For if we ignore the latter part of Howard's testimony, which was evidently a tissue of lies, what remains against him? Three things: his dogged persistency in not recognizing his wife in the murdered woman; the receiving of the house keys from his brother; and the fact that he was seen on the stoop of his father's house at an unusual hour in the morning following this murder. Now what have we against Franklin? Many things.

"First:

"That he can no more account for the hours between half-past eleven on Tuesday morning and five o'clock on the following Wednesday morning than his brother can. In one breath he declares that he was shut up in his rooms at the hotel, for which no corroborative evidence is forthcoming; and in another that he was on a tramp after his brother, which seems equally improbable and incapable of proof.

"Second:

"That he and not Howard was the man in a linen duster, and that he and not Howard was in possession of the keys that night. As these are serious statements to make, I will give you my reasons for them. They are distinct from the recognition of his person by the inmates of the Hotel D——, and added to that recognition, form a strong case against him. The janitor who has charge of the offices in Duane Street, happening to have a leisure moment on the morning of the day on which Mrs. Van Burnam was murdered, was making the most of it by watching the unloading of a huge boiler some four doors below the Van Burnam warehouse. He was consequently looking intently in that direction when Howard passed him, coming from the interview with his brother in which he had been given the keys. Mr. Van Burnam was walking briskly, but finding the sidewalk blocked by the boiler to which I have alluded, paused for a moment to let it pass, and being greatly heated, took out his handkerchief to wipe his forehead. This done, he moved on, just as a man dressed in a long duster came up behind him, stopping where he stopped and picking up from the ground something which the first gentleman had evidently dropped. This last man's figure looked more or less familiar to the janitor, so did the duster, and later he discovered that the latter was the one which he had seen hanging for so long a time in the little disused closet under the warehouse stairs. Its wearer was Franklin Van Burnam, who, as I took pains to learn, had left the office immediately in the wake of his brother, and the object he picked up was the bunch of keys which the latter had inadvertently dropped. He may have thought he lost them later, but it was then and there they slipped from his pocket. I will here add that the duster found by the hackman in his coach has been identified as the one missing from the closet just mentioned.

"Third:

"The keys with which Mr. Van Burnam's house was unlocked were found hanging in their usual place by noon of the next day. They could not have been taken there by Howard, for he was not seen at the office after the murder. By whom then were they returned, if not by Franklin?

"Fourth:

"The letter, for the possession of which I believe this crime to have been perpetrated, was found by us in a supposedly secret drawer of this gentleman's desk. It was much crumpled, and bore evidences of having been rather rudely dealt with since it was last seen in Mrs. Van Burnam's hand in that very office.

"But the fact which is most convincing, and which will tell most heavily against him, is the unexpected discovery of the murdered lady's rings, also in this same desk. How you became aware that anything of such importance could be found there, knowing even the exact place in which they were secreted, I will not stop to ask at this moment. Enough that when your maid entered the Van Burnam offices and insisted with so much ingenuousness that she was expected by Mr. Van Burnam and would wait for his return, the clerk most devoted to my interests became distrustful of her intentions, having been told to be on the look-out for a girl in gray or a lady in black with puffs on each side of two very sharp eyes. You will pardon me, Miss Butterworth. He therefore kept his eyes on the girl and presently espied her stretching out her hand towards a hook at the side of Mr. Franklin Van Burnam's desk. As it is upon this hook this gentleman strings his unanswered letters, the clerk rose from his place as quickly as possible, and coming forward with every appearance of polite solicitude,—did she not say he was polite, Miss Butterworth?—inquired what she wished, thinking she was after some letter, or possibly anxious for a specimen of some one's handwriting. But she gave him no other reply than a blush and a confused look, for which you must rebuke her, Miss Butterworth, if you are going to continue to employ her as your agent in these very delicate affairs. And she made another mistake. She should not have left so abruptly upon detection, for that gave the clerk an opportunity to telephone for me, which he immediately did. I was at liberty, and I came at once, and, after hearing his story, decided that what was of interest to you must be of interest to me, and so took a look at the letters she had handled, and discovered, what she also must have discovered before she let them slip from her hand, that the five missing rings we were all in search of were hanging on this same hook amid the sheets of Franklin's correspondence. You can imagine, madam, my satisfaction, and the gratitude which I felt towards my agent, who by his quickness had retained to me the honors of a discovery which it would have been injurious to my pride to have had confined entirely to yourself."

"I can understand," I repeated, and trusted myself to say no more, hot as my secret felt upon my lips.

"You have read Poe's story of the filigree basket?" he now suggested, running his finger up and down the filigree work he himself held.

I nodded. I saw what he meant at once.

"Well, the principle involved in that story explains the presence of the rings in the midst of this stack of letters. Franklin Van Burnam, if he is the murderer of his sister-in-law, is one of the subtlest villains this city has ever produced, and knowing that, if once suspected, every secret drawer and professed hiding-place within his reach would be searched, he put these dangerous evidences of his guilt in a place so conspicuous, and yet so little likely to attract attention, that even so old a hand as myself did not think of looking for them there."

He had finished, and the look he gave me was for myself alone.

"And now, madam," said he, "that I have stated the facts of the case against Franklin Van Burnam, has not the moment come for you to show your appreciation of my good nature by a corresponding show of confidence on your part?"

I answered with a distinct negative. "There is too much that is unexplained as yet in your case against Franklin," I objected. "You have shown that he had motive for the murder and that he was connected more or less intimately with the crime we are considering, but you have by no means explained all the phenomena accompanying this tragedy. How, for instance, do you account for Mrs. Van Burnam's whim in changing her clothing, if her brother-in-law, instead of her husband, was her companion at the Hotel D——?"

You see I was determined to know the whole story before introducing Miss Oliver's name into this complication.

He who had seen through the devices of so many women in his day did not see through mine, perhaps because he took a certain professional pleasure in making his views on this subject clear to the attentive Inspector. At all events, this is the way he responded to my half-curious, half-ironical question:

"A crime planned and perpetrated for the purpose I have just mentioned, Miss Butterworth, could not have been a simple one under any circumstances. But conceived as this one was by a man of more than ordinary intelligence, and carried out with a skill and precaution little short of marvellous, the features which it presents are of such a varying and subtle character that only by the exercise of a certain amount of imagination can they be understood at all. Such an imagination I possess, but how can I be sure that you do?"

"By testing it," I suggested.

"Very good, madam, I will. Not from actual knowledge, then, but from a certain insight I have acquired in my long dealing with such matters, I have come to the conclusion that Franklin Van Burnam did not in the beginning plan to kill this woman in his father's house.

"On the contrary, he had fixed upon a hotel room as the scene of the conflict he foresaw between them, and that he might carry it on without endangering their good names, had urged her to meet him the next morning in the semi-disguise of a gossamer over her fine dress and a heavy veil over her striking features; making the pretence, no doubt, of this being the more appropriate costume for her to appear in before the old gentleman should he so far concede to her demands as to take her to the steamer. For himself he had planned the adoption of a disfiguring duster which had been hanging for a long time in a closet on the ground-floor of the building in Duane Street. All this promised well, but when the time came and he was about to leave his office, his brother unexpectedly appeared and asked for the key to their father's house. Disconcerted no doubt by the appearance of the very person he least wished to see, and astonished by a request so out of keeping with all that had hitherto passed between them, he nevertheless was in too much haste to question him, so gave him what he wanted and Howard went away. As soon after as he could lock his desk and don his hat, Franklin followed, and merely stopping to cover his coat with the old duster, he went out and hastened towards the place of meeting. Under most circumstances all this might have happened without the brothers encountering each other again, but a temporary obstruction on the sidewalk having, as we know, detained Howard, Franklin was enabled to approach him sufficiently close to see him draw his pocket-handkerchief out of his pocket, and with it the keys which he had just given him. The latter fell, and as there was a great pounding of iron going on in the building just over their heads, Howard did not perceive his loss but went quickly on. Franklin coming up behind him picked up the keys, and with a thought, or perhaps as yet with no thought, of the use to which they might be applied, put them in his own pocket before proceeding on his way.

"New York is a large place, and much can take place in it without comment. Franklin Van Burnam and his sister-in-law met and went together to the Hotel D—— without being either recognized or suspected till later developments drew attention to them. That she should consent to accompany him to this place, and that after she was there should submit, as she did, to taking all the business of the scheme upon herself, would be inconceivable in a woman of a self-respecting character; but Louise Van Burnam cared for little save her own aggrandisement, and rather enjoyed, so far as we can see, this very doubtful escapade, whose real meaning and murderous purpose she was so far from understanding.

"As the steamer, contrary to all expectation, had not yet been sighted off Fire Island, they took a room and prepared to wait for it. That is, she prepared to wait. He had no intention of waiting for its arrival or of going to it when it came; he only wanted his letter. But Louise Van Burnam was not the woman to relinquish it till she had obtained the price she had put on it, and he becoming very soon aware of this fact, began to ask himself if he should not be obliged to resort to extreme measures in order to regain it. One chance only remained for avoiding these. He would seem to embrace her later and probably much-talked-of scheme of presenting herself before his father in his own house rather than at the steamer; and by urging her to make its success more certain by a different style of dress from that she wore, induce a change of clothing, during which he might come upon the letter he was more than confident she carried about her person. Had this plan worked; had he been able to seize upon this compromising bit of paper, even at the cost of a scratch or two from her vigorous fingers, we should not be sitting here at this moment trying to account for the most complicated crime on record. But Louise Van Burnam, while weak and volatile enough to enjoy the romantic features of this transformation scene, even going so far as to write out the order herself with the same effort at disguise she had used in registering their assumed names at the desk, was not entirely his dupe, and having hidden the letter in her shoe——"

"What!" I cried.

"Having hidden the letter in her shoe," repeated Mr. Gryce, with his finest smile, "she had but to signify that the boots sent by Altman were a size too small, for her to retain her secret and keep the one article she traded upon from his envious clutch. You seem struck dumb by this, Miss Butterworth. Have I enlightened you on a point that has hitherto troubled you?"

"Don't ask me; don't look at me." As if he ever looked at any one! "Your perspicacity is amazing, but I will try and not show my sense of it, if it is going to make you stop."

He smiled; the Inspector smiled: neither understood me.

"Very well then, I will go on; but the non-change of shoes had to be accounted for, Miss Butterworth."

"You are right; and it has been, of course."

"Have you any better explanation to give?"

I had, or thought I had, and the words trembled on my tongue. But I restrained myself under an air of great impatience. "Time is flying!" I urged, with as near a simulation of his own manner in saying the words as I could affect. "Go on, Mr. Gryce."

And he did, though my manner evidently puzzled him.

"Being foiled in this his last attempt, this smooth and diabolical villain hesitated no longer in carrying out the scheme which had doubtless been maturing in his mind ever since he dropped the key of his father's house into his own pocket. His brother's wife must die, but not in a hotel room with him for a companion. Though scorned, detested, and a stumbling-block in the way of the whole family's future happiness and prosperity, she still was a Van Burnam, and no shadow must fall upon her reputation. Further than this, for he loved life and his own reputation also, and did not mean to endanger either by this act of self-preservation, she must perish as if from accident, or by some blow so undiscoverable that it would be laid to natural causes. He thought he knew how this might be brought about. He had seen her put on her hat with a very thin and sharp pin, and he had heard how one thrust into a certain spot in the spine would effect death without a struggle. A wound like that would be small; almost indiscernible. True it would take skill to inflict it, and it would require dissimulation to bring her into the proper position for the contemplated thrust; but he was not lacking in either of these characteristics; and so he set himself to the task he had promised himself, and with such success that ere long the two left the hotel and proceeded to the house in Gramercy Park with all the caution necessary for preserving a secret which meant reputation to the one, and liberty, if not life, to the other. That he and not she felt the greater need of secrecy, witness their whole conduct, and when, their goal reached, she and not he put the money into the driver's hand, the last act of this curious drama of opposing motives was reached, and only the final catastrophe was wanting.

"With what arts he procured her hat-pin, and by what show of simulated passion he was able to approach near enough to her to inflict that cool and calculating thrust which resulted in her immediate death, I leave to your imagination. Enough that he compassed his ends, killing her and regaining the letter for the possession of which he had been willing to take a life. Afterwards——"

"Well, afterwards?"

"The deed he had thought so complete began to assume a different aspect. The pin had broken in the wound, and, knowing the scrutiny which the body would receive at the hands of a Coroner's jury, he began to see what consequences might follow its discovery. So to hide that wound and give to her death the wished-for appearance of accident, he went back and drew down the cabinet under which she was found. Had he done this at once his hand in the tragedy might have escaped detection, but he waited, and by waiting allowed the blood-vessels to stiffen and all that phenomena to become apparent by means of which the eyes of the physicians were opened to the fact that they must search deeper for the cause of death than the bruises she had received. Thus it is that Justice opens loop-holes in the finest web a criminal can weave."

"A just remark, Mr. Gryce, but in this fine-spun web of your weaving, you have not explained how the clock came to be running and to stop at five."

"Cannot you see? A man capable of such a crime would not forget to provide himself with an alibi. He expected to be in his rooms at five, so before pulling down the shelves at three or four, he wound the clock and set it at an hour when he could bring forward testimony to his being in another place. Is not such a theory consistent with his character and with the skill he has displayed from the beginning to the end of this woeful affair?"

Aghast at the deftness with which this able detective explained every detail of this crime by means of a theory necessarily hypothetical if the discoveries I had made in the matter were true, and for the moment subjected to the overwhelming influence of his enthusiasm, I sat in a maze, asking myself if all the seemingly irrefutable evidence upon which men had been convicted in times gone by was as false as this. To relieve myself and to gain renewed confidence in my own views and the discoveries I had made in this matter, I repeated the name of Howard, and asked how, in case the whole crime was conceived and perpetrated by his brother, he came to utter such equivocations and to assume that position of guilt which had led to his own arrest.

"Do you think," I inquired, "that he was aware of his brother's part in this affair, and that out of compassion for him he endeavored to take the crime upon his own shoulders?"

"No, madam. Men of the world do not carry their disinterestedness so far. He not only did not know the part his brother took in this crime, but did not even suspect it, or why acknowledge that he lost the key by which the house was entered?"

"I do not understand Howard's actions, even under these circumstances. They seem totally inconsistent to me."

"Madam, they are easily explainable to one who knows the character of his mind. He prizes his honor above every consideration, and regarded it as threatened by the suggestion that his wife had entered his father's empty house at midnight with another man. To save himself that shame, he was willing not only to perjure himself, but to take upon himself the consequences of his perjury. Quixotic, certainly, but some men are constituted that way, and he, for all his amiable characteristics, is the most dogged man I ever encountered. That he ran against snags in his attempted explanations, seemed to make no difference to him. He was bound that no one should accuse him of marrying a false woman, even if he must bear the opprobrium of her death. It is hard to understand such a nature, but re-read his testimony, and see if this explanation of his conduct is not correct."

And still I mechanically repeated: "I do not understand."

Mr. Gryce may not have been a patient man under all circumstances, but he was patient with me that day.

"It was his ignorance, Miss Butterworth, his total ignorance of the whole affair that led him into the inconsistencies he manifested. Let me present his case as I already have his brother's. He knew that his wife had come to New York to appeal to his father, and he gathered from what she said that she intended to do this either in his house or on the dock. To cut short any opportunity she might have for committing the first folly, he begged the key of the house from his brother, and, supposing that he had it all right, went to his rooms, not to Coney Island as he said, and began to pack up his trunks. For he meant to flee the country if his wife disgraced him. He was tired of her caprices and meant to cut them short as far as he was himself concerned. But the striking of the midnight hour brought better counsel. He began to wonder what she had been doing in his absence. Going out, he haunted the region of Gramercy Park for the better part of the night, and at daybreak actually mounted the steps of his father's house and prepared to enter it by means of the key he had obtained from his brother. But the key was not in his pocket, so he came down again and walked away, attracting the attention of Mr. Stone as he did so. The next day he heard of the tragedy which had taken place within those very walls; and though his first fears led him to believe that the victim was his wife, a sight of her clothes naturally dispelled this apprehension, for he knew nothing of her visit to the Hotel D—— or of the change in her habiliments which had taken place there. His father's persistent fears and the quiet pressure brought to bear upon him by the police only irritated him, and not until confronted by the hat found on the scene of death, an article only too well known as his wife's, did he yield to the accumulated evidence in support of her identity. Immediately he felt the full force of his unkindness towards her, and rushing to the Morgue had her poor body taken to that father's house and afterwards given a decent burial. But he could not accept the shame which this acknowledgment naturally brought with it, and, blind to all consequences, insisted, when brought up again for examination, that he was the man with whom she came to that lonely house. The difficulties into which this plunged him were partly foreseen and partly prepared for, and he showed some skill in surmounting them. But falsehoods never fit like truths, and we all felt the strain on our credulity as he met and attempted to parry the Coroner's questions.

"And now, Miss Butterworth, let me again ask if your turn has not come at last for adding the sum of your evidence to ours against Franklin Van Burnam?"

It had; I could not deny it, and as I realized that with it had also come the opportunity for justifying the pretensions I had made, I raised my head with suitable spirit and, after a momentary pause for the purpose of making my words the more impressive, I asked:

"And what has made you think that I was interested in fixing the guilt on Franklin Van Burnam?"

XXXIII   CONOCLASM

The surprise which this very simple question occasioned, showed itself differently in the two men who heard it. The Inspector, who had never seen me before, simply stared, while Mr. Gryce, with that admirable command over himself which has helped to make him the most successful man on the force, retained his impassibility, though I noticed a small corner drop from my filigree basket as if crushed off by an inadvertent pressure of his hand.

"I judged," was his calm reply, as he laid down the injured toy with an apologetic grunt, "that the clearing of Howard from suspicion meant the establishment of another man's guilt; and so far as we can see there has been no other party in the case besides these two brothers."

"No? Then I fear a great surprise awaits you, Mr. Gryce. This crime, which you have fixed with such care and seeming probability upon Franklin Van Burnam, was not, in my judgment, perpetrated either by him or any other man. It was the act of a woman."

"A WOMAN?"

Both men spoke: the Inspector, as if he thought me demented; Mr. Gryce, as if he would like to have considered me a fool but dared not.

"Yes, a woman," I repeated, dropping a quiet curtsey. It was a proper expression of respect when I was young, and I see no reason why it should not be a proper expression of respect now, except that we have lost our manners in gaining our independence, something which is to be regretted perhaps. "A woman whom I know; a woman whom I can lay my hands on at a half-hour's notice; a young woman, sirs; a pretty woman, the owner of one of the two hats found in the Van Burnam parlors."

Had I exploded a bomb-shell the Inspector could not have looked more astounded. The detective, who was a man of greater self-command, did not betray his feelings so plainly, though he was not entirely without them, for, as I made this statement, he turned and looked at me; Mr. Gryce looked at me.

"Both of those hats belonged to Mrs. Van Burnam," he protested; "the one she wore from Haddam; the other was in the order from Altman's."

"She never ordered anything from Altman's," was my uncompromising reply. "The woman whom I saw enter next door, and who was the same who left the Hotel D—— with the man in the linen duster, was not Louise Van Burnam. She was that lady's rival, and let me say it, for I dare to think it, not only her rival but the prospective taker of her life. O you need not shake your heads at each other so significantly, gentlemen. I have been collecting evidence as well as yourselves, and what I have learned is very much to the point; very much, indeed."

"The deuce you have!" muttered the Inspector, turning away from me; but Mr. Gryce continued to eye me like a man fascinated.

"Upon what," said he, "do you base these extraordinary assertions? I should like to hear what that evidence is."

"But first," said I, "I must take a few exceptions to certain points you consider yourself to have made against Franklin Van Burnam. You believe him to have committed this crime because you found in a secret drawer of his desk a letter known to have been in Mrs. Van Burnam's hands the day she was murdered, and which you, naturally enough, I acknowledge, conceive he could only have regained by murdering her. But have you not thought of another way in which he could have obtained it, a perfectly harmless way, involving no one either in deceit or crime? May it not have been in the little hand-bag returned by Mrs. Parker on the morning of the discovery, and may not its crumpled condition be accounted for by the haste with which Franklin might have thrust it into his secret drawer at the untoward entrance of some one into his office?"

"I acknowledge that I have not thought of such a possibility," growled the detective, below his breath, but I saw that his self-satisfaction had been shaken.

"As for any proof of complicity being given by the presence of the rings on the hook attached to his desk, I grieve for your sake to be obliged to dispel that illusion also. Those rings, Mr. Gryce and Mr. Inspector, were not discovered there by the girl in gray, but taken there; and hung there at the very moment your spy saw her hand fumbling with the papers."

"Taken there, and hung there by your maid! By the girl Lena, who has so evidently been working in your interests! What sort of a confession are you making, Miss Butterworth?"

"Ah, Mr. Gryce," I gently remonstrated, for I actually pitied the old man in his hour of humiliation, "other girls wear gray besides Lena. It was the woman of the Hotel D—— who played this trick in Mr. Van Burnam's office. Lena was not out of my house that day."

I had never thought Mr. Gryce feeble, though I knew he was over seventy if not very near the octogenarian age. But he drew up a chair at this and hastily sat down.

"Tell me about this other girl," said he.

But before I repeat what I said to him, I must explain by what reasoning I had arrived at the conclusion I have just mentioned. That Ruth Oliver was the visitor in Mr. Van Burnam's office there was but little reason to doubt; that her errand was one in connection with the rings was equally plain. What else would have driven her from her bed when she was hardly able to stand, and sent her in a state of fever, if not delirium, down town to this office?

She feared having these rings found in her possession, and she also cherished a desire to throw whatever suspicion was attached to them upon the man who was already compromised. She may have thought it was Howard's desk she approached, and she may have known it to be Franklin's. On that point I was in doubt, but the rest was clear to me from the moment Mr. Gryce mentioned the girl in gray; and even the spot where she had kept them in the interim since the murder was no longer an unsolved mystery to me. Her emotion when I touched her knitting-work and the shreds of unravelled wool I had found lying about after her departure, had set my wits working, and I comprehended now that they had been wound up in the ball of yarn I had so carelessly handled.

But what had I to say to Mr. Gryce in answer to his question. Much; and seeing that further delay was injudicious, I began my story then and there. Prefacing my tale with the suspicions I had always had of Mrs. Boppert, I told them of my interview with that woman and of the valuable clue she had given me by confessing that she had let Mrs. Van Burnam into the house prior to the visit of the couple who entered there at midnight. Knowing what an effect this must produce upon Mr. Gryce, utterly unprepared for it as he was, I looked for some burst of anger on his part, or at least some expression of self-reproach. But he only broke a second piece off my little filigree basket, and, totally unconscious of the demolition he was causing, cried out with true professional delight:

"Well! well! I've always said this was a remarkable case, a very remarkable case; but if we don't look out it will go ahead of that one at Sibley. Two women in the affair, and one of them in the house before the arrival of the so-called victim and her murderer! What do you think of that, Inspector? Rather late for us to find out so important a detail, eh?"

"Rather," was the dry reply. At which Mr. Gryce's face grew long and he exclaimed, half shamefacedly, half jocularly:

"Outwitted by a woman! Well, it's a new experience for me, Inspector, and you must not be surprised if it takes me a minute or so to get accustomed to it. A scrub-woman too! It cuts, Inspector, it cuts."

But as I went on, and he learned how I had obtained definite proof of the clock having been not only wound by the lady thus admitted to the house, but set also and that correctly, his face grew even longer, and he gazed quite dolefully at the small figure in the carpet to which he had transferred his attention.

"So! so!" came in almost indistinguishable murmur from his lips. "All my pretty theory in regard to its being set by the criminal for the purpose of confirming his attempt at a false alibi was but a figment of my imagination, eh? Sad! sad! But it was neat enough to have been true, was it not, Inspector?"

"Quite," that gentleman good-humoredly admitted, yet with a shade of irony in his tone that made me suspect that, for all his confidence in and evident admiration for this brilliant old detective, he felt a certain amount of pleasure at seeing him for once at fault.

Perhaps it gave him more confidence in his own judgment, seeing that their ideas on this case had been opposed from the start.

"Well! well! I'm getting old; that's what they'll say at Headquarters to-morrow. But go on, Miss Butterworth; let us hear what followed; for I am sure your investigations did not stop there."

I complied with his request with as much modesty as possible. But it was hard to suppress all triumph in face of the unrestrained enthusiasm with which he received my communication. When I told him of the doubts I had formed in regard to the disposal of the packages brought from the Hotel D———, and how to settle those doubts I had taken that midnight walk down Twenty-seventh Street, he looked astonished, his lips worked, and I really expected to see him try to pluck that flower up from the carpet, he ogled it so lovingly. But when I mentioned the lighted laundry and my discoveries there, his admiration burst all bounds, and he cried out, seemingly to the rose in the carpet, really to the Inspector:

"Didn't I tell you she was a woman in a thousand? See now! we ought to have thought of that laundry ourselves; but we didn't, none of us did; we were too credulous and too easily satisfied with the evidence given at the inquest. Well, I'm seventy-seven, but I'm not too old to learn. Proceed, Miss Butterworth."

I admired him and I was sorry for him, but I never enjoyed myself so much in my whole life. How could I help it, or how could I prevent myself from throwing a glance now and then at the picture of my father smiling upon me from the opposite wall?

It was my task now to mention the advertisement I had inserted in the newspapers, and the reflections which had led to my rather daring description of the wandering woman as one dressed thus and so, and without a hat. This seemed to strike him—as I had expected it would,—and he interrupted me with a quick slap of his leg, for which only that leg was prepared.

"Good!" he ejaculated; "a fine stroke! The work of a woman of genius! I could not have done better myself, Miss Butterworth. And what came of it? Something, I hope; talent like yours should not go unrewarded."

"Two letters came of it," said I. "One from Cox, the milliner, saying that a bareheaded girl had bought a hat in his shop early on the morning designated; and another from a Mrs. Desberger appointing a meeting at which I obtained a definite clue to this girl, who, notwithstanding she wore Mrs. Van Burnam's clothes from the scene of tragedy, is not Mrs. Van Burnam herself, but a person by the name of Oliver, now to be found at Miss Althorpe's house in Twenty-first Street."

As this was in a measure putting the matter into their hands, I saw them both grow impatient in their anxiety to see this girl for themselves. But I kept them for a few minutes longer while I related my discovery of the money in her shoes, and hinted at the explanation it afforded for her not changing those articles under the influence of the man who accompanied her.

This was the last blow I dealt to the pride of Mr. Gryce. He quivered under it, but soon recovered, and was able to enjoy what he called another fine point in this remarkable case.

But the acme of his delight was reached when I informed him of my ineffectual search for the rings, and my final conclusion that they had been wound up in the ball of yarn attached to her knitting-work.

Whether his pleasure lay chiefly in the talent shown by Miss Oliver in her choice of a hiding-place for these jewels, or in the acumen displayed by myself in discovering it, I do not know; but he evinced an unbounded satisfaction in my words, crying aloud:

"Beautiful! I don't know of anything more interesting! We have not seen the like in years! I can almost congratulate myself upon my mistakes, the features of the case they have brought out are so fine!"

But his satisfaction, great as it was, soon gave way to his anxiety to see this girl who, if not the criminal herself, was so important a factor in this great crime.

I was anxious myself to have him see her, though I feared her condition was not such as to promise him any immediate enlightenment on the doubtful portions of this far from thoroughly mastered problem. And I bade him interview the Chinaman also, and Mrs. Desberger, and even Mrs. Boppert, for I did not wish him to take for granted anything I had said, though I saw he had lost his attitude of disdain and was inclined to accept my opinions quite seriously.

He answered in quite an off-hand manner while the Inspector stood by, but when that gentleman had withdrawn towards the door, Mr. Gryce remarked with more earnestness than he had yet used:

"You have saved me from committing a folly, Miss Butterworth. If I had arrested Franklin Van Burnam to-day, and to-morrow all these facts had come to light, I should never have held up my head again. As it is, there will be numerous insinuations uttered by men on the force, and many a whisper will go about that Gryce is getting old, that Gryce has seen his best days."

"Nonsense!" was my vigorous rejoinder. "You didn't have the clue, that is all. Nor did I get it through any keenness on my part, but from the force of circumstances. Mrs. Boppert thought herself indebted to me, and so gave me her confidence. Your laurels are very safe yet. Besides, there is enough work left on this case to keep more than one great detective like you busy. While the Van Burnams have not been proved guilty, they are not so freed from suspicion that you can regard your task as completed. If Ruth Oliver committed this crime, which of these two brothers was involved in it with her? The facts seem to point towards Franklin, but not so unerringly that no doubt is possible on the subject."

"True, true. The mystery has deepened rather than cleared. Miss Butterworth, you will accompany me to Miss Althorpe's."

XXXIII   "KNOWN, KNOWN, ALL KNOWN."

Mr. Gryce possesses one faculty for which I envy him, and that is his skill in the management of people. He had not been in Miss Althorpe's house five minutes before he had won her confidence and had everything he wished at his command. I had to talk some time before getting so far, but he—a word and a look did it.

Miss Oliver, for whom I hesitated to inquire, lest I should again find her gone or in a worse condition than when I left, was in reality better, and as we went up-stairs I allowed myself to hope that the questions which had so troubled us would soon be answered and the mystery ended.

But Mr. Gryce evidently knew better, for when we reached her door he turned and said:

"Our task will not be an easy one. Go in first and attract her attention so that I can enter unobserved. I wish to study her before addressing her; but, mind, no words about the murder; leave that to me."

I nodded, feeling that I was falling back into my own place; and knocking softly entered the room.

A maid was sitting with her. Seeing me, she rose and advanced, saying:

"Miss Oliver is sleeping."

"Then I will relieve you," I returned, beckoning Mr. Gryce to come in.

The girl left us and we two contemplated the sick woman silently. Presently I saw Mr. Gryce shake his head. But he did not tell me what he meant by it.

Following the direction of his finger, I sat down in a chair at the head of the bed; he took his station at the side of it in a large arm-chair he saw there. As he did so I saw how fatherly and kind he really looked, and wondered if he was in the habit of so preparing himself to meet the eye of all the suspected criminals he encountered. The thought made me glance again her way. She lay like a statue, and her face, naturally round but now thinned out and hollow, looked up from the pillow in pitiful quiet, the long lashes accentuating the dark places under her eyes.

A sad face, the saddest I ever saw and one of the most haunting.

He seemed to find it so also, for his expression of benevolent interest deepened with every passing moment, till suddenly she stirred; then he gave me a warning glance, and stooping, took her by the wrist and pulled out his watch.

She was deceived by the action. Opening her eyes, she surveyed him languidly for a moment, then heaving a great sigh, turned aside her head.

"Don't tell me I am better, doctor. I do not want to live."

The plaintive tone, the refined accent, seemed to astonish him. Laying down her hand, he answered gently:

"I do not like to hear that from such young lips, but it assures me that I was correct in my first surmise, that it is not medicine you need but a friend. And I can be that friend if you will but allow me."

Moved, encouraged for the instant, she turned her head from side to side, probably to see if they were alone, and not observing me, answered softly:

"You are very good, very thoughtful, doctor, but"—and here her despair returned again—"it is useless; you can do nothing for me."

"You think so," remonstrated the old detective, "but you do not know me, child. Let me show you that I can be of benefit to you." And he drew from his pocket a little package which he opened before her astonished eyes. "Yesterday, in your delirium, you left these rings in an office down-town. As they are valuable, I have brought them back to you. Wasn't I right, my child?"

"No! no!" She started up, and her accents betrayed terror and anguish, "I do not want them; I cannot bear to see them; they do not belong to me; they belong to them."

"To them? Whom do you mean by them?" queried Mr. Gryce, insinuatingly.

"The—the Van Burnams. Is not that the name? Oh, do not make me talk; I am so weak! Only take the rings back."

"I will, child, I will." Mr. Gryce's voice was more than fatherly now, it was tender, really and sincerely tender. "I will take them back; but to which of the brothers shall I return them? To"—he hesitated softly—"to Franklin or to Howard?"

I expected to hear her respond, his manner was so gentle and apparently sincere. But though feverish and on the verge of wildness, she had still some command over herself, and after giving him a look, the intensity of which called out a corresponding expression on his face, she faltered out:

"I—I don't care; I don't know either of the gentlemen; but to the one you call Howard, I think."

The pause which followed was filled by the tap-tap of Mr. Gryce's fingers on his knee.

"That is the one who is in custody," he observed at last. "The other, that is Franklin, has gone scot-free thus far, I hear."

No answer from her close-shut lips.

He waited.

Still no answer.

"If you do not know either of these gentlemen," he insinuated at last, "how did you come to leave the rings at their office?"

"I knew their names—I inquired my way—It is all a dream now. Please, please do not ask me questions. O doctor! do you not see I cannot bear it?"

He smiled—I never could smile like that under any circumstances—and softly patted her hand.

"I see it makes you suffer," he acknowledged, "but I must make you suffer in order to do you any good. If you would tell me all you know about these rings——"

She passionately turned away her head.

"I might hope to restore you to health and happiness. You know with what they are associated?"

She made a slight motion.

"And that they are an invaluable clue to the murderer of Mrs. Van Burnam?"

Another motion.

"How then, my child, did you come to have them?"

Her head, which was rolling to and fro on the pillow, stopped and she gasped, rather than uttered:

"I was there."

He knew this, yet it was terrible to hear it from her lips; she was so young and had such an air of purity and innocence. But more heartrending yet was the groan with which she burst forth in another moment, as if impelled by conscience to unburden herself from some overwhelming load:

"I took them; I could not help it; but I did not keep them; you know that I did not keep them. I am no thief, doctor; whatever I am, I am no thief."

"Yes, yes, I see that. But why take them, child? What were you doing in that house, and whom were you with?"

She threw up her arms, but made no reply.

"Will you not tell?" he urged.

A short silence, then a low "No," evidently wrung from her by the deepest anguish.

Mr. Gryce heaved a sigh; the struggle was likely to be a more serious one than he had anticipated.

"Miss Oliver," said he, "more facts are known in relation to this affair than you imagine. Though unsuspected at first, it has secretly been proven that the man who accompanied the woman into the house where the crime took place, was Franklin Van Burnam."

A low gasp from the bed, and that was all.

"You know this to be correct, don't you, Miss Oliver?"

"O must you ask?" She was writhing now, and I thought he must desist out of pure compassion. But detectives are made out of very stern stuff, and though he looked sorry he went inexorably on.

"Justice and a sincere desire to help you, force me, my child. Were you not the woman who entered Mr. Van Burnam's house at midnight with this man?"

"I entered the house."

"At midnight?"

"Yes."

"And with this man?"

Silence.

"You do not speak, Miss Oliver."

Again silence.

"It was Franklin who was with you at the Hotel D———?"

She uttered a cry.

"And it was Franklin who connived at your change of clothing there, and advised or allowed you to dress yourself in a new suit from Altman's?"

"Oh!" she cried again.

"Then why should it not have been he who accompanied you to the Chinaman's, and afterwards took you in a second hack to the house in Gramercy Park?"

"Known, known, all known!" was her moan.

"Sin and crime cannot long remain hidden in this world, Miss Oliver. The police are acquainted with all your movements from the moment you left the Hotel D———. That is why I have compassion on you. I wish to save you from the consequences of a crime you saw committed, but in which you took no hand."

"O," she exclaimed in one involuntary burst, as she half rose to her knees, "if you could save me from appearing in the matter at all! If you would let me run away———"

But Mr. Gryce was not the man to give her hope on any such score.

"Impossible, Miss Oliver. You are the only person who can witness for the guilty. If I should let you go, the police would not. Then why not tell at once whose hand drew the hatpin from your hat and——"

"Stop!" she shrieked; "stop! you kill me! I cannot bear it! If you bring that moment back to my mind I shall go mad! I feel the horror of it rising in me now! Be still! I pray you, for God's sake, to be still!"

This was mortal anguish; there was no acting in this. Even he was startled by the emotion he had raised, and sat for a moment without speaking. Then the necessity of providing against all further mistakes by fixing the guilt where it belonged, drove him on again, and he said:

"Like many another woman before you, you are trying to shield a guilty man at your own expense. But it is useless, Miss Oliver; the truth always comes to light. Be advised, then, and make a confidant of one who understands you better than you think."

But she would not listen to this.

"No one understands me. I do not understand myself. I only know that I shall make a confidant of no one; that I shall never speak." And turning from him, she buried her head in the bedclothes.

To most men her tone and the action which accompanied it would have been final. But Mr. Gryce possessed great patience. Waiting for just a moment till she seemed more composed, he murmured gently:

"Not if you must suffer more from your silence than from speaking? Not if men—I do not mean myself, child, for I am your friend—will think that you are to blame for the death of the woman whom you saw fall under a cruel stab, and whose rings you have?"

"I!" Her horror was unmistakable; so were her surprise, her terror, and her shame, but she added nothing to the word she had uttered, and he was forced to say again:

"The world, and by that I mean both good people and bad, will believe all this. He will let them believe all this. Men have not the devotion of women."

"Alas! alas!" It was a murmur rather than a cry, and she trembled so the bed shook visibly under her. But she made no response to the entreaty in his look and gesture, and he was compelled to draw back unsatisfied.

When a few heavy minutes had passed, he spoke again, this time in a tone of sadness.

"Few men are worth such sacrifices, Miss Oliver, and a criminal never. But a woman is not moved by that thought. She should be moved by this, however. If either of these brothers is to blame in this matter, consideration for the guiltless one should lead you to mention the name of the guilty."

But even this did not visibly affect her.

"I shall mention no names," said she.

"A sign will answer."

"I shall make no sign."

"Then Howard must go to his trial?"

A gasp, but no words.

"And Franklin proceed on his way undisturbed?"

She tried not to answer, but the words would come. Pray God! I may never see such a struggle again.

"That is as God wills. I can do nothing in the matter." And she sank back crushed and wellnigh insensible.

Mr. Gryce made no further effort to influence her.

XXXIV   EXACTLY HALF-PAST THREE

"She is more unfortunate than wicked," was Mr. Gryce's comment as we stepped into the hall. "Nevertheless, watch her closely, for she is in just the mood to do herself a mischief. In an hour, or at the most two, I shall have a woman here to help you. You can stay till then?"

"All night, if you say so."

"That you must settle with Miss Althorpe. As soon as Miss Oliver is up I shall have a little scheme to propose, by means of which I hope to arrive at the truth of this affair. I must know which of these two men she is shielding."

"Then you think she did not kill Mrs. Van Burnam herself?"

"I think the whole matter one of the most puzzling mysteries that has ever come to the notice of the New York police. We are sure that the murdered woman was Mrs. Van Burnam, that this girl was present at her death, and that she availed herself of the opportunity afforded by that death to make the exchange of clothing which has given such a complicated twist to the whole affair. But beyond these facts, we know little more than that it was Franklin Van Burnam who took her to the Gramercy Park house, and Howard who was seen in that same vicinity some two or four hours later. But on which of these two to fix the responsibility of Mrs. Van Burnam's death, is the question."

"She had a hand in it herself," I persisted; "though it may have been without evil intent. No man ever carried that thing through without feminine help. To this opinion I shall stick, much as this girl draws upon my sympathies."

"I shall not try to persuade you to the contrary. But the point is to find out how much help, and to whom it was given."

"And your scheme for doing this?"

"Cannot be carried out till she is on her feet again. So cure her, Miss Butterworth, cure her. When she can go down-stairs, Ebenezer Gryce will be on the scene to test his little scheme."

I promised to do what I could, and when he was gone, I set diligently to work to soothe the child, as he had called her, and get her in trim for the delicate meal which had been sent up. And whether it was owing to a change in my own feelings, or whether the talk with Mr. Gryce had so unnerved her that any womanly ministration was welcome, she responded much more readily to my efforts than ever before, and in a little while lay in so calm and grateful a mood that I was actually sorry to see the nurse when she came. Hoping that something might spring from an interview with Miss Althorpe whereby my departure from the house might be delayed, I descended to the library, and was fortunate enough to find the mistress of the house there. She was sorting invitations, and looked anxious and worried.

"You see me in a difficulty, Miss Butterworth. I had relied on Miss Oliver to oversee this work, as well as to assist me in a great many other details, and I don't know of any one whom I can get on short notice to take her place. My own engagements are many and——"

"Let me help you," I put in, with that cheerfulness her presence invariably inspires. "I have nothing pressing calling me home, and for once in my life I should like to take an active part in wedding festivities. It would make me feel quite young again."

"But——" she began.

"Oh," I hastened to say, "you think I would be more of a hindrance to you than a help; that I would do the work, perhaps, but in my own way rather than in yours. Well, that would doubtless have been true of me a month since, but I have learned a great deal in the last few weeks,—you will not ask me how,—and now I stand ready to do your work in your way, and to take a great deal of pleasure in it too."

"Ah, Miss Butterworth," she exclaimed, with a burst of genuine feeling which I would not have lost for the world, "I always knew that you had a kind heart; and I am going to accept your offer in the same spirit in which it is made."

So that was settled, and with it the possibility of my spending another night in this house.

At ten o'clock I stole away from the library and the delightful company of Mr. Stone, who had insisted upon sharing my labors, and went up to Miss Oliver's room. I met the nurse at the door.

"You want to see her," said she. "She's asleep, but does not rest very easily. I don't think I ever saw so pitiful a case. She moans continually, but not with physical pain. Yet she seems to have courage too; for now and then she starts up with a loud cry. Listen."

I did so, and this is what I heard:

"I do not want to live; doctor, I do not want to live; why do you try to make me better?"

"That is what she is saying all the time. Sad, isn't it?"

I acknowledged it to be so, but at the same time wondered if the girl were not right in wishing for death as a relief from her troubles.

Early the next morning I inquired at her door again. Miss Oliver was better. Her fever had left her, and she wore a more natural look than at any time since I had seen her. But it was not an untroubled one, and it was with difficulty I met her eyes when she asked if they were coming for her that day, and if she could see Miss Althorpe before she left. As she was not yet able to leave her bed I could easily answer her first question, but I knew too little of Mr. Gryce's intentions to be able to reply to the second. But I was easy with this suffering woman, very easy, more easy than I ever supposed I could be with any one so intimately associated with crime.

She seemed to accept my explanations as readily as she already had my presence, and I was struck again with surprise as I considered that my name had never aroused in her the least emotion.

"Miss Althorpe has been so good to me I should like to thank her; from my despairing heart, I should like to thank her," she said to me as I stood by her side before leaving. "Do you know"—she went on, catching me by the dress as I was turning away—"what kind of a man she is going to marry? She has such a loving heart, and marriage is such a fearful risk."

"Fearful?" I repeated.

"Is it not fearful? To give one's whole soul to a man and be met by—I must not talk of it; I must not think of it—But is he a good man? Does he love Miss Althorpe? Will she be happy? I have no right to ask, perhaps, but my gratitude towards her is such that I wish her every joy and pleasure."

"Miss Althorpe has chosen well," I rejoined. "Mr. Stone is a man in ten thousand."

The sigh that answered me went to my heart.

"I will pray for her," she murmured; "that will be something to live for."

I did not know what reply to make to this. Everything which this girl said and did was so unexpected and so convincing in its sincerity, I felt moved by her even against my better judgment. I pitied her and yet I dared not urge her on to speak, lest I should fail in my task of making her well. I therefore confined myself to a few haphazard expressions of sympathy and encouragement, and left her in the hands of the nurse.

Next day Mr. Gryce called.

"Your patient is better," said he.

"Much better," was my cheerful reply. "This afternoon she will be able to leave the house."

"Very good; have her down at half-past three and I will be in front with a carriage."

"I dread it," I cried; "but I will have her there."

"You are beginning to like her, Miss Butterworth. Take care! You will lose your head if your sympathies become engaged."

"It sits pretty firmly on my shoulders yet," I retorted; "and as for sympathies, you are full of them yourself. I saw how you looked at her yesterday."

"Bah, my looks!"

"You cannot deceive me, Mr. Gryce; you are as sorry for the girl as you can be; and so am I too. By the way, I do not think I should speak of her as a girl. From something she said yesterday I am convinced she is a married woman; and that her husband——"

"Well, madam?"

"I will not give him a name, at least not before your scheme has been carried out. Are you ready for the undertaking?"

"I will be this afternoon. At half-past three she is to leave the house. Not a minute before and not a minute later. Remember."

XXXVA   RUSE

It was a new thing for me to enter into any scheme blindfold. But the past few weeks had taught me many lessons and among them to trust a little in the judgment of others.

Accordingly I was on hand with my patient at the hour designated, and, as I supported her trembling steps down the stairs, I endeavored not to betray the intense interest agitating me, or to awaken by my curiosity any further dread in her mind than that involved by her departure from this home of bounty and good feeling, and her entrance upon an unknown and possibly much to be apprehended future.

Mr. Gryce was awaiting us in the lower hall, and as he caught sight of her slender figure and anxious face his whole attitude became at once so protecting and so sympathetic, I did not wonder at her failure to associate him with the police.

As she stepped down to his side he gave her a genial nod.

"I am glad to see you so far on the road to recovery," he remarked. "It shows me that my prophecy is correct and that in a few days you will be quite yourself again."

She looked at him wistfully.

"You seem to know so much about me, doctor, perhaps you can tell me where they are going to take me."

He lifted a tassel from a curtain near by, looked at it, shook his head at it, and inquired quite irrelevantly:

"Have you bidden good-bye to Miss Althorpe?"

Her eyes stole towards the parlors and she whispered as if half in awe of the splendor everywhere surrounding her:

"I have not had the opportunity. But I should be sorry to go without a word of thanks for her goodness. Is she at home?"

The tassel slipped from his hand.

"You will find her in a carriage at the door. She has an engagement out this afternoon, but wishes to say good-bye to you before leaving."

"Oh, how kind she is!" burst from the girl's white lips; and with a hurried gesture she was making for the door when Mr. Gryce stepped before her and opened it.

Two carriages were drawn up in front, neither of which seemed to possess the elegance of so rich a woman's equipage. But Mr. Gryce appeared satisfied, and pointing to the nearest one, observed quietly:

"You are expected. If she does not open the carriage door for you, do not hesitate to do it yourself. She has something of importance to say to you."

Miss Oliver looked surprised, but prepared to obey him. Steadying herself by the stone balustrade, she slowly descended the steps and advanced towards the carriage. I watched her from the doorway and Mr. Gryce from the vestibule. It seemed an ordinary situation, but something in the latter's face convinced me that interests of no small moment depended upon the interview about to take place.

But before I could decide upon their nature or satisfy myself as to the full meaning of Mr. Gryce's manner, she had started back from the carriage door and was saying to him in a tone of modest embarrassment:

"There is a gentleman in the carriage; you must have made some mistake."

Mr. Gryce, who had evidently expected a different result from his stratagem, hesitated for a moment, during which I felt that he read her through and through; then he responded lightly:

"I made a mistake, eh? Oh, possibly. Look in the other carriage, my child."

With an unaffected air of confidence she turned to do so, and I turned to watch her, for I began to understand the "scheme" at which I was assisting, and foresaw that the emotion she had failed to betray at the door of the first carriage might not necessarily be lacking on the opening of the second.

I was all the more assured of this from the fact that Miss Althorpe's stately figure was very plainly to be seen at that moment, not in the coach Miss Oliver was approaching, but in an elegant victoria just turning the corner.

My expectations were realized; for no sooner had the poor girl swung open the door of the second hack, than her whole body succumbed to a shock so great that I expected to see her fall in a heap on the pavement. But she steadied herself up with a determined effort, and with a sudden movement full of subdued fury, jumped into the carriage and violently shut the door just as the first carriage drove off to give place to Miss Althorpe's turn-out.

"Humph!" sprang from Mr. Gryce's lips in a tone so full of varied emotions that it was with difficulty I refrained from rushing down the stoop to see for myself who was the occupant of the coach into which my late patient had so passionately precipitated herself. But the sight of Miss Althorpe being helped to the ground by her attendant lover, recalled me so suddenly to my own anomalous position on her stoop, that I let my first impulse pass and concerned myself instead with the formation of those apologies I thought necessary to the occasion. But those apologies were never uttered. Mr. Gryce, with the infinite tact he displays in all serious emergencies, came to my rescue, and so distracted Miss Althorpe's attention that she failed to observe that she had interrupted a situation of no small moment.

Meanwhile the coach containing Miss Oliver had, at a signal from the wary detective, drawn off in the wake of the first one, and I had the doubtful satisfaction of seeing them both roll down the street without my having penetrated the secret of either.

A glance from Mr. Stone, who had followed Miss Althorpe up the stoop, interrupted Mr. Gryce's flow of eloquence, and a few minutes later I found myself making those adieux which I had hoped to avoid by departing in Miss Althorpe's absence. Another instant and I was hastening down the street in the direction taken by the two carriages, one of which had paused at the corner a few rods off.

But, spry as I am for one of my settled habits and sedate character, I found myself passed by Mr. Gryce; and when I would have accelerated my steps, he darted forward quite like a boy and, without a word of explanation or any acknowledgment of the mutual understanding which certainly existed between us, leaped into the carriage I was endeavoring to reach, and was driven away. But not before I caught a glimpse of Miss Oliver's gray dress inside.

Determined not to be baffled by this man, I turned about and followed the other carriage. It was approaching a crowded part of the avenue, and in a few minutes I had the gratification of seeing it come to a standstill only a few feet from the curb-stone. The opportunity thus afforded me of satisfying my curiosity was not to be slighted. Without pausing to consider consequences or to question the propriety of my conduct, I stepped boldly up in front of its half-lowered window and looked in. There was but one person inside, and that person was Franklin Van Burnam.

What was I to conclude from this? That the occupant of the other carriage was Howard, and that Mr. Gryce now knew with which of the two brothers Miss Oliver's memories were associated.

BOOK IV   THE END OF A GREAT MYSTERY

XXXVI   THE RESULT

I was as much surprised at this result of Mr. Gryce's scheme as he was, and possibly I was more chagrined. But I shall not enter into my feelings on the subject, or weary you any further with my conjectures. You will be much more interested, I know, in learning what occurred to Mr. Gryce upon entering the carriage holding Miss Oliver.

He had expected, from the intense emotion she displayed at the sight of Howard Van Burnam (for I was not mistaken as to the identity of the person occupying the carriage with her), to find her flushed with the passions incident upon this meeting, and her companion in a condition of mind which would make it no longer possible for him to deny his connection with this woman and his consequently guilty complicity in a murder to which both were linked by so many incriminating circumstances.

But for all his experience, the detective was disappointed in this expectation, as he had been in so many others connected with this case. There was nothing in Miss Oliver's attitude to indicate that she had unburdened herself of any of the emotions with which she was so grievously agitated, nor was there on Mr. Van Burnam's part any deeper manifestation of feeling than a slight glow on his cheek, and even that disappeared under the detective's scrutiny, leaving him as composed and imperturbable as he had been in his memorable inquisition before the Coroner.

Disappointed, and yet in a measure exhilarated by this sudden check in plans he had thought too well laid for failure, Mr. Gryce surveyed the young girl more carefully, and saw that he had not been mistaken in regard to the force or extent of the feelings which had driven her into Mr. Van Burnam's presence; and turning back to that gentleman, was about to give utterance to some very pertinent remarks, when he was forestalled by Mr. Van Burnam inquiring, in his old calm way, which nothing seemed able to disturb:

"Who is this crazy girl you have forced upon me? If I had known I was to be subjected to such companionship I should not have regarded my outing so favorably."

Mr. Gryce, who never allowed himself to be surprised by anything a suspected criminal might do or say, surveyed him quietly for a moment, then turned towards Miss Oliver.

"You hear what this gentleman calls you?" said he.

Her face was hidden by her hands, but she dropped them as the detective addressed her, showing a countenance so distorted by passion that it stopped the current of his thoughts, and made him question whether the epithet bestowed upon her by their somewhat callous companion was entirely unjustified. But soon the something else which was in her face restored his confidence in her sanity, and he saw that while her reason might be shaken it was not yet dethroned, and that he had good cause to expect sooner or later some action from a woman whose misery could wear an aspect of such desperate resolution.

That he was not the only one affected by the force and desperate character of her glance became presently apparent, for Mr. Van Burnam, with a more kindly tone than he had previously used, observed quietly:

"I see the lady is suffering. I beg pardon for my inconsiderate words. I have no wish to insult the unhappy."

Never was Mr. Gryce so nonplussed. There was a mingled courtesy and composure in the speaker's manner which was as far removed as possible from that strained effort at self-possession which marks suppressed passion or secret fear; while in the vacant look with which she met these words there was neither anger nor scorn nor indeed any of the passions one would expect to see there. The detective consequently did not force the situation, but only watched her more and more attentively till her eyes fell and she crouched away from them both. Then he said:

"You can name this gentleman, can you not, Miss Oliver, even if he does not choose to recognize you?"

But her answer, if she made one, was inaudible, and the sole result which Mr. Gryce obtained from this venture was a quick look from Mr. Van Burnam and the following uncompromising words from his lips:

"If you think this young girl knows me, or that I know her, you are greatly mistaken.

She is as much of a stranger to me as I am to her, and I take this opportunity of saying so. I hope my liberty and good name are not to be made dependent upon the word of a miserable waif like this."

"Your liberty and your good name will depend upon your innocence," retorted Mr. Gryce, and said no more, feeling himself at a disadvantage before the imperturbability of this man and the silent, non-accusing attitude of this woman, from the shock of whose passions he had anticipated so much and obtained so little.

Meantime they were moving rapidly towards Police Headquarters, and fearing that the sight of that place might alarm Miss Oliver more than was well for her, he strove again to rouse her by a kindly word or so. But it was useless. She evidently tried to pay attention and follow the words he used, but her thoughts were too busy over the one great subject that engrossed her.

"A bad case!" murmured Mr. Van Burnam, and with the phrase seemed to dismiss all thought of her.

"A bad case!" echoed Mr. Gryce, "but," seeing how fast the look of resolution was replacing her previous aspect of frenzy, "one that will do mischief yet to the man who has deceived her."

The stopping of the carriage roused her. Looking up, she spoke for the first time.

"I want a police officer," she said.

Mr. Gryce, with all his assurance restored, leaped to the ground and held out his hand.

"I will take you into the presence of one," said he; and she, without a glance at Mr. Van Burnam, whose knee she brushed in passing, leaped to the ground, and turned her face towards Police Headquarters.

XXXVII   "TWO WEEKS!"

But before she was well in, her countenance changed.

"No," said she, "I want to think first. Give me time to think. I dare not say a word without thinking."

"Truth needs no consideration. If you wish to denounce this man——"

Her look said she did.

"Then now is the time."

She gave him a sharp glance; the first she had bestowed upon him since leaving Miss Althorpe's.

"You are no doctor," she declared. "Are you a police-officer?"

"I am a detective."

"Oh!" and she hesitated for a moment, shrinking from him with very natural distrust and aversion. "I have been in the toils then without knowing it; no wonder I am caught. But I am no criminal, sir; and if you are the one most in authority here, I beg the privilege of a few words with you before I am put into confinement."

"I will take you before the Superintendent," said Mr. Gryce. "But do you wish to go alone? Shall not Mr. Van Burnam accompany you?"

"Mr. Van Burnam?"

"Is it not he you wish to denounce?"

"I do not wish to denounce any one to-day."

"What do you wish?" asked Mr. Gryce.

"Let me see the man who has power to hold me here or let me go, and I will tell him."

"Very well," said Mr. Gryce, and led her into the presence of the Superintendent.

She was at this moment quite a different person from what she had been in the carriage. All that was girlish in her aspect or appealing in her bearing had faded away, evidently forever, and left in its place something at once so desperate and so deadly, that she seemed not only a woman but one of a very determined and dangerous nature. Her manner, however, was quiet, and it was only in her eye that one could see how near she was to frenzy.

She spoke before the Superintendent could address her.

"Sir," said she, "I have been brought here on account of a fearful crime I was unhappy enough to witness. I myself am innocent of that crime, but, so far as I know, there is no other person living save the guilty man who committed it, who can tell you how or why or by whom it was done. One man has been arrested for it and another has not. If you will give me two weeks of complete freedom, I will point out to you which is the veritable man of blood, and may Heaven have mercy on his soul!"

"She is mad," signified the Superintendent in by-play to Mr. Gryce.

But the latter shook his head; she was not mad yet.

"I know," she continued, without a hint of the timidity which seemed natural to her under other circumstances, "that this must seem a presumptuous request from one like me, but it is only by granting it that you will ever be able to lay your hand on the murderer of Mrs. Van Burnam. For I will never speak if I cannot speak in my own way and at my own time. The agonies I have suffered must have some compensation. Otherwise I should die of horror and my grief."

"And how do you hope to gain compensation by this delay?" expostulated the Superintendent. "Would you not meet with more satisfaction in denouncing him here and now before he can pass another night in fancied security?"

But she only repeated: "I have said two weeks, and two weeks I must have. Two weeks in which to come and go as I please. Two weeks!" And no argument they could advance succeeded in eliciting from her any other response or in altering in any way her air of quiet determination with its underlying suggestion of frenzy.

Acknowledging their mutual defeat by a look, the Superintendent and detective drew off to one side, and something like the following conversation took place between them.

"You think she's sane?"

"I do."

"And will remain so two weeks?"

"If humored."

"You are sure she is implicated in this crime?"

"She was a witness to it."

"And that she speaks the truth when she declares that she is the only person who can point out the criminal?"

"Yes; that is, she is the only one who will do it. The attitude taken by the Van Burnams, especially by Howard just now in the presence of this girl, shows how little we have to expect from them."

"Yet you think they know as much as she does about it?"

"I do not know what to think. For once I am baffled, Superintendent. Every passion which this woman possesses was roused by her unexpected meeting with Howard Van Burnam, and yet their indifference when confronted, as well as her present action, seems to argue a lack of connection between them which overthrows at once the theory of his guilt. Was it the sight of Franklin, then, which really affected her? and was her apparent indifference at meeting him only an evidence of her self-control? It seems an impossible conclusion to draw, and indeed there are nothing but hitches and improbable features in this case. Nothing fits; nothing jibes. I get just so far in it and then I run up against a wall. Either there is a superhuman power of duplicity in the persons who contrived this murder or we are on the wrong tack altogether."

"In other words, you have tried every means known to you to get at the truth of this matter, and failed."

"I have, sir; sorry as I may be to acknowledge it."

"Then we must accept her terms. She can be shadowed?"

"Every moment."

"Very well, then. Extreme cases must be met by extreme measures. We will let her have her swing, and see what comes of it. Revenge is a great weapon in the hands of a determined woman, and from her look I think she will make the most of it."

And returning to where the young girl stood, the Superintendent asked her whether she felt sure the murderer would not escape in the time that must elapse before his apprehension.

Instantly her cheek, which had looked as if it could never show color again, flushed a deep and painful scarlet, and she cried vehemently:

"If any hint of what is here passing should reach him I should be powerless to prevent his flight. Swear, then, that my very existence shall be kept a secret between you two, or I will do nothing towards his apprehension,—no, not even to save the innocent."

"We will not swear, but we will promise," returned the Superintendent. "And now, when may we expect to hear from you again?"

"Two weeks from to-night as the clock strikes eight. Be wherever I may chance to be at that hour, and see on whose arm I lay my hand. It will be that of the man who killed Mrs. Van Burnam."

XXXVIII   A WHITE SATIN GOWN

The events just related did not come to my knowledge for some days after they occurred, but I have recorded them at this time that I might in some way prepare you for an interview which shortly after took place between myself and Mr. Gryce.

I had not seen him since our rather unsatisfactory parting in front of Miss Althorpe's house, and the suspense which I had endured in the interim made my greeting unnecessarily warm. But he took it all very naturally.

"You are glad to see me," said he; "been wondering what has become of Miss Oliver. Well, she is in good hands; with Mrs. Desberger, in short; a woman whom I believe you know."

"With Mrs. Desberger?" I was surprised. "Why, I have been looking every day in the papers for an account of her arrest."

"No doubt," he answered. "But we police are slow; we are not ready to arrest her yet. Meanwhile you can do us a favor. She wants to see you; are you willing to visit her?"

My answer contained but little of the curiosity and eagerness I really felt.

"I am always at your command. Do you wish me to go now?"

"Miss Oliver is impatient," he admitted. "Her fever is better, but she is in an excited condition of mind which makes her a little unreasonable. To be plain, she is not quite herself, and while we still hope something from her testimony, we are leaving her very much to her own devices, and do not cross her in anything. You will therefore listen to what she says, and, if possible, aid her in anything she may undertake, unless it points directly towards self-destruction. My opinion is that she will surprise you. But you are becoming accustomed to surprises, are you not?"

"Thanks to you, I am."

"Very well, then, I have but one more suggestion to make. You are working for the police now, madam, and nothing that you see or learn in connection with this girl is to be kept back from us. Am I understood?"

"Perfectly; but it is only proper for me to retort that I am not entirely pleased with the part you assign me. Could you not have left thus much to my good sense, and not put it into so many words?"

"Ah, madam, the case at present is too serious for risks of that kind. Mr. Van Burnam's reputation, to say nothing of his life, depends upon our knowledge of this girl's secret; surely you can stretch a point in a matter of so much moment?"

"I have already stretched several, and I can stretch one more, but I hope the girl won't look at me too often with those miserable appealing eyes of hers; they make me feel like a traitor."

"You will not be troubled by any appeal in them. The appeal has vanished; something harder and even more difficult to meet is to be found in them now: wrath, purpose, and a desire for vengeance. She is not the same woman, I assure you."

"Well," I sighed, "I am sorry; there is something about the girl that lays hold of me, and I hate to see such a change in her. Did she ask for me by name?"

"I believe so."

"I cannot understand her wanting me, but I will go; and I won't leave her either till she shows me she is tired of me. I am as anxious to see the end of this matter as you are." Then, with some vague idea that I had earned a right to some show of confidence on his part, I added insinuatingly: "I supposed you would feel the case settled when she almost fainted at the sight of the younger Mr. Van Burnam."

The old ambiguous smile I remembered so well came to modify his brusque rejoinder.

"If she had been a woman like you, I should; but she is a deep one, Miss Butterworth; too deep for the success of a little ruse like mine. Are you ready?"

I was not, but it did not take me long to be so, and before an hour had elapsed I was seated in Mrs. Desberger's parlor in Ninth Street. Miss Oliver was in, and ere long made her appearance. She was dressed in street costume.

I was prepared for a change in her, and yet the shock I felt when I first saw her face must have been apparent, for she immediately remarked:

"You find me quite well, Miss Butterworth. For this I am partially indebted to you. You were very good to nurse me so carefully. Will you be still kinder, and help me in a new matter which I feel quite incompetent to undertake alone?"

Her face was flushed, her manner nervous, but her eyes had an extraordinary look in them which affected me most painfully, notwithstanding the additional effect it gave to her beauty.

"Certainly," said I. "What can I do for you?"

"I wish to buy me a dress," was her unexpected reply. "A handsome dress. Do you object to showing me the best shops? I am a stranger in New York."

More astonished than I can express, but carefully concealing it in remembrance of the caution received from Mr. Gryce, I replied that I would be only too happy to accompany her on such an errand. Upon which she lost her nervousness and prepared at once to go out with me.

"I would have asked Mrs. Desberger," she observed while fitting on her gloves, "but her taste"—here she cast a significant look about the room—"is not quiet enough for me."

"I should think not!" I cried.

"I shall be a trouble to you," the girl went on, with a gleam in her eye that spoke of the restless spirit within. "I have many things to buy, and they must all be rich and handsome."

"If you have money enough, there will be no trouble about that."

"Oh, I have money." She spoke like a millionaire's daughter. "Shall we go to Arnold's?"

As I always traded at Arnold's, I readily acquiesced, and we left the house. But not before she had tied a very thick veil over her face.

"If we meet any one, do not introduce me," she begged. "I cannot talk to people."

"You may rest easy," I assured her.

At the corner she stopped. "Is there any way of getting a carriage?" she asked.

"Do you want one?"

"Yes."

I signalled a hack.

"Now for the dress!" she cried.

We rode at once to Arnold's.

"What kind of a dress do you want?" I inquired as we entered the store.

"An evening one; a white satin, I think."

I could not help the exclamation which escaped me; but I covered it up as quickly as possible by a hurried remark in favor of white, and we proceeded at once to the silk counter.

"I will trust it all to you," she whispered in an odd, choked tone as the clerk approached us. "Get what you would for your daughter—no, no! for Mr. Van Burnam's daughter, if he has one, and do not spare expense. I have five hundred dollars in my pocket."

Mr. Van Burnam's daughter! Well, well! A tragedy of some kind was portending! But I bought the dress.

"Now," said she, "lace, and whatever else I need to make it up suitably. And I must have slippers and gloves. You know what a young girl requires to make her look like a lady. I want to look so well that the most critical eye will detect no fault in my appearance. It can be done, can it not, Miss Butterworth? My face and figure will not spoil the effect, will they?"

"No," said I; "you have a good face and a beautiful figure. You ought to look well. Are you going to a ball, my dear?"

"I am going to a ball," she answered; but her tone was so strange the people passing us turned to look at her.

"Let us have everything sent to the carriage," said she, and went with me from counter to counter with her ready purse in her hand, but not once lifting her veil to look at what was offered us, saying over and over as I sought to consult her in regard to some article: "Buy the richest; I leave it all to you."

Had Mr. Gryce not told me she must be humored, I could never have gone through this ordeal. To see a girl thus expend her hoarded savings on such frivolities was absolutely painful to me, and more than once I was tempted to decline any further participation in such extravagance. But a thought of my obligations to Mr. Gryce restrained me, and I went on spending the poor girl's dollars with more pain to myself than if I had taken them out of my own pocket.

Having purchased all the articles we thought necessary, we were turning towards the door when Miss Oliver whispered:

"Wait for me in the carriage for just a few minutes. I have one more thing to buy, and I must do it alone."

"But——" I began.

"I will do it, and I will not be followed," she insisted, in a shrill tone that made me jump.

And seeing no other way of preventing a scene, I let her leave me, though it cost me an anxious fifteen minutes.

When she rejoined me, as she did at the expiration of that time, I eyed the bundle she held with decided curiosity. But I could make no guess at its contents.

"Now," she cried, as she reseated herself and closed the carriage door, "where shall I find a dressmaker able and willing to make up this satin in five days?"

I could not tell her. But after some little search we succeeded in finding a woman who engaged to make an elegant costume in the time given her. The first measurements were taken, and we drove back to Ninth Street with a lasting memory in my mind of the cold and rigid form of Miss Oliver standing up in Madame's triangular parlor, submitting to the mechanical touches of the modiste with an outward composure, but with a brooding horror in her eyes that bespoke an inward torment.

XXXIX   THE WATCHFUL EYE

As I parted with Miss Oliver on Mrs. Desberger's stoop and did not visit her again in that house, I will introduce the report of a person better situated than myself to observe the girl during the next few days. That the person thus alluded to was a woman in the service of the police is evident, and as such may not meet with your approval, but her words are of interest, as witness:

"Friday P.M.

"Party went out to-day in company with an elderly female of respectable appearance. Said elderly female wears puffs, and moves with great precision. I say this in case her identification should prove necessary.

"I had been warned that Miss O. would probably go out, and as the man set to watch the front door was on duty, I occupied myself during her absence in making a neat little hole in the partitions between our two rooms, so that I should not be obliged to offend my next-door neighbor by too frequent visits to her apartment. This done, I awaited her return, which was delayed till it was almost dark. When she did come in, her arms were full of bundles. These she thrust into a bureau-drawer, with the exception of one, which she laid with great care under her pillow. I wondered what this one could be, but could get no inkling from its size or shape. Her manner when she took off her hat was fiercer than before, and a strange smile, which I had not previously observed on her lips, added force to her expression. But it paled after supper-time, and she had a restless night. I could hear her walk the floor long after I thought it prudent on my part to retire, and at intervals through the night I was disturbed by her moaning, which was not that of a sick person but of one very much afflicted in mind.

"Saturday.

"Party quiet. Sits most of the time with hands clasped on her knee before the fire. Given to quick starts as if suddenly awakened from an absorbing train of thought. A pitiful object, especially when seized by terror as she is at odd times. No walks, no visitors to-day. Once I heard her speak some words in a strange language, and once she drew herself up before the mirror in an attitude of so much dignity I was surprised at the fine appearance she made. The fire of her eyes at this moment was remarkable. I should not be surprised at any move she might make.

"Sunday.

"She has been writing to-day. But when she had filled several pages of letter paper she suddenly tore them all up and threw them into the fire. Time seems to drag with her, for she goes every few minutes to the window from which a distant church clock is visible, and sighs as she turns away. More writing in the evening and some tears. But the writing was burned as before, and the tears stopped by a laugh that augurs little good to the person who called it up. The package has been taken from under her pillow and put in some place not visible from my spy-hole.

"Monday.

"Party out again to-day, gone some two hours or more. When she returned she sat down before the mirror and began dressing her hair. She has fine hair, and she tried arranging it in several ways. None seemed to satisfy her, and she tore it down again and let it hang till supper-time, when she wound it up in its usual simple knot. Mrs. Desberger spent some minutes with her, but their talk was far from confidential, and therefore uninteresting. I wish people would speak louder when they talk to themselves.

"Tuesday.

"Great restlessness on the part of the young person I am watching. No quiet for her, no quiet for me, yet she accomplishes nothing, and as yet has furnished me no clue to her thoughts.

"A huge box was brought into the room to-night. It seemed to cause her dread rather than pleasure, for she shrank at sight of it, and has not yet attempted to open it. But her eyes have never left it since it was set down on the floor. It looks like a dressmaker's box, but why such emotion over a gown?

"Wednesday.

"This morning she opened the box but did not display its contents. I caught one glimpse of a mass of tissue paper, and then she put the cover on again, and for a good half hour sat crouching down beside it, shuddering like one in an ague-fit. I began to feel there was something deadly in the box, her eyes wandered towards it so frequently and with such contradictory looks of dread and savage determination. When she got up it was to see how many more minutes of the wretched day had passed.

"Thursday.

"Party sick; did not try to leave her bed. Breakfast brought up by Mrs. Desberger, who showed her every attention, but could not prevail upon her to eat. Yet she would not let the tray be taken away, and when she was alone again or thought herself alone, she let her eyes rest so long on the knife lying across her plate, that I grew nervous and could hardly restrain myself from rushing into the room. But I remembered my instructions, and kept still even when I saw her hand steal towards this possible weapon, though I kept my own on the bell-rope which fortunately hung at my side. She looked quite capable of wounding herself with the knife, but after balancing it a moment in her hand, she laid it down again and turned with a low moan to the wall. She will not attempt death till she has accomplished what is in her mind.

"Friday.

"All is right in the next room; that is, the young lady is up; but there is another change in her appearance since last night. She has grown contemptuous of herself and indulges less in brooding. But her impatience at the slow passage of time continues, and her interest in the box is even greater than before. She does not open it, however, only looks at it and lays her trembling hand now and then on the cover.

"Saturday.

"A blank day. Party dull and very quiet. Her eyes begin to look like ghastly hollows in her pale face. She talks to herself continually, but in a low mechanical way exceedingly wearing to the listener, especially as no word can be distinguished. Tried to see her in her own room to-day, but she would not admit me.

"Sunday.

"I have noticed from the first a Bible lying on one end of her mantel-shelf. To-day she noticed it also, and impulsively reached out her hand to take it down. But at the first word she read she gave a low cry and hastily closed the book and put it back. Later, however, she took it again and read several chapters. The result was a softening in her manner, but she went to bed as flushed and determined as ever.

"Monday.

"She has walked the floor all day. She has seen no one, and seems scarcely able to contain her impatience. She cannot stand this long.

"Tuesday.

"My surprises began in the morning. As soon as her room had been put in order, Miss O. locked the door and began to open her bundles. First she unrolled a pair of white silk stockings, which she carefully, but without any show of interest, laid on the bed; then she opened a package containing gloves. They were white also, and evidently of the finest quality. Then a lace handkerchief was brought to light, slippers, an evening fan, and a pair of fancy pins, and lastly she opened the mysterious box and took out a dress so rich in quality and of such simple elegance, it almost took my breath away. It was white, and made of the heaviest satin, and it looked as much out of place in that shabby room as its owner did in the moments of exaltation of which I have spoken.

"Though her face was flushed when she lifted out the gown, it became pale again when she saw it lying across her bed. Indeed, a look of passionate abhorrence characterized her features as she contemplated it, and her hands went up before her eyes and she reeled back uttering the first words I have been able to distinguish since I have been on duty. They were violent in character, and seemed to tear their way through her lips almost without her volition. 'It is hate I feel, nothing but hate. Ah, if it were only duty that animated me!'

"Later she grew calmer, and covering up the whole paraphernalia with a stray sheet she had evidently laid by for the purpose, she sent for Mrs. Desberger. When that lady came in she met her with a wan but by no means dubious smile, and ignoring with quiet dignity the very evident curiosity with which that good woman surveyed the bed, she said appealingly:

"'You have been so kind to me, Mrs. Desberger, that I am going to tell you a secret. Will it continue to remain a secret, or shall I see it in the faces of all my fellow-boarders tomorrow?' You can imagine Mrs. Desberger's reply, also the manner in which it was delivered, but not Miss Oliver's secret. She uttered it in these words: 'I am going out tonight, Mrs. Desberger. I am going into great society. I am going to attend Miss Althorpe's wedding.' Then, as the good woman stammered out some words of surprise and pleasure, she went on to say: 'I do not want any one to know it, and I would be so glad if I could slip out of the house without any one seeing me. I shall need a carriage, but you will get one for me, will you not, and let me know the moment it comes. I am shy of what folks may say, and besides, as you know, I am neither happy nor well, if I do go to weddings, and have new dresses, and——' She nearly broke down but collected herself with wonderful promptitude, and with a coaxing look that made her almost ghastly, so much it seemed out of accord with her strained and unnatural manner, she raised a corner of the sheet, saying, 'I will show you my gown, if you will promise to help me quietly out of the house,' which, of course, produced the desired effect upon Mrs. Desberger, that woman's greatest weakness being her love of dress.

"So from that hour I knew what to expect, and after sending precautionary advices to Police Headquarters, I set myself to watch her prepare for the evening. I saw her arrange her hair and put on her elegant gown, and was as much startled by the result as if I had not had the least premonition that she only needed rich clothes to look both beautiful and distinguished. The square parcel she had once hidden under her pillow was brought out and laid on the bed, and when Mrs. Desberger's low knock announced the arrival of the carriage, she caught it up and hid it under the cloak she hastily threw about her. Mrs. Desberger came in and put out the light, but before the room sank into darkness I caught one glimpse of Miss Oliver's face. Its expression was terrible beyond anything I had ever seen on any human countenance."

XL   AS THE CLOCK STRUCK

I do not attend weddings in general, but great as my suspense was in reference to Miss Oliver, I felt that I could not miss seeing Miss Althorpe married.

I had ordered a new dress for the occasion, and was in the best of spirits as I rode to the church in which the ceremony was to be performed. The excitement of a great social occasion was for once not disagreeable to me, nor did I mind the crowd, though it pushed me about rather uncomfortably till an usher came to my assistance and seated me in a pew, which I was happy to see commanded a fine view of the chancel.

I was early, but then I always am early, and having ample opportunity for observation, I noted every fine detail of ornamentation with approval, Miss Althorpe's taste being of that fine order which always falls short of ostentation. Her friends are in very many instances my friends, and it was no small part of my pleasure to note their well-known faces among the crowd of those that were strange to me. That the scene was brilliant, and that silks, satins, and diamonds abounded, goes without saying.

At last the church was full, and the hush which usually precedes the coming of the bride was settling over the whole assemblage, when I suddenly observed, in the person of a respectable-looking gentleman seated in a side pew, the form and features of Mr. Gryce, the detective. This was a shock to me, yet what was there in his presence there to alarm me? Might not Miss Althorpe have accorded him this pleasure out of the pure goodness of her heart? I did not look at anybody else, however, after once my eyes fell upon him, but continued to watch his expression, which was non-committal, though a little anxious for one engaged in a purely social function.

The entrance of the clergyman and the sudden peal of the organ in the well-known wedding march recalled my attention to the occasion itself, and as at that moment the bridegroom stepped from the vestry to await his bride at the altar, I was absorbed by his fine appearance and the air of mingled pride and happiness with which he watched the stately approach of the bridal procession.

But suddenly there was a stir through the whole glittering assemblage, and the clergyman made a move and the bridegroom gave a start, and the sound, slight as it was, of moving feet grew still, and I saw advancing from the door on the opposite side of the altar a second bride, clad in white and surrounded by a long veil which completely hid her face. A second bride! and the first was half-way up the aisle, and only one bridegroom stood ready!

The clergyman, who seemed to have as little command of his faculties as the rest of us, tried to speak; but the approaching woman, upon whom every regard was fixed, forestalled him by an authoritative gesture.

Advancing towards the chancel, she took her place on the spot reserved for Miss Althorpe.

Silence had filled the church up to this moment; but at this audacious move, a solitary wailing cry of mingled astonishment and despair went up behind us; but before any of us could turn, and while my own heart stood still, for I thought I recognized this veiled figure, the woman at the altar raised her hand and pointed towards the bridegroom.

"Why does he hesitate?" she cried. "Does he not recognize the only woman with whom he dare face God and man at the altar? Because I am already his wedded wife, and have been so for five long years, does that make my wearing of this veil amiss when he a husband, unreleased by the law, dares enter this sacred place with the hope and expectation of a bridegroom?"

It was Ruth Oliver who spoke. I recognized her voice as I had recognized her apparel; but the emotions aroused in me by her presence and the almost incredible claims she advanced were lost in the horror inspired by the man she thus vehemently accused. No lost spirit from the pit could have shown a more hideous commingling of the most terrible passions known to man than he did in the face of this terrible arraignment; and if Ella Althorpe, cowering in her shame and misery half-way up the aisle, saw him in all his depravity at that instant as I did, nothing could have saved her long-cherished love from immediate death.

Yet he tried to speak.

"It is false!" he cried; "all false! The woman I once called wife is dead."

"Dead, Olive Randolph? Murderer!" she exclaimed. "The blow struck in the dark found another victim!" And pulling the veil from her face, Ruth Oliver advanced to his side and laid her trembling hand with a firm and decisive movement on his arm.

Was it her words, her touch, or the sound of the clock striking eight in the great tower over our heads, which so totally overwhelmed him? As the last stroke of the hour which was to have seen him united with Miss Althorpe died out in the awed spaces above him, he gave a cry such as I am sure never resounded between those sacred walls before, and sank in a heap on the spot where but a few minutes previous he had lifted his head in all the glow and pride of a prospective bridegroom.

XLI   SECRET HISTORY

It was hours before I found myself able to realize that the scene I had just witnessed had a deeper and much more dreadful significance than appeared to the general eye, and that Ruth Oliver, in her desperate interruption of these treacherous nuptials, had not only made good her prior claim to Randolph Stone as her husband, but had pointed him out to all the world as the villainous author of that crime which for so long a time had occupied my own and the public's attention.

Thinking that you may find the same difficulty in grasping this terrible fact, and being anxious to save you from the suspense under which I myself labored for so many hours, I here subjoin a written statement made by this woman some weeks later, in which the whole mystery is explained. It is signed Olive Randolph; the name to which she evidently feels herself best entitled.

"The man known in New York City as Randolph Stone was first seen by me in Michigan five years ago. His name then was John Randolph, and how he has since come to add to this the further appellation of Stone, I must leave to himself to explain.

"I was born in Michigan myself, and till my eighteenth year I lived with my father, who was a widower without any other child, in a little low cottage amid the sand mounds that border the eastern side of the lake.

"I was not pretty, but every man who passed me on the beach or in the streets of the little town where we went to market and to church, stopped to look at me, and this I noticed, and from this perhaps my unhappiness arose.

"For before I was old enough to know the difference between poverty and riches, I began to lose all interest in my simple home duties, and to cast longing looks at the great school building where girls like myself learned to speak like ladies and play the piano. Yet these ambitious promptings might have come to nothing if I had never met him. I might have settled down in my own sphere and lived a useful if unsatisfied life like my mother and my mother's mother before her.

"But fate had reserved me for wretchedness, and one day just as I was on the verge of my eighteenth year, I saw John Randolph.

"I was coming out of church when our eyes first met, and I noticed after the first shock my simple heart received from his handsome face and elegant appearance, that he was surveying me with that strange look of admiration I had seen before on so many faces; and the joy this gave me, and the certainty which came with it of my seeing him again, made that moment quite unlike any other in my whole life, and was the beginning of that passion which has undone me, ruined him, and brought death and sorrow to many others of more worth than either of us.

"He was not a resident of the town, but a passing visitor; and his intention had been, as he has since told me, to leave the place on the following day. But the dart which had pierced my breast had not glanced entirely aside from his, and he remained, as he declared, to see what there was in this little country-girl's face to make it so unforgettable. We met first on the beach and afterwards under the strip of pines which separate our cottage from the sand mounds, and though I have no reason to believe he came to these interviews with any honest purpose or deep sincerity of feeling, it is certain he exerted all his powers to make them memorable to me, and that, in doing so, he awoke some of the fire in his own breast which he took such wicked pleasure in arousing in mine.

"In fact he soon showed that this was so, for I could take no step from the house without encountering him; and the one indelible impression remaining to me from those days is the expression his face wore as, one sunny afternoon, he laid my hand on his arm and drew me away to have a look at the lake booming on the beach below us. There was no love in it as I understand love now, but the passion which informed it almost amounted to intoxication, and if such a passion can be understood between a man already cultivated and a girl who hardly knew how to read, it may, in a measure, account for what followed.

"My father, who was no fool, and who saw the selfish quality in this attractive lover of mine, was alarmed by our growing intimacy. Taking an opportunity when we were both in a more sensible mood than common, he put the case before Mr. Randolph in a very decided way. He told him that either he must marry me at once or quit seeing me altogether. No delay was to be considered and no compromise allowed.

"As my father was a man with whom no one ever disputed, John Randolph prepared to leave the town, declaring that he could marry no one at that stage of his career. But before he could carry out his intention, the old intoxication returned, and he came back in a fever of love and impatience to marry me.

"Had I been older or more experienced in the ways of the world, I would have known that such passion as this evinced was short-lived; that there is no witchery in a smile lasting enough to make men like him forget the lack of those social graces to which they are accustomed. But I was mad with happiness, and was unconscious of any cloud lowering upon our future till the day of our first separation came, when an event occurred which showed me what I might expect if I could not speedily raise myself to his level.

"We were out walking, and we met a lady who had known Mr. Randolph elsewhere. She was well dressed, which I was not, though I had not realized it till I saw how attractive she looked in quiet colors and with only a simple ribbon on her hat; and she had, besides, a way of speaking which made my tones sound harsh, and robbed me of that feeling of superiority with which I had hitherto regarded all the girls of my acquaintance.

"But it was not her possession of these advantages, keenly as I felt them, which awakened me to the sense of my position. It was the surprise she showed (a surprise the source of which was not to be mistaken) when he introduced me to her as his wife; and though she recovered herself in a moment, and tried to be kind and gracious, I felt the sting of it and saw that he felt it too, and consequently was not at all astonished when, after she had passed us, he turned and looked at me critically for the first time.

"But his way of showing his dissatisfaction gave me a shock it took me years to recover from. 'Take off that hat,' he cried, and when I had obeyed him, he tore out the spray which to my eyes had been its chief adornment, and threw it into some bushes near by; then he gave me back the hat and asked for the silk neckerchief which I had regarded as the glory of my bridal costume. Giving it to him I saw him put it in his pocket, and understanding now that he was trying to make me look more like the lady we had passed, I cried out passionately: 'It is not these things that make the difference, John, but my voice and way of walking and speaking. Give me money and let me be educated, and then we will see if any other woman can draw your eyes away from me.'

"But he had received a shock that made him cruel. 'You cannot make a silk purse out of a sow's ear,' he sneered, and was silent all the rest of the way home. I was silent too, for I never talk when I am angry, but when we arrived in our own little room I confronted him.

"'Are you going to say any more such cruel things to me?' I asked, 'for if you are, I should like you to say them now and be done with it.'

"He looked desperately angry, but there was yet a little love left in his heart for me, for he laughed after he had looked at me for a minute, and took me in his arms and said some of the fine things with which he had previously won my heart, but not with the old fire and not with the old effect upon me. Yet my love had not grown cold, it had only changed from the unthinking stage to the thinking one, and I was quite in earnest when I said: 'I know I am not as pretty or as nice as the ladies you are accustomed to. But I have a heart that has never known any other passion than its love for you, and from such a heart you ought to expect a lady to grow, and there will. Only give me the chance, John; only let me learn to read and write.'

"But he was in an incredulous state of mind, and it ended in his going away without making any arrangements for my education. He was bound for San Francisco, where he had business to transact, and he promised to be back in four weeks, but before the four weeks elapsed, he wrote me that it would be five, and later on that it would be six, and afterwards that it would be when he had finished a big piece of work he was engaged upon, and which would bring him a large amount of money. I believed him and I doubted him at the same time, but I was not altogether sorry he delayed his return for I had begun school on my own account and was fast laying the foundation of a solid education.

"My means came from my father, who, now it was too late, saw the necessity of my improving myself. The amount of studying I did that first year was amazing, but it was nothing to what I went through the second, for my husband's letters had begun to fail me, and I was forced to work in order to drown grief and keep myself from despair. Finally no letters came at all, and when the second year was over, and I could at least express myself correctly, I woke to the realization that, so far as my husband was concerned, I had gone through all this labor for nothing, and that unless by some fortunate chance I could light upon some clue to his whereabouts in the great world beyond our little town, I would be likely to pass the remainder of my days in widowhood and desolation.

"My father dying at this time and leaving me a thousand dollars, I knew no better way of spending it than in the hopeless search I have just mentioned. Accordingly after his burial I started out on my travels, gaining experience with every mile. I had not been away a week before I realized what a folly I had indulged in in ever hoping to see John Randolph back at my side. I saw the homes in which such men as he lived, and met in cars and on steamboats the kind of people with whom he must associate to be happy, and a gulf seemed to open between us which even such love as mine would be powerless to bridge.

"But though hope thus sank in my breast, I did not lose my old ambition of making myself as worthy of him as circumstances would permit. I read only the best books and I allowed myself to become acquainted with only the best people, and as I saw myself liked by such the awkwardness of my manner gradually disappeared, and I began to feel that the day would come when I should be universally recognized as a lady.

"Meantime I did not advance an iota in the object of my journey; and at last, with every expectation gone of ever seeing my husband again, I made my way to Toledo. Here I speedily found employment, and what was better still to one of my ambitious tendencies, an opportunity to add to the sum of my accomplishments a knowledge of French and music. The French I learned from the family I lived with, and the music from a professor in the same house whose love for his pet art was so great that he found it simple happiness to impart it to one so greedy for improvement as myself.

"Here, in course of time, I also learned type-writing, and it was for the purpose of seeking employment in this capacity that I finally came to New York. This was three months ago.

"I was in complete ignorance of the city when I entered it, and for a day or two I wandered to and fro, searching for a suitable lodging-house. It was while I was on my way to Mrs. Desberger's that I saw advancing towards me a gentleman in whose air and manner I detected a resemblance to the husband who some five years since had deserted me. The shock was too much for my self-control. Quaking in every limb, I stood awaiting his approach, and when he came up to me, and I saw by his startled recognition of me that it was indeed he, I gave a loud cry and threw myself upon his arm. The start he gave was nothing to the frightful expression which crossed his face at this encounter, but I thought both due to his surprise, though now I am convinced they had their origin in the deepest and worst emotions of which a man is capable.

"'John! John!' I cried, and could say no more, for the agitations of five solitary, despairing years were choking me; but he was entirely voiceless, stricken, I have no doubt, beyond any power of mine to realize. How could I dream that in consideration, power, and prestige he had advanced even more rapidly than myself, and that at this very moment he was not only the idol of society, but on the verge of uniting himself to a woman—I will not say of marrying her, for marry her he could not while I lived—who would make him the envied possessor of millions. Such fortune, such daring, yes and such depravity, were beyond the reach of my imagination, and while I thought his pleasure less than mine, I did not dream that my existence was a menace to all his hopes, and that during this moment of speechlessness he was sounding his nature for means to rid himself of me even at the cost of my life.

"His first movement was to push me away, but I clung to him all the harder; at which his whole manner changed and he began to make futile efforts to calm me and lead me away from the spot. Seeing that these attempts were unavailing, he turned pale and raised his arm up passionately, but speedily dropped it again, and casting glances this way and that, broke suddenly into a loud laugh and became, as by the touch of a magician's wand, my old lover again.

"'Why, Olive!' he cried; 'why, Olive! is it you? (Did I say my name was Olive?) Happily met, my dear! I did not know what I had been missing all these years, but now I know it was you. Will you come with me, or shall I go home with you?'

"'I have no home,' said I, 'I have just come into town.'

"'Then I see but one alternative.' He smiled, and what a power there was in his smile when he chose to exert it! 'You must come to my apartments; are you willing?'

"'I am your wife,' I answered.

"He had taken me on his arm by this time and the recoil he made at these words was quite perceptible; but his face still smiled, and I was too mad with joy to be critical.

"'And a very pretty and charming wife you have become,' said he, drawing me on for a few steps. Suddenly he paused, and I felt the old shadow fall between us again. 'But your dress is very shabby,' he remarked.

"It was not; it was not near as shabby as the linen duster he himself wore.

"'Is that rain?' he inquired, looking up as a drop or two fell.

"'Yes, it is raining.'

"'Very well, let us go into this store we are coming to and buy a gossamer. That will cover up your gown. I cannot take you to my house dressed as you are now.'

"Surprised, for I had thought my dress very neat and lady-like, but never dreaming of questioning his taste any more than in the old days in Michigan, I went with him into the shop he had pointed out and bought me a gossamer, for which he paid. When he had helped me to put it on and had tied my veil well over my face, he seemed more at his ease and gave me his arm quite cheerfully.

"'Now,' said he, 'you look well, but how about the time when you will have to take the gossamer off? I tell you what it is, my dear, you will have to refit yourself entirely before I shall be satisfied.' And again I saw him cast about him that furtive and inquiring look which would have awakened more surprise in me than it did had I known that we were in a part of the city where he ran but little chance of meeting any one he knew.

"'This old duster I have on,' he suddenly laughed, 'is a very appropriate companion to your gossamer,' and though I did not agree with him, for my clothes were new, and his old and shabby, I laughed also and never dreamed of evil.

"As this garment which so disfigured him that morning has been the occasion of much false speculation on the part of those whose business it was to inquire into the crime with which it is in a most unhappy way connected, I may as well explain here and now why so fastidious a gentleman as Randolph Stone came to wear it. The gentleman called Howard Van Burnam was not the only person who visited the Van Burnam offices on the morning preceding the murder. Randolph Stone was there also, but he did not see the brothers, for finding them closeted together, he decided not to interrupt them. As he was a frequent visitor there, his presence created no remark nor was his departure noted. Descending the stairs separating the offices from the street, he was about to leave the building, when he noticed that the clouds looked ominous. Being dressed for a luncheon with Miss Althorpe, he felt averse to getting wet, so he stepped back into the adjoining hall and began groping for an umbrella in a little closet under the stairs where he had once before found such an article. While doing this he heard the younger Van Burnam descend and go out, and realizing that he could now see Franklin without difficulty, he was about to return up-stairs when he heard that gentleman also come down and follow his brother into the street.

"His first impulse was to join him, but finding nothing but an old duster in the closet, he gave up this intention, and putting on this shabby but protecting garment, started for his apartments, little realizing into what a course of duplicity and crime it was destined to lead him. For to the wearing of this old duster on this especial morning, innocent as the occasion was, I attribute John Randolph's temptation to murder. Had he gone out without it, he would have taken his usual course up Broadway and never met me; or even if he had taken the same roundabout way to his apartments as that which led to our encounter, he would never have dared, in his ordinary fine dress, conspicuous as it made him, to have entered upon those measures, which, as he is clever enough to know, lead to disgrace, if they do not end in a felon's cell. It was John Randolph, then, or Randolph Stone, as he is pleased to call himself in New York, and not Franklin Van Burnam (who had doubtless proceeded in another direction) who came up to where Howard had stood, saw the keys he had dropped, and put them in his own pocket. It was as innocent an action as the donning of the duster, and yet it was fraught with the worst consequences to himself and others.

"Being of the same height and complexion as Franklin Van Burnam, and both gentlemen wearing at that time a moustache (my husband shaved his off after the murder), the mistakes which arose out of this strange equipment were but natural. Seen from the rear or in the semi-darkness of a hotel-office they might look alike, though to me or to any one studying them well, their faces are really very different.

"But to return. Leading me through streets of which I knew nothing, he presently stopped before the entrance of a large hotel.

"'I tell you what, Olive,' said he, 'we had better go in here, take a room, and send for such things as you require to make you look like a lady.'

"As I had no objection to anything which kept me at his side, I told him that whatever suited him suited me, and followed him quite eagerly into the office. I did not know then that this hotel was a second-rate one, not having had experience with the best, but if I had, I should not have wondered at his choice, for there was nothing in his appearance, as I have already intimated, or in his manners up to this point, to lead me to think he was one of the city's great swells, and that it was only in such an unfashionable house as this he would be likely to pass unrecognized. How with his markedly handsome features and distinguished bearing he managed so to carry himself as to look like a man of inferior breeding, I can no more explain than I can the singular change which took place in him when once he found himself in the midst of the crowd which lounged about this office.

"From a man to attract all eyes he became at once a man to attract none, and slouched and looked so ordinary that I stared at him in astonishment, little thinking that he had assumed this manner as a disguise. Seeing me at a loss, he spoke up quite peremptorily:

"'Let us keep our secret, Olive, till you can appear in the world full-fledged. And look here, darling, won't you go to the desk and ask for a room? I am no hand at any such business.'

"Confounded at a proposition so unexpected, but too much under the spell of my feelings to dispute his wishes, I faltered out:

"'But supposing they ask me to register?'

"At which he gave me a look which recalled the old days in Michigan, and quietly sneered:

"'Give them a fictitious name. You have learned to write by this time, have you not?'

"Stung by his taunt, but more in love with him than ever, for his momentary display of passion had made him look both masterful and handsome, I went up to the desk to do his bidding.

"'A room!' said I; and when asked to write our names in the book that lay before me, I put down the first that suggested itself. I wrote with my gloves on, which was why the writing looked so queer that it was taken for a disguised hand.

"This done, he rejoined me, and we went up-stairs, and I was too happy to be in his company again to wonder at his peculiarities or weigh the consequences of the implicit confidence I accorded him. I was desperately in love once more, and entered into every plan he proposed without a thought beyond the joyous present. He was so handsome without his hat; and when after some short delay he threw aside the duster, I felt myself for the first time in my life in the presence of a finished gentleman. Then his manner was so changed. He was so like his oldest and best self, so dangerously like what he was in those long vanished hours under the pines in my sand-swept home on the shores of Lake Michigan. That he faltered at times and sank into strange spells of silence which had something in them that made my breath come fitfully, did not awaken my apprehension or rouse in me more than a passing curiosity. I thought he regretted the past, and when, after one such pause in our conversation, he drew out of his pocket a couple of keys tied together with a string, and surveyed the card attached to them with a strange look, easily enough to be understood by me now; I only laughed at his abstraction, and indulged in a fresh caress to make him more mindful of my presence.

"These keys were the ones which Mrs. Van Burnam's husband had dropped, and which he had picked up before meeting me; and after he had put them back into his pocket he became more talkative than before, and more systematically lover-like. I think he had not seen his way clearly till this moment, the dark and dreadful way which was to end, as he supposed, in my death.

"But I feared nothing, suspected nothing. Such deep and desperate wickedness as he was planning was beyond the wildest flight of my imagination. When he insisted upon sending for a complete set of clothing for me, and when at his dictation I wrote a list of the articles I wanted, I thought he was influenced by his wish as my husband to see me dressed in articles of his own buying. That it was all a plot to rob me of my identity could not strike such a mind as mine, and when the packages came and were received by him in the sly way already known to the public, I saw nothing in his caution but a playful display of mystery that was to end in my romantic establishment in a home of love and luxury.

"Or rather it is thus that I account for my conduct now, and yet the precaution I took not to change the shoes in which my money was hidden, may argue that I was not without some underlying doubt of his complete sincerity. But if so, I hid it from myself, and, as I have every reason to believe, from him also, doubtless excusing my action to myself by considering that I would be none the worse off for a few dollars of my own, even if he was my husband, and had promised me no end of pleasure and comfort.

"That he did intend to make me happy, he had assured me more than once. Indeed, before we had been long in this hotel room, he informed me that great experiences lay before me; that he had prospered much in the last five years and had now a house of his own to offer me and a large circle of friends to make our life in it agreeable.

"'We will go to our house to-night,' said he. 'I have not been living in it lately, and you may find it a little uncomfortable, but we will remedy that to-morrow. Anything is better than staying here under a false name and I cannot take you to my bachelor apartment.'

"I had doubted some of his previous statements, but this one I implicitly believed. Why should not so elegant a man have a house of his own; and if he had told me it was built of marble and hung with Florentine tapestries, I should still have credited it all. I was in fairy-land and he was my knight of romance, even when he again hung his head in leaving the hotel and looked at once so ordinary and uninteresting.

"The ruse he made use of to cut off all connection between ourselves and the Mr. and Mrs. James Pope who had registered at the Hotel D—— was accepted by me with the same lack of suspicion. That he should wish to carry no remembrance of our old life into our new home I thought a delightful piece of folly, and when he proposed that we should bequeath my gossamer and his own disfiguring duster to the coachman in whose hack we were then riding, I laughed gleefully and helped him fold them up and place them under the cushions, though I did wonder why he cut a piece out of the neck of the former, and pouted with the happy freedom of a self-confident woman when he said:

"'It is the first thing I ever bought for you, and I am just foolish enough to wish to preserve this much of it for a keepsake. Do you object, my dear?'

"As I was conscious of cherishing a similar folly in his regard, and could have pressed even that old duster of his to my heart, I offered him a kiss and said 'No,' and he put the scrap away in his pocket. That it was the portion on which was stamped the name of the firm from which it was bought did not occur to me.

"When the coach stopped, he urged me away on foot in a direction entirely strange to me, saying we would take another hack as soon as we had disposed of the bundles we were carrying. How he intended to do this, I did not know. But presently he drew me towards a Chinese laundry, where he bade me leave one of them as washing, and the other he dropped before the opening of a sewer as we stepped up a neighboring curb-stone."

"And still I did not suspect.

"Our ride to Gramercy Park was short, but during it he had time to put a bill in my hand and tell me I was to pay the driver. He had also time to secure the weapon upon which he had probably had his eye fixed from the first. His manner of doing this I can never forgive, for it was a lover's manner, and as such intended to deceive and cajole me. Drawing my head down on his shoulder, he drew off my veil, saying that it was the only article left of my own buying, and that we would leave it behind us in this coach as we had left the gossamer in the other. 'Only I will make sure that no other woman ever wears it,' he laughed, slitting it up and down with his knife. When this was done he kissed me, and then while my heart was tender and the warm tears stood in my eyes, he drew out the pin from my hat, meeting my remonstrances with the assurance that he hated to see my head covered, and that no hat was as pretty as my own brown hair.

"As this was nonsense, and as the coach was beginning to stop, I shook my head at him and put my hat on again, but he had dropped the pin, or so he said, and I had to alight without it.

"When I had paid the driver and the coach had driven off, I had a chance to look up at the house before which we had stopped. Its height and imposing appearance daunted me in spite of the great expectations I had formed, and I ran up the stoop after him in a condition of mingled awe and wild delight that was the poorest preparation possible for what lay before me in the dark interior we were entering.

"He was fumbling nervously in the keyhole with his key, and I heard a whispered oath escape him. But presently the door fell back, and we stepped in to what looked to me like a cavern of darkness.

"'Do not be frightened!' he admonished me. 'I will strike a light in a moment.' And after carefully closing the street door behind us, he stretched out his hand to take mine, or so I judge, for I heard him whisper impatiently, 'Where are you?'

"I was on the threshold of the parlor, to which I had groped my way while he was closing the front door, so I whispered back, 'Here!' but found voice for nothing further, for at that instant I heard a sound proceeding from the depths of darkness in front of me, and was so struck with terror that I fell back against the staircase, just as he passed me and entered the room from which that stealthy noise had issued.

"'Darling!' he whispered, 'darling!' and went stumbling on in the void of darkness before me, till suddenly by some power I cannot explain I seemed to see, faintly but distinctly, and as if with my mind's eye rather than with my bodily one.

"I perceived the shadowy form of a woman standing in the space before him, and beheld him suddenly grasp her with what he meant to be a loving cry, but which to my ears at that moment sounded strangely ferocious, and after holding her a moment suddenly release her, at which she uttered one low, curdling moan and sank at his feet. At the same instant I heard a click, which I did not understand then, but which I now know to have been the head of the hat-pin striking the register.

"Horrified past all power of speech and action, for I saw that he had intended this blow for me, I cowered against the stairs, waiting for him to pass out. This he did not do at once, though the delay must have been short. He stopped long enough by the prostrate form to stir it with his foot, probably to see if life was extinct, but no longer, yet it seemed an eternity before I perceived him groping his way over the threshold; an eternity in which every act of my life passed before me, and every word and every expression with which he had beguiled me came to rack my soul and made the horror of this mad awakening greater.

"No thought of her, or of the guilt with which he had forever damned his soul, came to me in that first moment of misery. My loss, my escape, and the danger in which I still stood if the least hint reached him of the mistake he had made, filled my mind too entirely for me to dwell on any less impersonal theme. His words, for he muttered several in that short passage out, showed me in what a fools' paradise I had been revelling, and how certainly I had turned his every thought towards murder when I seized him in the street and proclaimed myself his wife. The satisfaction with which he uttered, 'Well struck!' gave little hint of remorse; and the gloating delight with which he added something about the devil having assisted him to make it a safe blow as well as a deadly one, was proof not only of his having used all his cunning in planning this crime, but of his pleasure in its apparent success.

"That he continued in this frame of mind, and that he never lost confidence in the precautions he had taken and in the mystery with which the deed was surrounded, is apparent from the fact that he revisited the Van Burnam office on the following morning, and hung again on its accustomed nail the keys of the Gramercy Park house.

"When the front door had closed, and I knew that he had gone away in the full belief that it was my form he had left lying behind him on that midnight floor, all the accumulated terrors of the situation came to me in full force, and I began to think of her as well as of myself, and longed for courage to approach her or even the daring to call out for help. But the thought that it was my husband who had committed this crime held me tongue-tied, and though I soon began to move inch by inch in her direction, it was some time before I could so far overcome my terror as to enter the room where she lay.

"I had supposed, and still supposed (as was natural after seeing him open the door with the keys he took from his pocket), that the house was his, and the victim a member of his own household. But when, after innumerable hesitations and a bodily shrinking that was little short of torment, I managed to drag myself into the room and light a match which I found on a farther mantel-shelf, I saw enough in the general appearance of the rooms and of the figure at my feet to make me doubt the truth of both these suppositions. Yet no other explanation came to lighten the mystery of the occasion, and dazed as I was by the horror of my position and the mortal dread I felt of the man who in one instant had turned the heaven of my love into a hell of fathomless horrors, I soon had eyes for the one fact only, that the woman lying before me was sufficiently like myself to inspire me with the hope of preserving my secret and keeping from my would-be slayer the knowledge of my having escaped the doom he had prepared for me.

"For ascribe it to what motive you will, that was the one idea now dominating my mind. I wanted him to believe me dead. I wanted to feel that all connection between us was severed forever. He had killed me. By killing my love and faith in him he had murdered the better part of myself, and I shrank with inconceivable horror from anything that would bring me again under his eye, or force me to assert claims that it would be the future business of my life to forget.

"When the first match went out I had not courage to light another, so I crept away in the darkness to listen at the foot of the stairs. There was no sound from above, and a terrifying sense began to pervade me that I was in that house alone. Yet there was safety in the thought, and opportunity for what I was planning, and finally, under the stress of the purpose that was every moment developing within me, I went softly up-stairs and listened at all the doors till I was certain that the house was unoccupied. Then I came down and walked resolutely back into the parlor, for I knew if I allowed any time to pass I could never again summon up strength to cross its grisly threshold. Yet I did nothing for hours but crouch in one of its dismal corners, waiting for morning. That I did not go mad in that awful interval is a wonder. I must have been near it more than once.

"I have been asked, and Miss Butterworth has been asked, how in the light of what we now know concerning this poor victim's presence there, we account for her being in the darkness and showing so little terror at our entrance and Mr. Stone's approach. I account for it in this way: Two half-burned matches were found in the parlor grate. One I flung there; the other had probably been used by her to light the dining-room gas. If this was still lighted when we drove up, as it may have been, then, alarmed by the sound of the stopping coach, she had put it out, with a vague idea of hiding herself till she knew whether it was the old gentleman who was coming or only her suspicious and unreasonable husband. If it was not lighted then, she was probably aroused from a sleep on the parlor sofa, and was for the moment too dazed to cry out or resent an embrace she had not time to understand before she succumbed to the cruel stab that killed her. Miss Butterworth, however, thinks that the poor creature took the intruder for Franklin till she heard my voice, when she probably became so amazed that she was in a measure paralyzed and found it impossible to move or cry out. As Miss Butterworth is a woman of great discretion I should think her explanation the truest, if I did not consider her a little prejudiced against Mrs. Van Burnam.

"But to return to myself.

"With the first glimmer of light that came through the closed shutters I rose and began my dreadful task. Upheld by a purpose as relentless as that which drove the author of this horror into murder, I stripped the body and put upon it my own clothing, with the one exception of the shoes. Then, when I had re-dressed myself in hers, I steadied up my heart and with one wild pull dragged down the cabinet upon her so that her face might lose its traits and her identification become impossible.

"How I had strength to do this, and how I could contemplate the result without shrieking, I cannot now imagine. Perhaps I was hardly human at this crisis; perhaps something of the demon which had informed him in his awful work had entered into my breast, making this thing possible. I only know that I did what I have said and did it calmly. More than that, that I had mind and judgment left to give to my own appearance. Observing that the dress I had put on was of a conspicuous plaid, I exchanged the skirt portion with the brown silk petticoat under it, and when I observed that it hung below the other, as of course it would, I went through the house till I came upon some pins with which I pinned it up out of sight. Thus equipped, I was still a person to attract attention, especially as I had no hat to put on; my own having fallen from my head and been covered by the dead woman's body, which nothing would induce me to move again.

"But I had confidence in my own powers to escape question, toned up as I was in every nerve by the dreadfulness of my situation, and as soon as I was in decent shape for flight, I opened the front door and prepared to slip out.

"But here the intense dread I felt of my husband, a dread which had actuated all my movements and sustained me in as harrowing a task as ever woman performed, seized me with renewed force, and I quailed at the prospect of entering the streets alone. Supposing he should be on the stoop! Supposing he should be in an opposite window even! Could I encounter him again and live? He was not far away, or so I felt. A murderer, it is said, cannot help haunting the scene of his crime, and if he should see me alive and well, what might I not expect from his astonishment and alarm? I did not dare go out. But neither did I dare remain, so after quaking for a good five minutes on the threshold, I made one wild dash through the door.

"There was no one in sight, and I reached Broadway before I ran across a man or woman. Even then I got by without any one speaking to me, and, favored by Providence, found a nook at the end of an alley-way, where I remained undiscovered till it was late enough in the morning for me to enter a shop and buy a hat.

"The rest of my movements are known. I found my way to Mrs. Desberger's, this time without interruption; and from that place sought and found a situation with Miss Althorpe.

"That her fate was in any way connected with mine, or that the Randolph Stone she was engaged to marry was the John Randolph from whose clutches I had just escaped, was, of course, unsuspected by me, and, incredible as it may seem, continued to be unsuspected as long as I remained in the house. There was reason for this. My duties were such as I could well attend to in my own room, and feeling a horror of the world and everything in it, I kept my room as much as possible, and never went out of it when I knew that he was in the house. The very thought of love awakened intolerable emotions in me, and much as I admired and revered Miss Althorpe, I could not bring myself to meet or even talk of the man to whom she was in expectation of being so soon united. There was another thing of which I was ignorant, and that was the circumstances which had invested with so much interest the crime of which I had been witness. I did not know that the victim had been recognized, or that an innocent man had been arrested for her murder. In fact I knew nothing concerning the affair save what I had seen with my own eyes, no one having mentioned the murder in my presence, and I having religiously avoided the very sight of a paper for fear that I should see some account of the horrible affair, and so lose what small remnants of courage I still possessed.

"This apathy concerning a matter so important to myself, or rather this almost frenzied determination to cut myself loose from my dreadful past, may seem strange and unnatural; but it will seem stranger yet when I say that for all these efforts I was haunted night and day by one small fact connected with this past, which made forgetfulness impossible. I had taken the rings from the hands of the dead woman as I had taken away her clothes, and the possession of these valuables, probably because they represented so much money, weighed on my conscience and made me feel like a thief. The purse which I found in a pocket of the skirt I had put on was a trouble to me, but the rings were a source of constant terror and disturbance. I hid them finally in a ball of yarn I was using, but even then I experienced but little peace, for they were not mine, and I lacked the courage to avow it or seek out the person to whom they now rightfully belonged.

"When, therefore, in the intervals of fever which attacked me in Miss Althorpe's house, I overheard enough of a conversation between her and Miss Butterworth to learn that the murdered woman had been a Mrs. Van Burnam, and that her husband or relatives had an office somewhere downtown, I was so seized by the instinct of restitution, that I took the first opportunity that offered to leave my bed and hunt up these people.

"That I would injure them in any way by secretly restoring these jewels, I never dreamed. Indeed, I did not exercise my mind at all on the subject, but only followed the instincts of my delirium; and while to all appearance I showed all the cunning of an insane person, in the pursuit of my purpose, I fail to remember now how I found my way to Duane Street, or by what suggestion of my diseased brain I was induced to slip these rings upon the hook attached to Mr. Van Burnam's desk. Probably the mere utterance of this well-known name into the ears of the passers-by was enough to obtain for me such directions as I needed, but however that may be, the result was misapprehension, and the complications which followed, serious.

"Of the emotion caused in me by the unaccountable discovery of my connection with this crime I need not speak. The love which I at one time felt for John Randolph had turned to gall and bitterness, but enough sense of duty remained in my bruised and broken heart to keep me from denouncing him to the police, till by a sudden stroke of fate or Providence, I saw him in the carriage with Miss Althorpe, and realized that he was not only the man with whom she was upon the point of allying herself, but that it was to preserve his place in her regard and to attain the lofty position promised by this union, he had attempted to murder me, and had murdered another woman only less unfortunate and miserable than myself.

"It was the last and bitterest blow that could come from his hand; and though instinct led me to throw myself into the carriage before which I stood, and thus escape a meeting which I felt I could never survive, I was determined from that moment not only to save Miss Althorpe from an alliance with this villain, but to revenge myself upon him in some never-to-be-forgotten manner.

"That this revenge involved her in a public shame from which her angelic goodness to me should have saved her, I regret now as deeply as even she can wish. But the madness that was upon me made me blind to every other consideration than that of the boundless hatred I bore him; and while I can look for no forgiveness from her on that account, I still hope the day will come when she will see that in spite of my momentary disregard of her feelings, I cherish for her an affection that nothing can efface or make other than the ruling passion of my life."

XLII   WITH MISS BUTTERWORTH'S COMPLIMENTS

They tell me that Mr. Gryce has never been quite the same man since the clearing up of this mystery; that his confidence in his own powers is shaken, and that he hints, more often than is agreeable to his superiors, that when a man has passed his seventy-seventh year it is time for him to give up active connection with police matters. I do not agree with him. His mistakes, if we may call them such, were not those of failing faculties, but of a man made oversecure in his own conclusions by a series of old successes. Had he listened to me—But I will not pursue this suggestion. You will accuse me of egotism, an imputation I cannot bear with equanimity and will not risk; modest depreciation of myself being one of the chief attributes of my character.

Howard Van Burnam bore his release, as he had his arrest, with great outward composure. Mr. Gryce's explanation of his motives in perjuring himself before the Coroner was correct, and while the mass of people wondered at that instinct of pride which led him to risk the imputation of murder sooner than have the world accuse his wife of an unwomanly action, there were others who understood his peculiarities, and thought his conduct quite in keeping with what they knew of his warped and over-sensitive nature.

That he has been greatly moved by the unmerited fate of his weak but unfortunate wife, is evident from the sincerity with which he still mourns her.

I had always understood that Franklin had never been told of the peril in which his good name had stood for a few short hours. But since a certain confidential conversation which took place between us one evening, I have come to the conclusion that the police were not so reticent as they made themselves out to be. In that conversation he professed to thank me for certain good offices I had done him and his, and waxing warm in his gratitude, confessed that without my interference he would have found himself in a strait of no ordinary seriousness; "For," said he, "there has been no over-statement of the feelings I cherished toward my sister-in-law, nor was there any mistake made in thinking that she uttered some very desperate threats against me during the visit she paid me at my office on Monday. But I never thought of ridding myself of her in any way. I only thought of keeping her and my brother apart till I could escape the country. When therefore he came into the office on Tuesday morning for the keys of our father's house, I felt such a dread of the two meeting there, that I left immediately after my brother for the place where she had told me she would await a final message from me. I hoped to move her by one final plea, for I love my brother sincerely, notwithstanding the wrong I once did him. I was therefore with her in another place at the very time I was thought to be with her at the Hotel D——, a fact which greatly hampered me, as you can see, when I was requested by the police to give an account of how I spent that day. When I left her it was to seek my brother. She had told me of her deliberate intention of spending the night in the Gramercy Park house; and as I saw no way of her doing this without my brother's connivance, I started in search of him, meaning to stick to him when I found him, and keep him away from her till that night was over. I was not successful in my undertaking. He was locked in his rooms it seems, packing up his effects for flight,—we always had the same instincts even when boys,—and receiving no answer to my knock, I hastened away to Gramercy Park to keep a watch over the house against my brother coming there. This was early in the evening, and for hours afterwards I wandered like a restless spirit in and out of those streets, meeting no one I knew, not even my brother, though he was wandering about in very much the same manner, and with very much the same apprehensions.

"The duplicity of the woman became very evident to me the next morning. In my last interview with her she had shown no relenting in her purpose towards me, but when I entered my office after this restless night in the streets, I found lying on my desk her little hand-bag, which had been sent down from Mrs. Parker's. In it was the letter, just as you divined, Miss Butterworth. I had hardly got over the shock of this most unexpected good fortune when the news came that a woman had been found dead in my father's house. What was I to think? That it was she, of course, and that my brother had been the man to let her in there. Miss Butterworth," this is how he ended, "I make no demands upon you, as I have made no demands upon the police, to keep the secret contained in that letter from my much-abused brother. Or, rather, it is too late now to keep it, for I have told him all there was to tell, myself, and he has seen fit to overlook my fault, and to regard me with even more affection than he did before this dreadful tragedy came to harrow up our lives."

Do you wonder I like Franklin Van Burnam?

The Misses Van Burnam call upon me regularly, and when they say "Dear old thing!" now, they mean it.

Of Miss Althorpe I cannot trust myself to speak. She was, and is, the finest woman I know, and when the great shadow now hanging over her has lost some of its impenetrability, she will be a useful one again, or I do not rightly read the patient smile which makes her face so beautiful in its sadness.

Olive Randolph has, at my request, taken up her abode in my house. The charm which she seems to have exerted over others she has exerted over me, and I doubt if I shall ever wish to part with her again. In return she gives me an affection which I am now getting old enough to appreciate. Her feeling for me and her gratitude to Miss Althorpe are the only treasures left her out of the wreck of her life, and it shall be my business to make them lasting ones.

The fate of Randolph Stone is too well known for me to enlarge upon it. But before I bid farewell to his name, I must say that after that curt confession of his, "Yes, I did it, in the way and for the motive she alleged," I have often tried to imagine the contradictory feelings with which he must have listened to the facts as they came out at the inquest, and convinced, as he had every reason to be, that the victim was his wife, heard his friend Howard not only accept her for his, but insist that he was the man who accompanied her to that house of death. He has never lifted the veil from those hours, and he never will, but I would give much of the peace of mind which has lately come to me, to know what his sensations were, not only at that time, but when, on the evening, after the murder, he opened the papers and read that the woman whom he had left for dead with her brain pierced by a hat-pin, had been found on that same floor crushed under a fallen cabinet; and what explanation he was ever able to make to himself for a fact so inexplicable.

FOOTNOTES:

My attention has been called to the fact that I have not confessed whether it was owing to a mistake made by Mr. Gryce or myself, that Franklin Van Burnam was identified as the man who had entered the adjoining house on the night of the murder. Well, the truth is, neither of us was to blame for that. The man I identified (it was while watching the guests who attended Mrs. Van Burnam's funeral, you remember) was really Mr. Stone; but owing to the fact that this latter gentleman had lingered in the vestibule till he was joined by Franklin and that they had finally entered together, some confusion was created in the mind of the man on duty in the hall, so that when Mr. Gryce asked him who it was that came in immediately after the four who arrived together, he answered Mr. Franklin Van Burnam; being anxious to win his superior's applause and considering that person much more likely to merit the detective's attention than a mere friend of the family like Mr. Stone. In punishment for this momentary display of egotism, he has been discharged from the force, I believe.—A. B.

THE END

LOST MAN'S LANE

A SECOND EPISODE IN THE LIFE OF AMELIA BUTTERWORTH

PREFACE

A word to my readers before they begin these pages.
As a woman of inborn principle and strict Presbyterian training, I hate deception and cannot abide subterfuge. This is why, after a year or more of hesitation, I have felt myself constrained to put into words the true history of the events surrounding the solution of that great mystery which made Lost Man's Lane the dread of the neighboring country. Feminine delicacy, and a natural shrinking from revealing to the world certain weaknesses on my part, inseparable from a true relation of this tale, led me to consent to the publication of that meagre and decidedly falsified account of the matter which has appeared in some of our leading papers.
But conscience has regained its sway in my breast, and with all due confidence in your forbearance, I herein take my rightful place in these annals, of whose interest and importance I now leave you to judge.

AMELIA BUTTERWORTH.
GRAMERCY PARK, NEW YORK.

BOOK I: THE KNOLLYS FAMILY

I   A VISIT FROM MR. GRYCE

Ever since my fortunate—or shall I say unfortunate?—connection with that famous case of murder in Gramercy Park, I have had it intimated to me by many of my friends—and by some who were not my friends—that no woman who had met with such success as myself in detective work would ever be satisfied with a single display of her powers, and that sooner or later I would find myself again at work upon some other case of striking peculiarities.
As vanity has never been my foible, and as, moreover, I never have forsaken

and never am likely to forsake the plain path marked out for my sex, at any other call than that of duty, I invariably responded to these insinuations by an affable but incredulous smile, striving to excuse the presumption of my friends by remembering their ignorance of my nature and the very excellent reasons I had for my one notable interference in the police affairs of New York City.

Besides, though I appeared to be resting quietly, if not in entire contentment, on my laurels, I was not so utterly removed from the old atmosphere of crime and its detection as the world in general considered me to be. Mr. Gryce still visited me; not on business, of course, but as a friend, for whom I had some regard; and naturally our conversation was not always confined to the weather or even to city politics, provocative as the latter subject is of wholesome controversy.

Not that he ever betrayed any of the secrets of his office—oh no; that would have been too much to expect—but he did sometimes mention the outward aspects of some celebrated case, and though I never ventured upon advice—I know too much for that, I hope—I found my wits more or less exercised by a conversation in which he gained much without acknowledging it, and I gave much without appearing conscious of the fact.

I was therefore finding life pleasant and full of interest, when suddenly (I had no right to expect it, and I do not blame myself for not expecting it or for holding my head so high at the prognostications of my friends) an opportunity came for a direct exercise of my detective powers in a line seemingly so laid out for me by Providence that I felt I would be slighting the Powers above if I refused to enter upon it, though now I see that the line was laid out for me by Mr. Gryce, and that I was obeying anything but the call of duty in following it.

But this is not explicit. One night Mr. Gryce came to my house looking older and more feeble than usual. He was engaged in a perplexing case, he said, and missed his early vigor and persistency. Would I like to hear about it? It was not in the line of his usual work, yet it had points—and well!—it would do him good to talk about it to a non-professional who was capable of sympathizing with its baffling and worrisome features and yet would never have to be told to hold her peace.

I ought to have been on my guard. I ought to have known the old fox well enough to feel certain that when he went so manifestly out of his way to take me into his confidence he did it for a purpose. But Jove nods now and then—or so I have been assured on unimpeachable authority,—and if Jove has ever been caught napping, surely Amelia Butterworth may be pardoned a like inconsistency.

"It is not a city crime," Mr. Gryce went on to explain, and here he was base enough to sigh. "At my time of life this is an important consideration. It is no longer a simple matter for me to pack up a valise and go off to some distant village, way up in the mountains perhaps, where comforts are few and secrecy an impossibility. Comforts have become indispensable to my threescore years and ten, and secrecy—well, if ever there was an affair where one needs to go softly, it is this one; as you will see if you will allow me to give you the facts of the case as known at Headquarters to-day."

I bowed, trying not to show my surprise or my extreme satisfaction. Mr. Gryce assumed his most benignant aspect (always a dangerous one with him), and began his story.

II   I AM TEMPTED

"Some ninety miles from here, in a more or less inaccessible region, there is a small but interesting village, which has been the scene of so many unaccountable disappearances that the attention of the New York police has at last been directed to it. The village, which is at least two miles from any railroad, is one of those quiet, placid little spots found now and then among the mountains, where life is simple, and crime, to all appearance, an element so out of accord with every other characteristic of the place as to seem a complete anomaly. Yet crime, or some other hideous mystery almost equally revolting, has during the last five years been accountable for the disappearance in or about this village of four persons of various ages and occupations. Of these, three were strangers and one a well-known vagabond accustomed to tramp the hills and live on the bounty of farmers' wives. All were of the male sex, and in no case has any clue ever come to light as to their fate. That is the matter as it stands before the police to-day."

"A serious affair," I remarked. "Seems to me I have read of such things in novels. Is there a tumbled-down old inn in the vicinity where beds are made up over trap-doors?"

His smile was a mild protest against my flippancy.

"I have visited the town myself. There is no inn there, but a comfortable hotel of the most matter-of-fact sort, kept by the frankest and most open-minded of landlords. Besides, these disappearances, as a rule, did not take place at night, but in broad daylight. Imagine this street at noon. It is a short one, and you know every house on it, and you think you know every lurking-place. You see a man enter it at one end and you expect him to issue from it at the other. But suppose he never does. More than that, suppose he is never heard of again, and that this thing should happen in this one street four times during five years."

"I should move," I dryly responded.

"Would you? Many good people have moved from the place I speak of, but that has not helped matters. The disappearances go on just the same and the mystery continues."

"You interest me," I said. "Come to think of it, if this street were the scene of such an unexplained series of horrors as you have described, I do not think I should move."

"I thought not," he curtly rejoined. "But since you are interested in this matter, let me be more explicit in my statements. The first person whose disappearance was noted——"

"Wait," I interrupted. "Have you a map of the place?"

He smiled, nodded quite affectionately to a little statuette on the mantel-piece, which had had the honor of sharing his confidences in days gone by, but did not produce the map.

"That detail will keep," said he. "Let me go on with my story. As I was saying, madam, the first person whose disappearance was noted in this place was a peddler of small wares, accustomed to tramp the mountains. On this occasion he had been in town longer than usual, and was known to have sold fully half of his goods.

Consequently he must have had quite a sum of money upon him. One day his pack was found lying under a cluster of bushes in a wood, but of him nothing was ever again heard. It made an excitement for a few days while the woods were being searched for his body, but, nothing having been discovered, he was forgotten, and everything went on as before, till suddenly public attention was again aroused by the pouring in of letters containing inquiries in regard to a young man who had been sent there from Duluth to collect facts in a law case, and who after a certain date had failed to communicate with his firm or show up at any of the places where he was known. Instantly the village was in arms. Many remembered the young man, and some two or three of the villagers could recall the fact of having seen him go up the street with his hand-bag in his hand as if on his way to the Mountain-station. The landlord of the hotel could fix the very day at which he left his house, but inquiries at the station failed to establish the fact that he took train from there, nor were the most minute inquiries into his fate ever attended by the least result. He was not known to have carried much money, but he carried a very handsome watch and wore a ring of more than ordinary value, neither of which has ever shown up at any pawnbroker's known to the police. This was three years ago.

"The next occurrence of a like character did not take place till a year after. This time it was a poor old man from Hartford, who vanished almost as it were before the eyes of these astounded villagers. He had come to town to get subscriptions for a valuable book issued by a well-known publisher. He had been more or less successful, and was looking very cheerful and contented, when one morning, after making a sale at a certain farmhouse, he sat down to dine with the family, it being close on to noon. He had eaten several mouthfuls and was chatting quite freely, when suddenly they saw him pause, clap his hand to his pocket, and rise up very much disturbed. 'I have left my pocket-book behind me at Deacon Spear's,' he cried. 'I cannot eat with it out of my possession. Excuse me if I go for it.' And without any further apologies, he ran out of the house and down the road in the direction of Deacon Spear's. He never reached Deacon Spear's, nor was he ever seen in that village again or in his home in Hartford. This was the most astonishing mystery of all. Within a half-mile's radius, in a populous country town, this man disappeared as if the road had swallowed him and closed again. It was marvellous, it was incredible, and remained so even after the best efforts of the country police to solve the mystery had exhausted themselves. After this, the town began to acquire a bad name, and one or two families moved away. Yet no one was found who was willing to admit that these various persons had been the victims of foul play till a month later another case came to light of a young man who had left the village for the hillside station, and had never arrived at that or any other destination so far as could be learned. As he was a distant relative of a wealthy cattle owner in Iowa, who came on post-haste to inquire into his nephew's fate, the excitement ran high, and through his efforts and that of one of the town's leading citizens, the services of our office were called into play. But the result has been nil. We have found neither the bodies of these men nor any clue to their fate."

"Yet you have been there?" I suggested.

He nodded.

"Wonderful! And you came upon no suspicious house, no suspicious person?"

The finger with which he was rubbing his eyeglasses went round and round the rims with a slower and slower and still more thoughtful motion.

"Every town has its suspicious-looking houses," he slowly remarked, "and, as for persons, the most honest often wear a lowering look in which an unbridled imagination can see guilt. I never trust to appearances of that kind."

"What else can you trust in, when a case is as impenetrable as this one?" I asked.

His finger, going slower and slower, suddenly stopped.

"In my knowledge of persons," he replied. "In my knowledge of their fears, their hopes, and their individual concerns. If I were twenty years younger"—here he stole a glance at me in the mirror which made me bridle; did he think I was only twenty years younger than himself?—"I would," he went on, "make myself so acquainted with every man, woman, and child there, that—" Here he drew himself up with a jerk. "But the day for that is passed," said he. "I am too old and too crippled to succeed in such an undertaking. Having been there once, I am a marked man. My very walk betrays me. He whose good fortune it will be to get at the bottom of these people's hearts must awaken no suspicions as to his connection with the police. Indeed, I do not think that any man can succeed in doing this now."

I started. This was a frank showing of his hand at least. No man! It was then a woman's aid he was after. I laughed as I thought of it. I had not thought him either so presumptuous or so appreciative of talents of a character so directly in line with his own.

"Don't you agree with me, madam?"

I did agree with him; but I had a character of great dignity to maintain, so I simply surveyed him with an air of well-tempered severity.

"I do not know of any woman who would undertake such a task," I calmly observed.

"No?" he smiled with that air of forbearance which is so exasperating to me. "Well, perhaps there isn't any such woman to be found. It would take one of very uncommon characteristics, I own."

"Pish!" I cried. "Not so very!"

"Indeed, I think you have not fully taken in the case," he urged in quiet superiority. "The people there are of the higher order of country folk. Many of them are of extreme refinement. One family"—here his tone changed a trifle—"is poor enough and cultivated enough to interest even such a woman as yourself."

"Indeed!" I ejaculated, with just a touch of my father's hauteur to hide the stir of curiosity his words naturally evoked.

"It is in some such home," he continued with an ease that should have warned me he had started on this pursuit with a quiet determination to win, "that the clue will be found to the mystery we are considering. Yes, you may well look startled, but that conclusion is the one thing I brought away with me from—X., let us say. I regard it as one of some moment. What do you think of it?"

"Well," I admitted, "it makes me feel like recalling that pish I uttered a few minutes ago. It would take a woman of uncommon characteristics to assist you in this matter."

"I am glad we have got that far," said he.

"A lady," I went on.

"Most assuredly a lady."

I paused. Sometimes discreet silence is more sarcastic than speech.

"Well, what lady would lend herself to this scheme?" I demanded at last.

The tap, tap of his fingers on the rim of his glasses was my only answer.

"I do not know of any," said I.

His eyebrows rose perhaps a hair's-breadth, but I noted the implied sarcasm, and for an instant forgot my dignity.

"Now," said I, "this will not do. You mean me, Amelia Butterworth; a woman who—but I do not think it is necessary to tell you either who or what I am. You have presumed, sir—Now do not put on that look of innocence, and above all do not attempt to deny what is so manifestly in your thoughts, for that would make me feel like showing you the door."

"Then," he smiled, "I shall be sure to deny nothing. I am not anxious to leave—yet. Besides, whom could I mean but you? A lady visiting friends in this remote and beautiful region—what opportunities might she not have to probe this important mystery if, like yourself, she had tact, discretion, excellent understanding, and an experience which if not broad or deep is certainly such as to give her a certain confidence in herself, and an undoubted influence with the man fortunate enough to receive her advice."

"Bah!" I exclaimed. It was one of his favorite expressions. That was perhaps why I used it. "One would think I was a member of your police."

"You flatter us too deeply," was his deferential answer. "Such an honor as that would be beyond our deserts."

To this I gave but the faintest sniff. That he should think that I, Amelia Butterworth, could be amenable to such barefaced flattery! Then I faced him with some asperity, and said bluntly: "You waste your time. I have no more intention of meddling in another affair than——"

"You had in meddling in the first," he politely, too politely, interpolated. "I understand, madam."

I was angry, but made no show of being so. I was not willing he should see that I could be affected by anything he could say.

"The Van Burnams are my next-door neighbors," I remarked sweetly. "I had the best of excuses for the interest I took in their affairs."

"So you had," he acquiesced. "I am glad to be reminded of the fact. I wonder I was able to forget it."

Angry now to the point of not being able to hide it, I turned upon him with firm determination.

"Let us talk of something else," I said.

But he was equal to the occasion. Drawing a folded paper from his pocket, he opened it out before my eyes, observing quite naturally: "That is a happy thought. Let us look over this sketch you were sharp enough to ask for a few moments ago. It shows the streets of the village and the places where each of the persons I have mentioned was last seen. Is not that what you wanted?"

I know that I should have drawn back with a frown, that I never should have allowed myself the satisfaction of casting so much as a glance toward the paper, but the human nature which links me to my kind was too much for me, and with an involuntary "Exactly!" I leaned over it with an eagerness I strove hard, even at that exciting moment, to keep within the bounds I thought proper to my position as a non-professional, interested in the matter from curiosity alone.

This is what I saw:

"Mr. Gryce," said I, after a few minutes' close contemplation of this diagram, "I do not suppose you want any opinion from me."

"Madam," he retorted, "it is all you have left me free to ask for."

Receiving this as a permission to speak, I put my finger on the road marked with a cross.

"Then," said I, "so far as I can gather from this drawing, all the disappearances seem to have taken place in or about this especial road."

"You are as correct as usual," he returned. "What you have said is so true, that the people of the vicinity have already given to this winding way a special cognomen of its own. For two years now it has been called Lost Man's Lane."

"Indeed!" I cried. "They have got the matter down as close as that, and yet have not solved its mystery? How long is this road?"

"A half mile or so."

I must have looked my disgust, for his hands opened deprecatingly.

"The ground has undergone a thorough search," said he. "Not a square foot in those woods you see on either side of the road, but has been carefully examined."

"And the houses? I see there are three houses on this road."

"Oh, they are owned by most respectable people—most respectable people," he repeated, with a lingering emphasis that gave me an inward shudder. "I think I had the honor of intimating as much to you a few minutes ago."

I looked at him earnestly, and irresistibly drew a little nearer to him over the diagram.

"Have none of these houses been visited by you?" I asked. "Do you mean to say you have not seen the inside of them all?"

"Oh," he replied, "I have been in them all, of course; but a mystery such as we are investigating is not written upon the walls of parlors or halls."

"You freeze my blood," was my uncharacteristic rejoinder. Somehow the sight of the homes indicated on this diagram seemed to bring me into more intimate sympathy with the affair.

His shrug was significant.

"I told you that this was no vulgar mystery," he declared; "or why should I be considering it with you? It is quite worthy of your interest. Do you see that house marked A?"

"I do," I nodded.

"Well, that is a decayed mansion of imposing proportions, set in a forest of overgrown shrubbery. The ladies who inhabit it——"

"Ladies!" I put in, with a small shock of horror.

"Young ladies," he explained, "of a refined if not over-prosperous appearance. They are the interesting residue of a family of some repute. Their father was a judge, I believe."

"And do they live there alone," I asked,—"two young ladies in a house so large and in a neighborhood so full of mystery?"

"Oh, they have a brother with them, a lout of no great attractions," he responded carelessly—too carelessly, I thought.

I made a note of the house A in my mind.

"And who lives in the house marked B?" I now queried.

"A Mr. Trohm. You will remember that it was through his exertions the services of the New York police were secured. His place there is one of the most interesting in town, and he does not wish to be forced to leave it, but he will be obliged to do so if the road is not soon relieved of its bad name; and so will Deacon Spear. The very children shun the road now. I do not know of a lonelier place."

"I see a little mark made here on the verge of the woods. What does that mean?"

"That stands for a hut—it can hardly be called a cottage—where a poor old woman lives called Mother Jane. She is a harmless imbecile, against whom no one has ever directed a suspicion. You may take your finger off that mark, Miss Butterworth."

I did so, but I did not forget that it stood very near the footpath branching off to the station.

"You entered this hut as well as the big houses?" I intimated.

"And found," was his answer, "four walls; nothing more."

I let my finger travel along the footpath I have just mentioned.

"Steep," was his comment. "Up, up, all the way, but no precipices. Nothing but pine woods on either side, thickly carpeted with needles."

My finger came back and stopped at the house marked M.

"Why is a letter affixed to this spot?" I asked.

"Because it stands at the head of the lane. Any one sitting at the window L can see whoever enters or leaves the lane at this end. And some one is always sitting there. The house contains two crippled children, a boy and a girl. One of them is always in that window."

"I see," said I. Then abruptly: "What do you think of Deacon Spear?"

"Oh, he's a well-meaning man, none too fine in his feelings. He does not mind the neighborhood; likes quiet, he says. I hope you will know him for yourself some day," the detective slyly added.

At this return to the forbidden subject, I held myself very much aloof.

"Your diagram is interesting," I remarked, "but it has not in the least changed my determination. It is you who will return to X., and that, very soon."

"Very soon?" he repeated. "Whoever goes there on this errand must go at once; to-night, if possible; if not, to-morrow at the latest."

"To-night! to-morrow!" I expostulated. "And you thought——"

"No matter what I thought," he sighed. "It seems I had no reason for my hopes." And folding up the map, he slowly rose. "The young man we have left there is doing more harm than good. That is why I say that some one of real ability must replace him immediately. The detective from New York must seem to have left the place."

I made him my most ladylike bow of dismissal.

"I shall watch the papers," I said. "I have no doubt that I shall soon be gratified by seeing in them some token of your success."

He cast a rueful look at his hands, took a painful step toward the door, and dolefully shook his head.

I kept my silence undisturbed.

He took another painful step, then turned.

"By the way," he remarked, as I stood watching him with an uncompromising air, "I have forgotten to mention the name of the town in which these disappearances have occurred. It is called X., and it is to be found on one of the spurs of the Berkshire Hills." And, being by this time at the door, he bowed himself out with all the insinuating suavity which distinguishes him at certain critical moments. The old fox was so sure of his triumph that he did not wait to witness it. He knew—how, it is easy enough for me to understand now—that X. was a place I had often threatened to visit. The family of one of my dearest friends lived there, the children of Althea Knollys. She had been my chum at school, and when she died I had promised myself not to let many months go by without making the acquaintance of her children. Alas! I had allowed years to elapse.

III I SUCCUMB

That night the tempter had his own way with me. Without much difficulty he persuaded me that my neglect of Althea Burroughs' children was without any excuse; that what had been my duty toward them when I knew them to be left motherless and alone, had become an imperative demand upon me now that the town in which they lived had become overshadowed by a mystery which could not but affect the comfort and happiness of all its inhabitants. I could not wait a day. I recalled all that I had heard of poor Althea's short and none too happy marriage, and immediately felt such a burning desire to see if her dainty but spirited beauty—how well I remembered it—had been repeated in her daughters, that I found myself packing my trunk before I knew it.

I had not been from home for a long time—all the more reason why I should have a change now—and when I notified Mrs. Randolph and the servants of my intention of leaving on the early morning train, it created quite a sensation in the house.

But I had the best of explanations to offer. I had been thinking of my dead friend, and my conscience would not let me neglect her dear and possibly unhappy progeny any longer. I had purposed many times to visit X., and now I was going to do it. When I come to a decision, it is usually suddenly, and I never rest after having once made up my mind.

My sentiment went so far that I got down an old album and began hunting up the pictures I had brought away with me from boarding-school. Hers was among them, and I really did experience more or less compunction when I saw again the delicate yet daring features which had once had a very great influence over my mind. What a teasing sprite she was, yet what a will she had, and how strange it was that, having been so intimate as girls, we never knew anything of each other as women! Had it been her fault or mine? Was her marriage to blame for it or my spinsterhood? Difficult to tell then, impossible to tell now. I would not even think of it again, save as a warning. Nothing must stand between me and her children now that my attention has been called to them again.

I did not mean to take them by surprise—that is, not entirely. The invitation which they had sent me years ago was still in force, making it simply necessary for me to telegraph them that I had decided to make them a visit, and that they might expect me by the noon train. If in times gone by they had been properly instructed by their mother in regard to the character of her old friend, this need not put them out. I am not a woman of unbounded expectations. I do not look for the comforts abroad I am accustomed to find at home, and if, as I have reason to believe, their means are not of the greatest, they would only provoke me by any show of effort to make me feel at home in the humble cottage suited to their fortunes.

So the telegram was sent, and my preparations completed for an early departure.

But, resolved as I was to make this visit, my determination came near receiving a check. Just as I was leaving the house—at the very moment, in fact, when the hackman was carrying out my trunk, I perceived a man approaching me with every evidence of haste. He had a letter in his hand, which he held out to me as soon as he came within reach.

"For Miss Butterworth," he announced. "Private and immediate."

"Ah," thought I, "a communication from Mr. Gryce," and hesitated for a moment whether to open it on the spot or to wait and read it at my leisure on the cars. The latter course promised me less inconvenience than the first, for my hands were cumbered with the various small articles I consider indispensable to the comfortable enjoyment of the shortest journey, and the glasses without which I cannot read a word, were in the very bottom of my pocket under many other equally necessary articles.

But something in the man's expectant look warned me that he would never leave me till I had read the note, so with a sigh I called Lena to my aid, and after several vain attempts to reach my glasses, succeeded at last in pulling them out, and by their help reading the following hurried lines:

"DEAR MADAM:

"I send you this by a swifter messenger than myself. Do not let anything that I may have said last night influence you to leave your comfortable home. The adventure offers too many dangers for a woman. Read the inclosed. G."

The inclosed was a telegram from X., sent during the night, and evidently just received at Headquarters. Its contents were certainly not reassuring:

"Another person missing. Last seen in Lost Man's Lane. A harmless lad known as Silly Rufus. What's to be done? Wire orders. TROHM."

"Mr. Gryce bade me say that he would be up here some time before noon," said the man, seeing me look with some blankness at these words.

Nothing more was needed to restore my self-possession. Folding up the letter, I put it in my bag.

"Say to Mr. Gryce from me that my intended visit cannot be postponed," I replied. "I have telegraphed to my friends to expect me, and only a great emergency would lead me to disappoint them. I will be glad to receive Mr. Gryce on my return." And without further parley, I took my bundles back from Lena, and proceeded at once to the carriage. Why should I show any failure of courage at an event that was but a repetition of the very ones which made my visit necessary? Was I a likely person to fall victim to a mystery to which my eyes had been opened? Had I not been sufficiently warned of the dangers of Lost Man's Lane to keep myself at a respectable distance from the place of peril? I was going to visit the children of my once devoted friend. If there were perils of no ordinary nature to be encountered in so doing, was I not all the more called upon to lend them the support of my presence?

Yes, Mr. Gryce, and nothing now should hold me back. I even felt an increased desire to reach the scene of these mysteries, and chafed some at the length of the journey, which was of a more tedious character than I expected. A poor beginning for events requiring patience as well as great moral courage; but I little knew what was before me, and only considered that every moment spent on this hot and dusty train kept me thus much longer from the embraces of Althea's children.

I recovered my equanimity, however, as we approached X. The scenery was really beautiful, and the consciousness that I should soon alight at the mountain station which had played a more or less serious part in Mr. Gryce's narrative, awakened in me a pleasurable excitement which should have been a sufficient warning to me that the spirit of investigation which had led me so triumphantly through that affair next door had seized me again in a way that meant equal absorption if not equal success.

The number of small packages I carried gave me enough to think of at the moment of alighting, but as soon as I was safely again on terra firma I threw a hasty glance around to see if any of Althea's children were on hand to meet me.

I felt that I ought to know them at first glance. Their mother had been so characteristically pretty, she could not have failed to transmit some of her most charming traits to her offspring. But while there were two or three country maidens to be seen standing in and around the little pavilion known here as the Mountain-station, I saw no one who by any stretch of imagination could be regarded as of Althea Burroughs' blood or breeding.

Somewhat disappointed, for I had expected different results from my telegram, I stepped up to the station-master, and asked him whether I would have any difficulty in procuring a carriage to take me to Miss Knollys' house. He stared, it seemed to me, unnecessarily long, before replying.

"Waal," said he, "Simmons is usually here, but I don't see him around to-day. Perhaps some of these farmer lads will drive you in."

But they all drew back with a scared look, and I was beginning to tuck up my skirts preparatory to walking, when a little old man of exceedingly meek appearance drove up in a very old-fashioned coach, and with a hesitating air, springing entirely from bashfulness, managed to ask if I was Miss Butterworth. I hastened to assure him that I was that lady, whereupon he stammered out some words about Miss Knollys, and how sorry she was that she could not come for me herself. Then he pointed to his coach, and made me understand that I was to step into it and go with him.

This I had not counted upon doing, for I desired to both see and hear as much as possible before reaching my destination. There was but one way out of it. To his astonishment, I insisted that my belongings be put inside the coach, while I rode on the box.

It was an inauspicious beginning to a very doubtful adventure. I understood this when I saw the heads of the various onlookers draw together and many curious looks directed at both us and the conveyance that was to carry us. But I was in no mood to be daunted now, and mounting to the box with what grace I could, prepared myself for a ride into town.

But it seems I was not to be allowed to leave the spot without another warning. While the old man was engaged in fetching my trunk, the station-master approached me with great civility, and asked if it was my intention to spend a few days with the Misses Knollys. I told him that it was, and thinking it best to establish my position at once in the eyes of the whole town, added with a politeness equal to his own, that I was an old friend of the family, and had been coming to visit them for years, but had never found it convenient till now, and that I hoped they were all well and would be glad to see me.

His reply showed considerable embarrassment.

"Perhaps you have not heard that this village is under a cloud just now?"

"I have heard that one or two men have disappeared from here somewhat mysteriously," I returned. "Is that what you mean?"

"Yes, ma'am. One person, a boy, disappeared only two days ago."

"That's bad," I said. "But what has it to do with me?" I smilingly added, for I saw that he was not at the end of his talk.

"Oh, nothing," he eagerly replied, "only I didn't know but you might be timid——"

"Oh, I'm not at all timid," I hastened to interject. "If I were, I should not have come here at all. Such matters don't affect me." And I spread out my skirts and arranged myself for my ride with as much care and precision as if the horrors he had mentioned had made no more impression upon me than if his chat had been of the weather.

Perhaps I overdid it, for he looked at me for another moment in a curious, lingering way; then he walked off, and I saw him enter the circle of gossips on the platform, where he stood shaking his head as long as we were within sight.

My companion, who was the shyest man I ever saw, did not speak a word while we were descending the hill. I talked, and endeavored to make him follow my example, but his replies were mere grunts or half-syllables which conveyed no information whatever. As we cleared the thicket, however, he allowed himself an ejaculation or two as he pointed out the beauties of the landscape. And indeed it was well worth his admiration and mine had my mind been free to enjoy it. But the houses, which now began to appear on either side of the way, drew my attention from the mountains. Though still somewhat remote from the town, we were rapidly approaching the head of that lane of evil fame with whose awe-inspiring history my thoughts were at this time full. I was so anxious not to pass it without one look into its grewsome recesses that I kept my head persistently turned that way till I felt I was attracting the attention of my companion. As this was not desirable, I put on a nonchalant look and began chatting about what I saw. But he had lapsed into his early silence, and seemed wholly engrossed in his attempt to remove with the butt-end of his whip a bit of rag which had somehow become entangled in the spokes of one of the front wheels. The furtive look he cast me as he succeeded in doing this struck me oddly at the moment, but it was too small a matter to hold my attention long or to cause any cessation in the flow of small talk with which I was endeavoring to enliven the situation.

My desire for conversation lagged, however, as I saw rising up before us the dark boughs of a pine thicket. We were nearing Lost Man's Lane; we were abreast of it; we were—yes, we were turning into it!

I could not repress an exclamation of dismay.

"Where are we going?" I asked.

"To Miss Knollys' house," he found words to say, with a sidelong glance at me full of uneasy inquiry.

"Do they live on this road?" I cried, remembering with a certain shock Mr. Gryce's suspicious description of the two young ladies who with their brother inhabited the dilapidated mansion marked A in the map he had shown me.

"Where else?" was his laconic answer; and, obliged to be satisfied with this curtest of curt replies, I drew myself up with just one longing look behind me at the cheerful highway we were so rapidly leaving. A cottage, with an open window, in which a child's head could be seen nodding eagerly toward me, met my eyes and filled me with quite an odd sense of discomfort as I realized that I had caught the attention of one of the little cripples who, according to Mr. Gryce, always kept watch over this entrance into Lost Man's Lane. Another moment and the pine branches had shut the vision out, but I did not soon forget that eager, childish face and pointing hand, marking me out as a possible victim to the horrors of this ill-reputed lane. But I was aware of no secret flinching from the adventure into which I was plunging. On the contrary, I felt a strange and fierce delight in thus being thrust into the very heart of the mystery I had only expected to approach by degrees. The warning message sent me by Mr. Gryce had acquired a deeper and more significant meaning, as did the looks which had been cast me by the station-master and his gossips on the hillside, but in my present mood these very tokens of the serious nature of my undertaking only gave an added spur to my courage. I felt my brain clear and my heart expand, as if at this moment, before I had so much as set eyes on the faces of these young people, I recognized the fact that they were the victims of a web of circumstances so tragic and incomprehensible that only a woman like myself would be able to dissipate them and restore these girls to the confidence of the people around them.

I forgot that these girls had a brother and that—But not a word to forestall the truth. I wish this story to grow upon you just as it did upon me, and with just as little preparation.

The farmer who drove me, and who I afterwards learned was called Simsbury, showed a certain dogged interest in my behavior that would have amused me, or, at least, have awakened my disdain under circumstances of a less thrilling nature. I saw his eye roll in a sort of wonder over my person, which may have been held a little more stiffly than was necessary, and settle finally on my face, with a look I might have thought complimentary had I had any thought to bestow on such matters. Not till we had passed the path branching up through the woods toward the mountain did he see fit to withdraw it, nor did I fail to find it fixed again upon me as we rode by the little hut occupied by the old woman considered so harmless by Mr. Gryce.

Perhaps he had a reason for this, as I was very much interested in this hut and its occupant, about whom I felt free to cherish my own secret doubts—so interested that I cast it a very sharp glance, and was glad when I caught a glimpse through the doorway of the old crone mumbling over a piece of bread she was engaged in eating as we passed her.

"That's Mother Jane," explained my companion, breaking the silence of many minutes. "And yonder is Miss Knollys' house," he added, lifting his whip and pointing toward the half-concealed façade of a large and pretentious dwelling a few rods farther on down the road. "She will be powerful glad to see you, Miss. Company is scarce in these parts."

Astonished at this sudden launch into conversation by one whose reserve I had hitherto found it impossible to penetrate, I gave him the affable answer he evidently expected, and then looked eagerly toward the house. It was as Mr. Gryce had intimated, exceedingly forbidding even at that distance, and as we approached nearer and I was given a full view of its worn and discolored front, I felt myself forced to acknowledge that never in my life had my eyes fallen upon a habitation more given over to neglect or less promising in its hospitality.

Had it not been for the thin circle of smoke eddying up from one of its broken chimneys, I would have looked upon the place as one which had not known the care or presence of man for years. There was a riot of shrubbery in the yard, a lack of the commonest attention to order in the way the vines drooped in tangled masses over the face of the desolate porch, that gave to the broken pilasters and decayed window-frames of this dreariest of façades that look of abandonment which only becomes picturesque when nature has usurped the prerogative of man and taken entirely to herself the empty walls and falling casements of what was once a human dwelling. That any one should be living in it now and that I, who have never been able to see a chair standing crooked or a curtain awry, without a sensation of the keenest discomfort, should be on the point of deliberately entering its doors as an inmate, filled me at the moment with such a sense of unreality, that I descended from the carriage in a sort of a dream and was making my way through one of the gaps in the high antique fence that separated the yard from the gateway, when Mr. Simsbury stopped me and pointed out the gate.

I did not think it worth while to apologize for my mistake, for the broken palings certainly offered as good an entrance as the gate, which had slipped from its hinges and hung but a few inches open. But I took the course he indicated, holding up my skirts, and treading gingerly for fear of the snails and toads that incumbered such portions of the path as the weeds had left visible. As I proceeded on my way, something in the silence of the spot struck me. Was I becoming over-sensitive to impressions or was there something really uncanny in the absolute lack of sound or movement in a dwelling of such dimensions? But I should not have said movement, for at that instant I saw a flash in one of the upper windows as of a curtain being stealthily drawn and as stealthily let fall again, and though it gave me the promise of some sort of greeting, there was a furtiveness in the action, so in keeping with the suspicions of Mr. Gryce that I felt my nerves braced at once to mount the half-dozen uninviting-looking steps that led to the front door.

But no sooner had I done this, with what I am fain to consider my best air, than I suddenly collapsed with what I am bound to regard as a comprehensible and quite excusable fear; for, while I do not quail before men, and have a reasonable fortitude in the presence of most dangers, corporeal and moral, I am not quite myself in face of a rampant and barking dog. It is my one weakness, and while I usually can, and under most circumstances do, succeed in hiding my inner trepidation under the emergency just mentioned, I always feel that it would be a happy relief for me if the day should ever come when these so-called domestic animals would be banished from the affections and homes of men. Then I think I would begin to live in good earnest and perhaps enjoy trips into the country, which now, for all my apparent bravery, I regard more in the light of a penance than a pleasure.

Imagine, then, how hard I found it to retain my self-possession or even any appearance of dignity, when at the moment I was stretching forth my hand toward the knocker of this inhospitable mansion I heard rising from some unknown quarter a howl so keen, piercing, and prolonged that it frightened the very birds over my head and sent them flying from the vines in clouds.

It was the unhappiest kind of welcome for me. I did not know whether it came from within or without, and when after a moment of indecision I saw the door open, I am not sure whether the smile I called up to grace the occasion had any of the real Amelia Butterworth in it, so much was my mind divided between a desire to produce a favorable impression and a very decided and not-to-be-hidden fear of the dog who had greeted my arrival with such an ominous howl.

"Call off the dog!" I cried almost before I saw what sort of person I was addressing.

Mr. Gryce, when I saw him later, declared this to be the most significant introduction I could have made of myself upon entering the Knollys mansion.

IV   A GHOSTLY INTERIOR

The hall into which I had stepped was so dark that for a few minutes I could see nothing but the indistinct outline of a young woman with a very white face. She had uttered some sort of murmur at my words, but for some reason was strangely silent, and, if I could trust my eyes, seemed rather to be looking back over her shoulder than into the face of her advancing guest. This was odd, but before I could quite satisfy myself as to the cause of her abstraction, she suddenly bethought herself, and throwing open the door of an adjoining room, let in a stream of light by which we were enabled to see each other and exchange the greetings suitable to the occasion.

"Miss Butterworth, my mother's old friend," she murmured, with an almost pitiful effort to be cordial, "we are so glad to have you visit us. Won't you—won't you sit down?"

What did it mean? She had pointed to a chair in the sitting-room, but her face was turned away again as if drawn irresistibly toward some secret object of dread. Was there anyone or anything at the top of the dim staircase I could faintly see in the distance? It would not do for me to ask, nor was it wise for me to show that I thought this reception a strange one. Stepping into the room she pointed out, I waited for her to follow me, which she did with manifest reluctance. But when she was once out of the atmosphere of the hall, or out of reach of the sight or sound of whatever it was that frightened her, her face took on a smile that ingratiated her with me at once and gave to her very delicate aspect, which up to that moment had not suggested the remotest likeness to her mother, a piquant charm and subtle fascination that were not unworthy of the daughter of Althea Burroughs.

"You must not mind the poverty of your welcome," she said, with a half-proud, half-apologetic look around her, which I must say the bareness and shabby character of the room we were in fully justified. "We have not been very well off since father died and mother left us. Had you given us a chance we should have written you that our home would not offer many inducements to you after your own, but you have come unexpectedly and———"

"There, there," I put in, for I saw that her embarrassment would soon get the better of her, "do not speak of it. I did not come to enjoy your home, but to see you. Are you the eldest, my dear, and where are your sister and brother?"

"I am not the eldest," she said. "I am Lucetta. My sister"—here her head stole irresistibly back to its old position of listening—"will—will come soon. My brother is not in the house."

"Well," said I, astonished that she did not ask me to take off my things, "you are a pretty girl, but you do not look very strong. Are you quite well, my dear?"

She started, looked at me eagerly, almost anxiously, for a moment, then straightened herself and began to lose some of her abstraction.

"I am not a strong person," she smiled, "but neither am I so very weak either. I was always small. So was my mother, you know."

I was glad to have her talk of her mother. I therefore answered her in a way to prolong the conversation.

"Yes, your mother was small," I admitted, "but never thin or pallid. She was like a fairy among us schoolgirls. Does it seem odd to hear so old a woman as I speak of herself as a schoolgirl?"

"Oh, no!" she said, but there was no heart in her voice.

"I had almost forgotten those days till I happened to hear the name of Althea mentioned the other day," I proceeded, seeing I must keep up the conversation if we were not to sit in total silence. "Then my early friendship with your mother recurred to me, and I started up—as I always do when I come to any decision, my dear—and sent that telegram, which I hope I have not followed by an unwelcome presence."

"Oh, no," she repeated, but this time with some feeling; "we need friends, and if you will overlook our shortcomings—But you have not taken off your hat. What will Loreen say to me?"

And with a sudden nervous action as marked as her late listlessness, she jumped up and began busying herself over me, untying my bonnet and laying aside my bundles, which up to this moment I had held in my hands.

"I—I am so absent-minded," she murmured. "I—I did not think—I hope you will excuse me. Loreen would have given you a much better welcome."

"Then Loreen should have been here," I said, with a smile. I could not restrain this slight rebuke, yet I liked the girl; notwithstanding everything I had heard and her own odd and unaccountable behavior, there was a sweetness in her face, when she chose to smile, that proved an irresistible attraction. And then, for all her absent-mindedness and abstracted ways, she was such a lady! Her plain dress, her restrained manner, could not hide this fact. It was apparent in every line of her thin but graceful form and in every inflection of her musical but constrained voice. Had I seen her in my own parlor instead of between these bare and moldering walls, I should have said the same thing: "She is such a lady!" But this only passed through my mind at the time. I was not studying her personality, but trying to understand why my presence in the house had so visibly disturbed her. Was it the embarrassment of poverty, not knowing how to meet the call made so suddenly upon it? I hardly thought so. Fear would not enter into a sensation of this kind, and fear was what I had seen in her face before the front door had closed upon me. But that fear? Was it connected with me or with something threatening her from another portion of the house?

The latter supposition seemed the probable one. The way her ear was turned, the slight start she gave at every sound, convinced me that her cause of dread lay elsewhere than with myself, and therefore was worthy of my closest attention. Though I chatted and tried in every way to arouse her confidence, I could not help asking myself between the sentences, if the cause of her apprehension lay with her sister, her brother, or in something entirely apart from either, and connected with the dreadful matter which had drawn me to X. Or another supposition still, was it merely the sign of an habitual distemper which, misunderstood by Mr. Gryce, had given rise to the suspicions which it was my possible mission here to dispel?

Anxious to force things a little, I remarked, with a glance at the dismal branches that almost forced their way into the open casements: "What a scene for young eyes like yours! Do you never get tired of these pine-boughs and clustering shadows? Would not a little cottage in the sunnier part of the town be preferable to all this dreary grandeur?"

She looked up with sudden wistfulness that made her smile piteous.

"Some of my happiest days have been passed here and some of my saddest. I do not think I should like to leave it for any sunny cottage. We were not made for bonny homes," she continued. "The sombreness of this old house suits us."

"And of this road," I ventured. "It is the darkest and most picturesque I ever rode through. I thought I was threading a wilderness."

For a moment she forgot her cause of anxiety and looked at me quite intently, while a subtle shade of doubt passed slowly over her features.

"It is a solitary one," she acquiesced. "I do not wonder it struck you as dismal. Have you heard—has any one ever told you that—that it was not considered quite safe?"

"Safe?" I repeated, with—God forgive me!—an expression of mild wonder in my eyes.

"Yes, it has not the best of reputations. Strange things have happened in it. I thought that some one might have been kind enough to tell you this at the station."

There was a gentle sort of sarcasm in the tone; only that, or so it seemed to me at the time. I began to feel myself in a maze.

"Somebody—I suppose it was the station-master—did say something to me about a boy lost somewhere in this portion of the woods. Do you mean that, my dear?"

She nodded, glancing again over her shoulder and partly rising as if moved by some instinct of flight.

"They are dark enough, for more than one person to have been lost in their recesses," I observed with another look toward the heavily curtained windows.

"They certainly are," she assented, reseating herself and eying me nervously while she spoke. "We are used to the terrors they inspire in strangers, but if you"— she leaped to her feet in manifest eagerness and her whole face changed in a way she little realized herself—"if you have any fear of sleeping amid such gloomy surroundings, we can procure you a room in the village where you will be more comfortable, and where we can visit you almost as well as we can here. Shall I do it? Shall I call——"

My face must have assumed a very grim look, for her words tripped at that point, and a flush, the first I had seen on her cheek, suffused her face, giving her an appearance of great distress.

"Oh, I wish Loreen would come! I am not at all happy in my suggestions," she said, with a deprecatory twitch of her lip that was one of her subtle charms. "Oh, there she is! Now I may go," she cried; and without the least appearance of realizing that she had said anything out of place, she rushed from the room almost before her sister had entered it.

But not before their eyes had met in a look of unusual significance.

V A STRANGE HOUSEHOLD

Had I not surprised this look of mutual understanding, I might have received an impression of Miss Knollys which would in a measure have counteracted that made by the more nervous and less restrained Lucetta. The dignified reserve of her bearing, the quiet way in which she approached, and, above all, the even tones in which she uttered her welcome, were such as to win my confidence and put me at my ease in the house of which she was the nominal mistress. But that look! With that in my memory, I was enabled to pierce below the surface of this placid nature, and in the very constraint she put upon herself, detect the presence of the same secret uneasiness which had been so openly, if unconsciously, manifested by her sister.

She was more beautiful than Lucetta in form and feature, and even more markedly elegant in her plain black gown and fine lawn ruffles, but she lacked her sister's evanescent charm, and though admirable to all appearance, was less lovable on a short acquaintance.

But this delays my tale, which is one of action rather than reflection. I had naturally expected that with the appearance of the elder Miss Knollys I should be taken to my room; but, on the contrary, she sat down and with an apologetic air informed me that she was sorry she could not show me the customary attentions. Circumstances over which she had no control had made it impossible, she said, for her to offer me the guest-chamber, but if I would be so good as to accept another for this one night, she would endeavor to provide me with better accommodations on the morrow.

Satisfied of the almost painful nature of their poverty and determined to submit to privations rather than leave a house so imbued with mystery, I hastened to assure her that any room would be acceptable to me; and with a display of good feeling not wholly insincere, began to gather up my wraps in anticipation of being taken at once up-stairs.

But Miss Knollys again surprised me by saying that my room was not yet ready; that they had not been able to complete all their arrangements, and begged me to make myself at home in the room where I was till evening.

As this was asking a good deal of a woman of my years, fresh from a railroad journey and with natural habits of great neatness and order, I felt somewhat disconcerted, but hiding my feelings in consideration of reasons before given, replaced my bundles on the table and endeavored to make the best of a somewhat trying situation.

Launching at once into conversation, I began, as with Lucetta, to talk about her mother. I had never known, save in the vaguest way, why Mrs. Knollys had taken the journey which had ended in her death and burial in a foreign land. Rumor had it that she had gone abroad for her health which had begun to fail after the birth of Lucetta; but as Rumor had not added why she had gone unaccompanied by her husband or children, there remained much which these girls might willingly tell me, which would be of the greatest interest to me. But Miss Knollys, intentionally or unintentionally, assumed an air so cold at my well meant questions, that I desisted from pressing them, and began to talk about myself in a way which I hoped would establish really friendly relations between us and make it possible for her to tell me later, if not at the present moment, what it was that weighed so heavily upon the household, that no one could enter this home without feeling the shadow of the secret terror enveloping it.

But Miss Knollys, while more attentive to my remarks than her sister had been, showed, by certain unmistakable signs, that her heart and interest were anywhere but in that room; and while I could not regard this as throwing any discredit upon my powers of pleasing—which have rarely failed when I have exerted them to their utmost,—I still could not but experience the dampening effect of her manner. I went on chatting, but in a desultory way, noting all that was odd in her unaccountable reception of me, but giving, as I firmly believe, no evidence of my concern and rapidly increasing curiosity.

The peculiarities observable in this my first interview with these interesting but by no means easily-to-be-understood sisters continued all day. When one sister came in, the other stepped out, and when dinner was announced and I was ushered down the bare and dismal hall into an equally bare and unattractive dining-room, it was to find the chairs set for four, and Lucetta only seated at the table.

"Where is Loreen?" I asked wonderingly, as I took the seat she pointed out to me with one of her faint and quickly vanishing smiles.

"She cannot come at present," my young hostess stammered with an unmistakable glance of distress at the large, hearty-looking woman who had summoned me to the dining-room.

"Ah," I ejaculated, thinking that possibly Loreen had found it necessary to assist in the preparation of the meal, "and your brother?"

It was the first time he had been mentioned since my first inquiries. I had shrunk from the venture out of a motive of pure compassion, and they had not seen fit to introduce his name into any of our conversations. Consequently I awaited her response, with some anxiety, having a secret premonition that in some way he was at the bottom of my strange reception.

Her hasty answer, given, however, without any increase of embarrassment, somewhat dispelled this supposition.

"Oh, he will be in presently," said she. "William is never very punctual."

But when he did come in, I could not help seeing that her manner instantly changed and became almost painfully anxious. Though it was my first meeting with the real head of the house, she waited for an interchange of looks with him before giving me the necessary introduction, and when, this duty performed, he took his seat at the table, her thoughts and attention remained so fixed upon him that she well-nigh forgot the ordinary civilities of a hostess. Had it not been for the woman I have spoken of, who in her good-natured attention to my wants amply made up for the abstraction of her mistress, I should have fared ill at this meal, good and ample as it was, considering the resources of those who provided it.

She seemed to dread to have him speak, almost to have him move. She watched him with her lips half open, ready, as it appeared, to stop any inadvertent expression he might utter in his efforts to be agreeable. She even kept her left hand disengaged, with the evident intention of stretching it out in his direction if in his lumbering stupidity he should utter a sentence calculated to open my eyes to what she so passionately desired to have kept secret. I saw it all as plainly as I saw his heavy indifference to her anxiety; and knowing from experience that it is in just such stolid louts as these that the worst passions are often hidden, I took advantage of my years and forced a conversation in which I hoped some flash of his real self would appear, despite her wary watch upon him.

Not liking to renew the topic of the lane itself, I asked with a very natural show of interest, who was their nearest neighbor. It was William who looked up and William who answered.

"Old Mother Jane is the nearest," said he; "but she's no good. We never think of her. Mr. Trohm is the only neighbor I care for. Such peaches as the old fellow raises! Such grapes! Such melons! He gave me two of the nicest you ever saw this morning. By Jupiter, I taste them yet!"

Lucetta's face, which should have crimsoned with mortification, turned most unaccountably pale. Yet not so pale as it had previously done when, a few minutes before, he began to say, "Loreen wants some of this soup saved for"—and stopped awkwardly, conscious perhaps that Loreen's wants should not be mentioned before me.

"I thought you promised me that you would never again ask Mr. Trohm for any of his fruit," remonstrated Lucetta.

"Oh, I didn't ask! I just stood at the fence and looked over. Mr. Trohm and I are good friends. Why shouldn't I eat his fruit?"

The look she gave him might have moved a stone, but he seemed perfectly impervious to it. Seeing him so stolid, her head drooped, and she did not answer a word. Yet somehow I felt that even while she was so manifestly a prey to the deepest mortification, her attention was not wholly given over to this one emotion. There was something else she feared. Hoping to relieve her and lighten the situation, I forced myself to smile on the young man as I said:

"Why don't you raise melons yourself? I think if I possessed your land I should be anxious to raise everything I could on it."

"Oh, you're a woman!" he retorted, almost roughly. "It's good business for women; and for men, too, perhaps, who love to see fruit hang, but I only care to eat it."

"Don't," Lucetta put in, but not with the vigor I had expected.

"I like to hunt, train dogs, and enjoy other people's fruit," he laughed, with a nod at the blushing Lucetta. "I don't see any use in a man's putting himself out for things he can get for the asking. Life's too short for such folly. I mean to have a good time while I'm on this blessed sphere."

"William!"

The cry was irresistible, yet it was not the cry I had been looking for. Painful as was this exhibition of his stupidity and utter want of feeling, it was not the one thing she stood in dread of, or why was her protest so much weaker than her appearance had given token of?

"Oh!" he shouted in great amusement, while she shrunk back with a horrified look. "Lucetta don't like to hear me say that. She thinks a man ought to work, plow, harrow, dig, make a slave of himself, to keep up a place that's no good anyway. But I tell her that work is something she'll never get out of me. I was born a gentleman, and a gentleman I will live if the place tumbles down over our heads. Perhaps it would be the best way to get rid of it. Then I could go live with Mr. Trohm, and have melons from early morn till late at night." And again his coarse laugh rang out.

This, or was it his words, seemed to rouse her as nothing had done before. Thrusting out her hand, she laid it on his mouth, with a look of almost frenzied appeal at the woman who was standing at his back.

"Mr. William, how can you!" that woman protested; and when he would have turned upon her angrily, she leaned over and whispered in his ear a few words that seemed to cow him, for he gave a short grunt through his sister's trembling fingers and, with a shrug of his heavy shoulders, subsided into silence.

To all this I was a simple spectator, but I did not soon forget a single feature of the scene.

The remainder of the dinner passed quietly, William and myself eating with more or less heartiness, Lucetta tasting nothing at all. In mercy to her I declined coffee, and as soon as William gave token of being satisfied, we hurriedly rose. It was the most uncomfortable meal I ever ate in my life.

VI   A SOMBRE EVENING

The evening, like the afternoon, was spent in the sitting-room with one of the sisters. One event alone is worth recording. I had become excessively tired of a conversation that always languished, no matter on what topic it started, and, observing an old piano in one corner—I once played very well—I sat down before it and impulsively struck a few chords from the yellow keys. Instantly Lucetta—it was Lucetta who was with me then—bounded to my side with a look of horror.

"Don't do that!" she cried, laying her hand on mine to stop me. Then, seeing my look of dignified astonishment, she added with an appealing smile, "I beg pardon, but every sound goes through me to-night."

"Are you not well?" I asked.

"I am never very well," she returned, and we went back to the sofa and renewed our forced and pitiful attempts at conversation.

Promptly at nine o'clock Miss Knollys came in. She was very pale and cast, as usual, a sad and uneasy look at her sister before she spoke to me. Immediately Lucetta rose, and, becoming very pale herself, was hurrying toward the door when her sister stopped her.

"You have forgotten," she said, "to say good-night to our guest."

Instantly Lucetta turned, and, with a sudden, uncontrollable impulse, seized my hand and pressed it convulsively.

"Good-night," she cried. "I hope you will sleep well," and was gone before I could say a word in response.

"Why does Lucetta go out of the room when you come in?" I asked, determined to know the reason for this peculiar conduct. "Have you any other guests in the house?"

The reply came with unexpected vehemence. "No," she cried, "why should you think so? There is no one here but the family." And she turned away with a dignity she must have inherited from her father, for Althea Burroughs had every interesting quality but that. "You must be very tired," she remarked. "If you please we will go now to your room."

I rose at once, glad of the prospect of seeing the upper portion of the house. She took my wraps on her arm, and we passed immediately into the hall. As we did so, I heard voices, one of them shrill and full of distress; but the sound was so quickly smothered by a closing door that I failed to discover whether this tone of suffering proceeded from a man or a woman.

Miss Knollys, who was preceding me, glanced back in some alarm, but as I gave no token of having noticed anything out of the ordinary, she speedily resumed her way up-stairs. As the sounds I had heard proceeded from above, I followed her with alacrity, but felt my enthusiasm diminish somewhat when I found myself passing door after door down a long hall to a room as remote as possible from what seemed to be the living portion of the house.

"Is it necessary to put me off quite so far?" I asked, as my young hostess paused and waited for me to join her on the threshold of the most forbidding room it had ever been my fortune to enter.

The blush which mounted to her brow showed that she felt the situation keenly.

"I am sure," she said, "that it is a matter of great regret to me to be obliged to offer you so mean a lodging, but all our other rooms are out of order, and I cannot accommodate you with anything better to-night."

"But isn't there some spot nearer you?" I urged. "A couch in the same room with you would be more acceptable to me than this distant room."

"I—I hope you are not timid," she began, but I hastened to disabuse her mind on this score.

"I am not afraid of any earthly thing but dogs," I protested warmly. "But I do not like solitude. I came here for companionship, my dear. I really would like to sleep with one of you."

This, to see how she would meet such urgency. She met it, as I might have known she would, by a rebuff.

"I am very sorry," she again repeated, "but it is quite impossible. If I could give you the comforts you are accustomed to, I should be glad, but we are unfortunate, we girls, and—" She said no more, but began to busy herself about the room, which held but one object that had the least look of comfort in it. That was my trunk, which had been neatly placed in one corner.

"I suppose you are not used to candles," she remarked, lighting what struck me as a very short end, from the one she held in her hand.

"My dear," said I, "I can accommodate myself to much that I am not used to. I have very few old maid's ways or notions. You shall see that I am far from being a difficult guest."

She heaved a sigh, and then, seeing my eye travelling slowly over the gray discolored walls which were not relieved by so much as a solitary print, she pointed to a bell-rope near the head of the bed, and considerately remarked:

"If you wish anything in the night, or are disturbed in any way, pull that. It communicates with my room, and I will be only too glad to come to you."

I glanced up at the rope, ran my eye along the wire communicating with it, and saw that it was broken sheer off before it even entered into the wall.

"I am afraid you will not hear me," I answered, pointing to the break.

She flushed a deep scarlet, and for a moment looked as embarrassed as ever her sister had done.

"I did not know," she murmured. "The house is so old, everything is more or less out of repair." And she made haste to quit the room.

I stepped after her in grim determination.

"But there is no key to the door," I objected.

She came back with a look that was as nearly desperate as her placid features were capable of.

"I know," she said, "I know. We have nothing. But if you are not afraid—and of what could you be afraid in this house, under our protection, and with a good dog outside?—you will bear with things to-night, and—Good God!" she murmured, but not so low but that my excited sense caught every syllable, "can she have heard? Has the reputation of this place gone abroad? Miss Butterworth," she repeated earnestly, "the house contains no cause of terror for you. Nothing threatens our guest, nor need you have the least concern for yourself or us, whether the night passes in quiet or whether it is broken by unaccountable sounds. They will have no reference to anything in which you are interested."

"Ah, ha," thought I, "won't they! You give me credit for much indifference, my dear." But I said nothing beyond a few soothing phrases, which I made purposely short, seeing that every moment I detained her was just so much unnecessary torture to her. Then I went back to my room and carefully closed the door. My first night in this dismal and strangely ordered house had opened anything but propitiously.

VII   THE FIRST NIGHT

I spoke with a due regard to truth when I assured Miss Knollys that I entertained no fears at the prospect of sleeping apart from the rest of the family. I am a woman of courage—or so I have always believed—and at home occupy my second floor alone without the least apprehension. But there is a difference in these two abiding-places, as I think you are ready by this time to acknowledge, and, though I felt little of what is called fear, I certainly did not experience my usual satisfaction in the minute preparations with which I am accustomed to make myself comfortable for the night. There was a gloom both within and without the four bare walls between which I now found myself shut, which I would have been something less than human not to feel, and though I had no dread of being overcome by it, I was glad to add something to the cheer of the spot by opening my trunk and taking out a few of those little matters of personal equipment without which the brightest room looks barren and a den like this too desolate for habitation.

Then I took a good look about me to see how I could obtain for myself some sense of security. The bed was light and could be pulled in front of the door. This was something. There was but one window, and that was closely draped with some thick, dark stuff, very funereal in its appearance. Going to it, I pulled aside the thick folds and looked out. A mass of heavy foliage at once met my eye, obstructing the view of the sky and adding much to the lonesomeness of the situation. I let the curtain fall again and sat down in a chair to think.

The shortness of the candle-end with which I had been provided had struck me as significant, so significant that I had not allowed it to burn long after Miss Knollys had left me. If these girls, charming, no doubt, but sly, had thought to shorten my watch by shortening my candle, I would give them no cause to think but that their ruse had been successful. The foresight which causes me to add a winter wrap to my stock of clothing even when the weather is at the hottest, leads me to place a half dozen or so of candles in my travelling trunk, and so I had only to open a little oblong box in the upper tray to have the means at my disposal of keeping a light all night.

So far, so good. I had a light, but had I anything else in case William Knollys—but with this thought Miss Knollys's look and reassuring words recurred to me. "Whatever you may hear—if you hear anything—will have no reference to yourself and need not disturb you."

This was comforting certainly, from a selfish standpoint; but did it relieve my mind concerning others?

Not knowing what to think of it all, and fully conscious that sleep would not visit me under existing circumstances, I finally made up my mind not to lie down till better assured that sleep on my part would be desirable. So after making the various little arrangements already alluded to, I drew over my shoulders a comfortable shawl and set myself to listen for what I feared would be more than one dreary hour of this not to be envied night.

And here just let me stop to mention that, carefully considered as all my precautions were, I had forgotten one thing upon leaving home which at this minute made me very nearly miserable. I had not included among my effects the alcohol lamp and all the other private and particular conveniences which I possess for making tea in my own apartment. Had I but had them with me, and had I been able to make and sip a cup of my own delicious tea through the ordeal of listening for whatever sounds might come to disturb the midnight stillness of this house, what relief it would have been to my spirits and in what a different light I might have regarded Mr. Gryce and the mission with which I had been intrusted. But I not only lacked this element of comfort, but the satisfaction of thinking that it was any one's fault but my own. Lena had laid her hand on that teapot, but I had shaken my head, fearing that the sight of it might offend the eyes of my young hostesses. But I had not calculated upon being put in a remote corner like this of a house large enough to accommodate a dozen families, and if ever I travel again—

But this is a matter personal to Amelia Butterworth, and of no interest to you. I will not inflict my little foibles upon you again.

Eleven o'clock came and went. I had heard no sound. Twelve, and I began to think that all was not quite so still as before; that I certainly could hear now and then faint noises as of a door creaking on its hinges, or the smothered sound of stealthily moving feet. Yet all was so far from being distinct, that for some time I hesitated to acknowledge to myself that anything could be going on in the house, which was not to be looked for in a home professing to be simply the abode of a decent young man and two very quiet-appearing young ladies; and even after the noises and whispering had increased to such an extent that I could even distinguish the sullen tones of the brother from the softer and more carefully modulated accents of Lucetta and her sister, I found myself ready to explain the matter by any conjecture short of that which involved these delicate young ladies in any scheme of secret wickedness.

But when I found there was likely to be no diminution in the various noises and movements that were taking place in the front of the house, and that only something much out of the ordinary could account for so much disturbance in a country home so long after midnight, I decided that only a person insensible to all sight and sound could be expected to remain asleep under such circumstances, and that I would be perfectly justified in their eyes in opening my door and taking a peep down the corridor. So without further ado, I drew my bed aside and glanced out.

All was perfectly dark and silent in the great house. The only light visible came from the candle burning in the room behind me, and as for sound, it was almost too still—it was the stillness of intent rather than that of natural repose.

This was so unexpected that for an instant I stood baffled and wondering. Then my nose went up, and I laughed quietly to myself. I could see nothing and I could hear nothing; but Amelia Butterworth, like most of her kind, boasts of more than two senses, and happily there was something to smell. A quickly blown-out candle leaves a witness behind it to sensitive nostrils like mine, and this witness assured me that the darkness was deceptive. Some one had just passed the head of my corridor with a light, and because the light was extinguished it did not follow that the person who held it was far away. Indeed, I thought that now I heard a palpitating breath.

"Humph," I cried aloud, but as if in unconscious communion with myself, "it is not often I have so vivid a dream! I was sure that I heard steps in the hall. I fear

I'm growing nervous."

Nothing moved. No one answered me.

"Miss Knollys!" I called firmly.

No reply.

"Lucetta, dear!"

I thought this appeal would go unanswered also, but when I raised my voice for the third time, a sudden rushing sound took place down the corridor, and Lucetta's excited figure, fully dressed, appeared in the faint circle of light caused by my now rapidly waning candle.

"Miss Butterworth, what is the matter?" she asked, making as if she would draw me into my room—a proceeding which I took good care she should not succeed in.

Giving a glance at her dress, which was the same she had worn at the supper table, I laughingly retorted:

"Isn't that a question I might better ask you? It is two o'clock by my watch, and you, for all your apparent delicacy, are still up. What does it mean, my dear? Have I put you out so completely by my coming that none of you can sleep?"

Her eyes, which had fallen before mine, quickly looked up.

"I am sorry," she began, flushing and trying to take a peep into my room, possibly to see if I had been to bed. "We did not mean to disturb you, but—but—oh, Miss Butterworth, pray excuse our makeshifts and our poverty. We wished to fix up another room for you, and were ashamed to have you see how little we had to do it with, so we were moving some things out of our own room to-night, and——"

Here her voice broke, and she burst into an almost uncontrollable flood of tears.

"Don't," she entreated, "don't," as, quite thoroughly ashamed, I began to utter some excuses. "I shall be all right in a moment. I am used to humiliations. Only"—and her whole body seemed to join in the plea, it trembled so—"do not, I pray, speak quite so loud. My brother is more sensitive than even Loreen and myself about these things, and if he should hear——"

Here a suppressed oath from way down the hall assured me that he did hear, but I gave no sign of my recognition of this fact, and Lucetta added quickly: "He would not forgive us for our carelessness in waking you. He is rough sometimes, but so good at heart, so good."

This, with the other small matter I have just mentioned, caused a revulsion in my feelings. He good? I did not believe it. Yet her eyes showed no wavering when I interrogated them with mine, and feeling that I had perhaps been doing them all an injustice, and that what I had seen was, as she evidently meant to intimate, due to their efforts to make a sudden guest comfortable amid their poverty, I put the best face I could on the matter and gave the poor, pitiful, pleading face a kiss. I was startled to feel how cold her forehead was, and, more and more concerned, loaded her down with such assurances of appreciation as came to my lips, and sent her back to her own room with an injunction not to trouble herself any more about fixing up any other room for me. "Only," I added, as her whole face showed relief, "we will go to the locksmith to-morrow and get a key; and after to-night you will be kind enough to see that I have a cup of tea brought to my room just before I retire.

I am no good without my cup of tea, my dear. What keeps other people awake makes me sleep."

"Oh, you shall have your tea!" she cried, with an eagerness that was almost unnatural, and then, slipping from my grasp, she uttered another hasty apology for having roused me from my sleep and ran hastily back.

I stretched out my arm for the candle guttering in my room and held it up to light her. She seemed to shrink at sight of its rays, and the last vision I had of her speeding figure showed me that same look of dread on her pallid features which had aroused my interest in our first interview.

"She may have explained why the three of them are up at this time of night," I muttered, "but she has not explained why her every conversation is seasoned by an expression of fear."

And thus brooding, I went back to my room and, pushing the bed again against the door, lay down upon it and out of sheer chagrin fell fast asleep.

VIII   ON THE STAIRS

I did not wake up till morning. The room was so dark that in all probability I should not have wakened then, if my habits of exact punctuality had not been aided by a gentle knock at my door.

"Who's there?" I called, for I could not say "Come in" till I had moved my bed and made way for the door to open.

"Hannah with warm water," replied a voice, at which I made haste to rise. Hannah was the woman who had waited on us at dinner.

The sight of her pleasant countenance, which nevertheless looked a trifle haggard, was a welcome relief after the sombre features of the night. Addressing her with my usual brusqueness, but with quite my usual kindness, I asked how the young ladies were feeling this morning.

Her answer made a great show of frankness.

"Oh, they are much as usual," said she. "Miss Loreen is in the kitchen and Miss Lucetta will soon be here to inquire how you are. I hope you passed a good night yourself, ma'am."

I had slept more than I ought to, perhaps, and made haste to reassure her as to my own condition. Then seeing that a little talk would not be unwelcome to this hearty woman, tired to death possibly with life in this dreary house, I made some excuse for keeping her a few minutes, saying as I did so:

"What an immense dwelling this is for four persons to live in, or have you another inmate whom I have not seen?"

I thought her buxom color showed a momentary sign of failing, but it all came back with her answer, which was given in a round, hearty voice.

"Oh, I'm the only maid, ma'am. I cook and sweep and all. I couldn't abide another near me. Even Mr. Simsbury, who tends the cow and horse and who only comes in for his dinner, worries me by spells. I like to have my own way in the kitchen, except when the young ladies choose to come in. Is there anything more you want, ma'am, and do you prefer tea or coffee for breakfast?"

I told her that I always drank coffee in the morning, and would have liked to have added a question or two, but she gave me no chance. As she went out I saw her glance at my candlestick. There was only a half-burned end in it. She is calculating, too, how long I sat up, thought I.

Lucetta stood at the head of the stairs as I went down.

"Will you excuse me for a few moments?" said she. "I am not quite ready to follow you, but will be soon."

"I will take a look at the grounds."

I thought she hesitated for a moment; then her face lighted up. "Be sure you don't encounter the dog," she cried, and slipped hastily down a side hall I had not noticed the night before.

"Ah, a good way to keep me in," I reasoned. "But I shall see the grounds yet if I have to poison that dog." Notwithstanding, I made no haste to leave the house. I don't believe in tempting Providence, especially where a dog is concerned.

Instead of that, I stood still and looked up and down the halls, endeavoring to get some idea of their plan and of the location of my own room in reference to the rest.

I found that the main hall ran at right angles to the long corridor down which I had just come, and noting that the doors opening into it were of a size and finish vastly superior to those I had passed in the corridor just mentioned, I judged that the best bedrooms all lay front, and that I had been quartered at the end of what had once been considered as the servants' hall. At my right, as I looked down the stairs, ran a wall with a break, which looked like an opening into another corridor, and indeed I afterward learned that the long series of rooms of which mine was the last, had its counterpart on the other side of this enormous dwelling, giving to the house the shape of a long, square U.

I was looking in some wonderment at this opening and marvelling over the extravagant hospitality of those old days which necessitated such a number of rooms in a private gentleman's home, when I heard a door open and two voices speaking. One was rough and careless, unmistakably that of William Knollys. The other was slow and timid, and was just as unmistakably that of the man who had driven me to this house the day before. They were talking of some elderly person, and I had good sense enough not to allow my indignation to blind me to the fact that by that elderly person they meant me. This is important, for their words were not without significance.

"How shall we keep the old girl out of the house till it is all over?" was what I heard from William's surly lips.

"Lucetta has a plan," was the hardly distinguishable answer. "I am to take——"

That was all I could hear; a closing door shut off the remainder. Something, then, was going on in this house, of a dark if not mysterious character, and the attempts made by these two interesting and devoted girls to cover up the fact, by explanations founded on their poverty, had been but subterfuges after all. Grieved on their account, but inwardly grateful to the imprudence of their more than reckless brother, for this not-to-be-mistaken glimpse into the truth, I slowly descended the stairs, in that state of complete self-possession which is given by a secret knowledge of the intentions formed against us by those whose actions we have reason to suspect.

Henceforth I had but one duty—to penetrate the mystery of this household.

Whether it was the one suspected by Mr. Gryce or another of a less evil and dangerous character hardly mattered in my eyes. While the blight of it rested upon this family, eyes would be lowered and heads shaken at their name. This, if I could help it, must no longer be. If guilt lay at the bottom of all this fear, then this guilt must be known; if innocence—I thought of the brother's lowering brow and felt it incompatible with innocence, but remembering Mr. Gryce's remarks on this subject, read an instant lecture to myself and, putting all conclusions aside, devoted the few minutes in which I found myself alone in the dining-room to a careful preparation of my mind for its duty, which was not likely to be of the simplest character if Lucetta's keen wits were to be pitted against mine.

IX   A NEW ACQUAINTANCE

When my mind is set free from doubt and fully settled upon any course, I am capable of much good nature and seeming simplicity. I was therefore able to maintain my own at the breakfast-table with some success, so that the meal passed off without any of the disagreeable experiences of the night before. Perhaps the fact that Loreen presided at the coffee-urn instead of Lucetta had something to do with this. Her calm, even looks seemed to put some restraint upon the boisterous outbursts to which William was only too liable, while her less excitable nature suffered less if by any chance he did break out and startle the decorous silence by one of his rude guffaws.

I am a slow eater, but I felt forced to hurry through the meal or be left eating alone at the end. This did not put me in the best of humor, for I hated to risk an indigestion just when my faculties needed to be unusually alert. I compromised by leaving the board hungry, but I did it with such a smile that I do not think Miss Knollys knew I had not risen from any table so ill satisfied in years.

"I will leave you to my brother for a few minutes," said she, hastily tripping from the room. "I pray that you will not think of going to your room till we have had an opportunity of arranging it."

I instantly made up my mind to disobey this injunction. But first, it was necessary to see what I could make of William.

He was not a very promising subject as he turned and led the way toward the front of the house.

"I thought you might like to see the grounds," he growled, evidently not enjoying the rôle assigned him. "They are so attractive," he sneered. "Children hereabout call them the jungle."

"Who's to blame for that?" I asked, with only a partial humoring of his ill nature. "You have a sturdy pair of arms of your own, and a little trimming here and a little trimming there would have given quite a different appearance to this undergrowth. A gentleman usually takes pride in his place."

"Yes, when it's all his. This belongs to my sisters as much as to me. What's the use of my bothering myself about it?"

The man was so selfish he did not realize the extent of the exhibition he made of it. Indeed he seemed to take pride in what he probably called his independence. I began to feel the most intense aversion for him, and only with the greatest difficulty could prolong this conversation unmoved.

"I should think it would be a pleasure to give that much assistance to your sisters. They do not seem to be sparing in their attempts to please you."

He snapped his fingers, and I was afraid a dog or two would come leaping around the corner of the house. But it was only his way of expressing disdain.

"Oh, the girls are well enough," he grumbled; "but they will stick to the place. Lucetta might have married a half-dozen times, and once I thought she was going to, but suddenly she turned straight about and sent her lover packing, and that made me mad beyond everything. Why should she hang on to me like a burr when there are other folks willing to take on the burden?"

It was the most palpable display of egotism I had ever seen and one of the most revolting. I was so disgusted by it that I spoke up without any too much caution.

"Perhaps she thinks she can be useful to you," I said. "I have known sisters give up their own happiness on no better grounds."

"Useful?" he sneered. "It's a usefulness a man like me can dispense with. Do you know what I would like?"

We were standing in one of the tangled pathways, with our faces turned toward the house. As he spoke, he looked up and made a rude sort of gesture toward the blank expanse of empty and curtainless windows.

"I would like that great house all to myself, to make into one huge, bachelor's hall. I should like to feel that I could tramp from one end of it to the other without awakening an echo I did not choose to hear there. I should not find it too big. I should not find it too lonesome. I and my dogs would know how to fill it, wouldn't we, Saracen? Oh, I forgot, Saracen is locked up."

The way he mumbled the last sentence showed displeasure, but I gave little heed to that. The gloating way in which he said he and his dogs would fill it had given me a sort of turn. I began to have more than an aversion for the man. He inspired me with something like terror.

"Your wishes," said I, with as little expression as possible, "seem to leave your sisters entirely out of your calculations. How would your mother regard that if she could see you from the place where she is gone?"

He turned upon me with a look of anger that made his features positively ugly.

"What do you mean by speaking to me of my mother? Have I spoken of her to you? Is there any reason why you should lug my mother into this conversation? If so, say so, and be——"

He did not swear at me; he did not dare to, but he came precious near to it, and that was enough to make me recoil.

"She was my friend," said I. "I knew and loved her before you were born. That was why I spoke of her, and I think it very natural myself."

He seemed to feel ashamed. He grumbled out some sort of apology and looked about quite helplessly, possibly for the dog he manifestly was in the habit of seeing forever at his heels. I took advantage of this momentary abstraction on his part to smooth my own disturbed features.

"She was a beautiful girl," I remarked, on the principle that, the ice once broken, one should not hesitate about jumping in. "Was your father equally handsome for a man?"

"My father—yes, let's talk of father. He was a judge of horses, he was. When he died, there were three mares in the stable not to be beat this side of Albany, but those devils of executors sold them, and I—well, you had a chance to test the speed of old Bess yesterday. You weren't afraid of being thrown out, I take it. Great Scott, to think of a man of my tastes owning no other horse than that!"

"You have not answered my question," I suggested, turning him about and moving toward the gate.

"Oh, about the way my father looked! What does that matter? He was handsome, though. Folks say that I get whatever good looks I have from him. He was big—bigger than I am, and while he lived—What did you make a fellow talk for?"

I don't know why I did, but I was certainly astonished at the result. This great, huge lump of selfish clay had actually shown feeling and was ashamed of it, like the lout he was.

"Yesterday," said I, anxious to change the subject, "I had difficulty in getting in through that gate we are pointing for. Couldn't you set it straight, with just a little effort?"

He paused, looked at me to see if I were in earnest, then took a dogged step toward the gate I was still indicating with my resolute right hand, but before he could touch it he perceived something on that deserted and ominous highway which made him start in sudden surprise.

"Why, Trohm," he cried, "is that you? Well, it's an age since I have seen you turn that corner on a visit to us."

"Sometime, certainly," answered a hearty and pleasant voice, and before I could quite drop the look of severity with which I was endeavoring to shame this young man into some decent show of interest in this place, and assume the more becoming aspect of a lady caught unawares at an early morning hour plucking flowers from a stunted syringa, a gentleman stepped into sight on the other side of the fence with a look and a bow so genial and devoid of mystery that I experienced for the first time since entering the gloomy precincts of this town a decided sensation of pleasure.

"Miss Butterworth," explained Mr. Knollys with a somewhat forced gesture in my direction. "A guest of my sisters," he went on, and looked as if he hoped I would retire, though he made no motion to welcome Mr. Trohm in, but rather leaned a little conspicuously on the gate as if anxious to show that he had no idea that the other's intention went any further than the passing of a few neighborly comments at the gate.

I like to please the young even when they are no more agreeable than my surly host, and if the gentleman who had just shown himself had been equally immature, I would certainly have left them to have their talk out undisturbed. But he was not. He was older; he was even of sufficient years for his judgment to have become thoroughly matured and his every faculty developed. I therefore could not see why my society should be considered an intrusion by him, so I waited. His next sentence was addressed to me.

"I am happy," said he, "to have the pleasure of a personal introduction to Miss Butterworth. I did not expect it. The surprise is all the more agreeable. I only anticipated being allowed to leave this package and letter with the maid. They are addressed to you, madam, and were left at my house by mistake."

I could not hide my astonishment.

"I live in the next house below," said he. "The boy who brought these from the post office was a stupid lad, and I could not induce him to come any farther up the road. I hope you will excuse the present messenger and believe there has been no delay."

I bowed with what must have seemed an abstracted politeness. The letter was from New York, and, as I strongly suspected, from Mr. Gryce. Somehow this fact created in me an unmistakable embarrassment. I put both letter and package into my pocket and endeavored to meet the gentleman's eye with my accustomed ease in the presence of strangers. But, strange to say, I had no sooner done so than I saw that he was no more at his ease than myself. He smiled, glanced at William, made an offhand remark or so about the weather, but he could not deceive eyes sharpened by such experience as mine. Something disturbed him, something connected with me. It made my cheek a little hot to acknowledge this even to myself, but it was so very evident that I began to cast about for the means of ridding ourselves of William when that blundering youth suddenly spoke:

"I suppose he was afraid to come up the lane. Do you know, I think you're brave to attempt it, Trohm. We haven't a very good name here." And with a sudden, perfectly unnatural burst, he broke out into one of his huge guffaws that so shook the old gate on which he was leaning that I thought it would tumble down with him before our eyes.

I saw Mr. Trohm start and cast him a look in which I seemed to detect both surprise and horror, before he turned to me and with an air of polite deprecation anxiously said:

"I am afraid Miss Butterworth will not understand your allusions, Mr. Knollys. I hear this is her first visit in town."

As his manner showed even more feeling than the occasion seemed to warrant, I made haste to answer that I was well acquainted with the tradition of the lane; that its name alone showed what had happened here.

His bearing betrayed an instant relief.

"I am glad to find you so well informed," said he. "I was afraid"—here he cast another very strange glance at William—"that your young friends might have shrunk, from some sense of delicacy, from telling you what might frighten most guests from a lonely road like this. I compliment you upon their thoughtfulness."

William bowed as if the words of the other contained no other suggestion than that which was openly apparent. Was he so dull, or was he—I had not time to finish my conjectures even in my own mind, for at this moment a quick cry rose behind us, and Lucetta's light figure appeared running toward us with every indication of excitement.

"Ah," murmured Mr. Trohm, with an appearance of great respect, "your sister, Mr. Knollys. I had better be moving on. Good-morning, Miss Butterworth. I am sorry that circumstances make it impossible for me to offer you those civilities which you might reasonably expect from so near a neighbor. Miss Lucetta and I are at swords' points over a matter upon which I still insist she is to blame. See how shocked she is to see me even standing at her gate."

Shocked! I would have said terrified. Nothing but fear—her old fear aggravated to a point that made all attempt at concealment impossible—could account for her white, drawn features and trembling form. She looked as if her whole thought was, "Have I come in time?"

"What—what has procured us the honor of this visit?" she asked, moving up beside William as if she would add her slight frame to his bulky one to keep this intruder out.

"Nothing that need alarm you," said the other with a suggestive note in his kind and mellow voice. "I was rather unexpectedly intrusted this morning with a letter for your agreeable guest here, and I have merely come to deliver it."

Her look of astonishment passing from him to me, I thrust my hand into my pocket and drew out the letter which I had just received.

"From home," said I, without properly considering that this was in some measure an untruth.

"Oh!" she murmured as if but half convinced. "William could have gone for it," she added, still eying Mr. Trohm with a pitiful anxiety.

"I was only too happy," said the other, with a low and reassuring bow. Then, as if he saw that her distress would only be relieved by his departure, he raised his hat and stepped back into the open highway. "I will not intrude again, Miss Knollys," were his parting words. "If you want anything of Obadiah Trohm, you know where to find him. His doors will always be open to you."

Lucetta, with a start, laid her hand on her brother's arm as if to restrain the words she saw slowly laboring to his lips, and leaning breathlessly forward, watched the fine figure of this perfect country gentleman till it had withdrawn quite out of sight. Then she turned, and with a quick abandonment of all self-control, cried out with a pitiful gesture toward her brother, "I thought all was over; I feared he meant to come into the house," and fell stark and seemingly lifeless at our feet.

X   SECRET INSTRUCTIONS

For a moment William and myself stood looking at each other over this frail and prostrate figure. Then he stooped, and with an unexpected show of kindness raised her up and began carrying her toward the house.

"Lucetta is a fool," he cried suddenly, stopping and giving me a quick glance over his shoulder. "Because folks are terrified of this road and come to see us but seldom, she has got to feel a most unreasonable dread of visitors. She was even set against your coming till we showed her what folly it was for her to think we could always live here like hermits. Then she doesn't like Mr. Trohm; thinks he is altogether too friendly to me—as if that was any of her business. Am I an idiot? Have I no sense? Cannot I be trusted to take care of my own affairs and keep my own secrets? She's a weak, silly chit, to go and flop over like this when, d—n it, we have enough to look after without nursing her up and—I mean," he said, tripping himself up with an air of polite consideration so out of keeping with his usual churlishness as to be more than noticeable, "that it cannot add much to the pleasure of your visit to have such things happen as this."

"Oh, don't worry about me!" I curtly responded. "Get the poor girl in. I'll look after her."

But as if she heard these words and was startled by them, Lucetta roused in her brother's arms and struggled passionately to her feet. "Oh! what has happened to me?" she cried. "Have I said anything? William, have I said anything?" she asked wildly, clinging to her brother in terror.

He gave her a look and pushed her off.

"What are you talking about?" he cried. "One would think you had something to conceal."

She steadied herself up in an instant.

"I am the weakest of the family," said she, walking straight up to me and taking me affectionately by the arm. "All my life I have been delicate and these turns are nothing new to me. Sometimes I think I will die in one of them; but I am quite restored now," she hastily added, as I could not help showing my concern. "See! I can walk quite alone." And she ran, rather than walked, up the few short steps of the porch, at which we had now arrived. "Don't tell Loreen," she begged, as I followed her into the house. "She worries so about me, and it will do no good."

William had stalked off toward the stables. We were therefore alone. I turned and laid a finger on her arm.

"My dear," said I, "I never make foolish promises, but I can be trusted never to heedlessly slight any one's wishes. If I see no good reason why I should tell your sister of this fainting fit, I shall certainly hold my peace."

She seemed moved by my manner, if not by my words.

"Oh," she cried, seizing my hand and pressing it. "If I dared to tell you of my troubles! But it is impossible, quite impossible." And before I could urge a plea for her confidence she was gone, leaving me in the company of Hannah, who at this moment was busying herself with something at the other end of the hall.

I had no wish to interfere with Hannah just then. I had my letter to read, and did not wish to be disturbed. So I slipped into the sitting-room and carefully closed the door. Then I opened my letter.

It was, as I supposed, from Mr. Gryce, and ran thus:

"DEAR MISS BUTTERWORTH:

"I am astonished at your determination, but since your desire to visit your friends is such as to lead you to brave the dangers of Lost Man's Lane, allow me to suggest certain precautions.

"First.—Do not trust anybody.

"Second.—Do not proceed anywhere alone or on foot.

"Third.—If danger comes to you, and you find yourself in a condition of real peril, blow once shrilly on the whistle I inclose with this. If, however, the danger is slight, or you wish merely to call the attention of those who will be set to watch over you, let the blast be short, sharp, and repeated—twice to summon assistance, three times to call attention.

"I advise you to fasten this whistle about your neck in a way to make it easily obtainable.

"I have advised you to trust nobody. I should have excepted Mr. Trohm, but I do not think you will be given an opportunity to speak to him. Remember that all depends upon your not awakening suspicion. If, however, you wish advice or desire to make any communication to me or the man secretly holding charge over this affair in X., seek the first opportunity of riding into town and go at once to the hotel where you will ask for Room 3. It has been retained in your service, and once shown into it, you, may expect a visitor who will be the man you seek.

"As you will see, every confidence is put in your judgment."

There was no signature to this—it needed none—and in the packet which came with it was the whistle. I was glad to see it, and glad to hear that I was not left entirely without protection in my somewhat hazardous enterprise.

The events of the morning had been so unexpected that till this moment I had forgotten my early determination to go to my room before any change there could be made. Recalling it now, I started for the staircase, and did not stop though I heard Hannah calling me back. The consequence was that I ran full tilt against Miss Knollys coming down the hall with a tray in her hand.

"Ah," I cried; "some one sick in the house?"

The attack was too sudden. I saw her recoil and for one instant hesitate before replying. Then her natural self-possession came to her aid, and she placidly remarked:

"We were all up to a late hour last night, as you know. It was necessary for us to have some food."

I accepted the explanation and made no further remark, but as in passing her I had detected on this tray of food supposed to have been sent up the night before, the half-eaten portion of a certain dish we had had for breakfast, I reserved to myself the privilege of doubting her exact truthfulness. To me the sight of this partially consumed breakfast was proof positive of there being in the house some person of whose presence I was supposed to be ignorant—not a pleasant thought under the circumstances, but quite an important fact to have established. I felt that in this one discovery I had clutched the thread that would yet lead me out of the labyrinth of this mystery.

Miss Knollys, who was on her way down-stairs, called Hannah to take the tray, and, coming back, beckoned me toward a door opening into one of the front rooms.

"This is to be your room," she announced, "but I do not know that I can move you to-day."

She was so calm, so perfectly mistress of herself, that I could not but admire her. Lucetta would have flushed and fidgeted, but Loreen stood as erect and placid as if no trouble weighed upon her heart and the words were as unimportant in their character as they seemed.

"Do not distress yourself," said I. "I told Lucetta last night that I was perfectly comfortable and had no wish to change my quarters. I am sorry you should have thought it necessary to disturb yourself on my account last night. Don't do it again, I pray. A woman like myself had rather put herself to some slight inconvenience than move."

"I am much obliged to you," said she, and came at once from the door. I don't know but after all I like Lucetta's fidgety ways better than Loreen's unmovable self-possession.

"Shall I order the coach for you?" she suddenly asked, as I turned toward the corridor leading to my room.

"The coach?" I repeated.

"I thought that perhaps you might like to ride into town. Mr. Simsbury is at leisure this morning. I regret that neither Lucetta nor myself will be able to accompany you."

I thought what this same Mr. Simsbury had said about Lucetta's plan, and hesitated. It was evidently their wish to have me spend my morning elsewhere than with them. Should I humor them, or find excuses for remaining home? Either course had its difficulties. If I went, what might not take place in my absence! If I remained, what suspicions might I not rouse! I decided to compromise matters, and start for town even if I did not go there.

"I am hesitating," said I, "because of the two or three rather threatening-looking clouds toward the east. But if you are sure Mr. Simsbury can be spared, I think I will risk it. I really would like to get a key for my door; and then riding in the country is so pleasant."

Miss Knollys, with a bow, passed immediately down-stairs. I went in a state of some doubt toward my own room. "Am I surveying these occurrences through highly magnifying glasses?" thought I. It was very possible, yet not so possible but that I cast very curious glances at the various closed doors I had to pass before reaching my own. Such a little thing would make me feel like trying them. Such a little thing—that is, added to the other things which had struck me as unexplainable.

I found my bed made and everything in apple-pie order. I had therefore nothing to do but to prepare for going out. This I did quickly, and was down-stairs sooner perhaps than I was expected. At all events Lucetta and William parted very suddenly when they saw me, she in tears and he with a dogged shrug and some such word as this:

"You're a fool to take on so. Since it's got to be, the sooner the better, I say. Don't you see that every minute makes less our chances of concealment?"

It made me feel like changing my mind and staying home. But the habit of a lifetime is not easily broken into. I kept to my first decision.

XI   MEN, WOMEN, AND GHOSTS

Mr. Simsbury gave me quite an amiable bow as I entered the buggy. This made it easy for me to say:

"You are on hand early this morning. Do you sleep in the Knollys house?"

The stare he gave me had the least bit of suspicion in it.

"I live over yonder," he said, pointing with his whip across the intervening woods to the main road. "I come through the marshes to my breakfast; my old woman says they owes me three meals, and three meals I must have."

It was the longest sentence with which he had honored me. Finding him in a talkative mood, I prepared to make myself agreeable, a proceeding which he seemed to appreciate, for he began to sniff and pay great attention to his horse, which he was elaborately turning about.

"Why do you go that way?" I protested. "Isn't it the longest way to the village?"

"It's the way I'm most accustomed to," said he. "But we can go the other way if you like. Perhaps we will get a glimpse of Deacon Spear. He's a widower, you know."

The leer with which he said this was intolerable. I bridled up—but no, I will not admit that I so much as manifested by my manner that I understood him. I merely expressed my wish to go the old way.

He whipped up the horse at once, almost laughing outright. I began to think this man capable of most any wicked deed. He was forced, however, to pull up suddenly. Directly in our path was the stooping figure of a woman. She did not move as we advanced, and so we had no alternative but to stop. Not till the horse's head touched her shoulder did she move. Then she rose up and looked at us somewhat indignantly.

"Didn't you hear us?" I asked, willing to open conversation with the old crone, whom I had no difficulty in recognizing as Mother Jane.

"She's deaf—deaf, as a post," muttered Mr. Simsbury. "No use shouting at her." His tone was brusque, yet I noticed he waited with great patience for her to hobble out of the way.

Meanwhile I was watching the old creature with much interest. She had not a common face or a common manner. She was gray, she was toothless, she was haggard, and she was bent, but she was not ordinary or just one of the crowd of old women to be seen on country doorsteps. There was force in her aged movements and a strong individuality in the glances she shot at us as she backed slowly out of the roadway.

"Do they say she is imbecile?" I asked. "She looks far from foolish to me."

"Hearken a bit," said he. "Don't you see she is muttering? She talks to herself all the time." And in fact her lips were moving.

"I cannot hear her," I said. "Make her come nearer. Somehow the old creature interests me."

He at once beckoned to the crone; but he might as well have beckoned to the tree against which she had pushed herself. She neither answered him nor gave any indication that she understood the gesture he had made. Yet her eyes never moved from our faces.

"Well, well," said I, "she seems dull as well as deaf. You had better drive on." But before he could give the necessary jerk of the reins, I caught sight of some pennyroyal growing about the front of the cottage a few steps beyond, and, pointing to it with some eagerness, I cried: "If there isn't some of the very herb I want to take home with me! Do you think she would give me a handful of it if I paid her?"

With an obliging grunt he again pulled up. "If you can make her understand," said he.

I thought it worth the effort. Though Mr. Gryce had been at pains to tell me there was no harm in this woman and that I need not even consider her in any inquiries I might be called upon to make, I remembered that Mr. Gryce had sometimes made mistakes in just such matters as these, and that Amelia Butterworth had then felt herself called upon to set him right. If that could happen once, why not twice? At all events, I was not going to lose the least chance of making the acquaintance of the people living in this lane. Had he not himself said that only in this way could we hope to come upon the clue that had eluded all open efforts to find it?

Knowing that the sight of money is the strongest appeal that can be made to one living in such abject poverty as this woman, making the blind to see and the deaf to hear, I drew out my purse and held up before her a piece of silver. She bounded as if she had been shot, and when I held it toward her came greedily forward and stood close beside the wheels looking up.

"For you," I indicated, after making a motion toward the plant which had attracted my attention.

She glanced from me to the herb and nodded with quick appreciation. As in a flash she seemed to take in the fact that I was a stranger, a city lady with memories of the country and this humble plant, and hurrying to it with the same swiftness she had displayed in advancing to the carriage, she tore off several of the sprays and brought them back to me, holding out her hand for the money.

I had never seen greater eagerness, and I think even Mr. Simsbury was astonished at this proof of her poverty or her greed. I was inclined to think it the latter, for her portly figure was far from looking either ill-fed or poorly cared for. Her dress was of decent calico, and her pipe had evidently been lately filled, for I could smell the odor of tobacco about her. Indeed, as I afterward heard, the good people of X. had never allowed her to suffer. Yet her fingers closed upon that coin as if in it she grasped the salvation of her life, and into her eyes leaped a light that made her look almost young, though she must have been fully eighty.

"What do you suppose she will do with that?" I asked Mr. Simsbury, as she turned away in an evident fear I might repent of my bargain.

"Hark!" was his brief response. "She is talking now."

I did hearken, and heard these words fall from her quickly moving lips: "Seventy; twenty-eight; and now ten."

Jargon; for I had given her twenty-five cents, an amount quite different from any she had mentioned.

"Seventy!" She was repeating the figures again, this time in a tone of almost frenzied elation. "Seventy; twenty-eight; and now ten! Won't Lizzie be surprised! Seventy; twenty—" I heard no more—she had bounded into her cottage and shut the door.

"Waal, what do you think of her now?" chuckled Mr. Simsbury, touching up his horse. "She's always like that, saying over numbers, and muttering about Lizzie. Lizzie was her daughter. Forty years ago she ran off with a man from Boston, and for thirty-eight years she's been lying in a Massachusetts grave. But her mother still thinks she is alive and is coming back. Nothing will ever make her think different. But she's harmless, perfectly harmless. You needn't be afeard of her."

This, because I cast a look behind me of more than ordinary curiosity, I suppose. Why were they all so sure she was harmless? I had thought her expression a little alarming at times, especially when she took the money from my hand. If I had refused it or even held it back a little, I think she would have fallen upon me tooth and nail. I wished I could take a peep into her cottage. Mr. Gryce had described it as four walls and nothing more, and indeed it was small and of the humblest proportions; but the fluttering of some half-dozen pigeons about its eaves proved it to be a home and, as such, of interest to me, who am often able to read character from a person's habitual surroundings.

There was no yard attached to this simple building, only a small open place in front in which a few of the commonest vegetables grew, such as turnips, carrots, and onions. Elsewhere towered the forest—the great pine forest through which this portion of the road ran.

Mr. Simsbury had been so talkative up to now that I was in hope he would enter into some details about the persons and things we encountered, which might assist me in the acquaintanceship I was anxious to make. But his loquaciousness ended with this small adventure I have just described. Not till we were well quit of the pines and had entered into the main thoroughfare did he deign to respond to any of my suggestions, and then it was in a manner totally unsatisfactory and quite uncommunicative. The only time he deigned to offer a remark was when we emerged from the forest and came upon the little crippled child, looking from its window. Then he cried:

"Why, how's this? That's Sue you see there, and her time isn't till arternoon. Rob allers sits there of a mornin'. I wonder if the little chap's sick. S'pose I ask."

As this was just what I would have suggested if he had given me time, I nodded complacently, and we drove up and stopped.

The piping voice of the child at once spoke up:

"How d' ye do, Mr. Simsbury? Ma's in the kitchen. Rob isn't feelin' good to-day."

I thought her tone had a touch of mysteriousness in it. I greeted the pale little thing, and asked if Rob was often sick.

"Never," she answered, "except, like me, he can't walk. But I'm not to talk about it, ma says. I'd like to, but——"

Ma's face appearing at this moment over her shoulder put an end to her innocent garrulity.

"How d' ye do, Mr. Simsbury?" came a second time from the window, but this time in very different tones. "What's the child been saying? She's so sot up at being allowed to take her brother's place in the winder that she don't know how to keep her tongue still. Rob's a little languid, that's all. You'll see him in his old place to-morrow." And she drew back as if in polite intimation that we might drive on.

Mr. Simsbury responded to the suggestion, and in another moment we were trotting down the road. Had we stayed a minute longer, I think the child would have said something more or less interesting to hear.

The horse, which had brought us thus far at a pretty sharp trot, now began to lag, which so attracted Mr. Simsbury's attention, that he forgot to answer even by a grunt more than half of my questions. He spent most of his time looking at the nag's hind feet, and finally, just as we came in sight of the stores, he found his tongue sufficiently to announce that the horse was casting a shoe and that he would be obliged to go to the blacksmith's with her.

"Humph, and how long will that take?" I asked.

He hesitated so long, rubbing his nose with his finger, that I grew suspicious and cast a glance at the horse's foot myself. The shoe was loose. I began to hear it clang.

"Waal, it may be a matter of a couple of hours," he finally drawled. "We have no blacksmith in town, and the ride up there is two miles. Sorry it happened, ma'am, but there's all sorts of shops here, you see, and I've allers heard that a woman can easily spend two hours haggling away in shops."

I glanced at the two ill-furnished windows he pointed out, thought of Arnold & Constable's, Tiffany's, and the other New York establishments I had been in the habit of visiting, and suppressed my disdain. Either the man was a fool or he was acting a part in the interests of Lucetta and her family. I rather inclined to the latter supposition. If the plan was to keep me out most of the morning why could that shoe not have been loosened before the mare left the stable?

"I made all necessary purchases while in New York," said I, "but if you must get the horse shod, why, take her off and do it. I suppose there is a hotel parlor near here where I can sit."

"Oh, yes," and he made haste to point out to me where the hotel stood. "And it's a very nice place, ma'am. Mrs. Carter, the landlady, is the nicest sort of person. Only you won't try to go home, ma'am, on foot? You'll wait till I come back for you?"

"It isn't likely I'll go streaking through Lost Man's Lane alone," I exclaimed indignantly. "I'd rather sit in Mrs. Carter's parlor till night."

"And I would advise you to," he said. "No use making gossip for the village folks. They have enough to talk about as it is."

Not exactly seeing the force of this reasoning, but quite willing to be left to my own devices for a little while, I pointed to a locksmith's shop I saw near by, and bade him put me down there.

With a sniff I declined to interpret into a token of disapproval, he drove me up to the shop and awkwardly assisted me to alight.

"Trunk key missing?" he ventured to inquire before getting back into his seat.

I did not think it necessary to reply, but walked immediately into the shop. He looked dissatisfied at this, but whatever his feelings were he refrained from any expression of them, and presently mounted to his place and drove off. I was left confronting the decent man who represented the lock-fitting interests in X.

I found some difficulty in broaching my errand. Finally I said:

"Miss Knollys, who lives up the road, wishes a key fitted to one of her doors. Will you come or send a man to her house to-day? She is too occupied to see about it herself."

The man must have been struck by my appearance, for he stared at me quite curiously for a minute. Then he gave a hem and a haw and said:

"Certainly. What kind of a door is it?" When I had answered, he gave me another curious glance and seemed uneasy to step back to where his assistant was working with a file.

"You will be sure to come in time to have the lock fitted before night?" I said in that peremptory manner of mine which means simply, "I keep my promises and expect you to keep yours."

His "Certainly" struck me as a little weaker this time, possibly because his curiosity was excited. "Are you the lady from New York who is staying with them?" he asked, stepping back, seemingly quite unawed by my positive demeanor.

"Yes," said I, thawing a trifle; "I am Miss Butterworth."

He looked at me almost as if I were a curiosity.

"And did you sleep there last night?" he urged.

I thought it best to thaw still more.

"Of course," I said. "Where do you think I would sleep? The young ladies are friends of mine."

He rapped abstractedly on the counter with a small key he was holding.

"Excuse me," said he, with some remembrance of my position toward him as a stranger, "but weren't you afraid?"

"Afraid?" I echoed. "Afraid in Miss Knollys' house?"

"Why, then, do you want a key to your door?" he asked, with a slight appearance of excitement. "We don't lock doors here in the village; at least we didn't."

"I did not say it was my door," I began, but, feeling that this was a prevarication not only unworthy of me, but one that he was entirely too sharp to accept, I added stiffly: "It is for my door. I am not accustomed even at home to sleep with my room unlocked."

"Oh," he murmured, totally unconvinced, "I thought you might have got a scare. Folks somehow are afraid of that old place, it's so big and ghost-like. I don't think you would find any one in this village who would sleep there all night."

"A pleasing preparation for my rest to-night," I grimly laughed. "Dangers on the road and ghosts in the house. Happily I don't believe in the latter."

The gesture he made showed incredulity. He had ceased rapping with the key or even to show any wish to join his assistant. All his thoughts for the moment seemed to be concentrated on me.

"You don't know little Rob," he inquired, "the crippled lad who lives at the head of the lane?"

"No," I said; "I haven't been in town a day yet, but I mean to know Rob and his sister too. Two cripples in one family rouse my interest."

He did not say why he had spoken of the child, but began tapping with his key again.

"And you are sure you saw nothing?" he whispered. "Lots of things can happen in a lonely road like that."

"Not if everybody is as afraid to enter it as you say your villagers are," I retorted.

But he didn't yield a jot.

"Some folks don't mind present dangers," said he. "Spirits———"

But he received no encouragement in his return to this topic. "You don't believe in spirits?" said he. "Well, they are doubtful sort of folks, but when honest and respectable people such as live in this town, when children even, see what answers to nothing but phantoms, then I remember what a wiser man than any of us once said——But perhaps you don't read Shakespeare, madam?"

Nonplussed for the moment, but interested in the man's talk more than was consistent with my need of haste, I said with some spirit, for it struck me as very ridiculous that this country mechanic should question my knowledge of the greatest dramatist of all time, "Shakespeare and the Bible form the staple of my reading." At which he gave me a little nod of apology and hastened to say:

"Then you know what I mean—Hamlet's remark to Horatio, madam, 'There are more things,' etc. Your memory will readily supply you with the words."

I signified my satisfaction and perfect comprehension of his meaning, and, feeling that something important lay behind his words, I endeavored to make him speak more explicitly.

"The Misses Knollys show no terror of their home," I observed. "They cannot believe in spirits either."

"Miss Knollys is a woman of a great deal of character," said he. "But look at Lucetta. There is a face for you, for a girl not yet out of her twenties; and such a round-cheeked lass as she was once! Now what has made the change? The sights and sounds of that old house, I say. Nothing else would give her that scared look—nothing merely mortal, I mean."

This was going a step too far. I could not discuss Lucetta with this stranger, anxious as I was to hear what he had to say about her.

"I don't know," I remonstrated, taking up my black satin bag, without which I never stir. "One would think the terrors of the lane she lives in might account for some appearance of fear on her part."

"So it might," he assented, but with no great heartiness. "But Lucetta has never spoken of those dangers. The people in the lane do not seem to fear them. Even Deacon Spear says that, set aside the wickedness of the thing, he rather enjoys the quiet which the ill repute of the lane gives him. I don't understand this indifference myself. I have no relish for horrible mysteries or for ghosts either."

"You won't forget the key?" I suggested shortly, preparing to walk out, in my dread lest he should again introduce the subject of Lucetta.

"No," said he, "I won't forget it." His tone should have warned me that I need not expect to have a locked door that night.

XII   THE PHANTOM COACH

Ghosts! What could the fellow have meant? If I had pressed him he would have told me, but it did not seem quite a lady's business to pick up information in this way, especially when it involved a young lady like Lucetta. Yet did I think I would ever come to the end of this matter without involving Lucetta? No. Why, then, did I allow my instincts to triumph over my judgment? Let those answer who understand the workings of the human heart. I am simply stating facts.

Ghosts! Somehow the word startled me as if in some way it gave a rather unwelcome confirmation to my doubts. Apparitions seen in the Knollys mansion or in any of the houses bordering on this lane! That was a serious charge; how serious seemed to be but half comprehended by this man. But I comprehended it to the full, and wondered if it was on account of such gossip as this that Mr. Gryce had persuaded me to enter Miss Knollys' house as a guest.

I was crossing the street to the hotel as I indulged in these conjectures, and intent as my mind was upon them, I could not but note the curiosity and interest which my presence excited in the simple country folk invariably to be found lounging about a country tavern. Indeed, the whole neighborhood seemed agog, and though I would have thought it derogatory to my dignity to notice the fact, I could not but see how many faces were peering at me from store doors and the half-closed blinds of adjoining cottages. No young girl in the pride of her beauty could have awakened more interest, and this I attributed, as was no doubt right, not to my appearance, which would not perhaps be apt to strike these simple villagers as remarkable, or to my dress, which is rather rich than fashionable, but to the fact that I was a stranger in town, and, what was more extraordinary, a guest of the Misses Knollys.

My intention in approaching the hotel was not to spend a couple of dreary hours in the parlor with Mrs. Carter, as Mr. Simsbury had suggested, but to obtain if possible a conveyance to carry me immediately back to the Knollys mansion. But this, which would have been a simple matter in most towns, seemed well-nigh an impossibility in X. The landlord was away, and Mrs. Carter, who was very frank with me, told me it would be perfectly useless to ask one of the men to drive me through the lane. "It's an unwholesome spot," said she, "and only Mr. Carter and the police have the courage to brave it."

I suggested that I was willing to pay well, but it seemed to make very little difference to her. "Money won't hire them," said she, and I had the satisfaction of knowing that Lucetta had triumphed in her plan, and that, after all, I must sit out the morning in the precincts of the hotel parlor with Mrs. Carter.

It was my first signal defeat, but I was determined to make the best of it, and if possible glean such knowledge from the talk of this woman as would make me feel that I had lost nothing by my disappointment. She was only too ready to talk, and the first topic was little Rob.

I saw the moment I mentioned his name that I was introducing a subject which had already been well talked over by every eager gossip in the village.

Her attitude of importance, the air of mystery she assumed, were preparations I had long been accustomed to in women of this kind, and I was not at all surprised when she announced in a way that admitted of no dispute:

"Oh, there's no wonder the child is sick. We would be sick under the circumstances. He has seen the phantom coach."

The phantom coach! So that was what the locksmith meant. A phantom coach! I had heard of every kind of phantom but that. Somehow the idea was a thrilling one, or would have been to a nature less practical than mine.

"I don't know what you mean," said I. "Some superstition of the place? I never heard of a ghostly appearance of that nature before."

"No, I expect not. It belongs to X. I never heard of it beyond these mountains. Indeed, I have never known it to have been seen but upon one road. I need not mention what road, madam. You can guess."

Yes, I could guess, and the guessing made me set my lips a little grimly.

"Tell me more about this thing," I urged, half laughing. "It ought to be of some interest to me."

She nodded, drew her chair a trifle nearer, and impetuously began:

"You see this is a very old town. It has more than one ancient country house similar to the one you are now living in, and it has its early traditions. One is, that an old-fashioned coach, perfectly noiseless, drawn by horses through which you can see the moonlight, haunts the highroad at intervals and flies through the gloomy forest road we have christened of late years Lost Man's Lane. It is a superstition, possibly, but you cannot find many families in town but believe in it as a fact, for there is not an old man or woman in the place but has either seen it in the past or has had some relative who has seen it. It passes only at night, and it is thought to presage some disaster to those who see it. My husband's uncle died the next morning after it flew by him on the highway. Fortunately years elapse between its going and coming. It is ten years, I think they say, since it was last seen. Poor little Rob! It has frightened him almost out of his wits."

"I should think so," I cried with becoming credulity. "But how came he to see it? I thought you said it only passed at night."

"At midnight," she repeated. "But Rob, you see, is a nervous lad, and night before last he was so restless he could not sleep, so he begged to be put in the window to cool off. This his mother did, and he sat there for a good half-hour alone, looking out at the moonlight. As his mother is an economical woman there was no candle lit in the room, so he got his pleasure out of the shadows which the great trees made on the highroad, when suddenly—you ought to hear the little fellow tell it—he felt the hair rise on his forehead and all his body grow stiff with a terror that made his tongue feel like lead in his mouth. A something he would have called a horse and a carriage in the daytime, but which, in this light and under the influence of the mortal terror he was in, took on a distorted shape which made it unlike any team he was accustomed to, was going by, not as if being driven over the earth and stones of the road,—though there was a driver in front, a driver with an odd three-cornered hat on his head and a cloak about his shoulders, such as the little fellow remembered to have seen hanging in his grandmother's closet,—but as if it floated along without sound or stir; in fact, a spectre team which seemed to find its proper destination when it turned into Lost Man's Lane and was lost among the shadows of that ill-reputed road."

"Pshaw!" was my spirited comment as she paused to take her breath and see how I was affected by this grewsome tale. "A dream of the poor little lad! He had heard stories of this apparition and his imagination supplied the rest."

"No; excuse me, madam, he had been carefully kept from hearing all such tales. You could see this by the way he told his story. He hardly believed what he had himself seen. It was not till some foolish neighbor blurted out, 'Why, that was the phantom coach,' that he had any idea he was not relating a dream."

My second Pshaw! was no less marked than the first.

"He did know about it, notwithstanding," I insisted. "Only he had forgotten the fact. Sleep often supplies us with these lost memories."

"Very true, and your supposition is very plausible, Miss Butterworth, and might be regarded as correct, if he had been the only person to see this apparition. But Mrs. Jenkins saw it too, and she is a woman to be believed."

This was becoming serious.

"Saw it before he did or afterwards?" I asked. "Does she live on the highway or somewhere in Lost Man's Lane?"

"She lives on the highway about a half-mile from the station. She was sitting up with her sick husband and saw it just as it was going down the hill. She said it made no more noise than a cloud slipping by. She expects to lose old Rause. No one could behold such a thing as that and not have some misfortune follow."

I laid all this up in my mind. My hour of waiting was not likely to prove wholly unprofitable.

"You see," the good woman went on, with a relish for the marvellous that stood me in good stead, "there is an old tradition of that road connected with a coach. Years ago, before any of us were born, and the house where you are now staying was a gathering-place for all the gay young bloods of the county, a young man came up from New York to visit Mr. Knollys. I do not mean the father or even the grandfather of the folks you are visiting, ma'am. He was great-grandfather to Lucetta, and a very fine gentleman, if you can trust the pictures that are left of him. But my story has not to do with him. He had a daughter at that time, a widow of great and sparkling attractions, and though she was older than the young man I have mentioned, every one thought he would marry her, she was so handsome and such an heiress.

"But he failed to pay his court to her, and though he was handsome himself and made a fool of more than one girl in the town, every one thought he would return as he had come, a free-hearted bachelor, when suddenly one night the coach was missed from the stables and he from the company, which led to the discovery that the young widow's daughter was gone too, a chit who was barely fifteen, and without a hundredth part of the beauty of her mother. Love only could account for this, for in those days young ladies did not ride with gentlemen in the evening for pleasure, and when it came to the old gentleman's ears, and, what was worse, came to the mother's, there was a commotion in the great house, the echoes of which, some say, have never died out. Though the pipers were playing and the fiddles were squeaking in the great room where they used to dance the night away, Mrs. Knollys, with her white brocade tucked up about her waist, stood with her hand on the great front door, waiting for the horse upon which she was determined to follow the flying lovers. The father, who was a man of eighty years, stood by her side. He was too old to ride himself, but he made no effort to hold her back, though the jewels were tumbling from her hair and the moon had vanished from the highway.

"'I will bring her back or die!' the passionate beauty exclaimed, and not a lip said her nay, for they saw, what neither man nor woman had been able to see up to that moment, that her very life and soul were wrapped up in the man who had stolen away her daughter.

"Shrilly piped the pipes, squeak and hum went the fiddles, but the sound that was sweetest to her was the pound of the horses' hoofs on the road in front. That was music indeed, and as soon as she heard it she bestowed one wild kiss on her father and bounded from the house. An instant later and she was gone. One flash of her white robe at the gate, then all was dark on the highway, and only the old father stood in the wide-open door, waiting, as he vowed he would wait, till his daughter returned.

"She did not go alone. A faithful groom was behind her, and from him was learned the conclusion of that quest. For an hour and a half they rode; then they came upon a chapel in the mountains, in which were burning unwonted lights. At the sight the lady drew rein and almost fell from her horse into the arms of her lackey. 'A marriage!' she murmured; 'a marriage!' and pointed to an empty coach standing in the shadow of a wide-spreading tree. It was their family coach. How well she knew it! Rousing herself, she made for the chapel door. 'I will stop these unhallowed rites!' she cried! 'I am her mother, and she is not of age.' But the lackey drew her back by her rich white dress. 'Look!' he cried, pointing in at one of the windows, and she looked. The man she loved stood before the altar with her daughter. He was smiling in that daughter's face with a look of passionate devotion. It went like a dagger to her heart. Crushing her hands against her face, she wailed out some fearful protest; then she dashed toward the door with 'Stop! stop!' on her lips. But the faithful lackey at her side drew her back once more. 'Listen!' was his word, and she listened. The minister, whose form she had failed to note in her first hurried look, was uttering his benediction. She had come too late. The young couple were married.

"Her servant said, or so the tradition runs, that when she realized this she grew calm as walking death. Making her way into the chapel, she stood ready at the door to greet them as they issued forth, and when they saw her there, with her rich bedraggled robe and the gleam of jewels on a neck she had not even stopped to envelop in more than the veil from her hair, the bridegroom seemed to realize what he had done and stopped the bride, who in her confusion would have fled back to the altar where she had just been made a wife. 'Kneel!' he cried. 'Kneel, Amarynth! Only thus can we ask pardon of our mother.' But at that word, a word which seemed to push her a million miles away from these two beings who but two hours before had been the delight of her life, the unhappy woman gave a cry and fled from their presence. 'Go! go!' were her parting words. 'As you have chosen, you must abide. But let no tongue ever again call me mother.'

"They found her lying on the grass outside. As she could no longer sustain herself on a horse, they put her into the coach, gave the reins to her devoted lackey, and themselves rode off on horseback. One man, the fellow who had driven them to that place, said that the clock struck twelve from the chapel tower as the coach turned away and began its rapid journey home. This may and may not be so. We only know that its apparition always enters Lost Man's Lane a few minutes before one, which is the very hour at which the real coach came back and stopped before Mr. Knollys' gate. And now for the worst, Miss Butterworth. When the old gentleman went down to greet the runaways, he found the lackey on the box and his daughter sitting all alone in the coach. But the soil on the brocaded folds of her white dress was no longer that of mud only. She had stabbed herself to the heart with a bodkin she wore in her hair, and it was a corpse which the faithful negro had been driving down the highway that night."

I am not a sentimental woman, but this story as thus told gave me a thrill I do not know as I really regret experiencing.

"What was this unhappy mother's name?" I asked.

"Lucetta," was the unexpected and none too reassuring answer.

XIII   GOSSIP

This name once mentioned called for more gossip, but of a somewhat different nature.

"The Lucetta of to-day is not like her ancient namesake," observed Mrs. Carter. "She may have the heart to love, but she is not capable of showing that love by any act of daring."

"I don't know about that," I replied, astonished that I felt willing to enter into a discussion with this woman on the very subject I had just shrunk from talking over with the locksmith. "Girls as frail and nervous as she is, sometimes astonish one at a pinch. I do not think Lucetta lacks daring."

"You don't know her. Why, I have seen her jump at the sight of a spider, and heaven knows that they are common enough among the decaying walls in which she lives. A puny chit, Miss Butterworth; pretty enough, but weak. The very kind to draw lovers, but not to hold them. Yet every one pities her, her smile is so heart-broken."

"With ghosts to trouble her and a lover to bemoan, she has surely some excuse for that," said I.

"Yes, I don't deny it. But why has she a lover to bemoan? He seemed a proper man and much beyond the ordinary. Why let him go as she did? Even her sister admits that she loved him."

"I am not acquainted with the circumstances," I suggested.

"Well, there isn't much of a story to it. He is a young man from over the mountains, well educated, and with something of a fortune of his own. He came here to visit the Spears, I believe, and seeing Lucetta leaning one day on the gate in front of her house, he fell in love with her and began to pay her his attentions. That was before the lane got its present bad name, but not before one or two men had vanished from among us. William—that is her brother, you know—has always been anxious to have his sisters marry, so he did not stand in the way, and no more did Miss Knollys, but after two or three weeks of doubtful courtship, the young man went away, and that was the end of it. And a great pity, too, say I, for once clear of that house, Lucetta would grow into another person. Sunshine and love are necessities to most women, Miss Butterworth, especially to such as are weakly and timid."

I thought the qualification excellent.

"You are right," I assented, "and I should like to see the result of them upon Lucetta." Then, with an attempt to still further sound this woman's mind and with it the united mind of the whole village, I remarked: "The young do not usually throw aside such prospects without excellent reasons. Have you never thought that Lucetta was governed by principle in discarding this very excellent young man?"

"Principle? What principle could she have had in letting a desirable husband go?"

"She may have thought the match an undesirable one for him."

"For him? Well, I never thought of that. True, she may. They are known to be poor, but poverty don't count in such old families as theirs. I hardly think she would be influenced by any such consideration. Now, if this had happened since the lane got its bad name and all this stir had been made about the disappearance of certain folks within its precincts, I might have given some weight to your suggestion—women are so queer. But this happened long ago and at a time when the family was highly thought of, leastwise the girls, for William does not go for much, you know—too stupid and too brutal."

William! Would the utterance of that name heighten my suggestion? I surveyed her closely, but could detect no change in her somewhat puzzled countenance.

"My allusions were not in reference to the disappearances," said I. "I was thinking of something else. Lucetta is not well."

"Ah, I know! They say she has some kind of heart complaint, but that was not true then. Why, her cheeks were like roses in those days, and her figure as plump and pretty as any you could see among our village beauties. No, Miss Butterworth, it was through her weakness she lost him. She probably palled upon his taste. It was noticed that he held his head very high in going out of town."

"Has he married since?" I asked.

"Not to my knowledge, ma'am."

"Then he loved her," I declared.

She looked at me quite curiously. Doubtless that word sounds a little queer on my lips, but that shall not deter me from using it when the circumstances seem to require. Besides, there was once a time—But there, I promised to fall into no digressions.

"You should have been married yourself, Miss Butterworth," said she.

I was amazed, first at her daring, and secondly that I was so little angry at this sudden turning of the tables upon myself. But then the woman meant no offence, rather intended a compliment.

"I am very well contented as I am," I returned. "I am neither sickly nor timid."

She smiled, looked as if she thought it only common politeness to agree with me, and tried to say so, but finding the situation too much for her, coughed and discreetly held her peace. I came to her rescue with a new question:

"Have the women of the Knollys family ever been successful in love? The mother of these girls, say—she who was Miss Althea Burroughs—was her life with her husband happy? I have always been curious to know. She and I were schoolmates."

"You were? You knew Althea Knollys when she was a girl? Wasn't she charming, ma'am? Did you ever see a livelier girl or one with more knack at winning affection? Why, she couldn't sit down with you a half-hour before you felt like sharing everything you had with her. It made no difference whether you were man or woman, it was all the same. She had but to turn those mischievous, pleading eyes upon you for you to become a fool at once. Yet her end was sad, ma'am; too sad, when you remember that she died at the very height of her beauty alone and in a foreign land. But I have not answered your question. Were she and the judge happy together? I have never heard to the contrary, ma'am. I'm sure he mourned her faithfully enough. Some think that her loss killed him. He did not survive her more than three years."

"The children do not favor her much," said I, "but I see an expression now and then in Lucetta which reminds me of her mother."

"They are all Knollys," said she. "Even William has traits which, with a few more brains back of them, would remind you of his grandfather, who was the plainest of his race."

I was glad that the talk had reverted to William.

"He seems to lack heart, as well as brains," I said. "I marvel that his sisters put up with him as well as they do."

"They cannot help it. He is not a fellow to be fooled with. Besides, he holds third share in the house. If they could sell it! But, deary me, who would buy an old tumble-down place like that, on a road you cannot get folks who have any consideration for their lives to enter for love or money? But excuse me, ma'am; I forgot that you are living just now on that very road. I'm sure I beg a thousand pardons."

"I am living there as a guest," I returned. "I have nothing to do with its reputation—except to brave it."

"A courageous thing to do, ma'am, and one that may do the road some good. If you can spend a month with the Knollys girls and come out of their house at the end as hale and hearty as you entered it, it will be the best proof possible that there is less to be feared there than some people think. I shall be glad if you can do it, ma'am, for I like the girls and would be glad to have the reputation of the place restored."

"Pshaw!" was my final comment. "The credulity of the town has had as much to do with its loss as they themselves. That educated people such as I see here should believe in ghosts!"

I say final, for at this moment the good lady, springing up, put an end to our conversation. She had just seen a buggy pass the window.

"It's Mr. Trohm," she exclaimed. "Ma'am, if you wish to return home before Mr. Simsbury comes back you may be able to do so with this gentleman. He's a most obliging man, and lives less than a quarter of a mile from the Misses Knollys."

I did not say I had already met the gentleman. Why, I do not know. I only drew myself up and waited with some small inner perturbation for the result of the inquiry I saw she had gone to make.

XIV   I FORGET MY AGE, OR, RATHER, REMEMBER IT

Mr. Trohm did not disappoint my expectations. In another moment I perceived him standing in the open doorway with the most genial smile on his lips.

"Miss Butterworth," said he, "I feel too honored. If you will deign to accept a seat in my buggy, I shall only be too happy to drive you home."

I have always liked the manners of country gentlemen. There is just a touch of formality in their bearing which has been quite eliminated from that of their city brothers. I therefore became gracious at once and accepted the seat he offered me without any hesitation.

The heads that showed themselves at the neighboring windows warned us to hasten on our route. Mr. Trohm, with a snap of his whip, touched up his horse, and we rode in dignified calm away from the hotel steps into the wide village street known as the main road. The fact that Mr. Gryce had told me that this was the one man I could trust, joined to my own excellent knowledge of human nature and the persons in whom explicit confidence can be put, made the moment one of great satisfaction to me. I was about to make my appearance at the Knollys mansion two hours before I was expected, and thus outwit Lucetta by means of the one man whose assistance I could conscientiously accept.

We were not slow in beginning conversation. The fine air, the prosperous condition of the town offered themes upon which we found it quite easy to dilate, and so naturally and easily did our acquaintanceship progress that we had turned the corner into Lost Man's Lane before I quite realized it. The entrance from the village offered a sharp contrast to the one I had already traversed. There it was but a narrow opening between sombre and unduly crowding trees. Here it was the gradual melting of a village street into a narrow and less frequented road, which only after passing Deacon Spear's house assumed that aspect of wildness which a quarter of a mile farther on deepened into something positively sombre and repellent.

I speak of Deacon Spear because he was sitting on his front doorstep when we rode by. As he was a resident in the lane, I did not fail to take notice of him, though guardedly and with such restraint as a knowledge of his widowed condition rendered both wise and proper.

He was not an agreeable-looking person, at least to me. His hair was sleek, his beard well cared for, his whole person in good if not prosperous condition, but he had the self-satisfied expression I detest, and looked after us with an aspect of surprise I chose to consider a trifle impertinent. Perhaps he envied Mr. Trohm. If so, he may have had good reason for it—it is not for me to judge.

Up to now I had seen only a few scrub bushes at the side of the road, with here and there a solitary poplar to enliven the dead level on either side of us; but after we had ridden by the fence which sets the boundary to the good deacon's land, I noticed such a change in the appearance of the lane that I could not but exclaim over the natural as well as cultivated beauties which every passing moment was bringing before me.

Mr. Trohm could not conceal his pleasure.

"These are my lands," said he. "I have bestowed unremitting attention upon them for years. It is my hobby, madam. There is not a tree you see that has not received my careful attention. Yonder orchard was set out by me, and the fruit it yields—Madam, I hope you will remain long enough with us to taste a certain rare and luscious peach that I brought from France a few years ago. It gives promise of reaching its full perfection this year, and I shall be gratified indeed if you can give it your approval."

This was politeness indeed, especially as I knew what value men like him set upon each individual fruit they watch ripen under their care. Testifying my appreciation of his kindness, I endeavored to introduce another and less harmless and perhaps less personally interesting topic of conversation. The chimneys of his house were beginning to show over the trees, and I had heard nothing from this man on the subject which should have been the most interesting of all to me at this moment. And he was the only person in town I was at liberty to really confide in, and possibly the only man in town who could give me a reliable statement of the reasons why the family I was visiting was regarded in a doubtful light not only by the credulous villagers, but by the New York police. I began by an allusion to the phantom coach.

"I hear," said I, "that this lane has other claims to attention beyond those afforded by the mysteries connected with it. I hear that it has at times a ghostly visitant in the shape of a spectral horse and carriage."

"Yes," he replied, with a seeming understanding that was very flattering; "do not spare the lane one of its honors. It has its nightly horror as well as its daily fear. I wish the one were as unreal as the other."

"You act as if both were unreal to you," said I. "The contrast between your appearance and that of some other members of the lane is quite marked."

"You refer"—he seemed to hate to speak—"to the Misses Knollys, I presume."

I endeavored to treat the subject lightly.

"To your young enemy, Lucetta," I smilingly replied.

He had been looking at me in a perfectly modest and respectful manner, but he dropped his eyes at this and busied himself abstractedly, and yet I thought with some intention, in removing a fly from the horse's flank with the tip of his whip.

"I will not acknowledge her as an enemy," he quietly returned in strictly modulated tones. "I like the girl too well."

The fly had been by this time dislodged, but he did not look up.

"And William?" I suggested. "What do you think of William?"

Slowly he straightened himself. Slowly he dropped the whip back into its socket. I thought he was going to answer, when suddenly his whole attitude changed and he turned upon me a beaming face full of nothing but pleasure.

"The road takes a turn here. In another moment you will see my house." And even while he spoke it burst upon us, and I instantly forgot that I had just ventured on a somewhat hazardous question.

It was such a pretty place, and it was so beautifully and exquisitely kept. There was a charm about its rose-encircled porch that is only to be found in very old places that have been appreciatively cared for. A high fence painted white inclosed a lawn like velvet, and the house itself, shining with a fresh coat of yellow paint, bore signs of comfort in its white-curtained windows not usually to be found in the solitary dwelling of a bachelor. I found my eyes roving over each detail with delight, and almost blushed, or, rather, had I been twenty years younger might have been thought to blush, as I met his eyes and saw how much my pleasure gratified him.

"You must excuse me if I express too much admiration for what I see before me," I said, with what I have every reason to believe was a highly successful effort to hide my confusion. "I have always had a great leaning towards well-ordered walks and trimly kept flower-beds—a leaning, alas! which I have found myself unable to gratify."

"Do not apologize," he hastened to say. "You but redouble my own pleasure in thus honoring my poor efforts with your regard. I have spared no pains, madam, I have spared no pains to render this place beautiful, and most of what you see, I am proud to say, has been accomplished by my own hands."

"Indeed!" I cried in some surprise, letting my eye rest with satisfaction on the top of a long well-sweep that was one of the picturesque features of the place.

"It may have been folly," he remarked, with a gloating sweep of his eye over the velvet lawn and flowering shrubs—a peculiar look that seemed to express something more than the mere delight of possession, "but I seemed to begrudge any hired assistance in the tending of plants every one of which seems to me like a personal friend."

"I understand," was my somewhat un-Butterworthian reply. I really did not quite know myself. "What a contrast to the dismal grounds at the other end of the lane!"

This was more in my usual vein. He seemed to feel the difference, for his expression changed at my remark.

"Oh, that den!" he exclaimed, bitterly; then, seeing me look a little shocked, he added, with an admirable return to his old manner, "I call any place a den where flowers do not grow." And jumping from the buggy, he gathered an exquisite bunch of heliotrope, which he pressed upon me. "I love sunshine, beds of roses, fountains, and a sweep of lawn like this we see before us. But do not let me bore you. You have probably lingered long enough at the old bachelor's place and now would like to drive on. I will be with you in a moment. Doubtful as it is whether I shall soon again be so fortunate as to be able to offer you any hospitality, I would like to bring you a glass of wine—or, for I see your eyes roaming longingly toward my old-fashioned well, would you like a draft of water fresh from the bucket?"

I assured him I did not drink wine, at which I thought his eyes brightened, but that neither did I indulge in water when in a heat, as at present, at which he looked disappointed and came somewhat reluctantly back to the buggy.

He brightened up, however, the moment he was again at my side.

"Now for the woods," he exclaimed, with what was undoubtedly a forced laugh.

I thought the opportunity one I ought not to slight.

"Do you think," said I, "that it is in those woods the disappearances occur of which Miss Knollys has told me?"

He showed the same hesitancy as before to enter upon this subject.

"I think the less you allow your mind to dwell on this matter the better," said he—"that is, if you are going to remain long in this lane. I do not expend any more thought upon it than is barely necessary, or I should not retain sufficient courage to remain among my roses and my fruits. I wonder—pardon me the indiscretion—that you could bring yourself to enter so ill-reputed a neighborhood. You must be a very brave woman."

"I thought it my duty—" I began. "Althea Knollys was my friend, and I felt I owed a duty toward her children. Besides—" Should I tell Mr. Trohm my real errand in this place? Mr. Gryce had intimated that he was in the confidence of the police, and if so, his assistance in case of necessity might be of inestimable value to me. Yet if no such necessity should arise would I want this man to know that Amelia Butterworth—No, I would not take him into my confidence—not yet. I would only try to get at his idea of where the blame lay—that is, if he had any.

"Besides," he suggested in polite reminder, after waiting a minute or two for me to continue.

"Did I say besides?" was my innocent rejoinder. "I think I meant that after seeing them my sense of the importance of that duty had increased. William especially seems to be a young man of very doubtful amiability."

Immediately the non-commital look returned to Mr. Trohm's face.

"I have no fault to find with William," said he. "He's not the most agreeable companion in the world perhaps, but he has a pretty fancy for fruit—a very pretty fancy."

"One can hardly wonder at that in a neighbor of Mr. Trohm," said I, watching his look, which was fixed somewhat gloomily upon the forest of trees now rapidly closing in around us.

"Perhaps not, perhaps not, madam. The sight of a blossoming honeysuckle hanging from an arbor such as runs along my south walls is a great stimulant to one's taste, madam, I'll not deny that."

"But William?" I repeated, determined not to let the subject go; "have you never thought he was a little indifferent to his sisters?"

"A little, madam."

"And a trifle rough to everything but his dogs?"

"A trifle, madam."

Such reticence seemed unnecessary. I was almost angry, but restrained myself and pursued quietly, "The girls, on the contrary, seem devoted to him?"

"Women have that weakness."

"And act as if they would do—what would they not do for him?"

"Miss Butterworth, I have never seen a more amiable woman than yourself. Will you promise me one thing?"

His manner was respect itself, his smile genial and highly contagious. I could not help responding to it in the way he expected.

"Do not talk to me about this family. It is a painful subject to me. Lucetta—you know the girl, and I shall not be able to prejudice you against her—has conceived the idea that I encourage William in an intimacy of which she does not approve. She does not want him to talk to me. William has a loose tongue in his head and sometimes drops unguarded words about their doings, which if any but William spoke—But there, I am forgetting one of the most important rules of my own life, which is to keep my mouth from babbling and my tongue from guile. Influence of a congenial companion, madam; it is irresistible sometimes, especially to a man living so much alone as myself."

I considered his fault very pardonable, but did not say so lest I should frighten his confidences away.

"I thought there was something wrong between you," I said. "Lucetta acted almost afraid of you this morning. I should think she would be glad of the friendship of so good a neighbor."

His face took on a very sombre look.

"She is afraid of me," he admitted, "afraid of what I have seen or may see of—their poverty," he added, with an odd emphasis. I scarcely think he expected to deceive me.

I did not push the subject an inch farther. I saw it had gone as far as discretion permitted at this time.

We had reached the heart of the forest and were rapidly approaching the Knollys house. As the tops of its great chimneys rose above the foliage, I saw his aspect suddenly change.

"I don't know why I should so hate to leave you here," he remarked.

I myself thought the prospect of re-entering the Knollys mansion somewhat uninviting after the pleasant ride I had had and the glimpse which had been given me of a really cheery home and pleasant surroundings.

"This morning I looked upon you as a somewhat daring woman, the progress of whose stay here would be watched by me with interest, but after the companionship of the last half-hour I am conscious of an anxiety in your regard which makes me doubly wish that Miss Knollys had not shut me out from her home. Are you sure you wish to enter this house again, madam?"

I was surprised—really surprised—at the feeling he showed. If my well-disciplined heart had known how to flutter it would probably have fluttered then, but happily the restraint of years did not fail me in this emergency. Taking advantage of the emotion which had betrayed him into an acknowledgment of his real feelings regarding the dangers lurking in this home, despite the check he had endeavored to put upon his lips, I said, with an attempt at naïveté only to be excused by the exigencies of the occasion:

"Why, I thought you considered this domicile perfectly harmless. You like the girls and have no fault to find with William. Can it be that this great building has another occupant? I do not allude to ghosts. Neither of us are likely to believe in the supernatural."

"Miss Butterworth, you have me at a disadvantage. I do not know of any other occupant which the house can hold save the three young people you have mentioned. If I seem to feel any doubt of them—but I don't feel any doubt. I only dread any place for you which is not watched over by someone interested in your defence. The danger threatening the inhabitants of this lane is such a veiled one. If we knew where it lurked, we would no longer call it danger. Sometimes I think the ghosts you allude to are not as innocent as mere spectres usually are. But don't let me frighten you. Don't—" How quick his voice changed! "Ah, William, I have brought back your guest, you see! I couldn't let her sit out the noon hour in old Carter's parlor. That would be too much for even so amiable a person as Miss Butterworth to endure."

I had hardly realized we were so near the gate and certainly was surprised to find William anywhere within hearing. That his appearance at this moment was anything but welcome, must be evident to every one. The sentence which it interrupted might have contained the most important advice, or at the least a warning I could ill afford to lose. But destiny was against me, and being one who accepts the inevitable with good grace, I prepared to alight, with Mr. Trohm's assistance.

The bunch of heliotrope I held was a little in my way or I should have managed the jump with confidence and dignified agility. As it was, I tripped slightly, which brought out a chuckle from William that at the moment seemed more wicked to me than any crime. Meanwhile he had not let matters proceed thus far without putting more than one question.

"And where's Simsbury? And why did Miss Butterworth think she had got to sit in Carter's parlor?"

"Mr. Simsbury," said I as soon as I could recover from the mingled exertion and embarrassment of my descent to terra firma, "felt it necessary to take the horse to the shoer's. That is a half-day's work, as you know, and I felt confident that he and especially you would be glad to have me accept any means for escaping so dreary a waiting."

The grunt he uttered was eloquent of anything but satisfaction.

"I'll go tell the girls," he said. But he didn't go till he had seen Mr. Trohm enter his buggy and drive slowly off.

That all this did not add to my liking for William goes without saying.

BOOK II   THE FLOWER PARLOR

XV   LUCETTA FULFILS MY EXPECTATION OF HER

It was not till Mr. Trohm had driven away that I noticed, in the shadow of the trees on the opposite side of the road, a horse tied up, whose empty saddle bespoke a visitor within. At any other gate and on any other road this would not have struck me as worthy of notice, much less of comment. But here, and after all that I had heard during the morning, the circumstance was so unexpected I could not help showing my astonishment.

"A visitor?" I asked.

"Some one to see Lucetta."

William had no sooner said this than I saw he was in a state of high excitement. He had probably been in this condition when we drove up, but my attention being directed elsewhere I had not noticed it. Now, however, it was perfectly plain to me, and it did not seem quite the excitement of displeasure, though hardly that of joy.

"She doesn't expect you yet," he pursued, as I turned sharply toward the house, "and if you interrupt her—D—n it, if I thought you would interrupt her——"

I thought it time to teach him a lesson in manners.

"Mr. Knollys," I interposed somewhat severely, "I am a lady. Why should I interrupt your sister or give her or you a moment of pain?"

"I don't know," he muttered. "You are so very quick I was afraid you might think it necessary to join her in the parlor. She is perfectly able to take care of herself, Miss Butterworth, and if she don't do it—" The rest was lost in indistinct guttural sounds.

I made no effort to answer this tirade. I took my usual course in quite my usual way to the front steps and proceeded to mount them without so much as looking behind me to see whether or not this uncouth representative of the Knollys name had kept at my heels or not.

Entering the door, which was open, I came without any effort on my part upon Lucetta and her visitor, who proved to be a young gentleman. They were standing together in the middle of the hall and were so absorbed in what they were saying that they neither saw nor heard me. I was therefore enabled to catch the following sentences, which struck me as of some moment. The first was uttered by her, and in very pleading tones:

"A week—I only ask a week. Then perhaps I can give you an answer which will satisfy you."

His reply, in manner if not in matter, proclaimed him the lover of whom I had so lately heard.

"I cannot, dear girl; indeed, I cannot. My whole future depends upon my immediately making the move in which I have asked you to join me. If I wait a week, my opportunity will be gone, Lucetta. You know me and you know how I love you. Then come——"

A rude hand on my shoulder distracted my attention. William stood lowering behind me and, as I turned, whispered in my ear:

"You must come round the other way. Lucetta is so touchy, the sight of you will drive every sensible idea out of her head."

His blundering whisper did what my presence and by no means light footsteps had failed to do. With a start Lucetta turned and, meeting my eye, drew back in visible confusion. The young man followed her hastily.

"Is it good-by, Lucetta?" he pleaded, with a fine, manly ignoring of our presence that roused my admiration.

She did not answer. Her look was enough. William, seeing it, turned furious at once, and, bounding by me, faced the young man with an oath.

"You're a fool to take no from a silly chit like that," he vociferated. "If I loved a girl as you say you love Lucetta, I'd have her if I had to carry her away by force. She'd stop screaming before she was well out of the lane. I know women. While you listen to them they'll talk and talk; but once let a man take matters into his own hands and—" A snap of his fingers finished the sentence. I thought the fellow brutal, but scarcely so stupid as I had heretofore considered him.

His words, however, might just as well have been uttered into empty air. The young man he so violently addressed appeared hardly to have heard him, and as for Lucetta, she was so nearly insensible from misery that she had sufficient ado to keep herself from falling at her lover's feet.

"Lucetta, Lucetta, is it then good-by? You will not go with me?"

"I cannot. William, here, knows that I cannot. I must wait till——"

But here her brother seized her so violently by the wrist that she stopped from sheer pain, I fear. However that was, she turned pale as death under his clutch, and, when he tried to utter some hot, passionate words into her ear, shook her head, but did not speak, though her lover was gazing with a last, final appeal into her eyes. The delicate girl was bearing out my estimate of her.

Seeing her thus unresponsive, William flung her hand from him and turned upon me.

"It's your fault," he cried. "You would come in——"

But, at this, Lucetta, recovering her poise in a moment, cried out shrilly:

"For shame, William! What has Miss Butterworth to do with this? You are not helping me with your roughness. God knows I find this hour hard enough, without this show of anxiety on your part to be rid of me."

"There's woman's gratitude for you," was his snarling reply. "I offer to take all the responsibilities on my own shoulders and make it right with—with her sister, and all that, and she calls it desire to get rid of her. Well, have your own way," he growled, storming down the hall; "I'm done with it for one."

The young man, whose attitude of reserve, mixed with a strange and lingering tenderness for this girl, whom he evidently loved without fully understanding her, was every minute winning more and more of my admiration, had meanwhile raised her trembling hand to his lips in what was, as we all could see, a last farewell.

In another moment he was walking by us, giving me as he passed a low bow that for all its grace did not succeed in hiding from me the deep and heartfelt disappointment with which he quitted this house. As his figure passed through the door, hiding for one moment the sunshine, I felt an oppression such as has not often visited my healthy nature, and when it passed and disappeared, something like the good spirit of the place seemed to go with it, leaving in its place doubt, gloom, and a morbid apprehension of that unknown something which in Lucetta's eyes had rendered his dismissal necessary.

"Where's Saracen? I declare I'm nothing but a fool without that dog," shouted William. "If he has to be tied up another day—" But shame was not entirely eliminated from his breast, for at Lucetta's reproachful "William!" he sheepishly dropped his head and strode out, muttering some words I was fain to accept as an apology.

I had expected to encounter a wreck in Lucetta, as, this episode in her life closed, she turned toward me. But I did not yet know this girl, whose frailty seemed to lie mostly in her physique. Though she was suffering far more than her defence of me to her brother would seem to denote, there was a spirit in her approach and a steady look in her dark eye which assured me that I could not calculate upon any loss in Lucetta's keenness, in case we came to an issue over the mystery that was eating into the happiness as well as the honor of this household.

"I am glad to see you," were her unexpected words. "The gentleman who has just gone out was a lover of mine; at least he once professed to care for me very much, and I should have been glad to have married him, but there were reasons which I once thought most excellent why this seemed anything but expedient, and so I sent him away. To-day he came without warning to ask me to go away with him, after the hastiest of ceremonies, to South America, where a splendid prospect has suddenly opened for him. You see, don't you, that I could not do that; that it would be the height of selfishness in me to leave Loreen—to leave William——"

"Who seems only too anxious to be left," I put in, as her voice trailed off in the first evidence of embarrassment she had shown since she faced me.

"William is a difficult man to understand," was her firm but quiet retort. "From his talk you would judge him to be morose, if not positively unkind, but in action—" She did not tell me how he was in action. Perhaps her truthfulness got the better of her, or perhaps she saw it would be hard work to prejudice me now in his favor.

XVI   LOREEN

Lucetta had said to her departing lover, that in a week she might be able (were he willing or in a position to wait) to give him a more satisfactory answer. Why in a week?

That her hesitation sprang from the mere dislike of leaving her sister so suddenly, or that she had sacrificed her life's happiness to any childish idea of decorum, I did not think probable. The spirit she had shown, her immovable attitude under a temptation which had not only romance to recommend it, but everything else which could affect a young and sensitive woman, argued in my mind the existence of some uncompleted duty of so exacting and imperative a nature that she could not even consider the greatest interests of her own life until this one thing was out of her way. William's rude question of the morning, "What shall we do with the old girl till it is all over?" recurred to me in support of this theory, making me feel that I needed no further confirmation, to be quite certain that a crisis was approaching in this house which would tax my powers to the utmost and call perhaps for the use of the whistle which I had received from Mr. Gryce, and which, following his instructions, I had tied carefully about my neck. Yet how could I associate Lucetta with crime, or dream of the police in connection with the serene Loreen, whose every look was a rebuke to all that was false, vile, or even common? Easily, my readers, easily, with that great, hulking William in my remembrance. To shield him, to hide perhaps his deformity of soul from the world, even such gentle and gracious women as these have been known to enter into acts which to an unprejudiced eye and an unbiased conscience would seem little short of fiendish. Love for an unworthy relative, or rather the sense of duty toward those of one's own blood, has driven many a clear-minded woman to her ruin, as may be seen any day in the police annals.

I am quite aware that I have not as yet put into definite words the suspicion upon which I was now prepared to work. Up to this time it had been too vague, or rather of too monstrous a character for me not to consider other theories, such as, for instance, the possible connection of old Mother Jane with the unaccountable disappearances which had taken place in this lane. But after this scene, the increased assurance I was hourly receiving that something extraordinary and out of keeping with the customary appearances of the household was secretly going on in some one of the various chambers of that long corridor I had been prevented from entering, forced me to accept and act upon the belief that these young women held in charge a prisoner of some kind, of whose presence in the house they dreaded the discovery.

Now, who could this prisoner be?

Common sense supplied me with but one answer; Silly Rufus, the boy who within a few days had vanished from among the good people of this seemingly guileless community.

This theory once established in my mind, I applied myself to a consideration of the means at my disposal for determining its validity. The simplest, surest, but least satisfactory to one of my nature was to summon the police and have the house thoroughly searched, but this involved, in case I had been deceived by appearances—as was possible even to a woman of my experience and discrimination,—a scandal and an opprobrium which I would be the last to inflict upon Althea's children, unless justice to the rest of the world demanded it.

It was in consideration of this very fact, perhaps, that I had been chosen for this duty instead of some regular police spy. Mr. Gryce, as I very well knew, has made it his rule of life never to risk the reputation of any man or woman without reasons so excellent as to carry their own exoneration with them, and should I, a woman, with full as much heart as himself, if not quite as much brain (at least in the estimation of people in general), by any premature exposure of my suspicions, subject these young friends of mine to humiliations they are far too weak and too poor to rise above?

No, rather would I trust a little longer to my own perspicacity and make sure by the use of my own eyes that the situation called for the interference I had, as you may say, at the end of the cord I wore about my neck.

Lucetta had not asked me how I came to be back so much sooner than she had reason to expect me. The unlooked-for arrival of her lover had probably put all idea of her former plans out of her head. I therefore gave her the shortest of explanations when we met at the dinner table. Nothing further seemed to be necessary, for the girls were even more abstracted than before, and William positively boorish till a warning glance from Loreen recalled him to his better self, which meant silence.

The afternoon was spent in very much the same way as the evening before. Neither sister remained an instant with me after the other entered my company, and though the alternations were less frequent than at that time, their peculiarities were more marked and less naturally accounted for. It was while Loreen was with me that I made the suggestion which had been hovering on my lips ever since the noon.

"I consider this," I observed, in one of the pauses of our more than fitful conversation, "one of the most interesting houses it has ever been my good fortune to enter. Would you mind my roaming about a bit just to enjoy the old-time flavor of its great empty rooms? I know they are mostly closed and possibly unfurnished, but to a connoisseur like myself in colonial architecture, this rather adds to, than detracts from, their interest."

"Impossible," she was going to say, but caught herself back in time and changed the imperative word to one more conciliatory if equally unyielding.

"I am sorry, Miss Butterworth, to deny you this gratification, but the condition of the rooms and the unhappy excitement into which we have been thrown by the unfortunate visit paid to Lucetta by a gentleman to whom she is only too much attached, make it quite impossible for me to consider any such undertaking to-day. To-morrow I may find it easier; but, if not, be assured you shall see every nook and corner of this house before you finally leave it."

"Thank you. I will remember that. To one of my tastes an ancient room in a time-honored mansion like this, affords a delight not to be understood by one who knows less of the last century's life. The legends connected with your great drawing-room below [we were sitting in my room, I having refused to be cooped up in their dreary side parlor, and she not having offered me any other spot more cheerful] are sufficient in themselves to hold me entranced for an hour. I heard one of them to-day."

"Which?"

She spoke more quickly than usual, and for her quite sharply.

"That of Lucetta's namesake," I explained. "She who rode through the night after a daughter who had won her lover's heart away from her.

"Ah, it is a well-known tale, but I think Mrs. Carter might have left its relation to us. Did she tell you anything else?"

"No other tradition of this place," I assured her.

"I am glad she was so considerate. But why—if you will pardon me—did she happen to light upon that story? We have not heard those incidents spoken of for years."

"Not since the phantom coach flew through this road the last time," I ventured, with a smile that should have disarmed her from suspecting any ulterior motive on my part in thus introducing a subject which could not be altogether pleasing to her.

"The phantom coach! Have you heard of that?"

I wish it had been Lucetta who had said this and to whom my reply was due. The opportunities would have been much greater for an injudicious display of feeling on her part and for a suitable conclusion on mine.

But it was Loreen, and she never forgot herself. So I had to content myself with the persuasion that her voice was just a whit less clear than usual and her serenity enough impaired for her to look out of my one high and dismal window instead of into my face.

"My dear,"—I had not called her this before, though the term had frequently risen to my lips in answer to Lucetta—"you should have gone with me into the village to-day. Then you would not need to ask if I had heard of the phantom coach."

The probe had reached the quick at last. She looked quite startled.

"You amaze me," she said. "What do you mean, Miss Butterworth? Why should I not have needed to ask?"

"Because you would have heard it whispered about in every lane and corner. It is common talk in town to-day. You must know why, Miss Knollys."

She was not looking out of the window now. She was looking at me.

"I assure you," she murmured, "I do not know at all. Nothing could be more incomprehensible to me. Explain yourself, I entreat you. The phantom coach is but a myth to me, interesting only as involving certain long-vanished ancestors of mine."

"Of course," I assented. "No one of real sense could regard it in any other light. But villagers will talk, and they say—you will soon know what, if I do not tell you myself—that it passed through the lane on Tuesday night."

"Tuesday night!" Her composure had been regained, but not so entirely but that her voice slightly trembled. "That was before you came. I hope it was not an omen."

I was in no mood for pleasantry.

"They say that the passing of this apparition denotes misfortune to those who see it. I am therefore obviously exempt. But you—did you see it? I am just curious to know if it is visible to those who live in the lane. It ought to have turned in here. Were you fortunate enough to have been awake at that moment and to have seen this spectral appearance?"

She shuddered. I was not mistaken in believing I saw this sign of emotion, for I was watching her very closely, and the movement was unmistakable.

"I have never seen anything ghostly in my life," said she. "I am not at all superstitious."

If I had been ill-natured or if I had thought it wise to press her too closely, I might have inquired why she looked so pale and trembled so visibly.

But my natural kindness, together with an instinct of caution, restrained me, and I only remarked:

"There you are sensible, Miss Knollys—doubly so as a denizen of this house, which, Mrs. Carter was obliging enough to suggest to me, is considered by many as haunted."

The straightening of Miss Knollys' lips augured no good to Mrs. Carter.

"Now I only wish it was," I laughed dryly. "I should really like to meet a ghost, say, in your great drawing-room, which I am forbidden to enter."

"You are not forbidden," she hastily returned. "You may explore it now if you will excuse me from accompanying you; but you will meet no ghosts. The hour is not propitious."

Taken aback by her sudden amenity, I hesitated for a moment. Would it be worth while for me to search a room she was willing to have me enter? No, and yet any knowledge which could be obtained in regard to this house might be of use to me or to Mr. Gryce. I decided to embrace her offer, after first testing her with one other question.

"Would you prefer to have me steal down these corridors at night and dare their dusky recesses at a time when spectres are supposed to walk the halls they once flitted through in happy consciousness?"

"Hardly." She made the greatest effort to sustain the jest, but her concern and dread were manifest. "I think I had better give you the keys now, than subject you to the drafts and chilling discomforts of this old place at midnight."

I rose with a semblance of eager anticipation.

"I will take you at your word," said I. "The keys, my dear. I am going to visit a haunted room for the first time in my life."

I do not think she was deceived by this feigned ebullition. Perhaps it was too much out of keeping with my ordinary manner, but she gave no sign of surprise and rose in her turn with an air suggestive of relief.

"Excuse me, if I precede you," she begged. "I will meet you at the head of the corridor with the keys."

I was in hopes she would be long enough in obtaining them to allow me to stroll along the front hall to the opening into the corridor I was so anxious to enter. But the spryness I showed, seemed to have a corresponding effect upon her, for she almost flew down the passageway before me and was back at my side before I could take a step in the coveted direction.

"These will take you into any room on the first floor," said she. "You will meet with dust and Lucetta's abhorrence, spiders, but for these I shall make no apologies. Girls who cannot provide comforts for the few rooms they utilize, cannot be expected to keep in order the large and disused apartments of a former generation."

"I hate dirt and despise spiders," was my dry retort, "but I am willing to brave both for the pleasure of satisfying my love for the antique." At which she handed me the keys, with a calm smile which was not without its element of sadness.

"I will be here on your return," she said, leaning over the banisters to speak to me as I took my first steps down. "I shall want to hear whether you are repaid for your trouble."

I thanked her and proceeded on my way, somewhat doubtful whether by so doing I was making the best possible use of my opportunities.

XVII   THE FLOWER PARLOR

The lower hall did not correspond exactly with the one above. It was larger, and through its connection with the front door, presented the shape of a letter T— that is, to the superficial observer who was not acquainted with the size of the house and had not had the opportunity of remarking that at the extremities of the upper hall making this T, were two imposing doors usually found shut except at meal-times, when the left-hand one was thrown open, disclosing a long and dismal corridor similar to the ones above. Half-way down this corridor was the dining-room, into which I had now been taken three times.

The right-hand one, I had no doubt, led the way into the great drawing-room or dancing-hall which I had started out to see.

Proceeding first to the front of the house, where some glimmer of light penetrated from the open sitting-room door, I looked the keys over and read what was written on the several tags attached to them. They were seven in number, and bore some such names as these: "Blue Chamber," "Library," "Flower Parlor," "Shell Cabinet," "Dark Parlor"—all of which was very suggestive, and, to an antiquarian like myself, most alluring.

But it was upon a key marked "A" I first fixed my attention. This, I had been told, would open the large door at the extremity of the upper hall, and when I made a trial with it I found it to move easily, though somewhat gratingly, in the lock, releasing the great doors, which in another moment swung inward with a growling sound which might have been startling to a nervous person filled with the legends of the place.

But in me the only emotion awakened was one of disgust at the nauseous character of the air which instantly enveloped me. Had I wished for any further proof than was afforded by the warning given me by the condition of the hinges, that the foot of man had not lately invaded these precincts, I would have had it in the mouldy atmosphere and smell of dust that greeted me on the threshold. Neither human breath nor a ray of outdoor sunshine seemed to have disturbed its gloomy quiet for years, and when I moved, as I presently did, to open one of the windows I dimly discerned at my right, I felt such a movement of something foul and noisome amid the decaying rags of the carpet through which I was stumbling that I had to call into use the stronger elements of my character not to back out of a place so given over to rot and the creatures that infest it.

"What a spot," thought I, "for Amelia Butterworth to find herself in!" and wondered if I could ever wear again the three-dollar-a-yard silk dress in which I was then enveloped. Of my shoes I took no account. They were ruined, of course.

I reached the window in safety, but could not open it; neither could I move the adjoining one. There were sixteen in all, or so I afterwards found, and not till I reached the last (you see, I am very persistent) did I succeed in loosening the bar that held its inner shutter in place. This done, I was able to lift the window, and for the first time in years, perhaps, let in a ray of light into this desolated apartment.

The result was disappointing. Mouldy walls, worm-eaten hangings, two very ancient and quaint fireplaces, met my eyes, and nothing more. The room was absolutely empty. For a few minutes I allowed my eyes to roam over the great rectangular space in which so much that was curious and interesting had once taken place, and then, with a vague sense of defeat, turned my eyes outward, anxious to see what view could be obtained from the window I had opened. To my astonishment, I saw before me a high wall with here and there a window in it, all tightly barred and closed, till by a careful inspection about me I realized that I was looking upon the other wing of the building, and that between these wings extended a court so narrow and long that it gave to the building the shape, as I have before said, of the letter U. A dreary prospect, reminding one of the view from a prison, but it had its point of interest, for in the court below me, the brick pavement of which was half obliterated by grass, I caught sight of William in an attitude so different from any I had hitherto seen him assume that I found it difficult to account for it till I caught sight of the jaws of a dog protruding from under his arms, and then I realized he was hugging Saracen.

The dog was tied, but the comfort which William seemed to take in just this physical contact with his rough skin was something worth seeing. It made me quite thoughtful for a moment.

I detest dogs, and it gives me a creepy sensation to see them fondled, but sincerity of feeling appeals to me, and no one could watch William Knollys with his dogs without seeing that he really loved the brutes. Thus in one day I had witnessed the best and worst side of this man. But wait! Had I seen the worst? I was not so sure that I had.

He had not noticed my peering, for which I was duly thankful, and after another fruitless survey of the windows in the wall before me, I drew back and prepared to leave the place. This was by no means a pleasant undertaking. I could now see what I had only felt before, and to traverse the space before me amid beetles and spiders required a determination of no ordinary nature. I was glad when I reached the great doors and more than glad when they closed behind me.

"So much for Room A," thought I.

The next most promising apartment was in the same corridor as the diningroom. It was called the Dark Parlor. Entering it, I found it dark indeed, but not because of lack of light, but because its hangings were all of a dismal red and its furniture of the blackest ebony. As this mainly consisted of shelves and cabinets placed against three of its four walls, the effect was gloomy indeed, and fully accounted for the name which the room had received. I lingered in it, however, longer than I had in the big drawing-room, chiefly because the shelves contained books.

Had anything better offered I might not have continued my explorations, but not seeing exactly how I could pass away the time more profitably, I chose out another key and began to search for the Flower Parlor. I found it beyond the dining-room in the same hall as the Dark Parlor.

It was, as I might have expected from the name, the brightest and most cheerful spot I had yet found in the whole house. The air in it was even good, as if sunshine and breeze had not been altogether shut out of it, yet I had no sooner taken one look at its flower-painted walls and pretty furniture than I felt an oppression difficult to account for. Something was wrong about this room. I am not superstitious and have no faith in premonitions, but once seized by a conviction, I have never known myself to be mistaken as to its import. Something was wrong about this room—what, it was my business to discover.

Letting in more light, I took a closer survey of the objects I had hitherto seen but dimly. They were many and somewhat contradictory in character. The floor was bare—the first bare floor I had come upon—but the shades in the windows, the chintz-covered lounges drawn up beside tables bestrewn with books and other objects of comfort and luxury, bespoke a place in common if not every-day use.

A faint smell of tobacco assured me in whose use, and from the minute I recognized that this was William's sanctum, my curiosity grew unbounded and I neglected nothing which would be likely to attract the keenest-eyed detective in Mr. Gryce's force. There were several things to be noted there: First, that this lumbering lout of a man read, but only on one topic—vivisection; secondly, that he was not a reader merely, for there were instruments in the cases heaped up on the tables about me, and in one corner—it made me a little sick, but I persevered in searching out the corners—a glass case with certain horrors in it which I took care to note, but which it is not necessary for me to describe. Another corner was blocked up by a closet which stood out in the room in a way to convince me it had been built in after the room was otherwise finished. As I crossed over to examine the door, which did not appear to me to be quite closed, I noticed on the floor at my feet a huge discoloration. This was the worst thing I had yet encountered, and while I did not feel quite justified in giving it a name, I could not but feel some regret for the worm-eaten rags of the drawing-room, which, after all, are more comfortable underfoot than bare boards with such suggestive marks upon them as these.

The door to the closet was, as I had expected, slightly ajar, a fact for which I was profoundly grateful, for, set it down to breeding or a natural recognition of other people's rights, I would have found it most difficult to turn the knob of a closet door, inspection of which had not been offered me.

But finding it open, I gave it just a little pull and found—well, it was a surprise, much more so than the sight of a skeleton would have been—that the whole interior was taken up by a small circular staircase such as you find in public libraries where the books are piled up in tiers. It stretched from the floor to the ceiling, and dark as it was I thought I detected the outlines of a trap-door by means of which communication was established with the room above. Anxious to be convinced of this, I consulted with myself as to what a detective would do in my place. The answer came readily enough: "Mount the stairs and feel for yourself whether there is a lock there." But my delicacy or—shall I acknowledge it for once?—an instinct of timidity seemed to restrain me, till a remembrance of Mr. Gryce's sarcastic look which I had seen honoring lesser occasions than these, came to nerve me, and I put foot on the stairs which had last been trod—by whom, shall I say? William? Let us hope by William, and William only.

Being tall, I had to mount but a few steps before reaching the ceiling. Pausing for breath, the air being close and the stairs steep, I reached up and felt for the hinge or clasp I had every reason to expect to encounter. I found it almost immediately, and, satisfied now that nothing but a board separated me from the room above, I tried that board with my finger and was astonished to feel it yield. As this was a wholly unexpected discovery I drew back and asked myself if it would be wise to pursue it to the point of raising this door, and had hardly settled the question in my own mind, when the sound of a voice raised in a soothing murmur, revealed the fact that the room above was not empty, and that I would be committing a grave indiscretion in thus tampering with a means of entrance possibly under the very eye of the person speaking.

If the voice I had heard had been all that had come to my ears, I might have ventured after a moment of hesitation to brave the displeasure of Miss Knollys by an attempt which would have at once satisfied me as to the correctness of the suspicions which were congealing my blood as I stood there, but another voice—the heavy and threatening voice of William—had broken into this murmur, and I knew that if I so much as awakened in him the least suspicion of my whereabouts, I would have to dread an anger that might not know where to stop.

I therefore rested from further efforts in this direction, and fearing he might bethink him of some errand which would bring him to the trap-door himself, I began a retreat which I made slow only from my desire not to make any noise. I succeeded as well as if my feet had been shod in velvet and my dress had been made of wool instead of a rustling silk, and when once again I found myself planted in the centre of the Flower Parlor, the closet door closed, and no evidence remaining of my late attempt to probe this family secret, I drew a deep breath of relief that was but a symbol of my devout thankfulness.

I did not mean to remain much longer in this spot of evil suggestions, but spying the corner of a book protruding from under a cushion of one of the lounges, I had a curiosity to see if it were similar to the others I had handled. Drawing it out, I took one look at it.

I need not tell what it was, but after a hasty glance here and there through its pages, I put it back, shuddering. If any doubt remained in my breast that William was one of those monsters who feed their morbid cravings by experiments upon the weak and defenceless, it had been dispelled by what I had just seen in this book.

However, I did not leave the room immediately. As it was of the greatest importance that I should be able to locate in which of the many apartments on the floor above, the supposed prisoner was lodged, I cast about me for the means of doing this through the location of the room in which I then was. As this could only be done by affixing some token to the window, which could be recognized from without, I thought, first, of thrusting the end of my handkerchief through one of the slats of the outside blinds; secondly, of simply leaving one of these blinds ajar; and finally, of chipping off a piece with the penknife I always carry with innumerable other small things in the bag I invariably wear at my side. (Fashion, I hold, counts for nothing against convenience.)

This last seemed by much the best device. A handkerchief could be discovered and pulled out, an open blind could be shut, but a sliver once separated from the wood of the casement, nothing could replace it or even cover it up without itself attracting attention.

Taking out my knife, I glanced at the door leading into the hall, found it still shut and everything quiet behind it. Then I took a look into the shrubs and bushes of the yard outside, and, observing nothing to disturb me, snipped off a bit from one of the outer edges of the slats and then carefully reclosed the blinds and the window.

I was crossing the threshold when I heard a rapid footstep in the hall. Miss Knollys was hastening down the hall to my side.

"Oh, Miss Butterworth," she exclaimed, with one quick look into the room I was leaving, "this is William's den, the one spot he never allows any of us to enter. I don't know how the key came to be upon the string. It never was before, and I am afraid he never will forgive me."

"He need never know that I have been the victim of such a mistake," said I.

"My feet leave no trail, and as I use no perfumes he will never suspect that I have enjoyed a glimpse of these old-fashioned walls and ancient cabinets."

"The slats of the blinds are a little open," she remarked, her eyes searching my face for some sign that I am sure she did not find there. "Were they so when you came in?"

"I hardly think so; it was very dark. Shall I put them as I found them?"

"No. He will not notice." And she hurried me out, still eyeing me breathlessly as if she half distrusted my composure.

"Come, Amelia," I now whispered in self-admonition, "the time for exertion has come. Show this young woman, who is not much behind you in self-control, some of the lighter phases of your character. Charm her, Amelia, charm her, or you may live to rue this invasion into family secrets more than you may like to acknowledge at the present moment."

A task of some difficulty, but I rejoice in difficult tasks, and before another half-hour had passed, I had the satisfaction of seeing Miss Knollys entirely restored to that state of placid melancholy which was the natural expression of her calm but unhappy nature.

We visited the Shell Cabinet, the Blue Parlor, and another room, the peculiarities of which I have forgotten. Frightened by the result of leaving me to my own devices, she did not quit me for an instant, and when, my curiosity quite satisfied, I hinted that a short nap in my own room would rest me for the evening, she proceeded with me to the door of my apartment.

"The locksmith whom I saw this morning has not kept his word," I remarked as she was turning away.

"None of the tradesmen here do that," was her cold answer. "I have given up expecting having any attention paid to my wants."

"Humph," thought I. "Another pleasant admission. Amelia Butterworth, this has not been a cheerful day."

XVIII   THE SECOND NIGHT

I cannot say that I looked forward to the night with any very cheerful anticipations. The locksmith having failed to keep his appointment, I was likely to have no more protection against intrusion than I had had the night before, and while I cannot say that I especially feared any unwelcome entrance into my apartment, I should have gone to my rest with a greater sense of satisfaction if a key had been in the lock and that key had been turned by my own hand on my own side of the door.

The atmosphere of gloom which settled down over the household after the evening meal, seemed like the warning note of something strange and evil awaiting us. So marked was this, that many in my situation would have further disturbed these girls by some allusion to the fact. But that was not the rôle I had set myself to play at this crisis. I remembered what Mr. Gryce had said about winning their confidence, and though the turmoil evident in Lucetta's mind and the distraction visible even in the careful Miss Knollys led me to expect a culmination of some kind before the night was over, I not only hid my recognition of this fact, but succeeded in sufficiently impressing them with the contentment which my own petty employments afforded me (I am never idle even in other persons' houses) for them to spare me the harassment of their alternate visits, which, in their present mood and mine promised little in the way of increased knowledge of their purposes and much in the way of distraction and the loss of that nerve upon which I calculated for a successful issue out of the possible difficulties of this night.

Had I been a woman of ordinary courage, I would have sounded three premonitory notes upon my whistle before blowing out my candle, but while I am not lacking, I hope, in many of the finer feminine qualities which link me to my sex, I have but few of that sex's weaknesses and none of its instinctive reliance upon others which leads it so often to neglect its own resources. Till I saw good reasons for summoning the police, I proposed to preserve a discreet silence, a premature alarm being in their eyes, as I knew from many talks with Mr. Gryce, the one thing suggestive of a timid and inexperienced mind.

Hannah had brought me a delicious cup of tea at ten, the influence of which was to make me very drowsy at eleven, but I shook this weakness off and began my night's watch in a state of stern composure which I verily believe would have awakened Mr. Gryce's admiration had it been consonant with the proprieties for him to have seen it. Indeed the very seriousness of the occasion was such that I could not have trembled if I would, every nerve and faculty being strained to their utmost to make the most of every sound which might arise in the now silent and discreetly darkened house.

I had purposely omitted the precaution of pushing my bed against the door of my room, as I had done the night before, being anxious to find myself in a position to cross its threshold at the least alarm. That this would come, I felt positive, for Hannah in leaving my room had taken pains to say, in unconscious imitation of what Miss Knollys had remarked the night before:

"Don't let any queer sounds you may hear disturb you, Miss Butterworth. There's nothing to hurt you in this house; nothing at all." An admonition which I am sure her young mistresses would not have allowed her to utter if they had been made acquainted with her intention.

But though in a state of high expectation, and listening, as I supposed, with every faculty alert, the sounds I apprehended delayed so long that I began after an hour or two unaccountably to nod in my chair, and before I knew it I was asleep, with the whistle in my hand and my feet pressed against the panels of the door I had set myself to guard. How deep that sleep was or how long I indulged in it, I can only judge from the state of emotion in which I found myself when I suddenly woke. I was sitting there still, but my usually calm frame was in a violent tremble, and I found it difficult to stir, much more to speak. Some one or something was at my door.

An instant and my powerful nature would have asserted itself, but before this could happen the stealthy step drew nearer, and I heard the quiet, almost noiseless, insertion of a key into the lock, and the quick turn which made me a prisoner.

This, with the indignation it caused, brought me quickly to myself. So the door had a key after all, and this was the use it was reserved for. Rising quickly to my feet, I shouted out the names of Loreen, Lucetta, and William, but received no other response than the rapid withdrawal of feet down the corridor. Then I felt for the whistle, which had somehow slipped from my hand, but failed to find it in the darkness, nor when I went to search for the matches to relight the candle I had left standing on a table near by, could I by any means succeed in igniting one, so that I presently had the pleasure of finding myself shut up in my room, with no means of communicating with the world outside and with no light to render the situation tolerable. This was having the tables turned upon me with a vengeance and in a way for which I could not account. I could understand why they had locked me in the room and why they had not heeded my cry of indignant appeal, but I could not comprehend how my whistle came to be gone, nor why the matches, which were sufficiently plentiful in the safe, refused one and all to perform their office.

On these points I felt it necessary to come to some sort of conclusion before I proceeded to invent some way out of my difficulties. So, dropping on my knees by the chair in which I had been sitting, I began a quiet search for the petty object upon which, nevertheless, hung not my safety perhaps, but all chances of success in an undertaking which was every moment growing more serious. I did not find it, but I did find where it had gone. In the floor near the door, my hand encountered a hole which had been covered up by a rug early in the evening, but which I now distinctly remembered having pushed aside with my feet when I took my seat there. This aperture was not large, but it was so deep that my hand failed to reach to the bottom of it; and into this hole by some freak of chance had slipped the small whistle I had so indiscreetly taken into my hand. The mystery of the matches was less easy of solution; so I let it go after a moment of indecisive thought and bent my energies once again to listen, when suddenly and without the least warning there rose from somewhere in the house a cry so wild and unearthly that I started up appalled, and for a moment could not tell whether I was laboring under some fearful dream or a still more fearful reality.

A rushing of feet in the distance and an involuntary murmur of voices soon satisfied me, however, on this score, and drawing upon every energy I possessed, I listened for a renewal of the cry which was yet curdling my blood. But none came, and presently all was as still as if no sound had arisen to disturb the midnight, though every fibre in my body told me that the event I had feared—the event of which I hardly dared mention the character even to myself—had taken place, and that I, who was sent there to forestall it, was not only a prisoner in my room, but a prisoner through my own folly and my inordinate love of tea.

The anger with which I contemplated this fact, and the remorse I felt at the consequences which had befallen the innocent victim whose scream I had just heard, made me very wide-awake indeed, and after an ineffectual effort to make my voice heard from the window, I called my usual philosophy to my aid and decided that since the worst had happened and I, a prisoner, had to await events like any other weak and defenceless woman, I might as well do it with calmness and in a way to win my own approval at least. The dupe of William and his sisters, I would not be the dupe of my own fears or even of my own regrets.

The consequence was a renewed equanimity and a gentle brooding over the one event of the day which brought no regret in its train. The ride with Mr. Trohm, and the acquaintanceship to which it had led, were topics upon which I could rest with great soothing effect through the weary hours stretching between me and daylight. Consequently of Mr. Trohm I thought.

Whether the almost deathly quiet into which the house had now fallen, or the comforting nature of my meditations held inexorably to the topic I had chosen, acted as a soporific upon me I cannot tell, but greatly as I dislike to admit it, feeling sure that you will expect to hear I kept myself awake all that night, I insensibly sank from great alertness to an easy indifference to my surroundings, and from that to vague dreams in which beds of lilies and trellises covered with roses mingled strangely with narrow, winding staircases whose tops ended in the swaying branches of great trees; and so, into quiet and a nothingness that were only broken into by a rap at my door and a cheerful:

"Eight o'clock, ma'am. The young ladies are waiting."

I bounded, literally bounded from my chair. Such a summons, after such a night! What did it mean? I was sitting half dressed in my chair before my door in a straightened and uncomfortable attitude, and therefore had not dreamed that I had been upon the watch all night, yet the sunshine in the room, the cheery tones such as I had not heard even from this woman before, seemed to argue that my imagination had played me false and that no horrors had come to disturb my rest or render my waking distressing.

Stretching out my hand toward the door, I was about to open it, when I bethought me.

"Turn the key in the lock," said I. "Somebody was careful enough of my safety to fasten me in last night."

An exclamation of astonishment came from outside the door.

"There is no key here, ma'am. The door is not locked. Shall I open it and come in?"

I was about to say yes in my anxiety to talk to the woman, but remembering that nothing was to be gained by letting it be seen to what an extent I had carried my suspicions, I hastily disrobed and crept into bed. Pulling the coverings about me, I assumed a comfortable attitude and then cried:

"Come in."

The door immediately opened.

"There, ma'am! What did I tell you? Locked?—this door? Why, the key has been lost for months."

"I cannot help it," I protested, but with little if any asperity, for it did not suit me that she should see I was moved by any extraordinary feeling. "A key was put in that lock about midnight, and I was locked in. It was about the time some one screamed in your own part of the house."

"Screamed?" Her brows took a fine pucker of perplexity. "Oh, that must have been Miss Lucetta."

"Lucetta?"

"Yes, ma'am; she had an attack, I believe. Poor Miss Lucetta! She often has attacks like that."

Confounded, for the woman spoke so naturally that only a suspicious nature like mine would fail to have been deceived by it, I raised myself on my elbow and gave her an indignant look.

"Yet you said just now that the young ladies were expecting me to breakfast."

"Yes, and why not?" Her look was absolutely guileless. "Miss Lucetta sometimes keeps us up half the night, but she does not miss breakfast on that account. When the turn is over, she is as well as ever she was. A fine young lady, Miss Lucetta. I'd lose my two hands for her any day."

"She certainly is a remarkable girl," I declared, not, however, as dryly as I felt. "I can hardly believe I dreamed about the key. Let me feel of your pocket," I laughed.

She, without the smallest hesitancy, pulled aside her apron.

"I am sorry you put so little confidence in my word, ma'am, but Lor' me, what you heard is nothing to what some of our guests have complained of—in the days, I mean, when we did have guests. I have known them to scream out themselves in the middle of the night and vow they saw white figures creeping up and down the halls—all nonsense, ma'am, but believed in by some folks. You don't look as if you believed in ghosts."

"And I don't," I said, "not a whit. It would be a poor way to try to frighten me. How is Mr. William this morning?"

"Oh, he's well and feeding the dogs, ma'am. What made you think of him?"

"Politeness, Hannah," I found myself forced to say. "He's the only man in the house. Why shouldn't I think of him?"

She fingered her apron a minute and laughed.

"I didn't know you liked him. He's so rough, it isn't everybody who understands him," she said.

"Must one understand a person to like him?" I queried good-humoredly. I was beginning to think I might have dreamed about that key.

"I don't know," she said, "I don't always understand Miss Lucetta, but I like her through and through, ma'am, as I like this little finger," and holding up this member to my inspection, she crossed the room for my water-pitcher, which she proposed to fill with hot water.

I followed her closely with my eyes. When she came back, I saw her attention caught by the break in the flooring, which she had not noticed on entering.

"Oh," she exclaimed, "what a shame!" her honest face coloring as she drew the rug back over the small black gap. "I am sure, ma'am," she cried, "you must think very poorly of us. But I assure you, ma'am, it's honest poverty, nothing but honest poverty as makes them so neglectful," and with an air as far removed from mystery as her frank, good-natured manner seemed to be from falsehood, she slid from the room with a kind:

"Don't hurry, ma'am. It is Miss Knollys' turn in the kitchen, and she isn't as quick as Miss Lucetta."

"Humph," thought I, "supposing I had called in the police."

But by the time she had returned with the water, my doubts had reawakened. She was not changed in manner, though I have no doubt she had recounted all that I had said, below, but I was, for I remembered the matches and thought I saw a way of tripping her up in her self-complacency.

Just as she was leaving me for the second time I called her back.

"What is the matter with your matches?" I asked. "I couldn't make them light last night."

With a wholly undisturbed countenance she turned toward the bureau and took up the china trinket that held the few remaining matches I had not scraped on the piece of sandpaper I myself had fastened up alongside the door. A sheepish cry of dismay at once escaped her.

"Why, these are old matches!" she declared, showing me the box in which a half-dozen or so burned matches stood with their burned tops all turned down.

"I thought they were all right. I'm afraid we are a little short of matches."

I did not like to tell her what I thought about it, but it made me doubly anxious to join the young ladies at breakfast and judge for myself from their conduct and expression if I had been deceived by my own fears into taking for realities the phantasies of a nightmare, or whether I was correct in ascribing to fact that episode of the key with all the possibilities that lay behind it.

I did not let my anxiety, however, stand in the way of my duty. Mr. Gryce had bid me carry the whistle he had sent me constantly about my person, and I felt that he would have the right to reproach me if I left my room without making some endeavor to recover this lost article. How to do this without aid or appliances of any kind was a problem. I knew where it was, but I could not see it, much less reach it. Besides, they were waiting for me—never a pleasant thought. It occurred to me that I might lower into the hole a lighted candle hung by a string.

Looking over my effects, I chose out a hairpin, a candle, and two corset laces, (Pardon me. I am as modest as most of my sex, but I am not squeamish. Corset laces are strings, and as such only I present them to your notice.) I should like to have added a button-hook to my collection, but not having as yet discarded the neatly laced boot of my ancestor, I could only produce a small article from my toilet-service which shall remain unmentioned, as I presently discarded it and turned my whole attention to the other objects I have named. A poor array, but out of them I hoped to find the means of fishing up my lost whistle.

My intention was to lower first a lighted candle into the hole by means of a string tied about its middle, then to drop a line on the whistle thus discovered and draw it up with the point of a bent hairpin, which I fondly hoped I could make do the service of a hook. To think was to try. The candle was soon down in the hole, and by its light the whistle was easily seen. The string and bent hairpin went down next. I was successful in hooking the prize and proceeded to pull it up with great care. For an instant I realized what a ridiculous figure I was cutting, stooping over a hole in the floor on both knees, a string in each hand, leading apparently to nowhere, and I at work cautiously steadying one and as carefully pulling on the other. Having hooked the string holding the whistle over the first finger of the hand holding the candle, I may have become too self-conscious to notice the slight release of weight on the whistle hand. Whatever the reason, when the end of the string came in sight there was no whistle on it. The charred end showed me that the candle had burned the cord, letting the whistle fall again out of reach. Down went the candle again. It touched bottom, but no whistle was to be seen. After a long and fruitless search, I concluded to abandon my whistle-fishing excursion, and, rising from my cramped and undignified position, I proceeded to pull up the candle. To my surprise and delight, I found the whistle firmly stuck to the lower side of it. Some drops of candle grease had fallen upon the whistle where it lay. The candle coming in contact with it, the two had adhered, and I became indebted to accident rather than to acumen for the restoration of the precious article.

XIX   A KNOT OF CRAPE

I was prepared for some change in the appearance of my young hostesses, but not for so great a one as I saw on entering the dining-room that memorable morning. The blinds, which were always half closed, were now wide open, and under the cheerful influence of the light which was thus allowed to enter, the table and all its appointments had a much less dreary look than before. Behind the urn sat Miss Knollys, with a smile on her lips, and in the window William stood whistling a cheerful air, unrebuked. Lucetta was not present, but to my great astonishment she presently walked in with her hands laden with sprays of morning-glory, which she flung down in the centre of the board. It was the first time I had seen any attempt made by any of them to lighten the sombreness of their surroundings, and it was also the first time I had seen the three together.

I was more disconcerted by this simple show of improved spirits than I like to acknowledge. In the first place, they were natural and not forced; and, secondly, they were to all appearance unconscious.

They were not marked enough to show relief, and in Lucetta especially did not serve to hide the underlying melancholy of a disappointed girl, yet it was not what I expected from my supposed experiences of the night, and led me to answer a little warily when, with a frank laugh, Loreen exclaimed:

"So you have lost your character as a practical woman, Miss Butterworth? Hannah tells me you were the victim of a ghostly visit last night."

"Hannah gossips unmercifully," was my cautious and somewhat peevish reply. "If I chose to dream that I was locked into my room by some erratic spectre, I cannot see why she should take the confession of my folly out of my mouth. I was going to relate the fact myself, with all the accompaniments of rushing steps and wild and unearthly cries which are expected by the listeners to a veritable ghost story. But now I have simply to defend myself from a charge of credulity. It's too bad, Miss Knollys, much too bad. I did not come to a haunted house for this."

My manner, rather than my words, seemed to completely deceive them. Perhaps it deceived myself, for I began to feel a loss of the depression which had weighed upon me ever since that scream rang in my ears at midnight. It disappeared still further when Lucetta said:

"If your ramblings through the old rooms on this floor were the occasion of this nightmare, you must be prepared for a recurrence of the same to-night, for I am going to take you through the upper rooms myself this morning. Isn't that the programme, Loreen? Or have you changed your mind and planned a drive for Miss Butterworth?"

"She shall do both," Loreen answered. "When she is tired of tramping through dusty chambers and examining the decayed remnants of old furniture which encumber them, William stands ready to drive her over the hills, where she will find views well worth her attention."

"Thank you," said I. "It is a pleasant prospect." But inwardly I uttered anything but thanks; rather asked myself if I had not played the part of a fool in ascribing so much importance to the events of the past night, and decided almost without an argument that I had.

However, beliefs die hard in a mind like mine, and though I was ready to consider that an inflamed imagination may often carry us beyond the bounds of fact and even into the realm of fancy and misconception, I yet was not ready to give up my suspicions altogether, or to acknowledge that I had no foundation for the fear that something uncanny if not awful had taken place under this roof the night before. The very naturalness I observed in this hitherto restrained trio might be the result of the removal of some great strain, and if that was the case—Ah, well, alertness is the motto of the truly wise. It is when vigilance sleeps that the enemy gains the victory. I would not let myself be deceived even at the cost of a little ridicule. Amelia Butterworth was still awake, even under a semblance of well-laid suspicion.

My footsteps were not dogged after this as they had hitherto been in my movements about the house. I was allowed to go and come and even to stray into the second long corridor, without any other let than my own discretion and good breeding. Lucetta joined me, to be sure, after a while, but only as guide and companion. She took me into rooms I forgot the next minute, and into others I remember to this day as quaint memorials of a past ever and always interesting to me. We ransacked the house, yet after all was over and I sat down to rest in my own room, two formidable questions rose in my mind for which I found no satisfactory answer. Why, with so many more or less attractive bedchambers at their command, had they chosen to put me into a hole, where the very flooring was unsafe, and the outlook the most dismal that could be imagined? and why, in all our peregrinations in and out of rooms, had we always passed one door without entering? She had said that it was William's—a sufficient explanation, if true, and I have no doubt it was,—but the change of countenance with which she passed it and the sudden lightening of her tread (so instinctive that she was totally unconscious of it) marked that door as one it would be my duty to enter if fate should yet give me the opportunity. That it was the one in communication with the Flower Parlor I felt satisfied, but in order to make assurance doubly sure I resolved upon a tour through the shrubbery outside, that I might compare the location of the window having the chipped blind with that of this room, which was, as well as I could calculate, the third from the rear on the left-hand side.

When, therefore, William called up to know if I was ready for my drive, I answered back that I found myself very tired and would be glad to exchange the pleasure he offered, for a visit to the stables.

This, as I expected, caused considerable comment and some disturbance. They wanted me to repeat my experience of the day before and spend two if not more hours of the morning out of the house. But I did not mean to gratify them. Indeed I felt that my duty held me to the house, and was so persistent in my wishes, or rather in my declaration of them, that all opposition had to give way, even in the stubborn William.

"I thought you had a dread of dogs," was the final remark with which he endeavored to turn me aside from my purpose. "I have three in the barn and two in the stable, and they make a great fuss when I come around, I assure you."

"Then they will have enough to do without noticing me," said I, with a brazen assumption of courage sufficiently surprising if I had had any real intention of invading a place so guarded. But I had not. I no more meant to enter the stables than to jump off the housetop, but it was necessary that I should start for them and make the start from the left wing of the house.

How I managed the intractable William and led him as I did from bush to bush and shrub to shrub, up and down the length of that interminable façade of the left wing, would make an interesting story in itself. The curiosity I showed in plants, even such plants as had survived the neglect that had made a wilderness of this old-time garden; the indifference which, contrary to all my habits, I persisted in manifesting to every inconvenience I encountered in the way of straightforward walking to any object I set my fancy upon examining; the knowledge I exhibited, and the interest which I took it for granted he felt in all I discovered and all I imparted to him, would form the basis of a farce of no ordinary merit had it not had its birth in interests and intents bordering on the tragic.

A row of bushes of various species ran along the wall and covered in some instances the lower ledges of the first row of windows. As I made for a certain shrub which I had observed growing near what I supposed to be the casement from whose blind I had chipped a small sliver, I allowed my enthusiasm to bubble over, in my evident desire to display my erudition.

"This," said I, "is, without any doubt at all, a stunted but undoubted specimen of that rare tree found seldom north of the thirtieth degree, the Magnolia grandiflora. I have never seen it but once before, and that was in the botanical gardens in Washington. Note its leaves. You have noted its flowers, smaller undoubtedly than they should be—but then you must acknowledge it has been in a measure neglected—are they not fine?"

Here I pulled a branch down which interfered with my view of the window. There was no chip visible in the blinds thus discovered. Seeing this, I let the branch go. "But the oddest feature of this tree and one with which you are perhaps not acquainted" (I wonder if anybody is?) "is that it will not grow within twenty feet of any plant which scatters pollen. See for yourself. This next shrub bears no flower" (I was moving along the wall), "nor this." I drew down a branch as I spoke, caught sight of the mark I was looking for, and let the bough spring back. I had found the window I wanted.

His grunts and groans during all this formed a running accompaniment which would have afforded me great secret amusement had my purpose been less serious. As it was, I could pay but little attention to him, especially after I had stepped back far enough to take a glance at the window over the one I had just located as that of the Flower Parlor. It was, as I expected, the third one from the rear corner; but it was not this fact which gave me a thrill of feeling so strong that I have never had harder work to preserve my equanimity. It was the knot of black crape with which the shutters were tied together.

XX QUESTIONS

I kept the promise I had made to myself and did not go to the stables. Had I intended to go there, I could not have done so after the discovery I have just mentioned. It awakened too many thoughts and contradictory surmises. If this knot was a signal, for whom was this signal meant? If it was a mere acknowledgment of death, how reconcile the sentimentality which prompted such an acknowledgment with the monstrous and diseased passions lying at the base of the whole dreadful occurrence? Lastly, if it was the result of pure carelessness, a bit of crape having been caught up and used for a purpose for which any ordinary string would have answered, what a wonderful coincidence between it and my thoughts,—a coincidence, indeed, amounting almost to miracle!

Marvelling at the whole affair and deciding nothing, I allowed myself to stroll down alone to the gate, William having left me at my peremptory refusal to drag my skirts any longer through the briers. The day being bright and the sunshine warm, the road looked less gloomy than usual, especially in the direction of the village and Deacon Spear's cottage. The fact is, that anything seemed better than the grim and lowering walls of the house behind me. If my home was there, so was my dread, and I welcomed the sight of Mother Jane's heavy figure bent over her herbs at the door of her hut, a few paces to my left, where the road turned.

Had she not been deaf, I believed I would have called her. As it was, I contented myself with watching the awkward swayings of her body as she pottered to and fro among her turnips and carrots. My eyes were still on her when I suddenly heard the clatter of a horse's hoofs on the highway. Looking up, I encountered the trim figure of Mr. Trohm, bending to me from a fine sorrel.

"Good morning, Miss Butterworth. It's a great relief to me to see you in such good health and spirits this morning," were the pleasant words with which he endeavored, perhaps, to explain his presence in a spot more or less under a ban.

It was certainly a surprise. What right had I to look for such attentions from a man whose acquaintance I had made only the day before? It touched me, little as I am in the habit of allowing myself to be ruled by trivial sentimentalities, and though I was discreet enough to avoid any further recognition of his kindness than was his due from a lady of great self-respect, he was evidently sufficiently gratified by my response to draw rein and pause for a moment's conversation under the pine trees. This for the moment seemed so natural that I forgot that more than one pair of eyes might be watching me from the windows behind us—eyes which might wonder at a meeting which to the foolish understandings of the young might have the look of premeditation. But, pshaw! I am talking as if I were twenty instead of— Well, I will leave you to consult our family record on that point. There are certain secrets which even the wisest among us cannot be blamed for preserving.

"How did you pass the night?" was Mr. Trohm's first question. "I hope in all due peace and quiet."

"Thank you," I returned, not seeing why I should increase his anxiety in my regard. "I have nothing to complain of. I had a dream; but dreams are to be expected where one has to pass a half-dozen empty rooms to one's apartment."

He could not restrain his curiosity.

"A dream!" he repeated. "I do not believe in sleep that is broken by dreams, unless they are of the most cheerful sort possible. And I judge from what you say that yours were not cheerful."

I wanted to confide in him. I felt that in a way he had a right to know what had happened to me, or what I thought had happened to me, under this roof. And yet I did not speak. What I could tell would sound so puerile in the broad sunshine that enveloped us. I merely remarked that cheerfulness was not to be expected in a domicile so given over to the ravages of time, and then with that lightness and versatility which characterize me under certain exigencies, I introduced a topic we could discuss without any embarrassment to himself or me.

"Do you see Mother Jane over there?" I asked. "I had some talk with her yesterday. She seems like a harmless imbecile."

"Very harmless," he acquiesced; "her only fault is greed; that is insatiable. Yet it is not strong enough to take her a quarter of a mile from this place. Nothing could do that, I think. She believes that her daughter Lizzie is still alive and will come back to the hut some day. It's very sad when you think that the girl's dead, and has been dead nearly forty years."

"Why does she harp on numbers?" I asked. "I heard her mutter certain ones over and over."

"That is a mystery none of us have ever been able to solve," said he. "Possibly she has no reason for it. The vagaries of the witless are often quite unaccountable."

He remained looking at me long after he had finished speaking, not, I felt sure, from any connection he found between what he had just said and anything to be observed in me, but from—Well, I was glad that I had been carefully trained in my youth to pay the greatest attention to my morning toilets. Any woman can look well at night and many women in the flush of a bright afternoon, but the woman who looks well in the morning needs not always to be young to attract the appreciative gaze of a man of real penetration. Mr. Trohm was such a man, and I did not begrudge him the pleasure he showed in my neat gray silk and carefully adjusted collar. But he said nothing, and a short silence ensued, which was perhaps more of a compliment than otherwise. Then he uttered a short sigh and lifted the reins.

"If only I were not debarred from entering," he smiled, with a short gesture toward the house.

I did not answer. Even I understand that on occasion the tongue plays but a sorry part in interviews of this nature.

He sighed again and uttered some short encouragement to his horse, which started that animal up and sent him slowly pacing down the road toward the cheerful clearing whither my own eyes were looking with what I was determined should not be construed even by the most sanguine into a glance of anything like wistfulness. As he went he made a bow I have never seen surpassed in my own parlor in Gramercy Park, and upon my bestowing upon him a return nod, glanced up at the house with an intentness which seemed to increase as some object, invisible to me at that moment, caught his eye. As that eye was directed toward the left wing, and lifted as far as the second row of windows, I could not help asking myself if he had seen the knot of crape which had produced upon me so lugubrious an impression. Before I could make sure of this he had passed from sight, and the highway fell again into shadow—why, I hardly knew, for the sun certainly had been shining a few minutes before.

XXI   MOTHER JANE

"Well, well, what did Trohm want here this morning?" cried a harsh voice from amid the tangled walks behind me. "Seems to me he finds this place pretty interesting all of a sudden."

I turned upon the intruder with a look that should have daunted him. I had recognized William's courteous tones and was in no mood to endure a questioning so unbecoming in one of his age to one of mine. But as I met his eye, which had something in it besides anger and suspicion—something that was quizzical if not impertinent—I changed my intention and bestowed upon him a conciliatory smile, which I hope escaped the eye of the good angel who records against man all his small hypocrisies and petty deceits.

"Mr. Trohm rides for his health," said I. "Seeing me looking up the road at Mother Jane, he stopped to tell me some of the idiosyncrasies of that old woman. A very harmless courtesy, Mr. Knollys."

"Very," he echoed, not without a touch of sarcasm. "I only hope that is all," he muttered, with a sidelong look back at the house. "Lucetta hasn't a particle of belief in that man's friendship, or, rather, she believes he never goes anywhere without a particular intention, and I do believe she's right, or why should he come spying around here just at a time when"—he caught himself up with almost a look of terror—"when—when you are here?" he completed lamely.

"I do not think," I retorted, more angrily than the occasion perhaps warranted, "that the word spying applies to Mr. Trohm. But if it does, what has he to gain from a pause at the gate and a word to such a new acquaintance as I am?"

"I don't know," William persisted suspiciously. "Trohm's a sharp fellow. If there was anything to see, he would see it without half looking. But there isn't. You don't know of anything wrong here, do you, which such a man as that, hand in glove with the police as we know him to be, might consider himself interested in?"

Astonished both at this blundering committal of himself and at the certain sort of anxious confidence he showed in me, I hesitated for a moment, but only for a moment, since, if half my suspicions were true, this man must not know that my perspicacity was more to be feared than even Mr. Trohm's was.

"If Mr. Trohm shows an increased interest in this household during the last two days," said I, with a heroic defiance of ridicule which I hope Mr. Gryce has duly appreciated, "I beg leave to call your attention to the fact that on yesterday morning he came to deliver a letter addressed to me which had inadvertently been left at his house, and that this morning he called to inquire how I had spent the night, which, in consideration of the ghosts which are said to haunt this house and the strange and uncanny apparitions which only three nights ago made the entrance to this lane hideous to one pair of eyes at least, should not cause a gentleman's son like yourself any astonishment. It does not seem odd to me, I assure you."

He laughed. I meant he should, and, losing almost instantly his air of doubt and suspicion, turned toward the gate from which I had just moved away, muttering:

"Well, it's a small matter to me anyway. It's only the girls that are afraid of Mr. Trohm. I am not afraid of anything but losing Saracen, who has pined like the deuce at his long confinement in the court. Hear him now; just hear him."

And I could hear the low and unhappy moaning of the hound distinctly. It was not a pleasant sound, and I was almost tempted to bid William unloose the dog, but thought better of it.

"By the way," said he, "speaking of Mother Jane, I have a message to her from the girls. You will excuse me if I speak to the poor woman."

Alarmed by his politeness more than I ever have been by his roughness and inconsiderate sarcasms, I surveyed him inquiringly as he left the gate, and did not know whether to stand my ground or retreat to the house. I decided to stand my ground; a message to this woman seeming to me a matter of some interest.

I was glad I did, for after some five minutes' absence, during which he had followed her into the house, I saw him come back again in a state of sullen displeasure, which, however, partially disappeared when he saw me still standing by the gate.

"Ah, Miss Butterworth, you can do me a favor. The old creature is in one of her stubborn fits to-day, and won't give me a hearing. She may not be so deaf to you; she isn't apt to be to women. Will you cross the road and speak to her? I will go with you. You needn't be afraid."

The way he said this, the confidence he expected to inspire, had almost a ghastly effect upon me. Did he know or suspect that the only thing I feared in this lane was he? Evidently not, for he met my eye quite confidently.

It would not do to shake his faith at such a moment as this, so calling upon Providence to see me safely through this adventure, I stepped into the highway and went with him into Mother Jane's cottage.

Had I been favored with any other companion than himself, I should have been glad of this opportunity. As it was, I found myself ignoring any possible danger I might be running, in my interest in the remarkable interior to which I was thus introduced.

Having been told that Mother Jane was poor, I had expected to confront squalor and possibly filth, but I never have entered a cleaner place or one in which order made the poorest belongings look more decent. The four walls were unfinished, and so were the rafters which formed the ceiling, but the floor, neatly laid in brick, was spotless, and the fireplace, also of brick, was as deftly swept as one could expect from the little scrub I saw hanging by its side. Crouched within this fireplace sat the old woman we had come to interview. Her back was to us, and she looked helplessly and hopelessly deaf.

"Ask her," said William, pointing towards her with a rude gesture, "if she will come to the house at sunset. My sisters have some work for her to do. They will pay her well."

Advancing at his bidding, I passed a rocking-chair, in the cushion of which a dozen patches met my eye. This drew my eyes toward a bed, over which a counterpane was drawn, made up of a thousand or more pieces of colored calico, and noticing their varied shapes and the intricacy with which they were put together, I wondered whether she ever counted them. The next moment I was at her back.

"Seventy," burst from her lips as I leaned over her shoulder and showed her the coin which I had taken pains to have in my hand.

"Yours," I announced, pointing in the direction of the house, "if you will do some work for Miss Knollys to-night."

Slowly she shook her head before burying it deeper in the shawl she wore wrapped about her shoulders. Listening a minute, I thought I heard her mutter: "Twenty-eight, ten, but no more. I can count no more. Go away!"

But I'm nothing if not persistent. Feeling for her hands, which were hidden away somewhere under her shawl, I touched them with the coin and cried again:

"This and more for a small piece of work to-night. Come, you are strong; earn it."

"What kind of work is it?" I asked innocently, or it must have appeared innocently, of Mr. Knollys, who was standing at my back.

He frowned, all the black devils in his heart coming into his look at once.

"How do I know! Ask Loreen; she's the one who sent me. I don't take account of what goes on in the kitchen."

I begged his pardon, somewhat sarcastically I own, and made another attempt to attract the attention of the old crone, who had remained perfectly callous to my allurements.

"I thought you liked money," I said. "For Lizzie, you know, for Lizzie."

But she only muttered in lower and lower gutturals, "I can count no more"; and, disgusted at my failure, being one who accounts failure as little short of disgrace, I drew back and made my way toward the door, saying: "She's in a different mood from what she was yesterday when she snatched a quarter from me at the first intimation it was hers. I don't think you can get her to do any work to-night. Innocents take these freaks. Isn't there some one else you can call in?"

The scowl that disfigured his none too handsome features was a fitting prelude to his words.

"You talk," said he, "as if we had the whole village at our command. How did you succeed with the locksmith yesterday? Came, didn't he? Well, that's what we have to expect whenever we want any help."

Whirling on his heel, he led the way out of the hut, whither I would have immediately followed him if I had not stopped to take another look at the room, which struck me, even upon a second scrutiny, as one of the best ordered and best kept I had ever entered. Even the strings and strings of dried fruits and vegetables, which hung in festoons from every beam of the roof, were free from dust and cobwebs, and though the dishes were few and the pans scarce, they were bright and speckless, giving to the shelf along which they were ranged a semblance of ornament.

"Wise enough to keep her house in order," thought I, and actually found it hard to leave, so attractive to my eyes are absolute neatness and order.

William was pushing at his own gate when I joined him. He looked as if he wished I had spent the morning with Mother Jane, and was barely civil in our walk up to the house. I was not, therefore, surprised when he burst into a volley of oaths at the doorway and turned upon me almost as if he would forbid me the house, for tap, tap, tap, from some distant quarter came a distinct sound like that of nails being driven into a plank.

XXII   THE THIRD NIGHT

Mother Jane must have changed her mind after we left her. For late in the evening I caught a glimpse of her burly figure in the kitchen as I went to give Hannah some instructions concerning certain little changes in the housekeeping arrangements which the girls and I had agreed were necessary to our mutual comfort.

I wished to address the old crone, but warned, by the ill-concealed defiance with which Hannah met my advances, that any such attempt on my part would be met by anything but her accustomed good-nature, I refrained from showing my interest in her strange visitor, or from even appearing conscious of her own secret anxieties and evident preoccupation.

Loreen and Lucetta exchanged a meaning look as I rejoined them in the sitting-room; but my volubility in regard to the domestic affair which had just taken me to the kitchen seemed to speedily reassure them, and when a few minutes later I said good-night and prepared to leave the room, it was with the conviction that I had relieved their mind at the expense of my own. Mother Jane in the kitchen at this late hour meant business. What that business was, I seemed to know only too well.

I had formed a plan for the night which required some courage. Recalling Lucetta's expression of the morning, that I might expect a repetition of the former night's experiences, I prepared to profit by the warning in a way she little meant. Satisfied that if there was any truth in the suspicions I had formed, there would be an act performed in this house to-night which, if seen by me, would forever settle the question agitating the whole countryside, I made up my mind that no locked door should interfere with my opportunity of doing so. How I effected this result I will presently relate.

Lucetta had accompanied me to my door with a lighted candle.

"I hear you had some trouble with matches last night," said she. "You will find them all right now. Hannah must be blamed for some of this carelessness." Then as I began some reassuring reply, she turned upon me with a look that was almost fond, and, throwing out her arms, cried entreatingly: "Won't you give me a little kiss, Miss Butterworth? We have not given you the best of welcomes, but you are my mother's old friend, and sometimes I feel a little lonely."

I could easily believe that, and yet I found it hard to embrace her. Too many shadows swam between Althea's children and myself. She saw my hesitancy (a hesitancy I could not but have shown even at the risk of losing her confidence), and, paling slightly, dropped her hands with a pitiful smile.

"You don't like me," she said. "I do not wonder, but I was in hopes you would for my mother's sake. I have no claims myself."

"You are an interesting girl, and you have, what your mother had not, a serious side to your nature that is anything but displeasing to me. But my kisses, Lucetta, are as rare as my tears. I had rather give you good advice, and that is a fact. Perhaps it is as strong a proof of affection as any ordinary caress would be."

"Perhaps," she assented, but she did not encourage me to give it to her notwithstanding. Instead of that, she drew back and bade me a gentle good-night, which for some reason made me sadder than I wished to be at a crisis demanding so much nerve. Then she walked quickly away, and I was left to face the night alone.

Knowing that I should be rather weakened than helped by the omission of any of the little acts of preparation with which I am accustomed to calm my spirits for the night, I went through them all, with just as much precision as if I had expected to spend the ensuing hours in rest. When all was done and only my cup of tea remained to be quaffed, I had a little struggle with myself, which ended in my not drinking it at all. Nothing, not even this comfortable solace for an unsatisfactory day, should stand in the way of my being the complete mistress of my wits this night. Had I known that this tea contained a soporific in the shape of a little harmless morphine, I would have found this act of self-denial much easier.

It was now eleven. Confident that nothing would be done while my light was burning, I blew it out, and, taking a candle and some matches in my hand, softly opened my door and, after a moment of intense listening, stepped out and closed it carefully behind me. Nothing could be stiller than the house or darker than the corridor.

"Am I watched or am I not watched?" I queried, and for an instant stood undecided. Then, seeing nothing and hearing nothing, I slipped down the hall to the door beyond mine and, opening it with all the care possible, stepped inside.

I knew the room. I had taken especial note of it in my visit of the morning. I knew that it was nearly empty and that there was a key in the lock which I could turn. I therefore felt more or less safe in it, especially as its window was undarkened by the branches that hung so thickly across my own casement, shutting me in, or seeming to shut me in, from all communication with the outside world and the unknown guardian which I had been assured constantly attended my summons.

That I might strengthen my spirits by one glimpse of this same outside world, before settling down for the watch I had set for myself, I stepped softly to the window and took one lingering look without. A belt of forest illumined by a gibbous moon met my eyes; nothing else. Yet this sight was welcome, and it was only after I had been struck by the possibility of my own figure being seen at the casement by some possible watcher in the shadows below, that I found the hardihood necessary to withdraw into the darker precincts of the room, and begin that lonely watch which my doubts and expectations rendered necessary.

This was the third I had been forced to keep, and it was by far the most dismal; for though the bolted door between me and the hall promised me personal safety, there presently rose in some far-off place a smothered repetition of that same tap, tap, tap which had sent the shudders over me upon my sudden entrance into the house early in the morning. Heard now, it caused me to tremble in a way I had not supposed possible to one of my hardy nature, and while with this recognition of my feminine susceptibility to impressions there came a certain pride in the stanchness of purpose which led me to restrain all acknowledgment of fear, by any recourse to my whistle, I was more than glad when even this sound ceased, and I had only to expect the swishing noise of a skirt down the hall, and that stealthy locking of the door of the room I had taken the precaution of leaving.

It came sooner than I expected, came just in the way it had previously done, only that the person paused a moment to listen before hastening back. The silence within must have satisfied her, for I heard a low sigh like that of relief, before the steps took themselves back. That they would turn my way gave me a momentary concern, but I had too completely lulled my young hostesses' suspicions, or (let me be faithful to all the possibilities of the case) they had put too much confidence in the powder with which they had seasoned my nightly cup of tea, for them to doubt that I was soundly asleep in my own quarters.

Three minutes later I followed those steps as far down the corridor as I dared to go. For, since my last appearance in it, a candle had been lit in the main hall, and faint as was its glimmer, it was still a glimmer into the circle of which I felt it would be foolhardiness for me to step. At some twenty paces, then, from the opening, I paused and gave myself up to listening. Alas, there was plenty now for me to hear.

You have heard the sound; we all have heard the sound, but few of us in such a desolate structure and at the hour and under the influences of midnight! The measured tread of men struggling under a heavy weight, and that weight—how well I knew it! as well as if I had seen it, as I really did in my imagination.

They advanced from the adjoining corridor, from the room I had as yet found no opportunity of entering, and they approached surely and slowly the main hall near which I was standing in such a position as rendered it impossible for me to see anything if they took the direct course to the head of the stairs and so down, as there was every reason to expect they would. I did not dare to draw nearer, however, so concentrated my faculties anew upon listening, when suddenly I perceived on the great white wall in front of me—the wall of the main hall, I mean, toward which the opening looked—the shapeless outline of a drooping head, and realized that the candle had been placed in such a position that the wall must receive the full shadow of the passing cortège.

And thus it was I saw it, huge, distorted, and suggestive beyond any picture I ever beheld,—the passing of a body to its long home, carried by six anxious figures, four of which seemed to be those of women.

But that long home! Where was it located—in the house or in the grounds? It was a question so important that for a moment I could think of nothing but how I could follow the small procession, without running the risk of discovery. It had reached the head of the stairs by this time, and I heard Miss Knollys' low, firm voice enjoining silence. Then the six bearers began to descend with their burden.

Ere they reached the foot, a doubt struck me. Would it be better to follow them or to take the opportunity afforded by every member of the household being engaged in this task, to take a peep into the room where the death had occurred? I had not decided, when I heard them take the forward course from the foot of the stairs to what, to my straining ear, seemed to be the entrance to the dining-room corridor. But as in my anxiety to determine this fact I slipped far enough forward to make sure that their destination lay somewhere within reach of the Flower Parlor, I was so struck by the advantages to be gained by a cautious use of the trap-door in William's room, that I hesitated no longer, but sped with what swiftness I could toward the spot from which I had so lately heard this strange procession advance.

A narrow band of light lying across the upper end of the long corridor, proved that the door was not only ajar, but that a second candle was burning in the room I was about to invade; but this was scarcely to be regretted, since there could be no question of the emptiness of the room. The six figures I had seen go by embraced every one who by any possibility could be considered as having part in this transaction—William, Mr. Simsbury, Miss Knollys, Lucetta, Hannah, and Mother Jane. No one else was left to guard this room, so I pushed the door open quite boldly and entered.

What I saw there I will relate later, or, rather, I will but hint at now. A bed with a sheet thrown back, a stand covered with vials, a bureau with a man's shaving paraphernalia upon it, and on the wall such pictures as only sporting gentlemen delight in. The candle was guttering on a small table upon which, to my astonishment, a Bible lay open. Not having my glasses with me, I could not see what portion of the sacred word was thus disclosed, but I took the precaution to indent the upper leaf with my thumb-nail, so that I might find it again in case of future opportunity. My attention was attracted by other small matters that would be food for thought at a more propitious moment, but at that instant the sound of voices coming distinctly to my ear from below, warned me that a halt had been made at the Flower Parlor, and that the duty of the moment was to locate the trap-door and if possible determine the means of raising it.

This was less difficult than I anticipated. Either this room was regarded as so safe from intrusion that a secret like this could be safely left unguarded, or the door which was plainly to be seen in one corner had been so lately lifted, that it had hardly sunk back into its place. I found it, if the expression may be used of a horizontal object, slightly ajar and needing but the slightest pull to make it spring upright.

The hole thus disclosed was filled with the little staircase up which I had partly mounted in my daring explorations of the day before. It was dark now, darker than it was then, but I felt that I must descend by it, for plainly to be heard now through the crack in the closet door, which seemed to have a knack of standing partly open, I could hear the heavy tread of the six bearers as they entered the parlor below, still carrying their burden, concerning the destination of which I was so anxious to be informed.

That it could be in the room itself was too improbable for consideration. Yet if they took up their stand in this room it was for a purpose, and what that purpose was I was determined to know. The noise their feet made on the bare boards of the floor and the few words I now heard uttered in William's stolid tones and Lucetta's musical treble assured me that my own light steps would no more be heard, than my dark gown of quiet wool would be seen through the narrow slit through which I was preparing to peer. Yet it took no small degree of what my father used to call pluck, for me to put foot on this winding staircase and descend almost, as it were, into the midst of what I must regard as the last wicked act of a most cowardly and brutal murder.

I did it, however, and after a short but grim communion with my own heart, which would persist in beating somewhat noisily, I leaned forward with all the precaution possible and let my gaze traverse the chamber in which I had previously seen such horrors as should have prepared me for this last and greatest one.

In a moment I understood the whole. A long square hole in the floor, lately sawed, provided an opening through which the plain plank coffin, of which I now caught sight, was to be lowered into the cellar and so into the grave which had doubtless been dug there. The ropes in the hands of the six persons, in whose identity I had made no mistake, was proof enough of their intention; and, satisfied as I now was of the means and mode of the interment which had been such a boundless mystery to me, I shrank a step upward, fearing lest my indignation and the horror I could not but feel, from this moment on, of Althea's children, would betray me into some exclamation which might lead to my discovery and a similar fate.

One other short glance, in which I saw them all ranged around the dark opening, and I was up out of their reach, Lucetta's face and Lucetta's one sob as the ropes began to creak, being the one memory which followed me the most persistently. She, at least, was overwhelmed with remorse for a deed she was perhaps only answerable for in that she failed to make known to the world her brother's madness and the horrible crimes to which it gave rise.

I took one other look around his room before I fled to my own, or rather, to the one in which I had taken refuge while my own was under lock and key. That I spent the next two hours on my knees no one can wonder. When my own room was unlocked, as it was before the day broke, I hastened to enter it and lay my head with all its unhappy knowledge on my pillow. But I did not sleep; and, what was stranger still, never once thought of sounding a single note on the whistle which would have brought the police into this abode of crime. Perhaps it was a wise omission. I had seen enough that was horrible that night without beholding Althea's children arrested before my eyes.

BOOK III   FORWARD AND BACK

XXIII   ROOM 3, HOTEL CARTER

I rose at my usual hour. I dressed myself with my usual care. I was, to a superficial observer at least, in all respects my usual self when Hannah came to my door to ask what she could do for me. As there was nothing I wanted but to get out of this house, which had become unbearable to me, I replied with the utmost cheerfulness that my wants were all supplied and that I would soon be down, at which she answered that in that case she must bestir herself or the breakfast would not be ready, and hurried away.

There was no one in the dining-room when I entered, and judging from appearances that several minutes must elapse before breakfast would be ready, I took occasion to stroll through the grounds and glance up at the window of William's room. The knot of crape was gone.

I would have gone farther, but just then I heard a great rushing and scampering, and, looking up, saw an enormous dog approaching at full gallop from the stables. Saracen was loose.

I did not scream or give way to other feminine expressions of fear, but I did return as quickly as possible to the house, where I now saw I must remain till William chose to take me into town.

This I was determined should take place as soon after breakfast as practicable. The knowledge which I now possessed warranted, nay, demanded, instant consultation with the police, and as this could best be effected by following out the orders I had received from Mr. Gryce, I did not consider any other plan than that of meeting the man on duty in Room No. 3 at the hotel.

Loreen, Lucetta, and William were awaiting me in the hall, and made no apology for the flurry into which I had been thrown by my rapid escape from Saracen. Indeed I doubt if they noticed it, for with all the attempt they made to seem gay and at ease, the anxieties and fatigue of the foregoing nights were telling upon them, and from Miss Knollys down, they looked physically exhausted. But they also looked mentally relieved. In the clear depths of Lucetta's eye there was now no wavering, and the head which was always turning in anxious anticipation over her shoulder rested firm, though not as erect as her sister's, who had less cause perhaps for regret and sorrow.

William was joyful to a degree, but it was a forced joviality which only became real when he heard a sudden, quick bark under the window and the sound of scraping paws against the mastic coating of the wall outside. Then he broke out into a loud laugh of unrestrained pleasure, crying out thoughtlessly:

"There's Saracen. How quick he knows——"

A warning look from Lucetta stopped him.

"I mean," he stammered, "it's a dull dog that cannot find his master. Miss Butterworth, you will have to overcome your fear of dogs if you stay with us long. Saracen is unbound this morning, and"—he used a great oath—"he's going to remain so."

By which I came to understand that it was not out of consideration for me he had been tied up in the court till now, but for reasons connected with their own safety and the preservation of the secret which they so evidently believed had been buried with the body, which I did not like to remember lay at that very minute too nearly under our feet for my own individual comfort.

However, this has nothing to do with the reply I made to William.

"I hope he does not run with the buggy," I objected. "I want to take a ride very much this morning and could get small pleasure out of it if that dog must be our companion."

"I cannot go out this morning," William began, but changed his sentence, possibly at the touch of his sister's foot under the table, into: "But if you say I must, why, I must. You women folks are so plagued unreasonable."

Had he been ten years younger I would have boxed his ears; had he been that much older I would have taken cue and packed my trunk before he could have finished the cup of coffee he was drinking. But he was just too old to reprimand in the way just mentioned, and not old enough to appreciate any display of personal dignity or self-respect on the part of the person he had offended. Besides, he was a knave; so I just let his impertinence pass with the remark:

"I have purchases to make in the village": and so that matter ended, manifestly to the two girls' relief, who naturally did not like to see me insulted, even if they did not possess sufficient power over their brother to prevent it.

One other small episode and then I will take you with me to the village. As we were leaving the table, where I ate less than common, notwithstanding all my efforts to seem perfectly unconcerned, Lucetta, who had waited for her brother to go out, took me gently by the arm, and, eying me closely, said:

"Did you have any dreams last night, Miss Butterworth? You know I promised you some."

The question disconcerted me, and for a moment I felt like taking the two girls into my confidence and bidding them fly from the shame and doom so soon to fall upon their brother; but the real principle underlying all such momentary impulses on my part deterred me, and in as light a tone as I could command and not be an absolute hypocrite, I replied that I was sorry to disappoint her, but I had had no dreams, which seemed to please her more than it should, for if I had had no dreams I certainly had suffered from the most frightful realities.

I will not describe our ride into town. Saracen did go with us, and indignation not only rendered me speechless, but gave to my thoughts a turn which made that half-hour of very little value to me. Mother Jane's burly figure crouching in her doorway might otherwise have given me opportunity for remark, and so might the dubious looks of people we met on the highroad—looks to which I am so wholly unaccustomed that I had difficulty in recognizing myself as the butt of so much doubt and possibly dislike. I attributed this, however, all to the ill repute under which William so deservedly labored, and did not allow myself to more than notice it. Indeed, I could only be sorry for people who did not know in what consideration I was held at home, and who, either through ignorance or prejudice, allowed themselves privileges they would be the first to regret did they know the heart and mind of Amelia Butterworth.

Once in the village, I took the direction of affairs.

"Set me down at the hotel," I commanded, "and then go about such business as you may have here in town. I am not going to allow myself to be tracked all over by that dog."

"I have no business," was the surly reply.

"Then make some," was my sharp retort. "I want to see the locksmith—that locksmith who wouldn't come to do an honest piece of work for me in your house; and I want to buy dimities and wools and sewing silks at the dry-goods store over there. Indeed I have a thousand things to do, and expect to spend half the morning before the counters. Why, man, I haven't done any shopping for a week."

He gaped at me perfectly aghast (as I meant he should), and, having but little experience of city ladies, took me at my word and prepared to beat an honorable retreat. As a result, I found myself ten minutes later standing on the top step of the hotel porch, watching William driving away with Saracen perched on the seat beside him. Then I realized that the village held no companions for him, and did not know whether I felt glad or sorry.

To the clerk who came to meet me, I said quietly, "Room No. 3, if you please," at which he gave a nod of intelligence and led me as unostentatiously as possible into a small hall, at the end of which I saw a door with the aforesaid number on it.

"If you will take a seat inside," said he, "I will send you whatever you may desire for your comfort."

"I think you know what that is," I rejoined, at which he nodded again and left me, closing the door carefully behind him as he went.

The few minutes which elapsed before my quiet was disturbed were spent by me in thinking. There were many little questions to settle in my own mind, for which a spell of uninterrupted contemplation was necessary. One of these was whether, in the event of finding the police amenable, I should reveal or hide from these children of my old friend, the fact that it was through my instrumentality that their nefarious secret had been discovered. I wished—nay, I hoped—that the affair might be so concluded, but the possibility of doing so seemed so problematical, especially since Mr. Gryce was not on hand to direct matters, that I spent very little time on the subject, deep and important as it was to all concerned.

What most occupied me was the necessity of telling my story in such a way as to exonerate the girls as much as possible. They were mistaken in their devotion and most unhappy in the exercise of it, but they were not innately wicked and should not be made to appear so. Perhaps the one thing for which I should yet have the best cause to congratulate myself, would be the opportunity I had gained of giving to their connection with this affair its true and proper coloring.

I was still dwelling on this thought when there came a knock at my door which advised me that the visitor I expected had arrived. To open and admit him was the work of a moment, but it took more than a moment for me to overcome my surprise at seeing in my visitor no lesser person than Mr. Gryce himself, who in our parting interview had assured me he was too old and too feeble for further detective work and must therefore delegate it to me.

"Ah!" I ejaculated slowly. "It is you, is it? Well, I am not surprised." (I shouldn't have been.) "When you say you are old, you mean old enough to pull the wool over other people's eyes, and when you say you are lame, you mean that you only halt long enough to let others get far enough ahead for them not to see how fast you hobble up behind them. But do not think I am not happy to see you. I am, Mr. Gryce, for I have discovered the secret of Lost Man's Lane, and find it somewhat too heavy a one for my own handling."

To my surprise he showed this was more than he expected.

"You have?" he asked, with just that shade of incredulity which it is so tantalizing to encounter. "Then I suppose congratulations are in order. But are you sure, Miss Butterworth, that you really have obtained a clue to the many strange and fearful disappearances which have given to this lane its name?"

"Quite sure," I returned, nettled. "Why do you doubt it? Because I have kept so quiet and not sounded one note of alarm from my whistle?"

"No," said he. "Knowing your self-restraint so well, I cannot say that that is my reason."

"What is it, then?" I urged.

"Well," said he, "my real reason for doubting if you have been quite as successful as you think, is that we ourselves have come upon a clue about which there can be no question. Can you say the same of yours?"

You will expect my answer to have been a decided "Yes," uttered with all the positiveness of which you know me capable. But for some reason, perhaps because of the strange influence this man's personality exercises upon all—yes, all—who do not absolutely steel themselves against him, I faltered just long enough for him to cry:

"I thought not. The clue is outside the Knollys house, not in it, Miss Butterworth, for which, of course, you are not to be blamed or your services scorned. I have no doubt they have been invaluable in unearthing a secret, if not the secret."

"Thank you," was my quiet retort. I thought his presumption beyond all bounds, and would at that moment have felt justified in snapping my fingers at the clue he boasted of, had it not been for one thing. What that thing is I am not ready yet to state.

"You and I have come to issue over such matters before," said he, "and therefore need not take too much account of the feelings it is likely to engender. I will merely state that my clue points to Mother Jane, and ask if you have found in the visit she paid at the house last night anything which would go to strengthen the suspicion against her."

"Perhaps," said I, in a state of disdain that was more or less unpardonable, considering that my own suspicions previous to my discovery of the real tragedy enacted under my eyes at the Knollys mansion had played more or less about this old crone.

"Only perhaps?" He smiled, with a playful forbearance for which I should have been truly grateful to him.

"She was there for no good purpose," said I, "and yet if you had not characterized her as the person most responsible for the crimes we are here to investigate, I should have said from all that I then saw of her conduct that she acted as a supernumerary rather than principal, and that it is to me you should look for the correct clue to the criminal, notwithstanding your confidence in your own theories and my momentary hesitation to assert that there was no possible defect in mine."

"Miss Butterworth,"—I thought he looked a trifle shaken,—"what did Mother Jane do in that closely shuttered house last night?"

Mother Jane? Well! Did he think I was going to introduce my tragic story by telling what Mother Jane did? I must have looked irritated, and indeed I think I had cause.

"Mother Jane ate her supper," I snapped out angrily. "Miss Knollys gave it to her. Then she helped a little with a piece of work they had on hand. It will not interest you to know what. It has nothing to do with your clue, I warrant."

He did not get angry. He has an admirable temper, has Mr. Gryce, but he did stop a minute to consider.

"Miss Butterworth," he said at last, "most detectives would have held their peace and let you go on with what you have to tell without a hint that it was either unwelcome or unnecessary, but I have consideration for persons' feelings and for persons' secrets so long as they do not come in collision with the law, and my opinion is, or was when I entered this room, that such discoveries as you have made at your old friend's house" (Why need he emphasize friend—did he think I forgot for a moment that Althea was my friend?) "were connected rather with some family difficulty than with the dreadful affair we are considering. That is why I hastened to tell you that we had found a clue to the disappearances in Mother Jane's cottage. I wished to save the Misses Knollys."

If he had thought to mollify me by this assertion, he did not succeed. He saw it and made haste to say:

"Not that I doubt your consideration for them, only the justness of your conclusions."

"You have doubted those before and with more reason," I replied, "yet they were not altogether false."

"That I am willing to acknowledge, so willing that if you still think after I have told my story that yours is apropos, then I will listen to it only too eagerly. My object is to find the real criminal in this matter. I say at the present moment it is Mother Jane."

"God grant you are right," I said, influenced in spite of myself by the calm assurance of his manner. "If she was at the house night before last between eleven and twelve, then perhaps she is all you think her. But I see no reason to believe it—not yet, Mr. Gryce. Supposing you give me one. It would be better than all this controversy. One small reason, Mr. Gryce, as good as"—I did not say what, but the fillip it gave to his intention stood me in good stead, for he launched immediately into the matter with no further play upon my curiosity, which was now, as you can believe, thoroughly aroused, though I could not believe that anything he had to bring up against Mother Jane could for a moment stand against the death and the burial I had witnessed in Miss Knollys' house during the two previous nights.

XXIV THE ENIGMA OF NUMBERS

"When in our first conversation on this topic I told you that Mother Jane was not to be considered in this matter, I meant she was not to be considered by you. She was a subject to be handled by the police, and we have handled her. Yesterday afternoon I made a search of her cabin." Here Mr. Gryce paused and eyed me quizzically. He sometimes does eye me, which same I cannot regard as a compliment, considering how fond he is of concentrating all his wisdom upon small and insignificant objects.

"I wonder," said he, "what you would have done in such a search as that. It was no common one, I assure you. There are not many hiding-places between Mother Jane's four walls."

I felt myself begin to tremble, with eagerness, of course.

"I wish I had been given the opportunity," said I—"that is, if anything was to be found there."

He seemed to be in a sympathetic mood toward me, or perhaps—and this is the likelier supposition—he had a minute of leisure and thought he could afford to give himself a little quiet amusement. However that was, he answered me by saying:

"The opportunity is not lost. You have been in her cabin and have noted, I have no doubt, its extreme simplicity. Yet it contains, or rather did contain up till last night, distinct evidences of more than one of the crimes which have been perpetrated in this lane."

"Good! And you want me to guess where you found them? Well, it's not fair."

"Ah, and why not?"

"Because you probably did not find them on your first attempt. You had time to look about. I am asked to guess at once and without second trial what I warrant it took you several trials to determine."

He could not help but laugh. "And why do you think it took me several trials?"

"Because there is more than one thing in that room made up of parts."

"Parts?" He attempted to look puzzled, but I would not have it.

"You know what I mean," I declared; "seventy parts, twenty-eight, or whatever the numbers are she so constantly mutters."

His admiration was unqualified and sincere.

"Miss Butterworth," said he, "you are a woman after my own heart. How came you to think that her mutterings had anything to do with a hiding-place?"

"Because it did not have anything to do with the amount of money I gave her. When I handed her twenty-five cents, she cried, 'Seventy, twenty-eight, and now ten!' Ten what? Not ten cents or ten dollars, but ten———"

"Why do you stop?"

"I do not want to risk my reputation on a guess. There is a quilt on the bed made up of innumerable pieces. There is a floor of neatly laid brick———"

"And there is a Bible on the stand whose leaves number many over seventy."

"Ah, it was in the Bible you found———"

His smile put mine quite to shame.

"I must acknowledge," he cried, "that I looked in the Bible, but I found nothing there beyond what we all seek when we open its sacred covers. Shall I tell my story?"

He was evidently bursting with pride. You would think that after a half-century of just such successes, a man would take his honors more quietly. But pshaw! Human nature is just the same in the old as in the young. He was no more tired of compliment or of awakening the astonishment of those he confided in, than when he aroused the admiration of the force by his triumphant handling of the Leavenworth Case. Of course in presence of such weakness I could do nothing less than give him a sympathetic ear. I may be old myself some day. Besides, his story was likely to prove more or less interesting.

"Tell your story?" I repeated. "Don't you see that I am"—I was going to say "on pins and needles till I hear it," but the expression is too vulgar for a woman of my breeding; so I altered the words, happily before they were spoken, into "that I am in a state of the liveliest curiosity concerning the whole matter? Tell your story, of course."

"Well, Miss Butterworth, if I do, it is because I know you will appreciate it. You, like myself, placed weight upon the numbers she is forever running over, and you, like myself, have conceived the possibility of these numbers having reference to something in the one room she inhabits. At first glance the extreme bareness of the spot seemed to promise nothing to my curiosity. I looked at the floor and detected no signs of any disturbance having taken place in its symmetrically laid bricks for years. Yet I counted up to seventy one way and twenty-eight the other, and marking the brick thus selected, began to pry it out. It came with difficulty and showed me nothing underneath but green mold and innumerable frightened insects. Then I counted the bricks the other way, but nothing came of it. The floor does not appear to have been disturbed for years. Turning my attention away from the floor, I began upon the quilt. This was a worse job than the other, and it took me an hour to rip apart the block I settled upon as the suspicious one, but my labor was entirely wasted. There was no hidden treasure in the quilt. Then I searched the walls, using the measurements seventy by twenty-eight, but no result followed these endeavors, and—well, what do you think I did then?"

"You will tell me," I said, "if I give you one more minute to do it in."

"Very well," said he. "I see you do not know, madam. Having searched below and around me, I next turned my attention overhead. Do you remember the strings and strings of dried vegetables that decorate the beams above?"

"I do," I replied, not stinting any of the astonishment I really felt.

"Well, I began to count them next, and when I reached the seventieth onion from the open doorway, I crushed it between my fingers and—these fell out, madam—worthless trinkets, as you will immediately see, but——"

"Well, well," I urged.

"They have been identified as belonging to the peddler who was one of the victims in whose fate we are interested."

"Ah, ah!" I ejaculated, somewhat amazed, I own. "And number twenty-eight?"

"That was a carrot, and it held a really valuable ring—a ruby surrounded by diamonds. If you remember, I once spoke to you of this ring. It was the property of young Mr. Chittenden and worn by him while he was in this village. He disappeared on his way to the railway station, having taken, as many can vouch, the short detour by Lost Man's Lane, which would lead him directly by Mother Jane's cottage."

"You thrill me," said I, keeping down with admirable self-possession my own thoughts in regard to this matter. "And what of No. ten, beyond which she said she could not count?"

"In ten was your twenty-five-cent piece, and in various other vegetables, small coins, whose value taken collectively would not amount to a dollar. The only numbers which seemed to make any impression on her mind were those connected with these crimes. Very good evidence, Miss Butterworth, that Mother Jane holds the clue to this matter, even if she is not responsible for the death of the individuals represented by this property."

"Certainly," I acquiesced, "and if you examined her after her return from the Knollys mansion last night you would probably have found upon her some similar evidence of her complicity in the last crime of this terrible series. It would needs have been small, as Silly Rufus neither indulged in the brass trinkets sold by the old peddler nor the real jewelry of a well-to-do man like Mr. Chittenden."

"Silly Rufus?"

"He was the last to disappear from these parts, was he not?"

"Yes, madam."

"And as such, should have left some clue to his fate in the hands of this old crone, if her motive in removing him was, as you seem to think, entirely that of gain."

"I did not say it was entirely so. Silly Rufus would be the last person any one, even such a non compos mentis as Mother Jane, would destroy for hope of gain."

"But what other motive could she have? And, Mr. Gryce, where could she bestow the bodies of so many unfortunate victims, even if by her great strength she could succeed in killing them?"

"There you have me," said he. "We have not been able as yet to unearth any bodies. Have you?"

"No," said I, with some little show of triumph showing through my disdain, "but I can show you where to unearth one."

He should have been startled, profoundly startled. Why wasn't he? I asked this of myself over and over in the one instant he weighed his words before answering.

"You have made some definite discoveries, then," he declared. "You have come across a grave or a mound which you have taken for a grave."

I shook my head.

"No mound," said I. Why should I not play for an instant or more with his curiosity? He had with mine.

"Ah, then, why do you talk of unearthing? No one has told you where you can lay hand on Silly Rufus' body, I take it."

"No," said I. "The Knollys house is not inclined to give up its secrets."

He started, glancing almost remorsefully first at the tip, then at the head of the cane he was balancing in his hand.

"It's too bad," he muttered, "but you've been led astray, Miss Butterworth,— excusably, I acknowledge, quite excusably, but yet in a way to give you quite wrong conclusions. The secret of the Knollys house—But wait a moment. Then you were not locked up in your room last night?"

"Scarcely," I returned, wavering between the doubts he had awakened by his first sentence and the surprise which his last could not fail to give me.

"I might have known they would not be likely to catch you in a trap," he remarked. "So you were up and in the halls?"

"I was up," I acknowledged, "and in the halls. May I ask where you were?"

He paid no heed to the last sentence. "This complicates matters," said he, "and yet perhaps it is as well. I understand you now, and in a few minutes you will understand me. You thought it was Silly Rufus who was buried last night. That was rather an awful thought, Miss Butterworth. I wonder, with that in your mind, you look as well as you do this morning, madam. Truly you are a wonderful woman—a very wonderful woman."

"A truce to compliments," I begged. "If you know as much as your words imply of what went on in that ill-omened house last night, you ought to show some degree of emotion yourself, for if it was not Silly Rufus who was laid away under the Flower Parlor, who, then, was it? No one for whom tears could openly be shed or of whose death public acknowledgment could be made, or we would not be sitting here talking away at cross purposes the morning after his burial."

"Tears are not shed or public acknowledgment made for the subject of a half-crazy man's love for scientific investigation. It was no human being whom you saw buried, madam, but a victim of Mr. Knollys' passion for vivisection."

"You are playing with me," was my indignant answer; "outrageously and inexcusably playing with me. Only a human being would be laid away in such secrecy and with such manifestations of feeling as I was witness to. You must think me in my dotage, or else——"

"We will take the rest of the sentence for granted," he dryly interpolated. "You know that I can have no wish to insult your intelligence, Miss Butterworth, and that if I advance a theory on my own account I must have ample reasons for it. Now can you say the same for yours? Can you adduce irrefutable proof that the body we buried last night was that of a man? If you can, there is no more to be said, or, rather, there is everything to be said, for this would give to the transaction a very dreadful and tragic significance which at present I am not disposed to ascribe to it."

Taken aback by his persistence, but determined not to acknowledge defeat until forced to it, I stolidly replied: "You have made an assertion, and it is for you to adduce proof. It will be time enough for me to talk when your own theory is proved untenable."

He was not angry: fellow-feeling for my disappointment made him unusually gentle. His voice was therefore very kind when he said:

"Madam, if you know it to have been a man, say so. I do not wish to waste my time."

"I do not know it."

"Very well, then, I will tell you why I think my supposition true. Mr. Knollys, as you probably have already discovered, is a man with a secret passion for vivisection."

"Yes, I have discovered that."

"It is known to his family, and it is known to a very few others, but it is not known to the world at large, not even to his fellow-villagers.'

"I can believe it," said I.

"His sisters, who are gentle girls, regard the matter as the gentle-hearted usually do. They have tried in every way to influence him to abandon it, but unsuccessfully so far, for he is not only entirely unamenable to persuasion, but has a nature of such brutality he could not live without some such excitement to help away his life in this dreary house. All they can do, then, is to conceal these cruelties from the eyes of the people who already execrate him for his many roughnesses and the undoubted shadow under which he lives. Time was when I thought this shadow had a substance worth our investigation, but a further knowledge of his real fault and a completer knowledge of his sisters' virtues turned my inquiries in a new direction, where I have found, as I have told you, actual reason for arresting Mother Jane. Have you anything to say against these conclusions? Cannot you see that all your suspicions can be explained by the brother's cruel impulses and the sisters' horror of having those impulses known?"

I thought a moment; then I cried out boldly: "No, I cannot, Mr. Gryce. The anxiety, the fear, which I have seen depicted on these sisters' faces for days might be explained perhaps by this theory; but the knot of crape on the window-shutter, the open Bible in the room of death—William's room, Mr. Gryce,—proclaim that it was a human being, and nothing less, for whom Lucetta's sobs went up."

"I do not follow you," he said, moved for the first time from his composure. "What do you mean by a knot of crape, and when was it you obtained entrance into William's room?"

"Ah," I exclaimed in dry retort; "you are beginning to see that I have something as interesting to report as yourself. Did you think me a superficial egotist, without facts to back my assertions?"

"I should not have done you that injustice."

"I have penetrated, I think, deeper than even yourself, into William's character. I think him capable—But do satisfy my curiosity on one point first, Mr. Gryce. How came you to know as much as you do about last night's proceedings? You could not have been in the house. Did Mother Jane talk after she got back?"

The tip of his cane was up, and he frowned at it. Then the handle took its place, and he gave it a good-natured smile.

"Miss Butterworth," said he, "I have not succeeded in making Mother Jane at any time go beyond her numerical monologue. But you have been more successful." And with a sudden marvellous change of expression, pose, and manner he threw over his head my shawl, which had fallen to the floor in my astonishment, and, rocking himself to and fro before me, muttered grimly:

"Seventy! Twenty-eight! Ten! No more! I can count no more! Go."

"Mr. Gryce, it was you——"

"Whom you interviewed in Mother Jane's cottage with Mr. Knollys," he finished. "And it was I who helped to bury what you now declare, to my real terror and astonishment, to have been a human being. Miss Butterworth, what about the knot of crape? Tell me."

XXV   TRIFLES, BUT NOT TRIFLING

I was so astounded I hardly took in this final question.

He had been the sixth party in the funeral cortège I had seen pause in the Flower Parlor. Well, what might I not expect from this man next!

But I am methodical even under the greatest excitement and at the most critical instants, as those who have read That Affair Next Door have had ample opportunity to know. Once having taken in the startling fact he mentioned, I found it impossible to proceed to establish my standpoint till I knew a little more about his.

"Wait," I said; "tell me first if I have ever seen the real Mother Jane; or were you the person I saw stooping in the road, and of whom I bought the pennyroyal?"

"No," he replied; "that was the old woman herself. My appearance in the cottage dates from yesterday noon. I felt the need of being secretly near you, and I also wished for an opportunity to examine this humble interior unsuspected and unobserved. So I prevailed upon the old woman to exchange places with me; she taking up her abode in the woods for the night and I her old stool on the hearthstone. She was the more willing to do this from the promise I gave her to watch out for Lizzie. That I would don her own Sunday suit and personate her in her own home she evidently did not suspect. Had not wit enough, I suppose. At the present moment she is back in her old place."

I nodded my thanks for this explanation, but was not deterred from pressing the point I was anxious to have elucidated.

"If," I went on to urge, "you took advantage of your disguise to act as assistant in the burial which took place last night, you are in a much better situation than myself to decide the question we are at present considering. Was it because of any secret knowledge thus gained you declare so positively that it was not a human being you helped lower in its grave?"

"Partially. Having some skill in these disguises, especially where my own infirmities can have full play, as in the case of this strong but half-bent woman, I had no reason to think my own identity was suspected, much less discovered. Therefore I could trust to what I saw and heard as being just what Mother Jane herself would be allowed to see or hear under the same circumstances. If, therefore, these young people and this old crone had been, as you seem to think they are, in league for murder, Lucetta would hardly have greeted me as she did when she came down to meet me in the kitchen."

"And how was that? What did she say?"

"She said: 'Ah, Mother Jane, we have a piece of work for you. You are strong, are you not?'"

"Humph!"

"And then she commiserated me a bit and gave me food which, upon my word, I found hard to eat, though I had saved my appetite for the occasion. Before she left me she bade me sit in the inglenook till she wanted me, adding in Hannah's ear as she passed her: 'There is no use trying to explain anything to her. Show her when the time comes what there is to do and trust to her short memory to forget it before she leaves the house. She could not understand my brother's propensity or our shame in pandering to it. So attempt nothing, Hannah. Only keep the money in her view.'"

"So, and that gave you no idea?"

"It gave me the idea I have imparted to you, or, rather, added to the idea which had been instilled in me by others."

"And this idea was not affected by what you saw afterwards?"

"Not in the least—rather strengthened. Of the few words I overheard, one was uttered in reference to yourself by Miss Knollys. She said: 'I have locked Miss Butterworth again into her room. If she accuses me of having done so, I shall tell her our whole story. Better she should know the family's disgrace than imagine us guilty of crimes of which we are utterly incapable.'"

"So! so!" I cried, "you heard that?"

"Yes, madam, I heard that, and I do not think she knew she was dropping that word into the ear of a detective, but on this point you are, of course, at liberty to differ with me."

"I am not yet ready to avail myself of the privilege," I retorted. "What else did these girls let fall in your hearing?"

"Not much. It was Hannah who led me into the upper hall, and Hannah who by signs and signals rather than words showed me what was expected of me. However, when, after the box was lowered into the cellar, Hannah was drawing me away, Lucetta stepped up and whispered in her ear: 'Don't give her the biggest coin. Give her the little one, or she may mistake our reasons for secrecy. I wouldn't like even a fool to do that even for the moment it would remain lodged in Mother Jane's mind.'"

"Well, well," I again cried, certainly puzzled, for these stray expressions of the sisters were in a measure contradictory not only of the suspicions I entertained, but of the facts which had seemingly come to my attention.

Mr. Gryce, who was probably watching my face more closely than he did the cane with whose movements he was apparently engrossed, stopped to give a caressing rub to the knob of that same cane before remarking:

"One such peep behind the scenes is worth any amount of surmise expended on the wrong side of the curtain. I let you share my knowledge because it is your due. Now if you feel willing to explain what you mean by a knot of crape on the shutter, I am at your service, madam."

I felt that it would be cruel to delay my story longer, and so I began it. It was evidently more interesting than he expected, and as I dilated upon the special features which had led me to believe that it was a thinking, suffering mortal like ourselves who had been shut up in William's room and afterwards buried in the cellar under the Flower Parlor, I saw his face lengthen and doubt take the place of the quiet assurance with which he had received my various intimations up to this time. The cane was laid aside, and from the action of his right forefinger on the palm of his left hand I judged that I was making no small impression on his mind. When I had finished, he sat for a minute silent; then he said:

"Thanks, Miss Butterworth; you have more than fulfilled my hopes. What we buried was undoubtedly human, and the question now is, Who was it, and of what death did he die?" Then, after a meaning pause: "You think it was Silly Rufus."

I will astonish you with my reply. "No," said I, "I do not. That is where you make a mistake, Mr. Gryce."

XXVI   A POINT GAINED

He was surprised, for all his attempts to conceal it.

"No?" said he. "Who, then? You are becoming interesting, Miss Butterworth."

This I thought I could afford to ignore.

"Yesterday," I proceeded, "I would have declared it to be Silly Rufus, in the face of God and man, but after what I saw in William's room during the hurried survey I gave it, I am inclined to doubt if the explanation we have to give to this affair is so simple as that would make it. Mr. Gryce, in one corner of that room, from which the victim had so lately been carried, was a pair of shoes that could never have been worn by any boy-tramp I have ever seen or known of."

"They were Loreen's, or possibly Lucetta's."

"No, Loreen and Lucetta both have trim feet, but these were the shoes of a child of ten, very dainty at that, and of a cut and make worn by women, or rather, I should say, by girls. Now, what do you make of that?"

He did not seem to know what to make of it. Tap, tap went his finger on his seasoned palm, and as I watched the slowness with which it fell, I said to myself, "I have proposed a problem this time that will tax even Mr. Gryce's powers of deduction."

And I had. It was minutes before he ventured an opinion, and then it was with a shade of doubt in his tone that I acknowledge to have felt some pride in producing.

"They were Lucetta's shoes. The emotions under which you labored—very pardonable emotions, madam, considering the circumstances and the hour——"

"Excuse me," said I. "We do not want to waste a moment. I was excited, suitably and duly excited, or I would have been a stone. But I never lose my head under excitement, nor do I part with my sense of proportion. The shoes were not Lucetta's. She never wore any approaching them in smallness since her tenth year."

"Has Simsbury a daughter? Has there not been a child about the house some time to assist the cook in errands and so on?"

"No, or I should have seen her. Besides, how would the shoes of such a person come into William's room?"

"Easily. Secrecy was required. You were not to be disturbed; so shoes were taken off that quiet might result."

"Was Lucetta shoeless or William or even Mother Jane? You have not told me that you were requested to walk in stocking feet up the hall. No, Mr. Gryce, the shoes were the shoes of a girl. I know it because it was matched by a dress I saw hanging up in a sort of wardrobe."

"Ah! You looked into the wardrobe?"

"I did and felt justified in doing so. It was after I had spied the shoes."

"Very good. And you saw a dress?"

"A little dress; a dress with a short skirt. It was of silk too; another anomaly—and the color, I think, was blue, but I cannot swear to that point. I was in great haste and took the briefest glance. But my brief glances can be trusted, Mr. Gryce. That, I think, you are beginning to know."

"Certainly," said he, "and as proof of it we will now act upon these two premises—that the victim in whose burial I was an innocent partaker was a human being and that this human being was a girl-child who came into the house well dressed. Now where does that lead us? Into a maze, I fear."

"We are accustomed to mazes," I observed.

"Yes," he answered somewhat gloomily, "but they are not exactly desirable in this case. I want to find the Knollys family innocent."

"And I. But William's character, I fear, will make that impossible."

"But this girl? Who is she, and where did she come from? No girl has been reported to us as missing from this neighborhood."

"I supposed not."

"A visitor—But no visitor could enter this house without it being known far and wide. Why, I heard of your arrival here before I left the train on which I followed you. Had we allowed ourselves to be influenced by what the people about here say, we would have turned the Knollys house inside out a week ago. But I don't believe in putting too much confidence in the prejudice of country people. The idea they suggested, and which you suggest without putting it too clearly into words, is much too horrible to be acted upon without the best of reasons. Perhaps we have found those reasons, yet I still feel like asking, Where did this girl come from and how could she have become a prisoner in the Knollys house without the knowledge of—Madam, have you met Mr. Trohm?"

The question was so sudden I had not time to collect myself. But perhaps it was not necessary that I should, for the simple affirmation I used seemed to satisfy Mr. Gryce, who went on to say:

"It is he who first summoned us here, and it is he who has the greatest interest in locating the source of these disappearances, yet he has seen no child come here."

"Mr. Trohm is not a spy," said I, but the remark, happily, fell unheeded.

"No one has," he pursued. "We must give another turn to our suppositions."

Suddenly a silence fell upon us both. His finger ceased to lay down the law, and my gaze, which had been searching his face inquiringly, became fixed. At the same moment and in much the same tone of voice we both spoke, he saying, "Humph!" and I, "Ah!" as a prelude to the simultaneous exclamation:

"The phantom coach!"

We were so pleased with this discovery that we allowed a moment to pass in silent contemplation of each other's satisfaction. Then he quietly added: "Which on the evening preceding your arrival came from the mountains and passed into Lost Man's Lane, from which no one ever saw it emerge."

"It was no phantom," I put in.

"It was their own old coach bringing to the house a fresh victim."

This sounded so startling we both sat still for a moment, lost in the horror of it, then I spoke:

"People living in remote and isolated quarters like this are naturally superstitious. The Knollys family know this, and, remembering the old legend, forbore to contradict the conclusions of their neighbors. Loreen's emotion when the topic was broached to her is explained by this theory."

"It is not a pleasant one, but we cannot be wrong in contemplating it."

"Not at all. This apparition, as they call it, was seen by two persons; therefore it was no apparition but a real coach. It came from the mountains, that is, from the Mountain Station, and it glided—ah!"

"Well?"

"Mr. Gryce, it was its noiselessness that gave it its spectral appearance. Now I remember a petty circumstance which I dare you to match, in corroboration of our suspicions."

"You do?"

I could not repress a slight toss of my head. "Yes, I do," I repeated.

He smiled and made the slightest of deprecatory gestures.

"You have had advantages——" he began.

"And disadvantages," I finished, determined that he should award me my full meed of praise. "You are probably not afraid of dogs. I am. You could visit the stables."

"And did; but I found nothing there."

"I thought not!" I could not help the exclamation. It is so seldom one can really triumph over this man. "Not having the cue, you would not be apt to see what gives this whole thing away. I would never have thought of it again if we had not had this talk. Is Mr. Simsbury a neat man?"

"A neat man? Madam, what do you mean?"

"Something important, Mr. Gryce. If Mr. Simsbury is a neat man, he will have thrown away the old rags which, I dare promise you, cumbered his stable floor the morning after the phantom coach was seen to enter the lane. If he is not, you may still find them there. One of them, I know, you will not find. He pulled it off of his wheel with his whip the afternoon he drove me down from the station. I can see the sly look he gave me as he did it. It made no impression on me then, but now——"

"Madam, you have supplied the one link necessary to the establishment of this theory. Allow me to felicitate you upon it. But whatever our satisfaction may be from a professional standpoint, we cannot but feel the unhappy nature of the responsibility incurred by these discoveries. If this seemingly respectable family stooped to such subterfuge, going to the length of winding rags around the wheels of their lumbering old coach to make it noiseless, and even tying up their horse's feet for this same purpose, they must have had a motive dark enough to warrant your worst suspicions. And William was not the only one involved. Simsbury, at least, had a hand in it, nor does it look as if the girls were as innocent as we would like to consider them."

"I cannot stop to consider the girls," I declared. "I can no longer consider the girls."

"Nor I," he gloomily assented. "Our duty requires us to sift this matter, and it shall be sifted. We must first find if any child alighted from the cars at the Mountain Station on that especial night, or, what is more probable, from the little station at C., five miles farther back in the mountains."

"And—" I urged, seeing that he had still something to say.

"We must make sure who lies buried under the floor of the room you call the Flower Parlor. You may expect me at the Knollys house some time to-day. I shall come quietly, but in my own proper person. You are not to know me, and, unless you desire it, need not appear in the matter."

"I do not desire it."

"Then good-morning, Miss Butterworth. My respect for your abilities has risen even higher than before. We part in a similar frame of mind for once."

And this he expected me to regard as a compliment.

XXVII   THE TEXT WITNESSETH

I have a grim will when I choose to exert it. After Mr. Gryce left the hotel, I took a cup of tea with the landlady and then made a round of the stores. I bought dimity, sewing silk, and what not, as I said I would, but this did not occupy me long (to the regret probably of the country merchants, who expected to make a fool of me and found it a by no means easy task), and was quite ready for William when he finally drove up.

The ride home was a more or less silent one. I had conceived such a horror of the man beside me, that talking for talk's sake was impossible, while he was in a mood which it would be charity to call non-communicative. It may be that my own reticence was at the bottom of this, but I rather think not. The remark he made in passing Deacon Spear's house showed that something more than spite was working in his slow but vindictive brain.

"There's a man of your own sort," he cried. "You won't find him doing anything out of the way; oh, no. Pity your visit wasn't paid there. You'd have got a better impression of the lane."

To this I made no reply.

At Mr. Trohm's he spoke again:

"I suppose that you and Trohm had the devil of a say about Lucetta and the rest of us. I don't know why, but the whole neighborhood seems to feel they've a right to use our name as they choose. But it isn't going to be so, long. We have played poor and pinched and starved all I'm going to. I'm going to have a new horse, and Lucetta shall have a dress, and that mighty quick too. I'm tired of all this shabbiness, and mean to have a change."

I wanted to say, "No change yet; change under the present circumstances would be the worst thing possible for you all," but I felt that this would be treason to Mr. Gryce, and refrained, saying simply, as he looked sideways at me for a word:

"Lucetta needs a new dress. That no one can deny. But you had better let me get it for her, or perhaps that is what you mean."

The grunt which was my only answer might be interpreted in any way. I took it, however, for assent.

As soon as I was relieved of his presence and found myself again with the girls, I altered my whole manner and cried out in querulous tones:

"Mrs. Carter and I have had a difference." (This was true. We did have a difference over our cup of tea. I did not think it necessary to say this difference was a forced one. Some things we are perfectly justified in keeping to ourselves.) "She remembers a certain verse in the New Testament one way and I in another. We had not time to settle it by a consultation with the sacred word, but I cannot rest till it is settled, so will you bring your Bible to me, my dear, that I may look that verse up?"

We were in the upper hall, where I had taken a seat on the old-fashioned sofa there. Lucetta, who was standing before me, started immediately to do my bidding, without stopping to think, poor child, that it was very strange I did not go to my own room and consult my own Bible as any good Presbyterian would be expected to do. As she was turning toward the large front room I stopped her with the quiet injunction:

"Get me one with good print, Lucetta. My eyes won't bear much straining."

At which she turned and to my great relief hurried down the corridor toward William's room, from which she presently returned, bringing the very volume I was anxious to consult.

Meanwhile I had laid aside my hat. I felt flurried and unhappy, and showed it. Lucetta's pitiful face had a strange sweetness in it this morning, and I felt sure as I took the sacred book from her hand that her thoughts were all with the lover she had sent from her side and not at all with me or with what at the moment occupied me. Yet my thoughts at this moment involved, without doubt, the very deepest interests of her life, if not that very lover she was brooding over in her darkened and resigned mind. As I realized this I heaved an involuntary sigh, which seemed to startle her, for she turned and gave me a quick look as she was slipping away to join her sister, who was busy at the other end of the hall.

The Bible I held was an old one, of medium size and most excellent print. I had no difficulty in finding the text and settling the question which had been my ostensible reason for wanting the book, but it took me longer to discover the indentation which I had made in one of its pages; but when I did, you may imagine my awe and the turmoil into which my mind was cast, when I found that it marked those great verses in Corinthians which are so universally read at funerals:

"Behold I shew you a mystery. We shall not all sleep, but we shall all be changed."

"In a moment, in the twinkling of an eye———"

XXVIII   AN INTRUSION

I was so moved by this discovery that I was not myself for several moments.

The reading of these words over the body which had been laid away under the Flower Parlor was in keeping with the knot of crape on the window-shutter and argued something more than remorse on the part of some one of the Knollys family. Who was this one, and why, with such feelings in the breast of any of the three, had the deceit and crime to which I had been witness succeeded to such a point as to demand the attention of the police? An impossible problem of which I dared seek no solution, even in the faces of these seemingly innocent girls.

I was, of course, in no position to determine what plan Mr. Gryce intended to pursue. I only knew what course I myself meant to follow, which was to remain quiet and sustain the part I had already played in this house as visitor and friend. It was therefore as such both in heart and manner that I hastened from my room late in the afternoon to inquire the meaning of the cry I had just heard issue from Lucetta's lips. It had come from the front of the house, and, as I hastened thither, I met the two Misses Knollys, looking more openly anxious and distraught than at any former time of anxiety and trouble.

As they looked up and saw my face, Loreen paused and laid her hand on Lucetta's arm. But Lucetta was not to be restrained.

"He has dared to enter our gates, bringing a police officer with him," was her hoarse and almost unintelligible cry. "We know that the man with him is a police officer because he was here once before, and though he was kind enough then, he cannot have come the second time except to——"

Here the pressure of Loreen's hand was so strong as to make the feeble Lucetta quiver. She stopped, and Miss Knollys took up her words:

"Except to make us talk on subjects much better buried in oblivion. Miss Butterworth, will you go down with us? Your presence may act as a restraint. Mr. Trohm seems to have some respect for you."

"Mr. Trohm?"

"Yes. It is his coming which has so agitated Lucetta. He and a man named Gryce are just coming up the walk. There goes the knocker. Lucetta, you must control yourself or leave me to face these unwelcome visitors alone."

Lucetta, with a sudden fierce effort, subdued her trembling.

"If he must be met," said she, "my anger and disdain may give some weight to your quiet acceptance of the family's disgrace. I shall not accept his denunciations quietly, Loreen. You must expect me to show some of the feelings that I have held in check all these years." And without waiting for reply, without waiting even to see what effect these strange words might have upon me, she dashed down the stairs and pulled open the front door.

We had followed rapidly, too rapidly for speech ourselves, and were therefore in the hall when the door swung back, revealing the two persons I had been led to expect. Mr. Trohm spoke first, evidently in answer to the defiance to be seen in Lucetta's face.

"Miss Knollys, a thousand pardons. I know I am transgressing, but, I assure you, the occasion warrants it. I am certain you will acknowledge this when you hear what my errand is."

"Your errand? What can your errand be but to——"

Why did she pause? Mr. Gryce had not looked at her. Yet that it was under his influence she ceased to commit herself I am as convinced as we can be of anything in a world which is half deceit.

"Let us hear your errand," put in Loreen, with that gentle emphasis which is no sign of weakness.

"I will let this gentleman speak for me," returned Mr. Trohm. "You have seen him before—a New York detective of whose business in this town you cannot be ignorant."

Lucetta turned a cold eye upon Mr. Gryce and quietly remarked:

"When he visited this lane a few days ago, he professed to be seeking a clue to the many disappearances which have unfortunately taken place within its precincts."

Mr. Trohm's nod was one of acquiescence. But Lucetta was still looking at the detective.

"Is that your business now?" she asked, appealing directly to Mr. Gryce.

His fatherly accents when he answered her were a great relief after the alternate iciness and fire with which she had addressed his companion and himself.

"I hardly know how to reply without arousing your just anger. If your brother is in——"

"My brother would face you with less patience than we. Tell us your errand, Mr. Gryce, and do not think of calling in my brother till we have failed to answer your questions or satisfy your demands."

"Very well," said he. "The quickest explanation is the kindest in these cases. I merely wish, as a police officer whose business it is to locate the disappearances which have made this lane notorious, and who believes the surest way to do this is to find out once and for all where they did not and could not have taken place, to make an official search of these premises as I already have those of Mother Jane and of Deacon Spear."

"And my errand here," interposed Mr. Trohm, "is to make everything easier by the assurance that my house will be the next to undergo a complete investigation. As all the houses in the lane will be visited alike, none of us need complain or feel our good name attacked."

This was certainly thoughtful of him, but knowing how much they had to fear, I could not expect Loreen or Lucetta to show any great sense either of his kindness or Mr. Gryce's consideration. They were in no position to have a search made of their premises, and, serene as was Loreen's nature and powerful as was Lucetta's will, the apprehension under which they labored was evident to us all, though neither of them attempted either subterfuge or evasion.

"If the police wish to search this house, it is open to them," said Loreen.

"But not to Mr. Trohm," quoth Lucetta, quickly. "Our poverty should be our protection from the curiosity of neighbors."

"Mr. Trohm has no wish to intrude," was Mr. Gryce's conciliatory remark; but Mr. Trohm said nothing. He probably understood why Lucetta wished to curtail his stay in this house better than Mr. Gryce did.

XXIX   IN THE CELLAR

I had meanwhile stood silent. There was no reason for me to obtrude myself, and I was happy not to do so. This does not mean, however, that my presence was not noticed. Mr. Trohm honored me with more than one glance during these trying moments, in which I read the anxiety he felt lest my peace of mind should be too much disturbed, and when, in response to the undoubted dismissal he had received from Lucetta, he prepared to take his leave, it was upon me he bestowed his final look and most deferential bow. It was a tribute to my position and character which all seemed to feel, and I was not at all surprised when Lucetta, after carefully watching his departure, turned to me with childlike impetuosity, saying:

"This must be very unpleasant for you, Miss Butterworth, yet must we ask you to stand our friend. God knows we need one."

"I shall never forget I occupied that position toward your mother," was my straightforward reply, and I did not forget it, not for a moment.

"I shall begin with the cellar," Mr. Gryce announced.

Both girls quivered. Then Loreen lifted her proud head and said quietly:

"The whole house is at your disposal. Only I pray you to be as expeditious as possible. My sister is not well, and the sooner our humiliation is over, the better it will be for her."

And, indeed, Lucetta was in a state that aroused even Mr. Gryce's anxiety. But when she saw us all hovering over her she roused herself with an extraordinary effort, and, waving us aside, led the way to the kitchen, from which, as I gathered, the only direct access could be had to the cellar. Mr. Gryce immediately followed, and behind him came Loreen and myself, both too much agitated to speak. At the Flower Parlor Mr. Gryce paused as if he had forgotten something, but Lucetta urged him feverishly on, and before long we were all standing in the kitchen. Here a surprise awaited us. Two men were sitting there who appeared to be strangers to Hannah, from the lowering looks she cast them as she pretended to be busy over her stove. This was so out of keeping with her usual good humor as to attract the attention even of her young mistress.

"What is the matter, Hannah?" asked Lucetta. "And who are these men?"

"They are my men," said Mr. Gryce. "The job I have undertaken cannot be carried on alone."

The quick look the two sisters interchanged did not escape me, or the quiet air of resignation which was settling slowly over Loreen.

"Must they go into the cellar too?" she asked.

Mr. Gryce smiled his most fatherly smile as he said:

"My dear young ladies, these men are interested in but one thing; they are searching for a clue to the disappearances that have occurred in this lane. As they will not find this in your cellar, nothing else that they may see there will remain in their minds for a moment."

Lucetta said no more. Even her indomitable spirit was giving way before the inevitable discovery that threatened them.

"Do not let William know," were the low words with which she passed Hannah; but from the short glimpse I caught of William's burly figure standing in the stable door, under the guardianship of two detectives, I felt this injunction to be quite superfluous. William evidently did know.

I was not going to descend the cellar stairs, but the girls made me.

"We want you with us," Loreen declared in no ordinary tones, while Lucetta paused and would not go on till I followed. This surprised me. I no longer seemed to have any clue to their motives; but I was glad to be one of the party.

Hannah, under Loreen's orders, had furnished one of the men with a lighted lantern, and upon our descent into the dark labyrinth below, it became his duty to lead the way, which he did with due circumspection. What all this underground space into which we were thus introduced had ever been used for, it would be difficult to tell. At present it was mostly empty. After passing a small collection of stores, a wine-cellar, the very door of which was unhinged and lay across the cellar bottom, we struck into a hollow void, in which there was nothing worth an instant's investigation save the earth under our feet.

This the two foremost detectives examined very carefully, detaining us often longer, I thought, than Mr. Gryce desired or Lucetta had patience for. But nothing was said in protest nor did the older detective give an order or manifest any special interest in the investigation till he saw the men in front stoop and throw out of the way a coil of rope, when he immediately hurried forward and called upon the party to stop.

The girls, who were on either side of me, crossed glances at this command, and Lucetta, who had been tottering for the last few minutes, fell upon her knees and hid her face in the hollow of her two hands. Loreen came around and stood by her, and I do not know which of them presented the most striking picture of despair, the shrinking Lucetta or Loreen with her quivering form uplifted to meet the shafts of fate without a droop of her eyelids or a murmur from her lips. The light of the one lantern which, intentionally or unintentionally, was concentrated on this pathetic group, made it stand out from the midst of the surrounding darkness in a way to draw the gaze of Mr. Gryce upon them. He looked, and his own brow became overcast. Evidently we were not far from the cause of their fears.

Ordering the candle lifted, he surveyed the ceiling above, at which Loreen's lips opened slightly in secret dread and amazement. Then he commanded the men to move on slowly, while he himself looked overhead rather than underneath, which seemed to astonish his associates, who evidently had heard nothing of the hole which had been cut in the floor of the Flower Parlor.

Suddenly I heard a slight gasp from Lucetta, who had not moved forward with the rest of us. Then her rushing figure flew by us and took up its stand by Mr. Gryce, who had himself paused and was pointing with an imperious forefinger to the ground under his feet.

"You will dig here," said he, not heeding her, though I am sure he was as well acquainted with her proximity as we.

"Dig?" repeated Loreen, in what we all saw was a final effort to stave off disgrace and misery.

"My duty demands it," said he. "Some one else has been digging here within a very few days, Miss Knollys. That is as evident as is the fact that a communication has been made with this place through an opening into the room above. See!" And taking the lantern from the man at his side, he held it up toward the ceiling.

There was no hole there now, but there were ample evidences of there having been one, and that within a very short time. Loreen made no further attempt to stay him.

"The house is at your disposal," she reiterated, but I do not think she knew what she said. The man with the bundle in his arms was already unrolling it on the cellar bottom. A spade came to light, together with some other tools. Lifting the spade, he thrust it smartly into the ground toward which Mr. Gryce's inexorable finger still pointed. At the sight and the sound it made, a thrill passed through Lucetta which made her another creature. Dashing forward, she flung herself down upon the spot with lifted head and outstretched arms.

"Stop your desecrating hand!" she cried. "This is a grave—the grave, sirs, of our mother!"

XXX   INVESTIGATION

The shock of these words—if false, most horrible; if true, still more horrible—threw us all aback and made even Mr. Gryce's features assume an aspect quite uncommon to them.

"Your mother's grave?" said he, looking from her to Loreen with very evident doubt. "I thought your mother died seven or more years ago, and this grave has been dug within three days."

"I know," she whispered. "To the world my mother has been dead many, many years, but not to us. We closed her eyes night before last, and it was to preserve this secret, which involves others affecting our family honor, that we resorted to expedients which have perhaps attracted the notice of the police and drawn this humiliation down upon us. I can conceive no other reason for this visit, ushered in as it was by Mr. Trohm."

"Miss Lucetta"—Mr. Gryce spoke quickly; if he had not I certainly could not have restrained some expression of the emotions awakened in my own breast by this astounding revelation—"Miss Lucetta, it is not necessary to bring Mr. Trohm's name into this matter or that of any other person than myself. I saw the coffin lowered here, which you say contained the body of your mother. Thinking this a strange place of burial and not knowing it was your mother to whom you were paying these last dutiful rites, I took advantage of my position as detective to satisfy myself that nothing wrong lay behind so mysterious a death and burial. Can you blame me, Miss? Would I have been a man to trust if I had let such an event as this go by unchallenged?"

She did not answer. She had heard but one sentence of all this long speech.

"You saw my mother's coffin lowered? Where were you that you should see that? In some of these dark passages, let in by I know not what traitor to our peace of mind." And her eyes, which seemed to have grown almost supernaturally large and bright under her emotions, turned slowly in their sockets till they rested with something like doubtful accusation upon mine. But not to remain there, for Mr. Gryce recalled them almost instantly by this short, sharp negative.

"No, I was nearer than that. I lent my strength to this burial. If you had thought to look under Mother Jane's hood, you would have seen what would have forced these explanations then and there."

"And you——"

"I was Mother Jane for the nonce. Not from choice, Miss, but from necessity. I was impersonating the old woman when your brother came to the cottage. I could not give away my plans by refusing the task your brother offered me."

"It is well." Lucetta had risen and was now standing by the side of Loreen. "Such a secret as ours defies concealment. Even Providence takes part against us. What you want to know we must tell, but I assure you it has nothing to do with the business you profess to be chiefly interested in—nothing at all."

"Then perhaps you and your sister will retire," said he. "Distracted as you are by family griefs, I would not wish to add one iota to your distress. This lady, whom you seem to regard with more or less favor as friend or relative, will stay to see that no dishonor is paid to your mother's remains. But your mother's face we must see, Miss Lucetta, if only to lighten the explanations you will doubtless feel called upon to make."

It was Loreen who answered this.

"If it must be," said she, "remember your own mother and deal reverently with ours." Which entreaty and the way it was uttered, gave me my first distinct conviction that these girls were speaking the truth, and that the diminutive body we had come to unearth was that of Althea Knollys, whose fairy-like form I had so long supposed commingled with foreign soil.

The thought was almost too much for my self-possession, and I advanced upon Loreen with a dozen burning questions on my lips when the voice of Mr. Gryce stopped me.

"Explanations later," said he. "For the present we want you here."

It was no easy task for me to linger there with all my doubts unsolved, waiting for the decisive moment when Mr. Gryce should say: "Come! Look! Is it she?" But the will that had already sustained me through so many trying experiences did not fail me now, and, grievous as was the ordeal, I passed steadily through it, being able to say, though not without some emotion, I own: "It is Althea Knollys! Changed almost beyond conception, but still these girls' mother!" which was a happier end to this adventure than that we had first feared, mysterious as the event was, not only to myself, but, as I could see, to the acute detective as well.

The girls had withdrawn long before this, just as Mr. Gryce had desired, and I now expected to be allowed to join them, but Mr. Gryce detained me till the grave was refilled and made decent again, when he turned and to my intense astonishment—for I had thought the matter was all over and the exoneration of this household complete—said softly and with telling emphasis in my ear:

"Our work is not done yet. They who make graves so readily in cellars must have been more or less accustomed to the work. We have still some digging to do."

XXXI STRATEGY

I was overwhelmed.

"What," said I, "you still doubt?"

"I always doubt," he gravely replied. "This cellar bottom offers a wide field for speculation. Too wide, perhaps, but, then, I have a plan."

Here he leaned over and whispered a few concise sentences into my ear in a tone so low I should feel that I was betraying his confidence in repeating them. But their import will soon become apparent from what presently occurred.

"Light Miss Butterworth to the stairway," Mr. Gryce now commanded one of the men, and thus accompanied I found my way back to the kitchen, where Hannah was bemoaning uncomforted the shame which had come upon the house.

I did not stop to soothe her. That was not my cue, nor would it have answered my purpose. On the contrary, I broke into angry ejaculations as I passed her:

"What a shame! Those wretches cannot be got away from the cellar. What do you suppose they expect to find there? I left them poking hither and thither in a way that will be very irritating to Miss Knollys when she finds it out. I wonder William stands it."

What she said in reply I do not know. I was half way down the hall before my own words were finished.

My next move was to go to my room and take from my trunk a tiny hammer and some very small, sharp-pointed tacks. Curious articles, you will think, for a woman to carry on her travels, but I am a woman of experience, and have known only too often what it was to want these petty conveniences and not be able to get them. They were to serve me an odd turn now. Taking a half-dozen tacks in one hand and concealing the hammer in my bag, I started boldly for William's room. I knew that the girls were not there, for I had heard them talking together in the sitting-room as I came up. Besides, if they were, I had a ready answer for any demand they might make.

Searching out his boots, I turned them over, and into the sole of each I drove one of my small tacks. Then I put them back in the same place and position in which I found them. Task number one was accomplished.

When I issued from the room, I went as quickly as I could below. I was now ready for a talk with the girls, whom I found as I had anticipated, talking and weeping together in the sitting-room.

They rose as I came in, awaiting my first words in evident anxiety. They had not heard me go up-stairs. I immediately allowed my anxiety and profound interest in this matter to have full play.

"My poor girls! What is the meaning of this? Your mother just dead, and the matter kept from me, her friend! It is astounding—incomprehensible! I do not know what to make of it or of you."

"It has a strange look," Loreen gravely admitted; "but we had reasons for this deception, Miss Butterworth. Our mother, charming and sweet as you remember her, has not always done right, or, what you will better understand, she committed a criminal act against a person in this town, the penalty of which is state's prison."

With difficulty the words came out. With difficulty she kept down the flush of shame which threatened to overwhelm her and did overwhelm her more sensitive sister. But her self-control was great, and she went bravely on, while I, in faint imitation of her courage, restrained my own surprise and intolerable sense of shock and bitter sorrow under a guise of simple sympathy.

"It was forgery," she explained. "This has never before passed our lips. Though a cherished wife and a beloved mother, she longed for many things my father could not give her, and in an evil hour she imitated the name of a rich man here and took the check thus signed to New York. The fraud was not detected, and she received the money, but ultimately the rich man whose money she had spent, discovered the use she had made of his name, and, if she had not escaped, would have had her arrested. But she left the country, and the only revenge he took, was to swear that if she ever set foot again in X., he would call the police down upon her. Yes, if she were dying, and they had to drag her from the brink of the grave. And he would have done it; and knowing this, we have lived under the shadow of this fear for eleven years. My father died under it, and my mother—ah, she spent all the remaining years of her life under foreign skies, but when she felt the hand of death upon her, her affection for her own flesh and blood triumphed over her discretion, and she came, secretly, I own, but still with that horror menacing her, to these doors, and begging our forgiveness, lay down under the roof where we were born, and died with the halo of our love about her."

"Ah," said I, thinking of all that had happened since I had come into this house and finding nothing but confirmation of what she was saying, "I begin to understand."

But Lucetta shook her head.

"No," said she, "you cannot understand yet. We who had worn mourning for her because my father wished to make this very return impossible, knew nothing of what was in store for us till a letter came saying she would be at the C. station on the very night we received it. To acknowledge our deception, to seek and bring her home openly to this house, could not be thought of for a moment. How, then, could we satisfy her dying wishes without compromising her memory and ourselves? Perhaps you have guessed, Miss Butterworth. You have had time since we revealed the unhappy secret of this household."

"Yes," said I. "I have guessed."

Lucetta, with her hand laid on mine, looked wistfully into my face.

"Don't blame us!" she cried. "Our mother's good name is everything to us, and we knew no other way to preserve it than by making use of the one superstition of this place. Alas! our efforts were in vain. The phantom coach brought our mother safely to us, but the circumstances which led to our doors being opened to outsiders, rendered it impossible for us to carry out our plans unsuspected. Her grave has been discovered and desecrated, and we——"

She stopped, choked. Loreen took advantage of her silence to pursue the explanations she seemed to think necessary.

"It was Simsbury who undertook to bring our dying mother from C. station to our door. He has a crafty spirit under his meek ways, and dressed himself in a way to lend color to the superstition he hoped to awaken. William, who did not dare to accompany him for fear of arousing gossip, was at the gate when the coach drove in. It was he who lifted our mother out, and it was while she still clung to him with her face pressed close to his breast that we saw her first. Ah! what a pitiable sight it was! She was so wan, so feeble, and yet so radiantly happy.

"She looked up at Lucetta, and her face grew wonderful in its unearthly beauty. She was not the mother we remembered, but a mother whose life had culminated in the one desire to see and clasp her children again. When she could tear her eyes away from Lucetta, she looked at me, and then the tears came, and we all wept together, even William; and thus weeping and murmuring words of welcome and cheer, we carried her up-stairs and laid her in the great front chamber. Alas! we did not foresee what would happen the very next morning—I mean the arrival of your telegram, to be followed so soon by yourself."

"Poor girls! Poor girls!" It was all I could say. I was completely overwhelmed.

"The first night after your arrival we moved her into William's room as being more remote and thus a safer refuge for her. The next night she died. The dream which you had of being locked in your room was no dream. Lucetta did that in foolish precaution against your trying to search us out in the night. It would have been better if we had taken you into our confidence."

"Yes," I assented, "that would have been better." But I did not say how much better. That would have been giving away my secret.

Lucetta had now recovered sufficiently to go on with the story.

"William, who is naturally colder than we and less sensitive in regard to our mother's good name, has shown some little impatience at the restraint imposed upon him by her presence, and this was an extra burden, Miss Butterworth, but that and all the others we have been forced to bear" (the generous girl did not speak of her own special grief and loss) "have all been rendered useless by the unhappy chance which has brought into our midst this agent of the police. Ah, if I only knew whether this was the providence of God rebuking us for years of deception, or just the malice of man seeking to rob us of our one best treasure, a mother's untarnished name!"

"Mr. Gryce acts from no malice—" I began, but I saw they were not listening.

"Have they finished down below?" asked Lucetta.

"Does the man you call Gryce seem satisfied?" asked Loreen.

I drew myself up physically and mentally. My second task was about to begin.

"I do not understand those men," said I. "They seem to want to look farther than the sacred spot where we left them. If they are going through a form, they are doing it very thoroughly."

"That is their duty," observed Loreen, but Lucetta took it less calmly.

"It is an unhappy day for us!" cried she. "Shame after shame, disgrace upon disgrace! I wish we had all died in our childhood. Loreen, I must see William. He will be doing some foolish thing, swearing or——"

"My dear, let me go to William," I urgently put in. "He may not like me overmuch, but I will at least prove a restraint to him. You are too feeble. See, you ought to be lying on the couch instead of trying to drag yourself out to the stables."

And indeed at that moment Lucetta's strength gave suddenly out, and she sank into Loreen's arms insensible.

When she was restored, I hurried away to the stables, still in pursuit of the task which I had not yet completed. I found William sitting doggedly on a stool in the open doorway, grunting out short sentences to the two men who lounged in his vicinity on either side. He was angry, but not as angry as I had seen him many times before. The men were townsfolk and listened eagerly to his broken sentences. One or two of these reached my ears.

"Let 'em go it. It won't be now or to-day they'll settle this business. It's the devil's work, and devils are sly. My house won't give up that secret, or any other house they'll be likely to visit. The place I would ransack—But Loreen would say I was babbling. Goodness knows a fellow's got to talk about something when his fellow-townsfolk come to see him." And here his laugh broke in, harsh, cruel, and insulting. I felt it did him no good, and made haste to show myself.

Immediately his whole appearance changed. He was so astonished to see me there that for a moment he was absolutely silent; then he broke out again into another loud guffaw, but this time in a different tone.

"Why, it's Miss Butterworth," he laughed. "Here, Saracen! Come, pay your respects to the lady who likes you so well."

And Saracen came, but I did not forsake my ground. I had espied in one corner just what I had hoped to see there, and Saracen's presence afforded me the opportunity of indulging in one or two rather curious antics.

"I am not afraid of the dog," I declared, with marked loftiness, shrinking toward the pail of water I had already marked with my eye. "Not at all afraid," I continued, catching up the pail and putting it before me as the dog made a wild rush in my direction. "These gentlemen will not see me hurt." And though they all laughed—they would have been fools if they had not—and the dog jumped the pail and I jumped—not a pail, but a broom-handle that was lying amid all the rest of the disorder on the floor—they did not see that I had succeeded in doing what I wished, which was to place that pail so near to William's feet that—But wait a moment; everything in its own time. I escaped the dog, and next moment had my eye on him. He did not move after that, which rather put a stop to the laughter, which observing, I drew very near to William, and with a sly gesture to the two men, which for some reason they seemed to understand, whispered in the rude fellow's ear:

"They've found your mother's grave under the Flower Parlor. Your sisters told me to tell you. But that is not all. They're trampling hither and yon through all the secret places in the cellar, turning up the earth with their spades. I know they won't find anything, but we thought you ought to know——"

Here I made a feint of being startled, and ceased. My second task was done. The third only remained. Fortunately at that moment Mr. Gryce and his followers showed themselves in the garden. They had just come from the cellar and played their part in the same spirit I had mine. Though they were too far off for their words to be heard, the air of secrecy they maintained and the dubious looks they cast towards the stable, could not but evince even to William's dull understanding that their investigations had resulted in a doubt which left them far from satisfied; but, once this impression made, they did not linger long together. The man with the lantern moved off, and Mr. Gryce turned towards us, changing his whole appearance as he advanced, till no one could look more cheerful and good-humored.

"Well, that is over," he sighed, with a forced air of infinite relief. "Mere form, Mr. Knollys—mere form. We have to go through these pretended investigations at times, and good people like yourself have to submit; but I assure you it is not pleasant, and under the present circumstances—I am sure you understand me, Mr. Knollys—the task has occasioned me a feeling almost of remorse; but that is inseparable from a detective's life. He is obliged every day of his life to ride over the tenderest emotions. Forgive me! And now, boys, scatter till I call you together again. I hope our next search will be without such sorrowful accompaniments."

It succeeded. William stared at him and stared at the men slowly filing off down the yard, but was not for a moment deceived by these overflowing expressions. On the contrary, he looked more concerned than he had while seated between the two men manifestly set to guard him.

"The deuce!" he cried, with a shrug of his shoulders that expressed anything but satisfaction. "Lucetta always said—" But even he knew enough not to finish that sentence, low as he had mumbled it. Watching him and watching Mr. Gryce, who at that moment turned to follow his men, I thought the time had come for action. Making another spring as if in fresh terror of Saracen, who, by the way, was eying me with the meekness of a lamb, I tipped over that pail with such suddenness and with such dexterity that its whole contents poured in one flood over William's feet. My third task was accomplished.

The oath he uttered and the excuses which I volubly poured forth could not have reached Mr. Gryce's ears, for he did not return. And yet from the way his shoulders shook as he disappeared around the corner of the house, I judge that he was not entirely ignorant of the subterfuge by which I hoped to force this blundering booby of ours to change the boots he wore for one of the pairs into which I had driven those little tacks.

XXXII RELIEF

The plan succeeded. Mr. Gryce's plans usually do. William went immediately to his room, and in a little while came down and hastened into the cellar.

"I want to see what mischief they have done," said he.

When he came back, his face was beaming.

"All right," he shouted to his sisters, who had come into the hall to meet him. "Your secret's out, but mine——"

"There, there!" interposed Loreen, "you had better go up-stairs and prepare for supper. We must eat, William, or rather, Miss Butterworth must eat, whatever our sorrows or disappointments."

He took the rebuke with a grunt and relieved us of his company. Little did he think as he went whistling up the stairs that he had just shown Mr. Gryce where to search for whatever might be lying under the broad sweep of that cellar-bottom.

That night—it was after supper, which I did not eat for all my natural stoicism—Hannah came rushing in where we all sat silent, for the girls showed no disposition to enlarge their confidences in regard to their mother, and no other topic seemed possible, and, closing the door behind her, said quickly and with evident chagrin:

"Those men are here again. They say they forgot something. What do you think it means, Miss Loreen? They have spades and lanterns and——"

"They are the police, Hannah. If they forgot something, they have the right to return. Don't work yourself up about that. The secret they have already found out was our worst. There is nothing to fear after that." And she dismissed Hannah, merely bidding her let us know when the house was quite clear.

Was she right? Was there nothing worse for them to fear? I longed to leave these trembling sisters, longed to join the party below and follow in the track of the tiny impressions made by the tacks I had driven into William's soles. If there was anything hidden under the cellar-bottom, natural anxiety would carry him to the spot he had most to fear; so they would only have to dig at the places where these impressions took a sharp turn.

But was there anything hidden there? From the sisters' words and actions I judged there was nothing serious, but would they know? William was quite capable of deceiving them. Had he done so? It was a question.

It was solved for us by Mr. Gryce's reappearance in the room an hour or so later. From the moment the light fell upon his kindly features I knew that I might breathe again freely. It was not the face he showed in the house of a criminal, nor did his bow contain any of the false deference with which he sometimes tries to hide his secret doubt or contempt.

"I have come to trouble you for the last time, ladies. We have made a double search through this house and through the stables, and feel perfectly justified in saying that our duty henceforth will lead us elsewhere. The secrets we have surprised are your own, and if possible shall remain so. Your brother's propensity for vivisection and the return and death of your mother bear so little on the real question which interests this community that we may be able to prevent their spread as gossip through the town. That this may be done conscientiously, however, I ought to know something more of the latter circumstance. If Miss Butterworth will then be good enough to grant me a few minutes' conference with these ladies, I may be able to satisfy myself to such an extent as to let this matter rest where it is."

I rose with right good will. A mountain weight had been lifted from me, proof positive that I had really come to love these girls.

What they told him, whether it was less or more than they told me, I cannot say, and for the moment did not know. That it had not shaken his faith in them was evident, for when he came out to where I was waiting in the hall his aspect was even more encouraging than it had been before.

"No guile in those girls," he whispered as he passed me. "The clue given by what seemed mysterious in this house has come to naught. To-morrow we take up another. The trinkets found in Mother Jane's cottage are something real. You may sleep soundly to-night, Miss Butterworth. Your part has been well played, but I know you are glad that it has failed."

And I knew that I was glad, too, which is the best proof that there is something in me besides the detective instinct.

The front door had scarcely closed behind him when William came storming in. He had been gossiping over the fence with Mr. Trohm, and had been beguiled into taking a glass of wine in his house. This was evident without his speaking of it.

"Those sneaks!" cried he. "I hear they've been back again, digging and stirring up our cellar-bottom like mad. That's because you're so dreadful shy, you girls. You're afraid of this, you're afraid of that. You don't want folks to know that mother once—Well, well, there it is now! If you had not tried to keep this wretched secret, it would have been an old matter by this time, and my affairs would have been left untouched. But now every fool will cry out at me in this staid, puritanical old town, and all because a few bones have been found of animals which have died in the cause of science. I say it's all your fault! Not that I have anything to be ashamed of, because I haven't, but because this other thing, this d—d wicked series of disappearances, taking place, for aught we know, a dozen rods from our gates (though I think—but no matter what I think—you all like, or say you like, old

Deacon Spear), has made every one so touchy in this pharisaical town that to kill a fly has become a crime even if it is to save oneself from poison. I'm going to see if I cannot make folks blink askance at some other man than me. I'm going to find out who or what causes these disappearances."

This was a declaration to make us all stare and look a little bit foolish. William playing the detective! Well, what might I not live to see next! But the next moment an overpowering thought struck me. Might this Deacon Spear by any chance be the rich man whose animosity Althea Knollys had awakened?

BOOK IV   THE BIRDS OF THE AIR

XXXIII   LUCETTA

The next morning I rose with the lark. I had slept well, and all my old vigor had returned. A new problem was before me; a problem of surpassing interest, now that the Knollys family had been eliminated from the list of persons regarded with suspicion by the police. Mother Jane and the jewels were to be Mr. Gryce's starting-point for future investigation. Should they be mine? My decision on this point halted, and thinking it might be helped by a breath of fresh air, I decided upon an early stroll as a means of settling this momentous question.

There was silence in the house when I passed through it on my way to the front door. But that silence had lost its terrors and the old house its absorbing mystery. Yet it was not robbed of its interest. When I realized that Althea Knollys, the Althea of my youth, had just died within its walls as ignorant of my proximity as I of hers, I felt that no old-time romance, nor any terror brought by flitting ghost or stalking apparition, could compare with the wonder of this return and the strange and thrilling circumstances which had attended it. And the end was not yet. Peaceful as everything now looked, I still felt that the end had not come.

The fact that Saracen was loose in the yard gave me some slight concern as I opened the great front door and looked out. But the control under which I had held him the day before encouraged me in my venture, and after a few words with Hannah, who was careful not to let me slip away unnoticed, I boldly stepped forth and took my solitary way down to the gate.

It was not yet eight, and the grass was still heavy with dew. At the gate I paused. I wished to go farther, but Mr. Gryce's injunction had been imperative about venturing into the lane alone. Besides—No, that was not a horse's hoof. There could be no one on the road so early as this. I was alarming myself unnecessarily, yet—Well, I held my place, a little awkwardly, perhaps. Self-consciousness is always awkward, and I could not help being a trifle self-conscious at a meeting so unexpected and—But the more I attempt to explain, the more confused my expressions become, so I will just say that, by this very strange chance, I was leaning over the gate when Mr. Trohm rode up for the second time and found me there.

I did not attempt any excuses. He is gentleman enough to understand that a woman of my temperament rises early and must have the morning air. That he should feel the same necessity is a coincidence, natural perhaps, but still a coincidence. So there was nothing to be said about it.

But had there been, I would not have spoken, for he seemed so gratified at finding me enjoying nature at this early hour that any words from me would have been quite superfluous. He did not dismount—that would have shown intention—but he stopped, and—well, we have both passed the age of romance, and what he said cannot be of interest to the general public, especially as it did not deal with the disappearances or with the discoveries made in the Knollys house the day before, or with any of those questions which have absorbed our attention up to this time.

That we were engaged more than five minutes in this conversation I cannot believe. I have always been extremely accurate in regard to time, yet a good half-hour was lost by me that morning for which I have never been able to account. Perhaps it was spent in the short discussion which terminated our interview; a discussion which may be of interest to you, for it was upon the action of the police.

"Nothing came of the investigations made by Mr. Gryce yesterday, I perceive," Mr. Trohm had remarked, with some reluctance, as he gathered up his reins to depart. "Well, that is not strange. How could he have hoped to find any clue to such a mystery as he is engaged to unearth, in a house presided over by Miss Knollys?"

"How could he, indeed! Yet," I added, determined to allay this man's suspicions, which, notwithstanding the openness of his remark, were still observable in his tones, "you say that with an air I should hardly expect from so good a neighbor and friend. Why is this, Mr. Trohm? Surely you do not associate crime with the Misses Knollys?"

"Crime? Oh, no, certainly not. No one could associate crime with the Misses Knollys. If my tone was at fault, it was due perhaps to my embarrassment—this meeting, your kindness, the beauty of the day, and the feeling these all call forth. Well, I may be pardoned if my tones are not quite true in discussing other topics. My thoughts were with the one I addressed."

"Then that tone of doubt was all the more misplaced," I retorted. "I am so frank, I cannot bear innuendo in others. Besides, Mr. Trohm, the worst folly of this home was laid bare yesterday in a way to set at rest all darker suspicions. You knew that William indulged in vivisection. Well, that is bad, but it cannot be called criminal. Let us do him justice, then, and, for his sisters' sake, see how we can re-establish him in the good graces of the community."

But Mr. Trohm, who for all our short acquaintance was not without a very decided appreciation for certain points in my character, shook his head and with a smiling air returned:

"You are asking the impossible not only of the community, but yourself. William can never re-establish himself. He is of too rude a make. The girls may recover the esteem they seem to have lost, but William—Why, if the cause of those disappearances was found to-day, and found at the remotest end of this road or even up in the mountains, where no one seems to have looked for it, William would still be known throughout the county as a rough and cruel man. I have tried to stand his friend, but it's been against odds, Miss Butterworth. Even his sisters recognize this, and show their lack of confidence in our friendship. But I would like to oblige you."

I knew he ought to go. I knew that if he had simply lingered the five minutes which common courtesy allowed, that curious eyes would be looking from Loreen's window, and that at any minute I might expect some interference from Lucetta, who had read through this man's forbearance toward William the very natural distrust he could not but feel toward so uncertain a character. Yet with such an opportunity at my command, how could I let him go without another question?

"Mr. Trohm," said I, "you have the kindest heart and the closest lips, but have you ever thought that Deacon Spear———"

He stopped me with a really horrified look. "Deacon Spear's house was thoroughly examined yesterday," said he, "as mine will be to-day. Don't insinuate anything against him! Leave that for foolish William." Then with the most charming return to his old manner, for I felt myself in a measure rebuked, he lifted his hat and urged his horse forward. But, having withdrawn himself a step or two, he paused and with the slightest gesture toward the little hut he was facing, added in a much lower tone than any he had yet used: "Besides, Deacon Spear is much too far away from Mother Jane's cottage. Don't you remember that I told you she never could be got to go more than forty rods from her own doorstep?" And, breaking into a quick canter, he rode away.

I was left to think over his words and the impossibility of my picking up any other clue than that given me by Mr. Gryce.

I was turning toward the house when I heard a slight noise at my feet. Looking down, I encountered the eyes of Saracen. He was crouching at my side, and as I turned toward him, his tail actually wagged. It was a sight to call the color up to my cheek; not that I blushed at this sign of good-will, astonishing as it was, considering my feeling toward dogs, but at his being there at all without my knowing it. So palpable a proof that no woman—I make no exceptions—can listen more than one minute to the expressions of a man's sincere admiration without losing a little of her watchfulness, was not to be disregarded by one as inexorable to her own mistakes as to those of others. I saw myself the victim of vanity, and while somewhat abashed by the discovery, I could not but realize that this solitary proof of feminine weakness was not really to be deplored in one who has not yet passed the line beyond which any such display is ridiculous.

Lucetta met me at the door just as I had expected her to. Giving me a short look, she spoke eagerly but with a latent anxiety, for which I was more or less prepared.

"I am glad to see you looking so bright this morning," she declared. "We are all feeling better now that the incubus of secrecy is removed. But"—here she hesitated—"I would not like to think you told Mr. Trohm what happened to us yesterday."

"Lucetta," said I, "there may be women of my age who delight in gossiping about family affairs with comparative strangers, but I am not that kind of woman. Mr. Trohm, friendly as he has proved himself and worthy as he undoubtedly is of your confidence and trust, will have to learn from some other person than myself anything which you may wish to have withheld from him."

For reply she gave me an impulsive kiss. "I thought I could trust you," she cried. Then, with a dubious look, half daring, half shrinking, she added:

"When you come to know and like us better, you will not care so much to talk to neighbors. They never can understand us or do us justice, Mr. Trohm, especially."

This was a remark I could not let pass.

"Why?" I demanded. "Why do you think Mr. Trohm cherishes such animosity towards you? Has he ever——"

But Lucetta could exercise a repellent dignity when she chose. I did not finish my sentence, though I must have looked the inquiry I thought better not to put into words.

"Mr. Trohm is a man of blameless reputation," she avowed. "If he has allowed himself to cherish suspicions in our regard, he has doubtless had his reasons for it."

And with these quiet words she left me to my thoughts, and I must say to my doubts, which were all the more painful that I saw no immediate opportunity for clearing them up.

Late in the afternoon William burst in with news from the other end of the lane.

"Such a lark!" he cried. "The investigation at Deacon Spear's house was a mere farce, and I just made them repeat it with a few frills. They had dug up my cellar, and I was determined they should dig up his. Oh, the fun it was! The old fellow kicked, but I had my way. They couldn't refuse me, you know; I hadn't refused them. So that man's cellar-bottom has had a stir up. They didn't find anything, but it did me a lot of good, and that's something. I do hate Deacon Spear—couldn't hate him worse if he'd killed and buried ten men under his hearthstone."

"There is no harm in Deacon Spear," said Lucetta, quickly.

"Did they submit Mr. Trohm's house to a search also?" asked Loreen, ashamed of William's heat and anxious to avert any further display of it.

"Yes, they went through that too. I was with them. Glad I was too. I say, girls, I could have laughed to see all the comforts that old bachelor has about him. Never saw such fixings. Why, that house is as neat and pretty from top to bottom as any old maid's. It's silly, of course, for a man, and I'd rather live in an old rookery like this, where I can walk from room to room in muddy boots if I want to, and train my dogs and live in freedom like the man I am. Yet I couldn't help thinking it mighty comfortable, too, for an old fellow like him who likes such things and don't have chick or child to meddle. Why, he had pincushions on all his bureaus, and they had pins in them."

The laugh with which he delivered this last sentence might have been heard a quarter of a mile away. Lucetta looked at Loreen and Loreen looked at me, but none of us joined in the mirth, which seemed to me very ill-timed.

Suddenly Lucetta asked:

"Did they dig up Mr. Trohm's cellar?"

William stopped laughing long enough to say:

"His cellar? Why, it's cemented as hard as an oak floor. No, they didn't polish their spades in his house, which was another source of satisfaction to me. Deacon Spear hasn't even that to comfort him. Oh, how I did enjoy that old fellow's face when they began to root up his old fungi!"

Lucetta turned away with a certain odd constraint I could not but notice.

"It's a humiliating day for the lane," said she. "And what is worse," she suddenly added, "nothing will ever come of it. It will take more than a band of police to reach the root of this matter."

I thought her manner odd, and, moving towards her, took her by the hand with something of a relative's familiarity.

"What makes you say that? Mr. Gryce seems a very capable man."

"Yes, yes, but capability has nothing to do with it. Chance might and pluck might, but wit and experience not. Otherwise the mystery would have been settled long ago. I wish I———"

"Well?" Her hand was trembling violently.

"Nothing. I don't know why I have allowed myself to talk on this subject. Loreen and I once made a compact never to give any opinion upon it. You see how I have kept it."

She had drawn her hand away and suddenly had become quite composed. I turned my attention toward Loreen, but she was looking out of the window and showed no intention of further pursuing the conversation. William had strolled out.

"Well," said I, "if ever a girl had reason for breaking such a compact you are certainly that girl. I could never have been as silent as you have been—that is, if I had any suspicions on so serious a subject. Why, your own good name is impugned—yours and that of every other person living in this lane."

"Miss Butterworth," she replied, "I have gone too far. Besides, you have misunderstood me. I have no more knowledge than anybody else as to the source of these terrible tragedies. I only know that an almost superhuman cunning lies at the bottom of so many unaccountable disappearances, a cunning so great that only a crazy person———"

"Ah," I murmured eagerly, "Mother Jane!"

She did not answer. Instantly I took a resolution.

"Lucetta," said I, "is Deacon Spear a rich man?"

Starting violently, she looked at me amazed.

"If he is, I should like to hazard the guess that he is the man who has held you in such thraldom for years."

"And if he were?" said she.

"I could understand William's antipathy to him and also his suspicions."

She gave me a strange look, then without answering walked over and took Loreen by the hand. "Hush!" I thought I heard her whisper. At all events the two sisters were silent for more than a moment. Then Lucetta said:

"Deacon Spear is well off, but nothing will ever make me accuse living man of crime so dreadful." And she walked away, drawing Loreen after her. In another moment she was out of the room, leaving me in a state of great excitement.

"This girl holds the secret to the whole situation," I inwardly decided. "The belief that nothing more can be learned from her is a false one. I must see Mr. Gryce. William's rodomontades are so much empty air, but Lucetta's silence has a meaning we cannot afford to ignore."

So impressed was I by this, that I took the first opportunity which presented itself of seeing the detective. This was early the next morning. He and several of the townspeople had made their appearance at Mother Jane's cottage, with spades and picks, and the sight had naturally drawn us all down to the gate, where we stood watching operations in a silence which would have been considered unnatural by any one who did not realize the conflicting nature of the emotions underlying it. William, to whom the death of his mother seemed to be a great deliverance, had been inclined to be more or less jocular, but his sallies meeting with no response, he had sauntered away to have it out with his dogs, leaving me alone with the two girls and Hannah.

The latter seemed to be absorbed entirely by the aspect of Mother Jane, who stood upon her doorstep in an attitude so menacing that it was little short of tragic. Her hood, for the first time in the memory of those present, had fallen away from her head, revealing a wealth of gray hair which flew away from her head like a weird halo. Her features we could not distinguish, but the emotion which inspired her, breathed in every gesture of her uplifted arms and swaying body. It was wrath personified, and yet an unreasoning wrath. One could see she was as much dazed as outraged. Her lares and penates were being attacked, and she had come from the heart of her solitude to defend them.

"I declare!" Hannah protested. "It is pitiful. She has nothing in the world but that garden, and now they are going to root that up."

"Do you think that the sight of a little money would appease her?" I inquired, anxious for an excuse to drop a word into the ear of Mr. Gryce.

"Perhaps," said Hannah. "She dearly loves money, but it will not take away her fright."

"It will if she has nothing to be frightened about," said I; and turning to the girls, I asked them, somewhat mincingly for me, if they thought I would make myself conspicuous if I crossed the road on this errand, and when Loreen answered that that would not deter her if she had the money, and Lucetta added that the sight of such misery was too painful for any mere personal consideration, I took advantage of their complaisance, and hastily made my way over to the group, who were debating as to the point they would attack first.

"Gentlemen," said I, "good-morning. I am here on an errand of mercy. Poor old Mother Jane is half imbecile and does not understand why you invade her premises with these implements. Will you object if I endeavor to distract her mind with a little piece of gold I happen to have in my pocket? She may not deserve it, but it will make your task easier and save us some possible concern."

Half of the men at once took off their hats. The other half nudged each other's elbows, and whispered and grimaced like the fools they were. The first half were gentlemen, though not all of them wore gentlemen's clothes.

It was Mr. Gryce who spoke:

"Certainly, madam. Give the old woman anything you please, but—" And here he stepped up to me and began to whisper; "You have something to say. What is it?"

I answered in the same quick way: "The mine you thought exhausted has possibilities in it yet. Question Lucetta. It may prove a more fruitful task than turning up this soil."

The bow he made was more for the onlookers than for the suggestion I had given him. Yet he was not ungrateful for the latter, as I, who was beginning to understand him, could see.

"Be as generous as you please!" he cried aloud. "We would not disturb the old crone if it were not for one of her well-known follies. Nothing will take her over forty rods away from her home. Now what lies within those forty rods? These men think we ought to see."

The shrug I gave answered both the apparent and the concealed question. Satisfied that he would understand it so, I hurried away from him and approached Mother Jane.

"See!" said I, astonished at the regularity of her features, now that I had a good opportunity of observing them. "I have brought you money. Let them dig up your turnips if they will."

She did not seem to perceive me. Her eyes were wild with dismay and her lips trembling with a passion far beyond my power to comfort.

"Lizzie!" she cried. "Lizzie! She will come back and find no home. Oh, my poor girl! My poor, poor girl!"

It was pitiable. I could not doubt her anguish or her sincerity. The delirium of a broken heart cannot be simulated. And this heart was not controlled by reason; that was equally apparent. Immediately my heart, which goes out slowly, but none the less truly on that account, was touched by something more than the surface sympathy of the moment. She may have stolen, she may have done worse, she may even have been at the bottom of the horrible crimes which have given its name to the lane we were in, but her acts, if acts they were, were the result of a clouded mind fixed forever upon the fancied needs of another, and not the expression of personal turpitude or even of personal longing or avarice. Therefore I could pity her, and I did.

Making another appeal, I pressed the coin hard into one of her hands till the contact effected what my words had been unable to do, and she finally looked down and saw what she was clutching. Then indeed her aspect changed, and in a few minutes of slowly growing comprehension she became so quiet and absorbed that she forgot to look at the men and even forgot me, who was probably nothing more than a flitting shadow to her.

"A silk gown," she murmured. "It will buy Lizzie a silk gown. Oh! where did it come from, the good, good gold, the beautiful gold; such a little piece, yet enough to make her look fine, my Lizzie, my pretty, pretty Lizzie?"

No numbers this time. The gift was too overpowering for her even to remember that it must be hidden away.

I walked away while her delight was still voluble. Somehow it eased my mind to have done her this little act of kindness, and I think it eased the minds of the men too. At all events, every hat was off when I repassed them on my way back to the Knollys gateway.

I had left both the girls there, but I found only one awaiting me. Lucetta had gone in, and so had Hannah. On what errand I was soon to know.

"What do you suppose that detective wants of Lucetta now?" asked Loreen as I took my station again at her side. "While you were talking to Mother Jane he stepped over here, and with a word or two induced Lucetta to walk away with him toward the house. See, there they are in those thick shrubs near the right wing. He seems to be pleading with her. Do you think I ought to join them and find out what he is urging upon her so earnestly? I don't like to seem intrusive, but Lucetta is easily agitated, you know, and his business cannot be of an indifferent nature after all he has discovered concerning our affairs."

"No," I agreed, "and yet I think Lucetta will be strong enough to sustain the conversation, judging from the very erect attitude she is holding now. Perhaps he thinks she can tell him where to dig. They seem a little at sea over there, and living, as you do, a few rods from Mother Jane, he may imagine that Lucetta can direct him where to first plant the spade."

"It's an insult," Loreen protested. "All these talks and visits are insults. To be sure, this detective has some excuse, but——"

"Keep your eye on Lucetta," I interrupted. "She is shaking her head and looking very positive. She will prove to him it is an insult. We need not interfere, I think."

But Loreen had grown pensive and did not heed my suggestion. A look that was almost wistful had supplanted the expression of indignant revolt with which she had addressed me, and when next moment the two we had been watching turned and came slowly toward us, it was with decided energy she bounded forward and joined them.

"What is the matter now?" she asked. "What does Mr. Gryce want, Lucetta?"

Mr. Gryce himself spoke.

"I simply want her," said he, "to assist me with a clue from her inmost thoughts. When I was in your house," he explained with a praiseworthy consideration for me and my relations to these girls for which I cannot be too grateful, "I saw in this young lady something which convinced me that, as a dweller in this lane, she was not without her suspicions as to the secret cause of the fatal mysteries which I have been sent here to clear up. To-day I have frankly accused her of this, and asked her to confide in me. But she refuses to do so, Miss Loreen. Yet her face shows even at this moment that my old eyes were not at fault in my reading of her. She does suspect somebody, and it is not Mother Jane."

"How can you say that?" began Lucetta, but the eyes which Loreen that moment turned upon her seemed to trouble her, for she did not attempt to say any more—only looked equally obstinate and distressed.

"If Lucetta suspects any one," Loreen now steadily remarked, "then I think she ought to tell you who it is."

"You do. Then perhaps you—" commenced Mr. Gryce—"can persuade her as to her duty," he finished, as he saw her head rise in protest of what he evidently had intended to demand.

"Lucetta will not yield to persuasion," was her quiet reply. "Nothing short of conviction will move the sweetest-natured but the most determined of all my mother's children. What she thinks is right, she will do. I will not attempt to influence her."

Mr. Gryce, with one comprehensive survey of the two, hesitated no longer. I saw the rising of the blood into his forehead, which always precedes the beginning of one of his great moves, and, filled with a sudden excitement, I awaited his next words as a tyro awaits the first unfolding of the plan he has seen working in the brain of some famous strategist.

"Miss Lucetta,"—his very tone was changed, changed in a way to make us all start notwithstanding the preparation his momentary silence had given us—"I have been thus pressing and perhaps rude in my appeal, because of something which has come to my knowledge which cannot but make you of all persons extremely anxious as to the meaning of this terrible mystery. I am an old man, and you will not mind my bluntness. I have been told—and your agitation convinces me there is truth in the report—that you have a lover, a Mr. Ostrander——"

"Ah!" She had sunk as if crushed by one overwhelming blow to the earth. The eyes, the lips, the whole pitiful face that was upturned to us, remain in my memory to-day as the most terrible and yet the most moving spectacle that has come into my by no means uneventful life. "What has happened to him? Quick, quick, tell me!"

For answer Mr. Gryce drew out a telegram.

"From the master of the ship on which he was to sail," he explained. "It asks if Mr. Ostrander left this town on Tuesday last, as no news has been received of him."

"Loreen! Loreen! When he left us he passed down that way!" shrieked the girl, rising like a spirit and pointing east toward Deacon Spear's. "He is gone! He is lost! But his fate shall not remain a mystery. I will dare its solution. I—I—To-night you will hear from me again."

And without another glance at any of us she turned and fled toward the house.

XXXIV CONDITIONS

But in another moment she was back, her eyes dilated and her whole person exhaling a terrible purpose.

"Do not look at me, do not notice me!" she cried, but in a voice so hoarse no one but Mr. Gryce could fully understand her. "I am for no one's eyes but God's. Pray that he may have mercy upon me." Then as she saw us all instinctively fall back, she controlled herself, and, pointing toward Mother Jane's cottage, said more distinctly: "As for those men, let them dig. Let them dig the whole day long. Secrecy must be kept, a secrecy so absolute that not even the birds of the air must see that our thoughts range beyond the forty rods surrounding Mother Jane's cottage."

She turned and would have fled away for the second time, but Mr. Gryce stopped her. "You have set yourself a task beyond your strength. Can you perform it?"

"I can perform it," she said. "If Loreen does not talk, and I am allowed to spend the day in solitude."

I had never seen Mr. Gryce so agitated—no, not when he left Olive Randolph's bedside after an hour of vain pleading. "But to wait all day! Is it necessary for you to wait all day?"

"It is necessary." She spoke like an automaton. "To-night at twilight, when the sun is setting, meet me at the great tree just where the road turns. Not a minute sooner, not an hour later. I will be calmer then." And waiting now for nothing, not for a word from Loreen nor a detaining touch from Mr. Gryce, she flew away for the second time. This time Loreen followed her.

"Well, that is the hardest thing I ever had to do," said Mr. Gryce, wiping his forehead and speaking in a tone of real grief and anxiety. "Do you think her delicate frame can stand it? Will she survive this day and carry through whatever it is she has set herself to accomplish?"

"She has no organic disease," said I, "but she loved that young man very much, and the day will be a terrible one to her."

Mr. Gryce sighed.

"I wish I had not been obliged to resort to such means," said he, "but women like that only work under excitement, and she does know the secret of this affair."

"Do you mean," I demanded, almost aghast, "that you have deceived her with a false telegram; that that slip of paper you hold——"

"Read it," he cried, holding it out toward me.

I did read it. Alas, there was no deception in it. It read as he said.

"However—" I began.

But he had pocketed the telegram and was several steps away before I had finished my sentence.

"I am going to start these men up," said he. "You will breathe no word to Miss Lucetta of my sympathy nor let your own interests slack in the investigations which are going on under our noses."

And with a quick, sharp bow, he made his way to the gate, whither I followed him in time to see him set his foot upon a patch of sage.

"You will begin at this place," he cried, "and work east; and, gentlemen, something tells me that we shall be successful."

With almost a simultaneous sound a dozen spades and picks struck the ground. The digging up of Mother Jane's garden had begun in earnest.

XXXV   THE DOVE

I remained at the gate. I had been bidden to show my interest in what was going on in Mother Jane's garden, and this was the way I did it. But my thoughts were not with the diggers. I knew, as well then as later, that they would find nothing worth the trouble they were taking; and, having made up my mind to this, I was free to follow the lead of my own thoughts.

They were not happy ones; I was neither satisfied with myself nor with the prospect of the long day of cruel suspense that awaited us. When I undertook to come to X., it was with the latent expectation of making myself useful in ferreting out its mystery. And how had I succeeded? I had been the means through which one of its secrets had been discovered, but not the secret; and while Mr. Gryce was good enough, or wise enough, to show no diminution in his respect for me, I knew that I had sunk a peg in his estimation from the consciousness I had of having sunk two, if not three pegs, in my own.

This was a galling thought to me. But it was not the only one which disturbed me. Happily or unhappily, I have as much heart as pride, and Lucetta's despair, and the desperate resolve to which it had led, had made an impression upon me which I could not shake off.

Whether she knew the criminal or only suspected him; whether in the heat of her sudden anguish she had promised more or less than she could perform, the fact remained that we (by whom I mean first and above all, Mr. Gryce, the ablest detective on the New York force, and myself, who, if no detective, am at least a factor of more or less importance in an inquiry like this) were awaiting the action of a weak and suffering girl to discover what our own experience should be able to obtain for us unassisted.

That Mr. Gryce felt that he was playing a great card in thus enlisting her despair in our service, did not comfort me. I am not fond of games in which real hearts take the place of painted ones; and, besides, I was not ready to acknowledge that my own capacity for ferreting out this mystery was quite exhausted, or that I ought to remain idle while Lucetta bent under a task so much beyond her strength. So deeply was I impressed by this latter consideration, that I found myself, even in the midst of my apparent interest in what was going on at Mother Jane's cottage, asking if I was bound to accept the defeat pronounced upon my efforts by Mr. Gryce, and if there was not yet time to retrieve myself and save Lucetta. One happy thought, or clever linking of cause to effect, might lead me yet to the clue which we had hitherto sought in vain. And then who would have more right to triumph than Amelia Butterworth, or who more reason to apologize than Ebenezar Gryce! But where was I to get my happy thought, and by what stroke of fortune could I reasonably hope to light upon a clue which had escaped the penetrating eye of my quondam colleague? Lucetta's gesture and Lucetta's exclamation, "He passed that way!" indicated that her suspicions pointed in the direction of Deacon Spear's cottage; so did William's wandering accusations: but this was little help to me, confined as I was to the Knollys demesnes, both by Mr. Gryce's command and by my own sense of propriety. No, I must light on something more tangible; something practical enough to justify me in my own eyes for any interference I might meditate. In short, I must start from a fact, and not from a suspicion. But what fact? Why, there was but one, and that was the finding of certain indisputable tokens of crime in Mother Jane's keeping. That was a clue, a clue, to be sure, which Mr. Gryce, while ostensibly following it in his present action, really felt to lead nowhere, but which I—Here my thoughts paused. I dare not promise myself too satisfactory results to my efforts, even while conscious of that vague elation which presages success, and which I could only overcome by resorting again to reasoning. This time I started with a question. Had Mother Jane committed these crimes herself? I did not think so; neither did Mr. Gryce, for all the persistence he showed in having the ground about her humble dwelling-place turned over. Then, how had the ring of Mr. Chittenden come to be in her possession, when, as all agreed, she never was known to wander more than forty rods away from home? If the crime by which this young gentleman had perished had taken place up the road, as Lucetta's denouncing finger plainly indicated, then this token of Mother Jane's complicity in it had been carried across the intervening space by other means than Mother Jane herself. In other words, it was brought to her by the perpetrator, or it was placed where she could lay hand on it; neither supposition implying guilt on her part, she being in all probability as innocent of wrong as she was of sense. At all events, such should be my theory for the nonce, old theories having exploded or become of little avail in the present aspect of things. To discover, then, the source of crime, I must discover the means by which this ring reached Mother Jane—an almost hopeless task, but not to be despaired of on that account: had I not wrung the truth in times gone by from that piece of obstinate stolidity the Van Burnam scrub-woman? and if I could do this, might I not hope to win an equal confidence from this half-demented creature, with a heart so passionate it beat to but one tune, her Lizzie? I meant at least to try, and, under the impulse of this resolve, I left my position at the gate and recrossed the road to Mother Jane, whose figure I could dimly discern on the farther side of her little house.

Mr. Gryce barely looked up as I passed him, and the men not at all. They were deep in their work, and probably did not see me. Neither did Mother Jane at first. She had not yet wearied of the shining gold she held, though she had begun again upon that chanting of numbers the secret of which Mr. Gryce had discovered in his investigation of her house.

I therefore found it hard to make her hear me when I attempted to speak. She had fixed upon the new number fifteen and seemed never to tire of repeating it. At last I took cue from her speech, and shouted out the word ten. It was the number of the vegetable in which Mr. Chittenden's ring had been hidden, and it made her start violently.

"Ten! ten!" I reiterated, catching her eye. "He who brought it has carried it away; come into the house and look."

It was a desperate attempt. I felt myself quake inwardly as I realized how near Mr. Gryce was standing, and what his anger would be if he surprised me at this move after he had cried "Halt!"

But neither my own perturbation nor the thought of his possible anger could restrain the spirit of investigation which had returned to me with the above words; and when I saw that they had not fallen upon deaf ears, but that Mother Jane heard and in a measure understood them, I led the way into the hut and pointed to the string from which the one precious vegetable had been torn.

She gave a spring toward it that was well-nigh maniacal in its fury, and for an instant I thought she was going to rend the air with one of her wild yells, when there came a swishing of wings at one of the open windows, and a dove flew in and nestled in her breast, diverting her attention so, that she dropped the empty husk of the onion she had just grasped and seized the bird in its stead. It was a violent clutch, so violent that the poor dove panted and struggled under it till its head flopped over and I looked to see it die in her hands.

"Stop!" I cried, horrified at a sight I was so unprepared to expect from one who was supposed to cherish these birds most tenderly.

But she heard me no more than she saw the gesture of indignant appeal I made her. All her attention, as well as all her fury, was fixed upon the dove, over whose neck and under whose wings she ran her trembling fingers with the desperation of one looking for something he failed to find.

"Ten! ten!" it was now her turn to shout, as her eyes passed in angry menace from the bird to the empty husk that dangled over her head. "You brought it, did you, and you've taken it, have you? There, then! You'll never bring or carry any more!" And lifting up her hand, she flung the bird to the other side of the room, and would have turned upon me, in which contingency I would for once have met my match, if, in releasing the bird from her hands, she had not at the same time released the coin which she had hitherto managed to hold through all her passionate gestures.

The sight of this piece of gold, which she had evidently forgotten for the moment, turned her thoughts back to the joys it promised her. Recapturing it once more, she sank again into her old ecstasy, upon which I proceeded to pick up the poor, senseless dove, and leave the hut with a devout feeling of gratitude for my undoubted escape.

That I did this quietly and with the dove hidden under my little cape, no one who knows me well will doubt. I had brought something from the hut besides this victim of the old imbecile's fury, and I was no more willing that Mr. Gryce should see the one than detect the other. I had brought away a clue.

"The birds of the air shall carry it." So the Scripture runs. This bird, this pigeon, who now lay panting out his life in my arms had brought her the ring which in Mr. Gryce's eyes had seemed to connect her with the disappearance of young Mr. Chittenden.

XXXVI   AN HOUR OF STARTLING EXPERIENCES

Not till I was safely back in the Knollys grounds, not, indeed, till I had put one or two large and healthy shrubs between me and a certain pair of very prying eyes, did I bring the dove out from under my cape and examine the poor bird for any sign which might be of help to me in the search to which I was newly committed.

But I found nothing, and was obliged to resort to my old plan of reasoning to make anything out of the situation in which I thus so unexpectedly found myself. The dove had brought the ring into old Mother Jane's hands, but whence and through whose agency? This was as much a secret as before, but the longer I contemplated it, the more I realized that it need not remain a secret long; that we had simply to watch the other doves, note where they lighted, and in whose barn-doors they were welcome, for us to draw inferences that might lead to revelations before the day was out. If Deacon Spear—But Deacon Spear's house had been examined as well as that of every other resident in the lane. This I knew, but it had not been examined by me, and unwilling as I was to challenge the accuracy or thoroughness of a search led on by such a man as Mr. Gryce, I could not but feel that, with such a hint as I had received from the episode in the hut, it would be a great relief to my mind to submit these same premises to my own somewhat penetrating survey, no man in my judgment having the same quickness of eyesight in matters domestic as a woman trained to know every inch of a house and to measure by a hair's-breadth every fall of drapery within it.

But how in the name of goodness was I to obtain an opportunity for this survey. Had we not one and all been bidden to confine our attention to what was going on in Mother Jane's cottage, and would it not be treason to Lucetta to run the least risk of awakening apprehension in any possibly guilty mind at the other end of the road? Yes, but for all that I could not keep still if fate, or my own ingenuity, offered me the least chance of pursuing the clue I had wrung from our imbecile neighbor at the risk of my life. It was not in my nature to do so, any more than it was in my nature to yield up my present advantage to Mr. Gryce without making a personal effort to utilize it. I forgot that I failed in this once before in my career, or rather I recalled this failure, perhaps, and felt the great need of retrieving myself.

When, therefore, in my slow stroll towards the house I encountered William in the shrubbery, I could not forbear accosting him with a question or two.

"William," I remarked, gently rubbing the side of my nose with an irresolute forefinger and looking at him from under my lids, "that was a scurvy trick you played Deacon Spear yesterday."

He stood amazed, then burst into one of his loud laughs.

"You think so?" he cried. "Well, I don't. He only got what he deserved, the hard, sanctimonious sneak!"

"Do you say that," I inquired, with some spirit, "because you dislike the man, or because you really believe him to be worthy of hatred?"

William's amusement at this argued little for my hopes.

"We are very much interested in the Deacon," he suggested, with a leer; which insolence I allowed to pass unnoticed, because it best suited my plan.

"You have not answered my question," I remarked, with a forced air of anxiety.

"Oh, no," he cried, "so I haven't"; and he tried to look serious too. "Well, well, to be just, I have nothing really against the man but his mean ways. Still, if I were going to risk my life on a hazard as to who is the evil spirit of this lane, I should say Spear and done with it, he has such cursed small eyes."

"I don't think his eyes are too small," I returned loftily. Then with a sudden change of manner, I suggested anxiously: "And my opinion is shared by your sisters. They evidently think very well of him."

"Oh!" he sneered; "girls are no judges. They don't know a good man when they see him, and they don't know a bad. You mustn't go by what they say."

I had it on the tip of my tongue to ask if he did not think Lucetta sufficiently understood herself to be trusted in what she contemplated doing that night. But this was neither in accordance with my plan, nor did it seem quite loyal to Lucetta, who, so far as I knew, had not communicated her intentions to this booby brother. I therefore changed this question into a repetition of my first remark:

"Well, I still think the trick you played Deacon Spear yesterday a poor one; and I advise you, as a gentleman, to go and ask his pardon."

This was such a preposterous proposition, he could not hold his peace.

"I ask his pardon!" he snorted. "Well, Saracen, did you ever hear the like of that! I ask Deacon Spear's pardon for obliging him to be treated with as great attention as I had been myself."

"If you do not," I went on, unmoved, "I shall go and do it myself. I think that is what my friendship for you warrants. I am determined that while I am a visitor in your house no one shall be able to pick a flaw in your conduct."

He stared (as he might well do), tried to read my face, then my intentions, and failing to do both, which was not strange, broke into noisy mirth.

"Oh, ho!" he laughed. "So that is your game, is it! Well, I never! Saracen, Miss Butterworth wants to reform me; wants to make one of her sleek city chaps out of William Knollys. She'll have hard work of it, won't she? But then we're beginning to like her well enough to let her try. Miss Butterworth, I'll go with you to Deacon Spear. I haven't had so much chance for fun in a twelve-month."

I had not expected such success, and was duly thankful. But I made no reference to it aloud. On the contrary, I took his complaisance as a matter of course, and, hiding all token of triumph, suggested quietly that we should make as little ado as possible over our errand, seeing that Mr. Gryce was something of a meddler and might take it into his head to interfere. Which suggestion had all the effect I anticipated, for at the double prospect of amusing himself at the Deacon's expense, and of outwitting the man whose business it was to outwit us, he became not only willing but eager to undertake the adventure offered him. So with the understanding that I was to be ready to drive into town as soon as he could hitch up the horse, we parted on the most amicable terms, he proceeding towards the stable and I towards the house, where I hoped to learn something new about Lucetta.

But Loreen, from whom alone I could hope to glean any information, was shut in her room, and did not come out, though I called her more than once, which, if it left my curiosity unsatisfied, at least allowed me to quit the house without awakening hers.

William was waiting for me at the gate when I descended. He was in the best of humors, and helped me into the buggy he had resurrected from some corner of the old stable, with a grimace of suppressed mirth which argued well for the peace of our proposed drive. The horse's head was turned away from the quarter we were bound for, but as we were ostensibly on our way to the village, this showed but common prudence on William's part, and, as such, met with my entire approbation.

Mr. Gryce and his men were hard at work when we passed them. Knowing the detective so well, and rating at its full value his undoubted talent for reading the motives of those about him, I made no attempt at cajolery in the explanation I proffered of our sudden departure, but merely said, in my old, peremptory way, that I found waiting at the gate so tedious that I had accepted William's invitation to drive into town. Which, while it astonished the old gentleman, did not really arouse his suspicions, as a more conciliatory manner and speech might have done. This disposed of, we drove rapidly away.

William's sense of humor once aroused was not easily allayed. He seemed so pleased with his errand that he could talk of nothing else, and turned the subject over and over in his clumsy way, till I began to wonder if he had seen through the object of our proposed visit and was making me the butt of his none too brilliant wit.

But no, he was really amused at the part he was called upon to play, and, once convinced of this, I let his humor run on without check till we had re-entered Lost Man's Lane from the other end and were in sight of the low sloping roof of Deacon Spear's old-fashioned farmhouse.

Then I thought it time to speak.

"William," said I, "Deacon Spear is too good a man, and, as I take it, is in possession of too great worldly advantages for you to be at enmity with him. Remember that he is a neighbor, and that you are a landed proprietor in this lane."

"Good for you!" was the elegant reply with which this young boor honored me. "I didn't think you had such an eye for the main chance."

"Deacon Spear is rich, is he not?" I pursued, with an ulterior motive he was far from suspecting.

"Rich? Why, I don't know; that depends upon what you city ladies call rich; I shouldn't call him so, but then, as you say, I am a landed proprietor myself."

His laugh was boisterously loud, and as we were then nearly in front of the Deacon's house, it rang in through the open windows, causing such surprise, that more than one head bobbed up from within to see who dared to laugh like that in Lost Man's Lane. While I noted these heads and various other small matters about the house and place, William tied up the horse and held out his hand for me to descend.

"I begin to suspect," he whispered as he helped me out, "why you are so anxious to have me on good terms with the Deacon." At which insinuation I attempted to smile, but only succeeded in forcing a grim twitch or two to my lips, for at that moment and before I could take one step towards the house, a couple of pigeons rose up from behind the house and flew away in a bee-line for Mother Jane's cottage.

"Ha!" thought I; "my instinct has not failed me. Behold the link between this house and the hut in which those tokens of crime were found," and was for the moment so overwhelmed by this confirmation of my secret suspicions, that I quite forgot to advance, and stood stupidly staring after these birds now rapidly disappearing in the distance.

William's voice aroused me.

"Come!" he cried. "Don't be bashful. I don't think much of Deacon Spear myself, but if you do—Why, what's the matter now?" he asked, with a startled look at me. I had clutched him by the arm.

"Nothing," I protested, "only—you see that window over there? The one in the gable of the barn, I mean. I thought I saw a hand thrust out,—a white hand that dropped crumbs. Have they a child on this place?"

"No," replied William, in an odd voice and with an odd look toward the window I have mentioned. "Did you really see a hand there?"

"I most certainly did," I answered, with an air of indifference I was far from feeling. "Some one is up in the hay-loft; perhaps it is Deacon Spear himself. If so, he will have to come down, for now that we are here, I am determined you shall do your duty."

"Deacon Spear can't climb that hay-loft," was the perplexed answer I received in a hardly intelligible mutter. "I've been there, and I know; only a boy or a very agile young man could crawl along the beams that lead to that window. It is the one hiding-place in this part of the lane; and when I said yesterday that if I were the police and had the same search to make which they have, I knew where I would look, I meant that same little platform up behind the hay, whose only outlook is yonder window. But I forgot that you have no suspicions of our good Deacon; that you are here on quite a different errand than to search for Silly Rufus. So come along and——"

But I resisted his impelling hand. He was so much in earnest and so evidently under the excitement of what appeared to him a great discovery, that he seemed quite another man. This made my own suspicions less hazardous, and also added to the situation fresh difficulties which could only be met by an appearance on my part of perfect ingenuousness.

Turning back to the buggy as if I had forgotten something, and thus accounting to any one who might be watching us, for the delay we showed in entering the house, I said to William: "You have reasons for thinking this man a villain, or you wouldn't be so ready to suspect him. Now what if I should tell you that I agree with you, and that this is why I have dragged you here this fine morning?"

"I should say you were a deuced smart woman," was his ready answer. "But what can you do here?"

"What have we already done?" I asked. "Discovered that they have some one in hiding in what you call an inaccessible place in the barn. But didn't the police examine the whole place yesterday? They certainly told me they had searched the premises thoroughly."

"Yes," he repeated, with great disdain, "they said and they said; but they didn't climb up to the one hiding-place in sight. That old fellow Gryce declared it wasn't worth their while; that only birds could reach that loophole."

"Oh," I returned, somewhat taken aback; "you called his attention to it, then?"

To which William answered with a vigorous nod and the grumbling words:

"I don't believe in the police. I think they're often in league with the very rogues they——"

But here the necessity of approaching the house became too apparent for further delay. Deacon Spear had shown himself at the front door, and the sight of his astonished face twisted into a grimace of doubtful welcome drove every other thought away than how we were to acquit ourselves in the coming interview. Seeing that William was more or less nonplussed by the situation, I caught him by the arm, and whispering, "Let us keep to our first programme," led him up the walk with much the air of a triumphant captain bringing in a recalcitrant prisoner.

My introduction under these circumstances can be imagined by those who have followed William's awkward ways. But the Deacon, who was probably the most surprised, if not the most disconcerted member of the group, possessed a natural fund of conceit and self-complacency that prevented any outward manifestation of his feelings, though I could not help detecting a carefully suppressed antagonism in his eye when he allowed it to fall upon William, which warned me to exercise my full arts in the manipulation of the matter before me. I accordingly spoke first and with all the prim courtesy such a man might naturally expect from an intruder of my sex and appearance.

"Deacon Spear," said I, as soon as we were seated in his stiff old-fashioned parlor, "you are astonished to see us here, no doubt, especially after the display of animosity shown towards you yesterday by this graceless young friend of mine. But it is on account of this unfortunate occurrence that we are here. After a little reflection and a few hints, I may add, from one who has seen more of life than himself, William felt that he had cause to be ashamed of himself for his show of sport in yesterday's proceedings, and accordingly he has come in my company to tender his apologies and entreat your forbearance. Am I not right, William?"

The fellow is a clown under all and every circumstance, and serious as our real purpose was, and dreadful as was the suspicion he professed to cherish against the suave and seemingly respectable member of the community we were addressing, he could not help laughing, as he blunderingly replied:

"That you are, Miss Butterworth! She's always right, Deacon. I did act like a fool yesterday." And seeming to think that, with this one sentence he had played his part out to perfection, he jumped up and strolled out of the house, almost pushing down as he did so the two daughters of the house, who had crept into the hall from the sitting-room to listen.

"Well, well!" exclaimed the Deacon, "you have done wonders, Miss Butterworth, to bring him to even so small an acknowledgment as that! He's a vicious one, is William Knollys, and if I were not such a lover of peace and concord, he should not long be the only aggressive one. But I have no taste for strife, and so you may both regard his apology as accepted. But why do you rise, madam? Sit down, I pray, and let me do the honors. Martha! Jemima!"

But I would not allow him to summon his daughters. The man inspired me with too much dislike, if not fear; besides, I was anxious about William. What was he doing, and of what blunder might he not be guilty without my judicious guidance?

"I am obliged to you," I returned; "but I cannot wait to meet your daughters now. Another time, Deacon. There is important business going on at the other end of the lane, and William's presence there may be required."

"Ah," he observed, following me to the door, "they are digging up Mother Jane's garden."

I nodded, restraining myself with difficulty.

"Fool's work!" he muttered. Then with a curious look which made me instinctively draw back, he added, "These things must inconvenience you, madam. I wish you had made your visit to the lane in happier times."

There was a smirk on his face which made him positively repellent. I could scarcely bow my acknowledgments, his look and attitude made the interview so obnoxious. Looking about for William, I stepped down from the stoop. The Deacon followed me.

"Where is William?" I asked.

The Deacon ran his eye over the place, and suddenly frowned with ill-concealed vexation.

"The scapegrace!" he murmured. "What business has he in my barn?"

I immediately forced a smile which, in days long past (I've almost forgotten them now), used to do some execution.

"Oh, he's a boy!" I exclaimed. "Do not mind his pranks, I pray. What a comfortable place you have here!"

Instantly a change passed over the Deacon, and he turned to me with an air of great interest, broken now and then by an uneasy glance behind him at the barn.

"I am glad you like the place," he insinuated, keeping close at my side as I stepped somewhat briskly down the walk. "It is a nice place, worthy of the commendation of so competent a judge as yourself." (It was a barren, hard-worked farm, without one attractive feature.) "I have lived on it now forty years, thirty-two of them with my beloved wife Caroline, and two—" Here he stopped and wiped a tear from the driest eye I ever saw. "Miss Butterworth, I am a widower."

I hastened my steps. I here duly and with the strictest regard for the truth aver, that I decidedly hastened my steps at this very unnecessary announcement. But he, with another covert glance behind him towards the barn, from which, to my surprise and increasing anxiety, William had not yet emerged, kept well up to me, and only paused when I paused at the side of the road near the buggy.

"Miss Butterworth," he began, undeterred by the air of dignity I assumed, "I have been thinking that your visit here is a rebuke to my unneighborliness. But the business which has occupied the lane these last few days has put us all into such a state of unpleasantness that it was useless to attempt sociability."

His voice was so smooth, his eyes so small and twinkling, that if I could have thought of anything except William's possible discoveries in the barn, I should have taken delight in measuring my wits against his egotism.

But as it was, I said nothing, possibly because I only half heard what he was saying.

"I am no lady's man,"—these were the next words I heard,—"but then I judge you're not anxious for flattery, but prefer the square thing uttered by a square man without delay or circumlocution. Madam, I am fifty-three, and I have been a widower two years. I am not fitted for a solitary life, and I am fitted for the companionship of an affectionate wife who will keep my hearth clean and my affections in good working order. Will you be that wife? You see my home,"—here his eye stole behind him with that uneasy look towards the barn which William's presence in it certainly warranted,—"a home which I can offer you unencumbered, if you———"

"Desire to live in Lost Man's Lane," I put in, subduing both my surprise and my disgust at this preposterous proposal, in order to throw all the sarcasm of which I was capable into this single sentence.

"Oh!" he exclaimed, "you don't like the neighborhood. Well, we could go elsewhere. I am not set against the city myself———"

Astounded at his presumption, regarding him as a possible criminal, who was endeavoring to beguile me for purposes of his own, I could no longer repress either my indignation or the wrath with which such impromptu addresses naturally inspired me. Cutting him short with a gesture which made him open his small eyes, I exclaimed in continuation of his remark:

"Nor, as I take it, are you set against the comfortable little income somebody has told you I possessed. I see your disinterestedness, Deacon, but I should be sorry to profit by it. Why, man, I never spoke to you before in my life, and do you think———"

"Oh!" he suavely insinuated, with a suppressed chuckle which even his increasing uneasiness as to William could not altogether repress, "I see you are not above the flattery that pleases other women. Well, madam, I know a tremendous fine woman when I see her, and from the moment I saw you riding by the other day, I made up my mind I would have you for the second Mrs. Spear, if persistence and a proper advocacy of my cause could accomplish it. Madam, I was going to visit you with this proposal to-night, but seeing you here, the temptation was too great for my discretion, and so I have addressed you on the spot. But you need not answer me at once. I don't need to know any more about you than what I can take in with my two eyes, but if you would like a little more acquaintance with me, why I can wait a couple of weeks till we've rubbed the edges off our strangeness, when— —"

"When you think I will be so charmed with Deacon Spear that I will be ready to settle down with him in Lost Man's Lane, or if that will not do, carry him off to

Gramercy Park, where he will be the admiration of all New York and Brooklyn to boot. Why, man, if I was so easily satisfied as that, I would not be in a position to-day for you to honor me with this proposal. I am not easy to suit, so I advise you to turn your attention to some one much more anxious to be married than I am. But"—and here I allowed some of my real feelings to appear—"if you value your own reputation or the happiness of the lady you propose to inveigle into an union with you, do not venture too far in the matrimonial way till the mystery is dispelled which shrouds Lost Man's Lane in horror. If you were an honest man you would ask no one to share your fortunes whilst the least doubt rests upon your reputation."

"My reputation?" He had started very visibly at these words. "Madam, be careful. I admire you, but——"

"No offence," said I. "For a stranger I have been, perhaps, unduly frank. I only mean that any one who lives in this lane must feel himself more or less enveloped by the shadow which rests upon it. When that is lifted, each and every one of you will feel himself a man again. From indications to be seen in the lane to-day, that time may not be far distant. Mother Jane is a likely source for the mysteries that agitate us. She knows just enough to have no proper idea of the value of a human life."

The Deacon's retort was instantaneous. "Madam," said he, with a snap of his fingers, "I have not that much interest in what is going on down there. If men have been killed in this lane (which I do not believe), old Mother Jane has had no hand in it. My opinion is—and you may value it or not, just as you please—that what the people hereabout call crimes are so many coincidences, which some day or other will receive their due explanation. Every one who has disappeared in this vicinity has disappeared naturally. No one has been killed. That is my theory, and you will find it correct. On this point I have expended more than a little thought."

I was irate. I was also dumfounded at his audacity. Did he think I was the woman to be deceived by any such balderdash as that? But I shut my lips tightly lest I should say something, and he, not finding this agreeable, being no conversationalist himself, drew himself up with a pompously expressed hope that he would see me again after his reputation was cleared, when his attention as well as my own was diverted by seeing William's slouching figure appear in the barn door and make slowly towards us.

Instantly the Deacon forgot me in his interest in William's approach, which was so slow as to be tantalizing to us both.

When he was within speaking distance, Deacon Spear started towards him.

"Well!" he cried; "one would think you had gone back a dozen or so years and were again robbing your neighbor's hen-roosts. Been in the hay, eh?" he added, leaning forward and plucking a wisp or two from my companion's clothes. "Well, what did you find there?"

In trembling fear for what the lout might answer, I put my hand on the buggy rail and struggled anxiously to my seat. William stepped forward and loosened the horse before speaking. Then with a leer he dived into his pocket, and remarking slowly, "I found this," brought to light a small riding-whip which we both recognized as one he often carried. "I flung it up in the hay yesterday in one of my fits of laughing, so just thought I would bring it down to-day. You know it isn't the first time I've climbed about those rafters, Deacon, as you have been good enough to insinuate."

The Deacon, evidently taken aback, eyed the young fellow with a leer in which I saw something more serious than mere suspicion.

"Was that all?" he began, but evidently thought better than to finish, whilst William, with a nonchalance that surprised me, blunderingly avoided his eye, and, bounding into the buggy beside me, started up the horse and drove slowly off.

"Ta, ta, Deacon," he called back; "if you want to see fun, come up to our end of the lane; there's precious little here." And thus, with a laugh, terminated an interview which, all things considered, was the most exciting as well as the most humiliating I have ever taken part in.

"William," I began, but stopped. The two pigeons whose departure I had watched a little while before were coming back, and, as I spoke, fluttered up to the window before mentioned, where they alighted and began picking up the crumbs which I had seen scattered for them. "See!" I suddenly exclaimed, pointing them out to William. "Was I mistaken when I thought I saw a hand drop crumbs from that window?"

The answer was a very grave one for him.

"No," said he, "for I have seen more than a hand, through the loophole I made in the hay. I saw a man's leg stretched out as if he were lying on the floor with his head toward the window. It was but a glimpse I got, but the leg moved as I looked at it, and so I know that some one lies hid in that little nook up under the roof. Now it isn't any one belonging to the lane, for I know where every one of us is or ought to be at this blessed moment; and it isn't a detective, for I heard a sound like heavy sobbing as I crouched there. Then who is it? Silly Rufus, I say; and if that hay was all lifted, we would see sights that would make us ashamed of the apologies we uttered to the old sneak just now."

"I want to get home," said I. "Drive fast! Your sisters ought to know this."

"The girls?" he cried. "Yes, it will be a triumph over them. They never would believe I had an atom of judgment. But we'll show them, if William Knollys is altogether a fool."

We were now near to Mr. Trohm's hospitable gateway. Coming from the excitements of my late interview, it was a relief to perceive the genial owner of this beautiful place wandering among his vines and testing the condition of his fruit by a careful touch here and there. As he heard our wheels he turned, and seeing who we were, threw up his hands in ill-restrained pleasure, and came buoyantly forward. There was nothing to do but to stop, so we stopped.

"Why, William! Why, Miss Butterworth, what a pleasure!" Such was his amiable greeting. "I thought you were all busy at your end of the lane; but I see you have just come from town. Had an errand there, I suppose?"

"Yes," William grumbled, eying the luscious pear Mr. Trohm held in his hand.

The look drew a smile from that gentleman.

"Admiring the first fruits?" he observed. "Well, it is a handsome specimen," he admitted, handing it to me with his own peculiar grace. "I beg you will take it, Miss Butterworth. You look tired; pardon me if I mention it." (He is the only person I know who detects any signs of suffering or fatigue on my part.)

"I am worried by the mysteries of this lane," I ventured to remark. "I hate to see Mother Jane's garden uprooted."

"Ah!" he acquiesced, with much evidence of good feeling, "it is a distressing thing to witness. I wish she might have been spared. William, there are other pears on the tree this came from. Tie up the horse, I pray, and gather a dozen or so of these for your sisters. They will never be in better condition for plucking than they are to-day."

William, whose mouth and eyes were both watering for a taste of the fine fruit thus offered, moved with alacrity to obey this invitation, while I, more startled than pleased—or, rather, as much startled as pleased—by the prospect of a momentary tête-à-tête with our agreeable neighbor, sat uneasily eying the luscious fruit in my hand, and wishing I was ten years younger, that the blush I felt slowly stealing up my cheek might seem more appropriate to the occasion.

But Mr. Trohm appeared not to share my wish. He was evidently so satisfied with me as I was, that he found it difficult to speak at first, and when he did—But tut! tut! you have no desire to hear any such confidences as these, I am sure. A middle-aged gentleman's expressions of admiration for a middle-aged lady may savor of romance to her, but hardly to the rest of the world, so I will pass this conversation by, with the single admission that it ended in a question to which I felt obliged to return a reluctant No.

Mr. Trohm was just recovering from the disappointment of this, when William sauntered back with his hands and pockets full.

"Ah!" that graceless scamp chuckled, with a suspicious look at our downcast faces, "been improving the opportunity, eh?"

Mr. Trohm, who had fallen back against his old well-curb, surveyed his young neighbor for the first time with a look of anger. But it vanished almost as quickly as it appeared, and he contented himself with a low bow, in which I read real grief.

This was too much for me, and I was about to open my lips with a kind phrase or two, when a flutter took place over our heads, and the two pigeons whose flight I had watched more than once during the last hour, flew down and settled upon Mr. Trohm's arm and shoulders.

"Oh!" I exclaimed, with a sudden shrinking that I hardly understood myself. And though I covered up the exclamation with as brisk a good-by as my inward perturbation would allow, that sight and the involuntary ejaculation I had uttered, were all I saw or heard during our hasty drive homeward.

XXXVII I ASTONISH MR. GRYCE AND HE ASTONISHES ME

But as we approached the group of curious people which now filled up the whole highway in front of Mother Jane's cottage, I broke from the nightmare into which this last discovery had thrown me, and, turning to William, said with a resolute air:

"You and your sisters are not of one mind regarding these disappearances. You ascribe them to Deacon Spear, but they—whom do they ascribe them to?"

"I shouldn't think it would take a woman of your wit to answer that question."

The rebuke was deserved. I had wit, but I had refused to exercise it; my blind partiality for a man of pleasing exterior and magnetic address had prevented the cool play of my usual judgment, due to the occasion and the trust which had been imposed in me by Mr. Gryce. Resolved that this should end, no matter at what cost to my feelings, I quietly said:

"You allude to Mr. Trohm."

"That is the name," he carelessly assented. "Girls, you know, let their prejudices run away with them. An old grudge———"

"Yes," I tentatively put in; "he persecuted your mother, and so they think him capable of any wickedness."

The growl which William gave was not one of dissent.

"But I don't care what they think," said he, looking down at the heap of fruit which lay between us. "I'm Trohm's friend, and don't believe one word they choose to insinuate against him. What if he didn't like what my mother did! We didn't like it either, and———"

"William," I calmly remarked, "if your sisters knew that Silly Rufus had been found in Deacon Spear's barn they would no longer do Mr. Trohm this injustice."

"No; that would settle them; that would give me a triumph which would last long after this matter was out of the way."

"Very well, then," said I, "I am going to bring about this triumph. I am going to tell Mr. Gryce at once what we have discovered in Deacon Spear's barn."

And without waiting for his ah, yes, or no, I jumped from the buggy and made my way to the detective's side.

His welcome was somewhat unexpected. "Ah, fresh news!" he exclaimed. "I see it in your eye. What have you chanced upon, madam, in your disinterested drive into town?"

I thought I had eliminated all expression from my face, and that my words would bring a certain surprise with them. But it is useless to try to surprise Mr. Gryce.

"You read me like a book," said I; "I have something to add to the situation. Mr. Gryce, I have just come from the other end of the lane, where I found a clue which may shorten the suspense of this weary day, and possibly save Lucetta from the painful task she has undertaken in our interests. Mr. Chittenden's ring———"

I paused for the exclamation of encouragement he is accustomed to give on such occasions, and while I paused, prepared for my accustomed triumph. He did not fail me in the exclamation, nor did I miss my expected triumph.

"Was not found by Mother Jane, or even brought to her in any ordinary way or by any ordinary messenger. It came to her on a pigeon's neck, the pigeon you will find lying dead among the bushes in the Knollys yard."

He was amazed. He controlled himself, but he was very visibly amazed. His exclamations proved it.

"Madam! Miss Butterworth! This ring—Mr. Chittenden's ring, whose presence in her hut we thought an evidence of guilt, was brought to her by one of her pigeons?"

"So she told me. I aroused her fury by showing her the empty husk in which it had been concealed. In her rage at its loss, she revealed the fact I have just mentioned. It is a curious one, sir, and one I am a little proud to have discovered."

"Curious? It is more than curious; it is bizarre, and will rank, I am safe in prophesying, as one of the most remarkable facts that have ever adorned the annals of the police. Madam, when I say I envy you the honor of its discovery, you will appreciate my estimate of it—and you. But when did you find this out, and what explanation are you able to give of the presence of this ring on a pigeon's neck?"

"Sir, to your first question I need only reply that I was here two hours or so ago, and to the second that everything points to the fact that the ring was attached to the bird by the victim himself, as an appeal for succor to whoever might be fortunate enough to find it. Unhappily it fell into the wrong hands. That is the ill-luck which often befalls prisoners."

"Prisoners?"

"Yes. Cannot you imagine a person shut up in an inaccessible place making some such attempt to communicate with his fellow-creatures?"

"But what inaccessible place have we in——"

"Wait," said I. "You have been in Deacon Spear's barn."

"Certainly, many times." But the answer, glib as it was, showed shock. I began to gather courage.

"Well," said I, "there is a hiding-place in that barn which I dare declare you have not penetrated."

"Do you think so, madam?"

"A little loft way up under the eaves, which can only be reached by clambering over the rafters. Didn't Deacon Spear tell you there was such a place?"

"No, but——"

"William, then?" I inexorably pursued. "He says he pointed such a spot out to you, and that you pooh-poohed at it as inaccessible and not worth the searching."

"William is a—Madam, I beg your pardon, but William has just wit enough to make trouble."

"But there is such a place there," I urged; "and, what is more, there is some one hidden in it now. I saw him myself."

"You saw him?"

"Saw a part of him; in short, saw his hand. He was engaged in scattering crumbs for the pigeons."

"That does not look like starvation," smiled Mr. Gryce, with the first hint of sarcasm he had allowed himself to make use of in this interview.

"No," said I; "but the time may not have come to inflict this penalty on Silly Rufus. He has been there but a few days, and—well, what have I said now?"

"Nothing, ma'am, nothing. But what made you think the hand you saw belonged to Silly Rufus?"

"Because he was the last person to disappear from this lane. The last—what am I saying? He wasn't the last. Lucetta's lover was the last. Mr. Gryce, could that hand have belonged to Mr. Ostrander?"

I was intensely excited; so much so that Mr. Gryce made me a warning gesture.

"Hush!" he whispered; "you are attracting attention. That hand was the hand of Mr. Ostrander; and the reason why I did not accept William Knollys' suggestion to search the Deacon's barn-loft was because I knew it had been chosen as a place of refuge by this missing lover of Lucetta."

XXXVIII   A FEW WORDS

Never have keener or more conflicting emotions been awakened in my breast than by these simple words. But alive to the necessity of hiding my feelings from those about me, I gave no token of my surprise, but rather turned a stonier face than common upon the man who had caused it.

"Refuge?" I repeated. "He is there, then, of his own free will—or yours?" I sarcastically added, not being able to quite keep down this reproach as I remembered the deception practised upon Lucetta.

"Mr. Ostrander, madam, has been spending the week with Deacon Spear—they are old friends, you know. That he should spend it quietly and, to a degree, in hiding, was as much his plan as mine. For while he found it impossible to leave Lucetta in the doubtful position in which she and her family at present stand, he did not wish to aggravate her misery by the thought that he was thus jeopardizing the position on which all his hopes of future advancement depended. He preferred to watch and wait in secret, seeing which, I did what I could to further his wishes. His usual lodging was with the family, but when the search was instituted, I suggested that he should remove himself to that eyrie back of the hay where you were sharp enough to detect him to-day."

"Don't attempt any of your flatteries upon me," I protested. "They will not make me forget that I have not been treated fairly. And Lucetta—oh! may I not tell Lucetta——"

"And spoil our entire prospect of solving this mystery? No, madam, you may not tell Lucetta. When Fate has put such a card into our hands as I played with that telegram to-day, we would be flying in the face of Providence not to profit by it. Lucetta's despair makes her bold; upon that boldness we depend to discover and bring to justice a great criminal."

I felt myself turn pale; for that very reason, perhaps, I assumed a still sterner air, and composedly said:

"If Mr. Ostrander is in hiding at the Deacon's, and he and his host are both in your confidence, then the only man whom you can designate in your thoughts by this dreadful title must be Mr. Trohm."

I had perhaps hoped he would recoil at this or give some other evidence of his amazement at an assumption which to me seemed preposterous. But he did not, and I saw, with what feelings may be imagined, that this conclusion, which was half bravado with me, had been accepted by him long enough for no emotion to follow its utterance.

"Oh!" I exclaimed, "how can you reconcile such a suspicion with the attitude you have always preserved towards Mr. Trohm?"

"Madam," said he, "do not criticise my attitude without taking into account existing appearances. They are undoubtedly in Mr. Trohm's favor."

"I am glad to hear you say so," said I, "I am glad to hear you say so. Why, it was in response to his appeal that you came to X. at all."

Mr. Gryce's smile conveyed a reproach which I could not but acknowledge I amply merited. Had he spent evening after evening at my house, entertaining me with tales of the devices and the many inconsistencies of criminals, to be met now by such a puerile disclaimer as this? But beyond that smile he said nothing; on the contrary, he continued as if I had not spoken at all.

"But appearances," he declared, "will not stand before the insight of a girl like Lucetta. She has marked the man as guilty, and we will give her the opportunity of proving the correctness of her instinct."

"But Mr. Trohm's house has been searched, and you have found nothing—nothing," I argued somewhat feebly.

"That is the reason we find ourselves forced to yield our judgment to Lucetta's intuitions," was his quick reply. And smiling upon me with his blandest air, he obligingly added: "Miss Butterworth is a woman of too much character not to abide the event with all her accustomed composure." And with this final suggestion, I was as yet too crushed to resent, he dismissed me to an afternoon of unparalleled suspense and many contradictory emotions.

XXXIX   UNDER A CRIMSON SKY

When, in the course of events, the current of my thoughts receive a decided check and I find myself forced to change former conclusions or habituate myself to new ideas and a fresh standpoint, I do it, as I do everything else, with determination and a total disregard of my own previous predilections. Before the afternoon was well over I was ready for any revelations which might follow Lucetta's contemplated action, merely reserving a vague hope that my judgment would yet be found superior to her instinct.

At five o'clock the diggers began to go home. Nothing had been found under the soil of Mother Jane's garden, and the excitement of search which had animated them early in the day had given place to a dull resentment mainly directed towards the Knollys family, if one could judge of these men's feelings by the heavy scowls and significant gestures with which they passed our broken-down gateway.

By six the last man had filed by, leaving Mr. Gryce free for the work which lay before him.

I had retired long before this to my room, where I awaited the hour set by Lucetta with a feverish impatience quite new to me. As none of us could eat, the supper table had not been laid, and though I had no means of knowing what was in store for us, the sombre silence and oppression under which the whole house lay seemed a portent that was by no means encouraging.

Suddenly I heard a knock at my door. Rising hastily, I opened it. Loreen stood before me, with parted lips and terror in all her looks.

"Come!" she cried. "Come and see what I have found in Lucetta's room."

"Then she's gone?" I cried.

"Yes, she's gone, but come and see what she has left behind her."

Hastening after Loreen, who was by this time half-way down the hall, I soon found myself on the threshold of the room I knew to be Lucetta's.

"She made me promise," cried Loreen, halting to look back at me, "that I would let her go alone, and that I would not enter the highway till an hour after her departure. But with these evidences of the extent of her dread before us, how can we stay in this house?" And dragging me to a table, she showed me lying on its top a folded paper and two letters. The folded paper was Lucetta's Will, and the letters were directed severally to Loreen and to myself with the injunction that they were not to be read till she had been gone six hours.

"She has prepared herself for death!" I exclaimed, shocked to my heart's core, but determinedly hiding it. "But you need not fear any such event. Is she not accompanied by Mr. Gryce?"

"I do not know; I do not think so. How could she accomplish her task if not alone? Miss Butterworth, Miss Butterworth, she has gone to brave Mr. Trohm, our mother's persecutor and our life-long enemy, thinking, hoping, believing that in so doing she will rouse his criminal instincts, if he has them, and so lead to the discovery of his crimes and the means by which he has been enabled to carry them out so long undetected. It is noble, it is heroic, it is martyr-like, but—oh! Miss Butterworth, I have never broken a promise to any one before in all my life, but I am going to break the one I made her. Come, let us fly after her! She has her lover's memory, but I have nothing in all the world but her."

I immediately turned and hastened down the stairs in a state of humiliation which should have made ample amends for any show of arrogance I may have indulged in in my more fortunate moments.

Loreen followed me, and when we were in the lower hall she gave me a look and said:

"My promise was not to enter the highway. Would you be afraid to follow me by another road—a secret road—all overgrown with thistles and blackberry bushes which have not been trimmed up for years?"

I thought of my thin shoes, my neat silk dress, but only to forget them the next moment.

"I will go anywhere," said I.

But Loreen was already too far in advance of me to answer. She was young and lithe, and had reached the kitchen before I had passed the Flower Parlor. But when we had sped clear of the house I found that my progress bade fair to be as rapid as hers, for her agitation was a hindrance to her, while excitement always brings out my powers and heightens both my wits and my judgment.

Our way lay past the stables, from which I expected every minute to see two or three dogs jump. But William, who had been discreetly sent out of the way early in the afternoon, had taken Saracen with him, and possibly the rest, so our passing by disturbed nothing, not even ourselves. The next moment we were in a field of prickers, through which we both struggled till we came into a sort of swamp. Here was bad going, but we floundered on, edging continually toward a distant fence beyond which rose the symmetrical lines of an orchard—Mr. Trohm's orchard, in which those pleasant fruits grew which—Bah! should I ever be able to get the taste of them out of my mouth!

At a tiny gateway covered with vines, Loreen stopped.

"I do not believe this has been opened for years, but it must be opened now." And, throwing her whole weight against it, she burst it through, and bidding me pass, hastened after me over the trailing branches and made, without a word, for the winding path we now saw clearly defined on the edge of the orchard before us.

"Oh!" exclaimed Loreen, stopping one moment to catch her breath, "I do not know what I fear or to what our steps will bring us. I only know that I must hunt for Lucetta till I find her. If there is danger where she is, I must share it. You can rest here or come farther on."

I went farther on.

Suddenly we both started; a man had sprung up from behind the hedgerow that ran parallel with the fence that surrounded Mr. Trohm's place.

"Silence!" he whispered, putting his finger on his lips. "If you are looking for Miss Knollys," he added, seeing us both pause aghast, "she is on the lawn beyond, talking to Mr. Trohm. If you will step here, you can see her. She is in no kind of danger, but if she were, Mr. Gryce is in the first row of trees to the back there, and a call from me——"

That made me remember my whistle. It was still round my neck, but my hand, which had instinctively gone to it, fell again in extraordinary emotion as I realized the situation and compared it with that of the morning when, blinded by egotism and foolish prejudice in favor of this man, I ate of his fruit and hearkened to his outrageous addresses.

"Come!" beckoned Loreen, happily too absorbed in her own emotions to notice mine. "Let us get nearer. If Mr. Trohm is the wicked man we fear, there is no telling what the means are which he uses to get rid of his victims. There was nothing to be found in his house, but who knows where the danger may lurk, and that it may not be near her now? It was evidently to dare it she came, to offer herself as a martyr, that we might know——"

"Hush!" I whispered, controlling my own fears roused against my will by this display of terror in this usually calmest of natures. "No danger can menace her where they stand, unless he is a common assassin and carries a pistol——"

"No pistol," murmured the man, who had crept again near us. "Pistols make a noise. He will not use a pistol."

"Good God!" I whispered. "You do not share her sister's fears that it is in the heart of this man to kill Lucetta?"

"Five strong men have disappeared hereabout," said the fellow, never moving his eye from the couple before us. "Why not one weak girl?"

With a cry Loreen started forward. "Run!" she whispered. "Run!"

But as this word left her lips, a slight movement took place in the belt of trees where we had been told Mr. Gryce lay in hiding, and we could see him issue for a moment into sight with his finger like that of his man laid warningly on his lips. Loreen trembled and drew back, seeing which, the man beside us pointed to the hedge and whispered softly:

"There is just room between it and the fence for a person to pass sideways. If you and this lady want to get nearer to Miss Knollys, you might take that road. But Mr. Gryce will expect you to be very quiet. The young lady expressly said, before she came into this place, that she could do nothing if for any reason Mr. Trohm should suspect they were not alone."

"We will be quiet," I assured him, anxious to hide my face, which I felt twitch at every mention of Mr. Trohm's name. Loreen was already behind the hedge.

The evening was one of those which are made for peace. The sun, which had set in crimson, had left a glow on the branches of the forest which had not yet faded into the gray of twilight. The lawn, around which we were skirting, had not lost the mellow brilliancy which made it sparkle, nor had the cluster of varied-hued hollyhocks which set their gorgeousness against the neat yellow of the peaceful doorposts, shown any dimness in their glory, which was on a par with that of the setting sun. But though I saw all this, it no longer appeared to me desirable. Lucetta and Lucetta's fate, the mystery and the impossibility of its being explained out here in the midst of turf and blossoms, filled all my thoughts, and made me forget my own secret cause for shame and humiliation.

Loreen, who had wormed her way along till she crouched nearly opposite to the place where her sister stood, plucked me by the gown as I approached her, and, pointing to the hedge, which pressed up so close it nearly touched our faces, seemed to bid me look through. Searching for a spot where there was a small opening, I put my eye to this and immediately drew back.

"They are moving nearer the gate," I signalled to Loreen, at which she crept along a few paces, but with a stealth so great that, alert as I was, I could not hear a twig snap. I endeavored to imitate her, but not with as much success as I could wish. The sense of horror which had all at once settled upon me, the supernatural dread of something which I could not see, but which I felt, had seized me for the first time and made the ruddy sky and the broad stretch of velvet turf with the shadows playing over it of swaying tree-tops and clustered oleanders, more thrilling and awesome to me than the dim halls of the haunted house of the Knollys family in that midnight hour when I saw a body carried out for burial amid trouble and hush and a mystery so great it would have daunted most spirits for the remainder of their lives.

The very sweetness of the scene made its horror. Never have I had such sensations, never have I felt so deeply the power of the unseen, yet it seemed so impossible that anything could happen here, anything which would explain the total disappearance of several persons at different times, without a trace of their fate being left to the eye, that I could but liken my state to that of nightmare, where visions take the place of realities and often overwhelm them.

I had pressed too close against the hedge as I struggled with these feelings, and the sound I made struck me as distinct, if not alarming; but the tree-tops were rustling overhead, and, while Lucetta might have heard the hedge-branches crack, her companion gave no evidence of doing so. We could distinguish what they were saying now, and realizing this, we stopped moving and gave our whole attention to listening. Mr. Trohm was speaking. I could hardly believe it was his voice, it had so changed in tone, nor could I perceive in his features, distorted as they now were by every evil passion, the once quiet and dignified countenance which had so lately imposed upon me.

"Lucetta, my little Lucetta," he was saying, "so she has come to see me, come to taunt me with the loss of her lover, whom she says I have robbed her of almost before her eyes! I rob her! How can I rob her or any one of a man with a voice and arm of his own stronger than mine? Am I a wizard to dissipate his body in vapor? Yet can you find it in my house or on my lawn? You are a fool, Lucetta; so are all these men about here fools! It is in your house——"

"Hush!" she cried, her slight figure rising till we forgot it was the feeble Lucetta we were gazing at. "No more accusations directed against us. It is you who must expect them now. Mr. Trohm, your evil practices are discovered. To-morrow you will have the police here in earnest. They did but play with you when they were here before."

"You child!" he gasped, striving, however, to restrain all evidences of shock and terror. "Why, who was it called in the police and set them working in Lost Man's Lane? Was it not I——"

"Yes, that they might not suspect you, and perhaps that they might suspect us. But it was useless, Obadiah Trohm. Althea Knollys' children have been long-suffering, but the limit of their forbearance has been reached. When you laid your hand upon my lover, you roused a spirit in me that nothing but your own destruction can satisfy. Where is he, Mr. Trohm? and where is Silly Rufus and all the rest who have vanished between Deacon Spear's house and the little home of the cripples on the highroad? They have asked me this question, but if any one in Lost Man's Lane can answer, it is you, persecutor of my mother, and traducer of ourselves, whom I here denounce in face of these skies where God reigns and this earth where man lives to harry and condemn."

And then I saw that the instinct of this girl had accomplished what our united acumen and skill had failed to do. The old man—indeed he seemed an old man now—cringed, and the wrinkles came out in his face till he was demoniacally ugly.

"You viper!" he shrieked. "How dare you accuse me of crime—you whose mother would have died in jail but for my forbearance? Have you ever seen me set my foot upon a worm? Look at my fruit and flowers, look at my home, without a spot or blemish to mar its neatness and propriety. Can a man who loves these things stomach the destruction of a man, much less of a silly, yawping boy? Lucetta, you are mad!"

"Mad or sane, my accusation will have its results, Mr. Trohm. I believe too deeply in your guilt not to make others do so."

"Ah," said he, "then you have not done so yet? You believe this and that, but you have not told any one what your suspicions are?"

"No," she calmly returned, though her face blanched to the colorlessness of wax, "I have not said what I think of you yet."

Oh, the cunning that crept into his face!

"She has not said. Oh, the little Lucetta, the wise, the careful little Lucetta!"

"But I will," she cried, meeting his eye with the courage and constancy of a martyr, "though I bring destruction upon myself. I will denounce you and do it before the night has settled down upon us. I have a lover to avenge, a brother to defend. Besides, the earth should be rid of such a monster as you."

"Such a monster as I? Well, my pretty one,"—his voice grown suddenly wheedling, his face a study of mingled passions,—"we will see about that. Come just a step nearer, Lucetta. I want to see if you are really the little girl I used to dandle on my knee."

They were now near the gateway. They had been moving all this time. His hand was on the curb of the old well. His face, so turned that it caught the full glare of the setting sun, leaned toward the girl, exerting a fascinating influence upon her. She took the step he asked, and before we could shriek out "Beware!" we saw him bend forward with a sudden quick motion and then start upright again, while her form, which but an instant before had stood there in all its frail and inspired beauty, tottered as if the ground were bending under it, and in another moment disappeared from our appalled sight, swallowed in some dreadful cavern that for an instant yawned in the smoothly cut lawn before us, and then vanished again from sight as if it had never been.

A shriek from my whistle mingled with a simultaneous cry of agony from Loreen. We heard Mr. Gryce rush from behind us, but we ourselves found it impossible to stir, paralyzed as we were by the sight of the old man's demoniacal delight. He was leaping to and fro over the turf, holding up his fingers in the red sunset glare.

"Six!" he shrieked. "Six! and room for two more! Oh, it's a merry life I lead! Flowers and fruit and love-making" (oh, how I cringed at that!), "and now and then a little spice like this! But where is my pretty Lucetta? Surely she was here a moment ago. How could she have vanished, then, so quickly? I do not see her form amid the trees, there is no trace of her presence upon the lawn, and if they search the house from top to bottom and from bottom to top they will find nothing of her—no, not so much as a print of her footstep or the scent of the violets she so often wears tucked into her hair."

These last words, uttered in a different voice from the rest, gave the clue to the whole situation. We saw, even while we all bounded forward to the rescue of the devoted maiden, that he was one of those maniacs who have perfect control over themselves and pass for very decent sort of men except in the moment of triumph; and, noting his look of sinister delight, perceived that half his pleasure and almost his sole reward for the horrible crimes he had perpetrated, was in the mystery surrounding his victims and the entire immunity from suspicion which up to this time he had enjoyed.

Meantime Mr. Gryce had covered the wretch with his pistol, and his man, who succeeded in reaching the place even sooner than ourselves, hampered as we were by the almost impenetrable hedge behind which we had crouched, tried to lift the grass-covered lid we could faintly discern there. But this was impossible until I, with almost superhuman self-possession, considering the imperative nature of the emergency, found the spring hidden in the well-curb which worked the deadly mechanism. A yell from the writhing creature cowering under the detective's pistol guided me unconsciously in its action, and in another moment we saw the fatal lid tip and disclose what appeared to be the remains of a second well, long ago dried up and abandoned for the other.

The rescue of Lucetta followed. As she had fainted in falling she had not suffered much, and soon we had the supreme delight of seeing her eyes unclose.

"Ah," she murmured, in a voice whose echo pierced to every heart save that of the guilty wretch now lying handcuffed on the sward, "I thought I saw Albert! He was not dead, and I———"

But here Mr. Gryce, with an air at once contrite and yet strangely triumphant, interposed his benevolent face between hers and her weeping sister's and whispered something in her ear which turned her pallid cheek to a glowing scarlet. Rising up, she threw her arms around his neck and let him lift her. As he carried her—where was his rheumatism now?—out of those baleful grounds and away from the reach of the maniac's mingled laughs and cries, her face was peace itself. But his—well, his was a study.

XL   EXPLANATIONS

The hour we all spent together late that night in the old house was unlike any hour which that place had seen for years. Mr. Ostrander, Lucetta, Loreen, William, Mr. Gryce, and myself, all were there, and as an especial grace, Saracen was allowed to enter, that there might not be a cloud upon a single face there assembled. Though it is a small matter, I will add that this dog persisted in lying down by my side, not yielding even to the wiles of his master, whose amusement over this fact kept him good-natured to the last adieu.

There were too few candles in the house to make it bright, but Lucetta's unearthly beauty, the peace in Loreen's soft eyes, made us forget the sombreness of our surroundings and the meagreness of the entertainment Hannah attempted to offer us. It was the promise of coming joy, and when, our two guests departed, I bade good-night to the girls in their grim upper hall, it was with feelings which found their best expression in the two letters I hastened to write as soon as I gained the refuge of my own apartment. I will admit you sufficiently into my confidence to let you read those letters. The first of them ran thus:

"DEAR OLIVE:

"To make others happy is the best way to forget our own misfortunes. A sudden wedding is to take place in this house. Order at once for me from the shops you know me to be in the habit of patronizing, a wedding gown of dainty white taffeta [I did this not to recall too painfully to herself the wedding dress I helped her buy, and which was, as you may remember, of creamy satin], with chiffon trimmings, and a wedding veil of tulle. Add to this a dress suitable for ocean travel and a half-dozen costumes adapted to a southern climate. Let everything be suitable for a delicate but spirited girl who has seen trouble, but who is going to be happy now if a little attention and money can make her so. Do not spare expense, yet show no extravagance, for she is a shy bird, easily frightened. The measurements you will find enclosed; also those of another young lady, her sister, who must also be supplied with a white dress, the material of which, however, had better be of crape.

"All these things must be here by Wednesday evening, my own best dress included. On Saturday evening you may look for my return. I shall bring the latter young lady with me, so your present loneliness will be forgotten in the pleasure of entertaining an agreeable guest. Faithfully yours,

"AMELIA BUTTERWORTH."

The second letter was a longer and more important one. It was directed to the president of the company which had proposed to send Mr. Ostrander to South America. In it I related enough of the circumstances which had kept Mr. Ostrander in X. to interest him in the young couple personally, and then I told him that if he would forgive Mr. Ostrander this delay and allow him to sail with his young bride by the next steamer, I myself would undertake to advance whatever sums might have been lost by this change of arrangement.

I did not know then that Mr. Gryce had already made this matter good with this same gentleman.

The next morning we all took a walk in the lane. (I say nothing about the night. If I did not choose to sleep, or if I had any cause not to feel quite as elevated in spirit as the young people about me, there is surely no reason why I should dwell upon it with you or even apologize for a weakness which you will regard, I hope, as an exception setting off my customary strength.)

Now a walk in this lane was an event. To feel at liberty to stroll among its shadows without fear, to know that the danger had been so located that we all felt free to inhale the autumn air and to enjoy the beauties of the place without a thought of peril lurking in its sweetest nooks and most attractive coverts, gave to this short half-hour a distinctive delight aptly expressed by Loreen when she said:

"I never knew the place was so beautiful. Why, I think I can be happy here now." At which Lucetta grew pensive, till I roused her by saying:

"So much for a constitutional, girls. Now we must to work. This house, as you see it now, has to be prepared for a wedding. William, your business will be to see that these grounds are put in as good order as possible in the short time allotted to you. I will bear the expense, and Loreen———"

But William had a word to say for himself.

"Miss Butterworth," said he, "you're a right good sort of woman, as Saracen has found out, and we, too, in these last few plaguy days. But I'm not such a bad lot either, and if I do like my own way, which may not be other people's way, and if I am sometimes short with the girls for some of their d——d nonsense, I have a little decency about me, too, and I promise to fix these grounds, and out of my own money, too. Now that nine tenths of our income does not have to go abroad, we'll have chink enough to let us live in a respectable manner once more in a place where one horse, if he's good enough, will give a fellow a standing and make him the envy of those who, for some other pesky reasons, may think themselves called upon to fight shy of him. I don't begrudge the old place a few dollars, especially as I mean to live and die in it; so look out, you three women folks, and work as lively as you can on the inside of the old rookery, or the slickness of the outside will put you to open shame, and that would never please Loreen, nor, as I take it, Miss Butterworth either."

It was a challenge we were glad to accept, especially as from the number of persons we now saw come flocking into the lane, it was very apparent that we should experience no further difficulty in obtaining any help we might need to carry out our undertakings.

Meantime my thoughts were not altogether concentrated upon these pleasing plans for Lucetta's benefit. There were certain points yet to be made clear in the matter just terminated, and there was a confession for me to make, without which I could not face Mr. Gryce with all that unwavering composure which our peculiar relations seemed to demand.

The explanations came first. They were volunteered by Mr. Gryce, whom I met in the course of the morning at Mother Jane's cottage. That old crone had been perfectly happy all night, sleeping with the coin in her hand and waking to again devour it with her greedy but loving eyes. As I was alternately watching her and Mr. Gryce, who was directing with his hand the movements of the men who had come to smooth down her garden and make it presentable again, the detective spoke:

"I suppose you have found it difficult, in the light of these new discoveries, to explain to yourself how Mother Jane happened to have those trinkets from the peddler's pack, and also how the ring, which you very naturally thought must have been entrusted to the dove by Mr. Chittenden himself, came to be about its neck when it flew home that day of Mr. Chittenden's disappearance. Madam, we think old Mother Jane must have helped herself out of the peddler's pack before it was found in the woods there back of her hut, and of the other matter our explanation is this:

"One day a young man, equipped for travelling, paused for a glass of water at the famous well in Mr. Trohm's garden just as Mother Jane's pigeons were picking up the corn scattered for them by the former, whose tastes are not confined to the cultivation of fruits and flowers, but extend to dumb animals, to whom he is uniformly kind. The young man wore a ring, and, being nervous, was fiddling with it as he talked to the pleasant old gentleman who was lowering the bucket for him. As he fiddled with it, the earth fell from under him, and as the daylight vanished above his head, the ring flew from his up-thrown hand, and lay, the only token of his now blotted-out existence, upon the emerald sward he had but a moment before pressed with his unsuspicious feet. It burned—this ruby burned like a drop of blood in the grass, when that demon came again to his senses, and being a telltale evidence of crime in the eyes of one who had allowed nothing to ever speak against him in these matters, he stared at it as at a deadly thing directed against himself and to be got rid of at once and by means which by no possibility could recoil back upon himself as its author.

"The pigeons stalking near offered to his abnormally acute understanding the only solution which would leave him absolutely devoid of fear. He might have swung open the lid of the well once more and flung it after its owner, but this meant an aftermath of experience from which he shrank, his delight being in the thought that the victims he saw vanish before his eyes were so many encumbrances wiped off the face of the earth by a sweep of the hand. To see or hear them again would be destructive of this notion. He preferred the subtler way and to take advantage of old Mother Jane's characteristics, so he caught one of the pigeons (he has always been able to lure birds into his hands), and tying the ring around the neck of the bird with a blade of grass plucked up from the highway, he let it fly, and so was rid of the bauble which to Mother Jane's eyes, of course, was a direct gift from the heavens through which the bird had flown before lighting on her doorstep."

"Wonderful!" I exclaimed, almost overwhelmed with humiliation, but preserving a brave front. "What invention and what audacity!—the invention and the audacity of a man totally irresponsible for his deeds, was it not?" I asked. "There is no doubt, is there, about his being an absolute maniac?"

"No, madam." What a relief I felt at that word! "Since we entrapped him yesterday and he found himself fully discovered, he has lost all grip upon himself and fills the room we put him in with the unmistakable ravings of a madman. It was through these I learned the facts I have just mentioned."

I drew a deep breath. We were standing in the sight of several men, and their presence there seemed intolerable. Unconsciously I began to walk away. Unconsciously Mr. Gryce followed me. At the end of several paces we both stopped. We were no longer visible to the crowd, and I felt I could speak the words I had been burning to say ever since I saw the true nature of Mr. Trohm's character exposed.

"Mr. Gryce," said I, flushing scarlet—which I here solemnly declare is something which has not happened to me before in years, and if I can help it shall never happen to me again,—"I am interested in what you say, because yesterday, at his own gateway, Mr. Trohm proposed to me, and———"

"You did not accept him?"

"No. What do you think I am made of, Mr. Gryce? I did not accept him, but I made the refusal a gentle one, and—this is not easy work, Mr. Gryce," I interrupted myself to say with suitable grimness—"the same thing took place between me and Deacon Spear, and to him I gave a response such as I thought his presumption warranted. The discrimination does not argue well for my astuteness, Mr. Gryce. You see, I crave no credit that I do not deserve. Perhaps you cannot understand that, but it is a part of my nature."

"Madam," said he, and I must own I thought his conduct perfect, "had I not been as completely deceived as yourself I might find words of criticism for this possibly unprofessional partiality. But when an old hand like myself can listen to the insinuations of a maniac, and repose, as I must say I did repose, more or less confidence in the statements he chose to make me, and which were true enough as to the facts he mentioned, but wickedly false and preposterously wrong in suggestion, I can have no words of blame for a woman who, whatever her understanding and whatever her experience, necessarily has seen less of human nature and its incalculable surprises. As to the more delicate matter you have been good enough to confide to me, madam, I have but one remark to make. With such an example of womanhood suddenly brought to their notice in such a wild as this, how could you expect them, sane or insane, to do otherwise than they did? I know many a worthy man who would like to follow their example." And with a bow that left me speechless, Mr. Gryce laid his hand on his heart and softly withdrew.

EPILOGUE

SOME STRAY LEAFLETS FROM AN OLD DIARY OF ALTHEA KNOLLYS, FOUND BY ME IN THE PACKET LEFT IN MY CHARGE BY HER DAUGHTER LUCETTA.

I never thought I should do so foolish a thing as begin a diary. When in my boarding-school days (which I am very glad to be rid of) I used to see Meeley Butterworth sit down every night of her life over a little book which she called the repository of her daily actions, I thought that if ever I reached that point of imbecility I would deserve to have fewer lovers and more sense, just as she so frequently advised me to. And yet here I am, pencil in hand, jotting down the nothings of the moment, and with every prospect of continuing to do so for two weeks at least. For (why was I born such a chatterbox!) I have seen my fate, and must talk to some one about him, if only to myself, nature never having meant me to keep silence on any living topic that interests me.

Yes, with lovers in Boston, lovers in New York, and a most determined suitor on the other side of our own home-walls in Peekskill, I have fallen victim to the grave face and methodical ways of a person I need not name, since he is the only gentleman in this whole town, except—But I won't except anybody. Charles Knollys has no peer here or anywhere, and this I am ready to declare, after only one sight of his face and one look from his eye, though to no one but you, my secret, non-committal confidant—for to acknowledge to any human being that my admiration could be caught, or my heart touched, by a person who had not sued two years at my feet, would be to abdicate an ascendency I am so accustomed to I could not see it vanish without pain. Besides, who knows how I shall feel tomorrow? Meeley Butterworth never shows any hesitation in uttering her opinion either of men or things, but then her opinion never changes, whilst mine is a very thistle-down, blowing hither and thither till I cannot follow its wanderings myself. It is one of my charms, certain fools say, but that is nonsense. If my cheeks lacked color and my eyes were without sparkle, or even if I were two inches taller instead of being the tiniest bit of mortal flesh to be found amongst all the young ladies of my age in our so-called society, I doubt if the lightness of my mind would meet with the approbation of even the warmest woman-lovers of this time. As it is, it just passes, and sometimes, as to-night, for instance, when I can hardly see to inscribe these lines on this page for the vision of two grave, if not quietly reproving eyes which float between it and me, I almost wish I had some of Meeley's responsible characteristics, instead of being the airiest, merriest, and most volatile being that ever tried to laugh down the grandeur of this dreary old house with its century of memories.

Ah! that allusion has given me something to say. This house. What is there about it except its size to make a stranger like me look back continually over her shoulder in going down the long halls, or even when nestling comfortably by the great wood-fire in the immense drawing-room? I am not one of your fanciful ones; but I can no more help doing this, than I can help wishing Judge Knollys lived in a less roomy mansion with fewer echoing corners in its innumerable passages. I like brightness and cheer, at least in my surroundings. If I must have gloom, or a seriousness which some would call gloom, let me have it in individuals where there is some prospect of a blithe, careless-hearted little midget effecting a change, and not in great towering walls and endless floors which no amount of sunshine or laughter could ever render homelike, or even comfortable.

But there! If one has the man, one must have the home, so I had better say no more against the home till I am quite sure I do not want the man. For—Well, well, I am not a fool, but I did hear something just then, a something which makes me tremble yet, though I have spent five good minutes trilling the gayest songs I know.

I think it is very inconsiderate of the witches to bother thus a harmless mite like myself, who only asks for love, light, and money enough to buy a ribbon or a jewel when the fancy takes her, which is not as often as my enemies declare. And now a question! Why are my enemies always to be found among the girls, and among the plainest of them too? I never heard a man say anything against me, though I have sometimes surprised a look on their faces (I saw it to-day) which might signify reproof if it were not accompanied by a smile showing anything but displeasure.

But this is a digression, as Meeley would say. What I want to do, but which I seem to find it very difficult to do, is to tell how I came to be here, and what I have seen since I came. First, then, to be very short about the matter, I am here because the old folks—that is, my father and Mr. Knollys, have decided Charles and I should know each other. In thought, I courtesy to the decision; I think we ought to too. For while many other men are handsomer or better known, or have more money, alas! than he, he alone has a way of drawing up to one's side with an air that captivates the eye and sets the heart trembling, a heart, moreover, that never knew before it could tremble, except in the presence of great worldly prosperity and beautiful, beautiful things. So, as this experience is new, I am dutifully obliged for the excitement it gives me, and am glad to be here, awesome as the place is, and destitute of any such pleasures as I have been accustomed to in the gay cities where I have hitherto spent most of my time.

But there! I am rambling again. I have come to X., as you now see, for good and sufficient reasons, and while this house is one of consequence and has been the resort of many notable people, it is a little lonesome, our only neighbor being a young man who has a fine enough appearance, but who has already shown his admiration of me so plainly—of course he was in the road when I drove up to the house—that I lost all interest in him at once, such a nonsensical liking at first sight being, as I take it, a tribute only to my audacious little travelling bonnet and the curl or two which will fall out on my cheek when I move my head about too quickly, as I certainly could not be blamed for doing, in driving into a place where I was expected to make myself happy for two weeks.

He, then, is out of these chronicles. When I say his name is Obadiah Trohm, you will probably be duly thankful. But he is not as stiff and biblical as his name would lead you to expect. On the contrary, he is lithe, graceful, and suave to a point which makes Charles Knollys' judicial face a positive relief to the eye and such little understanding as has been accorded me.

I cannot write another word. It is twelve o'clock, and though I have the cosiest room in the house, all chintz and decorated china, I find myself listening and peering just as I did down-stairs in their great barn of a drawing-room. I wonder if any very dreadful things ever happened in this house? I will ask old Mr. Knollys to-morrow, or—or Mr. Charles.

I am sorry I was so inquisitive; for the stories Charles told me—I thought I had better not trouble the old gentleman—have only served to people the shadows of this rambling old house with figures of whose acquaintance I am likely to be more or less shy. One tale in particular gave me the shivers. It was about a mother and daughter who both loved the same man (it seems incredible, girls so seldom seeing with the eyes of their mothers), and it was the daughter who married him, while the mother, broken-hearted, fled from the wedding and was driven up to the great door, here, in a coach, dead. They say that the coach still travels the road just before some calamity to the family,—a phantom coach which floats along in shadow, turning the air about it to mist that chills the marrow in the bones of the unfortunate who sees it. I am going to see it myself some day, the real coach, I mean, in which this tragic event took place. It is still in the stable, Charles tells me.

I wonder if I will have the courage to sit where that poor devoted mother breathed out her miserable existence. I shall endeavor to do so if only to defy the fate which seems to be closing in upon me.

Charles is an able lawyer, but his argument in favor of close bonnets versus bewitching little pokes with a rose or two in front, was very weak, I thought, to-day. He seemed to think so himself, after a while; for when, as the only means of convincing him of the weakness of the cause he was advocating, I ran up-stairs and put on a poke similar to the aforesaid, he retracted at once and let the case go by default. For which I, and the poke, made suitable acknowledgments, to the great amusement of papa Knollys, who was on my side from the first.

Not much going on to-day. Yet I have never felt merrier. Oh, ye hideous, bare old walls! Won't I make you ring if——

I won't have it! I won't have that smooth, persistent hypocrite pushing his way into my presence, when my whole heart and attention belong to a man who would love me if he only could get his own leave to do so. Obadiah Trohm has been here to-day, on one pretext or another, three times. Once he came to bring some very choice apples—as if I cared for apples! The second time he had a question of great importance, no doubt, to put to Charles, and as Charles was in my company, the whole interview lasted, let us say, a good half-hour at least. The third time he came, it was to see me, which, as it was now evening, meant talk, talk, talk in the great drawing-room, with just a song interpolated now and then, instead of a cosy chat in the window-seat of the pretty Flower Parlor, with only one pair of ears to please and one pair of eyes to watch. Master Trohm was intrusive, and, if no one felt it but myself, it is because Charles Knollys has set himself up an ideal of womanhood to which I am a contradiction. But that will not affect the end. A woman may be such a contradiction and yet win, if her heart is in the struggle and she has, besides, a certain individuality of her own which appeals to the eye and heart if not to the understanding. I do not despair of seeing Charles Knollys' forehead taking a very deep frown at sight of his handsome and most attentive neighbor. Heigho! why don't I answer Meeley Butterworth's last letter? Am I ashamed to tell her that I have to limit my effusion to just four pages because I have commenced a diary?

I declare I begin to regard it a misfortune to have dimples. I never have regarded it so before when I have seen man after man succumb to them, but now they have become my bane, for they attract two admirers, just at the time they should attract but one, and it is upon the wrong man they flash the oftenest; why, I leave it to all true lovers to explain. As a consequence, Master Trohm is beginning to assume an air of superiority, and Charles, who may not believe in dimples, but who on that very account, perhaps, seems to be always on the lookout for them, shrinks more or less into the background, as is not becoming in a man with so many claims to respect, if not to love. I want to feel that each one of these precious fourteen days contains all that it can of delight and satisfaction, and how can I when Obadiah—oh, the charming and romantic name!—holds my crewels, instead of Charles, and whispers words which, coming from other lips, would do more than waken my dimples!

But if I must have a suitor, just when a suitor is not wanted, let me at least make him useful. Charles shall read his own heart in this man's passion.

I don't know why, but I have taken a dislike to the Flower Parlor. It now vies with the great drawing-room in my disregard. Yesterday, in crossing it, I felt a chill, so sudden and so penetrating, that I irresistibly thought of the old saying, "Some one is walking over my grave." My grave! where lies it, and why should I feel the shudder of it now? Am I destined to an early death? The bounding life in my veins says no. But I never again shall like that room. It has made me think.

I have not only sat in the old coach, but I had (let me drop the words slowly, they are so precious) I—I have had—a kiss—given me there. Charles gave me this kiss; he could not help it. I was sitting on the seat in front, in a sort of mock mirth he was endeavoring to frown upon, when suddenly I glanced up and our eyes met, and—He says it was the sauciness of my dimples (oh, those old dimples! they seem to have stood me in good stead after all); but I say it was my sincere affection which drew him, for he stooped like a man forgetful of everything in the whole wide world but the little trembling, panting being before him, and gave me one of those caresses which seals a woman's fate forever, and made me, the feather-brained and thoughtless coquette, a slave to this large-minded and true-hearted man for all my life hereafter.

Why I should be so happy over this event is beyond my understanding. That he should be in the seventh heaven of delight is only to be expected, but that I should find myself tripping through this gloomy old house like one treading on air is a mystery, to the elucidation of which I can only give my dimples. My reason can make nothing out of it. I, who thought of nothing short of a grand establishment in Boston, money, servants, and a husband who would love me blindly whatever my faults, have given my troth—you will say my lips, but the one means the other—to a man who will never be known outside of his own county, never be rich, never be blind even, for he frowns upon me as often as he smiles, and, worst of all, who lives in a house so vast and so full of tragic suggestion that it might well awaken doleful anticipations in much more serious-minded persons than myself.

And yet I am happy, so happy that I have even attempted to make the acquaintance of the grim old portraits and weak pastels which line the walls of many of these bedrooms. Old Mr. Knollys caught me courtesying just now before one of these ancestral beauties, whose face seemed to hold a faint prophecy of my own, and perceiving by my blushes that this was something more than a mere childish freak on my part, he chucked me under the chin and laughingly asked, how long it was likely to be before he might have the honor of adding my pretty face to the collection. Which should have made me indignant, only I am not in an indignant mood just now.

Why have I been so foolish? Why did I not let my over-fond neighbor know from the beginning that I detested him, instead of—But what have I done anyway? A smile, a nod, a laughing word mean nothing. When one has eyes which persist in dancing in spite of one's every effort to keep them demure, men who become fools are apt to call one a coquette, when a little good sense would teach them that the woman who smiles always has some other way of showing her regard to the man she really favors. I could not help being on merry terms with Mr. Trohm, if only to hide the effect another's presence has on me. But he thinks otherwise, and to-day I had ample reason for seeing why his good looks and easy manners have invariably awakened distrust in me rather than admiration. Master Trohm is vindictive, and I should be afraid of him, if I had not observed in him the presence of another passion which will soon engross all his attention and make him forget me as soon as ever I become Charles' wife. Money is his idol, and as fortune seems to favor him, he will soon be happy in the mere pleasure of accumulation. But this is not relating what happened to-day.

We were walking in the shrubbery (by we I naturally mean Charles and myself), and he was saying things which made me at the same time happy and a bit serious, when I suddenly felt myself under the spell of some baleful influence that filled me with a dismay I could neither understand nor escape from.

As this could not proceed from Charles, I turned to look about me, when I encountered the eyes of Obadiah Trohm, who was leaning on the fence separating his grounds from those of Mr. Knollys, looking directly at us. If I flinched at this surveillance, it was but the natural expression of my indignation. His face wore a look calculated to frighten any one, and though he did not respond to the gesture I made him, I felt that my only chance of escaping a scene was to induce Charles to leave me before he should see what I saw in the lowering countenance of his intrusive neighbor. As the situation demanded self-possession and the exercise of a ready wit, and as these are qualities in which I am not altogether deficient, I succeeded in carrying out my intention sooner even than I expected. Charles hurried from my presence at the first word, and proceeded towards the house without seeing Trohm, and I, quivering with dread, turned towards the man whom I felt, rather than saw, approaching me.

He met me with a look I shall never forget. I have had lovers—too many of them,—and this is not the first man I have been compelled to meet with rebuff and disdain, but never in the whole course of my none too extended existence have I been confronted by such passion or overwhelmed with such bitter recrimination. He seemed like a man beside himself, yet he was quiet, too quiet, and while his voice did not rise above a whisper, and he approached no nearer than the demands of courtesy required, he produced so terrifying an effect upon me that I longed to cry for help, and would have done so, but that my throat closed with fright, and I could only gurgle forth a remonstrance, too faint even for him to hear.

"You have played with a man's best feelings," he said. "You have led me to believe that I had only to speak to have you for my own. Are you simply foolish, or are you wicked? Did you care for me at all, or was it only your wish to increase the number of men in your train? This one" (here his hand pointed quiveringly towards the house) "has enjoyed a happiness denied me. His hand has touched yours, his lips—" Here his words became almost unintelligible till his purpose gave him strength, and he cried: "But notwithstanding this, notwithstanding any vows you may have exchanged, I have claims upon you that I will not yield. I who have loved no woman before you, will have such a hand in your fate that you will never be able to separate yourself from the influence I shall exert over you. I will not intrude between you and your lover; I will not affect dislike or disturb your outer life with any vain display of my hatred or my passion, but I will work upon your secret thoughts, and create a slowly increasing dread in the inner sanctuary of your heart till you wish you had called up the deadliest of serpents in your pathway rather than the latent fury of Obadiah Trohm. You are a girl now; when you are married and become a mother, you will understand me. For the present I leave you. The shadow of this old house which has never seen much happiness within it will soon rest upon your thoughtless head. What that will not do, your own inherent weakness will. The woman who trifles with a strong man's heart has a flaw in her nature which will work out her own destruction in time. I can afford to let you enjoy your prospective honeymoon in peace. Afterwards—" He cast a threatening look towards the decaying structure behind me, and was silent. But that silence did not unloose my tongue. I was absolutely speechless.

"Ten brides have crossed yonder threshold," he presently went on in a low musing tone freighted with horrible fatality. "One—and she was the girl whose mother was driven up to these doors dead—lived to take her grandchildren on her knees. The rest died early, and most of them unhappily. Oh, I have studied the traditions of your future home! You will live, but of all the brides who have triumphed in the honorable name of Knollys, you will lead the saddest life and meet the gloomiest end notwithstanding you stand before me now, with loose locks flying in the wind, and a heart so gay that even my despair can barely pale the roses on your cheek."

This was the raving of a madman. I recognized it as such, and took a little heart. How could he see into my future? How could he prophesy evil to one over whom he will have no control? to one watched over and beloved by a man like Charles? He is a dreamer, a fanatic. His talk about the flaw in my nature is nonsense, and as for the fate lowering over my head, in the shadows falling from the toppling old house in which I am likely to take up my abode—that is only frenzy, and I would be unworthy of happiness to heed it. As I realized this, my indignation grew, and, uttering a few contemptuous words, I was hurrying away when he stopped me with a final warning.

"Wait!" he said, "women like you cannot keep either their joys or their miseries to themselves. But I advise you not to take Charles Knollys into your confidence. If you do, a duel will follow, and if I have not the legal acumen of your intended, I have an eye and a hand before which he must fall, if our passions come to an issue. So beware! never while you live betray what has passed between us at this interview, unless the weariness of a misplaced affection should come to you, and with it the desire to be rid of your husband."

A frightful threat which, unfortunately perhaps, has sealed my lips. Oh, why should such monsters live!

I have been all through the house to-day with old Mr. Knollys. Every room was opened for my inspection, and I was bidden to choose which should be refurnished for my benefit. It was a gruesome trip, from which I have returned to my own little nook of chintz as to a refuge. Great rooms which for years have been the abode of spiders, are not much to my liking, but I chose out two which at least have fireplaces in them, and these are to be made as cheerful as circumstances will permit. I hope when I again see them, it will not be by the light of a waning November afternoon, when the few leaves still left to flutter from the trees blow, soggy and wet, against the panes of the solitary windows, or lie in sodden masses at the foot of the bare trunks, which cluster so thickly on the lawn as to hide all view of the highroad. I was meant for laughter and joy, flashing lights, and the splendors of ballrooms. Why have I chosen, then, to give up the great world and settle down in this grimmest of grim old houses in a none too lively village? I think it is because I love Charles Knollys, and so, no matter how my heart sinks in the dim shadows that haunt every spot I stray into, I will be merry, will think of Charles instead of myself, and so live down the unhappy prophecies uttered by the wretch who, with his venomous words, has robbed the future of whatever charm my love was likely to cast upon it. The fact that this man left the town to-day for a lengthy trip abroad should raise my spirits more than it has. If we were going now, Charles and I—But why dream of a Paradise whose doors remain closed to you? It is here our honeymoon is destined to be passed; within these walls and in sight of the bare boughs rattling at this moment against the panes.

I made a misstatement when I said that I had gone into all the rooms of the house this afternoon. I did not enter the Flower Parlor.

I had been married a month and had, as I thought, no further use for this foolish diary. So one evening when Charles was away, I attempted to burn it.

But when I had flung myself down before the blazing logs of my bedroom fire (I was then young enough to love to crouch for hours on the rug in my lonely room, seeking for all I delighted in and longed for in the glowing embers), some instinct, or was it a premonition? made me withhold from destruction a record which coming events might make worthy of preservation. That was five years ago, and to-day I have reopened the secret drawer in which this simple book has so long lain undisturbed, and am once more penning lines destined perhaps to pass into oblivion together with the others. Why? I do not know. There is no change in my married life. I have no trouble, no anxiety, no reason for dread; yet—Well, well, some women are made for the simple round of domestic duties, and others are as out of place in the nursery and kitchen as butterflies in a granary. I want just the things Charles cannot give me. I have home, love, children, all that some women most crave, and while I idolize my husband and know of nothing sweeter than my babies, I yet have spells of such wretched weariness, that it would be a relief to me to be a little less comfortable if only I might enjoy a more brilliant existence. But Charles is not rich; sometimes I think he is poor, and however much I may desire change, I cannot have it. Heigho! and, what is worse, I haven't had a new dress in a year; I who so love dress, and become it so well! Why, if it is my lot to go shabby, and tie up my dancing ringlets with faded ribbons, was I made with the figure of a fairy and given a temperament which, without any effort on my part, makes me, diminutive as I am, the centre of every group I enter? If I were plain, or shy, or even self-contained, I might be happy here, but now—There! there! I will go kiss little William, and lay Loreen's baby arm about my neck and see if the wicked demons will fly away. Charles is too busy for me to intrude upon him in that horrid Flower Parlor.

I was never superstitious till I entered this house; but now I believe in every sort of thing a sane woman should not. Yesterday, after a neglect of five years, I brought out my diary. To-day I have to record in it that there was a reason for my doing so. Obadiah Trohm has returned home. I saw him this morning leaning over his fence in the same place and in very much the same attitude as on that day when he frightened me so, a month before my wedding.

But he did not frighten me to-day. He merely looked at me very sharply and with a less offensive admiration than in the early days of our first acquaintance. At which I made him my best courtesy. I was not going to remind him of the past in our new relations, and he, thankful perhaps for this, took off his hat with a smile I am trying even yet to explain to myself. Then we began to talk. He had travelled everywhere and I had been nowhere; he wore the dress and displayed the manners of the great world, while I had only a hungry desire to do the same. As for fashion, I needed all my beauty and the fading sparkle of my old animation to enable me to hold up my head before him.

But as for liking him, I did not. I could admire his appearance, but he himself attracted me no more than when he had words of angry fury on his tongue. He is a gentleman, and one who has seen the world, but in other ways he is no more to be compared with my Charles than his pert new house, built in his absence, with the grand old structure with whose fatality he once threatened me.

I do not think he wants to threaten me with disaster now. Time closes such wounds as his very effectually. I wish we had some of his money.

I have always heard that the wives of the Knollys, whatever their misfortune, have always loved their husbands. I do not think I am any exception to the rule. When Charles has leisure to give me an hour from his musty old books, the place here seems lively enough, and the children's voices do not sound so shrill. But these hours are so infrequent. If it were not for Mr. Trohm's journal (Did I mention that he had lent me a journal of his travels?) I should often eat my heart out with loneliness. I am beginning to like the man better as I follow him from city to city of the old world. If he had ever mentioned me in its pages, I would not read another line in it, but he seems to have expended both his love and spite when he bade me farewell in the garden underlying these bleak old walls.

I am becoming as well acquainted with Mr. Trohm's handwriting as with my own. I read and read and read in his journal, and only stop when the dreaded midnight hour comes with its ghostly suggestions and the unaccountable noises which make this old dwelling so uncanny. Charles often finds me curled up over this book, and when he does he sighs. Why?

I have been teaching Loreen to dance. Oh, how merry it has made me! I think I will be happier now. We have the large upper hall to take steps in, and when she makes a misstep we laugh, and that is a good sound to hear in this old place. If I could only have a little money to buy her a fresh frock and some ribbons, I would feel perfectly satisfied; but I do believe Charles is getting poorer and poorer every day; the place costs so much to keep up, he says, and when his father died there were debts to be paid which leaves us, his innocent inheritors, very straitened. Master Trohm has no such difficulties. He has money enough. But I don't like the man for all that, polite as he is to us all. He seems to quite adore Loreen, and as to

William, he pets him till I feel almost uncomfortable at times.

What shall I do? I am invited to New York, I, and Charles says I may go, too—only I have nothing to wear. Oh, for some money! a little money! it is my right to have some money; but Charles tells me he can only spare enough to pay my expenses, that my Sunday frock looks very well, and that, even if it did not, I am pretty enough to do without fine clothes, and other nonsense like that,—sweet enough, but totally without point, in fact. If I am pretty, all the more I need a little finery to set me off, and, besides, to go to New York without money—why, I should be perfectly miserable. Charles himself ought to realize this, and be willing to sell his old books before he would let me go into this whirl of temptation without a dollar to spend. As he don't, I must devise some plan of my own for obtaining a little money, for I won't give up my trip—the first offered me since I was married,—and neither will I go away and come back without a gift for my two girls, who have grown to womanhood without a jewel to adorn them or a silk dress to make them look like gentlemen's children. But how get money without Charles knowing it? Mr. Trohm is such a good friend, he might lend me a little, but I don't know how to ask him without recalling to his mind certain words long since forgotten by him perhaps, but never to be forgotten by me, feather-brained as many people think me. Is there any one else?

I wonder if some things are as wicked as people say they are. I———

Here the diary breaks off abruptly. But we know what followed. The forgery, the discovery of it by her suave but secret enemy, his unnatural revenge, and the never-dying enmity which led to the tragic events it has been my unhappy fortune to relate at such length. Poor Althea! with thy name I write finis to these pages. May the dust lie lightly on thy breast under the shadow of the Flower Parlor, through which thy footsteps passed with such dread in the old days of thy youthful beauty and innocence!

THE END

Made in the USA
Lexington, KY
16 November 2014